Praise for New Wilderness

"[Matthews has] crafted the ultimate environmental nightmare."

—MACLEAN'S MAGAZINE

"A remarkably well-written novel that will leave you unable to stop reading."

—WINNIPEG FREE PRESS

"Matthews has created a world so realistic that you will look suspiciously at your pets."

— REGINA LEADER-POST

"[T]he interplay of gritty survivalism and rapid-fire action yields a page-turner, throughout which the author has also deftly woven themes of environmentalism and conservation."

—KIRKUS DISCOVERIES

City on the Currents

Brian S. Matthews

This novel is a work of fiction. Names, characters, places and incidents are the product of the author's imagination or are used fictitiously and any resemblance to actual persons living or dead, events or locales is entirely coincidental.

National Library of Canada Cataloguing in Publication

Matthews, Brian S., 1971-
New Wildernes / by Brian S. Matthews.

ISBN 1-897242-23-9

I.Title.

PS8576.A83123C57 2005 C813'.6 C2005-905960-5

Cover art by Bill Richards

Aydy Press
www.aydy.ca

For Fiona and Ron
and Tom

Synopsis of New Wilderness

June 10th of that first year seemed like any other summer day, until every animal and bird on the planet turned on mankind. From house pets to zoo creatures, wildlife to circus animals, everything that wasn't human wanted kill anything that was. Three days later, the hymenoptera—bees, wasps and ants—joined in. The death toll was immeasurable. Civilization collapsed.

Ten years later, humanity lives in fortified encampments. People venture out only when necessary, and then only in protective gear and heavily armed.

In what used to be British Columbia, Canada, the settlement of Compton Pit has found a way to protect itself against the animals and insects. Ultra-sonic projectors, called Screaming Mimis, surround the Pit and create a barrier repellent to aggressors.

Inside the Pit, Dr. Theodore Odega works feverishly to discover the cause of the Change.

Lena Wong runs communications, keeping contact with as much of the world as she can by bouncing signals off what few autonomous satellites still orbit the planet.

Darcy McCullough, chief of security, guards The Pit against two-legged predators.

Sid Halbert, known as the Boss, runs the show.

Ethan Toffee, chief of the hunters, supplies the Pit with meat while using the psyches of those around him as his personal game farm.

Richard "Caps" Scagling, auto-mechanic extraordinaire and cartoonist, tries to balance the world's horror with humour.

Noah Thurlow, electrical engineer, supplies them all with electricity by maintaining and improving the Pit's enormous solar panel array.

Noah is infatuated with Darcy, but she doesn't return his feelings. She's still in mourning for her lover, Travis Jones, who was killed by rats in caverns under the Pit.

Despite the security of the sound net, Compton Pit has its problems. People can go "tooth crazy" and foolishly leave the settlement. Others have to be locked outside. The Pit is waging a physical war with Fenwick Prison, a nearby settlement, and an economic war with the Reservoir, the region's chief stockpile of fuel and motor vehicles. Peter "Gascan" D'Abo, boss of the Reservoir, has long had his eye on Compton Pit's treasures.

October Neriah, the Pit's chief of transport, is ambushed and murdered on the highway by scavengers from Fenwick Prison.

Burle Campbell, chief of stores and one of the Pit's most trusted citizens, betrays them to Fenwick, but once discovered, turns double agent.

The Pit wins its war with Fenwick, but the conflict results in the destruction of the Pit's solar panel array and a number of vehicles. Desperate for trucks and new solar panels, Sid, Darcy, Noah, Caps, Lena and Toffee—dubbed the Deep Six—set out for the dreaded city of Vancouver, from which nobody has returned in the last decade. Enroute they encounter cartographer Donald Graff, who's traveling in the opposite direction.

The Deep Six penetrate Vancouver and acquire the materials they need. They plunder the University of British Columbia for an advanced solar panel prototype, and while there, discover the remains of a group of scientists who appear to have committed suicide subsequent to some intensive research.

Peter D'Abo learns from Donald Graff that the command core of Compton Pit is absent. D'Abo mobilizes an armored convoy with the intention of annexing the Pit.

As the Deep Six prepare to leave Vancouver, they're waylaid by silent people who abduct Noah and Lena and leave the rest for dead.

Inside Compton Pit, things are not going well. Without the trusted leaders to hold the place together, conflicts of personality escalate into a civil war.

Dr. Odega, on the verge of his greatest discovery, loses his mind and flees the Pit, stealing one of their best vehicles and indirectly killing a hunter.

Sid, Darcy, Toffee and Caps search the city to find their lost comrades.

Peter D'Abo arrives at Compton Pit, sets up a siege within the safety of the sound net and demands total surrender.

Lena and Noah suffer at the hands of their captors, a whale-worshipping cult who practice human sacrifice.

Sid, Darcy and Toffee rescue Noah and Lena. Caps is critically wounded.

Compton Pit turns off the sound net and the animals wipe out D'Abo and his crew.

The Deep Six return to Compton Pit with their bounty. Caps is taken to the infirmary, his chances of survival uncertain.

And I will send the beasts among you,
which shall rob you of your children...
and make you few in number;
and your ways shall become desolate.

Leviticus XXVI, 22

1. Yellow-Brick Road

They lay side by side on blankets, both naked save for the briefest of swimming apparel.

"You're in no hurry to go in yet?" asked Caps. His companion didn't answer. "Yeah, me neither. Pass the lotion?"

Noah tossed the bottle of deep-tanning oil onto Caps's blanket. The artist squeezed a small puddle of the stuff onto his belly and rubbed it into his skin.

"Oh, yeah," said Caps. "This is the life!" He stood up and applied a fresh coat to his legs. "It's not as good as Hawaii. You ever get out there? Guess you'd have been too young for surfing. Surfing, that's something I miss." He stretched his arms out and rode an imaginary wave, gyrating to keep his balance. "And the girls! All that heat and not a bead of sweat on 'em when they do that dance." He did a fair imitation of Hawaiian luau music and a graceless imitation of the dance. "They do at night, though. They sweat like crazy. Dancing around these huge bonfires. They really get moving then." Caps swung his arms up and down and jerked his pelvis from side to side.

"Okay!" Noah barked.

Caps stopped his prancing. "Okay as in 'I give?' "

"Yes! Uncle. You win."

"Double for a month. Yummy. Makes my nipples hard just thinking about it. Yours too I see."

Noah's teeth started to chatter. Far above the solar panels, uncontested in a cloudless sky, the November sun mocked them with light but no heat.

"I'm glad you caved," said Caps. "I'm freezing to death out here."

"You—" the rest of Noah's reply was cut off when a pair of coveralls hit him in the face. A moment later a similar projectile hit Caps.

"What the hell do you two think you're doing?" Sid Halbert demanded.

"Alright, the Boss." Caps jiggled his head in time with a Californian lilt. "Dude, grab some ground, catch some rays."

Noah struggled into the coveralls. The legs were twisted and his frantic kicking only made things worse.

"This isn't a joke, Richard," said Sid, made angrier by Caps's levity. "What happens when you both come down with pneumonia? Of all the stupid bets to make…" he trailed off as Caps, impossibly, turned paler than he already was.

"Damn it!" Noah had somehow managed to get one pant leg inside the other.

"Son of a bitch! Dogs!" yelled Caps.

"Nice try," said Noah.

Caps was already running.

Sid swiveled and looked behind him.

Still a distance away, through the panels, the shapes of three dogs trotted closer. The lead dog broke into a run. The access panel to the battery bay, and the safety of below, was between the three men and the animals. There was no chance of reaching it before the dogs did.

Sid ran after Caps. Noah, his legs still tangled in the coveralls, stood, took a step, and fell flat on his face.

"Noah, come on!" Caps yelled as he leapt for a panel mount.

The Boss pulled himself onto the same mount, then the two of them clambered up to a high support beam. Two thoughts struck Sid as he looked back for his chief electrical engineer: the first was that they weren't dogs, they were wolves; the second was that Noah wasn't going to make it.

Noah gave up on dressing and ran, his coveralls trailing from one hand, but the wolves were closing the distance too quickly for him to get to a support beam high enough. He could almost feel the teeth sinking into his legs. With less than twenty feet between himself and the lead wolf, he hooked his coveralls on a low-mounted panel and gave his legs everything he had. The wolf was fooled by the garment for only a moment, but that was all Noah needed. He jumped and grabbed the top edge of a large panel, then pulled himself up, throwing his leg over the top so he was lying on the edge of the frame, barely two inches thick. Two of the wolves stopped at Noah's panel. The third proceeded to the beam Caps and Sid sat on. Both men pulled their legs up as the creature jumped and missed.

"Shoot them," said Caps.

"With what?" Sid patted his empty hip. "If I'd brought a gun, I'd have already used it on you two."

There were no ground guards topside. Since the fall of both Fenwick Prison and Gascan D'Abo there was nothing even remotely close by to guard against, and of course the Screaming Mimis kept the teeth away. At least they were supposed to. Sid cast his eyes first at the southwest, then the northeast tower.

The lone wolf darted right and left, looking for a way to get at its prey. Noah's two were also pacing back and forth. Apart from an occasional low growl, none of the animals made much noise.

"HELP!" yelled Caps, waving at the towers. "HELP!"

"Stop that." Sid slapped Caps's arms down. "They can't hear you. Oh, no."

Two more wolves appeared through the panels, then another pair, until there was a total of seven wolves pacing and snarling.

The narrow frame Noah was on cut into his naked chest, and the warmth brought on by adrenaline was ebbing, sucked away by the cold air, but he had a more immediate problem. The panel he was on was a concentrator, one of many large, monochromatic cells designed to track the sun. To this end, it was mounted on a swivel, and Noah's additional weight was causing the panel to tilt down towards the wolves.

"Oh, shit…" breathed Caps.

Noah's scalp crawled and another surge of adrenaline burst through him. As the panel twisted, he let go of his tentative perch and pulled himself along to the opposite end that would soon be the high ground. The panel reached equilibrium parallel to the earth. Two wolves jumped onto it simultaneously, their combined weight enough to spur the panel into finishing its rotation. The wolves slid back to the ground, clawing at the panel's black surface as they went. Noah yanked himself up to the frame's new top edge and once again lay flat, his hands braced on either side. His eyes were huge with fear, and his trembling had nothing to do with the cold.

One of the wolves threw itself into the bottom of the panel. The frame couldn't turn anymore in that direction, but it lurched, nearly dislodging the young man.

"Noah, look at me," said Sid, his voice unnaturally calm. "You'll have to jump."

A ten-foot distance separated the top of the concentrator and the high beam the Boss and Caps were on.

"Don't look down. Just jump."

The wolf hit the concentrator again. Another wolf's ears perked up as it caught on.

Noah gripped the panel tightly with his hands as he brought his legs, then his feet, underneath him. If he'd been wearing boots, it would have been impossible, but bare soles made for better traction and soon he was poised on the frame like a monkey on a tree branch. Like a drunken monkey on a tree branch. His extremities were numb with the cold and three of the wolves were now doing their damnedest to shake him loose. Just as the largest of the three attackers smashed into the panel, Noah launched himself towards the beam. Panic had been kept in abeyance by the suddenness and sheer *unreality* of the situation—attacked by wolves amidst his own array, and so deep within the sound net—but in the fraction of the second in which he was airborne, he knew he was headed for the ground, not the beam. He could see each individual hair on the muzzle of the wolf rearing up at him.

Caps caught one arm, Sid the other, and as Noah slammed into the beam, they hauled him up onto it.

The wolves made a few more useless jumps, then surrounded the trio and growled.

Caps resumed waving his arms at the nearest tower and again the Boss slapped his arms down.

"I told you to stop that."

"Are you losing it?"

"What's going to happen? They can't see the wolves through the panels. Whoever's up there will think we've just locked ourselves out and send someone to open the hatch." He flicked his eyes at the animals.

"They'll be torn apart," said Caps. "So what do we do now?"

"You could give me your jacket," Noah stammered to the Boss.

"Sorry. Here."

Noah yanked the jacket on. Caps tried to pull his feet up into his pant legs without losing his perch. He failed. A quick grab from Sid saved him.

"Gershwin's gone," said Noah. "Our supercomputer finally fragged itself."

"Not necessarily," said Sid. "What if it's just lost power?"

"No way. No way! Everything else in the Pit would lose juice before Gershwin. I've got so many redundancies—"

"Alright, Noah. I believe you."

While five of the wolves set off down the length of the beam, most likely to look for a way up, two of them stayed guard. One sat down and whined.

"Oh, that creeps me out," Caps said. "This one's more disappointed than angry that it can't eat us yet. What's that one doing?"

One of the wolves had a cable in its teeth and was wrestling with it.

"It can't get us so he's ripping up my array," Noah said sullenly. "He'll never chew through that cable."

The wolf planted its feet, clamped down on the cable and pulled with all its might.

The Boss followed the cable with his eyes. It led up to a medium-sized panel mounted even higher than the beam they were sitting on.

"Noah, move!" Sid reached out, but Noah had already slid out of harm's way. The panel came loose and smashed into the beam before falling to the ground.

The wolf barked twice and the animals closest to it turned to face it, bodies in postures of attention. The wolf barked twice more then went to work on another cable.

"No way," said Caps, turning his head to follow the cable to another panel.

The wolves watched their cable-wrestling pack mate with curiosity. The three men slid a few feet down the beam. One wolf got bored and returned its gaze to the dinner hiding in the strange tree.

The panel came loose and cracked into the beam.

Noah cursed.

The instructing wolf looked at Noah and huffed a few times.

One by one, the wolves chose their cables.

"I'm very scared now," said Caps, eyeballing the canopy of panels above them.

Sid's head swung from left to right. There was nowhere to go.

Noah watched a cluster of wolves heading for cables in the distance. As a group they pulled up short and backed up a few steps. Noah searched frantically for whatever they'd found. He saw nothing in particular that would attract their attention. One of the creatures trotted forward only to lurch back again.

"Guy's, c'mon." Noah stood on the beam and walked along its length as quickly as he could and still keep his balance.

"What do you see?" Sid also rose to his feet.

A panel hit the beam, edge first. A brittle *snap* preceded shards of crystal tinkling to the ground.

"Each of the Mimis has a sphere of influence, right?" said Noah, wincing as another panel came loose. "Only one sphere actually crosses the fence into our topside. Gershwin's still online."

Sid and Caps caught on at the same time. The Screaming Mimis were set up so that their areas of effect overlapped and completely surrounded Compton Pit, but that was beyond the fence line. The limitations of geography forced one of the sound projectors to be set up close enough that it protected a small area within the perimeter, and that area included a portion of the array. If they could get to that area, then they could jump to the ground and still be safe. They could stay within the safety zone, and work their way to the southeast tower.

Three guard wolves kept pace with them as they shuffled along the beam. What few parts of his feet Noah could feel, felt like they were burning. He didn't know how much longer he could take it, and the safety zone was still a ways away.

"Just keep going, son."

"Th-that's easy for you to say. You've got boots on."

"I'll be happy to give them to you once we reach the ground."

Arms outstretched at their sides, they approached their goal. The larger group of wolves gave up on the cables and moved to intercept, and the closer they got, the louder they got. Soon all of the creatures were snarling and barking. One of them—the largest—made a last desperate jump, but fell short of the beam. When the wolves were thirty feet behind, and making no attempt to come closer, Sid lowered himself to hang from the beam by his hands, then dropped to the ground. When the animals didn't charge, Noah and Caps did the same. Frustrated beyond belief, the wolves began to howl.

"That'll do it," said Sid. He looked around. "Someone'll hear that. Good job, Noah."

"Thanks. About those boots?"

2. Bring the House Down

"Weren't you scared?" asked Darcy. The rifle she'd used to take down the last wolf lay across her lap. Five of the animals were already in Devon the tanner's possession. The other two were with Dr. Patel.

"Of course I was scared," replied Noah. He wore coveralls. And a sweater. And a coat. And on top of that he had a blanket wrapped around his shoulders. The only things bare were his feet and they were in a bucket of warm water.

"At least you didn't faint," said Caps with a chuckle. He also had his feet in water, but the coveralls were all he had for the rest of him.

"What were you doing out there in the first place?" Darcy asked.

"I'm going to kill you," snapped Lena as she pushed through the infirmary's plastic curtain.

"Crap." Caps lifted an implement tray and hid his face behind it. Lena smacked the tray with the flat of her hand, driving it into his forehead.

"Ouch! That hurt."

"Good. It was a bet, Darcy."

"A bet? What was it? Who could get the worst frostbite?"

"No." Noah jiggled his feat in the basin, making pleasant splashing sounds. "It's all Roshi's fault."

"Come again?"

"He pulled an ice-cream machine on his last wish list."

Since freeing Vancouver from the Children of Bjossa, the Pit made constant forays into the city for anything that wasn't nailed down. Each department head got to place a wish list with Daniel, the chief of transport. Not every item requested was found, or even looked for, but Roshi got top priority when it came to out-of-the-way, even frivolous items. It was best to keep the chef happy.

"So me and Caps got to test the first batch—"

"And he ate his too quickly," broke in Caps, "and got a headache. I ragged on him, of course. His first ice-cream in over a decade and he gets greedy. I—"

"He made fun of me. Said I couldn't handle the cold. I told him I could take cold longer than he could—"

"So we bet our milk for the month, threw on the Speedos and went topside."

"The suntan oil and the blankets were Caps's idea."

"We had to do something to justify why we were up there, otherwise we'd be just a couple of dimwits freezing our asses off."

Lena's mouth was caught between a frown and a grin. "You bought that? The tanning stuff was a clever disguise?"

"Didn't make it any more stupid," Noah mumbled.

"Did he rub a lot of lotion on? Do a stupid dance?"

"Yes," he looked up sharply at his friend

"He does that to keep warm." Lena bit her lip to keep from laughing. "I'd forgotten about that little con."

Far from looking guilty, Caps puffed up. He loved it when other people bespoke his brilliance.

"You dog." Noah wanted to throw something at him.

"Lena," said Darcy, "I think you missed the point in all this. Roshi has ice-cream." A short alarm sounded, one bell, pause, two bells, pause, repeat. Darcy pushed herself of the bed. "Guess it'll have to wait"

The meeting table was short a few bodies. There was no representative from the hunters. Daniel and Toffee were still away on their shopping spree—Caps's term for trips to the city—though if they were on schedule, they'd be back that night or the following day. It was to be the last such trip until April or so. Winter was almost on them and the Boss didn't want anyone snowbound away from home. In the middle of the table lay an odd device made up of plastic and wires.

"Anyone care to guess what that is?" offered Sid. "It's part radio," he hooked it with a finger and pulled it closer, "part Mimi."

There were murmurs around the table.

"I found it where Mimi Three was supposed to be. Someone hooked it up to fool Gershwin into thinking it still had a full projector there. The wolves burrowed under the fence. We had an open corridor, people, a yellow-brick road right into the Pit." He let that sink in before continuing. "The hole's filled in and perimeter guards are back up, two by two. If it wasn't for Archie and Jughead here, we might not have known about this for a while yet. Of the people who know the Mimis' locations, I can think of only five people that could do this. Sara and Seth, of course. Lena. And Noah I have a feeling you could do this, too."

"I couldn't," Noah said defensively.

"I'm not saying you did, I'm saying you could. I know you four didn't do it. That leaves only one person."

"Ted," Dr. Sara White said into the table.

"Mmhmm. Dr. Odega. When he 'left' us, a few of the spare Mimi components were lost. Now they're found. He knows the Mimis better than anyone else alive. He took the spare parts when he left, and in our last conversation prior to his unfortunate coma, he was desperate for a functioning Mimi to play with. I wouldn't give it to him. Darcy?"

Darcy picked up the radio-gizmo and tapped it against her palm. "We don't know how long ago this was done. There's no apparatus on Gershwin to tell us when the feed to Mimi three was interrupted. What we do know is that this had to be fairly recent, or the teeth would have come in before now. That means Odega got what he came for and split, or he's holed up somewhere. Either way, he needs fuel and supplies. The question is, where did he get them from?"

"He didn't get them from us," said Seth. "Everything in stores is accounted for."

"Most of the teeth have denned up," continued Darcy, "and those that haven't, as the wolves showed, are hungry. If he's camping, the only safe place is within the sound net. Our outer fringes are being swept by the hunters. I'm not crossing my fingers. Whether he still has our van, or if he's acquired a different vehicle is anybody's guess." She was very calm as she spoke, but her fingers tightened around the fake Mimi as if she was trying to choke it.

"The first priority," Sid took command of the meeting again, "is to plug up that hole in the sound net. To that end we'll pull one of the Mimis out of the caverns. I don't want any part of our underground unprotected, so whichever passage we pull the Mimi from, we're sealing for good. Seth, how are you at mining?"

In his old life, before the Change, Seth had been a demolitions expert for the United States Army. As such, he was the closest thing to a mining engineer in the Pit. "I don't think I could tap a vein for you, but if you just want me to collapse a tunnel…well, that I can do."

"Good. Darcy, you and Seth pick a tunnel to close."

"I'll need light in the caverns," said Seth. "The sooner the better."

***

Seth stared at a rough schematic of the caverns, weighing the pros and cons of which tunnel to close. Darcy didn't need anything to help her make the decision.

"That one," she pointed at the third passage from the left. It was where Travis Jones had died to a rat swarm.

Seth looked up, nodded, then tossed the map over his shoulder.

The group headed down the passage. Noah worked his way behind them, trying to follow the power cable that led to the Mimi. He'd find it, then lose it again under the stone-and-paint camouflage placed over the cable. At one point, he lost it for good.

"Oh, this is ridiculous. Caps!"

The artist dropped back from Seth and Darcy. "What?"

"I can't find the cable now. Your work is too damn good sometimes."

"I didn't do the cables. You, Darcy and Sara did. I just did the Mimi itself. We're pulling it out anyway, right?" He felt around the stone wall low to the ground. "There." He flicked some rock chips aside, found the cable underneath and gave it a hard pull. In a shower of dust and stone particles, a length of cable some twenty feet long burst into view. "Here," he handed the cable over, "just keep pulling, Jughead."

"Jughead? I don't think so. I'm Archie."

"Sorry. You can't be," Caps lowered his voice. "Archie likes girls."

"What's that supposed to mean?"

"I don't know, man. Ever since we got back from the city women have been throwing themselves at you."

"That's an exaggeration."

"Okay, maybe nudging themselves towards you, but you haven't taken advantage of any of 'em. If I were in your shoes, I'd be in a different bed every night. What about Eggerson's new assistant? I've seen the baby browns she flashes at you."

"Here, Seth." Darcy stopped at a point where a smaller passage forked away to the right. "Bring it down right here."

"Here?" Seth eyed the curving rock above him.

"Blast it. Wipe it away. Whatever it is you're going to do, do it here."

Dragging sounds and grunts of exertion echoed down the passage as Noah's conscripts lugged cables and fluorescents. Noah stopped ripping the Mimi's cable from the wall and took over installing the lights.

Seth wandered down the small fork. He turned his flashlight off as lights came on. One of the mules followed him into the passage.

"What are you doing?" Seth asked as the man hung the light from the ceiling. "I need it on the ground shining up."

The man gave him an irritated look as he repositioned the light. "I know that, but I saw the mount up there, so I thought that's where you wanted it."

Seth looked up at the metal hook driven into the cavern ceiling. "I didn't put that there."

When there was sufficient illumination, Darcy sent Noah away and hunkered down, keeping her back against the wall. She watched Seth as he wandered back and forth, occasionally tapping at the rock with a small hammer. Caps sat down beside her.

"How're you feeling?"

"I'm furious. Odega, or whoever, stealing from right under my nose. He better hope the teeth get him before I do."

"That's not what I meant."

"What? Oh," she waved her hand at the cave. "This? I'm fine. I don't even think about it anymore."

"No? Then why this passage? Makes more sense to me to close number six. It's the most convoluted. Or four. That one leads to our back door."

"It's good to have an escape route, so four's out. And six… okay. I'll be over it once we're done here."

"What the…" A chunk of rock crumbled under Seth's hammer, revealing a small cavity. He reached into the hole and pulled something out.

"Whatcha got there?" Caps asked, coming to his feet.

"I don't know. It's a piece of pipe, I think. PVC."

Darcy took it from him and looked inside. The pipe was about thirty centimeters in length, and ten or so centimeters in diameter. A ring of nails had been punched through the pipe at an angle so their points were all inside, and pointed to one end.

"There's something else in here." Seth pulled at a piece of fur until an entire pelt came from the hole. It was large, that of an elk or a deer.

Darcy handed Caps the pipe and slapped some dust off the pelt to examine it better. There were reinforced holes evenly spaced along the edges except at one corner where it had been chewed.

"Kinky sex," said Caps, waggling the pipe at Darcy. "Someone's been up to some kinky sex. The pelt's a blanket."

"At what part of the act is that pipe used?"

"I…uh…I'm not sure." He touched one of the nails with a finger. "I've never been this kinky."

"Sure." She snatched the pipe back. "Maybe Eggerson will know what it is."

***

"That sounded heavy," said Eggerson, his hands going to the box that had just landed on his desk.

"It's all there, and then some," said a rough voice.

"You don't usually make personal deliveries. What do you want?"

"This." Toffee plunked a fist-sized tooth down on the desk.

Eggerson blinked and picked it up, marveling at it. "What do you want me to do with this?"

"Carve something on it. An arctic landscape would be good."

"Not a request I'd expect from you. How did you…no, I don't want to know. I've never carved ivory before, I'd probably mess it up."

"So practice on this." Toffee placed a second huge tooth on the desk.

"I can give you a more immediate reward, if you'd like to try it on."

Toffee turned to leave. "No thanks. I'm just getting used to this one."

"You won't regret it."

"Fine." The chief of the hunters unhooked his prosthetic arm and traded it for the one Eggerson was holding up. After it was fitted, Toffee made a few practice movements. "It's heavier."

"Just a bit. It's worth it. Look." Eggerson took a hold on the prosthetic hand. "With The arm you've got now, you can make a fist by rotating the wrist wheel. This one does the same, but," he stroked the back of the hand, "you can also adjust the individual fingers."

Toffee jerked the prosthetic away from its creator. "I can barely see the wheels. You made this one look like a vein." He rolled the various dials, watching the wooden fingers move like the real thing. With a glove over them, they'd be almost indistinguishable. He pulled the arm off and looked inside. "More gears. Will my blade fit?"

"That's the best part, not only will it fit, but I put sharpening stones inside at an angle. Every time you slide the arm on and off, it hones the blade. The hole to oil the stones is on the underside, there's a panel." He grabbed the arm again and pushed on a spot near the top of the forearm. A square of wood sank in and slid back. "There's a small dropper of oil in a compartment here—"

"Eggerson, do you know what this—" Darcy stopped short upon seeing the hunter. "I heard you were back early."

"Daniel's trying to prove he can replace October."

"Any…"

"No. We all came back. What's that?"

"I was hoping he could tell me."

She handed the PVC pipe to Eggerson. He looked it over, slipped a finger inside and touched the tips of the nails. He offered it back. "Very medieval looking. Is it for torture?"

Darcy looked at the hunter. "You?"

"It could be for torture."

Darcy took it back and held it at her side. "Torture or kinky sex. Well, neither of you have been any help. Toffee, welcome back. Congratulations on bringing everyone home again."

It was just after dusk when Noah finished staking out the new trenches that needed to be dug. As Darcy had predicted, the hunters found nothing on their patrol. A Mimi had been moved up from below, which meant the unprotected passage in the tunnel would now be guarded twenty-four hours a day. Noah didn't envy anyone that duty. After looking over the battery bay, he headed to the motor pool. He found the man he was looking for under the massive front end of a semi.

"How's it going?" Noah asked, squatting down.

"Not good, buddy. You know the difference between Daniel and October? October brought her team in fast without wrecking the vehicles."

"Listen, about what you said earlier…"

"What did I say earlier?"

"That you think I don't like girls."

Caps nearly bashed his head sitting up, but stopped and slid out from under the truck. "…the hell are you talking about?"

"Archie, Jughead, you know."

"Having a low-self-esteem day are we? Heh. I just like making you sweat."

"So you were kidding?"

"No, I meant it. I really do like making you sweat."

Noah rolled his eyes.

Caps grinned. "You wanted to know when Darcy's birthday is? It's tomorrow."

"Yeah, sure."

"No, really. It's tomorrow."

"Tomorrow! You…that doesn't give me any time! Why didn't you tell me sooner? I could have ordered something on the last shopping spree. I could have—"

"You could have just asked her yourself, or Lena. You should know better than to rely on me for time-critical information. Happy hunting." He chuckled and pulled himself back under the truck.

Beside the wheel, Caps's wrench lay conveniently within his reach. Next to it was a bolt that looked important. Noah put the bolt in his pocket. *Happy hunting to you too.*

3. The Gift

Darcy pulled a fist full of red hair over the right side of her face and looked in the mirror. Hardly a wrinkle marred her skin.

Another year closer to thirty and she still would have been ID'd at most old-world bars. Until...she tilted her head and let her hair fall away. She covered the crescent-shaped scars on her cheek with her hand, leaving just the cicatrix around her eye naked for examination. The way it pulled the skin tight gave her eye an almost Asian slant. That in itself was a little exotic. She picked up an eyeliner pencil from her desk and drew delicate lines along the edge of her left eye, giving it the illusion of angle. The chief of security took her hand away. The scars ran to below the edge of her lips. She contemplated a jar of foundation, the plastic seal around the lid still unbroken. With a sigh she put the jar down and leaned back in her chair.

"What the Pit needs," she said to her reflection, "is a plastic surgeon."

There was a knock on the door.

"Just a minute." She dabbed at the eyeliner with a rag, then pulled her robe closed around her chest and legs. "Come in."

"I saw your light on under the door." Toffee waited in the hallway until Darcy gestured him in. He had a hide-wrapped bundle in his hand; thin and nearly four feet long. He shut the door behind him.

"What's that?"

"It's for you. I didn't want to wait until tomorrow. Happy Birthday."

Darcy made no move to take it. "Is it a rifle?"

"Open it."

Interested in spite of herself, Darcy accepted the bundle. It wasn't heavy enough to be a rifle. The hide was secured by ribbons at both ends. They were tied in bows.

"Did you wrap this?"

"Yes."

She fingered one of the bows. The ribbons came off easily and the hide fell away to reveal a staff, intricately engraved with Haida Indian-style figures.

"Wow," she breathed, touching a carving of Coyote near the top of the staff. "I wasn't expecting this. I don't know what I…wait." She looked intently at the topmost carving; it was of a killer whale. She took it in one hand and thrust it over her head, feeling its weight, looking at it from that angle. "Tell me this isn't the same staff."

"Then I'd be lying." His expression hadn't change, but somehow he'd taken on an air of self-satisfaction.

She threw it at his feet. "You got me. I fell for it. Happy?" Her anger's escalation was suddenly halted at the expression on his face. It was only there for a moment, but it was a look of genuine shock. "Wait. Why did you give this to me?"

For a moment, Toffee had no words. When he did speak, he almost stammered. "It's your birthday."

"And you thought I'd want…" she bent over and retrieved the staff, "this?"

"Hey, I nearly froze getting it."

He was angry. Darcy was immensely more comfortable with him this way.

"What about the whale? Did Bjossa just let you take it? How many of our people did you risk?"

"Just me. The whale was gull bait. The worst part was the smell. It was cold but those bodies had the whole summer to bloat and rot."

The extent to which he'd gone to obtain the staff suddenly became clear to her. Searching that huge corpse-laden pool. She could only get out one word: "Why?"

"Because it's important. You took care of the whole cult with that thing."

"I had nothing to do with it. They took care of themselves."

"No, that's not what happened. You commanded, they obeyed. This staff is a symbol of your power."

"It's a symbol of tragedy. You think I liked watching those kids jumping to their death? What Bjossa did to the first ones in? If I'd wanted it, I wouldn't have thrown it into the water. Here." She held it out to him. "I can only imagine what you went through, but I don't want it."

"Which? The staff or the effort?"

Darcy said nothing.

Reluctantly, Toffee took the staff. He worried it with his thumb and another unfamiliar expression gripped his face. On anyone else, Darcy would have described it as sheepish. "I have something else I can give you, but it won't be ready for a while. Do you like ivory?"

"Toffee, you're under no obligation to give me anything. I'm surprised you even knew tomorrow was my birthday."

"I have to give you something. I've got it. I'll give you the same thing Halbert gives you."

Darcy felt as if a bucket of cold water had been poured over her head.

"How do you know what Sid gives me?"

"He told me. How else? Oh, what are you getting pissed about now, Red?"

"What Sid gives me is private! You wouldn't understand. Fine. Gift accepted."

Toffee waited.

"What? Now? Forget it. It's late."

He abruptly broke eye contact, gazing about the room, evidently to find something else to look at. He nodded at the PVC pipe on Darcy's desk. "You figure out what that's for yet?"

"No, but I will. That's my new hobby."

"I'll let you get some sleep." He made as if to offer the staff to her again, then shook his head and left.

Darcy didn't sit at the head table at breakfast; she was angry at Sid. Instead she sat with Caps and Lena, who were pointedly not wishing her a happy birthday. Apparently they intended to surprise her later.

"Don't bother, guys," Darcy said around a mouthful of eggs. "I don't feel like pretending to be shocked."

Lena and Caps shared a glance. Caps smirked and gave a conceding nod.

"We don't have anything planned," said Lena. "Caps told me to leave it up to him."

"I figured I'd come up with something by this afternoon," said the artist. "Right now I'm drawing blanks. I've just had so much work to do lately, what with the new vehicles and all."

Darcy held her hands up. "God, don't make a big deal out of it. Toffee already did. He came to my room last night. He was acting really funny."

If Caps were a dog, his ears would have perked up. "Yeah? Funny how?"

"Just...he was really adamant about giving me this gift."

"What kind of gift?"

She glanced at Lena. "Something stupid. It's not important. Anyway, when I didn't want it...I think he was hurt."

"It's obvious." Caps grinned. "He's in love with you."

"It's my birthday, don't scare me like that. It's another one of his games. I was tired last night, but I'm awake now. Whatever he's trying to pull, I'll make sure it bites him in the ass. That'll be my real birthday present."

"Mine too," said Caps.

Darcy looked around the mess hall. "Where's Noah?"

"Probably off somewhere sweating."

Sid was in animal research when Darcy found him. The Boss had been spending most of his time there since the return from Vancouver. A new specialist, or even better, team of specialists would be brought in soon, but in the interim, Sid was trying to learn as much as he could himself. He'd waded through a great deal of Odega's books and notes, and was only recently beginning to make headway. Not much of it was written for the layman, and Dr. Patel could only spend so much time teaching Sid biology, biochemistry, zoology, entomology and a long list of other things that ended in "ology". The journal in front of Sid was way out there: two hundred and seventy-five pages of Odega's theories on lupine psychology.

"Happy birthday, Darce." They embraced and he kissed her cheek. "I missed you at breakfast."

"I'm mad at you." Contrary to her statement, she tightened her hug.

"So I see."

She pulled back a little. "No, really. Why did you tell Toffee what you give me for my birthday?"

"He asked. I'm sorry. I didn't realize it would upset you."

Sid gave her the same thing every year. After the Change, anything superfluous was just something more to haul when the two of them inevitably moved on. Joy was fleeting, so special food or drink was consumed on the spot, rarely saved for an occasion. On her birthday, Darcy was allowed to ask any question and have it answered completely and honestly, or make any request, and if it was within his power, Sid would grant it. One year, she had him sing to her, all night. Sid had a lovely voice, and he knew the words to lots of songs, but singing embarrassed him, and the odd times she heard his melodious baritone was when he'd drifted off on some memory and didn't realize he was singing.

Darcy broke completely out of the hug and took the stool next to him.

"Sid, everywhere we go, you always wind up taking charge. You're the Boss. So many people making demands of you…my birthday gift…it's mine. It's a part of you that belongs to just me. Telling other people lessens that."

"Darcy," he touched her cheek. "You have no idea how much of me belongs to you and only you. So have you thought of what you want?"

"Yes. Harp's made no secret of wanting another doctor here, and soon. Get a plastic surgeon."

Sid shook his head. "We'll take anyone who meets Harpreet's approval. If we get a choice we'll be leaning towards someone with an ER background."

"Any doctor today has an ER background. Hell, I've got an ER background."

"Honey, in a perfect world, but don't ask me for something I can't give you."

"Well, it was a long shot. Okay, here's the backup. I want to know about Toffee. The whole story, how you met, what possessed you to bring him here. Everything."

"You're kidding." He waited for her to smile or laugh. She didn't. "You get angry because I tell Ethan about the gift and then you want to waste it on talking about him?"

"It's not about him. It's about you. Why you chose him. Why you tolerate him."

"I would have thought his actions in Vancouver proved his worth. Please ask for something else."

"He saved Noah and Lena, he may even have saved us, but only because it benefited him in some way." She folded her arms, leaned back and propped her feet on the desk, shoving Sid's book away in the process. "I'm ready for my present now."

Sid was on his way to Mount Baker the day he first met Ethan Toffee. October drove the rig, blissfully unaware that in six months she'd be cat food, victim to the war between Fenwick Prison and Compton Pit.

The Mount Baker settlement was not in, or on, Mount Baker. It was actually miles away, but Mount Baker Resources Inc. was the last real owner of the silver mine prior to the Change, and when it was first settled, everything still inside and scattered around it bore the Mount Baker logo. The people who fled to the big hole in the ground were miners themselves, and their families. The process of shoring it up, and sealing it off was a terrible fight against time, and not many of the first people in were still around by the time the place was safe to inhabit. Gradually they expanded deeper into the mines and sent out the call that haven was waiting. They broadcast constantly on the radio, despite the drain it placed on their resources. They fired flares when they had them, and kept a floodlight going all night when they knew people were coming in. Nicholas Mayhew, thirty years a mining veteran in his former life, now the leader of his community, pushed relentlessly inward. He expanded the mines beyond those initially dug, keeping his people together as huge chambers were carved out, most times with nothing but pickaxes, and desperate missions were sent to the top to create ventilation shafts farther and farther up the mountain. That was the hardest part about living in a mine; getting air. Not just air a person could work in, but air a person could live in, twenty-four hours a day, forever. Nicholas Mayhew succeeded. The biggest innovation involved two huge funnels projecting from the side of the mountain to catch the canyon winds, and a series of smaller vents that allowed old air to be pushed out. From a distance, it looked like two robotic eyes over a mouth-like grid. Caps, if he'd ever seen it, would have called the face C3P0. October just called it ugly.

Shania Twain lilted from the speakers as the truck ground to a halt at the tip of the bowl before Mount Baker's entrance. Sid couldn't take his eyes off the face in the rock.

"It's not like it's the first time you've seen it," said October, begrudging even a few minutes' addition to the length of the trip, especially when their destination was right there.

"It's just as impressive the third time. Okay, carry on."

Sid's stomach lurched as October gunned the semi over the lip and into the bowl.

"Easy does it, please."

"Sorry, keep forgetting I have royalty on board."

The shakedown crew was as efficient as anything Sid could hope for at the Pit. He and October waited in the cab until signaled from outside that it was clear. No critters had unknowingly hitched a ride on either of the trucks. October was pulling the forty-footer, Craig had brought in the twenty. Mount Baker didn't have the huge airlock and motor pool the Pit enjoyed, instead there was an outdoor area surrounded by strong wire mesh on all sides and above. Wind and time had plugged most of the mesh with dirt, and lights were needed inside just as if they'd been underground. The same wind that had darkened the motor pool, drove towering silver-and-white windmills, generating a small amount of electricity to the settlement. Heating was managed through hot springs and geothermal energy, just like at the Pit.

Nicholas Mayhew greeted them personally. October received a hug, Sid, a cautious handshake.

"Good to see you again, Sid."

"The pleasure's all mine."

Mayhew had to look up. He was a full head shorter than Sid, but wider at the shoulders.

"Is that why you came? Pleasure?"

"I thought we could have a discussion."

"If it's concerning D'Abo, my position is still the same. But you'd know that, wouldn't you?"

"Maybe I just came for a drink, then." He held out a bell-shaped bottle of amber liquid.

Mayhew took the bottle and read the label. "Brandy. What a well-thought-out bribe."

"I won't lie to you, Nicholas. I'm here to recruit."

"I knew it." He grimaced. "What are you looking for?"

"I can always beef up my transport team, but mostly I'm after hunters."

Mayhew raised the brandy to the side of his head and shook it. "Thanks for this. It's a free country but you'll understand if I don't wish you luck."

"Your permission was all I wanted. Thank you."

"It's early yet, but I think I'll taste my bribe. Join me?"

"I'll drink after I've done my hunting."

Nicholas laughed. "Can't blame a man for trying. You know I'll be slandering you all the way back to my office."

"I'd do the same in your position."

"You wouldn't even let me through the front door."

It was an awkward moment, but both knew the truth of the situation; Mount Baker needed what Compton Pit had far more than the reverse. Sid and Burle took only slight advantage of this, and Mayhew couldn't afford to give them reason to change.

"I look forward to that drink," said Sid. "After you've got a few in you, you might be more susceptible to logic and reason. Underbel's coming around."

"Like hell. You'll swing me before you'll ever convince Beverly, and you'll never swing me. There's food waiting for you. I'll have Carmichael show you around, unless you'd like to play Theseus?"

"Did that last time. I'll pass."

Even those who lived in Mount Baker got lost occasionally when visiting an unfamiliar part of the settlement. Newcomers got lost for days, and were called T's, for Theseus, the mythological hero who'd challenged the minotaur's labyrinth.

"Carmichael," Mayhew called to a dark-haired, olive-skinned man in black coveralls. "You get to be tour guide. This is Sid Halbert, Boss of Compton Pit. Never forget he's a malicious tyrant lording over the rat-infested remains of a crumbling hotel."

"Just let me know when you're ready," said Carmichael, extending a hand.

Sid sent October inside to eat and stayed to watch the last of the unloading. He focussed on the chatter between the workers, listening for names: who was admired, who was disliked. As he watched, a tapping sound from beyond the mesh persisted long enough to become annoying. Sid shook a section of the mesh until enough dirt had been dislodged that he could see outside. On a ridge, high above the lip of the bowl, a simple wooden structure was being hastily erected. He caught the attention of a bearded man wearing a Seattle Mariner's jacket.

"Is that a gallows out there?"

"More like a bird feeder."

"It's barbaric," Sid said to October in one of the mess halls. He took another bite of meat. "Is this rat?"

"Marmoset. How is it different from what we do?"

"Are you sure? It tastes like rat. It's the...hands on approach."

"The result's the same."

"Yes, but we drive them out, drop them off, and leave them."

"You've never stayed to watch?" She moved her plate aside and placed a sheet of paper from her cargo manifest on the table.

"I know what it looks like."

"Yeah, but just to make sure. Just to know the bastard's dead."

"The bastard usually pounds on the car, crying and pleading. They cling to the bumper when we drive away and hold on for as long as they can. Staying would prolong everyone's agony."

"How is that not hands on? Because we don't stay around to watch it? Or because the condemned isn't tied up?"

Around them, people became more relaxed. All conversations became hushed, and about gentler topics. People relished their food more, or took more time to savor their drink. A slight breeze lifted one edge of the cargo list and pushed it towards October's plate.

"How long do you think they leave it up there?" Sid watched as a spot of reddish sauce on the edge of the plate made contact with the paper and leached into it. A bloodlike stain slowly inched towards printed words.

October didn't notice the growing blot in front of her. She was looking around the mess hall with a bemused look on her face. "Sometimes I really like it here. I don't know how long they leave it up. I doubt it's too long. Haven't you ever done something more than leave someone to nature? I have. I tied him to a tree. Her too. Me and some other people. They deserved it. I didn't stay to watch, but I did come back to make sure."

Sid let that absorb for a while. October was content to just sit and be still. She closed her eyes, the remains of her meal forgotten. After a while, he broke the silence. "What was their crime?"

"Oh," she waved a hand at him. "I don't want to talk about it. Maybe on the ride home."

Sid finished what he decided was rat. Good rat, but rat nonetheless. The volume of conversation in the room suddenly increased and a number of people got up and put their plates in bins by the door.

"Damn!" October finally noticed that gravy had invaded her neatly written cargo list.

Sid smiled and rapped the table a couple of times. "I'll have no problems negotiating here."

"Why do you say that? Oh! There he is." She pointed at a group of people who'd just entered.

"Gray Feather?"

"Both of them. The one on the left is Billy, the one in the middle is Paul."

The group sat down at two nearby tables. Food and drink was quickly served to them as if it had been waiting for their arrival.

"You're not going to go over there?" asked October once it became apparent Sid had no intention of introducing himself.

"I will, in good time." He tore a small piece from a dry corner of the page.

"Hey! Bad enough it's stained.

"You'll live." He placed the piece on the edge of the table.

"So, did you?"

"Did I what?"

"Ever tie a person to a tree, or something like that. Lock them in a room with a dog, maybe."

"I agree that sometimes it's in the best interests of the community to kill a man. I don't believe in … I suppose it's the rope. We don't tie our lockouts up. There's the choice."

"Some choice, teeth or gravity."

The curl of paper flipped off the table and drifted to the ground.

"That's my cue," said Sid. "Can you do me a favor and…"

"I know the routine. Go ahead."

Sid walked over to the hunters and extended his hand. "Paul Gray Feather? My name's Sid Halbert."

Paul turned and smiled at Billy. It was evident they were brothers, the same tan skin, the same high cheekbones, but whereas Billy wore his hair long and braided, Paul's was cut at the neckline and hung straight. In contrast to their more Indian features, Paul had a thick, neatly trimmed beard, while Billy had a pathetic scraggle on his chin. The elder Gray Feather nodded and took Sid's hand. "I was told you'd come looking for me."

"I assume you know the reason why, then. Do you know our chief of transport, October Neriah?" He gestured and Paul and Billy looked over. Without appearing to have noticed the attention being paid to her, October curled her bad leg under the chair and stretched her good one way out, under the guise of placing it on the chair across from her. The material of her pants pulled tight, outlining a calve that had once been highly sought after in the fashion industry. She flipped her hair casually and did a very good job of not laughing. Paul was the first to look back.

"I've made her acquaintance. I'm not going anywhere, Mr. Halbert, but you're welcome to make your pitch."

"*We're* not going anywhere," said Billy.

Sid took an empty chair and gently forced it between two other people so he could sit directly across from Paul.

"Compton Pit has a lot to offer you."

"I have everything I need right here."

"We have everything," said Billy.

"Maybe there are things you don't realize you need." Sid pursed his lips. "Competent medical care, for one thing." Sid heard two different jokes about Mount Baker's physician while he'd been watching the cargo being unloaded.

"Our doctor is good enough for me."

"But is he good enough for your little sister?"

Paul smiled and shook his finger. "Nicholas told me you were good."

"You tried, you failed," said Billy.

"Well, you might not like it, Billy." Sid motioned at the sparse growth on the young man's chin. "You'd have to shave your beard. Men can't have beards at Compton Pit."

Billy, affronted at first, looked at the lush shag on his brother's face. "No beards?" The hostility in his face ebbed a little. "What else is special about Compton Pit?"

"Why can't men have beards?" asked Paul.

"We've got lots of hot water. Pressurized showers too. After a hard day they rip the dirt right off you. Not just once a month, or anything like that. Twice a week, and hunters get to shower as soon as they come home. Those," he reached out and touched a bundle of feathers pinned to Billy's jacket, "are they grouse? Nice beadwork." He immediately turned his attention back to Paul. "We have a lot of electricity, almost more than we can use. There's stereos all over the place, any music you can think of. Why I bet October's got more CDs in her truck than you have in the whole settlement."

Paul kept his eyes on Sid, but Billy, as well as few other men at the table glanced over at her. She started to stretch her leg out again, then remembered she'd already used that move, and instead opted to let her head loll briefly to one side while she idly stroked her neck with one finger. Billy imagined that she might be thinking about him while her finger ran up and down, down and up her neck. What she was really thinking about was that Sid had had his freebie, and now every time he used her in this manner, was another time she was going scare the piss out him on the drive home.

The whole mess hall seemed to quiet and listen as Sid offered up one enticement after another, by the end of the night he'd have dozens of applicants, but right now he just wanted Paul Gray Feather, and Billy if that's what it took.

"And on top of all that," Sid leaned in close, so only the Gray Feathers could hear him, "We have birth control pills." The brothers looked at each other, then back at Sid. He gave them what was almost a wink, then slouched in his chair.

Paul mulled it over.

"Take it, buddy," said one of the hunters Sid wasn't interested in. "Hell, I'll go. Take me, I'm as good as he is."

"Shut up, Drew," said Paul, shaking his head in irritation.

"It sounds pretty good," said Billy.

Paul silenced his brother with a hand on his arm.

Sid gauged the feelings of the people around the table. At least one more of them was going to proposition him before he left. Two were ambivalent, and another two were barely concealing hostility, either because an outsider was trying to take their friends, or because they hadn't been chosen instead. Out of the corner of his eye the Boss watched the feathers on Billy's jacket.

Paul was right on the cusp. He'd heard many of the things that had been offered were true. The transport team loved going to Compton Pit. Sometimes they stayed. Sometimes they had to be forced out. The medical facilities were a point of fact. Two people that Paul knew of had made the trip to Compton Pit in terrible condition. Mount Baker had nothing to offer them. At Compton Pit, both had recovered. One of them hadn't returned: Chris Indred, a bald-headed nutcase who could hunt like a wolf, and sound just like one to boot.

The feathers ruffled a little bit. Sid closed his eyes.

"No, Mr. Halbert. I'm flattered, but I'll stay here."

Sid knew it was pointless, but he fired an ego-stroke as a parting shot. "We offer a lot, but my people are worth it. I only want the best for Compton Pit."

"That lets you off the hook," said Billy, punching his brother in the shoulder.

Paul scowled. Billy started to giggle.

Sid watched the interchange with slight confusion. "The word is you're the best hunter, Paul." He forced a laugh. "Have I been talking to the wrong person?"

"I still think you're the best," said Drew, nudging Paul with his shoulder.

Paul fixed Sid with a hard stare. "I am the best *man*. Him? He is like a spirit."

"Who is he? I'd like to talk to him."

"You'd have to get to him quick. Tomorrow he'll be feeding the birds."

4. Bladearm

Sid kept his face calm, but cursed inside. The best hunter in the place was a perpetrator of execution-worthy crimes, and the next best thing had just turned him down.

"So what did he do?" He knew he wouldn't get another crack at Gray Feather. Once they parted, Mayhew was sure to do his own bit of campaigning to ensure Paul's no vote held firm. There'd be a few bribes coming Paul's way, so at least he'd benefit a little bit.

"Ask around," said Paul. "I'm sure you'll hear lots of things. Talk to Brendan Mayhew, Nicholas's kid. You'll find him in the infirmary. He's the doctor's apprentice."

Sid excused himself, drew October out of her chair and led her out into the mine shaft. "Socialize a little," he said. "Find out if any of those other guys are worth having."

"What about the guy who's going to be dangled? Should I find out about him?"

"Might as well, his name's...uh..."

"His name's Toffee," said a voice behind them. Sid turned to find Billy Gray Feather leaning against the wall. "And if you really want to know what happened, talk to Natasha Rollins."

Sid had some papers for the doctor that Harpreet had asked be personally delivered. When he entered the infirmary, the doctor wasn't there; neither was the apprentice. The only person in the room was a patient recovering from what looked like a severe beating. Both eyes were black and one was swollen nearly closed. His nose was bandaged and his lip had taken a couple of stitches. The man's ribs were wrapped, but no extremities had been broken.

"Excuse me," Sid said quietly.

"Yes?" The man sat up.

"I didn't mean for you to get up. I was wondering if you know when Dr. Haines will return."

"Not today, unless there's an emergency." The man got out of bed, wincing as he did so.

"Oh, is his apprentice coming back then? Uh...Mayhew's son?"

"Brendan. That's me." He gave a self-depreciating laugh at Sid's surprise. "You thought I was a casualty. What can I do for you?" He peered at Sid's face through his good eye. "You're the Boss aren't you? Of Compton Pit, I mean."

"That's right. Sid Halbert."

"Yeah, I met you the last time you were here." He reached out to touch the twin scars that ran down Sid's left cheek. Sid kept still and allowed the examination. "You were very lucky." He was looking at the mass of scars on the left side of Sid's neck. "You could have died with so much damage to this area."

"Someone did some damage to your areas as well. The other guy look as bad as you?"

"Worse, but he looked that way before we fought."

"What started the fight?"

"It's personal." Brendan stood defiant, then crumbled a little, sitting down again with a sigh. "What did you want the doctor for, anyway?"

"These." he handed the papers over. "There's more." Sid began the laborious process of searching his pockets. Between his jacket, vest and cargo pants, there were a lot of them. "I've been known to get in a fist fight or two. Was it over a woman?"

"You could say that."

"They've got to be here somewhere. So, tell a fellow slugger," he favored the young doctor with a rakish grin, "did he make a pass at your lady, or sleep with her?"

"He raped my fiancée."

Sid felt his foot shoving into his mouth right up to the ankle. "I'm sorry. I didn't...I'm sorry." His fingers slipped out of the last pocket. "Nothing else. I guess that was all of it."

"Thanks."

That settles it, thought Sid as he exited the infirmary. *A rapist I might just tie up and watch die. Or kill him myself.*

People gave him directions to Nicholas Mayhew's office, he thought he followed them, but somehow wound up back at the mess hall. He shouldn't have dismissed Carmichael's services so quickly.

He was debating trying to scratch up a cup of coffee when October grabbed his arm. "There you are. I was hoping you'd come back here. Come with me, there's someone I want you to meet."

"Who is it?"

"You'll see."

***

Shortly after the meeting, Carmichael caught up with Sid.

"Nicholas wanted me to remind you of that drink."

"I hadn't forgotten."

"I think he'd like to see you now."

Sid made as if to go, then stopped, cursing his watch. "Carmichael, I'm sorry, I have to meet with my transport team, in fact I should have been there almost twenty minutes ago. Tell him I'll be there as soon as I can." Without giving the man a chance to argue, Sid set off in the opposite direction.

"Do you know where you're going?" Carmichael called after him.

"Believe it or not, I do."

"I don't know," said Gripe. His real name was Ivan Podirensko, but all he did was complain and gripe, so that's what people called him.

"What's the problem?" asked Paul Gray Feather. "You think we're going to break him out?"

"I really should get Mayhew's permission for this."

"Did he say no visitors?"

"Yes, he did actually. No matter who it was."

Paul said something quietly in Sid's ear, then took Gripe aside, pulling him by a beefy arm.

"You see the man I brought?"

Gripe nodded.

"Well, do you think Toffee just appeared out of nowhere when he showed up?"

"What do you mean?"

"He had to have been somewhere else before, right?"

"Sure."

"Sid over there, he never thought he'd find this guy. It's just plain luck that he came while we have the bladearm locked up. Sid's got a daughter. Who knows, she might recover one day."

Gripe peeked over Paul's shoulder. Sid was looking at the door to the lockup, an intense gleam in his eyes, fists at his sides. Gripe looked at the door with his own hate-filled expression, then turned back to Paul.

"I'm sorry, not without Mayhew's permission." He pushed past Gray Feather and stepped in front of Sid. "I sympathize, I really do, but I can't..."

Sid took Gripe's wrist and squeezed. "I promise I won't kill him. I won't even hit him in the face. Just give me five minutes."

"You've got a daughter, don't you, Ivan?" asked Paul.

After a few tense seconds, Gripe unlocked the door. Paul stayed back while Sid was led down a ten-meter passage, then right at a fork. Another ten meters led to a dead end with a grate in the floor.

"Prisoner will stand back," Gripe said into the grate. Propped up against the wall was a wooden ladder.

"What do you do if they don't want to come out of there?" asked Sid, considering the logistics of forcing a reluctant man up a ladder.

"We stun 'em with a taser and drag 'em out."

"Why do you have a taser?"

Gripe looked at Sid as if he was stupid. "To stun guys that don't want to come out of the hole." He opened the grate then eased the ladder down. Sid climbed down into the gloom, and the ladder was withdrawn. "I'll wait for you around the corner. Just yell when you want out."

At first Sid thought a trick had been played on him, he could see nothing but darkness. The air in the hole was as dank as it was opaque. He could hear water dripping, but nothing else.

"Who the fuck are you?"

Sid spun, thinking the voice had come from behind him.

"Ethan Toffee?" he asked the void. There was no reply. "I'm not here to hurt you."

"I wasn't worried about that."

This time Sid was sure the voice came from the left.

"You'll have to step out of the light if you want to see me."

Sid knew the man was right. Reluctantly, he stretched an arm out and moved two paces from the square of light that shone down from the corridor above. His hands encountered a chain pulled taut, then the bunk it was supporting. He sat down, placing his back firmly against the wall. He listened for the other man's breathing, but heard only the drip. Spirit indeed. Gradually the murk solidified into the shape of the hole, and the one-armed man sitting against the far wall. He had long silvery-gray, or possibly white hair, Sid couldn't tell for sure, and there was something odd about his profile. He looked at the stump of the man's right arm, where it ended just past the elbow

"You got a thing for amputees?" Toffee raised the stump.

"Nobody mentioned it to me. How do you hunt?"

"I get by. So?"

"My name's Sid Halbert. I'm the Boss of—"

"Compton Pit. I've heard of you. And?"

"What kind of man are you?"

Toffee scratched his stump. "I'm sure people must have told you things."

"Lots of things. What stands out is what you seem to be capable of. And that you're a man of your word. Are you a man of your word?" Sid dropped his voice to a whisper. "I can get you out of here."

"Uh-huh. What's the price tag?"

"Did you have to hurt Brendan Mayhew so badly?"

"Kid kept gettin' up. He's got sand. I'll give him that."

"If I free you, you'll owe me a life debt. You understand that?" Sid explained to him, briefly, what it was that he wanted from the man.

Toffee sat motionless for an entire minute and then nodded his head, once.

"I'm ready," Sid called, as he rose and stepped into the light.

After Gripe withdrew the ladder and secured the grate he turned to Sid. "You couldn't get him to scream, huh? Yeah, neither could we."

When Sid finally arrived at Nicholas Mayhew's office, he was forced to wait outside, a man named Burns insisting his boss was busy. Eventually, the door opened.

"Sid, come on in."

Mayhew's office was crammed. The desk was nothing special, but it was large. The walls held schematics of the mine, maps of the area and Old World newspaper clippings, mostly to do with mining accidents and bonanza-grade silver strikes. There was a comfortable chair in front of the desk, and beside it, another, not so comfortable. Mayhew gestured at the good chair. Sid took note of the brandy bottle. It was half empty.

"Skip pleasantries?" said Mayhew, pulling a glass over and pouring a couple fingers' worth. Sid nodded. The glass was pushed towards him.

"Does the quill work?" asked Sid, pointing to a feather pen in a stand near the left edge of the desk.

"Yes. If I have to use it."

Sid picked it up. The stand came with the quill. It was all of one piece, purely ornamental. Sid put it down and gently blew on the feather until it ruffled, then took the glass and smiled at Mayhew. "You only use this thing to guage air currents."

"Damn. Who told you? No, you figured that out by yourself, didn't you?"

Sid glanced at the vents on the walls, the only wall space not covered in maps or memorabilia. "Your home breathes."

"That she does. When the winds blow hard, she takes a deep breath. When the winds die down, she lets it out. It's a rhythm, everyone here falls into it even once they figure it out. In, attention, out, relax. Keeps me sane."

"An inhalation cost me Paul Gray Feather. I wanted him."

Mayhew smiled. "Score one for me. You could have used that by the way. Not told me that you knew. I'm surprised."

"I don't want to play games with you, Nicholas."

"I think you've been playing games all day." He glanced down at the floor. "Well, fair's fair." He reached behind his desk, then placed a jar nearly full of brandy on the desk and held up his glass. "This is my first one of the day."

Sid chuckled and said, "There's a different man I want."

"Here it comes."

"Ethan Toffee."

Nicholas almost choked on his drink, but regained his composure quickly. "There's a bit of a problem with that. Tomorrow he's going to—"

"I know, feed the birds. My taking him out of here also serves your purpose."

"The hell it does. That man—"

"Spare me the propaganda. I spoke with your future daughter-in-law. She begged me to save him."

Mayhew's eyes narrowed. "Who do you think you are? Who are you to come here and—"

"She lied out of fear. She hates you for making her stick to the lie, but not as much as she hates herself."

"The ends justify means. That…*monster* in the hole…there's not a person here who doesn't want to see him dangling."

"I met at least three who don't."

Nicholas slammed his hands down on the desk. His glass almost tipped over. "That's just because he hasn't screwed them over yet. If only that stupid girl hadn't been seen. He might have kept on going then. He's committed other crimes."

"What crimes?"

"Just because I can't prove a thing doesn't mean it isn't true. He gets into people's lives, Sid. He twists them. He disrupts the harmony of the community. That in itself is enough to punish him."

"But not enough to execute him."

"Tell that to my son."

"I spoke with witnesses. Brendan threw the first punch—"

"Why do you care?"

"I told you. I want him. From what I've heard, from people October vouches for, this man is the best hunter they've ever seen. He's also not very nice. But according to those same people, he doesn't tell bald-faced lies, and he keeps his word. I might also add that you've never lost a hunter from a squad he's been on. He seems quite capable of shit disturbing, but that's only if it's there to disturb in the first place."

Mayhew's voice grew quiet, his face stiff. "Are you questioning the morale of Mount Baker?"

"Nicholas, I'm sorry your son's fiancée wanted a last fling. I can understand you're horrified that she chose him of all people. You can't take your rage at her out on this man. No matter what else he's done, you can't execute him based on a lie. I'll cease trading with you if that's what it takes."

"You wouldn't."

"I can't trust a man who would pass a death sentence based on something he knows to be false. I wouldn't feel safe sending my transport team into your territory. Who knows when one of their deaths might not be used to save face?"

"You…you tyrant." Mayhew was on his feet. "You spew all your babble about the perils of D'Abo. The only reason you hate Gascan is because he's got more pull than you do." His fury suddenly abated. He sat down, a malicious smile playing at his lips. "You want Toffee? Take him. See how much shit you have lying around. You have a sort of daughter, don't you? She pretty?"

"If you think—"

"This is a temporary stay of execution. You'll see. You'll lock him outside yourself, if someone doesn't shoot him first. It's going to cost you."

Inside, Sid cheered. He didn't think he'd find what he was looking for so quickly.

"You'll take him out of here in chains, quietly. The story will be—"

"How about he has crimes against us and people back home who want to see him dead."

"Good. You paid for extradition rights."

"Paid…I don't—"

"Yes. Fifty percent of your barter, just for that."

"Ten."

"Twenty-five. No more haggling. And one other thing, you'll leave here with him, and only him, you understand? Whoever else has signed up with you, you tell them you made a mistake. You have no openings right now."

Sid chewed on that one. He had four bunks to fill, and he'd found the people he wanted in them. "Is this a deal breaker?"

"You crossed the line here. If I came to Compton Pit and talked to you the way you just talked to me, I'd be thrown out on my ass. I love to think about what Toffee'll do when he gets to your little so-called Utopia. But if you try to take one more of my people with you, I'll see him bird food by sunrise."

Sid finished his brandy and rolled the empty glass between his hands. "Fifteen percent on the barter, and we have a deal. And I'll want any personal possessions you've confiscated from Mr. Toffee."

Mayhew pulled open a deep drawer and removed a skinbag from it. He tossed it across the desk. Sid caught it and pulled the hide away to reveal, among other things, a long blade attached to a brace.

The leader of Mount Baker had one more thing to say before he let his visitor leave the office. He held up the brandy bottle. "Sid, when I'm proven right, do come for a visit, won't you? I'll buy you a drink."

Sid folded his hands together and looked at the floor. Throughout most of the story, Darcy had listened stolidly, though at some parts she had strained to maintain composure, and at one point asked Sid to stop a while before continuing.

They sat in silence until Darcy rubbed her left eye and said, "You knew what a raccoon he was. I don't understand."

"I needed him. I have faith in my people. I made him Chief of the Hunters to keep him busy until…"

"Sid, the whole story."

"I foresaw problems. I began to feel that Shangley and his scavengers were only puppets. D'Abo wanted what we have. He was only going to wait so long for it. I couldn't let that happen, so—"

"You bought an assassin. You were going to send Toffee off to kill D'Abo. That was the life debt. His for D'Abo's. You needed someone who could do it, someone who would do it. Paul Gray Feather?"

"No. I wanted him because he's a good hunter. We might get another shot at him, too. Mount Baker's finally reopened dealings with us. I was keeping an eye out for somebody like Toffee. When I found him in that hole, it was like striking gold."

"Fool's gold. You didn't mention this to me or anyone else. You never intended to put it up for discussion."

Sid took Darcy's hand in his. "It was for the good of the Pit. For the good of everyone. Now it's unnecessary, but look what Ethan's done for us. He still hasn't lost a hunter in the field, and he may have managed to start a few fights, but that's the most of it."

"You think so, don't you?"

"Darce, if you hadn't asked, you never would have known. Don't think less of me for this."

"Just like Brendan Mayhew never would have known about his fiancée cheating on him? If they hadn't got caught at it?"

"Honey, I know he gets under your skin, but has he ever…I mean has he…"

"Would you lock him outside if he did?"

Before Sid could answer, a voice crackled over the intercom. "Boss, are you there?"

"Go ahead, Lena."

"Get down to communications. We've got trouble."

5. So the Scorpion Rode the Frog

Sid and Darcy were a little breathless when they entered SatCom.

"What's going on?" asked Sid.

Lena offered up a pair of headphones. "Our noble hunter on the other end."

"Toffee?" Sid said into the mic. Silence. He looked at Lena.

"He was there a second ago. Said it was an emergency."

"Toffee," Sid repeated, "are you there? Over."

"Halbert," came the tense voice from the speaker, *"I'm at Lockout Point. Get out here or I'm dead."*

"What? What are you doing out at—"

"There's no time! A rock slide hit me. I'm in the Hummer. The Hummer's on the edge. If I get out, it goes over. If I don't get out, it's going over."

Sid snapped his fingers at Darcy. "We're on our way."

They sped along the broken pavement. Lockout Point was over twenty minutes away at a good speed, and Lena had already lost contact with Toffee by the time Sid and Darcy made it out of the airlock. The Jeep they took was a good vehicle, especially after some of Caps's enhancements, but it still wasn't as good as the Hummer. Sid didn't want to lose either the man or the vehicle.

"Do you care if we find him alive or not?" he asked Darcy.

"Honestly, I don't know."

Sid turned off the highway and onto a narrow road that wound around and up the mountain. After a few minutes they ascended above the tree line, pine and spruce giving way to barren rock and gravel all the way to a false top. Between clear-cut logging and a copper-gold mining venture that had violated just about every environmental law once in existence, this part of the range was incapable of supporting vegetation. Nothing lived up here, but that didn't make it safe. Drawn by the sound of the motor, the teeth would work their way up, and quickly. The road leveled out onto an oval-shaped plateau almost entirely surrounded by nearly-vertical rock face. The plateau had two exits: the first was the steep road; the second was a cliff overlooking a ravine. Normally flat, the plateau was now somewhat slanted and boulder strewn. Thick dust hung in the air. There was no sign of Toffee or the Hummer.

Sid brought the vehicle to a halt, but kept the motor revving.

A darting movement from near a boulder caught his attention. A cougar was making a beeline for the Jeep's driver's side. Sid opened the door and pushed back into his seat as Darcy leaned across him with her rifle up and put two rounds into the cougar's head. Sid slammed the door shut and the two of them waited. A minute ticked by. Nothing else moved.

"I'm getting out," said Darcy, zipping up her jacket and pulling gloves on.

"Be careful, that ground's not stable. There's probably more teeth on the way."

"I'm going to be more than careful."

She took her rifle as she left. She moved to the front of the vehicle, drew a few feet of cable from the winch and wrapped it around her waist. When the hook was securely threaded through her belt, she gave Sid the thumbs up. Sid played out some cable using a lever beside the stick shift. Darcy half jumped, half shuffled her way to the edge. When she got there she gave Sid the sign to stop feeding cable and leaned over at the edge.

At the bottom of the ravine, seventy, maybe eighty feet down, she could make out the side of the Hummer, or at least what part of it wasn't covered in dirt and rocks. Surviving a fall like that was impossible. The chief of the hunters was dead. A dozen emotions ran through Darcy's mind.

"Figures he'd bring you," said Toffee.

She nearly jumped out of her skin.

He was sitting, more like clinging, to a small, recessed ledge about three meters from the top of the cliff. He was doing so with one arm, his other had nothing on it but the stump.

"How'd you get down there?"

"I dangled and swung in. Only place I could reach where the teeth can't get me. There's no room for them to land."

"You're lucky it's not eagle season." She looked at Sid and pointed over the edge of the cliff. Between the distance and the motor, he wouldn't hear her if she yelled, so she signaled to him instead. She placed her rifle on the ground and held up her hands showing ten, meaning feet. Sid played out the requested amount of slack and watched Darcy go over the edge. The cable slackened a little, then jerked tight, twice. Sid flipped the lever and reeled the cable back in. Darcy appeared over the edge, with Toffee clinging to her. They disengaged the moment they had ground under their feet and wasted no time getting into the Jeep.

Toffee collapsed into the backseat as Darcy resumed her place in the front.

"Where's your arm?" asked Darcy

"It's all in the Hummer. My new arm, my blade, my rifle and my gun. Damn! Those were the best weapons I've ever had."

Sid worked the vehicle through a cautious three-point turn and started back down the road.

"What were you doing with your blade off?" Sid asked, waiting for something nasty to come charging up at them.

"My stump was itchy, I took my stuff off and the slide hit me. Didn't even feel it coming. I didn't get a chance to scoop anything before I bailed. I jumped down to that ledge to save my ass."

"Why were you here in the first place?"

"Lazy hunting. I figured I'd wait and shoot whatever came at me. Wasn't expecting it to be part of the mountain."

"You were very lucky," said Darcy.

"Don't run your mouths off about it." He stared out the window. "I'm supposed to be able to avoid this sort of thing."

The day shift was over and dinner was on the tables. Darcy knew there was a cake for her, but at her request Roshi wasn't going to bring it out publicly. It was just the one cake and not enough to serve everyone who'd want a piece. She was surprised not to see Noah again. She hadn't seen him all day.

Toffee's rock slide couldn't be kept completely secret; there was, after all, the Pit's Hummer to account for. The story had changed so that Toffee wasn't actually in the vehicle at the time. At least that way he didn't seem to have been caught napping, or scratching as the case may be.

After dinner, Darcy joined Caps and Lena in the Enchanted Forest, a pipe bay on the lower level decorated with Christmas lights. They gave her booze and chocolates. The chocolates were Old World, and although the plastic wrap was unbroken, they'd turned white inside the box. Darcy tried one and almost broke a tooth.

"Maybe they'll soften if you suck on them a while," said Lena hopefully.

The booze was one bottle of Bacardi rum and one bottle of Jose Cuervo tequila. Liquor was being passed around in the Pit so much now, it almost seemed to be a type of currency. Some people weren't even opening their bottles, instead hoarding them to pay for other services at a later date. So much of it was coming in from the city, a layer of dust had formed over Dr. Patel's still.

Darcy took a huge hit off Caps's pot pipe when it was offered to her. She'd decided she too would hoard her liquor, and so needed an alternative poison for the evening. She told them the truth about Toffee on the ridge, swearing them to secrecy of course.

"Awww," said Caps. "Did poor little baby lose his spider sense?"

Darcy was about to ask about Noah when he showed up, appearing through the steam to hunker down beside her. He handed her a fat skinbag.

"For me?" she said innocently, batting her eyelids. Then she giggled.

Noah looked at Caps and mimed taking a hit.

"Want some?" asked the artist. Noah shook his head.

Darcy tried to figure out what was inside by squeezing the object through the hide.

"Careful," said Noah. "It's delicate."

"I don't know if I should open this. Gifts have all been mean to me today."

"This one won't be."

She undid the thong and let the skin fall away. She held up the item inside. "It's…it's an ugly ball of glass on a stick."

"Wait. Here." Noah took it from her, stuck the opposite end of the stick into a base, then handed it back.

"Now it's an ugly ball of glass on a stand. Thank you, Noah, however did you know?"

"Very funny." He took it from her once more and placed it on the ground. From his pocket, he withdrew a small, but powerful flashlight. "This is a solar panel," he said, tapping the base. He shined the light directly on the panel. After a few seconds, the object made a tiny whirring noise, and the ball of glass began to move. Layers of it separated and swung down, until, when its metamorphosis was complete, it was no longer a lumpy ball, but a glass rose. "There's a switch on the side." He showed her. "Flip, shine the light on it again, and it'll close. I'll show you."

Darcy pulled the rose just out of his reach. "Don't. I like it open." She looked at it from every angle, allowing the light of the forest's colored bulbs to bleed through the glass petals. "It's beautiful. How long did it take you to make?"

"I made the motor. Neil made the rose."

"Who's Neil?"

"Eggerson. Neil Eggerson. You didn't know that?"

Darcy shook her head. She looked over at Caps and Lena. Lena shrugged but Caps claimed he knew.

Darcy returned her attention to the rose. "Thank you." She kissed Noah on the cheek. "It's the best gift I've gotten all day."

Later on, after Caps and Lena left, Noah and Darcy sat beside each other, not saying anything, just watching the lights change. For a few minutes, Darcy rested her head on Noah's shoulder. She said good night and left, but Noah stayed where he was, still feeling the weight of her head, the scent of her hair. Eventually he shut the lights off and turned in, but a full night's sleep was not to be his.

He didn't know how long he'd been out when Darcy woke him, it felt like only a few moments. She shook him gently with one hand. "Noah, wake up."

"I'm awake. You're supposed to knock."

He reached out and flipped on his light. Darcy was in a nightshirt, with a blanket draped over one arm. The look of pain on her face frightened him. "Darcy, what—" he stopped. There was blood on her leg, and on the floor, little splatters of it leading all the way to his door. He was fully alert in an eye blink. "What happened?"

"It's okay. I'm alright, mostly. Sorry about the mess." She pulled the blanket away. Dried blood stained her fingers where they peeked out from the end of a PVC pipe that encompassed her arm from palm to elbow. It appeared to be floating around her arm, rather than hanging from it. Noah looked in the pipe.

"What *is* this thing?" The illusion of floating was created by the ring of nails that kept Darcy's arm dead center in the pipe.

"I was trying to find out. I don't know why...probably the pot. I stuck my arm in it. As you can see..."

"You can't get it back out."

"I tried pulling on it. That didn't work." She left the weight of her arm in Noah's hands and sank into his rocking chair.

Noah wrapped his blanket around his waist to cover his nudity, then sat up, getting a better look at Darcy's predicament. "It's kind of like a Chinese finger trap, except it's got your arm." He pulled at it slightly. Darcy sucked air in through her teeth. A rivulet of blood ran down her arm and dripped into the bottom of the pipe. "Shouldn't we wake Dr. Patel? Or Caps?"

"Harp'll blab about it to everyone. Caps'll make a poster out of it. Would you stick your arm in this thing?"

"Hell no."

"Exactly, I feel like an idiot."

"But...those nails are really in there, I—"

"Noah, *please*, just get it off me. I know you can get it off me."

He turned the chair so she was facing the desk, then he placed the pipe on the desk and stacked books under her elbow and fingertips so she could relax without putting additional pressure on the nails in any direction. With her back to him, Noah doffed the sheet and pulled on a pair of coveralls. They still shared the same shower slot, were still naked before each other for a few minutes twice a week, but beyond the showers, it was inappropriate. He couldn't help but notice how her nightshirt had ridden up her thigh a little bit. The pale hair on her legs did nothing to deter from their shape.

Back to the task at hand, boy. Noah didn't have a tool kit in his room, but he did have a folding pair of pliers that contained screwdrivers and other tools within its handles. It was a Leatherman, one of many acquired during some shopping spree or another. Noah opened his up and steadied the PVC pipe with one hand while grasping at the head of one nail with the pliers. He pulled. The thin edge of the nail slipped out with a jerk. Noah tried to slip the edge of the knife under a nail head. A sliver of the knife's edge broke off.

"Those are really in there," he repeated.

Noah thought he'd cut himself, then realized it was her blood on his fingers. He looked inside the pipe and studied the nails. They were uniformly positioned. The angle of insertion was only slightly out of alignment, making for a near perfect circle of points in the pipe's middle. Those points were all embedded halfway up Darcy's forearm.

"I have to tinker a little. It'll probably hurt."

Darcy looked away and whispered, "Do what you have to do."

Noah reached in and jiggled a nail. He grasped it with the pliers and tried to force it out of the pipe. It wouldn't budge. "Man, what were these put in with? A sledgehammer?"

"Would a nail gun put them in that tight?"

"Do we have a nail gun?"

"Yes. Where are you going?"

Noah pulled his boots on over bare feet. "To my workshop. I'll be back in a few minutes."

He'd never forget the expression on her face when he returned with a hacksaw and bolt cutters. "Do you want something to bite down on?"

The first and second cuts with the hacksaw were easy, for Noah, anyway. Darcy just needed to rotate her arm. For the last cut, she had to kneel in order to expose the underside of the pipe. She clenched her teeth through the vibrations, but blood was now dripping from both ends of the pipe. With her sitting in the chair again, Noah slipped a section of the pipe off, exposing the nails. Darcy held the pipe while Noah snipped around her arm with the bolt cutters. When the last nail was cut, he slid the pipe off, leaving Darcy with thirteen short spikes sticking out of her arm. She reached to pull one out.

"Wait." Noah was headed for the door again. This time he returned with bandages and a bottle of booze. "Sorry, I should have grabbed these the first time out."

Noah pulled the nails out as quickly as he could. When they were all out, each making a light clink as they hit the bottom of an empty mug, he swabbed the wounds and then wrapped a bandage all the way around her arm. "You'll have to have Dr. Patel look at this tomorrow."

"Maybe. At least he won't see my arm stuck in the pipe. Go ahead, I know you've been holding back."

"Huh?"

"Don't you want to make fun of me?"

Noah hadn't even considered it. "I just want to know what you were thinking."

"I guess I wasn't."

"Anything going through that pipe, definitely a one-way trip."

"What did you say?"

"I said anything going through the pipe was a—"

"No." She was on her feet. Noah watched perplexed as Darcy mumbled to herself while making gestures in the air. She came to a decision and cupped her hands to her face. When she pulled them away, a tear glittered at the corner of one eye. "Come on, sun boy."

"Where do you want to go?"

"Into the caverns. I'll get dressed."

"Can't it wait until tomorrow? You should go to bed, and so should I."

"Seth brings the roof down tomorrow, and I couldn't sleep now if my life depended on it. You can't go to bed. I need you."

"Why?"

"I need the fork in cavern three lit up like daylight. You have to be my sun boy."

The cavern guards were surprised at the appearance of two chiefs hours before sunrise. They were even more surprised at being drafted into mule duty. Still, they were happy for the activity. The Mimi was gone from the cave but at this time of year, anything non-human in the caverns was taking a nice long nap. It didn't take long to have the section of cavern Darcy specified lit up, as she put it, like daylight.

"Each of you take a section of wall and search it," Darcy instructed her crew. "Push anything that looks like it will move. Loose rocks, cracks. If you find nothing, start prodding stuff that looks solid."

"Shouldn't at least one of us stand guard?" asked Patricia. She always seemed to pull the sunrise shift. "We'll be making a lot of noise. It might wake something up."

Darcy shook her head. "The teeth have been avoiding these caves for a long time now. They'll have a learned aversion to it."

"Wolves came in topside the first chance they got," said Noah.

Darcy gave a brisk nod. "Keep your weapons close."

"What are we looking for?"

"I don't know. Anything that doesn't belong, especially PVC pipes with nails in them. Let's get to it."

There were a lot of things that moved along the cavern walls. The first problem was not tripping over hastily-laid cables. The second was not tripping over the rocks and chunks of stone that quickly accrued on the ground as the searchers pulled at everything they could.

Noah looked at the grit wedged under his fingernails. Only the left thumb didn't have a dark ellipse at its end.

"Noah, come here." It was Darcy's voice, echoing a little.

At first he couldn't find her, then he saw a smear of light moving around deeper into the passage. She'd left the safely-lit area, and the protection of other guns. Noah motioned for a guard to join him. He took a flashlight and moved to where Darcy was playing with a pile of rocks.

"Do you think this looks natural?" she asked. The pile went almost to the ceiling.

"Looks like an old cave in. You're acting obsessive here, and you still haven't told me what this is about."

She shone her flashlight at the ceiling. "I don't think these stones came from up there." She pulled a few rocks away, then glanced over her shoulder. "Come on! Help me here."

"I'll help," said Noah, handing his flashlight to the guard. "You keep your eyes open."

The pile quickly diminished under their dual labor. None of the rocks were difficult to move. Soon it was evident there was an opening behind the pile. When a head-sized hole was cleared, Noah shone a beam through it.

"It looks like there's another passage here," he said.

Darcy tore at the pile until there was nothing left to bar their way. The passage opening was low. They had to crouch in order to enter. The flashlight's beam caught reflective metal. Darcy stoop-walked over to it, small pebbles making her footing unsure. There was a pair of identical objects, large metal tins. She picked one of them up.

"What do you make of this?" She held it out.

"It looks like one of Roshi's tins. Dry goods."

"How do you know what his tins look like?"

"You know how much time I spend in the kitchen trying to make him happy? I might as well move my bed in there sometimes. Ouch!" He was down on all fours. One of the pebbles dug painfully into this hand.

Darcy's beam swept along the passage wall, catching more metal. This turned out to be a jumble of mesh and a pile of PVC pipes. Each of the pipes was exactly alike, angled nails ringing the middle.

"These pebbles are all the same size," said Noah. "They look like…these aren't pebbles."

"They're rat droppings."

She moved back towards the small opening and ran her fingers along the stone. Metal fasteners were spaced intermittently all along the edge.

Noah had found the pile of PVC pipes and tried to remove one, but they were all stuck together by the mesh. He crawled out of the passage to find Darcy had sent the guard back to the pool of light.

"I shouldn't have pushed," she said. "I should have just waited until the roof was brought down and then I'd never have known."

Noah was standing, brushing petrified rat droppings off his legs. Darcy sat on the ground, her back against the wall and her knees hugged to her chest.

"Are you okay?"

"Noah, please, go away."

He hunkered down and put a hand on her arm. She shrank from his touch, didn't look at him as he left.

When Noah was a safe enough distance away, she pulled her legs tight and stared at nothing. It was too much. It was just too much.

"Return to your positions," she said as she rejoined the group. "Don't tell anyone what you've seen here. That's a serious order." Noah had waited for her and kept pace silently as they returned to the main cavern entrance. When they reached the door back into the Pit, he could no longer hold his tongue.

"I'm chief of photovoltaics, I think that gives me clearance to know what this about. Is it a leftover from Shangley?"

Darcy stopped for a moment, surprised she hadn't considered the possibility. No, that would be too easy. "Thanks for all your help. I need to talk to Sid. I'll… I'll explain everything later. Tell Eggerson he was right. The pipe was for torture.

Becoming instantly awake was a skill Sid would never lose. He'd acquired it as an RCMP officer in a tragically undermanned jurisdiction, and it served him well during the early years after the Change. That didn't stop him from being outraged, however, at being dragged from his bed and made to follow Darcy into the tiny passage without so much as a cup of coffee to get him started.

"What is all this?" He swung his light from the PVC to the tins.

"I wanted you to see it, so you didn't think I was crazy. Rat droppings." She let a small number of them tumble from her hand.

"So what? We're outside of Mimi range. There'll be rats here when it's warmer."

"These pipes are one-way traps. They were put up over there somewhere." She shone her light in the opposite direction from the opening. "There was a hide stretch across the hole, and grain or something like it scattered around in here. The rats—"

"I see it. The rats gathered in this cave. When all the food was gone, and they couldn't come back the way they'd come…"

Darcy had crawled back to the entrance. "They chewed their way through the hide and spilled out into passage three. Travis was…" her voice caught in her throat. "Travis was murdered." The flashlight fell from her hand. Saying it out loud broke the fragile dams she'd built against the tide. The anger would come later, and it would be like a force of nature, but right now the horror and loss was all she felt, as if her beloved Travis had just died that night. "Oh, God. Oh, God, Sid. He was murdered."

Sid rushed to embrace her. "Hold yourself together, kiddo. Those are your people back there. I'll get you back to your room."

Once in Darcy's quarters, Sid held her hand while she let it all go. When the tears had finally played themselves out, he asked her. "Do you have any suspects?"

The anger rose now, pushing her misery away, but it wasn't gone completely, and it never would be.

"As if you need to ask."

"What time is it?" asked Toffee in a foggy voice, sitting up in bed and pulling the sheets around him.

"Drop the act." Darcy knew the hunter could come awake as quickly, if not quicker, than she and Sid could. "I'm cashing in my birthday gift."

"Now?" He looked at Sid, who blocked the doorway. "You looking for some three-way action, Red? I don't swing that way. Tell Halbert to get lost and bring—"

"It's not just a request. I get any question answered, fully and truthfully."

"Are you a man of your word?" asked Sid.

Any pretense of fatigue dropped from Toffee's face. He sat up straight. "Yeah."

"Good," said Darcy. "Did you engineer the rat swarm that killed Travis Jones?"

Toffee's expression didn't change. "Red, can I speak to you alone?"

"Answer her," said Sid quietly.

Toffee kept his focus on Darcy. "Five minutes alone." His eyes seemed to say, *We all have secrets.*

"Five minutes. I'll be alright, Sid."

The Boss looked like he was going to argue, then he opened the door. "I'll be right outside."

"Sit down," the hunter gestured to the only chair in his room. Darcy didn't move. "Fine. This doesn't have to end like this."

"You mean like it always does for you? Sid told me everything."

"He doesn't know anywhere near everything. I didn't just go into the water for your staff. I went in for Bjossa's teeth. I wanted them as ornaments. I've never wanted ornaments before."

"So?"

His reply was so quiet she almost didn't hear him. "This feels like home to me."

"Don't you dare—"

"He wasn't supposed to die. It was just supposed to slow him down…turn a short patrol into a long one. He went into the caves early and without a burn team. Any idea why he did that?"

Because of me, Darcy thought, *because I yelled at him.*

It looked as if Toffee had read her mind. He leaned back and put his hand behind his head. "I just wanted him busy for the night. So we could be busy for the night."

Underneath the smugness, the air of contempt, Darcy thought she detected something else behind his eyes. It was almost like pleading. This tiny uncertainty kept her from killing him on the spot. Instead she opened the door. True to his word, Sid was right outside. She nodded. Sid stepped into the room and cleared the doorway. Four guards entered, one of them carried manacles.

"After sunrise," said Darcy, "we lock you outside. Nobody's coming to save you this time."

The six of them walked Toffee, clinking, to the cells. When the doors were closed and Sid and Darcy were alone, he put his hands on her shoulders. She pulled away.

"You knew what he was," she said, "and you brought him here anyway."

Toffee crossed his legs beneath him and tried for the umpteenth time to gain peace. He slowed his breathing, forgot the stone and bars around him and pictured ice. Of all the landscapes he'd traipsed across for fun and profit, it was the frozen wastelands that haunted him. The familiar and much needed serenity of the transcendental state hovered just out of reach. With a snarl he gave up. His mind was too busy. For the second time in his life, the hunter was tortured with ifs. *If* he hadn't left the one pipe and the hide outside the trap cave when he sealed the hole, choosing to hide them elsewhere; *if* guards hadn't been there to keep him from destroying the additional evidence once and for all; *if* Travis Jones hadn't gone into the caves alone...*if* Darcy McCullough didn't matter.

Seducing women had always been easy for him. Even after the fox had taken a piece of his nose and destroyed his looks forever, it was still easy. His presence was overwhelming, and the right thing to say always spilled out of his mouth. Toffee never seemed to be duplicitous, or needy, at least not to the prey. It was all so simple when he had nothing at stake. The only thing that had kept him from bedding the artist's darling Lena was that he hadn't gotten around to it yet. Besides, he was waiting for the two of them to get hitched. Wives were so much more fun to nail than girlfriends.

The hunter replayed his last conversation with Darcy repeatedly in his mind. Ten years earlier he'd been in a similar situation. Toffee didn't have the words then. He didn't have them now.

6. How to be Cold

July, Year of the Change

Toffee stared up pine board ceiling, watching the creeping shadows. They were cast by light coming through the steel mesh covering the bedroom window, reflected up by the windshield of a snowmobile outside. The snowmobile hadn't moved in a month, so if the sunlight was hitting it, it was time to get up. Actually, it had been time to get up when Toffee'd first opened his eyes an hour before. There was a noise from somewhere beyond the room, a distant scraping sound. Toffee winced, told himself not to wish, not to hope, threw off the covers and looked at his stump. The bandages had come off last week. He swung his legs out of bed and tried not to touch his nose. He knew what it felt like. He touched it anyway.

The floorboards creaked as he stood and within seconds the door swung open. The woman was short and round, brown skinned and today her long black hair was pinned back with whalebone combs. She stood there, smiling at him, always smiling, as if things were normal—as if there were more than three people alive in the village.

He envied her serenity. It had been so long since he'd smiled, his face had forgotten how.

The woman made a nonsense sound, pointed at his stomach and said, "*Naklisimayok.*"

He nodded. He was hungry this morning. That at least was a good sign.

Toffee pulled on a pair of jeans a half-size too large. That there'd once been somebody in the village close to his size was a stroke of luck, but not so great a stroke as Nutaraluk Inukpuk rescuing him in the first place from where he lay trapped in a knocked over sled-shack pinned down by the weight of a dead bear.

Toffee pulled on a shirt, then a sweater, then a jacket, almost managing to forget that the jacket's right cuff was pinned up at the shoulder.

The distant scraping noise became an incessant grinding.

The smell of boiled seal startled him. Not that seal meat would be a rare smell—the shock was that he could smell anything at all. He sniffed. It was a shallow, wheezing sniff, but that he'd managed it was a true victory. His nose was fixing itself, rebuilding nasal passages from within. Maybe soon sleep wouldn't involve mouth-breathing his way to a sore throat every morning.

Toffee's mouth watered. If he could smell again, maybe he could taste again.

He left behind the bare room and made his way to the kitchen, passing a hallway window that offered a good view of the snowed-in village. There wasn't much to it: three clapboard houses, a barn-like thing that served as town hall, school and church, and the trades building—the only building possessing a second floor. The place was called Kipingoyok, pop. 99; fifteen people, sixty-four dogs.

Each Husky was part of a sixteen-dog sled team. Each weighed between forty and fifty-five pounds, could individually pull twenty times its own weight and they all knew how to work as a unit.

Toffee entered the kitchen to find it empty. She'd gone somewhere else, but two pieces of seal lay steaming on a sideboard. Toffee picked one of them up and forgot to squeeze it before taking a bite. Oil dribbled down his lips as blubber and meat ignited his taste buds. He wiped his mouth with the back of his hand and started in on the second piece.

The grinding sound stopped.

Nutaraluk and Mayureak Inukpuk worked and lived in the trades building. It housed a generator, small machine shop, forge and anvil and the tools of a gunsmith. On the day of the Change, Mayureak huddled on the floor of a second floor room, pudgy hands over her ears, letting out tiny yelps each time her husband, leaning from a window, shot another dog. Fortunately for them only one team was at home. The rest were out there…somewhere.

"You come," said Nutaraluk, leaning into the kitchen. Metal filings glittered in his black hair and safety goggles dangled around his neck. Toffee gulped from a pitcher of water, then complied. They moved down a short corridor leading to the work area. Nutaraluk stopped suddenly and pivoted, slashing his hand through the air, making *whooshing* sounds with his mouth.

Toffee blinked at this impromptu Kung Fu movie impression.

Nutaraluk grinned and nodded. "Good for you," he said, in motion again, now tugging at the front of Toffee's jacket to hurry him along.

They entered the machine shop where Mayureak stood near a work bench and a pedal-driven grinding wheel.

"Sit," said Nutaraluk, indicating a stool near the bench.

The moment Toffee's butt hit the stool, Mayureak was working at his clothes, pushing off his jacket, tugging at his sweater.

"The hell are you doing?" Toffee protested.

The little Inuit man held up some implement of bondage, fashioned out of strips of metal and dog collars. He looked very satisfied with himself.

Mayureak giggled and in one hard yank had Toffee's sweater right over his head and down his arm. She skipped away as he recoiled and then her hands were inside his shirt.

Nutaraluk held up a length of chain, looking between it and Toffee as if measuring.

"Okay, you two have lost it," said Toffee, giving the woman a hard shove. "You come near me with—"

"It is good," said Nutaraluk. "You will be *kapvik*."

"I don't know that word. What are you doing?" The last was to Mayureak who held his half arm tenderly, one hand on his tricep the other cupping his stump. With one fingernail she scratched the lump of flesh, that unnatural dome, that abhorrent terminus. Toffee felt lightheaded; nauseous.

She eased his right arm from the shirt and Nutaraluk strapped the dog-collar-and-metal thing over Toffee's shoulder and around his upper arm. Next came a deerskin-padded metal cup that fit snug to the stump. Two chains and two straps, cinched tight, secured the cup to the dog collars. A metal sleeve four inches long and an inch-and-a-half wide projected from the center of the cup.

Nutaraluk wiggled his right arm up and down and nodded encouragingly.

Toffee mimicked the action, watching the cup hold firm to his stump.

"I get the idea," said Toffee. "Okay, I get the idea." He stared at the metal sleeve. "What am I supposed to do with this?"

The little man held up a long, slim blade.

Toffee smiled.

He was running, testing his stamina, speed and balance. More weight on the right arm was a must. The world couldn't seem to make up its mind about finally letting summer have a go and the ice shelf was both very sturdy and very fragile. Toffee veered left, because he felt that's what he should do. The most important thing about this run was getting in touch with his gut. Toffee lived by his gut. He'd learned to follow its counsel without hesitation, but since the day the animals got all frisky, he thought his gut was a damned liar.

Toffee came to an abrupt halt. To the south, a gray-blue strip of ocean nibbled at the edge of the ice shelf. His gut said hang a left, but his eyes showed him solid ground. He struggled with himself. Take a step or two, get some proof. He snarled and turned back towards the village. Faith, by definition, required no proof.

The smell of gasoline hung in the air of the trade building's foyer. Toffee kicked off his boots, pulled his glove off, finger by finger with his teeth, then shrugged out of his jacket and hung it on a wall-mounted peg. Nutaraluk was probably fueling up the generator. Toffee reached the room where the radio was stored about the same time the generator sputtered and roared into life somewhere deep in the machine shop. With a bit of awkwardness, he one-handed the headset over his ears and flicked the power toggle a few times until the indicator lights came on and static hissed.

Toffee sat down on a wooden stool, eyed the bikini-clad hoochie girl in the beer poster tacked to the wall, then turned the dial.

"Anybody out there?" he asked the static. "Anybody at all?"

Mayureak came into the room and sat down on the floor, back to the wall. She draped a pair of sealskin leggings across her lap and set to work on them with a needle. Nutaraluk came in a few moments later, chewing on something.

"Is that a power bar?" Toffee asked after eying the edge of the foil wrapper.

Nutaraluk nodded and held it out in offering.

"I'd rather eat tree bark." Toffee went back to twisting the dial, repeating his general broadcast.

Nothing was on the air. No emergency broadcasts, nothing. Toffee hated radio time. It was a waste of fuel. Worse, it was a chance to hope. Hope sucked.

After a while Toffee pulled off the headset and went to make some coffee. Behind him he could hear Nutaraluk speaking into the headset mic, talking in both English and Russian, trying not to plead.

The water in the kettle had nearly boiled when a scream from Mayureak brought Toffee running back.

"Hello, please repeat," said a voice through the static. *"Who is there? Is there somebody out there?"* A man's voice, slight Texas drawl.

Nutaraluk was dancing, stomping his feet. He planted the headset over Toffee's ears and scooped Mayureak up in his arms.

"We read you. Over," said Toffee.

"Goddamn. Who is this? Where are you? Over."

"We're..." Toffee paused, eyes narrowing. "Identify yourself. Over."

"Shawn Huggins. Facet Exploration. I'm on a boat. Over."

"I know this man," said Nutaraluk. "I know him."

Toffee ignored the Inuit. A boat. Escape. He shook his head. Get the facts first. "We're in a place called Kipingoyok. What is your status? Over."

"I know that place. Yeah, we've got some supplies stored there. Hey...don't you have a lot of dogs in that village? Over."

The man's question gave Toffee a thousand answers, not a single one of them wanted.

"The dogs are dead. What is your status? Over?"

"There's seven of us. We can make it to you. Goddamn it's good to hear another voice. We're almost out of gas. Over."

Out of gas. No escape. Seven more mouths to feed. Hope sucked.

Nutaraluk was already out the door. He'd have the snowmobiles ready to go in minutes.

"We'll meet you along the ice shelf," said Toffee. "Over."

The grimy thirty-six footer chugged towards them. It was a kind of grayish green with the name *Oklahoma Belle* painted on one side. People in filthy parkas leaned over the railings. Rifle barrels peeked over the shoulders of two of them. Mayureak waved. A few of the people waved back. As the boat pulled alongside the edge of the ice, Toffee noticed a pair of metal drums, on their sides, fixed to the stern. From small holes punched in the drum lids, a pinkish fluid dribbled out and down into the sea.

An anchor arced down from above and crunched into the ice.

"Goddamn!" said a ruddy face from deep inside a fur-lined hood. "Goddamn!" The man jumped from the side of the boat, landed in a stumbling crouch, and threw his arms around Toffee.

Another pair of people dropped down. One used a mallet to pound spikes into the ice while the other waited for lines to be thrown over.

As Toffee muscled his way out of the hug, he wished for a second that a deerskin sheath wasn't wrapped around his blade.

"Nuta, that you?" asked Shawn Huggins. "Nuta, you old sonofabitch!" He rushed to embrace the Inuit.

Five new people were now on the ice. Two more were still in the boat, handing down packs and boxes. All of them were men. Toffee glanced at Mayureak where she sat grinning from her snowmobile. *Nine men and one woman*, he thought. *You won't be grinning much longer.* He counted firearms; there were four visible rifles amongst the newcomers.

"Jason Beckworth," said a man with a thick brown moustache. He extended his right hand to Toffee, then pulled it back, studying the sheathed blade.

"How's the sea life been?" Toffee asked, keeping an eye on the water.

"Psychotic," said one of the men catching packs.

"What's that stuff you're leaking?" Toffee pointed at the barrels.

"That's our saving grace," said Shawn, pulling back his hood to reveal thick blond hair. "The stuff in the water hates it. They give us a wide berth. It's something we're not really supposed to have up here. Couldn't justify its need in an environmental impact study or some bullshit like that. I can sure justify it now."

The last two men dropped down and began loading things onto the sleds hooked to the snowmobiles.

"You see others?" asked Nutaraluk. "Which village you come from?"

"No village, Nuta," said Shawn. "Thompson Research Station. We held up there okay until we were overrun."

"Dogs?" asked Toffee. "Foxes?"

Shawn and Jason exchanged a look.

"Lemmings," said Shawn.

"Collared Lemmings to be specific," said Jason, forcing a laugh. "Almost makes a man want to jump off a cliff."

Toffee felt a headache coming on. Lemmings never committed mass suicide. That was one of Disney's big lies to the world. Humanity was screwed. They knew nothing about the enemy. "K" 'cause I'll kill you. Em oh yoo ess ee.

Ropes and tarps were thrown over the sleds. Three of the men climbed back on the boat.

There wasn't much wind. The sea was calm but something caused a long, low swell in the water to the south. The swell was gone as soon as it had appeared. If Toffee had blinked, he'd have missed it. His gaze returned to the metal drums.

"So you've been hugging the coast, trailing that toxic gunk behind you?"

"Yessir," said Shawn. "Our last two barrels there. Hey, Nuta, how much diesel we got stashed at your place?"

A vibration ran up Toffee's legs.

Nutaraluk looked down, face questioning.

The vibration came again.

"Get off the ice," said Toffee. "GET OFF THE BOAT!" he screamed.

The diamond explorers were staring at Toffee, looking in all directions, even out to sea. No animals were in sight.

"The ice is shifting some, that's all," said Shawn. "You kind of new in these parts or something? Not that I have a problem with paranoia, friend. Last week I saw a walrus..."

Toffee wasn't listening. He grabbed Nutaraluk under one arm and threw him onto one of the snowmobiles. "Move!"

Nutaraluk obeyed, not from fear of shifting ice, but from sudden fear of Toffee. Mayureak throttled up and followed after her husband. Toffee ran.

"Have you lost your minds?" Shawn called after them. "There's nothing out here!"

The ground exploded. Huge chunks of ice blasted into the air as a hundred tons of bowhead whale smashed up from below. Sixty feet long, with a sixteen-foot mouth, curved like an archer's bow, the leviathan shoved its head up into the air, a dark tower within a sparkling cloud of ice and water.

Three of the men who'd been standing on the ice were gone. The fourth, possibly Shawn, lay stunned a few feet from the new hole in the shelf. The whale sank out of sight.

The man—it *was* Shawn—rocked to one side then rolled to his knees. Water splashed him as a tail, twenty-five feet from fluke tip to fluke tip, rose up in the air. He had enough time to look at the tail before it slapped down like a hand squishing a bug. Shawn Huggins was not so much crushed into the ice as splattered across it.

The boat shuddered from bow to stern. One of the men tried to jump from it, but as he gripped the rail, the boat rolled. A tail rose near the now inverted prow. With a couple of loud crunches and a scream of metal, *Oklahoma Belle* was done for.

Nutaraluk stopped his snowmobile and Mayureak did the same. They looked past Toffee running towards them.

"Keep going," gasped Toffee.

All over the place, bits of ice jumped into the air.

"Dump the sleds. Forget them. We've got to move."

Another geyser of ice and water erupted near the first hole. This time only the tip of the whale's giant head poked up before disappearing. Almost as soon as the watery hole was clear, seals spat out onto the ice like giant mutant slugs.

"I figure there's less than ten thousand bowhead left," Toffee said as he unhitched the sled from Mayureak's snowmobile and dropped onto the seat behind her. "But right now, just about every one of them could be underneath us."

Nutaraluk stared at the seals barking and undulating their way up the ice. The vibrations in the ground had become a rhythmic thrum.

"They're destroying the shelf," said Toffee. "They're perforating it like toilet paper." He cuffed Mayureak across the back of the head. "Go!"

They hit the village but instead of going to ground, Nutaraluk refueled the snowmobiles and harnessed to one a sled bearing two barrels of gas. Mayureak grabbed survival packs from the trades building and, after helping Toffee into one of them, ran back inside.

The village of Kipingoyok was built right on the ice shelf, far enough from the sea that the coastal fauna wasn't an immediate threat. The bowheads were changing that. Shawn Huggins had united the pods, drawing their attention with a toxic pink trail.

Nutaraluk shrieked.

Toffee slid the sheath off his blade and looked around. There weren't any animals; it was worse than that. Nutaraluk's anguish was internal. His eyes gleamed then went empty. His moan became a chant, his hands beat on a fuel barrel. He called out to *Tulugaak*, the Creator.

A sharp *crack* followed by a muted rumble preceded a tremor that creaked the timbers of the village.

"This ain't the time, Nuta!" Toffee yelled. "Woman," he called to the trades building. "Get your ass out here!"

Of course they knew the ice. The bowheads would understand it the way a jewel cutter knew precious stones: every flaw, every weakness. They had the right tool for the job. The whales' triangle-shaped heads were designed to break through ice in order to breathe. It was a navy's wet dream—if the enemy is too far inland, move the coastline.

Nutaraluk paid no attention to what could only have been acres of the shelf becoming part of the ocean. His chant increased in fervor then abruptly broke off. His eyes fixed on Toffee. "It is you," he said.

There wasn't a word foul enough for what Toffee felt upon hearing this. It was something he'd been afraid of since the whole mess started, that his hosts would decide it wasn't man the animals were after, but white man.

Nutaraluk took a step back, startled by the buildings around him. He bumped into the snowmobile and jerked away as if burned.

"You really need to get a grip," said Toffee.

The Inuit's lips curled in disgust. It all had to go. The buildings, the machines, it all had to be pushed into the sea. He charged.

Toffee had to take the man down without hurting him. Height and reach made that easy. He threw a palm-strike at the centre of Nutaraluk's chest to plant him on his ass and knock some sense into him.

If Toffee's right arm still ended in a hand, maybe it would have worked out that way.

In a world of snow and ice, everything seemed to freeze just a little bit more.

Blood dripped from where the tip of the blade protruded from Nutaraluk's back.

From the distance came the barking of seals. From the trades building came a scream.

Toffee grabbed the man to keep him from falling, his mind running a hundred miles a minute. *Take the blade out? Leave it in? Was the heart nicked?* It was a distraction. He knew the anatomy of every mammal on the planet.

Lung.

Nutaraluk was a dead man.

Three loud *cracks* were quickly followed by a roar and tremor that made Toffee stumble and the Inuit slide off the blade.

Toffee went spinning as Mayureak smashed into him with her body. She recovered her balance and dove for her husband. She said his name over and over again. She shook him, squeezed his hands, his face. He did not look at her. He was staring at his hand, at the walrus tooth button he'd pulled off of Toffee's jacket. His hand went limp. The tooth fell.

While Mayureak keened, Toffee pulled the sheath snug around his blade and pondered the quickest way to get the woman off the corpse and onto a snowmobile. This was far beyond animals on a revenge binge. The ocean itself was coming for the village.

She looked at him and in her eyes he saw any connection between them was as gone as yesterday's coastline. The only way she'd go with him was bound hand and foot, lashed to a sled like a hunt's fresh kill.

She growled. It was a sound he'd only ever heard before from a mother wolf protecting its cubs.

His stomach lurched with a sudden and totally unexpected feeling of loss. A montage of recent memories flashed before his eyes: Mayureak cooking; her morning smile; her shuffling dance when something made her happy. He remembered her ministering to his wounds, bathing him, politely ignoring his occasional arousal, and the one time she didn't.

"I didn't mean to kill him. It was an accident." He'd meant to use a tone of apology, but it didn't come out that way.

Toffee took Nataraluk's survival pack and wedged it between fuel barrels on the sled. He stuffed two rifles in beside the pack. He eyed the right-side throttle on the snowmobile, but kept himself from turning back to the woman.

Slight vibrations found their way up through Toffee's boots. The whales were there, deep down. They were working an angle, a fault. Things bigger than city buses wanted him dead. He felt a touch of panic.

As a long staccato of *snaps* came from the east, Toffee yanked the kill switch up, tugged the pull cord to start the motor and sat down. It was going to be rough. His left arm would have to do all the work and controlling the throttle with the tip of his blade would be a task that just might break him. At least the thumb-controlled lever had an extension on it.

He took a few deep breaths, settled his feet and pushed the throttle.

Toffee didn't look back, not once, not even when the mother-of-all ripping sounds came from behind followed by a shudder that sent fissures racing past the snowmobile like bolts of frozen lightning.

7. Lockout

Noah sat in Caps's room, his chair perched on its back legs and his feet on the bed. Less than an hour before, in a quick and brutal meeting, Sid gave the word on the impending lockout. Lena had immediately gone off with Darcy, leaving Noah with Caps. However, as soon as they got to the artist's room, Caps split, claiming he'd be back quickly. Between everything that went on in the early hours of the morning, Noah'd had zero sleep, and zero preparation for what was happening.

"Miss me?" asked Caps, slipping into the room quietly. Most of the Pit was still in bed.

"Where'd you go?"

"To steal something. This." He held up a small skinbag on a leather thong.

"That's Toffee's."

"Yep." The little pouch made clicking sounds as Caps shook it. "His bag of magic teeth. You know there aren't even guards on his room?"

"Then why'd it take you so long? Toffee's room move to another settlement?"

"Hey, man," Caps flopped on the bed, "I didn't know what I wanted. I was going to take this cool staff, but it smelled funny, then I saw this hanging on the bed post. That's a real nice bed he's got. Oops. Had. Handmade by none other than Travis Jones. I wonder if anyone'll want to sleep in it now?"

"Travis Jones." Noah's expression was bleak.

"Yeah, Travis Jones. Why are you taking it so hard? It's not like you knew the guy."

"I feel like I do. I feel like I hate him."

The bag of teeth clicked as it hit the bedside table. "Wow. Where did that come from?"

Noah suddenly realized he'd spoken the thought out loud. "I'm so tired. Would you consider forgetting you heard that?"

"Like hell I will. Not even seven in the morning and already this is a great day. Crater-nose gets locked out and you've got a major hate-on for a dead guy." Caps shifted into a German accent. "Tell me, Mr. Zurlow, does it have someszing to do wisz your moszer?"

"Leave it alone. How can you make jokes at a time like this?"

"A time like this? Noah, unless you hadn't noticed, Christmas has come a full six weeks early. Anyway, don't tell me, let me guess. Do you hate the late Mr. Jones because…he was taller than you?"

Noah rose abruptly. "I have to talk to Darcy."

Caps grabbed his sleeve. "Not now. Trust me like you've never trusted before. Not now. Sit. Go on, sit."

Reluctantly, Noah sank back into the chair.

"Back to the problem at hand. Is it because he was better looking? Had style far in excess of your meager stock?"

Noah stared daggers at him.

"You're just no fun. I know you've been competing with his ghost for Darcy's affections, but that's no reason to hate him. He was a good man. One of the best."

"That's not why I…okay, a bit. Maybe a lot. Darcy and I are friends. Really good friends."

"So I've noticed. I'm a little shocked at how close you two have grown."

"She's cast me as her little brother. I know it's all I'll get, so I'm happy with it."

"Mmm. So what's the rest then?"

"The rest of what?"

"The rest of why you hate Mr. Jones."

Noah shrugged.

Caps stroked an imaginary beard and tsked a few times. His whole body seemed to come alert at once. "It's not…Noah, tell me it's not because of Toffee getting locked out."

Noah's eyes widened, but he didn't reply.

"You've got to be kidding me. You're blaming the victim for the murderer's punishment?"

"No!" Noah snapped forward in the chair, bringing the front legs down with a thump. Then he leaned back again. "Yes. I don't know. I guess I hate that Travis existed in the first place. I just can't believe…all the time I spent…"

Caps nodded to himself and contemplated having a hit. This was certainly a get-stoned discussion. He could never get away with being high in the morning, though. And besides, he wanted to be straight for Toffee's final exit.

"I warned you. Lena warned you. Heck, even Darcy warned you."

"He was different when we were alone."

"He was different when we were alone," Caps mimicked in a high-pitched voice. "You sound like a battered wife. Sometimes you look like one."

"He was teaching me to fight!"

"He was getting his rocks off smacking you around and having you come back for it three nights a week. You have some twisted hero worship going for him…I've got to admit I have a trace of it myself. When we were in the cab of that truck, his arm," Caps jerked his arm back and forth like a piston, "saved my life. All those critters…the way he just kept killing and killing and killing…it was poetry." Caps slumped, exhausted, as if he'd just relived the experience. "But, Noah, he rigged a rat swarm. How can you forgive that?"

"I'm not forgiving it. He saved my life too, y'know. And…never mind."

"What?"

"You're going to think I'm an asshole."

"That wouldn't exactly lower my opinion of you, buddy."

"Nice. How can I…" Noah trailed off.

"Just spit it out, boy."

"How can I," he took a deep breath and committed himself, "be completely angry at him for killing a man Darcy would have probably ended up marrying?"

There was a heavy silence in the room.

"You're right, Noah. You are an asshole. You're a dog's asshole. But I think I understand."

"You won't tell anyone about this conversation?"

"Nah. Too much damage to my reputation as your PR agent."

There was a rap at the door. Caps leaned over in the bed and yanked on the handle. It was Darcy. Noah looked at her, saw what lay beneath the composure on her face, and immediately felt like the world's biggest heel for everything he'd been thinking.

"It's time," she said. "If you want to join the send off, be in the motor pool in twenty minutes." She left.

"You coming, asshole?" asked Caps.

"No. I'll catch the next one."

"You're missing the best movie of the year." He clambered to his feet.

"Where are you going? She said twenty minutes."

"I want to get a good seat."

***

Purtricil stood by with a wooden club while Cheu-Keung unlocked the cell door.

"You won't need that," said Toffee, glancing at the club. "I'll come peaceably."

It was no good hoping for a bullet when being locked out of Compton Pit. A resisting prisoner would be beaten into submission, but never shot. Rules were rules.

Darcy stood rigid a few feet from the cell. Big Conrad and the Boss were on either side of her. Purtricil and Cheu-Keung manacled the hunter's ankles and wrist, then tied his right arm to his chest with a length of rope.

"Do I get a last request?"

"Not likely," said Darcy.

"There's bag hanging on the bedpost in my—"

"You have nothing. Everything in that room will go to the next Chief of the Hunters. Now," she tossed a furry strip to Purty. It was cut from the hide used to make the rat cave. "Gag him. No more words, prisoner. No parting shots from you."

Toffee shuffled between Cheu-Keung and Conrad as he was led to the motor pool. Bound as he was, he still thought he could take the two of them if he put his mind to it. Darcy and Sid were another matter, throw in Purty and there really was no point. The hunter bit down hard on the gag, but he wasn't getting through it that way. He had to hand it to the girl, she knew what she was doing. Of all the other things she could have done, gagging him was the meanest. He didn't even have the option to bite someone, but worse than that, he couldn't tell his secrets. Oh, he had lots of them, things he'd saved for a rainy day, little anecdotes guaranteed to enrage and dismay; going-away gifts that would have had people at each other's throats long after Toffee was just a memory.

Sara's face held a mixture of sorrow and determination. She felt it her duty, since temporarily leading the Pit, to be present at each lockout. Daniel looked a little regretful, as after going on so many shopping sprees with the man, he too had fallen under the hunter's spell.

"You're a very bad person," said Dr. Patel, the tone of his voice damning Toffee far more than adjectives ever could.

"Hey, Toffee," said Caps. "Tomorrow I'm going to find your head, then I'll put one of your teeth in here." He held up the skinbag, then slowly placed it around his neck. He expected the hunter to grunt, maybe jerk in his chains a little. Instead, Toffee gave him the coldest look Caps had ever seen. The artist had to stop himself from stepping back.

That was it. Ten people in total stood present at the lockout of Ethan Toffee. The rest of the Pit would be informed after the prisoner was well away. Sid had never had to deal with a lynch mob at Compton Pit, and he didn't want to start today.

"Watch your head," said Sid, pushing down on Toffee's skull as he loaded him into the jeep.

With Toffee safely in the back, still nestled between Chiu and Purty, Sid and Darcy climbed into the front while Daniel and Conrad got into a second vehicle.

Toffee craned his neck to take a last look around, then chided himself for doing so.

The journey took half an hour this time. Sid drove slowly, not wanting even the possibility of an accident to give Toffee an opportunity. Sid had no idea what the hunter could accomplish given the situation, but he wouldn't relax until this was over, and probably not even then. He felt a great gulf had opened between himself and Darcy. He had no idea how to close it.

When they reached the plateau, the three security guards and Daniel spilled out, rifles at the ready. The firearms were for the teeth. For the prisoner, each man now had a truncheon at his belt. Sid eyed Toffee, trying to figure out how to undo the man's chains without having to get close to him.

"Here, let me help," said Darcy. She punched Toffee in the nose. The hunter fell over backward and landed, spluttering.

"He'll be useless for a few minutes. Go ahead. Thought I'd forgotten that, didn't you, Toffee?"

Sid undid the fetters, then cut through the rope with a knife. He stood back immediately, leaving the gag for Toffee to undo. Darcy wasn't anywhere near as cautious, confident that the blow to his nose had disabled him the same as Noah's inadvertent punch had done so during the trip to Vancouver.

"You leave no mark on any of us," she said quietly. "No mark at all."

Toffee gained his feet in time to see both vehicles drive off. Two dogs were on him almost immediately. One was beige in color with floppy ears, scarred and bitten. Its thick coat hung loosely on a lean frame. The second dog was black, with a white stripe down the center of its muzzle. Toffee sidestepped to crouch beside a flat slab of rock lying across smaller stones. Full balance hadn't returned yet. Toffee pulled himself onto the sheet of rock and rested on his knees and elbows, his body listing to the right. The beige dog reached him first. As it leapt Toffee flung himself sideways. The dog landed on the slab and skidded to a stop. Toffee kicked both feet into one of the stones beneath the slab, knocking it free. The sheet of stone zipped down the pebble-strewn slope like a snowboard. The beige animal disappeared over the cliff's edge just as the black dog's teeth closed on Toffee's throat.

8. Sparring Partners

Seth brought the cavern down that afternoon, but not before Darcy placed an ornate wooden staff and a few vials of honey at the center of the blast zone.

At a meeting of the senior staff, Toffee's double room was given to Caps as he was next in line. To everyone's surprise, Lena passed up the chance to move in with him. "I'm not cleaning up after him," was her reply to all the raised eyebrows. Chris Indred, after serving as hunter third under three chiefs, and hunter second under one, finally became a chief himself. To show his joy, he thanked the Boss profusely then yipped like a coyote.

Dinner brought many boos in Noah's direction as he made a general announcement as to power cutbacks going into effect the next day. Further disapproval met the revelation that he'd installed secure breakers in the residential corridors, insuring that nobody would "accidentally" go over their share. Sara made everyone forget Noah completely when she announced it was time to cut showers back for the winter. Everyone went from ten minutes down to three. There would be some naked arguments for the next few weeks, and it wasn't going to help the Pit's aroma. "You smell like winter," was a common epitaph shot at people reeking from a long day's work.

It was the announcement of Toffee's lockout, made by Sid, that shut the house down.

The next day, Caps moved all his possessions, or rather browbeat his mechanic crew into moving all his possessions. In the end he succeeded in having to lift only a single bundle of posters.

Chris, as the new chief of the hunters, wasted no time in receiving Toffee's bed. Behind the privacy of his bedroom door he jumped up and down on his new prize, gleeful as a child. In the midst of his revelry, the weight of his new responsibility struck him like a punch to the stomach. Hunting was more fun than it had ever been because Toffee's eerie skill and deadly aim protected his crew. The fear involved, the foreboding the night before the hunt had become a vague memory. This was not the experience that awaited Chris. He spent the next few hours wrestling with the desire to abdicate.

At noon, Seth paid a visit to the security office.

"There's something I figured I should tell you," he said.

Darcy pulled off her headphones. She'd been listening to verbal logs made by Travis during his tenure as security chief. He only had six tapes, and thus recycled them each month. Darcy had all of them memorized. He never mentioned her unless it was in an official capacity, but she could hear what she wanted in the way he said her name.

"Go on."

"I did an inventory. I may be short a few sticks of dynamite."

"May be?"

"I didn't do the original accounting. We picked up this crate in Vancouver and I'm afraid I took it on faith the ticket held an accurate number." He shrugged his left arm and shoulder, still practically useless after being shot at Fenwick Prison. "If that number was accurate then we're three sticks short."

"When could they have been taken? If they were taken, I mean."

"Pretty much any time in the last four days. The crates have been in the caverns unattended, and one time they were left in the main corridor for a short duration."

"Attended?"

"Not the whole time. I can't be everywhere at once."

"How big...do you think..." She wiggled her bottom in the chair.

Seth looked confused for a moment, then gaped at her. "There is no way someone could kiester three sticks of dynamite. Maybe one, if they were really experienced."

"Or very determined." She shuddered. "No, it's not practical. He would have to have loaded it before he went to bed that night, too. He did know I had the PVC, though."

"Darcy, we might be short a few sticks. Emphasis on might. I spent more time with Toffee than...except for maybe when you guys went to the city. I've seen what he could do, but even if he made a smaller charge, he'd need a lighter, too. There's no way to extract both of those, then get the charge lit before you're food. Especially not with only one arm."

"There's a ledge, too small for anything to land on once a person's on it." Darcy moved to the intercom and reached for the button.

Seth stopped her. "This is insane. He's dead, hon." She was still trying to press the button. "Darcy, stop. By this time tomorrow he'll be nothing but fertilizer."

Three days after the lockout, Noah sat cross-legged in a room on the lower level. Musty-smelling mats covered the floor and a single, powerful bulb illuminated the gray concrete walls and rusted pipes that ran along the ceiling. He took deep breaths and tried to picture emptiness. He got nothing from this exercise, but did it because it was habit. At first he hated the hunter for declaring himself teacher, and the Boss for approving it. Noah came because he was worried what would happen to him if he didn't. As the months passed, and he gained competence and understanding of the way the body could be a weapon, he grew to look forward to his basement sessions. Caps was right, Toffee taught hard, it was the faster-learning-through-aversion-to-pain method. Noah stood, did some stretches, then commenced shadow boxing.

"Sorry I'm late," said Darcy. She was dressed the same as Noah, loose top and comfortable pants. She had a towel over her shoulders and her hair was tied back in a ponytail.

"Was I supposed to expect you?" He kept swinging.

"No, but I know you always start at seven. When Caps didn't know where you were, I figured it out."

He relaxed his fists and let them drop to his side. "You want to work out with me?"

"I thought I might take over your lessons."

"Uh..."

"I can use the exercise. What's the matter, afraid I'll hurt you?"

Noah chuckled. "Not really."

"You should be. Spar?"

"If that's what you really want."

She dropped into a fighting stance, hips slightly twisted, fists raised. "Don't hold back. You won't touch me. Aren't you going to change your stance?"

Noah kept his casual pose. "I'm ready."

"Let's go, then."

A second later Darcy was lying on her back with the wind knocked out of her while Noah brushed his hands off and looked very pleased with himself.

She rose to her feet and brought her fists up. "I guess that showed me." She'd expected him to be clumsy, instead he'd thrown her with an expert's ease. "Care to try that again?"

Noah tried it three more times. The first time Darcy took his legs out from under him. The second time she slapped him lightly on both sides of his face *then* took his legs out from under him. The third time she stepped inside his grab attempt and tossed him over her hip.

"Did you ever land a punch on him?" Darcy asked as she helped Noah to his feet.

"I came real close once. I didn't feel skin or anything, but I knew because he put me in a wristlock that I thought was going to break bone."

"Was it a hold like this?"

Noah yelped and dropped to one knee. Darcy released the pressure.

"Okay, sun boy. Do the same thing to me, and I'll show you how to counter it."

They tussled for a while. Darcy wanted to see his level of floor work before duking it out with punches and kicks. Noah was strong, but he had no sense of balance once he was taken down. Essentially Toffee had been teaching him a myriad of sucker-punch moves. Darcy released Noah from yet another mock chokehold. He stood and pulled off his shirt. Sweat glistened on his chest and arms. Darcy blinked in surprise. Sun boy was filling out. Months of hauling cables up and down the battery bay ladder had given him girth. His stomach was flat and with just a little work, he could have himself a six-pack.

"Is something wrong?" asked Noah, misunderstanding the expression on her face.

Darcy scooped her towel. "That's enough for me. I have time to do this with you twice a week."

"Okay. I'm going to stay here for a while."

She turned at the door. "You should add crunches to your warm-up."

The next two days brought a lot of cold-weather work as the entire senior staff and most of the seconds undertook the arduous task of relocating and re-camouflaging all the topside Screaming Mimis. It was an exhausted crew that sat around the table for a wrap-up meeting.

"Good work everyone," said the Boss. "We used up a lot of supplies doing this. I'll want a needs list from all departments."

"I can do mine right now," said Seth. "Construction material, obviously, flat timber, chicken wire, mesh, etc. Our only portable generator packed it in around four. Have you had a chance to look at it?" he asked Caps.

"An hour ago. It's cracked. I don't think I can improvise this time. Might as well grab a bunch of them on the next shopping spree, but that's not for months."

"We have two portable gennies," said Noah. "I experimented charging the main batteries with them. Not very efficient, but I can keep Gershwin and the Mimi's running in an emergency."

"The second genny was in the Hummer," said Seth. "The hunters always take one with them. A lot of field equipment was in that vehicle. We'll need to replace that, too."

"What about a recovery operation?" asked Noah.

Caps laughed. "What for? The Hummer fell almost a hundred feet. Boss, we've got some good Jeeps but they don't measure up."

Chris agreed with this quite strongly. Bad enough the hunters had lost their fairy godmother, they shouldn't have to do without the best vehicle as well.

"Underbel has two," said Seth. "They got them from the Reservoir.

"I don't think they'll give us too much trouble," said Sid. "Giving them half control of Gascan's palace earned us some favors, even if we couldn't run it by ourselves. Lena, get them on the horn tonight and have them send one up. Whatever they want in exchange, I'm sure we can supply it. Be discreet, of course."

The Pit's sudden wealth was being downplayed severely to the other settlements. What was revealed was attributed solely to the sacking of Gascan's Reservoir. It wasn't that Sid didn't trust the nearby settlements to come to a fair agreement concerning looting of the city, it was those who lay beyond that worried him. Word that Vancouver lay open and waiting would spread like wildfire. With D'Abo and Shangley both dead, the Pit faced nothing human to fear for a great distance. Farther south and east, however, were settlements that could match D'Abo play for play in mercenary tactics, and even outdo him on a few. Compton Pit alone was not worth the trip, but a prize like Vancouver was another thing entirely. Anyone massing such an expensive incursion wouldn't be satisfied simply bypassing the closer settlements. Compton Pit would be particularly attractive as a convenient base of operations. Diplomatic arrangements would never do either as the Pit couldn't rent itself out as stop-over. Sooner or later outsiders would uncover the secret of the Mimis, and then the Pit would again be under siege. At the same time, The Boss didn't want to completely cut off his neighbors from what the city had to offer. He trickled luxuries and Old World technology into the barter trucks, instructing Lena and Seth to trade hard for them, but not too hard.

"Unless there's anything else," Sid spread his arms.

"I say we hit the showers," said Caps. Paint stained his jacket, face and hands. His gloves had been soaked through with paint by the middle of the day, so he tossed them, thereby earning himself dirty hands that stung and burned as circulation returned.

"We can't break the water restrictions," said Sid.

"The hell we can't," said Sara. She'd also been working mostly gloveless because of the dexterity required in the final stages of the cover up. "We just can't be seen doing it."

"What do you suggest?"

Half an hour later, surly Comptonites were pushed down the residential corridors by Purtricil and Chris, while Daniel and Caps cordoned off an area of extreme heat with a pair of empty bed frames. Vicious steam blew from a pipe in the ceiling, completely obscuring what lay beyond.

"Hey, my room's up there," said one the men being turned away.

"We'll have the leak fixed as quickly as we can," said Caps, lining the second frame up with the first.

In the bathrooms beyond the steam, the first shift scrubbed themselves jubilantly beneath powerful streams of hot water.

"We're bad people," said Sara, peeling her lips back to allow the shower to act as a water pick.

"I think we'll learn to live with it," replied Sid.

9. Days of Custer

"What's so important that I had to come down here personally?" asked Sid, stepping into communications.

Lena sat in a chair. She had her foot in Caps's lap where it was receiving an expert massage.

"You're getting a call from Mon Mothma," said Caps.

"Who?"

"Seventeen hundred hours," said Lena. "Beverly Sanderson. She called earlier to make an appointment. Video transmission and your eyes only."

Sid glanced at his watch. "That's a minute away. What does she want?"

Lena shrugged and stood, pulling Caps up and towards the door. "No idea, Boss. I hope you get a cleaner transmission than I did."

Sid eased himself into the chair. The seat was still warm.

On one of the monitors, a blue box announced that somebody wanted to talk. Sid palmed the mouse and did the necessary clicking.

A woman's face appeared momentarily on the screen. It vanished, then reappeared.

"Sid?"

"I'm here, Beverly," he said. "What's up?"

Her brown hair hung limp on either side of her head. Her eyes were tired. *"Are you alone?"*

"Yes."

She winked out for a few seconds. When she came back, the top of her head was visible as she fiddled with something off screen. She looked up. *"We're in trouble."*

Sid folded his hands across his stomach and leaned back in the chair. "Who's 'we'?"

The picture vanished again. Sid waited. Nearly a minute went by. Beverly Sanderson reappeared, this time in a clear image. Smudges of dirt marred her chin and left cheek. *"I think that's got it fixed. Can you see me?"*

"Clearly."

When she pushed back her hair, Sid noticed a score of tiny cuts on the back of her hand.

"Sid, Underbel took a bad hit."

"Go on."

"We've lost a lot of people. Tunnels two and three are gone. Our infrastructure's—"

"Gone? What do you mean gone?"

She closed her eyes and tensed her shoulders. *"Ants, Sid. Ants got us bad."*

"Ants? It's November."

"Warmth from the settlement." She threw her hands up in the air. *"I don't know. They've been mining the concrete, the bedrock. We don't know for how long."*

"How many got in? You should have plenty of pesticide. How bad could—"

"Sid, listen to me. They've been mining the concrete. It's solid to us but to them it's just a big pile of stones. Tunnels two and three are gone. They fell apart. Caved in. It all happened in seconds. It happened at night."

Sid leaned forward and gripped the edge of the desk. "Aren't tunnels two and three residential areas?"

Sanderson looked away for a moment. When she turned back she said, *"Yes. Almost everybody was at home."*

"Survivors?"

"Everything's damaged. Water, power, ventilation. All our systems are broken. Tunnels are unstable. We've evacuated the lower level."

Sid's mouth went dry. He looked around for anything wet. A mug nearby held the dregs of tea. "How are you fighting the ants?" He reached for the mug.

Sanderson covered her eyes with one hand. The hand slid down to cover her mouth. When the hand came away, it looked as if she were chewing on her lips. *"There's not many to fight. They're getting smarter. They're not coming in, not giving us a shot at them. They're eating our home."*

Sid looked up, looked down, looked side to side. For a moment he had the urge to press his ear to the wall. The Mimis kept the ants away. The Mimis kept him safe. He drained the mug and put it down. He looked into the camera. Sanderson was looking into hers. Across the miles their eyes locked.

Sid's mind filled with images: the mess hall filled with cots; people sleeping in the corridors; the research animals killed for food. He accepted the horror but locked chains around his heart.

"I can't give you refuge. We don't have the space."

"We don't need refuge. We need help."

"Move to the Reservoir."

"It's not big enough to hold everybody."

"Prioritize."

Sanderson shook her head. *"Nicholas Mayhew's right about you sometimes."*

The leader of Mount Baker's warnings about Toffee echoed in Sid's head.

"We're desperate," she said. *"Help us or we're finished."*

Sid put his hands on either side of the monitor. "Beverly, I sympathize. Believe me, I do. You're asking for a humanitarian effort but we can't afford to give it. You're asking for an enormous chunk of our resources. How do you intend to pay?"

Sanderson nodded and took a deep breath. *"We have your van."*

"The hunters' van?" Sid jerked back. "Was—"

"By right of salvage it's ours. It and everything in it."

Sid forced himself to wear a poker face. What did she mean by that? Did she have a Mimi? Suspect what it was?

"What about Odega? Was he—"

"We have him." It was her turn to lean back and slip on a mask. *"We have him alive."*

"Why didn't you tell me this to begin with?"

Her mask slipped. She sniffed and rubbed at the corner of one eye. *"I was testing your generosity."*

"You still are. You're asking for the moon in exchange for one man, and one vehicle."

"And the contents of the vehicle." Her mask was back, this time to stay.

"You promised," said Lena. They were in SatCom. Lena was using the process of burning information to re-writable CDs to avoid making eye contact with Sid. "You said I'd never have to leave the Pit again."

"It's unavoidable, Lena—"

"You don't need me!" her hand jerked and a stack of CDs hit the floor.

"We both know I do. We have to get in and out. We have to be back before the snow cuts us off."

Lena stooped and collected some of the discs. "You promised. That supersedes any deal you made with *her*."

The chief of communications wasn't being stubborn, she was being realistic. The anxiety attacks she'd felt on the way to Vancouver were nothing compared to what she expected to go through if she ever stepped out of the Pit again. A phobia, generally, is an irrational fear, but her fear of leaving home had solid fact to rest upon. Not a week gone from Compton Pit, and she'd almost been breakfast for a whale. For Lena, it just didn't get any worse.

Sid reached for her shoulders, then thought better of it and let his hands drop. "We're taking four vehicles. It will be completely safe. Your boyfriend is coming. Darcy's coming. She wants to bring Dr. Odega home personally."

"I don't care. We're just going to lock him out anyway. You've got his notes. Let Underbel deal with him."

"His notes are incomprehensible."

"Probably, so is he."

"This isn't like Vancouver. We're just going to Underbel and back. A week at the most."

"That's what you said the last time." She shook her head, wringed her hands. "Rick's going. You're taking him. Alright. I'll go."

A few hours later, Sid had an opposite, but almost identical conversation with Noah.

"But, Boss..."

"No, it's too dangerous." They were in animal research. It had become as much an office to him as anything else.

"It's only to Underbel and back, it's not like I'd be going with you to the city."

"You're not needed. Underbel's electrical engineers aren't among the fatalities."

"Yeah, well, I need them."

This was an unexpected tack. "What for?"

"I've hit a plateau with my panels. The stuff I'm cranking out now isn't even as efficient as some of the panels we used to have. If I could go over Freeland's notes and schematics with Bacon for a few days—"

"I can arrange to have Bacon come here."

"Boss, Underbel was my home. I have to go. Please?"

Sid threw his hands up. "I'm going soft. Take me out and shoot me, someone, I'm going soft. You can come. Pack quickly."

Noah hastily stuffed a sack and headed for the armory where he checked out a sidearm. He considered the cumbersome .45 automatic that stood him so well in Vancouver, but chose instead a .38 revolver. It didn't have the stopping power of the larger handgun, but it fit much better into Noah's hand.

Caps was chewing out his second, Mickey Fornten, for something when Noah arrived at the motor pool.

"What was that all about?" Noah asked Caps, glancing over his shoulder at Mickey who'd gone off to the tool cage, muttering to himself.

"He screwed up. He has problems with calibration. I've nailed him on it before."

"Is one of our vehicles buggered?" Noah pictured them losing brakes and flying off into a ravine.

"Nah, nothing like that. We did an overhaul of the storage tank gauges last week. The settings were off and now we're coming up a little short on fuel. Not much, a drop in the bucket, really."

"Could Dr. Odega have stolen some of it?"

"Not a chance. Look, it's just lost in the paperwork somewhere. Don't tell the Boss or Darcy. We can worry about it when we get back."

Feet banged up and down a metal loading ramp attached to a forty-foot trailer. Equipment and materials came in on shoulders, on carts, on dollies. Chris Indred leaned by the door of a troop transport, mentally checking off names as people got on board. A twenty-foot trailer was quickly filling with mining tools and barrels of pesticide.

Sid stuck his head through the door of the troop transport, watched a cartload of metal pipes slam and rattle up into the forty-footer, then crossed the floor to Caps, pausing long enough to be joined by Darcy.

"Richard," said Sid, "where's your girlfriend."

"She's right here." Caps moved next to a Jeep and opened the front passenger door. Lena was slumped so far down in the seat, she couldn't be seen through the window. She turned her head to Sid and gave him a bleary-eyed grin.

"Are you drunk?" asked Darcy.

"Nope." Lena laughed and waved a hand in the air. "I passed drunk ages ago." Her other hand came up holding a pewter flask. "I would describe my present condition as wasted."

10. Underbel

Tents, crude lean-tos and hastily assembled shacks crowded the space within the barbed-wire perimeter. A thin layer of frost softened the rough edges, robbed it of color, made the settlement look as desperate as it was.

People wearing all they owned huddled around barrel fires, trembling beneath sparse clouds of steam.

"One step forward, ten steps back," said Sid, bringing the Jeep to a halt and letting the motor idle.

A section of the high fence rolled away and a dozen men and women came out, wearing armor made up of everything from hockey equipment to layers of carpet samples. With long sticks they probed the dark places around the vehicles, undersides and wheel wells.

They weren't being overly cautious. This was the primary method through which raccoons got in. Although the coons would have denned up by now, a seasonal insomniac was not unheard of.

Hand signals and calls of "all clear" became arms motioning to go on in. On the lead truck, an angled frame of steel and razor wire retracted until it was flush with the grill. The semi rumbled through the gate, going slowly to allow people to move out of the way.

Beyond the temporary dwelling lay the mall, pride of the town. A short drive south from the former Canadian border, the Bell Mall had been a bed of international commerce: the first one hit by Canucks seeking low American prices on the few occasions when Canadian currency was strong enough to justify the trip.

Today, the mall was a modern ruin. Not a sheet of glass remained in any frame. Entranceways, stripped of their doors, gaped black and empty. Bits of storefront signs dotted the exterior:

JC Penny, Bon Marche, Target. The signs were shot through with a hundred thousand cracks.

On a billboard above the cinema, three-quarters of Renée Zellweger's face smiled in perpetual cuteness; a twenty-first century Mona Lisa.

Noah, in the passenger seat of the Jeep, pressed his face against the window.

"Why don't they live in the mall?" asked Darcy. She put the vehicle into gear and followed the semi.

"Too unstable," said Noah. "Too many holes."

To the north, east and west, rubble and dark ground stretched out for miles. When the bugs started in on that fourth day, the city dwellers took refuge in fire. They burned it all. Only the mall had been spared, this their holy temple.

To the south, across the highway, what had once been a golf course was now a farm. Wire mesh cages sat atop soil beds lying in plastic and concrete basins. All the animals had gotten free, so humanity had imprisoned the vegetables.

When all vehicles were within the compound, the gate rolled shut and the inspection team traded in their sticks for rifles.

The larger vehicles were guided next to a ramp and a group of people waiting with strong backs and dollies. All vehicles were signaled to stop.

The door of the troop transporter swung open and Sid dropped down, almost immediately rubbing his hands together and blowing on them. "Why are we stopping here?" he asked a burly man who seemed to be in charge.

"There's no room downstairs. Motor pool is residential now."

At the bottom of the ramp, Beverly Sanderson, wearing a fur coat and hat, stood with her hands folded together at the waist. She met Sid halfway up the ramp.

"It feels like that first day all over again," she said.

Sid touched her shoulder, stroked the soft fur with his thumb. "It was a lot warmer back then."

Noah watched the doors at the bottom of the ramp roll up into the ceiling and disappear. He looked to his left, at the solar panel array he'd been weaned on. It looked so tiny, a third of the size of Compton Pit's, supplying a settlement that housed more than forty times the Pit's numbers.

Noah descended, entered the people-choked first level of what was once underground parking. He took a deep breath through his nose and grimaced.

"Hey, kid," Bacon offered a beefy hand.

Noah rushed forward and wrapped his arms around the bearded man. Bacon hesitated, then reluctantly returned the hug with one arm, while patting Noah's back with the other hand. Noah disengaged.

"You look good, kid. I hear you've been doing big things."

"Noah, welcome back." This came from Max Reagan, the second best electrician in Underbel. He had strong Greek features, with a thick mustache and bushy dark hair. He hugged Noah without any hesitation.

Noah pushed away from Max. The three men looked at each other.

"I know," offered Max.

"We took a bad hit, kid," said Bacon. "I couldn't believe it when I heard you were coming." He took Noah's pack. "You must have earned yourself some pull."

"Yeah, well." Noah searched nearby faces. How many of his friends were dead? "I've got some stuff to show you. Both of you, if I'm allowed."

"If you're allowed?" intoned Max.

"Hush hush, you know." Noah winked, then forced a huge grin. "I've got to get some more stuff from the Jeep, then I'll be right with you."

"Slow down, kid." Bacon held a hand up. "Don't you want to get settled in first? I made room for you in my digs."

"Maybe later. Let me show you this and then—"

"Not a chance," said Lena from the other side of the Jeep. She gripped tight at her pack, in a tug-of-war with one of the welcoming committee. "Take me straight to your SatCom. I'll sleep there if I have to."

Sanderson crooked a finger at one of her guards. "Take Miss Wong to SatCom. Scott and Naomi should already be there, if not, get them. If our guest changes her mind, take her to her quarters."

Lena followed the man a few paces then stopped. She looked at her boyfriend.

"I'll have to catch up with you," said Caps. In one hand he held his pack. In the other was a clipboard. He shrugged and waved the clipboard at the team moving supplies in.

A group of refugees being herded to somewhere shambled in front of Caps and Lena lost sight of him.

Sid touched Sanderson on the arm. "I'm also anxious."

"Yes," she said, nodding. "Dr. Odega. I'll take you to him personally."

Noah extracted a metal case from the back of the Jeep. A clatter of wood came from nearby. A soft body hit him and the case dropped from his fingers.

"Noah! You're back! You're back!"

Soft lips kissed him on his mouth, then his cheek, then his mouth again. Her arms were wrapped around his chest so tightly, he could barely breathe. He realized who she was half way through the first set of kisses. When her lips traveled from his neck back up to his mouth, he kissed back, then pushed her to arm's length.

"Jenny," he breathed. His former girlfriend's head was bandaged in cloth. Her left leg was splinted from ankle to knee. A crutch lay on the ground a few feet away. Moving feet kicked it under the Jeep. Besides the accoutrements of the injured, there was something else different about her. She'd covered the scars on her chin with makeup. He'd never seen her do that before.

"I came as soon as I heard you were here," she said into his chest. "I kept all your letters! Is there room for me yet? Can I go back with you?"

He looked down at the top of her head, completely stunned. What letters? Room for her? He hadn't even thought of her once on the drive in. That, more than anything, surprised him. On the trip to the Pit, Bacon had broken the news that Jenny wasn't a one-man type of gal. Noah had vented his anger, then written her off. Cass Owens had made that easy to do, teaching him bedroom skills far beyond Jenny's limited repertoire. Still, Jenny was his first love, of the physical kind at any rate, and his mind should have at least given her honorable mention as he anticipated his prodigal return.

Jenny looked up at him, her smile faltering at his blank look.

Bacon saved Noah from having to answer. He separated them with strong hands and scooped Jenny up into his arms. "You shouldn't be out of bed, girl. I know you two lovebirds want to be alone, but I need him first."

Jenny frowned, then nodded. She blew Noah a kiss. Bacon passed her off to Max, who carried her off without trying to find her crutch.

"What happened to her? What letters?" Noah demanded of Bacon.

Bacon rubbed his hands on the fronts of his pants. "Let's go get some food in you, I'll explain everything."

A man sloshed by with a bucket of pesticide balanced on his shoulder. Darcy counted it as number five and gave an in-a-minute hand sign to Sid.

Barrel number six sloshed by. Darcy stopped rubbing her hands and pulled her gloves on. "It's colder in here than it is outside," she said to no one in particular.

"It's colder deeper in," said a lean woman watching the procession of rescuers. A pattern of scars made a tic-tac-toe board on the left side of her forehead, incorporating her eyebrow as the bottom horizontal.

"Did you lose all heat? Everywhere?"

"Turned it off." She scratched her stomach. "We have to put the ants to sleep."

Darcy looked at the concrete pillars, at the distant walls and the tons of rock above their heads. In her mind, optimism had limited the hymenopteran activity to the collapsed tunnels. That wasn't the case. The whole settlement was shot through with them. She stopped counting barrels and started counting heads. The injured, the unhomed. How many of them were there? These people were on the verge of losing their minds.

A gaslight heater sat under the table. Another one sat on top. Noah stared at the contents of his plate and tried to remember how he had ever enjoyed a meal growing up in this place. Three strips of jerky and a daunting pile of root shavings. He hated root shavings.

"Not what you're used to is it, princess?" asked Max.

"Yeah," said Bacon. "You may be living the good life now, but don't forget your roots."

The joke squashed the fragment of appetite Noah had been able to summon.

"I told you he wouldn't laugh," said Max.

Noah looked up from his plate. He should have laughed. As bad as it was, it should have least merited a chuckle. Instead all he felt was annoyance. "What's going on with Jenny?"

"That's a king's feast right now," said Bacon. "But we weren't really going to make you eat that." The chair creaked as Bacon half turned and yelled at the kitchen doors. "Bring it out."

The doors banged open and David Grearson, the third member of Underbel's photovoltaic team wheeled in a rickety cart. On the cart was a serving platter covered in chocolate-chip cookies.

Noah's ire vanished. Just looking at the shape of the wondrous disks made his mouth water. He chose a large one, laden with chocolate and turned it back and forth in his hand, letting the anticipation of biting into it build until he couldn't resist it anymore. With his taste buds poised for a rocket trip back to childhood, he bit down. The first wave of sugar and chocolate rolled across his tongue, it was so good he could taste it in his knees. The morsel was swallowed involuntarily as the back of the tongue couldn't wait for its share of the pleasure. The aftertaste left much to be desired.

"Whilmsley baked them," said Bacon.

"You mean…"

"She said she only put a few root shavings in. You know, to improve the flavor."

Noah set into the cookies with a passion. He'd learned a long time ago that the best way to avoid the aftertaste was don't stop eating. At cookie number seven, his gluttony came to an abrupt stop when he realized the other three men weren't indulging themselves. They watched him, gentle smiles on their faces, as if they were gaining pleasure vicariously through him. It was weird.

Noah reluctantly put the cookie down and let the aftertaste take its course. "What is this? Is there laxatives in these or something?"

Max and Grearson adopted expressions of shocked innocence.

"He's not buying it," said Bacon.

"I'll get you something to drink," said Grearson and promptly left the table.

"We didn't expect to see you again," said Bacon. "At least, not here."

Noah took another bite of his cookie. He didn't think Grearson would be back anytime soon with an alternative method of banishing the sourness in his mouth.

His annoyance returned. He focused on Bacon. "Jenny said she kept all my letters. I only sent two letters, both to you. I didn't mean for her to read those."

"She didn't. After you left…she changed."

"Changed? Changed how?"

"I told you how she wasn't your girl alone? That wasn't entirely accurate."

Noah pushed the tray of cookies away. The aftertaste fit in perfectly with his mood. "We parted on lies, Bacon. Now there's more waiting for me on the return trip?"

"I did what I thought was right. You were leaving, end of story. Noah, she did sleep with me…"

"And me," said Max, as if to shoulder his share of the guilt.

"…and Max, and Grearson, but she only got giddy over you. I figured a clean break was best for both of you—"

"But she didn't—" broke in Max. Bacon silenced him with a look.

"I never saw it coming. She pined for you, Noah. Every time a convoy came back from Compton Pit, there she was banging on my door, asking if anything had come from you. She was so sad all the time, she…I'm not particularly proud of this, kid."

"What did you do?" Noah couldn't even imagine.

"She wanted a letter from you so…she got one."

"We wrote it together," said Max. "It was really good."

"It was okay," grunted Bacon. "It said you missed her, but it was unlikely you'd ever see her again. We made up some stuff, gave you some friends. Instead of making it better, it just made it worse."

"Made what worse?"

"She stopped sleeping with us," said Max.

"She was miserable," said Bacon. "She got so sad she was never in the mood. I thought the letter would make her happy and let you go. Instead she wrote back to you. Don't know what she did to get the paper and the ink. Nice stationary, not just scrap."

"I never got any letter."

"Of course you didn't," said Bacon. "Did Santa ever get a letter addressed to Santa? She admitted to being with us, begged your forgiveness and promised she'd save herself for you. So I wrote back to her, saying you forgave her but you didn't mind. She wrote back and—"

"How many letters?"

"A few," said Bacon.

"You've made a whore out of her."

"If you want to use that word, she's always been one."

"You made me her pimp."

"You wait one damn minute," started Max.

"He's right," said Bacon, staying Max with a hand on the shoulder. "Noah, we support her. She's got one thing to offer the community. Without us she'd be spreading her legs for anybody who'd give her a morsel of food. One of them legs won't be so pretty now. More than ever her life is in our hands. We did what we had to do."

Noah was on his feet. He didn't know what to do, scream, or storm out, or start throwing cookies at the two men.

"Read this," said Bacon, holding up a sheaf of papers. "Read any of them."

Noah snatched the bundle from Bacon's hand. He tore one of the pages a little in his anger. He glared at Bacon, then looked down at the page. Bacon was right; it *was* nice stationary. Light cream in color, with a green trim on the top and bottom. The script on the page was barely legible. Both the penmanship and choice of words were those of an infant. The spelling was so bad, it was more like deciphering than reading. He threw the letters on the table.

"These make her look like a retard."

"She's not that far off," said Bacon, retrieving the letters.

"Dogshit."

"She was your first fuck, Noah. Sorry to put it so bluntly, but you saw only what you wanted to see. She's almost completely stupid, but we think she's pretty and for some reason known only to God, the concept of electricity gets her horny."

"I hate you."

"No you don't. Aw, kid, where're you going?"

"To talk to Jenny. Don't get up, I'll find her. I'll look for the red light district."

11. Mistaken Identity

Caps stood before a concrete wall chalked with so many dotted lines and crosses, it looked like a giant treasure map. A team of seven men stood to one side. Two were from Compton Pit, the rest were natives.

"We're going in here," said a sour-faced man with brown hair in tight curls. He tapped an x-mark high on the wall.

Caps gave the man an appraising look. Was he a chief, or an apprentice with a battlefield promotion? So much knowledge had been lost to these people. All the dead filling their walls.

"This is deep, man," said Caps. "How are you going to drill in this deep?"

"That's our problem. Can you make the pumps?"

"I can draw up a prototype." Caps exhaled just to watch the cloud. He imagined it was pot smoke. He'd chosen poor gloves. He shoved his fingers under his armpits.

"We'll need twenty to start."

"What did you do before? I mean before you had to live here."

"Contractor. I built half this place."

"Isn't there some sort of building Hippocratic Oath about doing no harm?"

Two carts were pushed into the corridor. Men unloaded the carts and started assembling a machine. The sour-faced contractor lifted a drill bit longer than Caps's arm. They were going to give the place a new circulatory system, fill the walls and ceilings with thin pipes through which pesticide could be delivered, a hematoma of toxin.

A thin man, not part of the work crew, leaned against a wall a short distance away. He studied Caps, and not in a casual way. He was particularly interested in Caps's right hand, where only thumb, index and middle finger remained.

"Never seen one of these, buddy?" Caps raised and wiggled his hand, letting the empty fingers on the glove flop about.

"Are you Ricky Scagling?"

Caps studied the man's face. It wasn't the least bit familiar. "Nobody calls me that, but yeah."

"You make cartoons on T-shirts?"

Caps grinned, realizing what this was, enjoying the ego stroke. "I'm sorry, man, but I didn't bring any with me to sell. And I don't have time to make—"

"Gloria Rueben wants to see you," said the man as he pushed away from the wall. "Her digs are in Tunnel Nine."

Caps stood, mouth open, watching the messenger walk away. A kind of buzzing sound filled the artist's ears. His right hand, still held up for display, twitched.

"Excuse me," said Caps to a slack-jawed woman leaning in the doorway. Interior walls made of everything from handle-less doors to corrugated metal created rooms throughout the tunnel. Barrel fires placed intermittently beneath grated air vents provided enough light to make everybody want a whole lot more.

The woman shifted her glassy-eyed stare to Caps, but didn't reply.

"I'm looking for Gloria Rueben?"

She nodded at him.

"You know her?"

She shrugged and looked away.

Caps sighed and moved deeper into the tunnel. He didn't want to be here. He didn't want to deal with this.

Somebody both large and clumsy bumped into Caps, turning him around before moving on. For a moment the artist had no idea which way he was facing. Between darkness and bodies he was lost, cast away. He'd told nobody where he was going. He didn't want to have to explain.

He found the silent woman, used her as a landmark. She looked back at him and said, "I know where Jesus lives."

Caps winked and pointed a right-back-atcha. "I'm very happy for you."

"Down there," she waved a hand. "That way. It's a house made of shortbread."

"Riiight."

"Gloria lives there. She lives there with Jesus." She pulled back into the gloom of her home. A sheet of metal filled the doorway.

Caps looked in the direction she'd indicated. He passed a wall made of fence boards, another sheet metal thing, and came to an abrupt stop at a section of wall covered with lids from cookie tins. He pulled a glove off and rubbed the tartan of Royal Edinburgh.

"I guess you build with what you've got," Caps mumbled to himself.

The door was real. It came complete with hinges and a handle. He knocked. There was no answer. He stared at it, wrestling with indecision.

"Go on in," said a voice from behind. It was the messenger, watching from near a fire.

Caps touched the doorknob. He steadied himself and stepped inside.

"Hello?" he asked the darkness

"Is someone there?" asked a weak voice. A lantern ignited. The room was small. A padded chair sat beside a spindly table. A china cabinet, the glass intact on both doors, held a few pieces of Wedgwood dinnerware. Next to the cabinet was a wooden chest.

The chair was occupied. She was rail thin, with uneven, frazzled white hair. Her skin was deathly pale, and Caps could make out the shape of the woman's skull beneath her skin. A blanket was draped across legs that no doubt were barely thicker than the bones within.

The face was wasted but there was a familiarity in the eyes, the set of the mouth. And suddenly Caps felt eight years old, and he and his best friend were trying to explain exactly what they were doing in the back yard with a box of matches. Lying about it was that much more difficult because neither of them had a solid plan to deny in the first place. They'd simply come across the matches unattended and figured the fun would evolve from there.

Caps looked at the bed, considered kneeling beside the chair, but instead kept his distance and said, "Mrs. Rueben?"

"Ricky? Come closer. Let me see if that's really you."

His feet weighed a thousand pounds. He shuffled a little closer, then steeled himself and stepped forward until his legs were touching the arm of the chair.

"Come here," she said, gesturing impatiently.

Caps leaned down. She put her hands on either side of his face and gazed at his eyes. Wrinkles cracked her translucent skin as her lips curled into a smile. "Ricky. Little Ricky. It's so good to see you."

Her breath was appalling. Caps wanted to get away from it, get away from what was sure to come next.

Gloria Rueben rubbed a palm across his widow's peak. "You used to have so much hair." She reached for the length at the back, grabbed a lock and tugged. "Our little adopted hippie."

"I didn't know you were here," said Caps. "If I'd have known, I'd have come sooner." He was amazed by his capacity to lie so sincerely.

"Oh hush. Why would you know I was here? There's a T-shirt on the chest. I said I'd get it signed."

Caps turned and looked. It was a white shirt, silk-screened with Scooby Doo dabbing at his lips with Daphne's scarf. The caption read, "I would have gotten hungry if it wasn't for you darn kids."

"Nobody draws irreverence like you, Ricky. Do you remember the little comic book you made? Oh, what was it called?"

Caps's first glorious publication: he'd cut a standard size piece of paper into four parts and fold them together.

"It was absolutely awful. We thought you were disturbed. Oh what was it called?" She squeezed his wrist, urging him to answer.

"It was called 'The School of Severed Heads,' " said Caps.

"Yes! Horrible stuff. But then we saw the political commentary in it, and you were so young to have such thoughts."

"Oh, I ripped most of it off from *Mad* and *Cracked*. I didn't even get half the jokes, I just knew somehow they were funny."

"Give me the T-shirt." Her hands clamped on it. "I knew it was you. She visited me yesterday, said the artist was coming."

"How did it get here? I ran off the Scooby shirts for Mount Baker must be over a year ago."

"Sign it to Kathy. Ricky, do you know where your parents are?"

"No." He looked around the room. "Do you live here with someone?"

"No. I could never…after Chester."

"Mr. Reuben? When did he…?"

"He didn't make it past the first day." She offered the dry, cracked smile. "He told me he'd always be looking out for me even if I couldn't see him. Then he took a baseball bat and…the Millars from next door…you remember them? They pulled me into their station wagon. Chester was so brave. Are you looking for something?"

"Not really. The woman who told me how to find you said you live with Jesus. Thought there might be a painting or a—"

"He's here. He'll take me soon, but He knew it wasn't time yet." She pushed the T-Shirt into his hand. "Chester loved you, Ricky. He thought you were wild and a little lazy but you were a brother to our…"

In a second Caps was going to need the T-Shirt to wipe his eyes.

Gloria sniffed. "Do you know anything about Jamie?"

***

Ricky Scagling is in the back of a truck. It's a covered truck. This is a good thing. Birds tend to pick off people in the uncovered ones.

The truck is moving. This is also a good thing.

It was dimwit that brought them all here, the Arnold Rimmer wannabe with his blind confidence and constant misusage of military terminology. Not that the place wasn't everything he'd said it would be: vast stores of non-perishable food, bottled water, sanitation and first aid supplies, lots of concrete and thick doors.

What brain-dead neglected to mention, or perhaps simply hadn't taken into account, was that his "highly defensible position" was the concession storage warehouse at the dog track.

They'd driven right into the heart of the fastest canines on the continent.

Gamblers watching the races had probably thought the hounds were giving it all they had, but when the wooden bunny's job was handed to mankind, those dogs threw in a little extra mojo.

The vehicle is accelerating but the pack is closing in fast. The people who've survived long enough to make the truck have done so only thanks to human speed bumps. The dog that took down the blonde woman from Spring Street was still wearing its racing number.

Sleek and nasty, the pack's been a roving meat grinder. Their dark gray fur is stained black from so much dried blood.

Ricky is hanging out of the back of the truck, draped over the tailgate. His arms are stretched to their limit. He's about to fall.

A few yards behind the truck, Jamie Rueben is running. He's been Ricky's best friend since the second grade.

Jamie's not going to make it. He's too out of shape. Too many bags of Oreos, and too many bowls of weed. The pack's almost on him. This is it, the end. But Jamie, God bless him, finds one last reserve of energy. He's going to close the gap even if his heart explodes in the process. His fingertips touch Ricky's, and then there's palm, and wrist, glorious wrist, good strong grip, strong as oak. Ricky is pulling and it's going to be okay, everything's going to be okay.

Jamie is exhausted. Ricky's right hand is down two fingers and his left was never the muscle of the team. Oak isn't strong enough.

The best friends have a parting of the ways.

Ricky went north by truck, and Jamie went south by Greyhound.

"We got separated, Mrs. Rueben," was all Caps could say.

Her hand slid away from his just like Jamie's had. She coughed a few times, hollow and raspy. "I prayed that he was with you," she said. "On that day, I prayed he was with you even if you were loafing around and smoking drugs. If he was with you, he'd be okay. I know you'd never let anything happen to our Jamie."

There weren't a lot of cots. Mostly it was piles of blankets and mats on the floor. The infirmary wasn't large enough and the casualties had spilled out into a mess hall. Noah lingered at the doorway. He could see Jenny bunched beneath some blankets next to a man with both arms in splints. On her other side was a person bandaged head to toe and not moving. His chest didn't rise or fall.

Noah recognized Dr. Fellows, one of Underbel's own, walking between the wounded, but he waited until he could get the attention of Harpreet Patel.

Dr. Patel whispered something encouraging to a patient then joined Noah by the door.

"How's it going?" Noah asked.

"It's not good," said Dr. Patel. He glanced at the ceiling, folded his hands behind his back. "It could be worse, though. We're in a central location. Heat from this area won't spread too far."

Noah looked up as well. "You think there's ants up there?"

"I shouldn't think so. A hall full of incapacitated people would be too much of a temptation if I were an ant. I'd tuck in the moment the lights went out." His attention was drawn to a pair of men carrying a woman on a stretcher out of the hall. "Is there anything you need? It's just I've got to be in surgery in a moment."

"Have you had a chance to look at that girl over there?" Noah lifted his chin towards Jenny. "Splint on her leg? Head wound maybe?"

"Oh yes, nothing life threatening, I don't think. My fingers tell me it's a fractured tibia. Concussion as well."

"Mental capacity?"

"Oh, you've spoken with her? Don't worry. I've been informed she was dull witted prior to the injury. I really must go. Come find me later and tell me what your homecoming's been like."

Underbel's attitude was similar to Compton Pit's on the subject of incarceration. If someone needed to be locked up, generally it was better to lock them outside. Consequently Underbel's cages were for temporary occupants only. There were four cells defined by strong wire-mesh fencing. Only one had a tenant. In the farthest corner of the cell, a dark mass huddled beneath a blanket.

"Ted," said Sid quietly, hooking a finger through the mesh. The blanket didn't move. "Ted," he said a bit louder.

"That's not my name," said the shape beneath the blanket.

It was not the voice the Boss had been expecting. It wasn't deep enough and the vowels were missing the light kiss of Trinidad.

"Theodore?"

The blanket fell away as the man unfolded himself and rose to his full height. He was huge, very wide at the shoulders. "I'm sick of this crap!"

Sid shared a look of shock with Darcy, then turned to Sanderson. "What's the meaning of this?"

"I don't follow."

"This," he stabbed a finger at the man in the cage, "is not Dr. Odega."

"Damn rights," said the prisoner, snatching up his blanket and wrapping it around his shoulders.

"Are you sure?" asked Sanderson.

Sid's expression said, *Are you kidding me?*

"Of course he's sure." The prisoner grabbed the mesh, put his face to it.

Sanderson looked at the man, then back at Sid. Her surprise was genuine. "I thought he was lying. He fits the description; large, black. He was driving your van."

"Get me out of here, buddy," the prisoner said to Sid. "I'm freezing to death down here."

Darcy took a huge sidestep. The scars along Sid's neck were standing out and he was getting *that* face. The face he wore just before somebody started bleeding.

"You lied to me," Sid said from the back of his throat.

"If I was wanted for theft and murder by a settlement, I'd lie about who I was," Sanderson defended herself. "It's your van. This man matches the description you gave me."

"You bitch!" the prisoner shrieked. "Matching the description of…that's racial profiling." His tone changed as he turned back to Sid. "Come on, man," he said, as if he was asking for something simple like a glass of water. "Get me out of here."

"Where did you get that van?" asked Darcy.

Sanderson had taken a step back and two of her people had moved to stand between their boss and Sid.

"Where did you get the van?" Darcy repeated.

"I traded for it," said the prisoner, finally looking at her.

"With who?"

"With a guy. Big black fellah. He needed fuel, I wanted a better ride. I was headed here anyway but before I was even near the place these people ran me off the road and hauled me in."

"You questioned him," said Sid, "and *decided* he was lying."

"Man, they haven't asked me shit." The prisoner shook the mesh.

"Let's talk in private," said Sanderson.

Sid squeezed his left fist tight enough to draw blood with his nails. One of the guards was getting ready to throw a punch. Darcy stepped towards him.

"Question him," Sid said to Darcy. He looked at Sanderson and held out an arm as if to say, "After you."

Jenny perked right up when Noah sat on the stool beside her cot, though she didn't have the same strength she'd had in the motor pool.

"I've missed you so much," she said, grabbing his wrists and sitting up to kiss him.

He kissed her back, but instead of closing his eyes, Noah looked past her cheek to the bandage-wrapped man on the next cot. No doubt about it, the guy was dead.

"I don't like it here anymore," she said, nuzzling his neck. "There's bugs in the walls."

Noah tightened his arms around her. He had no idea what to say. The makeup on her face had been smeared some. He wondered where she got it from. Did Bacon or one of the others give it to her or did she screw somebody for it?

"Can you take me back with you?" she asked.

Noah lowered her back to the cot. He had to jerk a couple of times to break her embrace.

"Will we have a room together?" She caught both his hands between hers. "You said you have a big room. Is it big enough for both of us?"

Noah's grin was one of total discomfort but she took at it as a yes and sat up again, throwing her arms around his neck. She bit his earlobe and whispered, "If you want to cuddle you can take me somewhere. Don't worry about my leg. It only hurts a little."

She called it cuddling. That was her cute little word for it. All at once Noah felt sick. He remembered that first time. She'd been sitting naked on his bed, waiting for him. Her knees had been drawn up to her chest. He hadn't asked questions, he'd just climbed on board. Now he knew it wasn't some bold move on her part. Jenny was there because that's what she'd been told to do. *They're using you*, he wanted to say. Clear as bell, an image of Bacon and Max came to mind. They were working on the panels and one says to the other, "I think it's time we brought little Noah into the Jenny club."

"I have to go," said Noah, pulling at her arms, pushing her away.

"You just got here."

"I have work to do."

"When are you coming back?"

Noah broke off a piece of his soul and rubbed it in the dirt. “As soon as I can.” He kissed her forehead and left.

“You can’t just pack up and leave,” said Sanderson, her voice almost a shout.

“You don’t have your end of the deal,” Sid snarled back.

They stood glaring at each other across the desk in Sanderson’s office. It was a long, thin room that at one point had served as a security guard’s station. The walls were decorated with posters of tropical beaches. Most of them depicted golden, tanned, beautiful people frolicking in surf and white sands.

“There’s the van, and the contents,” said Sanderson.

“It was empty.”

“We needed the things in it. We kept an account.”

“Yes, yes,” Sid waved a hand, “fuel, first aid supplies. I don’t care about those.”

Her eyes narrowed. “Oh? What was in the van that you *would* care about?”

Inwardly, Sid cursed himself. He sucked his cheek for a few seconds before answering. “Odega. I care about Odega. We’ve fixed you up some. Tomorrow we’re leaving. We’re taking the van and one of your Hummers in payment.”

Sanderson lowered herself into her chair. “I have something else to sell.” She cocked an eyebrow. “My silence.”

Sid drummed his fingers a couple of times on her desk. “Apart from your husband, who would find that of value?”

“You’re not being very nice to me today, Sid.”

“You brought me and mine out here on false pretenses.”

She blew out a mouthful of air. “I didn’t know that. I didn’t even question him personally. He was unconscious when they brought him in.”

“Now there’s a surprise.”

“Vancouver,” she said and smiled. “Vancouver.”

It caught Sid cold. He was too tired, too far from home.

“Don’t try to bullshit me,” Sanderson continued. “Did you know one of those barrels of pesticide you brought along still had a shipping label on it? You broke the city. That’s where you were when D’Abo made his play. That’s where your latest trinkets have been coming from.”

“Beverly, listen to me—”

“Your people will stay.” From a drawer, Sanderson extracted two tin cups and a plastic bottle of water. “You’ll finish the work.” She filled both cups up halfway and pushed one towards Sid. “And I’ll keep my mouth shut until spring.”

“Permanently.”

“Not going to happen. Late spring.”

“Do you know what will happen if the word spreads about Vancouver?”

“Yes.” She sipped some water. “We’ll all get for free what you’re making us pay for.”

Sid flicked his cup. “You think Vancouver was free?”

Sanderson reached across the desk and patted his hand. “Don’t sulk. You can’t win every time.”

Sid picked up the cup and took a drink. “Give me a complete inventory on the van.”

12. Gone South

The Compton Pit chiefs met the next day at dawn in Sanderson's office. Caps was taken with a poster extolling the joys of Fiji. A pair of scuba divers swam beside a coral reef.

"I should have traveled more," said Caps. "If the world hadn't changed, I could be tripping across the globe right now."

Lena squeezed his arm. "If the world hadn't changed you'd be sitting around stoned all day watching Star Trek."

"Right now I'd settle for just sitting around stoned."

Sid pulled his eyes away from the scuba diving poster and cleared his throat. He held a dogskin pouch in his hand. The pouch jingled when he shook it. "This is money," he said.

"Whuhoo," said Caps, popping his cheek with a finger.

"It's money you can spend today," said Darcy, reaching into the pouch and pulling out a large copper coin. "New Portland money."

"New Portland," said Noah, reaching for the coin.

"The guy we came here for is actually named Remo Tyree. He's up from New Portland. He encountered Dr. Odega—"

"Or someone matching his description," cut in Sanderson.

"—to the southwest of here. Tyree was heading in this direction, Odega was going away. He traded Odega fuel and a smaller vehicle for our van." Darcy sat with her hip on the corner of the desk and turned to look at Sanderson. "Which means your people ran an innocent man off the road, beat him up and put him in a cage."

"Okay, so Odega's not here," said Lena. "When can we go? I'm finished my end. The rest of it is plug and play."

"I want to leave," said Caps.

"Me too," said Noah.

"How was Ted acting?" Dr. Patel asked Darcy. "Did this man say?"

"Normal," she replied. "Pleasant, even."

"So Odega's headed south," said Sid. "The nearest settlement in that direction is someplace called the Catacombs."

"Not 'the catacombs'," said Sanderson. "Just Catacombs."

"And you've been there?"

"Yes. Used to be you'd have to go down to the ruins of Seattle then back up again, but the earthquake all those years ago made a passable land bridge. It's…I'm too tired, Sid. Here," she reached over to a bookshelf, ran her finger along some spines, then pulled out a hardcover with red binding. "Read up on it yourself."

Sid took the book. Black print on the cover read; *Graff's Graphs Volume VII: The Pacific Coast.*

"We have this one," said Sid. "It's got Underbel in it, but he never made it as far as us for this edition. Can I borrow it? I'll return it on our way back."

"Back from where?" asked Lena.

"Darcy and I are going to Catacombs. It's our closest lead. If you three have really finished here, go home. You can drive the Hummer back."

"No they can't," said Sanderson.

"The Hummer's ours now."

"I'm not debating that. We can't let you go back to the Pit. We've closed the north road. Snow.

"It's too early for snow," said Lena with passion, as if she could manufacture fact from desire.

"We were closed off from Underbel by snow last November," said Sid. "Your scouts are sure?"

"They know snow." Sanderson sighed. "You'll have to stay until the pass clears."

"When will that be?" Caps was suddenly quite awake.

"Could be next week, could be spring. Whichever, we'll find room for you, and we can certainly use your skills." She stood. "Now if you'll excuse me I have to release a prisoner and see if I can put him to work."

"You're going to make him work?" Darcy was shocked.

Sanderson shrugged. "He has no vehicle. If he can't leave he has to earn his keep."

The moment the door closed behind her, Caps said to Sid, "I can't stay here. I'm coming with you."

Lena gaped at her lover.

"I don't want to stay either," said Noah.

"Unacceptable," said Sid. "Darcy and I have to go, but if we're snowbound from the Pit now, there's no guarantee we won't be snowbound from Underbel by the time we catch up with Odega. The answer is no. You three stay here until it's safe to—"

"Boss," Caps interrupted, "I really can't stay here."

Sid took a deep breath. "Is there something you want to tell me?"

"I'm not staying." He crossed his arms and clammed up.

"Everyone else out. Richard, a word with you."

Caps braced himself and turned to his girlfriend. He knew she was going to be angry, but the expression on her face made his heart drop to his stomach, then to his feet. His eyes lingered on the door as it closed behind her.

"What the hell is going on?" Sid demanded.

"I'll lose it here, Boss. I'm freaking out. I'm not kidding on this one."

"You don't freak out."

"Another day in this place and I will."

"Why?"

"What does it matter?" Caps cried, shaking his fists at the ceiling. "The cold, the ants in the walls, who cares? I can't be here anymore. Boss, I'm begging you. I'm an inch away from trying to walk home."

"You're not just being childish?" He lowered his voice and said, "Lena deserves better than this."

"Lena? I don't see how—"

"She'll have to come with us. I can't separate the two of you. Your presence is the only thing keeping her sane. If you make this choice, she has to take another road trip."

"Oh. Crap." He looked at the floor, then at his hands, and shuddered. "I can't stay here."

Sid nodded. "Move our stuff into the hunters' van. Send Noah in on your way out. I'm sure he's waiting outside."

Noah took the same chair Caps had been sitting in. Sid took a few deep breaths to prepare himself for the next disaster. "And you want to leave because?"

"I hate this place."

"You pleaded with me to come here. What happened with the meeting of the minds? You were supposed to be going over things with Underbel's panel jockeys."

"I did. Sort of. It was less productive than I'd hoped. Boss, I…I don't think I have any friends here." He laid it out for Sid, about Jenny, and her arrangement with Bacon and the others.

"You're tired, Noah, and I can appreciate how much this…disappoints you, but your value, both to the Pit and to—"

"I'm so tired of hearing about my value! Whatever you paid when you *bought* me, I've worked that off! In spades."

"I already gave out today's golden ticket. Richard beat you to it. You can do wonders for Underbel's array with a short stay, and I want Bacon's input on your new panels. Whatever your differences are, work them out. The community is more important than you are."

Noah understood from Sid's tone that arguing further was pointless. He stood. "Fine."

Sid waited a few moments. He should have known better than to think it would be so easy. He picked up the copy of *Graff's Graphs* and took a wistful glance at the poster of the scuba divers. He'd learned to dive while toying with the idea of transferring to the coast guard. How completely useless that training was to him now.

Lena was waiting for him in the hall.

"You promised."

Sid held his hands up. "You can't blame me for the weather, or for your boyfriend's whims."

" 'It's a safe trip,' you said. 'Back in a week,' you said. I knew this would happen." She yanked a pant leg up and rapped on her prosthetic. "How old is this?"

"How should I—"

"Six months. What happened to the one I had before it?"

"You lost it at the aquarium. That's not going to happen this time. We're going into some unfamiliar territory. It's just unfamiliar to us." He held up the book.

She yanked her pant leg down. "Do you know about Catacombs?"

"I haven't had a chance to read yet, but—"

"I have. I've read every edition of *Graff's* that we have. You know why? So I can be happy about all the places I'll never have to go."

"Lena, I am sorry. When we get home, you won't have to leave again. I'll make a general announcement, I'll add it to the Pit's charter, whatever it takes."

Her face emptied of emotion. No anger, no sorrow, only a terrible vacancy where one or both should have been. "I don't believe you."

13. View from Olympus

From the pages of *Graff's Graphs, Volume VII*

The settlement of Catacombs (map 14a) is the antithesis of all others listed to date. The people who live here are to be as lauded for their spirit as they should be lamented for their lunacy. Whereas most of us live under the ground with the animals above us, Catacombs is above ground, with the teeth below. So why such a contradictory name? It is not an irony. It is a play on words. Regrettably, space does not allow me to completely supply the settlement's history. For that, you should go there, if you have the courage. Suffice it to say, thanks to an earthquake, an abandoned mine and the sad end to a glorious family name, this settlement resides on ground beneath which run a thousand tunnels, and ten times as many cats. The people of Catacombs eat the cats, wear the cats, and trade the cats. The obvious drawback to this is that the cats ever struggle to do the same to the humans. The cat runs host some of the most interesting animal-proofing innovations you'll ever see. The town is quite traveler-friendly. Many needs can be supplied and the town readily accepts barter. New Portland dollars are also accepted. There is a capable mechanic, a secure birthing shelter and a more than adequate medical facility, as befits a community that farms cats. There is even a hotel and restaurant, called, as if there were any doubt, The Cat's Kills. Travelers along the continent's western coast should not miss out on this unique and exciting place.

Caps closed the book and placed it in the netting on the back of Darcy's seat. Lena was as far away from him as possible, squished into the far side of the van. He reached out and placed a hand on her leg. She didn't acknowledge him, but at least she didn't push his hand away.

"How much do you think this is worth?" Darcy asked Sid, hefting the pouch of coins.

"I haven't a clue. Doesn't matter. We've got enough incidental barter in the trunk to cover anything."

Darcy winced.

The sky was beginning to darken when the van reached the top of an incline and Catacombs spread out before them. Nestled inside a high wire-mesh fence stood a group of mostly single-level buildings joined together by mesh tunnels. In the distance, an unkempt mansion crumbled away on the edge of a cliff. Dead vines wrapped the edifice in a reddish, leafy embrace, looking as if one day they'd succeed in throwing the house over the edge once and for all.

A figure in a bulky fur coat came through a booth near the gate. "State your name and business," he called.

Sid shouted through his window. "My name's Sid. We're from Compton Pit, via Underbel."

"I know Underbel. Never heard of no Compton Pit."

"We're to the north aways," he held the copy of *Graff's* out the window. "We just had to check you out."

The man disappeared into his booth and the gate slid open. Sid pulled the van in, and the gate closed behind him. The man appeared again, this time coming right up to the window.

"I guess you'll be wanting the hotel, then." He looked past Sid as he spoke, taking in the van's other occupants.

"You guessed right."

"Go straight until you can't anymore, turn right. You can't miss it. Visitor's rules are posted in the lobby. Make sure you read them."

"Will do." Sid rolled the window up and drove slowly past the other buildings. The ground within the fence was dead. The buildings were mostly repaired Old World structures. There wasn't enough of them to justify a town, but possibly the site had once been a secluded convention center. As they drove, Lena looked out her window and shuddered every time they passed over a grate. There were a lot of them. She could picture the cats in the tunnels beneath them, sharpening their claws on stone and making special plans just for her.

All the buildings were the same color, dull brown with yellow trimmings and hints of rust. A long segmented building had the look of a pre-Change motel, but the Cat's Kills turned out to be an old three-story house. The windows on all floors were covered with both bars and mesh. Brown-painted sheet metal was bolted to the house all around to a height of ten feet. The sloping roof was likewise reinforced. Christmas lights hung under the eaves, though they weren't on. A pair of cat pelts were affixed to either side of the front door, and the welcome mat was made up of the combined skins of three felines, two tabby, one gray. Above the door, a wooden sign proclaiming the establishment's name also bore the likeness of a cat with a rat in its mouth.

The door swung open and a rotund man stepped out. He was nearly bald, with a few strands of black hair clinging to his head above the ears. His entire outfit consisted of a hodgepodge of cat fur. Even his boots were made of the stuff.

"I'm George Douglas. Welcome to the Cat's Kills," he said, "the best hotel this side of the Columbia River."

Sid dropped out of the van and shook the man's hand. "I'm Sid. That's Darcy, and there's two more in the back.

"Well, come in, you must be hungry. Four of 'em!" This last was yelled at the open door. "Will you be staying long?"

"At least for the night."

"Good, good," he kept his grip on Sid's hand, using it to pull the man up the steps. "How many rooms will you need? There are four rooms available, three doubles and a single."

"We'll take two…uh…" A strange joy started in Sid's stomach and spread through his entire body, "…doubles."

George's smile swelled as if he too was struck by the sudden mirth. "Been underground a long time, huh? Feels good to book a hotel room, doesn't it? Feels right. That's our motto, 'The Cat's Kills, where it feels right.' " They were at the door when George stopped. "There is of course, the matter of payment."

"We have money," said Sid. From beside the van, Darcy shook the coin pouch. "New Portland dollars."

"Excellent. Rooms are twenty a night. Booze is a dollar a cup, coffee is two. The dinner special'll run you two bucks a head, but I'll knock a dollar off if all four of you have a drink with dinner."

Sid did some quick math. They had fifty-two dollars in that pouch. Food and lodgings for all of them would leave him with just a single dollar. Maybe if they all bunked in the same room…he shook his head and laughed inwardly. The first cash in over a decade, and already he wanted to hoard it. On the other hand, if their search for Odega took them farther south, he'd need fuel and other supplies.

"Do I get fuel from you?"

"Nope, you get that from Grady down by the gate. Two hundred bucks a gallon. You need travelin' food? Got that, and ammo. We also have—"

"Stop." Sid pulled his sleeve out the innkeeper's grasp. "My cash just ran out. Why don't I get the rooms on barter?"

George's smile dimmed, but only a little. "Sure, sure. No offense, but I'll have to see what you're offering first."

Caps stood at the bottom of the steps. Lena, upon realizing they weren't going in yet, jumped back into the van and shut the door. The Boss, with George in tow, moved to the van's rear and opened the doors. He shoved a few skinbags off the large metal trunk. The lock hung open. He was sure he'd closed it. Maybe it was broken. The trunk lid lifted with a tiny creek and the two men looked inside. George took two steps back, eyes wide in outrage.

"I don't know what type of town you think this is, stranger, but you and yours can just get on out of here."

Sid barely heard him. He was too busy being swept up in his own outrage. He'd packed the trunk himself: a selection of pelts, mostly to cover what lay beneath; six bottles of booze; four portable water purifiers with extra cartridges; disposable pens that still worked and beneath it all, the crown jewel, a 2.4 gigahertz laptop computer. That wasn't what was in the trunk now.

"Hi," said Noah, squinting at the light and waving feebly.

"Sid!" shouted Darcy.

The innkeeper had fished a long-barreled pistol out his pants and had it pointed at the back of Sid's head. "You let that boy on out of there. He's staying here."

Sid spun. "Darcy, no!" He threw himself into her path and she had to pull up short to keep from running into him. "That idiot," he jerked his thumb at Noah, "is not a slave."

George's eyes narrowed. "What's he doing in the trunk, then?"

"I'm a stowaway," said Noah, easing his stiff legs to the ground.

"Right on, man!" Caps clapped his hands together.

George looked at all their faces, especially Noah's. His thumb gently released the gun's hammer, then the whole pistol vanished into his cat suit. "I guess you'll be wanting another room."

Sid caught movement in windows, and from the corners of buildings, as people stepped into the open, letting their own firearms rest easy. Of course the other townsfolk would be keeping a careful eye on newcomers. "I'll just stick with the two rooms. Noah there can sleep on the floor."

"I swear," George winked at Noah, "that just about ruined my good mood. What are you all waiting for? Inside, inside."

"What about the bill?" asked Sid.

"I spotted a thing or two in your van. I'm sure we can accommodate each other."

The other townsfolk, taking their cue from George, went about their business.

As the group filed into the hotel, Sid pulled Darcy aside.

"Where's the barter?"

"How should I know? Ask Noah."

"Don't start. I locked that trunk. You're the only one besides me who knows the combination."

Darcy scratched her forearm. Beneath her sleeve, a ring of small wounds itched as they healed. "I owed him one, Sid. He really didn't want to stay there. We've still got the laptop, the booze and the box of pens. The rest is stowed in Underbel."

"This is direct insubordination. I can't believe—"

"I smuggled an angel out of hell. You smuggled the devil into paradise."

Sid put a hand on her shoulder and squeezed hard. "I'm going to give you this one. But this is the last one. The *last* one! I'm done apologizing and you're not going to milk this for the next twenty years. Am I understood?" His hand left her shoulder and cupped her jaw, he lifted her head until they were eye to eye. "Am I understood?"

She twisted out of his grip. "Yes." Her face softened. "Let's not be mad, okay? I'm even with Noah, and we're even with each other. Forgive me?"

Sid nodded. He moved to close the van but caught sight of something in trunk. "There's a jug. I'm guessing it's not booze."

Darcy bit her lip. "He was in there a long time, Sid."

The lobby of the Cat's Kills was little more than enough space for a closet. Beyond was the restaurant. Faded red carpet stretched between the walls, a myriad of stains joining Persian swirls. The walls were decorated with landscape paintings, animal heads—a moose, a fox and three cats arranged in a triangle—a rifle rack and a collection of pictures, framed black-and-whites.

There were six tables, square, each seating four. A long bookshelf, shelves stuffed to the max, occupied the far wall. Near the stairs was a model under a glass case, and beside that, a rack of thick fishing poles.

Sid peered at the model. Wooden blocks had been carved to represent buildings. The largest building was a four-story affair in the shape of a horseshoe embracing a host of smaller buildings. A swimming pool lay behind that, and to the right was a parking lot and helicopter pad.

"That was going to be the new Olympus View Convention Retreat," said George. "It was going to replace the old Olympus View Convention Retreat, which is what you're in now."

"Olympus View?"

George pointed out the south window. "That's Mount Olympus. Been living here, or close by almost all my life. Never once saw old Zeus coming down, but he still likes to toss a thunderbolt or two our way."

"If you expect to feed our guests," said a woman's voice from behind them, "you'll have to get something to eat." She took Sid's hand and shook it firmly. "I'm Renatta Douglas, and this oaf here was supposed to go fishing first thing in the morning."

"I got busy," said George. "I swear, I don't know if taking a long walk outside might not be better than staying home sometimes. Alright," he held his hands up in surrender, "I'm going. If one of you lot would tote my gear, I'll knock the price down a bit."

"I'll go," said Caps, crossing to the rack of poles. "I used to love fishing."

"Don't be stupid," Renatta said to her husband. "Take the harpoons."

"I'll get dinner my own way, woman. Now get our guests settled in."

Lena watched with pensive eyes as her man left the dubious security of the hotel.

"Don't worry, dear, it's perfectly safe." Renatta appeared at her elbow.

Mrs. Douglas was a stout woman a little over five feet high. She wore a blue cardigan over an even bluer dress. A woolen cap was pulled down to just above her eyebrows and what hair that showed was dark, with gray streaks. With her husband gone, delight burst from her face, as if she had to take over being ridiculously happy. "My, aren't you a pretty thing," she said to Darcy. "And you're a looker yourself." Her eyes lingered on Noah. "Such a fine young man. Was it uncomfortable in the trunk, dear?"

"I've had better accommodations."

"And you will again. Oh…" a thirtyish man was half way down the stairs. His features were similar to George's, same rounded cheeks, same sunken eyes. "This is our son, Francis."

"Call me Frank. Never seen you bunch before."

"We read about your town in *Graff's Graphs*," said Darcy, sticking with Sid's story.

"Oh. Graffers," he nodded as if it explained everything.

"Graffers?"

Renatta walked over to the bookcase and tapped a red book on the top shelf. "Lots of people come here since that nice man wrote about us. We have all his books. Autographed. He signed the lot of them when he came through the last time. There's the man himself." She turned and admired a photograph in a brown frame. The group immediately recognized Donald Graff. He was sitting in a chair beneath the collection of cat heads, a pipe clenched between his teeth. "Frank took the picture. That's what he loves, taking pictures. He'll take yours if you like."

"Twenty dollars or equivalent a picture," said Frank, "more if you want it bigger than the ones over there."

Darcy took a closer look at the photograph. Graff wore the same bemused look he'd held as he'd regaled them with tales at Camper World. It seemed like a lifetime had passed since then. Graff had asked her to go with him when he'd left. As if.

"We'll be waiting a while for dinner," said Renatta. "Frank, if you're not going to help in the house, why don't you show our guests around?"

"I suppose I could do that." said Frank, as if he had a choice in the matter.

"I could do with a walk," said Noah, still working kinks out of his back and shoulders.

Surprisingly, Lena joined them. Sid, tired from driving and the sudden excitement of being treated as a slaver, opted out, choosing instead to have Renatta show him his room.

Frank led them out of the Cat's Kills and down the steps. "That's what's left of Delancey Manor," he said pointing to the right. "Beneath your feet was the Fool's Head Mine. To the north—it's overgrown now—was the Olympus View Fairgrounds. The mansion's not part of the tour—"

"Pretty soon it won't even be part of the cliff," Noah said under his breath.

"—for a very good reason. That house over there was the final residence of Christina Delancey, of the Mississippi Delanceys…"

"She never had kids, and her husband died back in the early aughts." George Douglas stopped walking long enough to tap his chin a couple of times, then his pace resumed with the history lesson. "Aught two, I think it was. She sold off all her southern holdings and retreated to the mansion. Kept a few servants—"

"Let me guess," said Caps, "and a lot of cats. How far to the river? Is it over the cliff?"

"Over the cliff? We're not leaving the fence line, son."

Caps shrugged and kept in step. Maybe their destination was an underground river accessed within the town limits. George carried one pole, while Caps had somehow wound up carrying everything else: another pole, two tackle boxes, two folding chairs and a large, empty sack. The pole threatened to slip from his grasp. His half hand wasn't used to such unwieldy cargo. Caps stooped to recover the pole's balance, almost stepping on a grate in the process. He jigged sideways.

"Don't worry, you can step on the grates." George turned and did just that. "They're strong." He waited on the grate. Seeing that Caps was not going to accept the implied invitation to do the same, he set off once again towards their destination.

"What you said about Christine, you're sort of right. Everyone thought she lived with a million cats, but she didn't. She only kept three in the house. Queenie, Smoke and Miss Posey. I loved Miss Posey. I'm not ashamed to admit it. There was a cat that walked in joy. Cute as a button and always rubbing up against you like she was an itchy buffalo and you was a rock. The thing was, Christine would accept any cat brought to her. And people did. They'd drive up out of the blue because they didn't want their pet no more, or couldn't have it, and they'd heard about good old Christine Delancey. My son did up a website for her. She loved cats. Had big old cat shows twice yearly. October and June."

"June?"

"Mmhmm. Ninth to eleventh, every year, like clockwork. Not like dog shows. No obedience stuff. Just lots of plump women saying 'Look how pretty my pussy is!' " He nudged Caps with an elbow. "I don't tell that one to the ladies.

"But that weren't the only place the cats came from. Y'see, Christine took in every cat sent her way, she just didn't keep them in the house. Down there." He tapped the ground with the end of his pole. "The cat runs used to be Fool's Head Mine. First guy to own it, way back before my daddy's time, was Jeremy Head. He got a little gold out of it, very little, just enough to seed the thing so he could sell the claim to a sucker. The sucker in turn found himself another sucker and so on. The mine changed hands nine times all told, and every time it was dug a little deeper. The Delanceys were the final owners and they closed it up for good back when I was just a little kid. That last January 'fore the Change, the earth rolled a bit—"

"I remember that. I was living in Seattle. It rattled some dishes and took out a house of cards I'd spent five hours building."

George laughed. "You must have had some time on your hands. It may have been a dish rattler for you, but for us, well, it was like we'd woken Zeus up with our New Year's party and he was none too happy about it. Dropped a ton of dirt into the ground. Set the construction back something awful. The quake a few years after was worse, but we recovered from it and it did give us the northern land bridge.

" Both quakes killed a lot of cats, too. We thought that was the worst part of the first one. Funny, huh?

"That's where they all was. Every cat that Christine ever got, 'sides her own three, she put them in the mine. There was always mice around, and she'd put out clean water here and there. Kept them bowls full, too. The cats thrived or they died, and let me tell you, they thrived. So now here we are, all we know, 'cause me and Renatta been runnin' the Olympus View for most of our lives, sitting on top of a bunch of tunnels full of cats that just ain't friendly. There's holes all over the place, but fortunately, 'cause

Zeus ain't a complete jerk, not a lot of places they could get out. The folks at the show…it was a mess, let me tell you. But me and Natta weren't leaving. No way. We caved in the mine entrance, holed up in the house and fought our way back out again bit by bit. The cats from the show, one by one, they jumped into the holes to see what all them other cats were up to. Big old cat trap." He stopped and planted one end of his pole in the ground. "Drop the chairs, we're here."

Caps dumped his cargo. "Is the water under that grate?"

"Water? Son, ain't you figured it out? Only fish around here are catfish."

"Over there is Grady. He's our mechanic and supplies the fuel. You'll see him at dinner. Everyone comes to the Kills for dinner." Frank led his group a few more strides. "This the birthing house, we call it the Cradle." He stopped beside a square building swathed in sheet metal and coils of barbed wire. A mesh tunnel led to another building of the same size. "That's the hospital. Our doctor's over in Ketchikaw right now, so don't get sick. Hey," he noticed he'd lost one of the group.

Darcy was a bit back, standing by one of the grates. The sun shone directly into it, illuminating a wide strip of the tunnel beneath. A pair of kittens, one gray with orange spots on its face, the other nearly solid black, were wrestling. They pounced and rolled, batted and bit. They were gangly, their legs too long and their ears too big for their heads.

Conflicted, she watched the kittens frolic in the pool of cold sunlight, and another kitten came back to life. Bono, her fluffy ball of happiness.

Every morning, an hour before the sun came up, Bono would slip under the sheets and nestle in the hollow of her throat. The soft fur, the sensual throbbing as the creature purred its way deeper into her heart each time.

"Don't watch too long," said Frank.

The kittens scattered as a large gray cat with orange splotches all along its body darted into the light. It looked up at Darcy and hissed. Another cat joined it, this one lean with short hair. Its attention was on Darcy, but it looked at the tunnel walls, intent on finding a way up.

"Come on." Frank pulled on her arm. "Come on before it's ruined for you."

She didn't fight him as he led her away the vent. The group proceeded eastward, towards Catacombs's main gate.

"This building is the mouse farm."

"Mouse farm." Lena found the concept disgusting. "Is that a euphemism? We call our research lab the zoo."

"No. It's just as it sounds. Beneath you are generations of cats born to the runs. They know all the hiding places, every nook and cranny. If we didn't restock the supply, the mice would run out."

"You people are insane," said Lena. "The cats might not be able to get out of those tunnels, but mice…" She looked at the ground. "Oh my God!"

A concrete block, housing some sort of plumbing, was to her left. She scrabbled on top of it, pulling her limbs up as if something were about to get her. "Darcy, get up here. Get up here! Mice can burrow straight up!" She turned to the Cat's Kills. It was over two hundred meters to the front steps. Two hundred meters of dirt from which a million mice could suddenly pop out like an upside-down rainstorm. The mesh tunnels that connected the buildings looked safe. She pointed at the nearest one. "How do I get in there? How? Tell me! Noah, why are you still on the ground?" Hysteria was well on its way.

Frank dropped to one knee and started digging with his hands.

"What are you doing?" Lena shrieked.

Noah heard laughter come from within one of the buildings.

"Darcy, get away from him! Stop digging! Someone stop him digging! Rick! Where's Rick?"

The laughter peaked and choked off from lack of oxygen. Noah could picture someone gripping their sides for the painful silent end of an uncontrollable laughing fit. Caps called them mirth quakes.

Frank stopped digging and pointed. "Concrete. Solid. Under everything, all the way to the fence. You have nothing to worry about."

Lena's mouth moved wordlessly as she looked at the patch Frank had uncovered. "Then why all the dirt?"

"Dirt's softer to walk on. We stay outside as much as we can. The covered walkways are only for wasp season or when the birds act up. Come down, miss. I didn't mean to scare you."

From within the wall, Noah heard someone aping Lena's screams. The laughter renewed.

Frank cast his eyes at the last building on the tour. "I think we'll leave out the inside of the mouse farm, hmm? If you want souvenirs we sell stuff at the hotel. Oh, and we've got three flavors of cat jerky: original, hickory and hot 'n' spicy." He laughed at himself. "There you go. I'm heading in."

Gingerly, Lena climbed down from her perch. "Sounds good to me."

"Can I stay out for a bit?" asked Darcy.

"Sure," replied Frank, surprised at being asked. "This is a free town. Just don't be climbing into the cat runs."

"I promise," she said cooly.

Noah, hesitated. He looked at the hotel, then fell into step beside Darcy.

George produced a small crank handle from a pocket in his suit. He fitted it to a slot next to the grate and turned. Slowly, the grate tilted up on one side, dust slid off, creating a small cloud in the still air. From a pouch he took a handful of what looked like marijuana. He sprinkled it into the grate saying, "Catnip. Stay back, don't let them see you. Open up one of them boxes."

Caps planted himself in one of the chairs and placed a tackle box on his lap. Opening the cover allowed three trays to float up and separate. Only the bottom tray held hooks, big hooks with vicious barbs. The other two trays contained a multitude of colorful rubber lures.

"Gimme this one," said George, scooping a dayglow squid and hooking it to the end of his line. Only then did Caps notice the reels held steel cable.

"Don't you want a hook?" Caps asked as George flicked his wrists and sent the squid hurtling into the blackness.

"Not at first. Just watch me for the first one."

They sat quietly, watching the end of the rod. It didn't budge. The minutes passed.

"How long does this take," asked Caps, getting a little fidgety.

"Take out the bottom tray of that basket and give me what's underneath it." Caps did as instructed, handing over a small flask. George unscrewed the cap one handed and took a long pull. "Fish don't bite if you're not drinking." He held the flask out. "Home brew. Good stuff."

"I'm not much for booze. I don't suppose you've got any smoke?"

George snorted. "Doper, huh? We don't keep no peoplenip around here."

"Peoplenip? That's good. I like that."

"If you use it, make sure you give credit where it's due, son." He winked. The tip of the pole dipped and sprung up. "Here we go." His relaxed grip became one of practiced efficiency. He bobbed the rod a few times then snapped his wrists back, making the little rubber squid nearly clear the hole before dropping back down again. "Gotta keep it moving, make it interesting to them. Hey! Get back here!" Caps had left his seat and taken a step towards the hole. "If it sees you it won't care about no lure. Mind me now, or there's no dinner. In the box is another squid just like this one. Get it and hook it. You can do that right?"

"Yeah. It's not like it's rocket science." He sheathed the hook in the little squid.

"Okay, now hook it to your rod. Good. Now…trade!" He grabbed the second rod and shoved the first into Caps's startled hands. "Keep it moving, mister. Same ways as I did, back and forth then jump it, back and forth then jump it!"

Caps tried to do as he was told, but it wasn't as easy as the innkeeper had made it look. The line jerked and pulled as he tried to maneuver it, the lure a victim to swats and bites.

George extended the second rod over the hole. "Okay, the next time you snap it, bring it all the way out."

Caps flicked his wrists and swung his arms. The instant his lure cleared the hole, George cast the hooked one in. Caps wasn't prepared for the scream. He almost fell out of his chair. A shriek maybe, a whine of pain, that he would have expected, but not the guttural howl of agony that blasted out of the grate. "Jesus! I thought you had like, house cats down there! What is that? A bobcat? A cougar?"

"Echoes," said George. "Get the club out of the sack. I'm not wasting time on this one." He grunted and spun the reel. The end of his pole dipped and shimmied.

The dreadful howl continued, and beneath it, the plaintive mewing of another cat's distress. The reel spun, relentlessly hauling the animal up from the depths. A paw was the first thing to appear. The hook had not gone through the animal's mouth, but through the chest. The cat must have been crouched over the plaything-turned-deadly when the line snapped the hook up. It was gray and white, short-haired, and every one of those hairs was standing straight out. Its back legs wheeled in air as it tried to disembowel its attacker. With a frenzy it bit and clawed at the steel wire, working the hook deeper with every thrash.

"Cool," said Caps, leaning back and putting his hands behind his head.

"You think this is easy?" George clenched around the pole. "Hit it!"

Caps snatched the club and jumped out of his chair. This was just like the head room back home, only better. He swung, catching the animal on the side. The momentum almost knocked the rod free. With a wrench of his back, George kept the cat from touching the ground and held the rod steady.

"In the head! Hit it in the head!"

The cat struggled with far less vigor. Blood dripped from saturated fur around the hook's entry point. Its ears were back and its hazel eyes were glossing over. Caps cracked its skull.

"Bag it." With a sigh of relief, George let the rod go. "You don't ever want one of those suckers to hit the ground. Once they get their legs under them, they forget all about the hook."

"How dangerous can they be once they're hooked?" He slit the skin around the hook with a sharp knife, then threw the animal in the sack.

"How dangerous? If it's not hooked too bad, it'll drag that rod from here to Mexico to get at you, or just rip the hook out altogether. Here." He leaned forward in the chair, pulled at his pant cuff and yanked the boot down a bit, exposing a slanted scar above the ankle. "That's how dangerous a hooked cat can be."

The mewling from below had gotten louder. It was so sad, so mournful. In spite of himself, Caps felt a heartstring being plucked. "I don't believe you."

"Come again?"

"That scar's too wide for a claw mark, 'less it was a cougar. It's too straight for a bite. That's a scar you use anytime you're trying to make a point. I bet you don't even remember what it's really from."

George's eyes widened in affront, then a smile forced its way past anger and he laughed, long and hard. "I like you, son. I like you fine. It's from a motorcycle accident. I was twenty and I was drunk. I was riding…no wait a minute. Well I'll be. Damned if I'm not a hundred percent sure on that."

Caps looked at the hole and considered putting his fingers in his ears. "How long is that crying going to last?"

George picked up his rod. "Hand me a feather lure and we'll put a stop to it right now."

"By the way, you're all crazy," said Caps, opening the second tackle box.

"Just because you got away with being fresh once doesn't mean you should make a habit of it. The red and black one. Thanks."

"No I mean it. One day you'll wake up and this entire town will be down there with the teeth. It could happen any second, I figure."

"The big one? Yeah, could happen at any second for decades. Nothing anybody can do about it. Zeus'll crack the earth when he's good and ready."

"You do know the real Zeus would be on the Mt. Olympus in Greece, not that Olympus over there."

"Way I figure it, Zeus can be on any damn Mt. Olympus he wants to." George released the reel. Rather than dropping straight like the squid did, the feathers spun, slowly descending into the cat runs like a tiny helicopter. "Here we go. Get your rod ready."

Caps looked past the rod to the crumbling mansion beyond the fence. "I assume Delancey was eaten by her cats?"

"Nope. Christine was in the town. Wasn't cats on us, neither. Those were way out on the fairgrounds. Can't says I ever seen so many mice. I guess I always knew there were that many of 'em around, but seeing them…" He looked off in the distance. "Our house was already as mouse-proofed as a place could get. So were most of the Olympus View buildings. That's what saved us in the first few hours, gave us time to get our heads straight. Christine Delancey died of a heart attack. She passed on 'bout a minute after I pulled her in and shut the door."

"If all the buildings were mouse-proofed, why'd you let the mansion go?"

"I said all the buildings of Olympus View. The mansion was anything but mouse-proof. Christine said killing mice gave her cats something to do."

14. Something to Do

"Darcy, get off that thing!" said Noah.

She was lying on a grate. At first she'd just looked down through it, but the longer she watched, the less rational she'd become.

It started with just one cat, pure white, lying in the pool of light. Front legs straight out, tail curled under, covering the back legs. The little pinkness of its ears and nose, and the scowl on its face, made it look like a grumpy bunny, like Easter gone bad. Into the light stepped another cat, this one ginger, with big ears and a triangular head. At first it bit the white cat. Then it began licking, starting at the white cat's head, then working its way down the flank, a luxurious bath. That was when Darcy melted to the ground, sprawled across the rusting metal. The white cat batted the ginger's head, then rolled over, offering the unbathed side.

Of its own volition, Darcy's right arm snaked through the grate and reached out, not for the cats themselves, but for the once-world they represented.

"Darcy!" Noah grabbed her leg. "Get your arm out of there!"

Her eyes went wide as she came to her senses. She pulled away, but stopped as her elbow jammed against the metal.

"Shit. I'm stuck." She glanced at the tunnel below.

The white cat was gone, but the ginger remained. It stood in the middle of the light, looking up at her with big green eyes. It stood on its hind legs and made a sound, more like a raccoon's chirp than a cat's meow. Darcy tugged at her trapped limb, heard material rip.

In a blur the white cat flew beneath the grate and landed on Darcy's arm. Its teeth and front claws sank into her flesh at the same time. Instantly its back claws were at work, shredding sleeve to get at skin.

"Aaaghh!" Darcy yanked hard. Her elbow came free, but she couldn't get her arm out. The cat's grip was too powerful. She pulled, banging the cat's head into the underside of the grate again and again. Noah landed on the grate beside her, gripping her under the shoulder, adding his strength to hers. With a *snap,* the grate opened beneath them.

They fell, screaming and grabbing, an eye blink that lasted an hour. The grate's hinges held. Darcy's trapped arm kept her from falling, Noah's grip on the bottom edge of the grate saved him. The white cat hung from Darcy's arm by its front claws, but quickly pulled up enough to get its teeth in again. Darcy clenched her jaw against the pain. It was a miracle her arm hadn't broken. She looked down. The ground was about two meters below their feet. The ginger was gone. To her left, a series of thin ledges stood out from the wall, allowing the cats to climb high enough to attack her. The white cat had used the ledges first. Now the ginger followed suit. It launched itself from the top ledge, landing and fastening itself to Darcy's hip. She thrashed. The grate let go completely and all of them crashed to the floor of the cat runs.

Noah was up immediately, moving despite the pain in his chest. His lungs struggled to regain breath as he kicked as hard as he could at the cat on Darcy's hip. It flew off her.

Darcy pulled her arm free of the grate and turned to see the ginger already recovered and swatting at her face. Her head jerked away, the claws caught hair. Noah grabbed the cat in both hands. It twisted and clawed open a bloody weal on Noah's cheek. He dropped it and it wrapped itself around his leg, sinking in with all four claws and vicious teeth. The white cat lay beneath the grate, its neck broken, blue eyes vacant and blood dribbling from its mouth. Darcy didn't know if the blood was hers or the cat's. She worked her hand around the throat of the ginger and crushed its windpipe. It shuddered and convulsed as she threw it down the tunnel.

They both looked up. The opening might as well have been a mile away. The ledges the cats used were too narrow for a person.

"Darcy, climb me." Noah positioned himself directly under the opening.

"What?"

"Just do it. We have seconds here."

She stepped in the stirrup he'd made with his hands, put her hands on his head and climbed up to his shoulders. He was remarkably steady. When both her feet were on his shoulders, with his hands gripping her ankles, she stood straight and stretched out her arms. "I can't reach it."

"Jump."

"My arm's weak. I might not be able to hold on."

"When I let go of your ankles, jump."

She crouched, nearly fell, steadied herself, then he let go and she launched herself upward, catching the edge of the opening. Her arm didn't betray her and in a moment she was up and out. She pulled over to the edge and stuck out her good arm. There was no way he could jump that high.

"Noah, I can't reach you."

"I know.

Their eyes locked. Something passed between them, something she didn't understand at first

"I have to go now." Noah looked one way and ran the other. A second later a dozen cats, meowing and chirping, sped through the pool of light.

Noah had no delusions of being able to outrun the cats. Far ahead of him, small bodies darted through another pool of light. He was *so* dead. Then he saw the mine cart. It was off to one side, nowhere near a track. He grabbed its edge, hauling with all his might. The cart teetered, then crashed down on its side. He hauled again, dropping under it as the cart upended, surrounding him with metal walls. Immediately thumps and scratching assaulted him as cats from all directions attacked the cart.

A scratching sound from above him sounded like it was inside rather than out. He looked up. Dim light penetrated the cart from a myriad of tiny holes. Most of them weren't large enough to allow even a paw's entry, but the one on the cart's bottom, now his roof, was. A furry leg stretched through the hole, scooped up and scratched the inside of the cart. The claw withdrew, then returned. Noah turned as best he could in the cramped space. It was like being back in the trunk, except in there his only fear was the Boss finding him before it was too late to go back to Underbel. If only Sid had.

From its holster on his belt, Noah pulled his folding pliers. He extended one of the knife blades, then grabbed the searching cat leg. It yanked out of his grasp, claws tearing the skin on his palm as it went. Noah waited. The claw returned. This time he grabbed it with resolve, prepared for it to jerk away. He pulled hard, yanking the cat against the cart. Noah slid the blade up the leg until it was pressed against the joint, then he forced it home. Warm blood trickled down his fingers and the cat screamed. He gave the leg one more yank then let it go. Would the wound be fatal? Did it matter? Even if every cat in the runs lined up and offered him a leg, how many would he have to kill? A thousand? Ten thousand? Around him, the tone of the scratching had changed. There were still claws on metal, but now there was a softer sound. Digging. The hard-packed earth of the floor could only delay the animals, not stop them.

Fear clenched his stomach and his bowels, but he bit his lip to keep from screaming and gripped his stomach with his arms. He refused to foul himself. His body could let go of its functions when he was dead, then and only then. A claw nicked his ear, patted around, then found his scalp. Noah grabbed the leg and ran it through with his knife. Toffee's rough voice whispered in his mind; *Stick and pull. Only the dead leave the blade in*. No sooner had the claw retreated through the small hole in the dirt, then another was through. Noah stabbed this one too, and the next. Light appeared by his legs as a gap opened large enough to admit a head, then a leg, then a whole cat. He gave up on the spot by his head and brought the knife to bear on this new danger, slamming his leg against the hole to keep another cat from entering.

The cat inside was a dark shape, landing on his chest, going for his neck. Its teeth sank into his thumb as he pushed at it. He drew his arm back for a swing, banged it into the cart and lost the knife. He felt claws pierce his pant leg and enter flesh. The digging was from all around now. Claws reached for him as soon as holes were big enough. The cat was folded over his arm now, bringing its back claws up. Noah grabbed a leg, he didn't know which one, and twisted as hard as he could, popping it out of joint and tearing skin. The cat let go of one hand to attack the other. With a roll he put the animal directly under him and crushed its neck with his forearm. In moving he opened the large hole, and two cats wedged themselves together, both trying to get in at the same time.

Noah kicked at them as hard as he could in the limited space. Flecks of metal fell on his face, then with a snap, a portion of the cart's bottom gave out and a cat landed on his head. It was too surprised to attack right away. Noah grabbed it and threw it up as hard as he could, then something acrid filled his nose and mouth and he couldn't breath. His eyes squeezed shut, stinging and burning. His lungs yearned for oxygen and tried again to get it. A wracking cough ripped at the back of his throat.

"He's alive, that's one for the books," said a muffled voice.

"Get him! Let's move," a different voice, lower pitched.

The cart was lifted and moved aside, hands grabbed for him and something wet was pressed over his face.

"Can you walk?"

Noah got his legs under him, steadied by people on either side. What happened to the cats?

"Keep moving. Almost there. Don't open your eyes."

The wetness against his face fell away. He opened his eyes. In the instant before the stinging closed them, he saw his benefactors. They had the bodies of men, but the heads of cats. He screamed, or tried to. His throat burned anew. The wetness was back, then he felt something squeeze him tightly around the chest and his feet left the ground.

"Got him, okay, got him!"

Then he was lying down, the wetness disappeared and hands gripped the side of his face.

"Noah! Noah, speak to me!"

He opened his eyes and caught a glimpse of pale skin surrounded by red hair.

"He can't speak, and put the towel back," said a man's voice, both angered and amused.

When Noah could open his eyes again, he discovered he was lying on a cot in the infirmary. His lips felt dry, and all his limbs stung and burned as Darcy and a man with a shaggy brown beard cleaned his various wounds.

"You earned yourself some scars, boy," said the bearded man. "I'm Grady. Good move getting under that mine cart. I thought I was going in for a corpse." On the table beside Grady was a gas mask. Two huge glass eyes over a fat muzzle. Noah understood how his mind had seen a cat head.

Noah looked all around him. The room was lit by an oil lamp and a meshed-over skylight. It had windows, but they were boarded up. A trunk and some standing lockers were against one wall, with another cot, and a smaller table upon which were bottles of antiseptic, needles and sutures. He scanned his body. He was stripped to his shorts, and his hands were wrapped in cloth. His gaze settled on Darcy. Her face was covered in dirt, but she was looking at him in a way he'd only fantasized about; adoration with a hint of awe. The moment she became aware of his scrutiny, she turned away.

The door opened and Sid came in, followed by two other people. One of them had a gas mask under one arm.

"How is he?" Sid asked Darcy.

"Fine. He's going to be fine."

Sid clucked his tongue. "Noah, you've got as many lives as a cat, you know that? Try not to lose any more, 'kay?" He turned to the man with the gas mask. "I thought you people said this place was safe."

"It is when people aren't jumping up and down on the grates," said Grady.

Darcy told Sid exactly what had happened.

"They're not the first ones to go in," said Grady. "Just the first one's to come out."

George pushed through the door, adding congestion to an already crowed infirmary. "I don't believe it! A mine cart, yet."

"We should have a party," said Grady. "What do you think, George? We should mark this occasion."

"It's his decision," George pointed at Sid.

"Why is it my decision? You want a party, have a party."

After suffering through getting stitches on both legs and one arm, Noah was helped back to the Cat's Kills and the entire town crowded into the hotel. Noah tried to tell his tale but was too ill to do it justice, so Caps took over for him. By the fifth rendition, the telling of it was nine times longer than the actual event. Noah tried to talk to Darcy, but it was as if she was avoiding him and he didn't have the strength to pursue. He begged off, leaving Caps to keep his spirit alive.

George caught Sid's arm and nodded at the wounded hero plodding up the staircase. "You'll need another room."

"Just another bed. Can you shove a cot into one of the rooms?"

George gave a thumbs-up. "Sure thing. Two bucks."

Renatta had been cooking all day. She already had meat but didn't want to go through nagging her husband for the next day's dinner. He always left it till late, not giving her much time to cook. There was more than one way to skin a cat, but all of them were time consuming. When all the people stomped up her front steps, she conscripted the first two in to help out with cleaning and gutting, then set to work on the catch of the day. George and Frank disappeared into the back room a few times, always reappearing laden with smoked meats, canned pickles and booze. Lots of booze.

Darcy realized one of the townsfolk was hitting on her. He was very drunk, and the smell coming off him made her wonder if his pants were cat fur, or denim he'd really let go. When he doffed his jacket to show her his scars, she packed it in. She didn't even dismiss herself, turning her back on him just as he moved his arm to flex a bicep while pretending he wasn't. He shambled after her a few steps but was intercepted by Caps, who asked the man how many cats it took to make his boots. She walked away when the man bent down to look.

Lena caught Darcy at the stairs. "What's the matter with you?"

"If I wanted to be slobbered over by walking stenches, I'd go drinking with tanners."

"You do go drinking with tanners."

"Just Devon, and he knows better than to slobber."

"Anyway, that's not what I meant. You hardly spoke two words to Noah. If he'd saved me like that, I'd be kissing him head to toe."

"Wouldn't that make Caps jealous?"

Lena shot a glance at her boyfriend who was trying to tell his one-and-only cat fishing story to people who were veterans of the game. "You know what I mean," she said, but Darcy was already gone.

Sid leaned on a wall next to George and asked casually, "How many travelers do you get through here?"

"Not a lot. Most people stop at Ketchikaw. Until Donald Graff spread the word about us, we pretty much kept to ourselves, trading with Ketchikaw and New Portland. A few other places. Why do you ask?"

"I was wondering if a friend of ours might have passed through here."

"Graffers, huh? The others maybe, 'specially the redhead, but you didn't figure as a tourist. Too much purpose about you. What's this friend's name?"

"Theodore Odega."

"Never heard of him."

"Maybe he used a different name. He's tall, and big, really big. Not fat, big boned. Black. Skin darker than mine."

"And he's a friend, huh?" George took a pull from his bottle. He mulled it over. "He was here for a spell."

"How long did he stay here?"

"Couple months I suppose. Earned his keep. Strong fellah, good worker. But he weren't calling himself no Theodore. Eric. Called himself Eric."

"That's his middle name."

"Guess he's your man. He headed out over a month ago. Came back here last week with a different car. Ate a meal, said hello, and took off again."

"Did he say where he was going?"

George motioned at Sid's empty cup. When the cup was raised, he filled it from his bottle. "You looking to do right by him or wrong by him?

Sid had to think that one over. "I'm looking to do as right by him as I can."

"He was looking at some map, asking about bridges in the Peninsula. I'd say he was headed to New Portland."

Hovering at the edge of the conversation, Lena watched Sid's face. She didn't like what she saw.

"Do you have a SatCom?" Sid asked

George laughed. "Now what the hell would we do with a SatCom? Spend what electricity we've got on yackin' on the phone? While we're on the subject of spending, and I hate to bring this up, but we do have to discuss your bill."

Sid put his cup down. "I thought that was settled."

"Oh the rooms, sure. And you know what, dinner's on the house. Your eight-fingered friend there was so helpful while we was fishin'. But there's the other things."

"What other things?"

"The grate we'll have to fix. Those things open up, not down, you know. Your kids broke it good. The gas grenades we used. Those don't grow on trees. The antiseptic, antibiotics, bandages, sutures, plus there's the danger pay to the men who had to go in after your boy. That's a big one. And of course, the party."

"The party? I never..." Comprehension hit him. *It's his decision.* "This is a shakedown."

"I prefer to think of it as a closing-for-winter sale with you buying everything."

"What do you want?"

"That laptop working?"

"Yes."

George grinned. "I'll have to see it of course, but that'll do just fine. Natta, get us another bottle."

"It'll do just fine and change," said Sid. "A lot of change. I'll want fuel and supplies, plus a message taken to Underbel, and maybe a person."

"Now hold on a sec..."

Lena sidled away and turned her back on Sid. He was going on. Maybe a person? He was sending her back to Underbel with strangers. A foul smell hit her and a fur-clad shoulder pressed up against hers.

"Hi there, China Doll. You're as pretty as a china doll. Do you like the fur? I've got fur all over my place."

Caps appeared at her side and whispered in her ear.

"I do like fur," Lena said with smile. "How many cats did it take to make your boots?"

"People keep asking me that." He stooped to look at them, having forgotten the number he'd already come up with. While he strained to separate the different shades, his China Doll was whisked away to the upper regions of the establishment.

Lena kissed Caps goodnight. She was still mad at him, but he'd been wonderful tonight. She entered the room she shared with Darcy. She could tell from the breathing that her friend wasn't really asleep, but allowed her to get away with the pretense.

On the ground floor, Walter, the stinking Casanova, shouted at the top of his lungs, "There are seven cats in my boots!"

Grady, equally drunk, shouted, "We'd better get 'em out of there!" He tackled Walter and yanked at the footwear. A clumsy fight ensued, resulting in both men being tossed bodily from the Cat's Kills. Sobered by the flight, or more exactly, the landing, they went their separate ways, Walter to his room in the main building, and Grady shuffling towards his digs on the other side of the small town. On the way he dropped to his knees by a grate.

"Sorry about the gas," he said.

A plaintive mew drifted up from the darkness. Grady reached out and stroked the grate, feeling warm fur beneath his hand instead of cold metal. Then he rose, knowing better than to stay any longer.

15. Checks and Balances

Awake first, Sid scrubbed himself in a cramped tub filled with tepid water. He missed the Pit intensely, more for its comforts than its securities.

The door to the bathroom opened and Lena walked in. True, the showers at home were unisex, but the unfamiliar environment made the Boss self-conscious. He yanked the curtain shut.

"You could have knocked."

"You're not sending me back."

"Excuse me?" He pulled the curtain aside enough to stick his head out.

"I know what you're planning and I heard your deal with George."

Sid winced and let the curtain close. "I had no intention of sending you. I was going to send Noah back."

"Oh." She yanked the curtain open. "You're not doing that either."

"Lena!" his hands moved to cover his crotch, then instead he lay back, as best he could, and rested his arms on the side of the tub.

"I'm serious," her eyes never left his. "He saved Darcy's life. I like having him around. He helps keep me sane. I could have cheered when he popped out of the trunk. And don't say he's too important to risk. How do you think that makes the rest of us feel?"

"I don't mean—"

"And if your inner alpha male is bruised because he disobeyed your orders, get over it. If not for him, then for me. You owe me."

"I owe you? What do I—" his eyes widened as her arm shot into the tub. It came out holding the plug. The pipes gurgled as water drained away

"To Underbel and back, a quick visit. Then it was a 'jaunt' to Catacombs. Now I think we're going even farther. You owe me."

She yanked the curtain closed and left the bathroom. The door shut with a satisfying *thud* and she leaned against it and smiled, picturing the Boss watching his bathwater slurp down the drain. Burle Campbell had once told her that one way to come out ahead in a negotiation was to make your opponent feel naked. It was so much easier when the opponent actually was naked.

One down, one to go. She returned to her room and shook Darcy awake. "Good morning."

"What time is it?" She knuckled the corners of her eyes.

"No idea. The sun's been up for about half an hour. Breakfast?"

"Not if it's cat meat."

"I doubt it'll be eggs and bacon. I'm going to wake Noah. Are you going to sit with your savior and be nice?"

"Oh, God," Darcy tossed her blankets aside and scanned for her clothing. "Can't this wait for later?"

"Nope. We're going for a long trip and I don't want any tension. All of you are going to have your hands full looking after my needs."

"Aren't we full of ourself this morning."

"There's only two ways I'm not going to lose it out there. One of them is dead drunk and I don't need the hangover. The other way is everyone talking and happy. So give."

Lena sat on her own bed and quietly slid Darcy's coveralls under it with her foot.

In a muscle shirt and shorts, Darcy plodded around the room. She had other clothes, but they were down in the van. Puzzled, she looked beneath her own bed, then yanked a blanket from it to wear against the cold. She dropped into the room's only chair and looked at the floor, a little lost. "He looked at me."

"People have been known to do that."

"The way he looked at me…"

"If you think he's mad at you because your arm isn't ten feet long—"

"No. Not mad. He…I don't…I wouldn't have…" Her eyes narrowed. "Are you hiding my clothes?"

Dogshit! Lena hooked the coveralls with her foot and slid them out into the open.

"Thanks," Darcy retrieved the garment. "You're right, I need to talk to him. I will before we leave. I guess you know where we're going, then. Sid told you?"

"He didn't have to. Has he planned this since Underbel?"

"If we didn't find Odega here, yes."

Darcy skipped breakfast, it was pickles and cat hash. She stayed in her room until she heard plates being cleared, then braved the downstairs. Sid nodded to her from where he sat, arguing with George while the laptop sat on the table between them. She went outside to find Noah and Caps loading the van.

"Morning," she said grabbing a skinbag and falling into step beside Noah. "How are you feeling?" The scratches on his face and hands looked itchy, but not infected. There was still a little dried blood in his hair.

"I'm fine, but my throat hurts…and everything else. How are you doing?"

"Better. I need to talk to you."

Caps, waiting inside to receive cargo, caught her look and stretched out on the van's back seat. She took Noah's arm and pulled him a few steps from the van.

"I know I was acting funny last night. I was ashamed."

"Ashamed? Why?"

"You put my life before your own."

"Not really. Better one of us live than both of us die."

"You could have climbed me."

"No, I don't think that would have worked."

"Why not? I'm stronger than you are. Here," she cupped her hands into a stirrup and bent a little. Noah held a hand up in refusal but Darcy insisted. "Come on, climb me."

With an air of resignation, he put one foot in her hands and stepped up to her shoulder. The moment he put weight on her shoulder, she leaned to the side and he fell to the dirt.

"Okay," she said, helping him up. "It's harder than I thought it was. Again."

He tried again, this time they both went down. From the van, Caps laughed and hooted.

"I'm ready this time," she offered the stirrup again.

Noah took her wrists and pushed them apart. "Too late. We're out of time."

"We've got plenty of…oh, you mean the cats get us. Okay, so how did you know you could do it?"

"Balance. It was an exercise Toffee put me through."

"You let Toffee climb you?"

Noah chuckled. "No. I'd hold a barbell across my shoulders and he'd pull weights on and off. If I started to lean in any direction, he'd pile more weights on that side until I fell over."

"Why did you put up with that?"

"I wanted to learn what he had to teach. Lucky for us, huh? Anyway, it's not just you. Even if you stood stalk still, I don't think I could jump from your shoulders. That takes a different type of balance."

"How did you know I could do it?"

"I…you know, it just didn't occur to me that you couldn't."

Her eyes changed. A glimmer appeared, a fragment of the way she'd looked at him the night before. "I almost killed us. When you disappeared into the tunnel…then the cats…" Her hand rose up and delicately touched the largest scratch on his face, a thin red line from beside his nose to the corner of his mouth. He reached up to take her hand but she pulled it away. Her mouth tightened and her eyes went dead. "I'm sorry. Thank you for saving my life."

Noah watched her disappear into the house. He didn't understand. As near as he could tell, she resented him for what he'd done.

"Tell me the truth," said Caps, dropping an arm across Noah's shoulders. "How many times have you fantasized about rescuing her from animals?"

"Countless."

"You actually do it, and you still get no play. That's our Darcy. Hey," he punched Noah in the arm, "I love you for it. Now that you're not in shock or nauseous any more, you feeling macho? Huh? All manly?"

"Like you wouldn't believe." Noah beat his chest.

Striking a bodybuilder's pose, arms flexed on either side, Caps growled. Noah aped the posture and growled back. Strutting and growling they finished loading the van.

Renatta caught Darcy at the foot of the stairs. "I heard what you said out there. I wasn't eavesdropping, but grown men and women throwing themselves to the ground." Laughter escaped her lips and was quickly hidden behind a hand. "Well, that's something you can never get enough of. You're wrong, you know. You saved him as much as he saved you."

"How do you figure?"

"Ordinarily, Grady would never jump into the runs right away, but he'll do anything for a pretty face."

"My face isn't pretty."

"Oh, these?" Renatta patted the scars on Darcy's cheek. She reached up and pulled off her knit cap. The hair that peeked out when the hat was on was the only hair the woman had. The top of her head was a gnarled landscape, the aftermath of a large cat nearly ripping her scalp off. "Girl, worry about scars when you've got scars to worry about."

Darcy appreciated what the woman was trying to do, but Renatta's scars didn't lessen her own. "Thanks, Mrs. Douglas, but even if I did save Noah, he saved me first."

The envoys to Underbel left, carrying with them Sid's message to be relayed to Compton Pit, but no extra passengers.

George reached out to Sid as he climbed into the van. "Empty roads."

"Thanks."

"You ever in the neighborhood again, you stop on by. You bring another laptop with you, I'll feed you on the house."

As the van pulled off the side road and onto the remains of the main highway, Noah leaned forward and put a hand on the Sid's shoulder. "I know I was in the trunk on the way in, but I think you're going in the wrong direction."

Sid pulled the van over and turned in his seat so he could address all of his subordinates. "Here's the deal. We're going to New Portland, not to Underbel."

Lena sighed and bumped her head against her window.

"Odega stole a Mimi from us. If he intends to do anything with it, he'll need a lab and the proper equipment. Outside of the Pit or the Reservoir, New Portland is the closest place to find those things. Furthermore," his expression darkened, "all of you, in your own way, seems to have forgotten who's in charge here.

"What did I do?" asked Caps defensively.

"Shut up, Richard. This isn't the same as our trip to Vancouver, but we have to treat it with the same vigilance. You will do as I say, all of you. Just because we're outside the Pit doesn't change the facts. I'm still the boss of you, all of you. Do I make myself clear?"

"What if..." Lena steeled herself. "What if we have to go farther than New Portland?"

"We'll cross that bridge when I get to it." He watched their reaction to that one. His chief concern was Lena. He never would have thought of her as a threat to the chain of command, but her play in the bathroom had completely disarmed him. He'd decided to keep Noah with the group before her little stunt, but there was no way she would believe that now. Maybe it was for the best. The drive ahead of them would surely tax her nerves to the fullest. A boost of confidence might go a long way in preventing an anxiety attack.

"According to *Graff's* the next settlement isn't until Kelso. We have to take Highway 101 to get to the I-5, and it's going to be hard driving. Just stick together, do as I tell you and we'll have something new to brag about when we get home."

"And we're going south?" asked Lena. "Boss, that takes us right across the Olympic Peninsula."

"To back track would add two extra days. George says the road is passable. Hard, but passable."

16. Encroachment

Bounded by the Straight of Juan de Fuca on the north and Puget Sound on the east, the Olympic Peninsula swelled with nature's bounty long before the Change. The Olympic Mountains trapped clouds from the Pacific, causing a rain forest to the west and a dry, rain-sheltered area to the east. This conjunction of both extremely wet and extremely dry climates resulted in an ecosystem populated by a whole bunch of different ways to die.

Teaming with squirrels, rabbits, elk, bear, wolves, mice, rats, wasps, hornets, and of course, ants, it was road Sid would never have attempted during the warmer months. Even with a number of animals asleep, the biggest threat to the road was the forest itself. Forced up by roots, split asunder by saplings germinated in cracks and crevices, Highway 101 was as broken a stretch of blacktop as Sid had ever navigated, but true to George's words, the road was passable. The hunters' van was an armored Ford converted to off-road suspension and tires. It had once borne the logo of Parks and Recreations. An ordinary van could never have traversed the potholed, uneven highway. In many places overhanging branches narrowed the road to a single lane, barely wide enough for a tractor-trailer rig, and evidence of failed trips dotted the roadside, rusted hulks gone green with moss and lichen. The forest pressed close to both sides, obscuring from view the Hood Canal, and creating a claustrophobic tunnel of green and brown. The first break in the tree line was the town of Quilcene, not much more than a gas station and general store in its heyday, now much less than that.

It must have been over for them quickly, decided Noah, gazing at crumbling buildings overgrown with plant life.

There was even less of Brinnon. Only a signpost and a slight recession in the forest gave evidence that the town had even been there at all.

"Fifty klicks to Hoodsport," said Lena flipping through a dog-eared map book. Her tension had eased over the hours. They hadn't seen any teeth yet, and without them to validate her fear, she'd been free to watch hour after hour of beautiful scenery.

"We should get some up-to-date maps in New Portland," said Sid. "I wonder if they still use imperial instead of metric."

"A century of common sense didn't make us gringos change," said Caps. "I don't see how a decade of chaos would. Only metric I knew before moving north was how to cut ounces into grams."

The map book Lena had, taken from Underbel, was printed in 1999. The maps were speckled with numbered red stars. The stars referred to places where coupons from the middle of the book could be used. She flipped to the coupons and pulled one out, handing it up to the front of the van. "Hamma Hamma Oysters. Look, buy two or more pounds of oysters or mussels and get an additional pound free. I wonder how hostile the oysters are."

Sid laughed a bit more than he should have. They all did. It was the first joke she'd made since leaving Catacombs; the first since leaving the Pit.

It took almost three hours to negotiate the fifty kilometers to the remains of Hoodsport.

"I bought nacho chips and a first aid kit here," said Caps. "It would have been that building there." He pointed at what looked like a disordered pile of bricks. "We shot the rapids on the Skokomish."

"Was that with Emma?" asked Lena.

"Yeah, Miss Fitness. Don't know what I was thinking."

"You liked her well enough to remember the name of the river."

"I remember the name of the river because I made a joke out of it. I said the river was named Skokomish 'cause that's the sound your head makes when you fly out of the raft and hit a rock. I hated that trip. Soaking wet for three days, these black flies freakin' everywhere."

He'd never mentioned that the sex had been amazing. Invigorated by the great outdoors, Emma had pummeled his exhausted body with her pelvis until he was sure he'd have to be pulled from the ground by an excavation team.

The rough clearing that had once been Hoodsport disappeared behind them. The Boss stopped the van on the bridge over the Skokomish for refueling and to allow Caps to inspect the van's underbody. It had taken a nasty thump while shuddering over a fallen tree. Since then, the steering pulled a bit to the left. They were all armed now, sidearms in holsters, Sid and Darcy shouldering rifles.

Caps pulled himself out from under the van. "I don't see anything critical. How much farther to the I-5?"

"Another seventy or eighty klicks," said Lena.

"We'll be fine," he said loudly for Lena's benefit, but he shot a warning glance at Sid.

They took the next stretch of road even easier, slowing to a crawl for six bone-rattling kilometers of broken seams and raised blacktop that was more like an indecisive staircase than any road. Here the trees were so high and thick, it seemed like night, though sunset was still hours away. Caps took over in the driver's seat and the Boss stretched out on the van's rearmost seat, evicting Noah to the middle bench.

"You want to switch?" Lena asked Darcy.

Noah patted the seat beside him.

"It's okay," said Darcy. "I'll keep shotgun."

True night was setting in when the van passed a large sign, welcoming travelers to Washington's state capital, Olympia. Even from the outskirts of town, the legislative building was visible, a domed white structure in the neo-classical style, a miniature version of the same building that presumably still stood in Washington, D.C.

"We'll bunk down here. Richard, I'll take over." Sid pulled off the I-5 at an exit and the road took them down and below an underpass. "One of these buildings must be securable."

The city streets were far worse-off than the interstate. Wrecked vehicles and overgrown pavement forced them towards the city center. They passed motels and fast food joints, all broken, all empty. It gave Noah a hollow ache in his stomach. A car lot was next, two actually, one on either side of the road. Noah could see dozens of vehicles, dark outlines in dusk's fading light.

"Church up ahead," said Darcy.

Sid slowed the van to a crawl and Darcy turned on a spotlight mounted in a turret on the vehicle's roof. Using a handle in the ceiling she tracked the beam of light across the front of the temple.

"Stone walls," said Caps. "Good. High windows, good. Splintered doors. Bad."

The bottoms of both high wooden doors were staved in, jagged wood around dark holes.

"I think that's a new car over there," said Noah. "To the right. It's got spikes on it."

The spotlight's beam drifted down the wall and over the ground to an armor-plated station wagon on off-road suspension. The tires were flat, the doors caved in. Spikes lined the trunk and roof. Spikes on the back bumper were bent or broken. The metal grate over the back window was deeply dented and the windshield was gone, mesh and all.

"Looks like somebody took a giant sledgehammer to it," said Caps. "They must have rolled it."

Darcy moved the light back to the doors of the church. "Maybe whoever was in that car tried to hole up in there."

"That station wagon's been here a while," said Sid. "Look at the vines wrapped around the suspension. This is no good. No place to put the van. I don't want to leave it exposed." He sped up and put the church behind them. "Here looks good."

They pulled into the parking lot of a service station with an attached garage. Four pumps grew moss beneath a thick metal canopy. A flatbed truck sat on rotted tires. The building was cinderblock and the only visible window was of the bulletproof service type.

Sid turned the spotlight on. "Darcy, Noah, see if you can get that door open. Richard, cover them."

The front door's window was intact, as were the bars over it. A ring of keys dangled from the handle. Darcy tried the handle first. It was locked, but she jiggled the key and, luckily, the lock wasn't seized. The door opened but the key snapped as she tried to remove it.

Revolver in one hand, flashlight in the other, Noah lit the way for Darcy as they passed a dust-covered desk and cash register and reached a doorway beside a Pepsi machine. Noah shone his light on a rack of tourist brochures, motel coupons and pleas from various charitable organizations.

"Get that light back here," said Darcy. She fiddled with the handle of a metal door. She found the right key and opened the way to the service bay.

Noah's beam swept through the darkness. They listened for the sounds of any animals and checked the ceiling for bats.

"Roof access," said Noah, drifting his light beam from the trap door in the ceiling down a ladder and to the floor, where a skeleton lay wrapped in rags.

Flashlight and gun barrels poking at every corner, they crossed into the service bay and approached the skeleton.

"No broken bones," said Darcy. "No tooth or claw marks."

"Ants," said Noah.

"Probably. He comes running in here, forgets his keys at the door. He locks the connecting door from the inside. He's safe from the teeth, but the mandibles are a different story."

"What makes you so sure it's a he?"

Darcy pointed at a large metal oval grown tarnished amidst the rags. "No woman would ever wear that belt buckle."

"How's it coming?" called Caps from the retail foyer.

"Tell Sid it's a go," Darcy called back. "Let's pop this open."

The service bay door was a galvanized steel roll-up. The flashlight traced the track to the left of the door until it found a release pin. Noah pulled at it, but wound up having to give it a good kick. Darcy released the pin on the other side and together they hauled the door up. The van eased inside and they yanked the door down, slamming the locks in place simultaneously. More flashlights came out, and Sid lit a gas lantern, placing it on top of the van.

"Oh the humanity," Caps extolled from a work bench, picking up and dropping one corroded tool after another. "I swear, there's just no pride anymore. Imagine a man keeping his tools like this and having the nerve to call himself a professional. I wouldn't hire you." He shook a screwdriver at the skeleton.

"Have some respect," Lena said quietly.

Sid dumped sleeping bags from the van. "We'll sleep in threes. Noah, Richard take first watch. Anybody hungry?"

They ate a sparse meal of jerky. Lena and Caps both opted for the hot 'n' spicy cat jerky and were soon hacking and drinking more than their share of the water to drown the burn. With the three lucky sleepers bunked down, Caps and Noah pushed the Pepsi machine in front of the foyer door and took positions near the service window.

"Think there's anything in this?" asked Caps, tapping the drink machine with his rifle.

"Does it take New Portland coins?"

"I'm serious." Caps put his rifle down.

"I don't think we should be messing with our first line of defense."

Caps shifted the drink machine, scraping it across the floor. "How do we open this thing?"

A distant *crack* sounded from somewhere outside.

"What was that?" Noah brought his rifle up.

"Sounded like a tree branch snapping."

They listened for a while.

"Probably some piece of a house falling off," said Caps. "You know, if a roof falls in a forest and nobody's around to—"

Crack!

"That was closer," said Noah. "Did that sound closer to you?"

From down the street, something clattered on concrete.

Caps put his back to the drink machine and shoved it tight against the door. "Let's wake the Boss."

They moved into the garage. Sid was awake and sitting up. Caps hunkered down and whispered, "There's movement outside."

"What kind?"

"Sounds like stuff getting broken. A late-season bear maybe."

Sid pulled on his boots. There were three windows in the garage door, narrow strips of glass. Sid put his face close to one of them, but saw nothing. He closed his eyes and listened. The air was still. No signs creaked on rusty chains. No broken doors banged against their frames.

"I hear something," said Noah.

"Yes." Sid held up a finger. "I hear it too. It sounds like…it sounds like…"

"Heels," said Caps. "Like a woman in high heels."

Sid nodded, and a small part of his brain despaired at how long it had been since he'd even seen a woman in high heels.

"It's getting closer," said Noah.

Caps looked out the window. "Now it sounds like hooves. A pig? Pig or boar."

"Charging boar," said Sid. He pushed Caps away from the window and lurched back. The sound of trotting hooves had become a gallop.

With a tremendous *bang* the rollup door shook and rattled. Dirt and rust fell from above and one of the windows cracked.

Darcy was instantly awake. Lena's eyes opened but it would take a few seconds for her brain to engage.

The garage door took another hard hit. It was like standing under a gong. The bottom panels bent inwards and a gap appeared between the two lowest sections. Caps turned his flashlight on the gap and found an eye looking back at him.

Sid dove for a rifle.

Caps flinched.

Noah took aim and fired. The eye burst in a spray of blood and brain tissue. Sid looked through the gap, then out the window again, but couldn't see what they'd just killed.

"Good shot," said Caps.

Noah edged towards the door. "It was like three feet away."

"It's alone, right?" asked Lena. "Tell me it's alone."

Darcy was at the door beside Sid. Even with the flashlight shining straight down, all they could make out was a patch of faded brown fur, like that of a deer.

"I hear more high heels," said Caps.

Sid stood up. "Load the van. We're leaving."

Pack up was fast. Less than a minute passed before the engine was running and Noah and Darcy stood by the door pins.

"Go," said Sid from the driver's window.

Noah pulled. So did Darcy.

Sid checked his side mirror, then called out. "What's going on?"

"Jammed," said Darcy.

"Mine too," said Noah. "The door's bent."

With a clatter of hooves and what sounded like a grunt, another creature slammed into the door. Metal crunched and two of the windows broke out completely.

"Get in," Sid ordered. The moment they'd complied he floored it in reverse, but the van didn't have enough lead up. It hit the door, bent it back towards its original shape, but didn't break through. Sid leaned on the gas and tires squealed. The smell of burning rubber filled the air. The garage door strained against its guides but held.

Impact from behind sent a shudder through the van and jerked everybody in their seats.

"It's not alone," said Lena. "It's not alone. It's not alone. It's not alone."

Caps threw his arms around her and pulled her against his chest. He squeezed her tight, whispered into her ear.

Sid jumped from the van and put rifle and flashlight through the window. The animal had backed up for another charge. It had a slim, pointed muzzle and patches of white around its eyes and mouth. "I've got bad news and I've got bad news," said Sid as he took aim. "The bad news is it's a bighorn sheep." The creature lowered its head. "The other bad news is…" It charged. Sid fired. "These things travel in herds." A smoking hole dead centre between its thick, curving horns, the ram fell over on its side.

"Okay," Sid chambered another round, "what do we know about bighorn sheep? Talk to me, people."

Darcy examined the door guides. "Could we shoot these apart?"

Sid looked at the van. Caps had turned himself into a padded room around Lena's hysteria.

"The bighorn sheep," said Noah, "grows to a height of forty inches at the shoulder and can weigh up to two-hundred-and-eighty pounds. They reach sexual maturity at age two and have a lifespan of ten to fifteen years."

"Since when are you a zoologist?" asked Darcy, sounding a little amazed.

Noah held up a pamphlet. "It was on the rack over there. It's a conservation thing. Save our dwindling wild sheep."

Sid looked at the pushed-in metal and thought about the smashed doors at the church. "Let's hope they've stayed dwindled. Keep reading." He could hear more heels. Now that Caps had put that association in his head, he couldn't get rid of it.

"Bighorn sheep engage in head-butting contests to establish mating rights. These contests can last for over a day. Impacts reach speeds of up to seventy miles per hour and can generate forces of over two-thousand pounds."

"Noah!" Caps shouted through a window. "Shut the hell up! Lena? Lena? Lena, honey?" She'd stopped thrashing. Now she just leaned against him and made a sort of cooing noise. He'd suffered through her attacks time and time again and it never got any easier. "Oh great! She's gone coma pigeon."

"Count your blessings," said Darcy. "Tie her wrists and ankles and get a gun." She loathed herself for the comment but this was crunch time.

"Noah," said Sid. "Herd size? Anything? I'm hearing multiples out there."

"Mature males commonly travel in bachelor groups of eight to ten."

"That's not too bad. We've got the ammo for that. Richard, get the spotlight going."

"Except during mating season, when the males unite with the females, and herds can reach sizes of over a hundred."

"Sid," Darcy pushed her rifle barrel farther out the window. "I hear way more than ten."

Sid flexed his trigger finger. "And mating season is?" It wasn't just a few pairs of pumps out there. It was an entire shoe convention.

"Uh…" Noah turned to the last page of the pamphlet. "Mating season is October to December. We're right in the middle of it."

17. Ba Ram Ewe

"The roof," shouted Sid. "Darce, get that trapdoor open."

"No way," said Caps. "We're not leaving Lena down here alone."

The overlapping clopping from outside coalesced into a pounding roar. Darcy was already on the ladder. Sid pulled his rifle from the window and fell back. Noah squeezed off one shot, then did the same.

The rollup door clanged as if struck by a locomotive. The tracks bent and reverberated, the remaining glass shattered and a guide-wheel rod snapped in half. Thousands of pounds of mutton pushed against the galvanized steel. Sid stuck his rifle through a window and emptied the clip.

Darcy climbed the ladder as quickly as she could while still testing each rung before putting weight on it.

"There's bolts pushed out of the concrete," said Noah. "The door won't take another hit like that."

The baaing and snorting outside was getting louder by the minute and the air was thick with the musk of damp animals.

Sid shone a flashlight out his window. Brown fur filled the parking lot. Wide-spaced eyes winked red and gold. "It'll take them a while to figure out they all have to back up."

"I feel like I'm in the anti-nativity scene," said Caps.

The garage door rattled from dozens of bumps and kicks. Noah fired a few shots into the herd. Sid slotted a fresh clip into his rifle. "Darce, how's it coming with that roof hatch?"

"Working on it." She grunted and cursed. "Latch is stiff. What's the plan?"

"We go topside to get a proper shooting angle and we kill all the mature males. With any ammo we have left, we start killing lambs. Maybe the females will back off."

With a screech, the hatch opened and Darcy climbed through it and onto the flat gravel-topped roof.

"I'm staying right here," said Caps, shouldering his rifle as if he could stop the herd by himself.

"Fine," said Sid. "Noah, let's go."

They ascended and joined Darcy at the roof's edge. They stared in awe at the murderous herd. Sid was the first to snap out of it, drawing a bead on the biggest set of horns he could find. He dropped it in two shots and every one of those sheep looked up. The shorter, slimmer horns of the ewes quivered like antennae.

Noah's rifle bucked and a large male's head snapped to one side as a chunk flew out of one of its horns.

The herd started milling, the garage door forgotten.

Darcy put three slugs into a ram that just wouldn't lie down and die.

The sheep surrounded the building, rearing up and clopping their hooves against it. This unexpected behavior had the three of them running the circumference of the roof, trying to keep track of the rams.

"What are they doing?" asked Noah, finding his target, then losing it again.

Sid found a male looking straight up at him. "Honestly?" He shot the thing through the nose. "I think they're trying to find a way up."

Darcy fired two quick shots and looked at the darkness beyond the herd. "Sid, this is so noisy. We'll be getting mountain lions soon. Wolves."

With a thump and a snort, a ram landed on the roof and charged at Sid. Stunned by the impossibility of a sheep scaling a flat concrete wall, he stood the way deer used to when they saw headlights.

At the last possible moment he dove to the side. The ram's horns clipped his lower leg and he spun like a top.

Noah fired but the shot went high. The ram skidded to a halt near the roof's edge and turned towards Darcy. She shot it in the face and it tumbled to the street below.

Sid's foot hurt so much he had to look at it to confirm it was still attached. He looked at where the animal had come from. "How did that..."

A female sailed up and landed on the gravel. Noah's rifle clacked on an empty chamber. Sid and Darcy shot the ewe at the same time. It stumbled and collapsed. Noah dropped his rifle, pulled his revolver and moved to where the sheep were somehow getting up. When he arrived, he got his gun up in time to blast a ewe in mid-flight.

A ram jumped from the ground to the flatbed truck, bounced to the metal canopy over the fuel pumps and bounced again all the way to the roof.

Noah fired three times, missing each time. Darcy grabbed Noah by the back of the collar and yanked him out of the way as the sheep landed and Sid shot out its legs.

"Inside!" Sid yelled. He clenched his teeth against a scream as he put weight on the injured foot. They ran for the hatch, practically dove through it. "Go, go!" Sid acted as rear guard. There were already three sheep on the roof, all ewes, all charging. Sid shot the lead sheep, dropped his rifle through the open hatch and rolled after it, grabbing the ladder as he dropped into space.

Darcy gasped in fear as Sid swung in and smashed into the rungs, but he held on. A ewe looked down from above. She reached a foreleg out into space. A bullet zipped through the air, the ewe lurched back and Sid reached up and pulled the hatch closed.

"This is a real shitty place you brought us to," shouted Caps without his usual sarcastic air.

"Everybody get in the van," Sid ordered, descending as fast as he could. "Richard, take the wheel."

The clattering on the roof was getting to be as loud as the hoof beats from the ground.

They're mountain sheep, thought Sid. *Of course they could make jumps like that.* He suddenly remembered some nature show where he'd seen a mountain goat bounce its way up a crevice like a wooly Jackie Chan.

Lena lay across the van's rearmost seat. Her wrists and ankles were tied and seatbelts were wrapped around her torso and legs.

Sid opened the sun roof. "Darcy, help me."

"What am I doing, Boss?" Caps asked, revving the motor in neutral.

"Put her in reverse and get ready to use every trick we've got."

Caps slid open the cover on a row of switches. "A lot of stuff was stripped off by Underbel."

Sid and Darcy stood with their heads and shoulders through the open sunroof.

The crunching from above lessened. It sounded like there were more hooves moving away from the building than around it.

"Shoot the top three wheels on either side," said Sid, raising his rifle. He blew one of the door's guide-wheels right out of the track. The targets were at short range, but they were small. There were more misses than hits, but in seconds the wheels were destroyed and the top of the door folded in on itself.

"Everybody buckle in," said Sid as he closed the sunroof. "Tell me there's fuel in the firebursts."

"Like, maybe three seconds' worth," said Caps.

Darcy took the front passenger seat. Noah and Sid strapped themselves into the middle bench.

The baaing quieted down and was replaced by galloping. The stampede was incoming, headed up by a vanguard of nature's best battering rams; organic siege engines.

Caps took a deep breath and stamped down on both clutch and accelerator peddles.

The rams hit the door. Hinges snapped, bolts popped from the walls and the lower guide wheels broke free of the tracks. The roll-up door swung like a teeter-totter. Momentum cracked the folded top sections like a whip.

Caps took his foot off the clutch.

The garage door left the tracks completely and fell on the sheep like a steel blanket. The van squealed backwards onto and over the door, crushing sheep beneath it.

Darcy flipped one of the dashboard switches and jets of fire whooshed out on either side of the van. Mounds of sheep flesh shuddered under the wheels and the dominant aromas became burnt fur and roast lamb. The firebursts spluttered empty.

The van rocked as a ram T-boned it on the right side. Caps flipped another switch, but nothing happened. He flipped the next four switches simultaneously. Small, one-shot fletchet guns fired in all directions from the van's undercarriage. Tiny shards of metal and glass ripped through legs and flanks.

A ram struck the back doors, shaking them against the frame. Noah reached for the sunroof.

"Don't do that," said Sid. A second later, one of the sheep landed on the roof.

Darcy spun the searchlight. They were moving, but hemmed in by the sheer size of the herd. Caps jinked the van right and left but the sheep on top held its ground and started stamping.

In the headlights, ewes cleared a path and a ram came barreling for the front bumper. Caps hit the last switch. He was so proud of this one. After all this time he'd finally know what it felt like to actually *use* it. A pair of mechanisms whirred to life and twin circular-saw blades protruded from beneath the bumper and cut the ram's forelegs off as it smashed into the bars protecting the grill.

"That rocked!" said Caps. "Hunters get all the fun."

Noah held his revolver pointed at the sun roof. Sid counted to three by flicking fingers. He flipped the latch and Noah fired until the hammer fell on empty shells. The sheep tumbled from the roof.

"Get into that alley," said Sid. "Cut off the runs at our sides."

Still going backwards, Caps angled at a fire lane between two buildings. Ewes butted at the back of the van with their smaller horns and the budding headgear of lambs tapped the paneling.

"Are we down to just the females?" asked Sid as he looked out the windows.

The van made it a hundred feet down the alley and stopped. Caps shifted into forward gear as ewes sidestepped or backed away.

"Where was he hiding?" breathed Darcy.

A huge ram faced them down from the mouth of the alley. Its horns had spiraled through a complete circle and were working on a second.

"Hello, prime alpha," said Caps, stepping on the gas. "Y'know, after we squish this guy, the van gets to hump all the ewes."

The ram thundered towards them in what appeared to be the most mismatched game of chicken since a ship once ordered a lighthouse to alter course. But the ram had no intention of taking on the armored grill. Moments before impact it jumped, cleared the saw blades and steel bars, and smashed into the mesh-covered windshield.

The glass caved in, spilling across the dash top and covering Caps and Darcy from lap to chest. The mesh stretched and split. Cold, damp air rushed into the van and for eternal seconds the vehicle fishtailed from side to side while the ram, head and one leg inside the van, twisted its massive head and strained to chomp Darcy's face in half.

With no clue where he was going, Caps kept the peddle to the metal.

Darcy pushed as far away in her seat as the door would allow. Her rifle was on the floorboards somewhere but going for it would put her in range of the snapping teeth.

Noah brought his gun up and clicked away, forgetting the chambers were spent.

Sid undid his seatbelt, rocked forward and grabbed the sheep by the horns. He tried to push it away from the Darcy but it was far too strong for him. It snapped at him and he pulled his hands back just fast enough to avoid losing fingers.

Using focus bordering on lunacy, Caps watched the road as best he could and turned the van towards a wide, empty street.

Darcy had her sidearm up, a short-barreled Smith & Wesson .44. "Fire in the hole!" she cried, and blew the ram's brains out all over Caps.

The animal thrashed a few times, its back legs kicking the grill, then it went limp.

The herd quickly thinned out and then became pursuing shadows in the mirrors. Noah gaped at the dead ram staring back at him with open, empty eyes.

Caps rubbed a sleeve across his face and picked bone fragments off his cheek. "I swear, every time I go on a drive with you people, I end up covered in animal bits."

Lena woke, but didn't thrash. She had only a dim memory of her panic attack, but her hands and legs were tied. It wasn't the first time she'd found herself that way. She was on the backseat of the van, wrapped in blankets but still cold. A small hooded lantern hung from the suicide handle above her head. From somewhere behind the van, a rifle fired.

Lena brought her wrists up and sighed with relief that it was her boyfriend who'd tied the knots. There was one loop that made the whole thing fall apart. She tugged it with her teeth and rubbed her wrists as the rope slid off. Not having to ask for help gave her back a sliver of dignity. She untied her ankles and looked at the mesh over the windshield, now held together in the middle by twisted wires. There was no glass at all. No wonder it was so cold.

Her heavy jacket had been left in easy reach. She pulled it on and tried the side door, but it wouldn't open. The back doors, bent in a little, were likewise seized. The front doors worked and she exited from the passenger side.

The van was in the middle of a long bridge. Caps was on his back, reloading the fletchet guns. Sid held guard at one end of the bridge while Darcy and Noah were positioned at the other.

"Hi," said Caps, coming to his feet. "How are you feeling?" He pulled her into a hug, relief emanating from his body into hers.

Lena rubbed her face in his neck, not for a second minding the raspy stubble on his cheek. "I'm okay." She stepped away from him, surveyed the van's exterior and gave a low whistle. "You've got a lot of work to do when we get home."

"Going to have to do it in New Portland. Without a windshield it's going to be a cold ride. The Boss's all freaked about how little barter we have." He turned towards Sid and called, "All loaded."

"All in, then," said Sid, limping to the van's side. "Darcy, Noah, take first watch."

He climbed into the van and lay down on the back seat. Caps and Lena somehow managed to snuggle together on the middle seat, while Noah and Darcy stayed in the front. In a remarkably short time Caps was snoring. Lena elbowed him without waking up.

Quiet settled in, stretched out, became heavy.

Darcy bit her lower lip. She'd tried to avoid sharing a watch with Noah, but Sid was out and Lena wasn't going to sleep without Caps wrapped around her like a blanket.

"I hate being cold," Noah said quietly. "Do you think we'll find a replacement windshield?"

Her mind teetered between optimism and pessimism. "I think we'll be lucky to find clear enough plastic."

Moonlight through the mesh showed only silhouettes. Darcy was grateful for this. She didn't want to see that look again from him. She didn't think she could stand it.

"My dad used to tell me this story," said Noah. "These Spanish sailors came to America and Indians met them at the shore with blankets. The Indians asked the sailors to get on the blankets and then carried them to the tribal chief like royalty. The chief says, 'It is said that anything a white man's feet touch becomes his. You have touched only these blankets.' Then the Indians carried the sailors back to the shore, threw them and the blankets into the ocean and told them to go back where they came from."

Darcy poked at a loose-looking part of the mesh. "What made you think of that?"

"The pamphlet about the sheep. It was talking about how man's encroachment was killing the population. So they spend all these years building back up and we ride in and in one night waste all the mature males."

"Noah, you're not turning into a sympathizer on us are you?"

"Nah. Sometimes I just think that we've always been at war with the animals and it's only this last decade or so they started fighting back."

"I was never at war with the animals. I was an environmental activist."

"Maybe, but you were only trying to save the animals you didn't feel like eating or wearing."

Darcy turned in her seat to face him. "Uhm, this is kind of a pointless conversation, isn't it?"

"Yeah, but if I talk about what's really on my mind you'll get mad or bail from the van."

Darcy was immediately taken aback. It wasn't like him to be so confrontational. The last thing she needed was for him to suddenly force the issue. The way he sat, it looked as if he might reach out to her at any second and she wasn't entirely sure she'd push him away if he did.

"I thought we'd discussed this," she said, a tinge of anger in her voice.

"Not with words we haven't."

"Why ruin a good thing?"

Noah twisted in his seat, putting his back to her and looking out the side window. For the rest of the watch they sat in obstinate silence, but when the time came to bed down, Darcy found herself taking a spot beside Noah in the back of the van instead of waiting for someone to vacate a seat.

They lay with their backs to each other and at one point she heard him scratching at a spot on his arm where a wound was healing.

He'd have scars now. Noah's first animal scars ever and he had them because of her. She realized with sad acceptance that she was going to have to give him at least one more.

18. Traffic Jam

Noah awoke at the break of dawn. The jacket bunched under his head had put a crick in his neck, and his ass and hips were numb from the van's hard floor, but the weight on his torso was delicious. Darcy was curled into his side, head on his chest, red hair splayed, one arm draped over him with her hand resting on his bicep. Her smell filled his nostrils; wonderful, pungent, unwashed Darcy. From one of the seats came Caps's snore. He knew it was Caps, because Sid's snore was a staggered series of hacks and grunts, while Caps's was a low, steady drone.

Shut up, Noah thought angrily.

She moved, snuggling in a little tighter. Noah placed a hand on her head, and when she didn't awake, gently stroked her hair.

Illumination grew within in the van, and then the sun came clear into the sky.

"Wake up," said Sid from the front seat. He thumped the ceiling with a fist. "Wake up, time to go."

Noah pulled his hand away as Darcy's head rose. She looked blearily at him, knuckled her eyes, pulled herself up and staggered to the front of the van without saying a word.

"Water," croaked Caps. "My mouth tastes like a dog—"

"Mine too," said Lena, hands and face appearing over the back of the seat. "Noah, give us some water."

Noah pulled a flask from one of the skinbags and handed it up. Lena's hair was doing a fair impression of the Statue of Liberty's crown. One hand automatically pushed it into place as she took a long swig from the flask.

"Bathroom break," said Darcy, shouldering a rifle. "C'mon, Lena."

"Stay on the bridge," said Sid.

"But modesty is so important to a proper lady," Lena fluttered her eyes at him.

Sid winced. A panic attack the night before and now she was perky and playful. Not for the first time, Sid wondered how truly unbalanced she just might be.

"Yeah," Darcy joined in, "no peeking, boys." They left the van.

Caps sat up and the three men looked at each other. They all had the same expression of weariness, though Sid looked by far the worst. Scabbed-over abrasions covered one cheek and his foot ached abominably.

"I can't drive," said Sid. "Can't clutch."

Caps didn't reply. He'd taken a mouthful of water and was looking for somewhere to spit it out. Cheeks bulging, he opened the passenger door and expectorated onto the bridge.

Noah opened a small canister and dipped his finger in the white powder within, then passed it to Caps, who also took some before handing it to the Boss. They rubbed their teeth with the powder, scrubbing as best they could.

"Do you remember toothpaste?" asked Caps around a finger. "I'd kill for toothpaste. I'd eat toothpaste."

"Be happy we have the baking soda," said Sid, motioning for the flask of water.

"All done," Darcy clambered into the van. "Your turn. We took the left, so the little boy's room is to the right."

"And try to clean up after yourselves," added Lena. "Your mother doesn't live here."

"None of our mothers live at all," said Noah. He meant nothing by it, but the comment succeeded in all but killing the lighthearted mood established by the women.

As Caps relieved himself over the side of the bridge, he tried to think of a single person close to him who could still count even one of their parents among the living. Nobody came to mind.

The van checked out and refueled, Caps took them south, out of the Olympic Peninsula and onto clearer, more traveled roads. The section of the I-5 south of Olympia was nearly clear of debris and it was fairly smooth sailing, past the ruins of Chehalis, past overgrown farms and a collection of rotting timber that at one time had been a common market. A tilted sign, nearly fallen, announced that they were leaving the great state of Washington. Another sign past it gave them a distance to Portland—thirty-two miles.

"Lena, care to tell us about our destination?" Sid asked.

Lena started to recite from memory, then thought better of it, took the copy of *Graff's* from the pocket on the back of the front seat and flipped to the requested section. She read in a clear, slightly animated tone.

" 'At the confluence of the Columbia and Willamette rivers, New Portland sits now on the remnants of Old Portland, just as Portland itself grew from the remains of an even older Portland in

1878. From Stumptown to White City to River City to the City of Roses, Portland has had many names, including the one she has now; the Birdcage. New Portland has the distinction of being one of the few large city-states to exist more above ground than below. The Birdcage, at this writing, stretches north from Salmon Street (though Burnside and Morrison bridge are impassable) and east from 21st avenue. As time goes by, more and more of the city is reclaimed, though at some cost in both materials and people.

" 'Sitting against two rivers, one of which supplies electricity, New Portland's worst enemy is the birds. Strong on environmental issues long before the Change, NP's founders, or if you prefer, rebuilders, saw the importance of not wiping out their avian neighbors, so great a role do they play in the local ecology. Instead, every strong net, bit of mesh or fencing available was scavenged from those areas not settled and placed way up in the sky. That's right, forty feet up, fastened to buildings and poles, the entire sky over New Portland is covered over. A year-round, full-time crew of hundreds of people is constantly on the go, cleaning and maintaining the city's roof. Buildings that rise above the cage are sealed off at the fourth floor, with the exception of the earthquake-proof Manhaus Tower at the corner of 19th and Lovejoy. From there, city officials and privileged visitors may walk as high as the twentieth floor to look out over the Birdcage and ruins of the Tri-state area. The roof observation deck is, of course, off limits.

" 'During wasp season, the city is active mostly at night, and since municipal workers do their best to eliminate hymenopteran intrusion, volunteers facilitate pollination of the many beautiful trees and flowers that still grow within the city. New Portland is a staggering vision of human achievement. Many of the city's old traditions still continue, including the summer Shakespeare festival.

" 'New Portland is the epicenter of trade for the area, and has its own currency and credit system. So well received is the city's coin, it can be used at other settlements as far north as Catacombs, and as far south as Albany Pit, though the farther you go, the less power your dollar has. The same ammunition that will cost you a mere $50.00 in New Portland, can cost up to a hundred times as much in Albany Pit. Since hard cash is in coin only, it's best to carry large denominations when shopping outside the city, unless you wish to bring a trolley for your purse. Coins are one, two, five, ten, twenty, fifty, seventy-five, one hundred and two hundred dollar denominations. The faces that appear on them (in order from lowest to highest) are—' "

"You can skip that part," said Sid. "We're not applying for citizenship."

"Sorry, I thought you might be interested. Okay, where was I? So-and-so on the fifty, blah blah blah, here we are. 'Portland can supply just about any need you have if you have the cash or the barter. All the necessities are available, though ammunition is dear and explosives entirely consumed by the burgeoning coal mining industry. Jobs are available in all fields from scientific research to general labor. There's always room for new people on the cage-maintenance crews or in the coal mines. Government is through elected officials, although strong-arm tactics abound in local politics and the process may not be as democratic as New Portlanders would like outsiders to believe.

" 'Where the Birdcage truly exceeds is in luxuries. The corner of Raleigh Street and 14th Ave is the nexus for an impressive market district, which includes among other things, a music store, a book store and an art gallery offering masterpieces recovered from mansions in the unclaimed cityscape. Dining is available to suit all palates, provided you like fish and fowl.

" 'As a final note on the thriving community of New Portland, the city operates a twenty-four hour radio station found at 650 on the AM dial. If you have a radio in your vehicle, and it works, turn it on, tune in, and pretend we're still living in a world where pet food comes in cans, not clothing.' "

Lena closed the book. "The rest is more addresses and the usual maps."

"Who cares about maps," said Darcy, nearly pushing Noah out of his seat in her haste to turn on the radio. Familiar white static, the only language spoken by radios for that last ten years, filled the van. Darcy toggled the AM/FM switch and played with the dial. She passed it going up the dial—the tuner knob worked but the plastic channel indicator did not, forever frozen at eleven hundred—then caught a snippet of voice on the way back down. With another slight twist, the static dropped away, and the smooth voice of a male announcer flowed from the speakers.

"...That's right, up to fifty percent off on most stock until the end of the festival. How can MacMurty's do it you ask? They scavenge themselves and pass the savings on to you. That's MacMurty's Outfitters on Hoyte, west of the fountain. MacMurty's Outfitters accepts letters of credit from both of New Portland's banks." A few bars of piano music played before an excited woman's voice exclaimed the wonders of KNPR 650, New Portland's best radio station. After a few seconds of dead air, a slow, steady drum beat made the speakers throb. The drums were joined by bass guitar and finally a synthesizer, set low and powerful, brought in the melody. The synthesizer had an oddly familiar tone to Darcy. The man's voice that eased in a second later was totally recognizable.

Darcy cupped her hands to her face and closed her eyes, trying to soak the music in with her skin.

"Isn't that Peter Gabriel?" said Caps.

"It sure is," breathed Darcy. "Shush." She hugged herself and rocked side to side as Gabriel's voice slid into her, infusing her muscles, easing along her bones.

Caps kept his mouth shut for as long as he could, then said, "I don't recognize this one. I thought I knew all of Gabriel's stuff. It must be off a soundtrack or something."

As the song reached its climax, Darcy realized she didn't recognize it either, and she didn't think she was familiar with all of Gabriel's work, she *knew* she was.

The radio announcer couldn't let the song end in peace either. Some things never changed. As the last of the lyrics faded away, he spoke over the song. "That was Pete's newest, 'Twilight Iron.' He'll be off for the rest of the week, but you can catch him again next Tuesday at Coppola's where he'll be resuming his regular schedule—"

"Ohmygod! Ohmygod!" Darcy bounced in her seat. "He's still alive! He's still performing! Sid, how long are we staying? We have to stay! We have to go to Coppola's!"

The Boss replied, but his voice was drowned out by that of the announcer. He gestured to have the volume reduced, then spoke again. "When we find Odega, we're leaving. If we find he's moved on, we follow."

"But, Sid, it's *Peter Gabriel*! Peter. Gabriel. New songs. Ten years worth of new songs. How can we—"

"If it was Queen Latifah, we still wouldn't be staying. Hey, turn it up again."

"…last night of the Wonders of the World Show at Coppola's. If you haven't seen it yet, don't miss it. Who knows when it'll come around again. And now twenty minutes of uninterrupted music on KNPR 650, New Portland's best and only radio station."

Darcy held her breath, anticipating the next miracle to come from the speakers, but she was disappointed. There was nothing particularly special about the George Michaels tune that poured out, imploring teacher to give him one more try. Her eyes narrowed and she shot a covert look at Sid. It didn't matter to her if they found out Odega had gone off in a space ship, they were going to see a concert. She'd sabotage the van if she had to.

"Uh, Boss," Caps said, concern edging his voice, "we've got company."

"This is a busy city, there's bound to be other travelers," replied Sid, turning in his seat to look out the rear windows. "Well. Well, well."

There were dozens of vehicles behind them, cars, vans, trucks, of all colors and in all conditions.

The van crested a hill, and Caps slammed on the brakes. South of them was the Fremont bridge, the best access into New Portland. From the front gates of the city, across the bridge and almost up to the I-5 exit was a queue of cars and trucks, as mottled as those that were coming in from behind. Caps sat, mouth gaping, foot on the brake, until the vehicle behind them, a reconditioned Jeep Wrangler, and the one behind it, began honking their horns. Caps eased the van forward the thirty feet to the closest car, and stopped again. The line didn't seem to be moving.

All five of them looked around in wonder. The Birdcage lay before them, less than a kilometer away, but it might as well have been across the ocean for all the likeliness that they'd see the inside of it before nightfall. The car in front of Caps pulled forward five or six feet and immediately the Wrangler started honking. Caps closed the gap. "Jeez. I don't believe it. First vacation in ten years and we're stuck in traffic."

"It's…fantastic," said Lena, a tear forming at the corner of her left eye.

"And now traffic and weather," came the bubbling voice of the announcer. "It's a shade over sixty-five degrees out there, with clear skies, but our cricket in the box swears we've got rain coming tomorrow and for the next few days. Periodic showers and a drop in temperature are in the forecast for tonight so if you're out enjoying the last night of the festival, make sure you've got some warm clothes. Now here's Janice Roguna with traffic in New Portland's only traffic helicopter."

The announcer's voice was replaced by a woman's deep alto over the rhythmic *thwop* of a helicopter's rotor.

"I'm just outside the cage, Gary, and the lineup for entrance is as bad today as it's been for the last week. Seems everyone in the Tri-State area and beyond is here to visit our little town."

"Helicopter?" Sid moved to the front of the van and pushed his head between Darcy's and Noah's as all three of them stared up at the sky through the mesh. There was no chopper in sight. Though the rotors were coming in clear through the radio, there was no sound of it from outside.

"How high could it be?" asked Sid. He opened the side door and hopped to the road, pausing a moment before putting weight on his left foot. It hurt, but didn't give out. He looked on all sides. Lena joined him.

"Do you see anything?" she asked.

"No…do you…oh." His heart fell.

Coming up the road was a flatbed truck. On the back of the truck, held down by ropes and chains, was a battered helicopter with only one of its blades still intact. The front end of the chopper was bashed in, and the whole craft listed to the right as one of the landing skids was bent out. In the cockpit of the chopper, a woman with curly, black hair spoke into a microphone while rapidly beating her chest with one fist. She smiled at Sid as the truck passed.

From within the van the woman's voice flowed out in synch with the moving lips in the helicopter. "We've got people from all over, Gary. Welcome all to New Portland." In the chopper, she stopped beating her chest long enough to wave. Arms snaked out of numerous vehicles in the line up and waved back. "We're going to do one more pass of the I-5, and then we're cruising back in."

"Good plan, Janice," resumed the announcer. "Wouldn't want you getting caught in any of that weather."

Shaking his head, Sid pulled himself back into the van.

"Boss?" said Caps.

"No, Richard, you can't have a broken helicopter."

"That's such a good joke, though."

The car in front pulled ahead once more, and Caps followed suit, not wanting to be honked at.

As late morning passed into early afternoon, the van managed to move a full fifty feet. Sid noticed that ahead of them, in order to conserve gas, many people left their motors off and pushed from the outside when it came time to creep forward. The closer they got to the city, the more industry was in action. Cage-covered ATV's sped up and down the side of the interstate, sporting the crest of the New Portland Police Department. Guns were fired at the occasional animal to rush the line up of vehicles, and the radio cautioned all travelers to refrain from using their own weapons, saying that the NPPD would take care of any and all intrusions, and to endanger the officers with window hunting might invite return fire. Lena took the driver's seat and Caps, Noah and Darcy took turns pushing the van when the opportunity arose. A pick-up truck loaded with animal carcasses passed a couple of times. A meshed-off golf cart worked its way up the line from the city. A man with a clipboard walked alongside it, stopping to speak with the driver of each vehicle. When it arrived at the van, Lena gestured to Sid.

"Welcome to New Portland," said the man. He had thin strands of hair drifting up from a comb-over and his cheeks were rosy with the chill. "Secure parking or free parking?"

"Excuse me?"

"Cars aren't allowed into city limits during the festival. You have to park and be ferried inside. Secure parking is patrolled by the NPPD, free parking isn't." He pointed at the land just outside the Birdcage. To the right of the road was a staggering number of vehicles, all parked in orderly columns, to the left, an equal number of vehicles spread out, pointed in every direction. "Your choice. I'll also need how many of you there are, proof of means, and how long you plan to stay."

"Proof of means?"

"Cash or barter."

Sid handed him the bag of coins, both those from Remo Tyree's stash, and the extras he'd picked up in Catacombs.

"I see," said the man, fingering aside a few of the coins. "This won't go very far, but it's enough to get you inside. How many and how long?"

"Five of us. I'm not sure how long we're staying. Couple of days I suppose."

The man handed the pouch back and made a notation on his clipboard.

"Secure or free?"

"How much is secure parking?"

"Twenty-five dollars per day. If your ticket runs out, you're towed to the free lot, and it's ten dollars to get your keys back."

"There much theft over in the free parking?"

"I wouldn't leave a rotting dog in my car if I wanted it to be there when I got back."

"I see."

"It's another five a head for city entrance. You can pay that now or at the gate."

"Okay, we'll go with the secure lot. I'll pay that now. Is there…uh…" Sid almost laughed, "tax on that?"

"Are you kidding? This is the tax."

Sid dumped seventy-five dollars worth of coins in the man's hands. He in turn dropped them into a metal box in the back of the cart, then gave Sid a yellow placard for the dashboard of the van.

Sid tried to ask a couple of questions, but the man waved him off and strode to the next vehicle.

"How much money do we have left?" asked Lena

"Not much."

"Where are we sleeping tonight? Can we stay in a hotel?"

"I doubt we can afford it. We'll probably have to hump it back to the van."

"How far can you walk?"

Sid wiggled his foot. "I'll manage."

From behind the van, Darcy turned to Noah. "Sid's going to be more pissed than ever at me for leaving all that barter in Underbel."

"Forget about it. We're still pissed at him for dragging us out here."

"Oh, yeah. I forgot," she giggled. "You know, I'm never going to bitch about my job again."

"How's that?"

"Policing Compton Pit can be a pain, but look at this." She gestured at the Birdcage and the surrounding area. "I wouldn't want this job for…all the cash in New Portland."

By the middle of the afternoon, they were well within gun range of the city's outer gates. Trading booths were set up on either side of the road, trying to be the first to suck barter out of newcomers, or drain the last few coins out of the departing. A pickup truck with a tank on its back drove up and down, hawking fuel at outrageous prices. Vehicles leaving both the secure and free parking were routed off the I-5 down a side road, disappearing past the tree line. Horns honked, radios blared, people got out of their vehicles to converse with those in front and behind them. Only the diligence of the NPPD and the cool of the season kept the gathering from becoming a massacre. Noah couldn't remember the last time he'd seen so many people in one place. It filled him with joy and hope, warmed him from belly to chest and tingled in the ends of his fingertips.

Caps got into a screaming match with the driver of the Wrangler. It ended suddenly when Wrangler man wiggled a pot pipe under Caps's nose. Caps climbed into the Jeep for a few minutes, then exited with a puff of smoke behind him.

"His name's Carey," the artist said to Noah. "He's not a bad guy. This is the first chance he's had to be belligerent to other drivers in ten years and he was milking it for all its worth." He added as an afterthought, "One of his eyes is fake."

At last they reached the entrance to the secure parking. Sid presented the placard, handed over the keys and the group loaded supplies into backpacks, armed themselves and prepared to join the line up for the bus into the city.

"No guns," said one of the lot attendants.

Sid blinked at him in surprise.

"Sorry, no guns during the festival. It's okay to leave them in the van. They'll be safe. If you prefer, we have secure lockup with some space left in it, but it'll be another ten dollars a day."

"We'll risk the van."

After an announcement that the next city bus wouldn't be for at least another hour, and the city was no longer allowing entry on foot, a grumbling crowd dispersed to examine the merchants' booths.

Darcy made a beeline for a stand declaring advanced ticket sales. "How much for Gabriel tickets?"

"You mean Pete?" asked the man behind the counter, he was average looking with short brown hair and matching beard, the type of face you'd forget the moment your eyes left it. "I'd like to make money off of that but it's free."

"Free?"

"Yep. First come, first serve, four nights a week, though the band only joins him on Fridays. I've got a few tickets left for the last Wonders of the World show, though. Last night. You shouldn't miss it."

The edges of her mouth turned down. "Wonders of the World? What is it? A slide show of statues and castles?"

"You've never heard of the Wonders of the World show? Dancers, acrobats… straight from Terpris. The magician has to be seen to be believed."

"I love magicians," said Noah, appearing at Darcy's shoulder.

"Terpris…" Darcy breathed. "So that's what all this is about. I thought you were like this all the time."

"You didn't know about Terpris?" The scalper laughed. "What are you here for then?"

"We just…Terpris. Wow."

"I love magicians," Noah repeated.

Darcy looked at him. She couldn't help smiling. Either he didn't know about Terpris, or he just didn't care. She turned back to the scalper. "Okay, my friend here loves magicians. How much are tickets?"

"Sixty per. They're cheap because they're at the back. All I've got left."

"Sixty per?" She didn't know exactly how much coin was in Sid's bag, but she doubted it was enough to cover that.

"Sorry, can't afford it."

Noah's disappointment was palpable.

"We take barter," said the scalper, indicating a few crates behind with various odds and ends in them.

Darcy considered. When would they ever get to see another variety show? She undid her watchstrap and dropped the timepiece on the counter. The scalper looked at it, tested the strap, then held it up to his ear. "How many tickets do you want?"

"Five."

The scalper offered the watch back. "Sorry. This just begins to cover it."

Darcy raised an eyebrow at Noah.

"What?"

"Your watch."

"But…but you gave this to me."

"I can always give you another. How badly do you want to see this show?"

Noah handed over the watch. It was steel, and the imprint on the back claimed it was waterproof to sixty meters, not that anybody was likely to test it.

The scalper looked at the second watch front and back. "Excuse me for a moment," he had a quick conference with a woman in the next booth, then returned. "Five tickets. Here you go."

Darcy accepted the tickets. They were pressed, not written, on medium card stock with perforations to allow for a souvenir stub. Even though they weren't for Peter Gabriel, just holding tickets in her hands again made her feel giddy as a child.

"Are you even a little mad at Sid for dragging us out here?" she asked Noah.

"Nope, not a bit."

"Me neither. Let's go give him a hug."

Sid stood away from the booths, looking at prices, thinking about how little their money was going to stretch.

"Foot bothering you?" asked Caps.

"Finances bothering me."

"Your problem, not mine, oh fearless leader. I'm going to browse."

"Don't stray too far."

"Yes, Mother."

Caps moved from booth to booth, eyeing the wares. There were knives and kitchen tools, hand-made toys, maps, spices and all manner of things. It was too bad they didn't have Eggerson with him. The toy maker could have made a fortune. He stopped at a booth marked "Charms and Curses". The proprietor was an old Asian woman with gold-capped teeth and small round-framed glasses.

"You're kidding me," said Caps, gesturing at her wares.

"No joke. All real. Good luck. You want good luck? How 'bout be big man in bed? Bird charm…" she held out a pierced beak on a leather thong. "You wear this, be invisible to birds." She sniffed the air. "You like to grow things?" She smiled and her eyes twinkled behind the lenses. A small skinbag appeared on the counter. "Green thumb charm, make your crazy weed grow big and strong." She tapped the pouch. "Real thumb in there."

"No way," Caps reached for the bag.

"No, don't open," she slapped his hand away. "Let magic out if you open the bag."

"Excuse me," said a tall, beefy man as he pushed past Caps, "are you Miss Hong?" The woman nodded. "Do you remember Robin Pryce?"

"I know Robin. He know me."

"He told me I could get a dog charm from you. Are those them?" he pointed at necklaces of strung teeth hanging from hooks on one side of the stand.

"Those weak," said Miss Hong. "Friend of Robin, you want this." She lifted a necklace from around her own neck and placed it on the counter. As near as Caps could tell, it was identical to the ones on open display.

"How much?"

"Friend of Robin? One hundred twenty-five dollar. Price firm. Price for Pryce," she cackled at her own joke.

The man clunked a skinbag on the counter without a second's hesitation. Miss Hong hefted the bag in one hand. "Already counted?"

"Robin said it would be that much."

"You not try to cheat Miss Hong?"

He gave her a wary smile. "That would be kind of stupid, wouldn't it?"

The skinbag disappeared behind the counter. He dropped the necklace over his head and walked away.

"Do you buy, or just sell?" asked Caps, fingering the supposedly weak charms.

"What you have I want to buy?"

Caps fished Toffee's tooth bag from within his shirt, opened it up and spilled a sample of its contents into the palm of his hand. He held them out for the woman's inspection. She spread a red silk cloth across the counter and tapped it with a stubby finger. Caps spread the teeth out on the cloth, then at a glance from the witch, upended the pouch and spilled the rest of its booty out for her inspection. The woman lifted a few of the teeth, turned them this way and that, then placed a small number of them in one corner of the cloth. She picked up another tooth, then dropped it dismissively into the main pile.

"Some okay, most filler," she said. "Give you…oh…fifty dollars for whole lot."

Caps turned and put on his most contemplative expression. He hadn't clue one what fifty dollars was worth. He rubbed his chin with his finger and thumb, hmmed a couple of times and glanced down to find Lena looking up at him.

"Lame," she said.

"Hey, the Boss said we need money. She'll give me fifty bucks for the whole lot. What do you think?"

Lena picked up the tooth Miss Hong had discarded so casually. "I think she'll give us fifty for this one tooth alone." She turned to face the charm dealer. "Won't you?"

Behind the lenses, Miss Hong's eyes narrowed and flashed, then a grim smile stretched her face. "Men so easy," she said. "Better for me you stay at home, eh?"

"Would if I could." Lena pulled the smaller pile of teeth back towards the main pile. "I think we should talk about these on an individual basis."

And so it went. Miss Hong offered, Lena counter-offered. They laughed, sometimes maliciously, sometimes like they were lifelong friends trying to put one over on the other. The longer the haggling went on, the more English was replaced by Mandarin, until at the end both women jabbered at each other in what sounded to Caps more like a pair of geese fighting than a human discussion.

Finally, all of the teeth vanished into Miss Hong's coffers. Caps offered her Toffee's pouch, but her hand stopped inches before touching it, and she wrinkled her nose. "No want that. You smart, you throw away."

A chill ran down his spine, then he realized Lena must have told her about the hunter while they were talking in Chinese. It was all a show, even after the deal had been struck. He shrugged and returned the empty bag to its place around his neck.

Miss Hong scrawled a signature across the bottom of an embossed piece of paper, and handed it over Lena.

"What's this?"

"Letter of credit. Good as money. Much lighter."

Lena looked at the voucher dubiously. "You not try to cheat Lena Wong?"

The witch cracked a smile, gold teeth flashing, "That would be stupid, wouldn't it?"

Then to Lena's amazement, the witch came around the counter and gave her a hug. Miss Hong flicked her eyes at Caps, and in Mandarin asked, "*He's yours*?"

"*Every bit him.*"

"*You can do better.*"

"*I'm a charitable soul.*"

"*You're a big liar.*"

When they were well away from the booth, Caps took Lena by the shoulders. "How on Earth did you learn so much about teeth?"

"I know jack squat about teeth. I know a lot about body language, particularly when it comes to what somebody wants."

"And what's my body language telling you right now?"

"That you better hope we have enough money to get our own hotel room."

"I love you so much. I'm so sorry I—"

She touched the tips of her fingers to Caps mouth. "Look around you. All these people. Listen to the hawkers. I wouldn't have missed this for the world."

"Well I have to apologize for something. I'm sorry I had to tie you up."

"Maybe I liked it."

An air horn's blast announced the arrival of the buses. The group gathered at the appointed place, a booth hawking goods made of turtle shell. Sid looked at the happy faces of his subordinates and cursed himself for not enjoying the moment as they were.

"What's wrong?" asked Darcy.

"I've been checking prices here. We don't have enough money. We can't even afford to leave."

"Will this help?" asked Lena, holding out the letter of credit.

Sid's eyes widened at the figure on it. "It's a hell of a good start. How'd you get this?"

"It wasn't easy," said Caps. "It was like pulling teeth."

Sid turned to Noah and Darcy. "Did you guys get anything?"

Darcy looked at the letter of credit, then held out the tickets. "Maybe we can sell these."

Sid looked at the tickets, looked at his people, and bent one of the tickets between his fingers at the perforated seam. "Been a long time since I've seen a show. But Darcy, the midnight show? Why so late?"

"Midnight show?" she snatched one of the tickets and looked at the time on it. "I guess we've got a few hours to kill."

19. Under the Madding Crowd

It took four busloads to ferry the people into the city. It wasn't a great distance, but it allowed for a contained environment in which officials could count heads.

"Do you know what's really going on here?" Darcy asked Sid quietly.

"You mean Terpris?"

"Can we?"

"We'll see. Don't get your hopes up."

The bus spilled them out en masse in a square that made the market outside seem barren by comparison. Stalls crammed both sides of the street, and the street was peopled from side to side, hustling and bustling. The calls of the hawkers intermingled, one call ending as another began to the point where it sounded like a person could purchase steel-plated dog on a stick, genuine pre-Change stained-glass scarves, bearskin silverware, or thirty-eight caliber winter boots. Throughout it all, the tan uniforms of the NPPD appeared and disappeared, watching for pickpockets and other potential problems.

The only mode of travel besides on foot were rickshaw-like contraptions that pushed and shoved through the throng.

The buildings surrounding the square were a mixture of semi-modern architecture, brown stone and red brick, colonial houses reinforced with steel, like doll houses wrapped in tinfoil.

Every building that wasn't a store seemed to be a hotel. Hastily handmade signs of wood and sheets joined more professional renderings in proclaiming the virtues of booking rooms within. Anything was an enticement. A tool shed was labeled as a swank hotel, a leaky hot-water pipe billed as an indoor sauna.

Despite the number of visitors to the town, there was a quite a turnover at the various hotels. People came for the day, left or got kicked out.

After checking a few establishments, Sid settled on two rooms in a tin-plated colonial, blue and white with a shrub at the foot of the path pruned to look like an open hand. The amount of money they had left once the rooms were paid for was essentially nil.

"I'm going to grab one of those rickshaws and head over to the animal research center," said Sid. "If Odega stopped anywhere in the town, it would be there. Richard, do you have that sketch I asked for?"

"Hang on a sec." Caps flipped through his sketchbook and tore a page out, handing over a drawing of Dr. Odega face-on and in three-quarter profile.

"The rest of you are free to explore the market, or whatever. Coppola's is only a block from here…a block from here. Never thought I'd be measuring distances in blocks again. Let's all meet at, say, eleven-thirty. If by some chance you spot Odega, follow him, but don't make contact."

At first the four of them wandered together, but soon Darcy split from the group, and Noah naturally followed her, leaving Caps and Lena to browse the stalls at the market. At one booth, a rotund Mexican was earning his coin doing hand-drawn portraits. The subject had to sit still for a long time. The price was twenty dollars per. Caps perused the man's work, nodding appreciatively. "He's good."

"You're better," said Lena.

"That goes without saying, but he is good."

The sketch artist finished and handed his drawing to the dark-haired customer in the chair opposite. The man looked at the picture and beamed. "It looks just like me!" He held the picture up for his companions to admire. To a man, his friends insulted the image, saying that it didn't look anything like him and he was dreaming. Caps had to agree. It was a flattering image, the type he often made himself.

"Come on," said Lena, grabbing her man by the wrist and dragging him back the way they'd come. She stopped by a woodcrafter's booth that sold, among other things, picture frames. A father and son, dark-skinned with the same short hair cut worked the wood together.

"If we send a lot of business your way, will you give us a cut?" she asked the father.

"Depends on how much business."

"We need to borrow a couple of your chairs. The most comfortable you've got."

"I don't think so."

"We're not going anywhere. We'll park them right in front. You don't see results in fifteen minutes, we walk." She dropped a few coins on the counter. "A deposit against possible damage to the chairs."

The man nodded to his son who set a couple of chairs out in front of the booth.

"Give me your sketchbook," she said to Caps.

Caps pulled the pad out of his pack and handed it to her. She flipped through a few pages, then ripped one of them out.

"Hey!" Caps tried to grab the book back from her but she dodged him.

"May I?" she asked the father while reaching for a hammer and a small nail. Without waiting for a reply, she hammered the nail through the page so it hung from one side of the stall. It was a thoroughly insulting sketch of the Boss, eyes looking maniacal, scars twice as wide as they actually were.

"Portraits!" She screamed, slapping the book into Caps's stomach. "Get your portraits here!"

The same group that had surrounded the Mexican stopped in front of the woodcrafter's booth. One of them fingered the sketch of Sid. "How much do you charge?"

"Twelve dollars. Ten apiece if all four of you get one."

"We don't have the time," said the man who already had a sketch.

"My man here works fast," countered Lena.

"What the hell," said the friend who'd been first to ridicule the portrait. He sat down.

Caps sat opposite him and opened the sketchpad to a blank page.

"Quick and dirty," Lena whispered in his ear.

He began with the shape of the head, then worked the eyes, and added hair, a little more than the man actually had.

"No," said Lena, "quick and *dirty*. Trust me."

So Caps turned the extra hair into a dirty grease line. He made the eyes droopy and the ears too big. The man's lips weren't the best pair a person was ever born with, and Caps made them look even worse. When he was done, he tore the page out and handed it over.

"This looks nothing like me," said the dissatisfied customer.

"It looks exactly like you," said one of the friends, then burst into laughter. "If you don't pay for it, Doug, I will."

"Yeah? I'd like to see how he makes you look."

The man sat down in the chair Doug had just vacated and turned to Caps. "Take your best shot, buddy."

So Caps splayed the man's nostrils a little wider, drew eyes closer together and gave the face an overall expression of dazed stupidity.

"Perfect," was Doug's comment.

All four of them did take their turn, and while one sat, the other three browsed the woodcrafter's stall. Other people stopped to look at the mockery Caps was making of anyone willing. Soon they were lined up. People were buying from the woodcrafter just for something to do. After each caricature was complete, Lena would recommend having the woodcrafter frame it, and a few did.

"You don't really want to watch more of this?" asked Noah. It was interesting, even exciting at first, but after the last couple, it had become unpleasant.

"Just one more," said Darcy. "I promise."

They stood amongst a mob surrounding a plywood boxing ring with a three-foot apron. The ropes surrounding the ring were tied directly to the posts, rather than fixed to turnbuckles. A fresh splotch of blood stained the mat near one post.

"Who's next?" called a wiry man with white gloves and a black tuxedo jacket. "Who's next to prove their manhood and maybe win the prize? You?" He looked at one of the crowd. "You? You're a big fellah!" He strode to the other side of the ring. "Come on people, the longer you let Ripper rest, the harder he'll be to beat."

That did it. A barrel-chested man with long arms and a black woolen cap pulled himself into the ring and stood before the barker. "I'll do it," he said.

The barker whispered in the man's ear, got some whispered replies, pointed to a corner and moved to the center of the ring.

"In this corner of the ring," the barker pointed at the newcomer, "weighing in at approximately two hundred and sixty pounds, from the settlement of Ketchikaw, Mike Foster!"

Cheers went up from the crowd, encouraging Mike to kick some ass. For his part, he dropped his jacket through the ropes and pulled off his shirt.

"And in this corner of the ring, at a definite two hundred and eighty pounds, the undisputed champion of bare-chested fighting, Ripper!" He dragged the name out like it was spelled with nine times as many letters as it had.

Ripper would have been imposing had he been only half as large; tall, with a wide chest and arms as thick as Noah's legs. His head was bald and nose flat, as if after being broken so many times, it had given up trying to heal out again. He was hairy, front and back and tattoos of matching dragons twisted around both arms. He wore red, tightly laced boots over black leggings.

Two men and a woman moved around the ring, giving odds and taking bets.

The barker motioned the fighters towards the center of the ring and spieled out the rules, instructions the crowd had heard many times this day.

"No biting, scratching or eye-gouging. Everything else is fair game. The fight's over when someone is knocked out, gives up, or taps out. Are you ready? Are you ready? Fight!"

Mike Foster wrapped his arms around Ripper's waist, planted his feet and tried to lift the man of the ground. Ripper didn't budge. He slammed his elbow into the middle of his opponent's back and watched him hit the mat. He stood his ground and waited for the man to get back up. Mike crawled to the ropes and pulled himself up, shook his head at the barker's query of submission, and raised his fists. He approached Ripper like a boxer, and from his movements it appeared he had some experience with the art. He threw a couple of experimental jabs and backed off when they were easily blocked.

He moved in again, feinted with his left and landed a solid right hook on Ripper's chin, but he didn't follow up. He stood blinking at the uninjured Ripper, and a second later lay face down on the mat, eyes glassy, his lips a bloody mess.

The barker counted to ten, raised a bored Ripper's arm in victory and returned to calling for a new challenger.

Mike Foster was pulled from the ring by a pair of ring attendants—not small men themselves—a few feet from Noah and Darcy.

Noah looked at the man's face as he was slapped awake by a third man with a doctor's bag.

"Okay, can we go now?" Noah asked Darcy, but her attention was elsewhere.

"...A challenge this time, a real challenge for the Ripper!" called the barker. "Imagine the bragging rights! Imagine the jingle of coin in your pocket!"

"I can take him," said Darcy.

"Mmhmm," was Noah's reply.

"His best punch is an overhand right. It's fast for an overhand, but I can dodge it. His defense isn't strong, he can just absorb a lot of punishment. I can get inside."

"That's nice. There's an electronics booth I want to check out."

"So go check it out. You know where I'll be."

"No way. You can't be serious."

"Sid said we needed money. The prize is five-hundred dollars."

"He'll kill you."

Darcy jumped to the ring apron and called to the barker. "I'll challenge him." The barker ignored her and continued his tirade. "Hey, shorty! I said I'll challenge him."

The barker sidestepped to her and spoke quietly. "Madam, I believe you are embarrassing yourself."

Only half the crowd agreed with him. The other half yelled on her behalf. Cries of "Let her try!" overlapped with "Get off the ring!"

Noah pulled at Darcy's pant cuff. She shook him off. Big monster and a bloodthirsty crowd under a metal sky. It was a nightmare.

"May I remind the crowd," yelled the barker, "this is *bare-chested* fighting!" He pointed at a large sign beyond the ring that said just that.

A short hush fell over the crowd before someone yelled, "Take it off," then the cacophony resumed.

The thundercloud in Noah's head vanished and his whole body drooped with relief.

Darcy looked at the crowd. The women seemed to be mostly in favor of her giving up. *Thanks for the support, sisters*. She looked at the bloodstain left by Mike Foster's lips, then she looked at Noah. A thought tripped through her head. A vicious idea that seduced with the simplicity it offered.

When Darcy's jacket hit the ring apron, Noah felt like he'd gone a round with Ripper himself. As it slid off the apron and onto the ground, a cheer went up far louder than any the crowd had offered before.

Noah grabbed her ankle and squeezed. "Darcy, don't do this."

She pulled off her sweater and dropped it on his face. "Why not? I know you watch me in the showers. You think you've got a monopoly on seeing my tits?"

Aghast, she thought, looking at his face. For the rest of her life, when she heard the word aghast, that's what she'd see. Surprise, indignation and awful hurt all rolled into one. A part of her nodded in satisfaction while another part, forced down, kicked and screamed and screamed some more.

She stepped into the ring, away from Noah's clawing hands. He tried to follow her in, but the ring attendants pulled him back, holding him easily despite his struggle.

"Wait," cried the barker, quieting the crowd with a sweep of his arms. "I see we have a member of the local constabulary in attendance." Eyes turned towards an officer on one side of the ring. "I'll not be arrested for promoting indecent exposure."

The officer checked Darcy out head to toe. "Don't let anybody say I stand in the way of equality."

The noise picked up, and the officer got his share of back pats.

Her shirt and bra came off. The chill instantly goose pimpled her skin. She ignored the crowd and focused on Ripper, willing him to be the only thing in existence. The catcalls were numerous, as were the propositions. It was as if none of these men had seen breasts before. She deep-breathed her way to a calm place, but a few things said by those closest to the ring penetrated.

A man told her she had a nice rack. A woman asked her how much she wanted for the bra. An Australian accent told her to kick some ass. Another Australian accent told her to give him a piece of hers. The one that broke right through was relatively quiet, spoken as if in answer to a question. "Sure. Put a paper bag over her head and I'd fuck her."

For an insane moment, Toffee's voice rang in her head. *Good. Now you're angry instead of pathetic.*

"Let's do this," she said to the barker.

She moved to her corner. Ripper had never left his.

"Ladies and gentlemen ..." He turned to Darcy and asked quietly, "I'm sorry, what is your name?"

"Sandra. Sandra Jones."

"Thank you. Ladies and gentlemen, in this corner of the ring, and you know it's never polite to ask a lady's weight." He paused for a laugh. "The challenger, Sandra Jones. And we all know the champion...Ripperrrrrr!"

As the combatants approached the ring's center, the barker whispered to Ripper, "Try not to mess her up too badly." He looked at them both. "No biting, scratching or eye-gouging. Anything else is fair game. The fight is over when someone is unconscious, submits, or taps out. Fight."

Ripper threw a right at the top of her head. She dodged, stepped inside the arm and threw three quick lefts to his side and a right to his jaw. He took the body blows, but bobbed away from the right. His eyes brightened with curiosity. He threw the right again. This time Darcy caught his wrist and tried to step into a throw, but he shifted his weight, twisted his arm and Darcy had to move quickly not to be thrown herself.

His face split in a wolfish grin as he danced back and dropped into a proper fighting stance.

At ringside Noah realized what Darcy had just become aware of herself. Ripper wasn't slow, or clumsy, he just hadn't had to exert himself yet. *I hope he knocks your head off,* Noah thought, then hated himself for it.

Darcy now had two fights, one with the Ripper, the other with fear that was threatening to shatter her composure. Instead of triumphantly handing Sid five hundred dollars, humiliation would be her reward, and a lot of pain.

Ripper came in fast, but still went for a knockout punch. Darcy sidestepped, threw a kick that was blocked, then the man's arms were around her. She head-butted the ruin of his nose, dropped and rolled from his embrace and onto her feet, kicked out at his knee, but missed. He'd lifted her target out of harm's way with an economy of movement, and as he stepped down, spun and threw a blow at her side that she took on her shoulder. It knocked her halfway across the ring. The pain of it surprised her. Ripper closed the distance between them.

Darcy wrapped her arms around her stomach and wailed, "Don't hurt my baby!"

Horrified, Ripper froze, which was exactly the desired result. Darcy's palm snapped up and caught him under the chin, heel to jaw, solid connection. Ripper's head rocked back and Darcy was behind him and on him, locking in her chokehold. He didn't try to pull her arms. He launched himself backwards to crush her to the mat with his weight. Darcy let go and twisted, landing beside him instead of under him. She rolled, momentum swinging her fist to a hammer blow right between Ripper's eyes. She stood up, he didn't.

Amazement growing with every number, the barker counted the champion out.

The crowd went wild. Gamblers screamed for their winnings, and some cheered her on, but the catcalls continued, and if anything, the proposals increased in number and vulgarity.

The moment the barker raised her hand in victory she snatched it away and grabbed a towel from Ripper's corner. She wrapped it around herself and looked for her clothes to find an attendant handing them to her in a bundle. Her bra was missing. That was a shame. Straight from Vancouver and in excellent condition, good support. She only had one other like it, and it was back at the Pit. At a signal from the barker, the attendants surrounded her, broad backs inwards, providing a human curtain for her to dress behind. That's it folks, show's over.

Ripper sat up. The barker asked him something too quietly to hear, and the former champion shook his head.

"Ladies and Gentlemen, thank you for your patronage. The prize is won, and this night of bare-chested fighting is over." He pronounced it "ovah," and dragged it out almost as long as he did with Ripper's name.

With Darcy dressed, the attendants moved to disperse the crowd.

"You're not really pregnant, are you?" asked the barker, offering a letter of credit.

"No. But you said anything was fair game."

He smirked and said, "Deadlier of the species." Then he walked away.

Darcy looked for Noah, but he was nowhere to be seen, not at ringside, or anywhere in the vicinity.

Ripper was leaning on the corner post nearest her and misunderstood her change in expression. “Yes, I know,” he said in a deep voice more cultured than she would have expected. “There were a lot of guys out there. Do you want an escort?”

Darcy gave him a slight smile. “No thank you. I doubt any of them will mess with me. How’s your head?”

“Hurts.”

“That won’t last long.”

“I know.”

“My hand feels like it’s broken.”

“Good.”

The ring attendants cleared a path for her as she left. Ripper helped. He may have been defeated, but he could still kick anyone else’s ass.

She made her way back to where they’d first approached the ring, then to the electronics booth but Noah wasn’t there either. She looked at her wrist, but her watch wasn’t there anymore. She stepped out into the street and Noah was standing right in front of her. He had bruising and a little gravel on his left cheek.

“Here.” He held out her bra. “I had to chase a guy down for this.”

“How did you find me?”

“Just lucky.” He pushed the bra into her hands and turned away. “I’m going to browse by myself for a bit.”

“Wait,” she called to his retreating back. “I have your ticket.” But he was gone.

20. Scars

"I'm running out of paper," said Caps when he had just two pages left.

Lena relayed this information to the father, who sent his son scurrying off into the market. Caps was on the last page, and looking forward to resting his hand, when the boy dropped three blank pads at his feet, along with some freshly sharpened pencils and a bottle with a foul-smelling liquor in it.

"I don't really drink," said Caps.

"I do," said Lena. She took a long pull. "Gack! That's awful." She took another pull.

Caps settled into a trance. His thought process shut down until only what was needed to connect eye to hand functioned. As the hours and people went by, the drawings became more and more offensive. It seemed the more he insulted, the more he was appreciated. Towards the end, Caps would have made Helen of Troy look like a bulldog. One sketch faded into the next, a montage of crescents and shade lines, gawky ears and huge noses. Caps had no idea how long he'd been at it when Lena finally said, "Last one," to a pretty woman who would soon have ridiculously thick eyebrows and a prodigious chin.

The drawing done, the woman laughed in spite of herself. She paid and walked away, unconsciously smoothing her eyebrows with moistened finger tips. Caps flexed his fingers and wrist, moaning for an icepack.

Lena settled out with the father, leaving him most of the cash and procuring another letter of credit. The man was very happy. Just as they were getting ready to leave, one of the people already sketched came back and bought the chairs. The woodcrafter gave Lena a cut of that, and asked them if they had somewhere to eat dinner.

"Coppola's," said Lena. "We're seeing the last show."

"It's excellent," said the boy, then clamped his hand over his mouth.

"I knew it!" roared the father. "Held up at the tool shop you told me. You went to see the show!" he raised his large hand and the boy cringed.

"We can miss this part," said Lena, dragging Caps away, but when she looked back, the man was only berating his son, not beating him.

Darcy was the first to arrive at Coppola's. She had tickets, but waited outside despite the increasing chill. She had to force herself not to look around every time blond hair appeared on the street. She was torn between believing she'd done the right thing and being convinced she'd gone too far. In her mind, Noah looked up at her from the cat tunnel, a last glimpse before running for his life. She didn't want him to be in love with her. Couldn't have him in love with her. His friendship, however, she wanted, and wanted desperately now that there was a chance she'd thrown it away.

Coppola's was a long, single story building with faded red brick showing between sheets of metal polished to a nearly mirror shine. The metal reflected the streetlights—streetlights!—as did the glass set behind steel mesh in windows near the top of the wall. She looked at the streetlights and remembered Noah's shock at how many fluorescent lights Compton Pit had when he'd first arrived so many months ago.

"Stop it," she commanded herself.

A side door opened and a man stepped out and lit a pipe, the bowl glowing cheerily in the dim light near the alley. At first she thought he might be smoking pot, but the way he puffed told her it was tobacco, or a similar substance. The man's head swung lazily in her direction, then his body came to attention and he moved in her direction. Her left side towards him, and thinking from the purpose in his stride that he might be coming to hit on her, she turned to face him, assuming her scars would put a damper on his desires. If anything, he moved a bit faster.

"Hello, Sandra," he said, his face still not fully illuminated. "Fancy meeting you here."

Great, she thought. *He's seen my tits and doesn't care about my face.* It amazed her. Whoever this guy was, he had to know she could pound him into the ground if she wanted, and still he came. Men.

As soon as he pierced the circle of light from the street lamp, she recognized him. It was the barker. Still, that didn't mean he wasn't going to hit on her.

"Coming to see the show?" he asked, frowning at his pipe which had gone out.

"Yes. With friends."

"Ah," he looked around. "That young man who was with you…I don't see him. Is he inside already?"

"No."

In his favor, the barker wasn't eyeing her. Instead he was trying to relight his pipe with a silver lighter. "So…impressive. Both taking Ripper down and being willing to show off your attributes. Not a choice I would have made."

"Wasn't my choice. It was your idea."

"No, my idea was to keep you from getting into the ring in the first place. If I'd known what you were capable of, I wouldn't have insisted on that particular clause. Once your course was evident…even with Ripper, the crowd could not be dissuaded. There." The warm glow from the pipe resumed. "I've only a couple of minutes, then I have to get back inside."

"Are you a part of the show?"

"I am the master of ceremonies, young tigress. Horatio K. Trafalgar, at your service."

A laugh burst from her throat. She stifled it. "Is that your real name?"

"Is Sandra *your* real name?"

"No. I didn't want—"

"A gaggle of lust-struck ruffians to know your real name? I understand. So what do you normally go by?"

"Darcy."

"Yes. More suited to you. My name…" he leaned closer to her and dropped his voice to a conspirator's whisper, "…really is Horatio K. Trafalgar. Don't tell anyone." He moved back and lay one finger along the side of his nose.

In the brief moment he'd been close to her, she saw the man had an awful complexion, pocked cheeks and nose, artfully covered with blush.

"How could you be at the ring and work this show? Doesn't it run all night?"

"Oh no." He cursed quietly as the pipe went out again. "There's only two shows. The first at six, and the midnight show. The latter is more for the adults, of course. Racier, scarier. In all, it's the better of the two. I'd better get in. Where are you sitting?"

She fumbled the two tickets out of her pocket and showed them to him.

"Nosebleeds? Hardly worthy of this night's champion. Just the two of you?"

"Five."

"I see. Shouldn't be a problem. I'll leave word with the doorman. Identify yourself to him and I'm sure he can accommodate you better. Quite impressive, young tigress. Quite impressive."

Horatio disappeared back through the side door, leaving Darcy alone, but not for long. She heard Caps before she saw him, complaining about his wrist, and how he'd had no time to browse the market. Lena preceded him around the corner of Coppola's, looking exasperated at her lover's bitching.

"Hi, Darcy." Lena looked up and down the street. "Noah with you?"

"He's meeting us here. I think."

"You think?"

Caps stopped bemoaning his wrist long enough to give Darcy a condescending look. "You have another fight with him?"

"We may have had a disagreement."

People were starting to line up at the door and approach from all sides. She didn't want to have this discussion at all, never mind in front of strangers. Sid's rickshaw chose that moment to pull up at the curb. He stepped off and approached them, moving better than he had earlier in the day.

"Any luck?" asked Darcy.

"Yes. Let's get inside. Uh, where's Noah?"

"Right here." His voice seemed to come from nowhere, then the rickshaw pulled away, revealing Noah standing behind it. He stepped up on the curb and Sid gripped his chin, turning his head to one side to look at the bruise.

"I fell in the street," he said. "I'm fine."

"You pop any stitches?" Sid asked.

"No."

Darcy collected the tickets, and spoke quietly to the doorman who, in turn, gestured to a woman in a sequined tuxedo jacket. She led them from the front door down to a table a few feet from the stage.

The interior of Coppola's was a marriage of gigolo and opera, dark walls hung with thick, red drapes. Mirrored pillars halfway along each wall stood flanked by matching stone busts on wooden pedestals. The tables were all round, and all of the same size. About thirty of them were spread out before a high stage at the far end of the room. There was no bar apparent, but men and women appeared and disappeared behind one of the drapes carrying either full or empty glasses and bottles depending on what direction they were going.

"Hidden bar," Caps said to Noah. "That's the sign of a good venue. Doesn't detract from the show. I haven't been in a place like this since..." he drifted off, eyes going everywhere.

Between the drapes, pictures hung on the walls, photographs from concerts and plays, caricatures of celebrities, old movie posters. The scent of cooking meat mixed with smells of sweat, unwashed clothing and pungent smoke. Each table had a candle in the center, though none of them were lit. Along the walls were electric lights designed to look like kerosene lamps.

"Good seats," said Caps, pulling a chair out for Lena.

When everyone was sitting Sid leaned forward a little to gain their attention, and pitched his voice so that only they could hear him. "Ted was here. He talked to the scientists, checked out their research center. He seemed disappointed in their analytical equipment and left. We do have one more lead. One man at animal research believes he may have gone to Terpris."

Darcy's face cracked in a wide grin. "So we're going? We're really going?"

"Tomorrow. Last day, too. Darcy and I will go. I'll use what means we have to buy our passage, then, success or failure, we're going home."

Darcy slapped her letter of credit onto the table at the same time as Lena produced hers. After seeing the figure on Darcy's note, Lena added a skinbag of coins.

Sid scooped the money in his hands. "What have you lot been doing?"

"She did nothing," said Caps. "Me, I've got chronic tendonitis."

"Poor baby," Lena patted his leg under the table. She looked around the table, eyes bright with pride for her boyfriend. "Rick…" she looked past Darcy's shoulder and clapped her hands. "Darcy, behind you. That's what we were doing."

Darcy turned to look at a caricature on the wall behind her.

"That is one of mine. It's up already," said Caps quietly, "and framed. Too cool."

"You drew this?" Darcy demanded.

"Yeah. Why?"

"When did you draw this?"

"I don't know. Sometime today. I drew a thousand of them. What's the big deal?"

"This," Darcy stabbed the picture with a finger, "is Peter Gabriel."

"No way!" Caps beamed at Lena. "Peter Gabriel modeled for me!" He reached over his shoulder and patted himself on the back. "I'm loving every minute of this trip."

"I guess your wrist stopped hurting," said Lena.

"You didn't know?" Darcy's jaw dropped. "How could you not know it was Peter Gabriel? I thought you were a fan."

"I listened to him," Caps shrugged, "I didn't spend hours staring at his picture."

"Ooohhh," Darcy snarled. "I should have stayed with you guys today instead of hanging out with Noah." She meant nothing by it, nothing at all, but the moment the words were out of her mouth, she knew how someone would receive them.

She took a quick look at him, but Noah's face was turned towards the empty stage.

"Where'd you get this?" Sid waved the credit note at Darcy.

"I won a prize fight."

That made her the center of attention.

"You what?" Sid was not impressed.

"Not the bald guy," said Lena. "The big, bald guy crushing people in the ring by the curried rat vendor?"

"I didn't see any curried rat," Darcy arched an eyebrow, "but he was big and bald."

"Good job," announced Caps as if it didn't surprise him in the least. "Anyway, he was probably too busy staring at your legs to fight back."

Darcy cringed in expectation of what would come out of Noah's mouth. It was the perfect time for a taunt, and the more time he spent with Caps, the better he'd become at them. He said nothing. Instead of relief, she felt worse than if he'd taken the bait.

"I wouldn't have let you do it," said Sid. "How big?" he asked Lena, then without waiting for an answer, turned to Noah. "Where were you when all this was going on?"

"I was shopping for lingerie."

"Well," exclaimed a waitress, looking at the pile of money on the table, "I guess you guys are drinking tonight."

"Here, here," Lena thumped the table.

"You have food, right?" Darcy took the waitress's elbow.

The waitress produced a filthy, cracked menu from her apron and held it out in the open position. Darcy reached for it, but the girl woman pulled it away. "Sorry, can't. It's my only one."

"You can print tickets," said Caps, "but you've only got one menu?"

"People keep stealing the menus for souvenirs."

"Order for us," said Sid.

Darcy rattled off some choices, Lena ordered the drinks and Sid sorted through coins.

"I've got it," said Noah. He dropped a pouch on the waitress's tray. She pulled it open and fingered the contents.

"Keep the change," said Noah.

"All of it?" the waitress's eyes grew wide.

"Yeah ..." he paused, wondering just how much money was in the pouch. "Well, whatever's left once we're done tonight."

"Oh," her eyes fell a bit. "You guys turn heavy drinkers later on?"

"Only me," said Lena. She caught a reproachful look from the Boss. "I won't be guzzling tonight, though."

The waitress's face brightened again. "Okay then. I'll be back soon."

With all the other cash hitting the table, only Darcy thought to wonder where Noah had gotten his coin from. Maybe he did some work for the people at the electronics booth. She leaned over and punched Caps in the shoulder.

"Hey," he flinched.

"That's for drawing Peter Gabriel while I wasn't around."

"We're coming too," said Caps, throwing an arm around Lena. "To Terpris, I mean. We've got enough cash there for all of us to go."

"No." Sid shook his head, "We need the rest to outfit our trip home. If weather prevents us, we'll need it even more."

"Wait a minute." Caps shook a finger at Sid. "You've got another source of moola. You told us to have a good time today, not to scrub up supplies. Something hidden in the van?"

"I have nothing physical. I was going to borrow what we needed against future trade. It would have taken time and wheedling. This stuff is cash in hand."

"I'm not going," Lena said simply. "So there's some money back in our pocket."

"Lena," Caps squeezed her shoulder. "You have to come. Why wouldn't you… oh come on now, it's not the same thing."

"Size doesn't change a thing."

Now what on Earth did that mean? Noah fumed inside. Up until this point he thought Terpris was the name of the festival. Everything was Terpris. Terpris drink specials, Terpris merchandise, last days of Terpris, this, that and the other thing. Now it turned out Terpris was a settlement and everyone had known it all along. He could hear the Boss talking about Odega again, but he ignored the words, phasing out everything but the stage and select memories of the day. Though the table was round, they'd gathered around it in a semi-circle. Noah was at the end on the left side of the table. By shifting his chair he effectively turned his back on the group. The stage was deep, with lots of places for people to enter from the wings. Apart from a black backdrop, the stage was bare. He'd expected a little scenery at least.

Occasionally a group at Underbel put on a play; Shakespeare a few times, maybe a musical, but in all of Underbel, there had been one capable actor, and only two actresses of equal skill. It was impossible for these three to hold a serious show together amid other performers so bad, even the greatest tragedy was reduced to a long, unbroken stream of derisive laughter. By the time Noah was fifteen, the actor had gone to the teeth. By sixteen, one of the actresses had drank herself to death, and the other had lost her spark, both for the stage and for life. It wasn't the end of her theatrical career, however. Shortly after Noah's seventeenth birthday the woman went tooth crazy. Her days were spent shambling pointlessly from place to place, occasionally delivering loud monologues from plays or movies, dance numbers from musicals, or dramatic scenes in which the supporting cast was seen only by her. People started calling her Baby Jane. Eventually, she'd been tossed out the door.

"Here you go," said the waitress, unloading wooden mugs and plates from her tray. Darcy had chosen Coppola's answer to finger food. Sauce dripped from skewers of meat and strips of fried fish surrounded by small boiled potatoes.

"The show's going to start soon." The waitress pushed a glass of water in front of Sid. "We don't serve while it's on, so if you want more drinks, you should order them now."

Noah took a meat skewer and absently bit off of chunk. Dog. Always dog. You could spice it, batter it, didn't matter. Everything else might taste like chicken, but you couldn't disguise the taste of dog.

Darcy stood and scanned the room.

"The bathroom's that way," said the waitress, tilting a finger. "It's kinda stinky."

"Thanks."

"I'll join you," said Lena, pushing back from the table.

They worked their way along the wall, offering excuse-me's as they pushed the backs of chairs. The place had filled up. At the table farthest from the stage, a man with an air of management apologized to a group who were wholly dissatisfied with their seats. The bathrooms were near the back, opposite the entrance doors, which were now closed. The bathroom did stink. Out-of-order signs hung from all but one of the five stalls. Fortunately, there was no line up.

"Go ahead," said Lena. "I just want to wash my hands."

Lena eyed sinks, grimy with all manner of substances, lifted the edge of a filthy towel that hung between them, and decided her hands were clean enough as they were. "What did you do to Noah?" she asked through the stall door.

"What are you talking about?"

"You're not speaking, you're not looking at each other. Not at the same time, anyway."

"Do you mind, I'm on the toilet here. Damn. There's no paper. Could you—"

"On it." Lena looked in two stalls, then found success in the third. The pail beside the toilet had a few scraps of paper in it, some torn from books, others that looked like bits of paper towel. "Got some."

Darcy's hand appeared under the stall door.

"So what did you do to Noah?" Lena kept the handful of paper at her side.

"That's not fair."

Lena waited.

"How do you know he didn't do something to me?"

Still, Lena waited.

"Okay," Darcy's voice was suddenly very tired. "I'll spill. Just give, will you?"

She finished in the stall, noting with a small amount of bitter amusement that one of the book pages contained romantic poetry. The water that came from the bathroom faucet was crystal clear. She rubbed her hands thoroughly under the stream, as if the action could also wash her clean of what she was feeling. Lena waited silently, leaning against the wall, arms folded across her chest.

"He loves me," said Darcy, then took a deep breath. "It's not a crush, it's not lust in the loins. He truly loves me."

Lena raised an eyebrow.

Darcy tsked. "At least try to look surprised."

"Welcome to six months ago."

"You act like I should be returning the feeling."

"He's a genius. He's caring. And if that isn't enough for you, he's toning up into a total hunk. Oh, and one other thing. He can put up with you."

Darcy rubbed her forehead and sniffed.

"You could at least take him out for a test drive."

"A test drive? You mean sleep with him?" Darcy shuddered. "I'd never get rid of him if I did that."

"Why do you want to get rid of him?"

A woman entered. She wore a half veil over the left side of her face, and the left arm, bare in the sleeveless yellow shirt carried a multitude of small bite scars. She used a stall briefly, then exited without looking at the two women.

"Did you see that veil?" asked Darcy. "That's not a bad idea."

"Nice try. Let's keep to the subject."

"The last man who loved me was rat swarmed while I was screwing the prick who murdered him. How's that? When Noah looks at me the way…the way he looks at me…"

"So that's it? You see Noah and think about Travis?"

"I don't deserve to be loved. Not in that way. I don't deserve to be loved by any man."

21. Wonders of the World

Noah didn't notice the women return. He was too busy tracing the snaking cables that ran across the ceiling in front of the stage. As darkness claimed the room, he calculated there were at least thirty different lights pointed at the stage.

A bright white spot hit center stage and the crowd erupted in a thunder of applause. Into the light stepped a man in a tuxedo, puffed shirt, top hat, and a white mask covering his face to below the nose.

"Ladies and Gentlemen, hunters and farmers, miscreants of all ages, welcome to the *Wonders of the World*!"

Caught up in the spectacle, Noah didn't recognize the voice as the same one that had adjudicated the prize fight.

"Our tale begins in ancient Baghdad," continued the announcer, "where Ali Mustafa Ahmen visits his beloved Jaramina."

The spot went out, then reappeared on the other side of the stage on a nearly skeletal East Indian man wearing only a white turban and a loincloth. A white backdrop lit up, and projected from behind came the silhouette of a curvaceous woman, one arm beckoning to Ali Mustafa. Ali approached the silhouette, looking in every direction in a comic combination of fear and desire.

"Unfortunately," came the barker's voice from offstage, "Jaramina is newly wed to the jealous Sultan Vihja."

The silhouette began to undulate, and Ali mimicked the undulation as he moved across the stage. The way he moved made it look as if all his limbs had extra joints and his spine was made of rubber. When he was close enough, he reached out and seemed to embrace the shadow of Jaramina. He bent his head and soon was wrapped in a passionate kiss with empty air, but it coordinated with the shadow so well, the illusion was nearly perfect. He tightened his arms and the shadow moved closer. He bent forward, the shadow bent back. Suddenly the shadow pushed and Ali threw his arms out as if something had really shoved him away. A new silhouette appeared on the backdrop, this one seven feet tall, its arms raised menacingly. The Jaramina-shadow fell to its knees in a position of supplication and Ali looked this way and that for a place to hide.

The hulking shadow turned towards Ali and drew a long blade. It swung the blade and Ali did a standing back flip. The blade swung again and Ali dropped to his belly. He rolled and twisted as the blade swung down again and again. The choreography was so tight, Noah forgot for a moment it was all illusion. Ali sprang to his feet and ran this way and that as the shadow chased him across the stage. The performer's facial expressions were exaggerated, eyes bulging, mouth twisting. Ali turned his back to the crowd and as the blade swung at his neck, pulled his head down so low, it looked as if it had come off his shoulders, then his head popped back up and he jumped and landed on his back as the blade swung for his midriff. The shadow man chopped at the prone man's legs, and Ali brought his legs up, folding himself in half. The scimitar came down again, and Ali the contortionist rolled backwards, still bent in half, then came up on his hands, ankles locked behind his head. In this position, he ran on his hands across the stage and off, the sword barely missing him the whole way. Noah laughed so hard his stomach hurt.

The sitar music ceased, and the barker returned to his spot on the stage amidst heavy applause.

"We hope you enjoyed this display of ancient love and jealousy. Now, for your pleasure, the power and majesty of … *Totep*!"

The barker disappeared, the stage was lit in full, and the backdrop went up to reveal a large wooden model of an Aztec pyramid. A muscular man with tanned skin stepped out from behind the pyramid and performed a number of feats of juggling with a variety of sharp blades. The act culminated with four long daggers thudding into the stage and the fifth going straight down the juggler's gullet.

The curtain dropped, the lights went down, and the barker returned to announce the next act.

The juggler was followed by an acrobat, then Ali returned once more with another man and the two had an amazing sword fight while insulting each other at the top of their lungs. At the end of the duel, the barker announced a fifteen-minute intermission.

The house lights came up and servers rushed around, getting orders and clearing empties.

"Earth to Noah," said Caps, snapping his fingers at his friend who was staring at the empty stage.

"Thank you so much for getting these tickets," Sid said to Darcy.

"It was Noah's idea," she replied.

Caps leaned close to Noah and whispered, "Ali Mustafa's a fake."

"Come again?"

"That East Indian accent he was using during the duel. It was fake."

"So what?"

"So…it's a fake accent, that's all."

Noah smirked. Caps was somehow threatened by the little man's talents and had to make himself feel better by getting something on the guy. "Have you ever seen anything like that?" he asked to change the subject.

"Sure. I had a buddy who was a juggler. He didn't do sword swallowing though.

"How far to Terpris?" Noah asked casually.

"Hmmm. I guess Astoria's about a hundred miles from here."

"So…how far to Terpris?"

"I just told you." Caps gave Noah a strange look.

Noah was even more confused. Was Astoria Terpris? If so, why not just call it Astoria?

The lights went down, the crowd hushed, and the barker appeared in his spotlight.

"The preamble done with, we get to the real show. Those of the faint of heart should leave now." The curtain went up. Behind it was a wide cage of chicken wire. Within the cage was a small table, a wooden trunk, and a man-sized shape under a white drop cloth. "The cage, ladies and gentlemen, is not for the performer's safety, but for that of the audience. Ladies and Gentlemen, I give you Mephisto, master of the black arts." With an exagerated gesture he sidestepped to the wings and the spotlight moved to the drop cloth. The cloth fell, revealing a man with dark skin, his face painted like a skull. He wore an open black vest, loose black pants that stopped at the knees, white gloves and no shoes. He was the most tattooed man Noah had ever seen. Every visible inch of Mephisto was inked with intricate patterns of circles and whorls. It looked familiar, and in a few seconds, Noah's mind supplied the word Maori, of New Zealand origin.

Music faded in. Not the twang of a sitar, but the moody tone of a woodwind, low and haunting. Mephisto spread his arms and fingers wide to show they were empty, then with a flourish, produced a large black silk out of thin air. He showed both sides of the silk, draped it over one hand, then snatched it away to reveal a small human skull. He draped the silk over the skull, then brought his hand out from beneath. The skull appeared to stay in place, under the silk, but with no visible means of support. Grasping the silk at both ends, he moved it back and forth, the levitating skull bobbing and weaving beneath, until the skull rose up and peeked from behind the silk. Mephisto moved to the music, seemingly pulled by the skull.

Caps leaned close to Lena's ear and whispered, "The gimmick's called a zombie. The way it works is—"

Lena elbowed him. "Shush. I haven't seen a magic show since I was a kid. You're not going to ruin it for me." After a pause she whispered, "Tell me later."

The skull disappeared fully under the silk again and Mephisto crumpled the silk into a ball, as if there had never been a skull there in the first place. The audience applauded, but instead of bowing, the magician acted as if it were merely his due. The silk vanished into his hand, he opened the trunk and withdrew a black sheet. He displayed both sides of the sheet, much as he had with silk.

"Now," said Caps, "he's going to do the same trick with a whole skeleton."

Mephisto held the sheet up, then let it drop. Standing in the circle of his arms was a veiled woman a head shorter than the magician. She wore a form-fitting emerald body suit that showed off a slim, boyish figure.

The woman stooped to retrieve the sheet and dropped it in the trunk, then withdrew a piece of rope and handed it over. The magician pulled the rope taught to show its strength, then the woman cut it in the middle with a flashing stroke of a knife. The magician held both lengths taut, and she cut again, leaving him with four pieces. He tied the ends of each piece of rope to another, and held it out. The woman blew on each knot, and as she did so, the knots pulled free, until Mephisto held once more a whole piece of rope.

"Bad pacing," said Caps. "Cut-and-restored-rope should have been at the start, not after the other two tricks."

Mephisto threw one end of the rope up and it stopped at the apex of its flight. He released the other end and the rope hung straight up and down in midair. The woman leapt on the rope and climbed nearly to the top.

"You were saying," Sid said quietly, a smile stretching his face.

The woman slid down the rope and Mephisto clapped his hands. The rope disappeared in a burst of flame.

Applause started once more, but the woman gestured for silence.

The woman moved to the back of the stage, and Mephisto once more showed his empty hands, then he clapped them together and a flash of light momentarily blinded most everyone in the audience. When their vision returned, the magician stood with a white dove cupped in his hands. He opened his hands a bit, and the dove climbed to the edge of his thumb and looked about.

Quiet murmurs came from various tables. "It's a fake," once voice said. "Is he insane?" asked another.

The woman approached, Mephisto flicked his wrist, and the bird hopped from his hand to hers. She placed the bird on a stand she'd erected while the audience was watching the magician. Almost immediately, Mephisto was holding another dove. This too was taken and placed on the stand. The birds made no attempt to fly at the audience.

"Lobotomized?" asked Caps.

"Could be," said Sid. "Or drugged."

Mephisto produced a third dove, then a fourth. Both were taken and placed on the stand. Finally, the magician brought his hands to his mouth and appeared to regurgitate a fifth dove. With the dove gripped in one hand, he spread his arms and gave his first bow of the performance. The applause he received dwarfed any that had been given earlier. The woman placed all five doves in a wooden cage and deposited it offstage.

Mephisto and his assistant moved through a series of tricks, all of which Noah had seen before, but not for so long, they amazed anew. Mephisto put the woman into a trance and levitated her, put her in a standing box and pulled sections away so it looked like he was separating her torso away from the rest of her body, shoved her in another box and ran swords through it, only to open the box to reveal her unharmed and wearing a top hat. With an evil grin, he took the top hat, and yanked a rabbit out of it. A living, honest-to-goodness-rabbit. He held it up by its ears and incredibly, scratched its belly before allowing his assistant to take it.

Now the magician sat cross-legged on the stage and rolled his eyes back into his head as if going into a trance. A few people undid clamps on the sides of the cage and removed it in sections.

A large, transparent box was wheeled in from the wings, and something waist-high, covered with a tarp, was brought in from the opposite side. The stage hands vacated, leaving only the meditating magician, and his assistant.

"Ladies and gentlemen," the woman spoke for the first time, "this case," she gestured with a hand at the see-through box, "is air tight. It is important that you keep absolutely quiet, for my master needs his utmost concentration for this final act. Once again, I remind you, the case is air tight. You are in absolutely no danger."

Mephisto stood and his assistant removed a straightjacket from the trunk and buckled him into it. The magician stepped into the case, and his assistant closed and sealed the door. She wheeled the smaller object to the side of the case and secured it somehow, then she removed enough tarp to uncover a large clock sitting on a clear surface.

"When I say start," she announced, "Mephisto has thirty seconds to get out of his straightjacket and escape before a panel opens and his case fills with..." she pulled the tarp away, "... these!"

Under the tarp was a smaller transparent box on a stand. The box was filled with bees. There was only one visible way out of the box—through a closed panel and into Mephisto's prison.

Someone screamed. A man close to the stage jumped from his chair and ran towards the exit, tripping over someone else who was doing exactly the same thing. The atmosphere in the room was electric. Nobody else attempted to flee, but the fear was tangible. Greater than the fear was desire to see this man, this tattooed, painted man, pit himself against a swarm of bees.

"Am I the only one," said Lena, "who realizes that the minute that guy opens the door, all those bees are going to come out here?"

"Relax," said Caps, "he'll be out with the door shut by twenty seconds." An edge to his voice belied his confidence.

The woman set the timer, knocked on the front of the case and said, "Start," then she ran from the stage as if the bees were already in the air.

Mephisto struggled. He jerked and pulled, his head turning every few seconds towards the opening that would supply his doom. At ten seconds he'd made no progress. At twenty he was no closer to freeing himself than he was at ten.

"Get him out of there," someone yelled.

Twenty-five seconds. Each tick of the clock seemed to be an hour apart. Twenty-eight seconds. People got out of their chairs, others turned their heads away. Mephisto hadn't so much as loosened a strap. Sweat stood out on his forehead and his eyes bulged.

Thirty seconds. There was a click, and the connecting panel fell open. The bees flowed from their box into the case, completely covering the magician.

Sid came to his feet, not sure of what to do, but there had to be something.

Amid the bees, the straightjacket hit the floor, and Mephisto, crawling with insects, placed his hands on the front of the case and grinned at the audience. Though he was absolutely covered, it appeared as if he was in no pain, as if not a single bee stung him.

As the audience came aware of the miracle they were witnessing, a pair of men entered from the wings and wheeled the grinning magician offstage, case, bees and all.

One person started clapping, slow and loud. Another pair of hands joined in, and soon the thunder of applause threatened to bring the roof down.

"How did he do that?" Lena shouted at Caps over the din.

"I haven't a clue," the artist shook his head. "I haven't the slightest clue."

The barker took the stage and silenced the crowd with a few gestures. "We thank you, we thank you. Please, quiet now. Quiet. Please. And now we bring you the final act of the evening."

"That wasn't it?" asked Caps aloud. "What the hell are they going to follow that with?"

The barker smiled, waiting for absolute silence. "From the amusing to the terrifying, from the exotic to the erotic, ladies you may want to leave, lest jealousy consume you. Married men, hurry home or fear your betrothed may never satisfy again. More beautiful than Desdemona, more sumptuous than an entire harem, I give you…Sampson and Delilah."

The lights went out, and faded in again to show a tall man standing stock still in the middle of the stage. As the light grew brighter, it became clear it wasn't a real man, but a well-carved statue, dark brown, with no facial features. The music started, a serpentine melody of woodwind and string with just a hint of percussion. From the left wing, a woman wrapped in silks eased to center stage, hips swinging subtly, arms writhing more like tentacles than human limbs. The silks were translucent, hinting at, but not revealing what lay beneath. The woman, Delilah, swayed until she was in front of the statue. A thin veil, not unlike that worn by the magician's assistant, covered her face. With her back to the statue she gripped its wrists and moved its hands up her body starting at the hips. Arms twisted on articulated joints. When the hands reached her face, she tilted her head, pressing it to the statue's fingers. She jerked the hands away, and one of them took the veil with it.

Her face was young and perfectly symmetrical; golden hair tied in a knot, thin eyebrows over almond-shaped eyes, small nose and rosebud of a mouth. From his vantage point close to the stage, Noah could see her eyes were sky blue.

Her head bobbed on her neck as she executed a series of pirouettes, then raised one leg ever so slowly, and placed it on the shoulder of the statue. She brought one of the hands up to cup her buttock, then whirled away, leaving behind the silk that had acted as a skirt. Her legs were tanned to a golden brown, clean-shaven and free of scars. She bent forward at the waist and stood, running her hands up her legs. The music increased in tempo and she undulated faster, adding more movement to her pelvis and shoulders. Far from being tawdry, the effect was erotic, even elegant.

Darcy looked away from the dancer and scanned the crowd. All eyes, male and female were on Delilah. As her gaze came back to her own table, she was surprised to see Sid, who normally favored larger, fuller-bodied women, pursing his lips in appreciation.

Delilah put her back against the statue and once more ran its hands up her body, this time stopping them at her chest. She stepped forward, and the silk wrapping her torso pulled away, exposing her midriff and silks wrapped around her breasts and pelvis. Her eyes closed and the music slowed again. She stroked herself and writhed, reveling in her own physical being.

For the first time, Darcy noticed the two men who'd taken positions on the floor in front of the stage, facing the crowd. One of them was Ripper, looking none the worse for wear for Darcy's knockout punch. the second man was even larger than Ripper, wider in the shoulders with brooding eyes and dark hair. Their job was obvious; to stop lusting viewers from making the stage.

Delilah embraced the statue and rubbed herself up and down against one side of it, then pressed her stomach to it and pushed away, leaving behind the silk that wrapped her breasts. Darcy couldn't help but compare. The dancer's were smaller than hers, but appeared firmer, and sat higher on the chest.

She scanned the audience again. Whereas her own little strip show earlier had brought catcalls and lascivious shouts, the men in this audience were silent, sitting in rapt attention. When she looked at the stage again, Delilah had unpinned her hair and the cascade of gold fell to her waist.

A beat came from the audience as men began stomping their feet or banging mugs on tables in time to the music. Delilah had lost the silk at her waist, leaving only a pink g-string between herself and complete nudity. She arched her back and ran her hands through her hair, bending and twisting with liquid grace. Smoke of some sort poured in from the wings, and colored lights flashed and moved about the stage.

Delilah suddenly stopped, placed her back to the statue and moved one of its hands to the g-string. The music fell silent. The drum beat from the crowd continued. Delilah eyed her audience almost defiantly, then jerked the statue's hand away at the same moment as she bent her head forward. The g-string dangled from the hand, her hair fell to cover the front of her body, the music started again. Delilah snapped her head back and for a second stood exposed in all her glory, then the lights went out.

The audience held its breath. When the lights came back on, the barker stood in the middle of the stage. There were a few boos, but the barker laughed them off.

"Ladies and Gentlemen, thank you for coming. You have been a remarkable audience. We're off for distant lands on the morrow.

We have enjoyed both this city and her people. Ladies and Gentlemen, the *Wonders of the World*."

One by one, the performers assembled on the stage, Ali, Totep, the acrobat, the swordsman, then Mephisto and assistant, and finally, Delilah in a garment not unlike a toga. They bowed to the audience, and filed off the stage, not returning for a curtain call. Eventually the noise died down and people began to gather their belongings.

Ripper had disappeared, but the larger man stood by the door to backstage, discouraging audience members who wanted to go back and express their appreciation.

"That was something," said Caps. "I'd have never put a strip act after a magician, especially not that magician, but…wow."

"So you think she was prettier than me?" asked Lena, a little menace in her voice.

"Whoa, look at the time," Caps stood. "Boss, we should be getting back to the hotel."

"Darcy and me'll share a room," said Lena.

"Hey," Caps started, "I thought—"

"You can just close your eyes," Lena kissed his nose, "and pretend Noah's that dancer, 'kay?"

She sidled past him towards the door.

Caps looked at her back, then groaned at Noah.

"So was she prettier than me?" asked Noah, fluttering his eyelids.

"Buddy, nobody's prettier than you."

22. Road to Astoria

The crowd was cheering, Ripper was bleeding and one of Darcy's arms was raised in victory while the other was clasped across her breasts. Noah wasn't disappointed. He was furious and confused, humiliated and hurt. At the same time as his cheeks burned with shame at being so easily manhandled by the ring attendants, his heart leapt with pride at Darcy's incredible achievement.

In contrast, his own confidence took a blow every bit as hard as the one Ripper's face had just received. If Darcy could do what she'd done to that monster, how did she truly view Noah? A joke, that's how she saw him. It would be more likely for her to have fallen for Toffee than it ever was for her to think of Noah as a man. At least the late Chief of the Hunters could hold his own in a fight.

On the ring apron, just outside the ropes, Darcy's clothes sat in a pile. As Noah moved towards them—the ring attendants let him go the moment the fight was over—a hand darted out from the crowd, snatched the bra and disappeared. For an instant, Noah thought of letting the theft go unpunished. He pushed through the crowd. He didn't have a face to look for, but the arm had been clothed in a bright green sleeve. At the periphery of the audience, Noah spotted a jacket of the same color on a man moving casually away from the ring towards the darker streets of the inner city. Noah cast his eyes about, making sure there weren't other jackets of similar color, then set off after the man, walking just a little faster than his quarry.

The man looked back. He had long dark hair under a knit cap, and watery eyes. He quickened his pace. He looked back again, decided he was being followed, and took off at a run. Noah pounded after him. The sounds of the market faded away and the man twisted and turned, possibly familiar with the layout of the streets, but Noah was faster and his limbs were charged with rage.

He tackled the man from behind and both of them crashed to the pavement.

"Give me the bra," said Noah a little breathless, locking his arms around the man's torso.

The thief twisted and smashed an elbow into Noah's cheek, jarring his head to one side and momentarily darkening his vision. The thief slithered out of Noah's grasp and tried to gain his feet, but Noah spun on the ground, used his legs to scissor and sweep the thief's legs out from under him, sending him face first to the ground. The thief tried to get up but Noah drove a knee into his lower back, then pulled his head up by a handful of hair and punched him hard in the side of the face, once, twice, three times. On the third punch, the man gurgled and went limp. Noah rolled him over, dusted himself off and looked about, suddenly aware that he was the outsider here.

The street was empty. The thief's lips were a mess, either from the punches or the initial takedown, and shallow breath caused pink bubbles to froth at the corners of the mouth. The jaw was already swelling, and under the layers of clothing the man turned out to be quite thin. The bra was stuffed into the inside pocket of the jacket. Noah retrieved Darcy's undergarment and noticed a pouch lying a few feet away. He lifted it, feeling the heft and jingle. It was a money pouch, probably lifted from other people in the crowd, or an amalgamation of the day's pickpocketing. That the coin could legitimately belong to the man didn't occur to Noah until much later, when he was back at the colonial hotel. Possibly the man wasn't a thief at all, but an aroused fight fan seeing an opportunity for an intimate souvenir of an anonymous redhead with a beautiful body.

Great, Noah thought guiltily, *I'm a mugger.* He was also offended by the level of violence he'd visited on the man. Rationally, he could have subdued the man in a more genteel manner. Other options were at his disposal, any number of debilitating arm or leg locks that would have granted pain-induced cooperation. But no, he'd been quick and dirty, just the way Toffee had taught him. *If you can't end a guy in three seconds, you'd better stick with using a gun.* Those were the hunter's words of wisdom. He hadn't woken the man up or even alerted another soul to his presence, just left him there for another mugger to happen across, or…rats.

"Oh, God," Noah groaned and wrapped his arms around his stomach which suddenly threatened to disgorge its contents. "And then I went to a show."

"Come again?" Caps looked up from the sketchpad. Despite his earlier complaints of wrist pain, the moment they got to their room, Caps lay down on the bed and scribbled furiously. Sid collapsed on the other bed and was almost instantly asleep.

Noah was sitting on the floor beside the bed he was going to share with the painter, head-to-foot, with Caps no doubt kicking him multiple times through the course of the night.

"Nothing," Noah didn't want to talk about it. It was just too awful. Especially since underneath it all was a giddy satisfaction at beating the hell out of another human being. *He's fine,* he rationalized. Knockouts to the jaw don't last that long. "How rat-free do you think the city is?"

"Y'know, I asked a guy about that while I was drawing him. Normally I wouldn't let the subject speak, but this guy's lower face was pretty ordinary. The top of his head, though? Wow, nature just wasn't kind to this guy."

"All scarred? You were making fun of people's scars?"

"At-birth nature, not tooth nature. Actually I downplayed people's facial scars as much as possible. I worked with head and face shapes people came into this world with. Or tried to, on a couple of folks it was hard to tell. Anyway, this guy said larger animal activity is pretty low, what with the cage and all. Rats and mice do get in during the warmer months, but in fall and winter they're cleared out pretty quick. They never hide long enough to grow into a swarm."

"And this guy was reliable? Like he lives here, not another visitor."

"He lives here alright …"

Noah shuddered in relief. At least his victim wasn't something's meal.

"… and as reliable as you could get. He was one of the cops."

Noah's relief vanished and his stomach lurched again. A scenario sprang to his mind. The guy's legit, goes to the cops … no, not scary enough. The guy's legit and a relative of somebody important, goes to the cops, gives a description, and the next thing Noah knows, he's being dragged off to some spot in the woods and left to the teeth, and not a damn thing Sid or the others could do about it.

"What do you think?" Caps held his pad out for Noah's inspection. "I scrapped the others, they were too complicated."

On the page was a three-dimensional drawing of a cube within a cube. "What is it?"

"The dude's bee-box. Look," Caps indicated one edge of the cube with the tip of the pencil. "There's a hidden layer. He stands in the middle, right? The bees fly into this gap. You can't see the inner lining, so it looks like the bees are all over the guy."

Noah shook his head ruefully. Here he was, charging, trying and convicting himself, while right next to him, the artist spent his energy so frivolously, blissfully unaware that cops would be breaking down the door at any moment.

"Caps, the bees didn't look like they were all over the guy, they *were* all over him. You saw the same thing I did."

"Did we? Did we really? Okay, what if he had some plastic bees on invisible strings he could pop out all over the place, while the real ones went into the protective layer?"

"Caps..."

"Bah, you're right." He tossed the pad aside in frustration. "I can't figure out how he did it and it's bugging the heck out of me. The birds and the rabbit were doped. How do you dope a bee? They die if they lose their stingers, so that's not it. How do you dope it so it can still fly and stuff, but won't sting? Shit, how do you even practice the trick in the first place? That's all magic really is."

"Bees?"

"Practice. I wanted to be one once."

"A bee?"

"Shut up. A magician. I forked out a pile of cash for books and gimmicks, and not dime-store crap either. The good stuff."

"So what happened?"

"I tell everybody I got turned off by how geeky the magicians I hung out with were, but the truth is, I couldn't hack the practice. Hours man, hours. Sore hands, sore wrists, aching fingers, day after day. You've got to hand it to magicians for that if nothing else. Hey," he snapped his fingers, "could it be a hologram? The bees I mean."

Noah gave an exaggerated nod. "Suurre. Project multiple complex holograms on a moving object to that degree. Wait, if the whole thing was a hologram, including the magician, that could be done."

"You mean from the moment he stepped into the box?"

"Uh-huh, from that moment. Micro-light emitters coupled with projectors from above working on some sort of transparent lattice. You've nailed it."

"Ah. You're shining me on. I'll sleep on it. You staying on the floor?"

"You should be so lucky. You crashing now?"

"Yeah. Last bus to Terpris is first thing in the morning and we'll have to get up when the Boss does to convince him to take us. You are coming aren't you?

"Couldn't we just go later in the van?"

"Nah, the road to Astoria's closed to traffic except the buses. Won't be open again till after the festival."

"So what's so special about Terpris? I mean apart from the fact that Dr. Odega might be there?"

"What's so special about...you're kidding me, right? You're not kidding me...oh my. You didn't hear about Terpris in Underbel?"

"Not that I can remember."

"And all this time...whoo boy." Caps, already naked to the waist, pulled off his pants and socks and slid under the covers. "You'll see tomorrow. G'night."

"The way I see it ..." Lena paused and took a deep breath.

"Yes?" Darcy rolled over. They were each lying with their heads at the foot of their beds. The lamp mounted on the wall between them made it impossible to make eye contact from the headboards.

"You can't accept love. That'll take some time to get over. You know Caps is awesome at therapy—"

"Lena..." Her voice was filled with warning.

"Okay, okay. Just thought I'd take another shot at it. This is what you need to do. You need to get laid."

"We already went over this."

"I don't mean Noah. Just grab some guy and get with it."

"Some guy?"

"Well not just anybody. Someone who gets your juices going. You know, put some loving between you and the memory of...the memory of *him*. A little friction to get the bad taste out of your mouth. Oh, sorry. I didn't mean that the way it sounded."

"A sex sorbet? So who? My options are limited. It can't be anyone at the Pit."

"Why not? Chiu-Keung wouldn't put up a fight I'm sure. He's a well put-together guy."

"He's my subordinate. How could I have a professional relationship with him afterwards?"

"You had a professional relationship with Travis when you were on duty. You were his subordinate."

"Like hell professional. He'd be giving briefings, orders, I'd be looking him up and down thinking about getting him out of his coveralls. And anyway, it's different. Word would get around, and once you've had sex with a man, he always feels like he's one up on you."

"Caps used to think like that. Why not somebody here? Before we go, pick up a stud and get it on."

Darcy leaned on one elbow and pulled the skin tight around her scars. "Just pick up some stud."

"Nice try. We both know how easy it is for you. Just think about it."

***

It was simple work for Caps to talk Sid into allowing all of them to go. Sid's protest was more for show than anything else. Convincing Lena was the difficult part, but in the end, she caved and the artist beamed as all five of them climbed onto the last bus. The road to Astoria was as clear as Compton Pit's driveway. NPPD vehicles patrolled at intervals, and vast sections of the road had rows of sharpened poles pointed outwards, as if some feudal lord feared attack from mounted cavalry.

Noah kept silent about his ignorance. No place called Terpris was on the map, so at least he knew it was a post-Change settlement. The real mystery was why the bus they were on was the last bus going there. On a lot of booths were signs stating sales due to the last day of Terpris. That would suggest the settlement was being abandoned, but the place being uninhabitable didn't jibe with how many people wanted to go there. The bus was packed.

Caps and Lena sat in the seat ahead of Noah, talking quietly. In the seat behind him, Sid and Darcy discussed various methods to bring Odega home via bus, or perhaps a bribe to the NPPD would be necessary to obtain transportation. They didn't mention the doctor's name, and spoke in a semi-code of references, but Noah was able to understand them. He had the window seat, and since he was on the side towards the river, this was a grand thing. The Columbia River rolled along, carrying bits of detritus and foaming over rocks close to the shore.

Sitting next to him was a portly man with an unkempt beard who occasionally picked his teeth with what appeared to be a raccoon's claw. After each mining foray, the man would examine what he'd recovered, wipe the claw on the sleeve of his dogskin coat and pocket the implement, only to withdraw it and repeat the process a few minutes later.

"Going to Terpris?" the dentist-in-training asked.

"Yes."

"Hmm."

The claw came out, and Noah turned away.

Sid had told them to bring only those items it would break their hearts to have stolen. Noah tried not to look too directly at any police officers on the way to the bus, or any police vehicles on the way to Astoria. Though nothing had happened to justify his fears, he was convinced there'd be a posse waiting for him the minute they got back from Terpris. In a way, being arrested would be a positive thing, because it would mean his victim was healthy enough to make a complaint.

The river disappeared behind a clump of trees. They'd been on the road over an hour now, and a man with a red vest over his jacket was making his way towards the back of the bus, speaking with each passenger.

"Terpris?" he asked Lena when he was beside the seat she shared with Caps.

"Yes, five of us. He's got the money." She jerked her thumb over her shoulder.

"Got mine," said the hygienist, pulling a yellow-painted wooden card from his pocket.

The man in the vest looked at Noah.

"One more back." He also jerked a thumb.

Sid haggled briefly with the man, then handed over some money and received five wooden cards for his efforts.

The river reappeared, far wider than it had been prior to being obscured by the trees.

"Look at that," said Caps, leaning over the back of the seat. "Almost half a mile wide now. We're almost there."

"Delightful," said Lena, in a tone that suggested she thought it was anything but.

The drive lasted a few more minutes, then they passed a newly-made sign that welcomed travelers to Astoria. The sign was hanging from the observation tower of a submarine, now sitting on the ground. The periscope rotated to follow the bus as it passed. Noah pressed his face to the window, keeping the strange sight in view for as long as he could. Parked next to the tower was a police jeep.

From *Graff's Graphs Vol VII*

> …the observation tower, formally of the Columbia River Maritime Museum, and prior to that of the World War II submarine USS *Rasher,* was moved to the outskirts of town to provide a secure watch station for Astoria's outermost guard detail. The museum itself has long since been scavenged for materials, as has most of the town.
>
> Established in 1811, and named for John Jacob Astor who established a fur-trading colony at the mouth of the Columbia, Astoria was a thriving tourist community rarely visited by anybody who actually lived in Oregon.
>
> A jovial mix of modern and colonial architecture, the town was in many ways a miniature version of Portland. In its current incarnation, the settlement sticks to this pattern, as its few inhabited buildings sit within a high cage very much like New Portland's. Outside the cage, a mile or so from what was once the downtown core, stands the 125-foot-high Romanesque Astoria column.

Rising from Coxcomb Hill, the column once commanded a glorious view of the river, town and coast. Now it is unused and in a state of disrepair.

The Astorians learned quickly that to climb to its observation deck invited death by birds. A cage was erected over the deck, but so many birds threw themselves into the mesh in suicidal diving runs, the cage was soon clogged with feathers and carcasses, as opaque as a brick wall. Cleaning the cage from within is a pointless task, as birds will smash into whatever area of the cage a person is cleaning. It is no longer called the Astoria Column. It is now called the Featherdome.

Today, Astoria is nothing more than a desperate fishing community, cursing the cold and the rain in the winter months, and heading underground to curse the insects and animals in the spring and summer. However, every few years, Astoria briefly becomes a thriving community once more, host to throngs of tourists, but not for anything the town itself has to offer.

The bus bypassed the cage-covered buildings and proceeded along the waterfront, passing the 17th Street docks, now naught but rotting timbers barely attached to the land, and on to the Port of Astoria.

The first thing Noah saw was the twenty-foot metal waste bin nearly full with dead gulls. The next thing he saw was the crowd of people at the base of the dock, loading and unloading trucks that must have come up earlier or been there already because he'd seen no such traffic during the drive. As the bus pulled to a stop, Noah's eyes followed the length of the dock to a pair of sixty-foot boats, bristling with pedestal-mounted guns, and beyond that…

"Terpris," he breathed.

"Now you get it," said Caps.

23. The Legend of Bertram Wallis

June 10th, New Wilderness Day

Captain Gerard "Kings" Ransom strode the deck, non-skid surface springy under his feet. His hands were clasped behind his back as he silently fumed at what was happening aboard his command. The whole concept was a waste of time and energy and he thought it a joke when it was first presented to him, and an even bigger one when his superiors had told him the event was a go.

It was a beautiful day for it, there was no doubt about that. Cloudless sky, bit of wind made stronger by the passage of his vessel, some gulls swooping and diving a hundred feet off the port bow. Then the sound came, the unmistakable sound of an emptying bladder.

Ransom turned to see the apologetic expression on his brother's face as the man's Alsatian, leg raised, piddled against a guard rail.

"Sorry," Gregory Ransom shrugged. "I did walk him before we came on board."

"Why did you...never mind." It was a useless question. Gregory never went anywhere without his stupid dog, and the man had gone through proper channels to get permission to bring the cur with him. The captain had argued against this, too. He didn't even want his brother around in the first place, but with so many other civilians in attendance, there was no possible excuse to keep him from coming on board.

"At least put him on a leash. I can't have a loose dog on the flight deck."

"I don't know where it is. You know how I'm always losing things." It was a lie. The leash was in his pocket, but Alf hated his leash, and besides the dog wouldn't do anything wrong. Alf was a good boy. He was the best boy. Gregory lightly gripped the dog's collar.

By all rights, Ransom should have been on the bridge, or even the Primary Flight Control gallery of the island tower, known as the Pri-Fly. He couldn't stay there, however. With all the reporters on the Pri-Fly's aft balcony—Vulture's Row—and even more reporters on the bridge, a place civilians had no right to be, the captain thought he could at least get some peace on the flight deck.

"It's okay," said Gregory. "The rain'll take care of it? Right?"

"You shouldn't be up here," Ransom made as if to grab his brother's sleeve.

"I got permission. I have this," he held up a helmet with ear protectors in it. "Now what's up with you, Gerry? It's not everyday you get to work with a living legend, and look at all the cameras. You'll be famous."

Ransom clenched his teeth against a reply and scanned the flight deck, but this only exacerbated things. Every available parking space was filled, but not with the carrier's usual air wing. There wasn't an F-14B Tomcat or F/A-18 Hornet anywhere in sight. The deck looked like an open-air museum, like an airplane graveyard forced out to sea. Single-prop TBD Dauntlesses sat alongside gray SBD Devastators and a few F4F-3 Wildcats. Relics, some of which hadn't seen airtime since Ransom watched new episodes of Hogan's Heroes. His eyes could see through the fresh coat of paint to the rust beneath. They didn't belong on his ship, they were memories, keepsakes of an ancient war. His real air wing was split between assignment on the *Kitty Hawk* and stowed at two different airports on the mainland. The room on the hangar deck—two football field's worth of it—was needed for the press conference, and the pavilions.

"Bloody pavilions," he said out loud.

"Huh? You say something?" Gregory stopped baby-talking to his dog and moved a few steps closer to his brother.

"The pavilions. You should visit the pavilions."

"Oh, most of them aren't open yet, and besides, they won't let me take Alf down there." He ruffled the dog's head.

"Won't they?" He tried to keep the sarcasm out of his voice. He failed.

"No. I don't know why. There's all those giant parrots in the Amazon display. They crap all over the place. And that magician guy brought a tiger with him."

"Gregory, go down, will you? Tell anyone who tries to stop you that I okayed it. Make sure Alf gets a good look at the tiger."

"Hey, is that him?" Gregory pointed over Ransom's shoulder.

On the far side of the deck, a man posed in archaic flight gear before a cluster of photographers. One hand on his hip, the other grasping the prop of a Dauntless, he looked like the cover of a dime-paperback war novel. Bertram Wallis. This was all his fault. Admiral Emeritus Wallis. Ambassador Wallis. Richer than an oil sheik and at least three-hundred-years-old Wallis. Okay, closer to ninety, and he didn't even look it. No, Wallis must have thrown enough money at wrinkles to feed a country in Africa. Bertram Wallis was like his planes, rust hiding under a fresh coat of paint. Ransom didn't begrudge the gray that crept into the dark brown of his own mustache and all but claimed the hair up top. He'd have a few more gray hairs after this was over. A United Nations Gala event, culture, entertainment, fine dining…but a cruise ship wasn't good enough.

"I wish I could do what he's going to do," said Gregory. "Look at him, Alf." He stooped and grabbed the dog's head, pointing it in the direction of Bertram Wallis. "Look at him. He's a great man."

There were at least a dozen places the carrier should be: the South Pacific, the Mediterranean, pick a conflict. Instead she was sitting a few miles from Norfolk, prepared to defend the completely safe Virginia shoreline with antiquated aircraft. Why? So Bertram Bloody Fucking Wallis could kick things off by climbing in the same plane—at least he claimed it was the same plane—he flew at Guadalcanal and Midway, and lead Fighting Six, Torpedo Six and Bombing Six on one last Combat Air Patrol. But who knew, maybe there were some subversive gulls preparing to wreak havoc on America's tenth state. Bertram Wallis had somehow managed to qualify as a pilot. A hefty chunk of money must have opened that door. His money was behind most of this.

Ransom had argued long and hard. Why my command? Why my boat? There were smaller carriers more suited for this debacle. But Ransom's was the carrier from which Bertram Wallis had flown his historic missions back in World War II. No it wasn't, that was the CV6, Ransom's command was the CVN-65. Wallis's carrier was scrapped in New Jersey in 1959. They just had the same name.

His arguments were irrelevant to the brass. They sympathized, but the decision had been made at the top. Each time they turned their backs on him, Ransom imagined they were practicing puckering up to kiss Wallis's wrinkled ass. Unless he'd poured money into that part of his body as well. So the captain followed his orders, but logged an official protest. It would serve them right if war broke out while he was playing gracious host to civilians and the flying geezers. The time it would take to offload all this garbage, and get his birds back onboard, and his crew—over two thousand of them were on liberty—Ransom didn't even want to think about it.

"Excuse me, sir," a young sailor, wearing the blue jersey/white helmet of a messenger, approached with a pair of ear protectors in one hand. "They're getting ready to launch. Are you planning to stay down here, sir?"

Ransom looked at his brother. "Yes, I suppose so." He took the ear protectors and returned the sailor's salute.

The photographers were ushered off the flight deck and suddenly Bertram Wallis wasn't the only relic beside the planes. Only Wallis was going to fly, but the other surviving members who could still make it appeared in uniform, if only to further Bertram's moment. In place of his wing mates, Wallis had tracked down their sons and grandsons who could fly. Two were Navy, one was Air Force, one was commercial. Rounding out the rest of the crew was any pilot who'd flown anything off the CV6 before she'd been mothballed in '51. They'd all qualified for deck landings and takeoffs, though. At least the practice and drills had been performed on a different vessel. Ransom might have resigned if he'd been forced to put up with that mess.

As handshakes and hugs were exchanged by the pilots. Bertram Wallis climbed into his Dauntless, and struck a few more poses. He was lit by brief flashes of light as a crewman took his own personal photographs.

Ransom briefly considered punitive measures for that breach in protocol, but discarded the idea. To discipline a sailor for something as tiny as that when a troop of half-naked acrobats was making human pyramids on the hangar deck...no point in taking his wrath out on the crew.

"Do you think it's safe for him to fly?" asked Gregory, the sound of his voice muffled by the ear protectors. "What if he has a heart attack?"

"It'll renew my belief in birthday wishes."

And that was the icing on the cake, wasn't it? That Bertram Wallis shared Captain Ransom's birthday. He didn't care much for birthdays, but this one was important to him. It was not only his forty-seventh year on the planet, it was also a year to the day he'd taken command of the carrier. It was a year-and-and-month to the day a Navy optometrist initialed a report and took away Ransom's flying days forever.

That's where the anger really came from. Ransom couldn't launch from his own carrier, but a man nearly twice his age was about to kiss the sky.

"Shouldn't Alf have ear protectors?" Gregory asked in alarm. He knelt and cupped his hands over the dog's ears. The dog wiggled free.

If it was a regular launch, with proper aircraft, the dog would have been deafened by the sounds of the jet engines and catapults that flung the birds into the wind. But then the animal wouldn't be there in the first place.

The catapults had to be tuned way down to accommodate the lighter planes. At full strength, the modern catapults would have flipped the Wildcats end over end like throwing knives.

Arms waved. Green, blue and yellow-jacketed sailors moved through their assigned tasks, treating the launch as seriously as if in actual combat. The carrier executed a gentle turn into the wind, and one by one, engines droning, the Dauntlesses leapt to the sky, followed by Devastators and finally the Wildcats. The intricate clockwork dance of man and machine performed so expertly by the deck crew filled Ransom's heart with pride each and every time he watched it. Not a single mistake. Basketball teams only dreamed of working this well together.

The planes banked and came together in a three-layered V formation. The cheers from Vulture's Row rang down from six stories up and penetrated Ransom's ear protectors.

Ransom's pride in his crew temporarily banished his ire, and with a light heart, he watched the three wings pass high on the port side, bank and dive to do a near fly-by of the island. It didn't even bother him when elevator one, forward from the island, rose from below carrying with it a full brass band. Navy men, sailors all, blasted away on trumpets, trombones and tubas and thumped on drums in tribute to the vintage planes and geriatric pilots.

It was a wonder to behold. For everything Ransom disliked about the man, there he was, survivor of twenty-seven missions against the Japanese, victor in both the financial and political arenas, almost a century old and still flying, still tasting the wind.

One of the planes, a Wildcat in the lowest of the three V's, dropped from formation and splashed into the ocean.

The screams were immediate. A thousand things needed to be done at exactly this moment and Ransom sprinted for the stairway that would take him to the bridge. His elation vanished. Not even vindication of his protests mitigated the stress he was under. Launching old men from a carrier was as bad an idea as he'd ever heard. None of that mattered now. One of those codgers was potentially dead out there; dead on Ransom's watch.

Gregory and Alf were running behind him, but he barely noticed. A voice exploded from the loudspeakers, ordering the deck crew to prepare to recover the planes. This air patrol was over. Another plane dropped from formation, a Devastator from the middle tier. It veered sharply to the left, then dove, its wing clipping the stabilizer of a Wildcat and both planes went into the sea.

The screams had changed in pitch. They were not the cries of horrified onlookers, but the terror of those themselves in peril.

A body slammed to the deck scant feet away. Ransom froze with his hand on the stanchion at the bottom of the steps. The man had landed on his back but his face was a mess of blood and torn flesh.

Gunfire erupted from above, but it wasn't the sound of a military issue weapon. It was the loud boom of a .45. The captain looked up. Someone, he thought it was a man, was leaning over the rail of the Pri-Fly gallery, shooting uselessly at a flock of gulls that swarmed Vulture's Row like it was a fishing boat.

The screams weren't just coming from above either. Across the whole flight deck, sailors ducked and ran, arms flailing to fend off gulls that dropped from the sky like a thousand feathered bombs. Ransom watched, dumbfounded, as a purple-clad fueling crewman—a grape—leapt over the starboard side. Surrounding the flight deck were a series of nets to save people blown over by jet wash or weather. The grape landed in one of those nets and was instantly savaged by a pair of gulls that landed on his chest.

If a wing of planes, anything from Japanese Zeros to Russian MiGs, had appeared out of the clear blue sky in an attack run, Captain Ransom could have dealt with it. Despite the shock, he would have known what to do, what orders to give, but nothing had prepared him for this. A pile of brass instruments lay scattered on and around the number one elevator. Fighting, Bombing and Torpedo Six had broken apart, each plane flew its own course, each pursued by a black cloud.

No, Ransom realized, not clouds…gulls. The birds were deliberately flying into the planes, smashing props and cockpit hoods. The birds were everywhere, sweeping the deck, clogging the sky, and he saw in his mind what would occur as clearly as if it had already happened. All the pilots would have but one thought—land. Some might head for the mainland, but they'd all want to get out of the sky, and the closest strip was the one they'd left just minutes before. No landing patterns, no Landing Signal Officers to guide them in…they'd crash, each and every one, either into the sea, or into the ship.

Stunned birds thumped to the deck after bouncing off the thick glass of the island's windows. In the midst of it all was another noise, one completely alien to the sounds of the ocean. Less than ten feet away, Alf ripped Gregory's throat open. The captain's brother lay thrashing on the deck, the protective helmet he'd so proudly held up just minutes before, was half off his head and turned, obscuring the top of his face. A flap of skin stretched from just below his chin to the mouth of the Alsatian.

Across the deck a siren blared general quarters.

Ransom ran forward and kicked at the animal as hard as he could, but the dog jumped aside and launched itself at him. He got his arm under the dog's throat, but the force and weight of the animal knocked him over backward. His ear protectors flew from his head and he screamed as teeth closed around his right wrist. He punched at the animal with his other hand, but the dog ignored the blows. There was too much noise: the alarm, a voice booming from the speakers, making sounds but no sense; the cries of gulls, and above it all, a droning that was growing ever louder. The dog was going to have Ransom's hand off in a minute, but that droning demanded the captain turn his head and find the source.

A Dauntless was less than sixty feet from the ocean's surface, and headed straight for the carrier. Doubtless the pilot wanted to land, but he was coming in amidships, impossible from his direction and location to trap one of the arresting wires with his tail hook. Even if he made the deck, he'd go right over it and into the water on the other side, killing Lord knew how many people in the process.

Ransom's wrist was free. His cheek was now the dog's chew toy. The pain was incredible, as was the horror as he felt skin pull from his face. Then the sun was blocked out and the terrible pulling was gone. An officer, white uniform stained with blood and grease, stood over the captain, a blood-and-fur-matted wrench in his hand. His mouth moved, but Ransom couldn't understand the words. Then the officer was pulling at him, pulling him by the damaged wrist.

The Dauntless sounded as if it was on top of them. Ransom saw the spinning prop, saw right through the cockpit's canopy and knew without a shadow of a doubt it was Bertram Wallis, his expression more confused than horrified as he banked right and crashed into the side of the carrier. The deck lurched violently, throwing people off their feet and sending a few of them into the deathtrap of the safety nets. And still the gulls came.

Other sailors had made their way to the captain, surrounding him, protecting him with their bodies. As Ransom gained his feet, one of his protectors literally flew away from him, so great was the impact as the gull struck the man in the chest. The officer—Lieutenant Davis—pulled him aft, away from the bridge, towards an open hatch to the lower decks, then Davis was gone, squashed under a mass of feathers as if gulls had just appeared on him like magic.

The captain stared as all about him, chaos unlike anything he'd ever dreamed of, washed the deck in blood and feathers. His hand found the torn flap of his cheek and pushed it up, willing it to stay in place. His mouth filled with blood and he had to swallow to keep from gagging. One of the gulls had Davis's eye in its beak.

A Wildcat caught the number three wire with its tail hook, but it had come in at too oblique an angle. The plane swung sideways, the tail hook couldn't handle the torque and snapped off, sending the Wildcat spinning and grinding along the deck. A Devastator came straight down and exploded on the deck just in front of elevator four, the only one on the port side.

The deck heaved, tossing Ransom and the sailors like so many bowling pins.

Any hope the captain had for the pilots died right there. He could only pray the rest of them would ditch in the sea instead of trying to make the deck. The crew had enough to worry about without adding more fire and shrapnel to the mix.

The captain rolled to his stomach, put his hands under him, excruciating right wrist notwithstanding, and pushed himself up to his knees amidst a wave of dizziness and nausea.

Alf was inches away, seemingly fully recovered from the wrench blow. Blood trickled from a wound behind the ear, but otherwise the dog was alert and completely focused. Ransom's arms and legs went out from under him, and he lay helpless beneath canine and birds alike.

24. Terpris

She was over a thousand feet long, over two-hundred-and-fifty feet wide and she was anchored less than a hundred meters from the Port of Astoria. Her paint was faded, gone in some places but regardless, she was the most incredible thing Noah had ever seen.

The boxy island tower, bristling with antennae, was her highest point, rising two-hundred-and-fifty feet from the waterline. Behind, half the height of the island, a massive funnel trickled grey smoke. Shorter than the funnel, a small forest of masts spread out across the flight deck, protruding from the myriad of boats that had, for whatever reason, been deprived of their keels and bolted to the flight deck. The flags of a hundred erstwhile nations flew from those masts. Propellers on high posts—wind generators—lined the rails and a phalanx of them stood at the very front of the ship. Black solar panels topped some of the masts and flanked a greenhouse erected near the stern. Pedestal-mounted guns vied with other projections for space along the sides: nets hung, hooks dangled. Two long cables extended to gondola towers on the shore, and cars ran back and forth, carrying cargo and people to and from a location so fantastic as to be something out of a fairy tale.

As a teenager, Noah had heard about *Terpris* from Bacon, but it had been so long ago, the memory of the tale had been buried until now. Home to thousands, Bacon hadn't refer to it as a vessel, but as a place.

"Come on," said Caps. "We're taking the boat."

Noah looked down the length of the dock, then he cast a covetous eye on the cage around Astoria. He checked the horizon in all directions. There were clouds out at sea, but inland it was clear.

"Sky's empty, buddy." Caps tugged at Noah's sleeve. "There's more shotguns here than at a Moony wedding in Alabama."

"Huh?"

"Moonies had mass weddings, southern weddings were shotgun…forget it. It's never funny if I have to explain it. Every bird that comes close gets shredded. You see that guy in the khaki with the bags over both shoulders? I've been watching him. His whole job is to feed ammo to the guys with the guns."

Caps was right. There were a lot of armed people protecting the docks. Noah looked at the ocean. The tide was just on its way back in and the pilings stood a few feet clear of the water.

"How high can sharks jump?"

"Don't you start. I'm going to have a hard enough time with Lena."

Noah followed the artist. The docks were as packed as the market streets in New Portland. More so even. Men loaded cargo onto one of the two boats, crates and barrels mostly. The boats themselves were nearly identical. Painted a uniform dull gray, long davits for fishing, steel cage covering most of what once would have been open deck. Pedestal-mounted large-bore rifles were placed along the sides as casually as dollar-per-minute binoculars perched at Old World points of interest. Guns were more important than life jackets on boats like these. A man in the water wouldn't live long enough for anything but the speediest rescue, and all a life jacket did was keep the top half of the body afloat while the bottom half disappeared, sometimes in one or two big bites, other times in a series of nibbles.

Noah pushed and shoved his way past people. He'd lost sight of Sid and Darcy, but knew they were ahead of him. Fragments of a hundred different discussions and arguments assaulted his ears from every direction, many of them in languages he didn't understand. That was a new experience. Everyone he knew in Underbel spoke English. It was the same with Compton Pit. It had been a while since Noah had even heard another language.

The crowd suddenly parted, and the reason was obvious. Along one side of the dock was a row of cages, each with a dog in it.

A pair of men in dogskin dusters, looking like the world's poorest cowboys, grimaced as a man in a sharp uniform bent to examine each dog in turn.

"Too young," he said and moved to the next cage. "Too young. Too young. This one. Too young. I will take this one."

The pants were white, the jacket blue, with strong lines and gold bands at the cuffs. Noah grinned. These guys pulled out all the stops when it came to costumes for the festival. It was clearly an authentic Navy uniform, but it looked brand new. The man wearing it, if it did indeed belong to him, knew how to take care of his clothes.

"Too young. Too young. Too…" he paused, then gingerly extended a finger through the cage and poked the animal within. "Too dead. This one. That is all of them."

"That's only three you've picked," said one of the dogskin cowboys.

"There is only three I want. About our requirements, we were very clear, yes?" The discussion finished, the sailor pulled his hat from where he'd stowed it under his arm, placed it smartly on his head and strode off.

"About our requirements, we were very clear," mimicked the cowboy, approximating the Navy man's Russian accent.

"Better than nothing," said his partner.

"Noah, come on." Caps grabbed his arm and yanked him into the throng.

At the foot of the gangway, Lena stopped and refused to budge. "I can't."

"You can," Caps urged.

"No I can't. You don't know what I'm feeling right now."

"You're not going to flip out. Look at all the people. Look at all the guns." He put his arms around her from behind. "These people live their life on the water. Since they're still breathing, they're probably pretty good at it."

"I'm sorry, sweetheart. You go. I'll find something to do in Astoria. You can—"

"Lena, this is a once in a lifetime thing. It's *Terpris*! How can you not want to see it?"

"I can see it fine from here. Look. It's a big boat with some little boats piled on top of it. See ya." She tried to pull out of Caps's arms, but he held firm.

"Hey," the artist yelled up to a man in khaki watching people board the gray-and-black vessel. "Tell my lady here why your boat is safe."

The man folded his arms across the railing and leaned over. "Short or long?"

"Brag your heart out."

"Well," he ran one hand lovingly across the rail. "She's triple-hulled. Guard-covered screws, sixteen guns, six each side, two by two on front and back, wider'n your average cutter, she'll speed through Sea State Five and you won't even spill your beer." He winked on that one. "Holds seal airtight; they're self-fumigating. For ram protection, three layers of blades along the hull, you can't see any of them 'cause we're riding low, and punchers."

"Okay," said Lena. "Okay."

Caps squeezed her tighter. "I'm glad that convinced you, because I didn't understand a word he said."

"How many punchers?" Noah called up.

The man shrugged. "A bunch. Never counted."

One step at a time, as if the gangplank might collapse from beneath her at any moment, Lena ascended. Caps kept his hands on her hips in case she changed her mind again.

"What the heck's a puncher?" Caps asked over his shoulder.

Noah looked down at the water hoping to see one, but the surface was opaque. "They're just what they sound like. Pistons mounted on the bottom of the boat. Turn them on and they start punching."

"Cool. We could use a couple of those on the van."

At the top of the gangway they stepped under a cage that stood twelve feet high and covered two-thirds of the deck, from the fat, squat pilot house to the davits at the stern supporting a sixteen-foot semi-rigid launch.

"There you are," said Sid as the trio boarded. "Here," he turned to a full-figured black woman in an elegant red coat. "These are the other three in my party."

Noah goggled at all the Navy uniforms, whites mixed with less glamorous khakis of servicemen. The officer he'd seen inspecting the dogs wasn't in a costume at all. He was in his everyday clothes.

The hatches to below deck were closed, and the door to the pilot house was guarded, so the tourists milled around under the cage, until the woman called for their attention.

"Hello? Hello? Thank you. In a few minutes we'll be boarding *Terpris*. You each have a visitor's card. Please wear them around your neck, displayed openly at all times. If you don't have a string with yours, you can get one from me. Please wait until I'm finished." She held a hand up to stop a few people who moved towards her. "Thank you. My name is Stephanie and I'll be your guide once we're aboard. You do not have to take the tour, but if you choose not to, you will be limited to the Street and the Valley. That is to say the flight deck, not including the island, and a portion of the hangar deck. The shops on the Street will not accept New Portland currency today." There was a collective groan from people familiar with *Terpris*. "However, you may exchange for ship's currency immediately upon boarding." She smiled. "As this is our last day, you might find the exchange rate prohibitive." She shrugged an apology. "Before we embark, I need you to line up and sign my register. If you write a false name, please use one you'll remember. If I have to call for any of you, it would be best that you answer."

She held the register up and waited for the tourists to comply.

"Amazing, isn't it?" Caps nudged Noah with an elbow. "That speech is commonplace to her. She makes it all the time. Hey, did anyone catch the name of this boat?"

"Her name's the *Hugin*," said the sailor who'd boasted of the boat's prowess earlier. "Her sister boat's the *Munin.*" He nodded at the second boat on the other side of the dock. "So, you want to see the motors for the punchers?"

"You bet, sign in for me, sweetheart, would you? The names are familiar. What do they mean?" he asked as the sailor opened a hatch to below deck.

"Thought and memory."

"Oh yeah. Hugin and Munin were Odin's ravens. I would have thought it'd be bad luck to name a boat after a bird or animal."

"Dunno. The Navy already had the boats when I enlisted a few years back." He dropped his legs into the hatch and climbed down the ladder.

"The boats belong to *Terpris*?"

"They belong to the sea."

Caps followed him down the ladder, his half-hand a little awkward on the rungs. "Come again?"

"All boats belong to the sea. Just a matter of time before she claims 'em."

"That's pessimistic. Might as well say all people belong to the teeth."

"Don't we?"

When Caps disappeared from sight, it was if the *Hugin* had tipped to one side for Lena. She could feel the anxiety rising. In her mind she was already in the water, flailing about as those around her disappeared, pulled from beneath. She had to make an effort not to hyperventilate. Noah was beside her, staring at everything and nothing. She took his hand and squeezed it. He was startled at first, then gave her a reassuring smile and squeezed back. The deck vibrated beneath their feet, and the *Munin* pulled away from the dock just as the *Hugin's* lines were tossed to her deck.

"Is that everybody?" Stephanie called. "Everybody?" Nobody gave her a contradictory response so she nodded at a deckhand who entered the door to the pilot house. With a gentle lurch, the eighty-seven-footer left the safety of her moorings and headed for the carrier.

By the time the dock was fifty feet behind them, Lena was squeezing Noah's hand so hard he thought she was going to break his fingers. He pulled, but she wasn't going to relinquish her hold, so instead he moved behind her and wrapped her in his arms much the same way Caps had. Her grip on his hand eased a bit and she leaned into his chest, making small gasping noises.

Caps was taller than Noah, but Lena was a head shorter than both of them. She fit perfectly into the circle of his arms. Noah felt a familiar stab of envy. Not for possession of Lena herself, but for the love the artist had found. Her head was right below his nose and he sniffed it involuntarily. Her hair was soft and sweet. She must have washed it that morning, using some sort of floral shampoo.

Noah jerked his head back, realizing the impropriety of what he'd just done, but Lena didn't seem to notice, she just leaned harder into him as the dock receded and *Terpris* grew ever larger.

The carrier was anchored with her bow facing west. The *Hugin* turned to port, coming parallel with *Terpris* and running the full length of her to give the passengers a chance to admire the floating city's true size.

Over a dozen times longer than the *Hugin* and five times as high, Noah felt like he was cruising beside a fortress. The only things missing were battlements and cannons. Actually, just the battlements were missing, but applicable substitutions were in place everywhere.

A mesh-covered catwalk lined with safety nets hugged the external perimeter of the top deck. Past that, countless lines, chains and ropes hung over a short metal wall, more an armored fence. On one rope, pulled taught between a pair of davits, someone's laundry was hanging out to dry. The head of a gigantic anchor protruded from a hole under on the port side of the tapered bow. From an identical orifice on the starboard side, the thickest chain Noah had ever seen, taut and rusty, angled into the sea.

"The anchors each weigh thirty-two tons," said Stephanie. "Each link of the anchor chain weighs three hundred and fifty pounds."

A pair of long boats hung from davits along the starboard side, their keel blades dull and weathered. Conical protrusions between the blades housed the punchers. Empty davits showed where *Hugin* and *Munin* spent their time when not deployed. They chugged past two enormous openings outside of which were elevator platforms, each with almost as much floor space as Compton Pit's motor pool.

Noah stared up at the number sixty-five painted on the island. Holes surrounding the numbers looked like light sockets, and taking the size of the ship into consideration, each digit was over twenty feet in height. Further scrutiny told him that that parts of the island had recently been painted. Below and a few meters aft of the island was a patch of blackened metal as if from some long ago explosion. From the slightly different shades in the gray, he could tell the area had been deliberately avoided during repainting. He disengaged himself from Lena and walked towards the tour guide. Lena hooked a finger in his belt and allowed herself to be tugged along after him.

"Excuse me," he said to Stephanie. "Why haven't they cleaned and painted over the blast mark?"

"It's not a mark," she replied. "It's a grave. That will be covered in the tour."

"Do you make your own paint?"

"No need. There's an unlimited supply of it cached around the world if you know where to look."

Sid asked the tour guide if he could look at the guest register, or if she'd seen a man matching Odega's description. She answered no to both questions.

Munin appeared around the stern of the ship, and headed out to sea.

"Where's that one going?" Noah asked. "Is there another carrier farther out?"

Stephanie laughed. She had crinkle lines around her eyes and mouth. "No. There's a barge. All your questions will be covered in the tour."

Caps appeared on deck just as the boat drew along side a cage-covered floating platform at the carrier's stern and reversed engines to stop. The ship's name was painted on the hull in black letters, in the middle of a V formed by net-enshrouded steps leading up from the cage-covered platform.

Sailors cast lines and the *Hugin* was tied off.

"It's so huge," said Darcy, enthralled with the carrier to the point of hardly noticing she was on the ocean for the first time since she'd been thirteen.

The cage door opened, the gangway clanked down.

"No way," said Lena, looking down at the platform. It was wide, and attached to the carrier, but only a few feet thick. "I'm not standing on that thing. No way, forget it." Her apprehension spread to a few of the other tourists.

"Ma'am," said the sailor who'd opened the cage, "we have so much sonar going right now, if you dropped an eyelash in the water, we could track it all the way to the bottom."

Stephanie walked down to the platform. "People," she called up, "anything ramming this platform would really get the short end of the stick. Or rather, the long end of some spikes."

Gingerly, Lena put a foot on the gangway.

"Ma'am?" The sailor indicated the lineup behind her.

"Come on," said Caps, gently pushing her down the ramp.

Stephanie herded the group up the steps to the fantail, an open-air area at the rear of the hangar deck. A woman gave each tourist a hardhat while another woman looked at visitors' tags and noted numbers in a log.

"Please wear your hats at all times while on the flight deck," said Stephanie, putting on one of her own. "We've been in port a week, so we've pretty much cleared the air, but there are always exceptions. Forget what you know of bogies—birds—from landlocked settlements. Bogies at sea always attack. Always."

Navy guards looked on as she held the group together, forestalling all questions and moving them up to the flight deck. She led them past various structures including the greenhouse and brought them to a stop at a spot shaded by ten stories of island control tower.

"Okay. Welcome to *Terpris*. Those of you not staying with the tour, off you go. Just remember to be back here in two hours. If you leave by gondola, make sure you sign out. I wasn't kidding when I said I hate having to look for people."

"Do we take the tour?" Darcy asked Sid.

"I'm not sure. Excuse me," he interrupted the tour guide just as she was about to speak. "Is animal research on this tour?"

"I'm afraid not. That's a secure area."

"I see. How long is the tour?"

"About forty-five minutes."

Sid nodded and stepped back into the crowd. He turned to Darcy. "We'll take it to begin with at least. We can always leave."

"In a few minutes I'll be leading you below deck. I know some of you are anxious to do some shopping but we'll end our tour here on the Street. First, a very brief history. On Fubar Day—that's what it's generally called here—the carrier was operating off of Norfolk, Virginia. Instead of performing military operations, she was host to a United Nations gala event, including an air display from some of America's most respected pilots. The bogies brought down every single plane. A few of them crashed into the carrier, most notably one on the starboard side, as some of you have noticed. The impact mark is left as it is, to honor all those lost that day.

"A few weeks later," Stephanie continued, "the carrier was now far enough from land to avoid the birds, and moving at a steady clip so as not to be bothered by whales. And before anyone asks, even an entire pod of blue whales is incapable of sinking *Terpris*. Believe me, they've tried. The carrier had been out of contact with the land due to severe damage to the antennae arrays from the sheer number of bogie impacts and yet another plane. When she reestablished communications…well, we all know what the world had become.

"Because of her unique position on Fubar Day, *Terpris* had on board an almost equal population of Navy and civilians." She looked around. "We appear to be waiting for someone. Feel free to look around for a minute, but if you're staying with the tour, don't stray too far."

A number of people split off from the group and headed for a booth with a sign reading "Exchange" at the top.

Lena was still uncomfortable, but faring better on the deck of *Terpris* than she had on the smaller vessel.

A short distance down the deck, a group of men were catching cargo from a hoist and stacking it on pallets. Whatever they were loading in the wooden crates was heavy. Often enough, two men would share a load. Darcy drifted a bit closer. One of the men was bare-chested despite the cold. He handled each crate by himself, muscles straining, but little exertion showing on his face. His arms were well-muscled without being grotesque, his chest was scar-free and covered with a fine coat of fair hair. His chin was strong with a little dimple. He had no beard, but a day's worth of scrub surrounded a small but well-shaped mouth.

"Hello, sailor," Darcy said without meaning to.

The man looked right at her. In reflex she turned the right side of her face away from him.

"Hello, yourself," he said, a broad grin making his eyes twinkle. "You with the tour?"

"Aren't you going to get in trouble if you stop working?" He was coming around a large crate towards her, so she turned again and flicked her head to bring her hair over her scars.

"I'm not Navy. See," he thumped his chest. "No uniform."

"You don't live here, then?"

"I do. I'm a civy." He was past the crate, almost within arm's reach. "Why don't you ditch this bunch and I'll give you a much better tour."

Darcy stepped back and put her hands up. "You always come on this strong?"

"Life's short. And I really meant a tour of the ship. The name's David. Hey, Winch," he called to a swarthy man still at work, "toss me my shirt."

Winch was as ugly as David was handsome. Winch's prodigious gut hid his belt. His jacket hung open because closing it probably put too much strain on the seams. His thick forehead protruded a little farther than the average man's. Winch had a dark, spiky beard and beneath bushy eyebrows, eyes that were both too small and too close together, as if they were trying to snuggle up to the misshapen nose between them.

Winch gave David a look of disgust, then glanced at Darcy and smacked his lips. "We're losing Romeo," he announced to the other workers before tossing a gray pullover over the crates and into David's waiting hand.

Darcy still had her hand up. "Sorry, I don't think I should leave my group."

David's blond head popped through the sweater's neck hole, then his hands appeared and he tugged the garment into place. It had horizontal lines, making his chest seem even wider.

"Look…you didn't say your name."

"Darcy," her mouth spouted off without her permission. It was followed by a nervous giggle, which she hated even more. Her hair fluttered in the breeze. She caught the ends of it to hold it in place. She realized what she must look like: a dimwitted girl in awe of the great man-thing in front of her. But still, he was a hunk, and to top it all off, there was something familiar about him.

David postured with all the confidence of a lion crouched behind an oblivious zebra. He lifted her yellow boarding card and used its string to pull her closer. She reached out with both hands to pull it away from him and her hair drifted to the side, exposing her scars. David dropped the card and his eyes grew wide.

Darcy turned and walked away.

"Hey, I don't mind," David called after her. "I mean, I've seen worse. Okay. Enjoy the tour, Darcy."

There's a moment I'll be proud of, she thought bitterly.

She rejoined the tour at the same time as another person, a man who towered over the rest of the group. He didn't wear a Navy uniform, but his clothing was uniform-like; black pants with a single gray stripe down each leg, black shirt and jacket of a gray matching the pant stripes. On the left front pocket of the vest was a police officer's badge, but not of any type that Darcy recognized. Though his uniform was sharp, his hair was anything but. Dark and lanky, with bangs hanging down almost to his eyes, and a few streaks of grayish-white along the sides. She recognized him as the man who'd stood guard beside Ripper during the strip show.

"Group, before we continue," Stephanie said, one hand resting on the policeman's arm. "This is Mark. As I was saying, two factions live here. The Navy, those people you see that look like they're doing all the work, and the civies, which is short for civilians. Tourism falls under the responsibility of us, the civies. Mark here is our chief lawman. The Navy calls him the Marshal. We call him the Old Bull, or just Bull. He's got a very short speech to make, and then we'll be on our way."

"He doesn't look that old," Noah whispered to Caps.

"He's old enough."

"Listen carefully," stated Mark. His voice was low, but it carried well. "You're restricted to the Street, that's residential and commercial areas of this deck; and the Valley, that's zone two of the hangar deck, and certain other areas only in the presence of Stephanie here, or someone she appoints to accompany you. If you are found in *any other* area, you will be immediately ejected from *Terpris*. And, this is important, do not miss your ride home, either intentionally or unintentionally. That is all."

"So with that out of the way, please follow me." Stephanie gestured with her hand and led them to an oval-ish door at the base of the island. It didn't go all the way to the floor and when opened, left a high lip to step over. "We'll begin in the p-ways, which we call cramps because of how tight they are. The cramps include nearly every corridor in *Terpris*. Watch your step. Come along single file, keep one shoulder pressed against the right wall as much as possible. And please try not to get in anyone's way."

Noah was shocked at how narrow the corridors were when his turn came to step through the door. On a vessel this size he'd expected hallways wide enough to drive a car through.

"Now, we get our exercise." Stephanie stopped at another oval door at the end of a short section of corridor. "These," she pointed to the door's threshold, "are called knee knockers, and you're all going to hit quite a few of them before you get used to it. Follow, please." She continued leading them through corridors and over knee knockers, relentless with her spiel. History was left behind in favor of factual information concerning the structure of *Terpris*, materials used and how safe she was from anything the sea could throw at her. "Careful," she said, descending the first of a series of steep, narrow steps that were closer to ladders than stairs. At the bottom, and through another hatch, and everything looked both familiar and new. "This is the Valley."

The ceiling was only twenty-five feet up, but beneath that steel sky sat what could be fallout from every major city in the Old World smashing into each other at the same time. The buildings were all of similar size, but no two architectures were alike. There was a pagoda, bright orange and red, a red brick building that looked like a miniature fire hall, a white sandstone rectangle peaked by a golden dome, a cottage with a thatched roof, an Eiffel Tower that nearly reached the ceiling, and farther down, a fifteen-foot-high windmill built near the gigantic oval opening on the starboard side..

Quietly, Caps began to sing 'It's a Small World After All'. He earned a few appreciative laughs, and a couple of people actually joined in. Stephanie allowed herself a smile, which was replaced by a look of slowly dawning horror when she realized Caps intended to sing the whole song, even though his impromptu accompaniers backed out of the gig after a few words.

It might have been a go if he wasn't such a bad singer. In sympathy, an older woman who could carry a tune started up, singing just a bit louder and feeling just a bit uncomfortable. Like something out of a badly directed musical, other voices joined in. Apparently only Caps and his first supporter knew all the words, and the others hashed it or dropped out only to come back at twice the volume once they returned to the comfort zone of the chorus.

Lena felt ill.

The song ended with some clapping and a few back slaps, and the energy changed. Instead of an assortment of individuals, they were now a group, bonded by something as tenuous as a half-remembered song, and the nervous tension of singing with strangers. For one man in the group, it was the first time he'd sang anything since the Change. For almost everybody it was the first time in a while that they'd had prolonged exposure to masses of people they didn't know.

"That was new," said Stephanie, and she meant it. "Yes, I suppose it is a bit like Disneyland."

"It's like a drug trip," Caps said loudly. "Somewhere here there's a poster of Keith Richards that says, 'You must be at least as high as this man to board the ride.' "

Stephanie cleared her throat. "If I may continue? The United Nations event scheduled for the evening of Fubar Day had at its heart a series of pavilions, one from nearly every country attending, and the party wasn't limited to UN members. We've added a great deal over the years. Each of these buildings is sound, no matter how flimsy they appear. Their cultural architecture is a façade, built around walls strong enough never to buckle, no matter how rough the seas might get. Since the Old World is gone, we do our best to preserve as much of it as we can. We would love to have this upstairs but the winds on the Street can get high enough to turn the façades into kites. The Valley is a hundred-and-twelve meters long, and thirty-three meters wide. The hangar deck itself is much longer, but the Valley only occupies zone two and part of zone one. Zone three is taken up by the boilers that power the screws and most of *Terpris*, and most of zone one acts as our motor pool. This bulkhead to your left, is actually one of the biggest doors you'll ever see. These buildings are both decorative and functional. Some of them are administrative buildings, others are workshops, or residences. Now if you'll come this way..."

She brought the group a few paces forward to a damaged life preserver in a glass case. "Re-christening the carrier was a political circus but eventually a suggestion was made acceptable to all parties. This life preserver was found on the first day. The first two letters and the last letter of the name were burned away. As you can see, the remaining letters spell out *Terpris*."

Caps played word-puzzle in his head for a few seconds, then his jaw dropped. "We're on *that* carrier? Wow! I feel like I've...come home."

"Let's go." Sid squeezed Darcy's arm. He turned to the others. "Stay with the tour. We'll meet you back on the flight deck."

"What if we see Odega?" asked Noah.

"Follow him as much as you can. He may have charmed his way in with the scientists here and have access you don't. If he does leave, stay by the last hatch or whatever he goes through that you can't, and do whatever it takes to have me paged."

"Paged?"

"Look around. There's speakers everywhere. Don't use my name, that'll spook Ted. Page…Bruce Banner. I know at least you can remember that, Richard."

"Don't make me angry." Caps tried to sound like Bill Bixby. "You wouldn't like me when I'm angry."

Sid walked away quickly. Darcy had to trot to catch up with him. Stephanie called after them to stick to the Valley and the Street.

"Why are we walking so fast?" asked Darcy. "Did you see him?"

"Not Ted, but someone we need to talk to."

They rounded the Eiffel Tower and almost ran into Mark, the Old Bull.

"Excuse me," said Sid, "we're—"

"You left the tour," Mark cut him off. "Remember to stick to the—"

"Yes we know, you've all made that quite clear. We're looking for someone that may have come aboard."

"Not today I take it?" He gave Darcy a speculative look.

"No. Not from our group. Do you inspect everyone who comes aboard?"

"Not everyone. I do inspect all the tour groups. Why are you looking for this person?"

"What other ways are there to come aboard besides on the tour group?"

"Answer my question, I'll answer yours."

"He's a friend. He's unbalanced and he needs our help."

"If you say so. The other ways to come aboard are to apply for citizenship, or buy passage. What does he look like?"

Sid patted his pockets for the sketch and then grunted when he remembered it was in the pack Caps was carrying. "He's black, like me—"

"As opposed to black like an orange?"

"Marshal, I didn't mean to insult your intelligence."

"You didn't. I hate redundant speech. Go on.

"He's bald, my height, very broad in the chest and shoulders. Wide nose, big arms, bite scars on left forearm, tip of right pinky absent."

"Nope. Haven't seen anybody like that."

"Who would have? Is there one person that logs in all guests or new…citizens? Could I check the registers for these? Also the registers for all the tour groups."

"Is this guy running from you?"

Sid pondered a moment. It was all the answer the Old Bull needed.

"The registers won't do you any good. I doubt he would use his real name. We have to take identity at face value. Immigration and passage go through the XO, but you can't see him. He's busy. So am I."

"Go get the sketch from Richard," Sid instructed Darcy. "Marshal, please, another minute. Could you take us to animal research, or allow me to speak with any of your research department? I believe our friend would go straight to those people."

"He couldn't go straight to those people, he'd have to go through channels and I don't have time to get you started. You should have come yesterday. Good day."

When Darcy returned with the sketch, Sid was grinding his fists into his hips.

"Sid, miniature Aztec pyramid over by the far wall—"

"Port side, not far wall."

"Whatever. A family of four lives in it. That juggler we saw last night, his wife and kids. Sid, have you noticed how many children there are here? They're everywhere."

"Delightful. How many of these, uh, buildings can we walk into? How many are private homes?"

"I don't know. Should we rejoin the tour?"

"No. Do you want to?"

"Yes. I'll stick with you though."

"You don't think he's here, do you?"

"I think he's long gone, or holed up somewhere in New Portland."

"You may be right, but New Portland isn't going anywhere and this place is. Let's go topside." He stopped mid-stride and looked around regretfully.

"You sure you don't want to just take thc tour?" Darcy urged.

"We don't have that luxury. Maybe next time."

"Next time?"

"Don't you want to come back to New Portland? I know I do. I want to be here without a specific agenda so I can get all giddy like the rest of you. We'll skip the Peninsula, though."

"You're walking almost normally today.

"It's tender, but not painful. Let's go."

The Street was as surreal as the village below, but for different reasons. There were a number of squat, sloped roof buildings with slanted walls, but mostly there were boats: fishing boats, small pleasure boats and houseboats. They were welded to the flight deck with additional stabilization coming from steel cables running from the deck to hulls and masts.

"Makes sense, I guess," said Sid. "If you're going to build a traveling village, why not use things already built to take on the sea?"

The Street was larger than the Valley, having four and a half acres to play with, minus space used for the greenhouse, loading zones, cranes, gun mounts and the island tower. In the center of buildings that were obviously dwellings, was a row of shops that ended at a bar with an etched metal sign proclaiming its name; Tanzers.

Tanzers was a large, two-story houseboat. The interior was lit by sunlight through a number of thick windows, and at night by a score of light fixtures that hung from the ceiling.

The tables were round, like the ones at Coppola's, but these were bolted to the floor. A baby grand piano was secured to a small, low stage against one wall. The bar was mahogany, long and scratched along its dark surface. Behind the bar was a selection of bottles, each seated in its own depression in a rack, rather than sitting loose on a shelf. Glasses hung from above the bar, with a catch at the end of each rack to keep the glassware from sliding out when the seas made level a relative term.

A few people were sitting at the tables, none of them Navy. Behind the bar was a man with a mop of hair as red as it could naturally get. His beard, which dropped below his face almost as low as his hair was piled high, was of the same extreme color.

"Only taking ship's currency today," said the barkeep as they approached. "Not New Portland dollars."

"We don't want a drink, just some information." Sid reached up and flicked a glass with his finger, pleased by the tone it produced.

"Like I said, just taking ship's currency today."

"If I give you New Portland money, you could exchange it, couldn't you?"

"It's not worth much right now."

"Very small piece of information. Have you seen this man?" He produced the sketch.

"That's not bad. Look at this." He put one of Caps's caricatures on the bar top. "One of my waitresses got it in the city yesterday. I'm going to put it up."

"Our boy goes international," said Darcy.

"Would you like one done of yourself?" Sid asked.

"You telling me you drew this?"

"No. The man who did is on board. He's taking the tour right now, but I can have him come here if you'll look at this sketch."

"Deal." He looked at the drawing. "Nope. Haven't seen him. I still get mine, right?"

"Do you mind if I show this around to your patrons?"

"Not after I get my drawing I won't. Till then, leave them alone."

They visited the shops, and Sid had to drag Darcy out of each of them. The wares ranged from the useful to the useless, and Sid doubted a few of the stores did much trade when limited to the occupants of *Terpris* as a customer base. Some of the materials used were quite exotic, as the crafters had the whole world to scavenge. As each successive person replied in the negative to questions of Odega, Sid regretted more and more spending so much time on his quest, and not appreciating the diverse society that surrounded him. With the last shop behind them, a store that sold knives, sewing supplies and hand-crafted jewelry, the Boss decided it was time to pester some officers. There were enough of them about near the cargo cranes.

"Hey, you looking for a big black guy?" asked a short man with scruffy gray hair and a salt-and-pepper beard. His dun-colored jacket was a little too large for his frame and only his fingers peaked out from the sleeves. "I can take you to him."

"Can you now?"

"Off the beaten track, so it'll cost you."

"Does he look like this?" he held out the sketch.

The man only glanced at it. "That's him. Not much time. We should go now."

"How do we know you're telling us the truth?" asked Darcy. "You barely looked at the sketch."

"I know your scars, you're Halbert right? Right?"

"You could have gotten that off the register," said Darcy. "We used our real names."

"Compton Pit, right? How would I know that, huh? You're Darlene. Know your scars, too."

"Darcy, not Darlene. If you do know our friend, why would he describe our scars to you?"

"Not scars. *Scars*," he held his hands wide as if the word meant something else entirely. "Figure of speech. I know your scars. I recognize you. He talks 'bout you. Time's a'wasting."

"Now that we know he's here, we can go to the authorities," said Darcy. "Once we've explained how dangerous he might be—"

"He's down deep," said the man. "Take forever to go through the bureaucrats. And if you does get them to help you, it's the barge for him."

"The barge?"

"Stowaways go on the barge. No exceptions. They'll never give him up to you."

"What's this barge?"

"Anchored beyond the river. They never dock it near shore. Worse than any prison you ever heard of. Lotta folk jump. I would. Make up your mind."

"Stay here," Sid ordered Darcy. "Tell the others what's happened. I knew he was here."

"No way," Darcy shook her head. "You can't handle Odega by yourself and you know it. Not if he doesn't want to come with you."

Sid nodded. "Okay, take us to him."

"Money first."

Sid opened his money pouch and spilled a few coins into the man's waiting hands, then a few more when the hands did not withdraw.

"Not even close," the man offered Sid's coins back. Sid withdrew a letter of credit from his pocket, Darcy didn't know which one, and offered it up.

The man jiggled the coins and said, "Do you want this or not?"

Sid pulled the second letter of credit out and fanned it with the first. "You'll get this only when we see Odega."

Darcy was incensed. Ripper could have broken her face. She hadn't risked what was left of her looks for the benefit of this grimy opportunist.

The man led them to the outskirts of the village on the port side and signaled for them to hide behind a building's edge. He approached a sailor guarding a hatch and whispered in his ear. The sailor's eyes filled with alarm and he took off towards the stern. Responding to a frantic gesture, Sid and Darcy sprinted across the deck and to the now open hatch.

"What did you say to him?" Sid asked as they descended a ladder to more of the so-called cramps.

"Just somethin'. Just somethin'."

"Will he come after us?"

"No. He shouldn't have left his post in the first place. Hey, hide your tags, hide your tags."

"Are we going to animal research?" asked Sid. "How do we get past any further guards?" His common sense was waking up. They were going to be caught and ejected from the ship, all their effort gone for naught.

"Leave that to me. Leave that to me. Left aways, left aways. Going down now. Going deeper."

"Figures," said Caps. "The Boss has all our money."

They were standing on the Street, near the exchange booth. Time was getting short and Caps just had to have a scratched Monty Python DVD.

"Calm down," said Lena. "You've got that tape from Vancouver, the Holy Grail, or whatever."

"Tape broke."

"Already?"

"Old tape. It got watched a lot, even if you didn't like it."

"I never said I didn't like it. I just don't think it's worth starting a religion over, like you do."

"I don't know about that," offered Noah. "The bit with the rabbit was kind of prophetic."

"I know your scars," said a short, ragged-looking man, appearing at Noah's elbow. "Noah, Lena, Caps," he pointed at each of them, then shook his fists as if some minor victory had been achieved.

"How do you know us?" demanded Lena.

"Boss Halbert. You follow me. Come on, he wants to show you."

"Show us what?"

The man's face pinched up. "He said to tell you…tell you Bruce Banner said it was okay. Alright? You follow me now."

Caps shrugged. "That seems legit."

Lena still had some doubts, and they showed in her body language.

"It's okay," said the man, misunderstanding her reluctance. "Halbert already paid me. Paid me extra."

"There goes my DVD," Caps grumbled and followed the man as he moved quickly between the buildings.

When he gestured at them to hide, they obeyed, but Lena put her mouth close to Caps's ear.

"I don't like this. Now we're sneaking around?"

"You didn't think we'd make it through this trip without having to sneak somewhere did you? Look, the Boss found a way to slip us in. The worst that can happen is we'll be kicked off, and it's almost time to leave anyhow."

The man approached a sailor guarding a hatch and whispered in his ear.

"For real this time," said the sailor, both excited and skeptical at the same time.

The little man shrugged, but whatever it was they were talking about, the sailor was more eager to believe than disbelieve, and took off at a run.

"Let's go," said Caps, running for the hatch.

25. Down Deep

They moved at a quick pace down the narrow passage. The knee knockers earned their names anew as the three of them banged themselves trying to keep up. Their guide had no such problem and stepped over them as if they weren't even there. A few times they were brought up short as the little man halted them to scout an intersection. They did encounter people moving in the opposite direction, both Navy and civilian, but nobody that paid attention to them more than was necessary to avoid collisions. The cramps seemed to go on forever, and steep stairways only led to more cramps. Their path was a maze, up, along, down, up again. All three of them were nearly out of breath when the ragged man, eyes full of fear, jumped back from an intersection.

"Come, quickly, quickly!" he did a shuffling run as he lead them back the way they'd come and down a corridor they'd passed the first time. He stopped and listened at a T-junction. Loud footsteps were coming towards them. "Here, hide in here." He yanked a hatch open. "Quickly!"

When all three of them were through the hatch, it slammed shut.

"The Boss better have a good reason for this," said Lena. "You know what he'd do if he caught visitors poking around in the back corridors of the Pit?"

"He'd kick them out," said Caps. "Oh, boohoo."

"What if the boat leaves without us?"

"Then we get a gondola ride."

Time passed. Caps put his ear to the door, but could hear nothing through the thick steel. He tried the handle. "Hmm. It's locked."

"That's not funny," said Lena.

"I agree," said Caps strained at the door. "Dogshit."

Caps gave up and Noah tried for himself.

Lena's spine turned ice cold and her stomach flipped over. "Please tell me you're taking the joke too far." She looked hard at Noah. Caps could keep a straight face telling the most ludicrous lies, but Noah would crack. He didn't.

"Oh no. Oh please no." She shouldered Noah out of the way and pulled at the handle.

"He must have been snatched," said Caps. "Or maybe he had to lead someone away. He'll be back."

"Why did he lock the door then?"

"Maybe it's jammed," said Noah.

They looked around the room. The ceiling was low enough that it could be touched with just a short jump. Pipes ran along the ceilings and walls through the length of the room and around a corner.

"There must be another way out of here," said Caps.

As a group they turned the corner and that's when Lena screamed.

Sid and Darcy lay on their stomachs on the floor, their legs tied together, their wrists bound behind their backs. There was an ugly lump on the back of Sid's head, and a trickle of dried blood down the side of his neck. Darcy had no apparent injury.

Caps rushed to Sid's side, Noah and Lena to Darcy's.

"He's alive," said Caps, checking Sid's carotid artery.

"So's she," said Lena. "What's going on?" she asked desperately.

"Odega," said Caps. "He's crazier than we thought."

"How crazier?" Lena demanded. "He assaulted Harpreet, he killed Senna."

"There's no proof he killed Senna. She could have just wiped out."

Noah slapped Darcy's cheek, gently at first, then harder. "C'mon, Darcy, wake up."

Though Darcy didn't respond, Sid did to similar treatment from Caps. He groaned, his eyes flickered open, and he tried to move. "What…what's going on?"

"What happened?" asked Caps, working at the rope binding Sid's wrists. "We were locked in here by this little guy in clothes too big for him. He knew our names.

"Darce!" Sid wiggled closer to his adopted daughter, hampering Caps's efforts at untying him.

"She's breathing," said Noah, "but I can't wake her. She doesn't look like she was hit."

The Boss pulled his hands free of the loosened rope and went to work on Darcy's bonds, dragging his legs behind him. When her hands were free he ordered, “Roll her over. I take it that hatch won’t open?”

“Nope,” said Caps, untying Sid’s legs.

“Is there another hatch?”

“Nope.”

Sid checked Darcy’s pulse for himself, then put an ear close to her mouth. He turned his head and sniffed. “Chloroform, or something like it. He could have taken us both out himself. Hit me, chloroform her…how could I…” *have been so stupid*, he finished in his head.

He tried to stand, and when his vision returned, he was lying on the floor again.

“Watch it,” said Caps. “You’ve got quite a bump back there. Your eyes are bloodshot.”

“Get us out of here,” said Lena. She grabbed Sid by the front of his jacket and pulled him into a sitting position. “Get us out of here now!”

“Calm down. We’ll make some noise and face the music when the guards find us.” He dragged himself against a wall and pulled Darcy’s head into his lap. “Start screaming, people.”

So Caps screamed for help, loudly, but not as loud as Lena who really let rip, as if she could tear down the bulkheads with her voice alone.

“Stop. Stop, stop, stop!” yelled Sid after a few seconds. The screams were echoing back on themselves in the small L-shaped room, threatening to make his head explode. “Hit the walls.”

Caps slammed his fist into the door, then winced and cradled it in his half hand.

“I meant with a pipe or something.”

They did a hasty search of the room, then one by one took off their hardhats and used those.

“It’ll carry farther if you hit a pipe,” said Lena.

“Is it getting warmer in here?” Caps pulled at the neck of his shirt.

Noah hit the pipe with a steady rhythm, but his eyes were on Darcy the whole time. “When will she wake up?”

“Don’t just bang the pipe,” said Sid. “Do any of you know Morse code?”

“Well, duh.” Lena found time amidst her panic to feel insulted.

“Sorry. I took a…something…to the back of the head. Darce, any guesses?” He looked down at her, expecting an answer, then he remembered. “Send an SOS.”

Lena taught Noah by punching out the beat on her palm. While Noah tried, she shrugged out of her jacket and dropped it to the floor.

The banging was only slightly better on Sid's head than the yelling. He struggled out of his jacket, then without thinking, pulled Darcy's off as well.

Noah's chosen pipe banged back and he flinched in surprise.

"Thank God," breathed Lena. She undid the top two buttons of her shirt. "Noah, I'll take over." The pipe banged again as she stepped up to it. "Yes, we're here." She banged the SOS one more time, then changed pattern. "Locked in room."

The pipe banged once.

"That's it?" She repeated her message.

One bang.

"Okay, buddy," she said to the pipe, "if you don't know Morse code, go find someone who does. It shouldn't be too hard, you're on a boat full of sailors.

Bang.

Lena tried again, SOS, then "trapped in room," instead of "locked in room."

Bang.

"Lena, stop," said Caps. He tapped his foot and held his finger up for silence. Bang. Still he kept his finger up. Bang. "It's not a person. It's machinery. Probably something stoking up."

"Pick another pipe," said the Boss.

Two bangs, then a third from a different pipe. Then there was a hiss of steam and a gurgle of fluid and four or five pipes sounded out a steady tempo.

Sid clamped his hands over his ears, pain burst in his head and it felt like his teeth were dissolving.

Caps was down to an undershirt, and with his shirt wrapped around his hand, he patted pipes to test for heat. "Boss, we've got to get out of here now." He had to repeat himself loudly to be heard over the banging from the pipes. He tried the door handle again but it remained stuck fast.

"Richard," the Boss yelled, despite what it cost him. "What are these pipes? What kind of room are we in?"

"I know cars, not ships! Okay, okay. Hot, hot, not hot..." he patted pipes and studied their layout. "Steam. lots of steam, water for...cooling. No electrical conduits except the one for the light." His eyes darted. There wasn't even a light switch. "It's like a maintenance access, but there's no valves or gauges or cutoffs."

It was really heating up. Noah was naked to the waist, Lena still had on her shirt, but it hung open. Sid kicked off his boots.

"I think it's a leftover." Caps said. "That wall's been modified, or added. The fixtures around the pipes aren't constant."

"Can we mess with the pipes?" Noah yelled.

"Not with any tools we've got. Even if we could, we'd either flood the chamber with steam under pressure, or water. Drown or scald."

Sid screamed inside his head. It was the perfect trap. No way out, no way to signal for help. If the heat didn't level out, it could kill them before they were found. The bait was shamefully weak but the cage was impeccable.

The few people that saw them on the way in had paid no attention. The sailor certainly wouldn't report absences from his post, wouldn't even think of them as such. Stephanie would notice they were missing, though. "Security will do a pre-departure sweep of all areas. We'll be found." He hoped he said it with conviction. He hoped the Marshal's men were thorough.

Caps unbuckled his belt and was about to unbutton his trousers, but Noah stopped him.

"I'll make you a bet." He pulled his shirt back on. "I take the heat better than you can."

"What're the stakes?" Caps yelled.

"A gallon of ice cream."

"Where the hell do we get…Roshi's got an ice cream maker!" He cinched his belt. "You're on."

Lena threw herself at the hatch, she tugged and pulled, smashed her fists against it and screamed in three different languages for someone to open the door.

Noah and Caps grabbed an arm apiece and hauled her back.

"Lemme go!" she insisted. "I'm not hysterical I just want out of here!" She stopped struggling and they let her go.

"You're right. You're not hysterical," shouted Caps. "*Why* aren't you hysterical?"

"Figure it out. Why did you talk me into coming here?"

Sid cut open his jacket with the blade from a pocketknife and yanked stuffing from it to shove in his ears. His vision was closing in from the edges, and he feared he would pass out again. He tried to think, but nothing would stay in focus.

The temperature peaked at three degrees higher than intolerable. Noah gained a sliver of satisfaction when Caps pulled off his shirt. The artist's decision was based on getting the clothes off before he lost the energy to do so. They made piles with their clothes and lay on them. Caps went through the backpack again as if a miraculous inventory item might have been overlooked the first time.

Darcy's eyes fluttered open as her pants were worked down her legs by Lena. Her eyes went in and out of focus, then she drifted off into what appeared to be normal sleep, except no amount of coaxing would wake her.

Time passed. The noise had subsided to an occasional clank and Noah, Lena and Caps took turns banging out the SOS, but none of them could do it very loudly, or for very long. Sid was in a fugue state. It took all his will power to just to keep his eyes open.

"Is this room air tight?" Noah asked Caps.

"It could be."

"There's five of us. I'm trying to calculate oxygen…consumption rate…but I can't…my head won't…"

"We'll be found."

"Cool."

"Say that word again."

At some point Noah realized he was the only one conscious. Nobody to talk to. Not that they'd done much talking as the time had dragged out. Opening the mouth only invited more precious body fluid to escape. In Noah's heat-addled brain, he wasn't frightened, he was bored. He'd forgotten about the SOS completely. The only thing on his mind was that someone, he wasn't quite sure who, but definitely someone was supposed to open the hatch and let them out. He knew because both the Boss and Caps had said so.

From where he lay Noah could see what looked like a small shower head, barely noticeable between two pipes. It was high up. Clambering to his feet, he moved under it and cocked his head to one side. Fire suppression. If it was functional, it could make water. It might even set off an alarm. Maybe that's what the guy who opened the door was waiting for.

Noah bent over for his hardhat, thinking he might be able to bash the spout open. The hardhat slipped from his fingers. He lay down. Just a quick rest then he'd…then he'd do something. He shrugged it off; it probably wasn't that important.

Every thing that may abide the fire,
ye shall make to go through the fire…
…and all that abideth not the fire,
ye shall make go through the water.

Numbers XXXI, 23

26. Making a Splash

Noah awakened instantly, spitting ice cold water out of his mouth and blinking it out of his eyes. There was a face right in his, and then he was being yanked to his feet as if he weighed nothing.

"Fill this," said the angry face, holding a bucket out to a man dressed in khaki.

Nothing made any sense. Noah didn't have anything on save his shorts. His friends were in a similar state of undress, their clothes strewn across the floor.

"There's nothing on this planet as stupid as people," said angry man. "Hey, you with me, idiot?"

Men in black and gray were coming through the hatch. The hatch. It was open.

"You're the guy," Noah croaked. "You're the guy who opens the hatch. We've been waiting for you."

"He's delirious," said the sailor, handing over the bucket.

Then it all came back to him. It was over. There'd be some unpleasantness, but then they were going home. "I guess we're getting kicked off the boat, huh?"

"That's right, you are," said the Old Bull, looming over Noah.

"What a relief."

"You're messed up." Mark tapped him in the middle of his forehead. It was a hard tap. "Can you walk?"

"Yes. Could I get a drink—" Hands grabbed him and hauled him through the hatch. "Wait…my friends."

"They'll be right after you. And you'll get more to drink than you can handle. Let's wake the redhead next."

"You don't have to be so rough," Noah stumbled, pushed along by the security officer. He earned a slap in the back of the head for his protest.

"Shut up, keep moving. Idiot, why'nt you just stay on shore and shoot y'seff?"

He wasn't expecting this level of abuse. Sure, they'd strayed from the open areas, but no harm done, right? A little sympathy for what they'd been through would have been nice.

People pressed against the walls of the cramps to get out of the way of the procession. He heard Darcy voicing complaints from behind him. She shut up abruptly, obviously getting the same treatment he was.

Noah wondered about their stuff. It would suck having to ride back to New Portland in his underwear. "You're not going to kick us off without our clothes, are you?"

"What difference does it make?" The guard pushed him again, sending him sprawling over a knee knocker.

"Hey," Mark's voice blasted down the corridor, "don't break him till the captain says so."

Noah was given a large glass of water after a long and humiliating trip through the cramps. People shook their heads, or clucked their tongues. One guy laughed and called him a splasher, whatever that meant. Every time he tried to speak he was told to shut up. It seemed he'd climbed a hundred ladders and instead of being taken to the flight deck or the brow, he was guided through a hatch and pushed into a chair in a room about the size of their hotel room in New Portland. As soon as he drained the glass, his arms were yanked behind him, through the back of the chair and handcuffed at the wrists.

Darcy gasped as the drained glass was yanked from her hands, and grunted as her arms were secured. She looked at Noah with wide, confused eyes.

Noah shrugged with his eyebrows. *I don't know either.*

When all of them were given water and locked down, the Old Bull moved before them and sat down on the edge of a desk in the middle of the room. Two flags, draped from poles, hung in the room at either corner of the wall behind the desk. One of them was the Stars and Stripes. The other was red, blue and yellow, but it was impossible to tell anything besides that, hanging folded as it was. Beside the mystery flag was another hatch. Like the cramps and the furnace trap, the walls were a dull gray.

The other black-and-gray civies left, and were replaced by Navy security personnel.

Sid opened his mouth, but shut it at a warning glance from Mark. He didn't need another slap to the head.

Two men entered from the inner hatch. Both of them wore whites, though one was more decorated than the other. The taller of the two Noah recognized as the man who'd inspected the dogs on the docks. The second man he hadn't seen before, but he could guess who he was based on the deference being given him. His face may have been gentle at one time, but the ragged scars on the left side, shaped like they traced the dorsal fin of a shark, gave the visage a sinister cast.

Mark got off the desk.

The captain looked the group over, took a chair behind the desk, and raised his eyes to Mark. "Go ahead, Marshal." His words were slightly distorted. The right side of his mouth moved while the left did not.

"Yes, Captain. They were in a maintenance access on 03 deck, port side. That access gets pretty hot, so I guess they took their clothes off and figured they could wait it out."

"Wait it out—" blustered Sid.

"Why don't you just kick us off?" asked Noah. The captain looked at him in surprise.

"Can't you feel it?" said Lena miserably. "We're moving."

"Interesting performance," said the captain. "We've seen it before. Marshal, how did you find them?"

"There was a visitor's tag on the floor outside the hatch. I guess they dropped one when they ditched the rest of them. One of my boys found it."

"Ditched…Captain, may I please speak?" Sid clenched his teeth in anticipation of a slap, but it didn't come. The captain smiled wryly, then inclined his head.

"We are not stowaways. Neither did we stay in that furnace by choice. We were lured there and locked in. We did not dispose of our visitor's cards. If you didn't see them then they must be buried under our clothes. We're victims here, not perpetrators."

The captain looked askance at Mark.

"Just the one tag. Door wasn't locked."

"Then they were taken while we were unconscious by the man who locked us in."

"You reached that area how?" asked the taller officer. He rolled his r's lightly.

"We got help from a small man in ragged clothes. He distracted a guard."

"Which guard?"

"It doesn't matter, look, I was knocked unconscious from behind—"

The officer put his face close to Sid's and asked again, very calmly, "Which guard?"

"Near the jewelry store," said Darcy. "Hatch on the left…port side. The man told the guard something and he left his post."

"Ah. That should narrow it down."

"He does have a contusion on the back of his head," said Mark.

"Why did this man help you?" Ransom asked Sid.

"I paid him. But that's not the—"

"Describe him to me."

"Look, I'm trying to tell you—" Sid's head snapped back from Mark's backhanded cuff. It was an easy motion, delivered with no more emotion than he'd use to swat a fly.

"Five two, maybe five three," said Caps. "Gray hair, dirty and uneven. Blue eyes. Thin nose slightly bent to the left. Greyish beard. Nails were really short. Bitten. His clothes were too big. If you want, I can draw you a picture."

"He might be telling the truth on that one," said Mark. "There was a sketchpad in their stuff. The bag's at your feet, Captain. I don't need a picture, though. Seaman Veccio," he spoke to the man directly behind Noah. "Go find Spider and bring his ass in here. Get my boys to help you. They know where he hides."

"Spider," Ransom sighed. "You've suspected him of conning stowaways in the past, haven't you?"

"Among other things. No proof, though. I doubt Spider could overpower even the kid," he pointed to Noah.

"Captain," Sid took a deep breath. "The man you want is named Dr. Theodore Odega. We came here looking for him. There's a sketch amongst our things. This man Spider knew our names and used that information to lure us to that room. If Odega is not a stowaway himself, then he may be a passenger, or a new citizen."

Ransom, who'd been pawing through the backpack, upended it on the desk, then looked at Mark.

"I didn't take it. Sir, two of them approached me earlier asking me about this guy. They mentioned the sketch, but claimed not to have it with them."

"All immigration goes through Commander Stukov," said the Captain. "Commander?"

"Nobody by that name, sir," said Stukov.

"Large black man," said Sid. "Bald. He may have used his middle name, Eric."

The commander shook his head.

"We've heard every story possible," said the captain. "Yours is better thought out than others, and staying in the compartment until you all passed out was a daring touch, but it doesn't wash. My guess is one of your own people gave you that bump on your head. Whatever you're running from—"

"We have no reason to run from anything. My name is Sid Halbert. I'm the leader of a settlement called Compton Pit. These people with me are my Chief of Security, chief mechanic, Chief of Photovoltaics and Chief of Communications. If you have SatCom capability, and I assume you do, you can verify all of it. Lena can give you the contact coordinates."

Ransom laughed. "Oh that's rich. If you are the leader of this settlement, why would you bring most of your senior staff to chase somebody? Hmm? I'd have gone with less ambitious identities."

"Captain Ransom, excuse me for eavesdropping." The hatch swung all the way open and a man stepped in. "I heard about some naked stowaways and that always peaks my interest." His voice was familiar, right down to the smooth, southern accent. "Shocking as it may be, I know these people, and they are exactly who they say they are. Hello, Darcy. How've you been?"

Darcy's jaw dropped. Of course he was here. He'd told her this was where he was going when he'd driven out of their lives so many months ago. "Donald. Donald Graff."

"Nice to be remembered."

He nodded a greeting to each of them, and in their surprise, they forgot their situation for a moment, and nodded back.

"How do you know these people, Donald?" asked Ransom.

"They were on their way to Vancouver. The big one in Canada, not the little one in Washington. I was on my way back from surveying the outskirts. We met at a safe house. An old camper lot."

"I thought Vancouver was a dead town," said Ransom.

"It is. Or perhaps *was*," he raised a conspirator's eyebrow at Sid. "I never expected to see you again as long as I lived. The captain's right, though. For people of your importance you do seem to take a lot of long trips."

"There," Sid fixed his eyes on Ransom. "Are you satisfied? If you remove these cu—"

"This changes nothing. Donald, do you know for certain these people aren't running from something?"

"I'm sure that…ah…" he looked at Darcy apologetically. "No. In all honesty, I can't vouch for that."

"What would we be running from?" Sid asked, exasperation in his voice despite his best efforts to appear calm.

"A coup," Mark offered indifferently. "Or another settlement annexing yours and wanting to tie up loose ends."

"Just what I was thinking," said Ransom.

"It started out as a short trip," said Noah. "Underbel and back. It grew from there."

"A three hour tour," sang Caps, "a three hour tour."

Sid tried to ignite the artist with the power of his eyes.

"I do not think you should be making light of these proceedings," Stukov said quietly.

"Why not?" said Caps. "This whole thing has been a joke. On us, I mean. You guys are sailors, right? Sailors like a good yarn. We'll tell you exactly how we got here. Lena?"

Lena's eyes went wide. She shook her head. "You've got the floor."

"If I tell it, it'll take six hours. I don't think they'll give us that long."

So Lena told them everything, haltingly at first, but then with confidence when no one stopped her. She was concise as possible, making sure to include every twist, with the exception of specifying what Odega's stolen piece of technology was.

"Wonderful," said Graff when she was finished. He turned to Caps. "Later on, I'd like to hear your version of it. I'll bring my notebook."

"Mr. Graff," Ransom snapped. "I told you I would extend every courtesy to you in order to help your book. However, you just stepped over the line of protocol. It hasn't been decided yet whether these people have a 'later on.' Dismissed."

"But…" He choked off whatever else he was going to say. "Yes, Captain."

The hatch closed behind the cartographer and a sailor moved to prevent it from being opened again.

"Take them away," said Ransom. "We'll resume this once I've had a talk with Spider."

"Wait," said Sid. "If you take Mr. Graff at his word, then take me at mine now. Unless he disembarked, somewhere on board is a totally insane and very dangerous man. The sooner you find him the better. The longer you wait before turning around, the farther you'll have to go to take us back."

"Take you…back? To where?"

"Astoria."

Ransom's eyes narrowed. "Marshal, get these people out of my sight."

27. The Stowaways

Instead of a ship's brig, they were taken to a jail in the Valley that wouldn't have looked out of place in a cowboy movie. Although the brick facing and interior were fake, the steel walls beneath were every bit as secure, if not more so, than the real thing. It allowed the civilians to build a functional jail in the Valley without breaking with the theme of preserving the past.

Initial attempts to build a scaled-down Tower of London failed due to spatial limitations.

Temporary incarceration of stowaways from the tours fell under the jurisdiction of the civies, and as such, they belonged to the Old Bull until the captain declared otherwise.

They were given their clothes, minus their boots. They were given water, but no food. Donald Graff tried to visit them, but was turned away.

There was a single window in the back of the cell, four bars prevented escape. Caps pushed his face against the bars and, in his best Clint Eastwood, said to a passerby, "Hey pardner, reckon I can git a word in with you?"

"What do you want, splasher?" the man asked, approaching the bars. He appeared young, tousled blond hair and no beard, but his eyes were old. He wore a sailor's khaki shirt with faded jeans for trousers.

"Me 'n' mine's bin wrongly accused. You find a way to spring us, I'll make it worth yer while."

The man smiled a little. He came a little closer and looked through the window at the other prisoners, then did an impression of his own. "Well, you jest sitcherself a spell, pilgrim. Ah'll get a rope and mah horse."

"Was that supposed to be John Wayne?" asked Caps.

"Don't know. Was yours supposed to be Clint Eastwood? Either you're watered or you're the most centered guy I've ever met." He shook his head and walked away.

"Why do people keep calling us splashers?" asked Noah. He sat on the edge of one of the two bunks.

"How do you make a splash?" asked Lena.

"Throw something in water."

"There you go, genius."

"Wait," he rounded on Darcy, "you said the punishment for stowing away was being put on some barge."

"That's what Spider told us."

"He lied." Lena gave a fake laugh. "Imagine that. A stand-up guy like Spider lying to us."

"The guy called me 'watered,' " said Caps, completely avoiding the subject. "Do you think that's their word for tooth crazy?"

"Well it fits," said Darcy. "You're certainly not centered. Lena over there, she's centered."

"Yeah," agreed Caps, moving to sit on the bunk next to his girlfriend. "You're taking this amazingly well."

"Am I?"

"You may be worried, but you're not—"

"Flipping out?" She leaned forward and looked at everyone. "Would you all like me to flip out? A little seizure to break the monotony?"

"That's not what I meant," said Caps.

"You know what happens to me during my attacks." She looked at Noah. "*You* don't. When I'm the thrashing she-demon, as Caps likes to call it, I'm not incoherent. I'm clawing at water. When I have an attack, I'm not thinking dogs, or raccoons. I think I'm drowning. I'm being pulled under by a whale. I'm not just afraid of it happening, I'm actually *there.* It's irrational. Right now it's very rational. I knew it from the moment we couldn't open that hatch. I've always known I was going to die in the water. Sometimes it's an effort just to step into the showers. Well. I don't have to worry about it anymore."

"You're not going to be eaten by a whale," said Caps.

"They're out there right now, waiting, Rick. I can feel them. They've been cheated twice. Third time's the charm."

"I'll enjoy disappointing them again," said Sid. His headache was down to a low, steady throb. The guard had laughed at him when he asked for ice. The lump on the back of his head was sensitive, delivering a burning pain when touched. Nevertheless, his hand still drifted up by itself to prod it once in a while. "The worst-case scenario is we have to make land at the next port and work our way home from there. True, we have nothing, but you've all proven yourselves resourceful. The question is, is Ted still on board? What we do next is—"

"You and your stupid obsession," Lena spat.

"Lena, I give you my word—"

"Shut up! To Underbel and back. I shouldn't even have had to do that. We had an agreement after Vancouver. Your word is worthless."

Caps was torn. His loyalty to Sid had been earned time and time again, but to choose between Sid and Lena…there wasn't much choice. His eyes found the floor and he put an arm over his girlfriend's shoulders.

"Are you finished?" asked Sid. "If you have nothing positive to contribute, keep quiet. Any signs of dissention will weigh against us in this situation. We have to prove our side with nothing but our sincerity and our demeanor. You may want to go for a swim, but I have other plans." He held back on apologizing to her. She wouldn't accept it anyway. "We also need answers to some questions that I'm still hazy about. How did Ted know about the Bruce Banner code? Either he was so close he could hear us, or someone working for him was. I don't know about you lot, but when Spider came to us topside, it was the first time I'd laid eyes on him. Ted is a brilliant man, but I have difficulty with him being this devious."

"He could have been listening to us on the ship's internal communication system," said Darcy. "If he knew the path of the tour, it must be mapped out somewhere. Maybe he could hear every word we said just by flipping switches."

"You had to make it easy for him, didn't you … Boss." Lena pushed herself off the bunk and took a step towards Sid.

Darcy moved to intercept her. "I take it back," said Darcy. "You're not centered. You're forgetting who the real enemy is, here."

"Oh, I remember. His name's Bruce Banner."

"I liked it better when you were having seizures," mumbled Darcy.

"That's enough!" Caps snapped, moving between the two women and pushing them apart. "This is so messed up." He sat on the cot, took Lena by the wrist and pulled her down next to him. "Oh, man. I really need to get stoned."

"Can you say that a bit louder?" snapped Darcy. "I think there were security personal on the lower decks who didn't hear you. It's a wonder you weren't in jail on New Wilderness Day."

"It's a wonder you weren't pregnant on New Wilderness Day," said Lena.

Noah bunched his fists and in a child's voice cried, "Mommy and Daddy, please stop fighting!"

All four of them turned to stare at him. Then the door to the outer office banged open. Their guard admitted the blond man who'd bantered through the window, followed by a man in a dark blue suit. The suited man had more hair than Noah had ever seen on a single head. It didn't drop far past his neck, but on the top and sides it swelled out like the cloud from an explosion. And the color! It made Darcy seem a brunette by comparison. If the man's shoulders and chest weren't so wide, it would have looked completely freakish.

"Which one of you is the artist?" asked the cloud of hair.

"That would be me," said Caps.

"Thought as much," said the blond man. "Name's Tivoli." He made as if to stick his hand through the bars, then thought better of it. "This is Tanzer."

"I've come for my drawing," said the bartender.

Tivoli held out a sketchpad and some pencils just close enough to the bars for Caps to take them.

"Hey," said the guard, slapping Tivoli's arms down. "You didn't say anything about sharp pencils."

"Are they going to cut through the bars with them?" Tanzer asked. "Not even you could nap long enough for them to manage that."

"Okay. Don't get too close to the bars though."

"How come he's allowed in but Donald Graff wasn't?" asked Darcy.

"Graff? That the writer?" Tanzer gave a cruel little chuckle. "The writer can't cut off the guard's liquor, can he?"

"You don't have the only still on the boat," the guard said defensively.

"No, but I do have the best one."

"What's this about a drawing?" asked Caps.

"I told him you'd come by and do a caricature of him in exchange for some information," said Sid. "He didn't give me any."

"No," corrected Tanzer. "You told me I'd get my drawing if I looked at your sketch."

Sid looked around the cell. "This isn't exactly the time—"

"Excuse me," Tivoli smiled. It was a gentle smile, and oddly calming. "You made a deal with Tanzer. I don't know how it is where you come from, but here in *Terpris*, a deal's a deal, even a crazy one. You're already a stowaway. You don't want to add welching to the charges." After getting a nod from the guard, he held up the pad and pencils. "And besides, you have no idea how hard it is to get Tanzer here to come below deck."

"No offence," said Sid, "but considering our situation, that sounds rather flimsy."

"Flimsy or not, I want my drawing." Tanzer folded his arms. "Should I sit down?"

"Yes," Caps took the pad and pencils.

Tanzer looked at the guard as if there was something he should be doing. The guard grimaced, then fetched a chair from the front office.

"I'd expect a Scottish accent to go with that hair," said Caps. "You sound more like New York. Where're you from."

"I lived in New York for twenty years. Good ear. No Scots in my family."

"Why the suit?"

"I want it classy. And don't make my head look like an apple on a stick. That's too predictable."

"So you want something more serious? Like the sketch the Boss showed you?"

"Halfway in between. Get to it."

"If you have to exaggerate something," said Tivoli, "give him an enormous prick."

"I've already got one," said Tanzer. "And if he doesn't shut up, I'll break his fingers." He turned to the guard. "Get out of here, would you? They're not going to try anything."

The guard grumbled, but returned to the outer office. Through the barred door, he could still see, if not hear everything.

"Pssst," it came from the window.

Tanzer flicked his eyebrows. *Go ahead.*

There was nobody at the window, so Sid stepped up to it and looked out. Donald Graff was crouched just below it.

"I'm not supposed to have any contact with you," he said quietly.

Sid gripped the bars and pushed himself against them, blocking as much of the window as possible. "Why not?"

"I tried talking to the captain about you. I think he's suspicious about why I'm making the effort for people I've only met once. Here," he offered up a pair of white pills. "Analgesic. And here," he held out a small skinbag. "Ice."

Sid dry-swallowed the pills, then palmed the bag. "I won't ask how you got this."

"From my bar," said Tanzer. "Where do you think?"

"No talking, please," said Caps.

"How does it look, Mr. Graff?" Sid whispered.

"Donald. I'm sorry to say, it doesn't look good. Someone's come forward who says you're lying about everything."

"Spider."

"I have to go. I'll do what I can."

Sid dropped to the bunk, placed the ice against the back of his head and leaned back, using the wall to keep the skinbag in place. "Thank heavens for small mercies."

"Why are you helping us?" asked Noah.

"It's all his idea." Tanzer jerked a hand at his companion. "He'd be nice to animals if I let him."

"No talking, please." Caps worked slowly, for a number of reasons. The work distracted him from their situation. As long as the two men were outside the cell, it was unlikely hostilities within it would resume. Finally, it could be the last Richard Scagling original, ever. So it might as well be a good one.

Lena sat on the floor against the wall, eyes glazed, like those of Eggerson's puppets.

Tanzer was getting fidgety, and Caps could only drag it out for so long. He signed his name and handed the pad and pencils back through the bars. In the drawing, he'd hidden the man's hair under a horned helmet, and added braids to the beard. Gone was the suit, and in its place was a thick coat and kilt, with a sword slung from a wide sash.

"You made me a Viking," said Tanzer.

"It's in your cheekbones. You're not a Scott. You're a Nord."

"It was a few generations back, but yes. You've satisfied your end of the deal. Good luck." He looked at Sid when he stuck his hand close to the bars for a shake. Sid fitted the skinbag into Tanzer's hand during the exchange with a nod of thanks.

"Wait," said Caps. "All the people on this ship, there's no artists?"

"There's a few," said Tivoli.

"So, if you wanted a picture so badly, why didn't you get one of them to do it?"

"Because," Tanzer waved the pad, "they would have charged me."

"There is a *bit* of Scot in him." Tivoli smirked.

The two men left and there was quiet in the cell. Noah glanced furtively back and forth, hoping Sid would come up with the magic words to make everything okay.

The barred door opened again. This time their visitor was Stephanie. She sat down in the chair vacated by Tanzer. She'd changed out of the red outfit, and the loose cream-colored drape she wore now was less flattering to the lines of her body. She was quite chubby. Sid sat up a bit straighter.

"Why didn't you just stay with the tour?" she asked at last.

"Why didn't you look for us earlier, when we didn't show up at the boat?" returned Darcy.

"Your names were signed out in the gondola logs. Your hardhats were returned. I had no *need* to look for you." Gone was the bubbly demeanor of the tour guide. This woman not only wore a different outfit, she wore a different face.

"The same man who locked us in that room must have signed us out," Sid smoothed his hair, running his hand firmly over his bump in the process. The small relief brought on by the ice vanished in an instant. He kept the pain from his face, but his toes curled so tightly his feet cramped up.

"Normally you'd have already been sentenced. Women in the water, men on the barge or in the water depending on the captain's or the XO's mood."

"We get automatic death sentences because we're women?" said Darcy.

"There's no women's prison facility. Getting splashed is more humane than putting a woman on the barge."

"So you, like, tow another boat around just to use as a prison?" Caps rubbed his forehead. "Isn't that a waste of resources?"

"The barge is our resources. It's a floating coal refinery. In absence of fancy machines and chemicals, prisoners do the work. So, the skipper feels there's enough inconsistencies that you merit representation. That's why I'm here. "

"No offence," said Darcy, "but a tour guide?"

"I act as tour guide sometimes because I enjoy it. I'm a member of the diplomatic committee and I'm also the civilian public defender."

A high-pitched whistle that echoed through the Valley was followed by an announcement requesting Robert Keller to report to either civilian or Navy security. It went on to instruct anyone who knew of Mr. Keller's whereabouts to also come forward.

"Hear that?" said Stephanie. "Robert Keller is Spider. That announcement means they haven't found him yet. That could work for us or against us. Tell me everything."

28. The State of the Navy

June 22, Year of the Change

The ocean was gentle; swells so low, they were hardly worth mentioning. There hadn't been a bird sighting in over a day, and for the first time since everything started, Captain Ransom stood on his flight deck. His face was stitched and bandaged. His right arm hung in a sling. Comparatively, he was better off than most others. The casualties were many, and astounding. The huge parrots brought on board for the rainforest pavilion had done a lot of damage, but nothing in comparison to the tiger. The cat had killed nine people and injured six others by itself, but the stampede it caused on the hangar deck had resulted in multiple tramplings. The lucky ones got off with concussions or broken bones. Two people had died, crushed over the knee knockers while people ran over their backs. One of the deceased was the French Ambassador. The other was the XO's wife. Captain Huff was all but useless now. Ransom was disappointed in the man. He thought he was made of sterner stuff.

Thank God for the Marines. Saddled with the task of providing security for the gala, it was they who'd brought down the tiger. It was they who'd quelled the stampede, and a few days later, the riot. It had been a little odd, once more having a detachment of Marines aboard the carrier, and it raised old rivalries between the "squids" and the "gyrenes", but in this case they'd earned their due in Ransom's eyes. He'd be recommending them all for commendations once this was over. The Marines had stayed true to their uniform, every single one of them, even when a number of sailors hadn't. Over three hundred people were being detained in zone one of the hangar deck. Mostly, but not all, civilians.

They'd tried to return to Norfolk, but the carrier's home, pier eleven, was no more. As near as they could tell, something had ignited a tanker carrying jet fuel. The resulting explosion had decimated the docks. With nobody to do damage control, the fires had spread, finding more things to ignite and detonate. The black smoke over Norfolk could still be seen miles away. Two attempts at making landfall had cost four boats and twenty-four men. A whale got one of the boats. They didn't know what got the others.

"Captain to the bridge," boomed a voice. At least the loudspeaker still worked.

On top of the damage to the antennae array, there'd been a few internal fires and a massive electrical surge from one disaster or another. Order had taken time to restore. Systems were out all over the place. Ransom headed towards the bridge, trailed at a respectful distance by a petty officer and a Marine.

He climbed the six ladders up to the bridge and was greeted by a flush-faced officer holding out a mic. "Communications are back online, sir. I have Rear Admiral White on the horn."

"Admiral," Ransom grunted through his teeth with a profound sense of relief. The damn doctor had wired his jaw shut to keep him from ripping out the stitches with a tirade. At least he could move his lips.

"Captain, what is your position?"

"Thirty-four degrees east, forty-two degrees north, sir." That was at least close to where they were. The GPS was out, so was Loran—a simpler system that bounced radio signals off landside receivers. They'd been doing it the old fashioned way, dead reckoning, for ten days. "Sir, what is—"

"What is your status?"

"We're as stable as can be expected under the—"

"How's your air wing?"

"All dead, such as it was. We had six ramp strikes, one to the island, one starboard. The rest went into the ocean. Sir, what the hell is going on?"

"How fares your battle group?"

"I have none. Admiral, are you familiar with our last assignment? We were hosting the UN gala."

"Oh. That debacle. So you're loaded with civilians. No. Not just any old civilians. Under no circumstances are you to attempt to dock or land. What I'm sure you've been experiencing...look, I'm sending you some things." There was a pause. *"Are you getting it?"*

Ransom looked at one of his officers. The man glanced up from a screen and nodded.

"Yes. Admiral, did I hear you right? Are you instructing me not to make for land? As in anywhere?"

"Read everything I've sent you. Captain, you're the best news I've had since... you realize the importance of the people you've got on board?"

Beside him, the communications officer watching the monitor, broke down crying.

"Lieutenant, you're dismissed," hissed Ransom, forgetting to cut the mic.

"Don't be so hasty," came Admiral White's voice.

"Sir, we have casualties far in excess of our capabilities to render proper care. Morale is at a dangerous low. We have insurgents on board and we're not supplied for an indefinite stay at sea. If we cannot make land, request we rendezvous with the fleet, sir."

"Captain, as of this moment, in the Atlantic, you are *the fleet. Read what I've sent you. I'll be waiting for your call. White out."*

"Admiral? Admiral!"

"Cut off at his end," said a man with red-framed glasses. He wasn't Navy, but a tech rep, Vincent McCabe, a civilian sent out by his company to assist the military with the complex systems on board.

"Get him back. Now." A gob of saliva dribbled down Ransom's chin and soaked into the bandages. In a few minutes, the damp spot would start to itch.

The communications officer, Lieutenant Keiths, was no longer sobbing audibly, but he trembled in his chair and tears ran down his cheeks.

"Did we get it all?" Ransom asked.

"Yes, sir."

"Put it through to my chair." The captain dropped heavily into the raised leather seat from which he commanded the ship. Computer screens were mounted on either side. On one to his right began a slow scroll of information, communiqués—the word mayday proceeded nearly every one—ships' positions, notices of lost contact. The carriers on operations had faced far worse problems than Ransom's. Their planes were heavier, with far more powerful jet fuel and loaded to the teeth with missiles and bombs. Crashes both during launching and recovering had led to daisy chain effects catastrophic to the carrier's personnel. The birds however, were only the beginning. Ransom froze the screen on one dispatch he had to reread three times.

> Whales and dolphins are no longer acting with simple hostility but in clearly premeditated, intelligent attack patterns. The nature of these strategies show the cetaceans are cognizant of telemetry, sonar, causal relationships, and to a degree, our weapons capabilities. It is also possible the cetaceans are utilizing psychological warfare, as behavior has been observed that can only be described as taunting.

The whales couldn't damage the hull of the larger ships in the Navy. They'd tried repeatedly with Ransom's command. Though no significant physical damage had occurred, the sound of the impacts resounding through the hull had threatened to drive his people mad. Within clusters of ships, however, the whales found that if they couldn't sink a ship, they could guide it by bashing the keel and rudders. In this way, smaller ships were forced to collide with larger ones. In more than one case, angles of impact seemed to be directed such that triple collisions occurred. The mammals had also appeared to trick ships into firing torpedoes and other armament into each other. The submarines were no better off.

> They stopped ramming us and started rubbing. By accident or design, the whales have inverted us. I'm standing on the ceiling of my bridge. We are grounded at a depth of 420 meters. Without immediate assistance, we will not survive.

A grim realization spread through the captain. Bertram Wallis had saved them all: because of him there was no proper air wing on board, no surrounding battle group of cruisers, tankers and destroyers to use against them.

The dispatches were followed by similar information from both Army and Air Force. The whales were not the only ones with a grasp of geometry and physics. The birds were capable of throwing themselves into the flight path of planes traveling at nearly any speed. The knack which predatory avians had for power diving hundreds of feet to snatch a smaller bird from the air was simply being applied on a grander scale. According to the dispatches, there was no knowledge of currently-airborne craft of any kind, anywhere.

The Army's reports ran the entire length of the animal kingdom, from the tiniest ant to the largest elephant.

Lastly, the captain was subjected to miscellaneous information; sound bites from news stations, municipal damage reports, government press releases.

He stabbed a button that patched him through to the entire ship. "This is the captain. All senior officers report to my wardroom." He released the button. "Mr. Keiths…"

"Hailing, Captain."

"You've read it all?" asked Admiral White.

"Yes. What are your orders, sir?"

"Orders. Yes, what are my orders?" What followed sounded like a barely restrained giggle. *"Nuke the unborn gay whales."*

"Sir?"

"It's a bumper sticker on my grandson's car. Captain, I've had a very sudden change of heart. I still have family surviving. I'm going to go to them."

"Admiral, what are you telling me?"

"I'm telling you to get to like the taste of fish. I'm telling you you're on your own. I know you want me to direct you, give you a plan of action. You've been a credit to your uniform and have served your country well, but that country is no longer.

"You have on board diplomats, heads of state, artists and academics from all over the world. You also have a lot of reporters, which is good because it means you'll have no shortage of bait." This time the Admiral's laughter came through loud and clear.

"Admiral," desperation flooded Ransom's senses. The chain of command was the only thing that kept firm ground under his feet, a chain for which he was not the anchor. "I don't think this is the time to be making jokes."

"I think it's exactly the time to be making jokes, son. Keep that in mind. We've had no contact with the President. I've had no contact with a superior in five days."

"Sir, how can that be? There are multiple locations where our president and leaders can be kept safe from a nuclear event. How could—"

"Standard procedure, Captain. Immediately upon confirmation of crisis, the president et al are to be evacuated by the quickest means possible."

"Helicopters."

"Possibly. Or Air Force One. Who knows? They might all be safe and sound, they just can't talk to us. As far as I'm concerned, I'm the Commander in Chief of the whole damn Navy. I'm sorry to say I'm abandoning my post. If you want it, the job's yours. I suggest you keep moving, Captain. There doesn't seem to be anyplace safe to stay. White out."

A tear ran down Ransom's cheek as he pushed himself out of the chair. He'd have to have his bandages changed soon. They were going to itch like hell.

29. Probetur Malus

Stephanie had changed into a blue dress that might have come straight from the Aretha Franklin formal collection. Its lines did much to hide her girth, but Sid could imagine the abundant curves that lay beneath as she preceded him down the cramps. He wasn't deliberately thinking lustful thoughts, and felt childish for doing so, but the brain did what the brain did. Ahead of Stephanie was her assistant, a middle-aged Jamaican woman with cornrows curled tight to her head and a perpetual frown on her face.

Noah was sick to death of the narrow passages and knee knockers. The narrowest maintenance access in Compton Pit was easier to navigate than these steel tunnels, yet somehow the *Terpris* people did it everyday.

They were taken to a different room than the one in which they'd been first interrogated. This one was larger, with benches and a screen along the back wall. In front of the screen was a metal desk, with a gavel and its strike plate sitting near one edge. The chair behind the desk was comfortable leather, the chair beside the desk was hard metal. They still had to wear cuffs, but at least their wrists were shackled in front of them this time.

Gray steel. Noah winced. The walls in this room were also gray steel. With all the color in the Valley, couldn't someone have wandered in here with a paintbrush?

Four sailors guarded the only exit: two inside, two out. Another pair were at the front wall. They had no sidearms, but their nightsticks looked sturdy.

The alleged stowaways were seated on a bench, Stephanie on a chair in front. "Remember what I told you," she said, turning to face them. She gave Caps a particularly stern look. "I do all the talking."

They waited. Stephanie began to tap her foot. Boredom set into Noah like a monkey on his back. A guard's mask slipped and his agitation showed through. It was highly irregular for the captain or the XO to be late for a trial.

Finally the sailors snapped to attention as Ransom and Stukov entered the room, followed immediately by Mark.

"As you were," said the XO.

The captain wore judge's robes.

"I was hoping for Judge Judy," Caps whispered to Noah.

Stukov took the chair adjacent to Stephanie. Apparently he would be the prosecution. The Old Bull sat behind him.

Ransom took his seat behind the desk and composed himself. "Marshal, have you succeeded in locating Mr. Keller?"

"No, sir. Spider has blackmailed and defrauded a number of people over the years. He knows how to go to ground, so it's possible he's still onboard, but I think it's more likely he snuck off at Astoria."

"Fine. Sid Halbert, Darcy McCullough, Noah Thurlow, Richard Scagling, Lena Wong, you are charged with unauthorized entry, and embarking upon this vessel without leave. How do you plead?"

"The defendants plead not guilty," said Stephanie.

It was simple. The prosecution would present his case, then Stephanie would present hers. Either side could call anyone to the stand and there was no such thing as the fifth amendment. Refusal to answer questions was an indication of guilt. A sailor was admitted; it was the man Spider had distracted on the Street.

"Go ahead, commander," Ransom folded his hands.

"Yes, sir. I call Richard Scagling."

Caps crossed to the chair and sat down. There was no swearing in.

"Mr. Scagling, the sailor who gave you access to secure areas, he is in this room?"

"Yes, he's—"

"You will point him out to us, please?"

"I was just about to do that." He raised his cuffed hands and pointed at the sailor.

"Thank you. No more questions."

"Cross?" Ransom asked Stephanie. When she shook her head, he said to Caps, "You may step down."

"Wait, that's it?"

"Step down, Mr. Scagling," said Commander Stukov.

"Aren't you supposed to say something like, 'Let the record show so-and-so indicated so-and-so,' or something like that?"

"Richard," hissed Stephanie.

Caps returned to his bench.

"Call Seaman First Class Stuart Reid."

The sailor took the chair.

"Mr. Reid, where were you posted from 08:00 hours to 16:00 hours on November 21st?"

"I was posted at hatch seven, port side, the Street, sir."

"At any time, did you leave your post?"

"Once, to relieve myself at 11:52. Deputy Hillerman of the civilian guard held my post, sir."

"And that was it? You were, at no other time, vacant from your post?"

"No, sir."

"Captain," Stephanie said as she stood up. "Request a recess to find witnesses to speak to the contrary."

"Denied. This man is not on trial. Continue, Commander."

"No further questions."

Stephanie whispered to her assistant, who rose and exited the room.

"Stuart," Stephanie began, without rising from her seat. "Do you know a man named Robert Keller?"

"I know of him, ma'am. Up until today I didn't know that was his name."

"So you've always known your associate as Spider."

"Objection," said Stukov.

"That one was a little crass," said Ransom. "Sustained."

"Stuart, what is the punishment for being absent from your post without leave or extenuating circumstances?"

"Maximum penalty of twenty lashes at the Captain's Mast, ma'am."

Caps gasped. Twenty lashes. This was anything but a progressive Navy.

Stephanie stood and approached the witness. "Would you do anything to avoid receiving twenty lashes?"

"Within the bounds of following my orders, yes ma'am."

"But not beyond those limits."

"No."

"Lieutenant, would you lie to avoid twenty lashes?"

"No ma'am. The maximum penalty for lying to your superiors is immediate expulsion from *Terpris*, whether in port or not."

"Did you have any discussions with Robert Keller on November 21st?"

"No ma'am."

"Are you a strong swimmer, Stuart?"

"Objection."

"Withdrawn. No further questions." She returned to her seat.

"Lt. Reid, dismissed," said Ransom. "But keep yourself available."

"Yes, sir."

"He's lying," Sid whispered at the back of Stephanie's head. She didn't respond.

"Call Donald Graff," said Stukov.

The hatch opened and Graff was let in. He took his seat confidently, but looked confused when the XO rose to begin questioning.

"Excuse me," said Graff, "I thought I was a witness for the defense."

"You may still be. Mr. Graff," Stukov removed a hardcover book from his briefcase and handed it to the witness. "You could identify this book, please?"

"This is one of my journals." He turned to Ransom. "I didn't say you could go through my things."

"Captain," Stephanie rose. "It is illegal for the Navy to perform a search and seizure of a civilian's property without due cause."

"That is correct," said Ransom, "but Mr. Graff is a guest under the auspices of the Navy, not the Merchants Guild, and as such, he and his possessions are subject to our regulations."

Stephanie took her chair. She didn't know what was in the journal, but whatever it was, Donald Graff wasn't happy about it.

"Mr. Graff," Stukov continued, "in our initial discovery, you claimed contact with the defendants prior to their arrival in *Terpris*. That is correct?"

"Yes."

"And in that same statement, you indicated knowledge of their identities?"

"Yes."

"And did you have this knowledge prior to meeting them for the first time?"

Graff chewed his cheek. "Yes."

Sid and Darcy exchanged a look.

Stukov clasped his hands behind his back. "Elaborate, please, on that prior knowledge?"

"I had...physical descriptions and some comments as to their personalities. Well, a few of them. The young man, there, Noah Thurlow, and the mechanic, Richard Scagling, I knew next to nothing about them."

"At the time you met them, the information you had at hand, they confirmed it?"

Donald clearly didn't want to answer.

"Objection, relevance," fired Stephanie.

"The defense intends to call Mr. Graff as a character witness, sir. I merely ask what he has seen of their character."

"Oh, come on," Stephanie banged a pen on the table like it was her own gavel. "You're crossing my witness before I get a chance to present."

"I am establishing a pattern of behavior, sir." Stukov stood stock still as he waited.

"Overruled."

Stukov smiled. "Do I need to repeat the question, Mr. Graff?"

"No. Ah, did you read all my journals then?"

"Only the one containing the relevant dates. Answer the question, Mr. Graff."

"No. They did not confirm their identities."

"In fact, they lied about who they were, yes?"

"They didn't give me false names, if that's what you're asking."

"Did they lie about their current place of residence and positions therein?"

"Not lie, exactly. They were…evasive. But you have to understand—"

"Mr. Graff, it was your intention to visit the settlement Compton Pit immediately after surveying the outskirts of Vancouver, yes?"

"You've read my journal. You already—"

"Answer the question."

"Yes."

"The defendants were aware of your intentions?"

"Yes."

"And did they, considering their lofty positions at that settlement, offer to assist you in gaining entry to Compton Pit?"

"No. But if—"

"Mr. Graff, they sought to dissuade you from your objective, yes? Informing you that the road was blocked and therefore inaccessible?"

"Look, between settlements in that area—"

"Captain, please direct the witness to answer the question."

"Mr. Graff," Ransom raised an eyebrow.

"Alright. Yes. They told me the road was blocked."

"Did you take them at face value?" Stukov's smile dimmed a little.

Graff squeezed the journal tightly with both hands. "I took a look for myself. I always do."

"The road was blocked?"

"No."

"There was evidence that the road had been recently cleared?"

"Not that I saw. No."

"No further questions."

Stephanie stood and turned her back to the captain under the guise of straightening her dress, in actuality she did it to cast an accusing glare at Sid. He shrugged. She whispered a question in his ear. He replied quickly and she nodded.

"Mr. Graff, can you think of a reason as to why the defendants would not want you to visit their home?"

"Objection," Stukov said. "Calls for speculation."

"Captain, Donald Graff has traveled across North America. He's visited and studied hundreds of settlements. His works are the definitive authority on that continent. As such I'd like him declared an expert on inter-settlement politics."

"That's fair." Ransom nodded. "Any objections, Commander?"

Stukov shook his head.

Graff let out the breath he'd been holding. "I can think of some excellent reasons. Political instability abounded in Compton Pit's vicinity. I can name two settlements at the time that would use certain developments as an excuse to stage an attack."

"Could you be more specific?" Stephanie asked.

"It would be my pleasure. If I was in the defendants' position, I would not want it getting out that..." he smiled at the judge and prosecution, "...the captain and executive officer were absent from home."

"No further questions."

"Redirect?" asked Stukov. He stood when the captain nodded. "Mr. Graff you made the accused aware of your suspicions as to their true identities?"

"No."

"Why?"

"If they didn't want to tell me, that was their business."

"Would you like me to read a passage from your journal?" Stukov reached for the book.

Graff wrapped his arms around the book protectively. "That won't be necessary."

"Good."

"I...you people. It's like the world hasn't changed a bit."

"Why did you not tell them you knew who they were?"

"I didn't let on that I knew because...because I didn't know how far they would go to protect their settlement and their identities."

"How far did you think they might go?"

"Objection," Stephanie shouted. "Calls for—"

"You already had me declare him an expert," said the Captain. "Overruled."

"Mr. Graff," Stukov urged.

"I thought they might seek to detain me. Either force me to go with them or disable my vehicle."

"Since you were far from any settlement, either option was tantamount in your mind to killing you, yes?"

"Yes."

"No more questions."

"You may step down, Mr. Graff." said Ransom.

He was as reluctant to stand as he'd been eager to sit only a few minutes earlier. "Can I stay?" he asked.

"No, you may not. Dismissed."

"Call Master Chief Petty Officer William Porter," said Stukov.

A slightly chubby man of average height was admitted. He had sparse black hair in a comb over, and darkly tanned skin.

"Chief, as highest ranking non-commissioned officer, you have the right to approve immigration applications?"

"Yes I do. Although primarily, that's your responsibility."

"During our stay at Astoria, you admitted new citizens to *Terpris*?"

"I did."

"Did you inform me, or register these new citizens with me prior to this afternoon?"

"Not all of them, no."

"Thank you, Chief. No further questions."

"Cross?" Ransom offered Stephanie.

She shook her head, a little confused.

"Call your next witness, Commander."

"Yes, sir. Call Dr. Theodore Odega."

30. Salvage

July 3, Year of the Change

"She's dead in the water sir," said Petty Officer William Porter. He ran a hand through his thick, black hair and turned back to his conning station. He raised his binoculars again. "Listing to starboard. No signs of life."

"Hail them again," Ransom ordered.

"Still no response," replied Keiths.

"Reverse engines, one third."

"Aye, sir, engines one third."

"Image on your monitor now, sir," said one of the tech reps.

On one of the screens beside the captain's chair appeared the enhanced image of the vessel. It was a Russian destroyer. Her deck was at a forty degree angle, with the stern lying lower than the bow. The destroyer wasn't moving, but she had been a few hours before when she first appeared on the surface radar.

"It's clear, sir," said the man at Sonar. "Nothing big enough to register."

"Bring us alongside."

Orders were repeated across the bridge, spoken into mics and sent with runners. The bridge was crowded, alive again now that they had a purpose. After much debate, the captain had ordered the data package from Admiral White displayed on all ships monitors, on all decks. There were no need-to-know limitations on this one. What had happened to the world, every person on board needed to know.

Already amongst the civilians the political bandying had begun. There were people on board who were used to piloting countries and it didn't sit well with them to be told what to do by the captain of a mere ship. A human storm was brewing, but in the meantime, Ransom had to give his men a job to do, an objective, or watch what was left of his Navy fall apart.

In a way, it was Admiral White's idea. Ransom was going to locate and pull together every ship he could find, from other carriers to the smallest sloop. A unified Navy, cognizant of the threat they faced. They'd modify their weapons; the carrier's Sea Sparrow SAM missiles weren't much use against dolphins. The rifles of the Marines could easily be avoided simply by diving deep below the surface. Already the spare 20mm Gatling guns had been pedestal-mounted on the back of cargo carts and the Close-In Weapon Systems—antiaircraft machineguns—were now pointed at the sea.

"It's the *Rybinsk,* sir. Correlating with data now." It was the tech rep with the red glasses. Vincent Mcabe. "Commanding officer Captain Mikhail Stukov. Last known position was twenty-two south, sixty-four west. Where do you think she was headed?"

"Maybe she was coming to America," said Porter. "Drawing alongside, Captain."

Through the actions of the crew, the four gigantic propellers completed their task of slowing, then stopping the massive ship, bringing her to a standstill next to the sloping ship.

They watched for a short while, both with eyes and cameras, waiting to see if the carrier's wake would further the demise of the destroyer.

"She seems to have stabilized," said Porter. "That may change once we've men aboard. Wait, there are men aboard."

There was at least one man. A Russian officer had clawed his way up the deck and was waving his arms frantically.

"Are our translators in position?" asked Ransom.

Lieutenant Colonel Fred Mills, commanding officer of the Marine detachment, pulled his headset askew. "Captain, he's demanding we get away from the *Rybinsk*. He's insists—"

"Colonel, tell your man to inform the Russian the *Rybinsk* is ours by right of salvage and that survivors will be treated as well as our own crew."

"No, captain, he's telling us to get away because of dolphins. He says there's hundreds of them. "

"Sonar?" Ransom spun in his chair.

"Nothing, Captain."

"Mr. Allen, if there's even a school of minnows, I want to know about it."

"No schools, sir. Nothing dense enough to register."

"Colonel, have the Russian brought aboard, along with any other survivors. If their sonar's out, which it most likely is, he doesn't know we're safe for the moment. Lower the lines, away the boats."

Grapples were thrown from the hangar deck, boats descended to the water and the docking platform on the stern lowered into position. When six lines were secure, Marines slid down the ropes to the capsizing vessel. Boson chairs—planks of wood—were lowered along with rigged pallets. Ladders followed. Three boats tied off to the destroyer while a swarm of Marines and sailors descended to her deck. All the while, the Russian officer screamed and gestured at the water.

Russian sailors came out of hatches, not to greet or obstruct the boarding party, but to push past them in haste to get at the boats. An unconscious man, already secured to a stretcher, was brought out and hauled up the side of the carrier. Bucket brigades were established, quickly filling cargo nets and the boats with supplies: canned goods, bottled water, armament and other sundries, anything that wasn't nailed down or below water.

The angry Russian gave up struggling with his two Marine "escorts" as they dragged him to an incoming boat. He jerked away from them, and in the process, toppled over the railing and into the ocean.

A disturbance in an otherwise calm sea appeared immediately surrounding the *Rybinsk's* sunken stern. Instantly it spread to surround the entire hull.

"Captain, multiple contacts," snapped Lt. Allen. "Possibly dolphins."

"How did they get so close without us detecting them?"

"I don't know sir, maybe...Sir, I've just lost Sonar."

"Col. Mills, abort. Mister Keiths, you have the con." The captain was already through the hatch. Ransom was becoming a different type of commander. In a performance review, it would look very bad for him to have left the bridge at a crisis moment, but he wouldn't have to suffer those anymore.

All around the *Rybinsk,* dark gray backs broke the surface and submerged, dorsal fins briefly flashing in the spray, then the air was filled with dolphins. They were large, ranging from six to nine feet in length, dark gray with white bellies and yellow patches along their flanks. They snatched men from the deck, pulled the ropes, fouled rigging and smashed into the boats.

The Gatling guns were useless. They couldn't open fire without hitting men. The Marines on the destroyer were better able to defend themselves, but from many positions they couldn't fire either.

The *Rybinsk* lurched, and her stern dropped farther below the surface. Sailors on the small boats rushed to untie the lines, dolphins prevented them. Five-hundred-pound living missiles with short beaks filled with pointed teeth severed limbs and dragged men into the water. The destroyer began to roll, completing its list to starboard, hauling the carrier's boats right out of the water, to drag across the *Rybinsk's* port side. Marines and sailors alike slid down the deck and into the dolphin-infested water.

On the hangar deck, cables were hauled up and the securing lines were cut. Marines fired angry bursts into the water. Cetacean blood mingled with human as fat chunks of tissue were blasted off the dolphins. Men disappeared under the water, only to be rocketed back to the surface by their float coats once either the dolphins had let go or their limbs had. Screams, the likes of which hadn't been heard since the first day, came from both above and below.

Men who'd scrambled up the destroyer's deck, now almost perpendicular to the sea, and onto the port side, made for the boats and the tie lines. The boats slid down the side and into the water. One of them upended, but the other two kept their keels. A group of dolphins launched themselves simultaneously onto one side of one of the boats, their additional weight flipping the vessel over. Almost immediately, they did the same to the second boat.

Ransom made it to the opening off the hangar deck in time to see the carnage, and be able to do nothing about it. A few feet away from him, his XO, Captain Huff, fell to his knees and soiled himself.

Major Dawson, Col. Mills's man on deck, called for a cease fire. His men were wasting precious ammunition for no real gain. On board the destroyer, a few men were left clutching at the railing on the port side. There was no way to rescue them.

A pair of headphones were snapped onto Ransom's head by persons unknown.

"This is the captain," he said into the mouthpiece. "Ahead full. The *Rybinsk* is going under."

Along the bow of the destroyer, dolphins reared on their tails and skipped the water backwards, squeaking and cackling at the carrier.

"Let them have it," Ransom ordered one of the Gatling guns. The 20 mm opened fire and a dolphin exploded in a spray of red. The other wave dancers disappeared below the surface.

As the carrier pulled away, the destroyer's bow lifted completely out of the water, sailors still clinging to the rails. Dolphins jabbered from below, waiting for the last of their victims.

On the bridge, Lt. Allen stared at his blank sonar screen and said, "We have to come up with something better than a towed array."

In all, seventy-one men and three boats were lost for less supplies than could fit in the back of a large van.

Hours later, when the Russian captain came awake in a wardroom converted into a sick bay, the first person he saw was a young, blond man, formally of Scranton, Pennsylvania. His name was Laurence Tivoli, a correspondent for the *Herald*, onboard a ship for the first time since his discharge from the Navy two years previous.

Tivoli had been pressed into service as an intern because he'd been standing at the right place at the wrong time. He helped Captain Stukov drink some water, and because the Russian spoke fluent English, answered a few questions, and then summoned an officer. That officer spoke briefly with Stukov, and summoned the captain.

"You rescued how many men from my ship?" Stukov asked when Ransom arrived at his bedside.

"Sixteen including yourself."

"Where are they?"

"Secure. They were in your brig when we found them, so I felt it best to lock them up until you recovered. One of them claimed to be you, but we have your picture in our database. Captain Stukov, my boarding party was attacked by a large pod of dolphins that slipped through our sonar undetected. Did they pull the same thing with you? The *Rybinsk* was nearly deserted and all your boats were away."

"Yes. We kept moving though we were taking on water. The dolphins, they harried us. When our sonar was clear we…the men were in my brig because they did not…conduct themselves well. I had every intention of letting them out once all my…" he looked at the occupants of the cots around him. "You said sixteen men? There were fifteen in the brig. Does that mean…" he was overcome with a racking cough.

"There was another officer at first. He told us about the dolphins, but we didn't believe him. He didn't make it."

"Ah. Alexei. He was my chief navigator, and a friend. When our sonar was clear, we floated the boats. Myself and Alexei, a few others were the last onboard when the dolphins appeared again. My men…so many men."

A look passed between them, a moment of empathy.

"We saw no evidence of this on our approach," said Ransom.

"After the dolphins killed them, they ripped apart the flotation jackets. So the bodies would sink, yes? They knew you were coming before we did. Had I not been in this condition, I would have come up to warn you, instead of Alexei. Perhaps I could have been more clear."

"Captain Stukov—"

"Call me Mikhail. I am hardly a captain now."

"According to your service record you're a former aviator. That qualifies you for command aboard a carrier, but we'll talk about that later. Captain Stukov, do you know how they did it? How did they evade our sonar?"

"They pressed themselves against our hull. They hid in the thermal layer. Once they'd taken our men from the lifeboats, they came inside, through the holes in the port side. The few men that stayed on board to help with the prisoners, they were taken when they went below for more ammunition. I would guess that many of yours were taken in the same way." Stukov coughed again, long and hard.

Ransom wanted to end it there, but he pushed his way past this new horror, and prepared for the bigger one coming. "Mikhail, one more question, then I'll let you rest. How did the dolphins do so much damage to your ship?"

"Captain, I owe you and your country a great apology. We were fired upon by one of your submarines." The cold war was long over, but the Russian and American Navy still played tag with each other in the spirit of competitiveness. "There was great confusion, I could not establish contact with my superiors and all our lines of communication were clogged with outlandish reports of...well, I am sure you know. I gave the order to return fire. There was an exchange. Before we killed it, the submarine did a great deal of damage to my *Rybinsk*. My hat's off, as you say, to the submarine's captain and crew. Our repairs were not sufficient for any duration. I now believe the first torpedo that struck my ship was not meant for us, but instead for a whale that appeared in our sonar log."

They were silent for a few minutes.

"I was hosting a UN gala," said Ransom. "We had a tiger on board."

"Ah. It is as if our time on this planet is over, Captain. Like the dinosaurs, yes? It is something else's turn now."

31. Fugitive

Sid, Darcy and Stephanie came to their feet, all talking at the same time. The gavel banged and Ransom spoke above all of them. "The accused will be silent! Sit down, Mr. Halbert, Miss McCullough."

"Captain," said Stephanie, "I was not informed that Dr. Odega was on board *Terpris*, furthermore—"

"We did not know ourselves until shortly before the proceedings, counselor. Chief Porter was lax in his paperwork and will be disciplined accordingly."

"That's why all of you were late. Request a continuance."

"Denied."

"Request a recess."

"Denied."

"Captain I strongly object."

"Objection noted. Commander, please continue."

Dr. Odega entered the room. It showed in his face that he'd lost some weight, but other than that, he was unchanged. He wore a dark gray sweater that stretched tight across his chest. When his eyes fell upon Sid and the others, every feature he had went wide in surprise. It was as if his whole face had dropped open.

"Nice try, Ted," said Sid.

"The accused will be silent." Ransom banged his gavel.

Odega stood frozen in place until one of the guards took his elbow and pushed him forward. As he was led to the chair, his eyes stayed on the group, head turning as his body passed them. "What are you doing here?" he asked, voice choked with surprise.

"I don't know," Caps whispered to Lena. "I'm kind of buying it."

"I think I am, too," she replied. The shock on Odega's face was mirrored on her own.

"Dr. Odega..." Stukov began.

"What are they doing here? I told you everything when I was admitted. Whatever they've said—"

"Dr. Odega, you are not on trial here. They are."

"They are…ah, that would explain the cuffs. What did they do?"

"Dr. Odega, these first two questions may seem moot, but I'm going to ask them anyway. You are familiar with the accused?"

"Yes. Very familiar. Not so much with young…Thurlow, isn't it? Accused of what?"

"You were aware of their presence on board *Terpris* prior to entering these proceedings?"

"No. Certainly not."

"You were aware of their intention to come aboard?"

"No. I'm surprised to see any of them south of Underbel. Lena," he looked right at her, "I can't believe you left the Pit in the first place."

"Please do not address the defendants," instructed Ransom.

"Dr. Odega, you have been aboard *Terpris* how long?"

"Four days."

"You arrived under what circumstances?"

"I arrived on the *Munin* and immediately set about making contact with the animal research department. After a long wait I was met by Dr. Leighton. After a discussion, he introduced me to Dr. Chen. After another discussion, they suggested I apply for citizenship. I did so, and with their sponsorship, was quickly accepted."

"Dr. Odega, between 08:00 and 16:00 today, you were where?"

"I spent most of my time in animal research. I had lunch in mess hall two at around two o'clock…14:00. After that I returned to the research labs."

"There is someone who can verify this?"

"Either Dr. Leighton or Dr. Chen were with me at all times."

"I see. At some point you ascended to the Street or Valley?"

"No."

"At some point you were on the 02 deck, or the second deck?"

"No."

"Dr. Odega, do you know a man named Robert Keller, aka Spider?"

"Not to the best of my knowledge."

"At any time did you contact a person or persons with the intention of assaulting and trapping the defendants?"

Odega's eyes grew wide. "Certainly not."

"Thank you, Doctor. No further questions."

Sid tried to whisper in Stephanie's ear, but she waved him off. She composed herself, rose, and moved to stand directly in front of Odega.

"Dr. Odega, may I call you Ted?" He nodded. "Ted, prior to immigrating to *Terpris*, was your prior residence a settlement called Compton Pit?"

"My prior permanent residence, yes."

"Could you please describe the circumstances under which you left Compton Pit?" She waited for Stukov to object. To her surprise, he didn't.

"I'd been in a coma. When I came to I was...disorientated. I took a vehicle and left."

"Did you have permission to leave?"

"No. I didn't need it. Compton Pit is a settlement, not a prison."

"Did you have permission to take the vehicle?"

"No, I did not."

"Did you assault both the settlement's physician and a security officer?"

"Yes."

"Was the vehicle the only thing you stole?"

"Yes."

"Did you not return later and steal something else? Something Mr. Halbert describes as a piece of audio equipment?"

"Yes. I've been up front about this from the beginning."

Stephanie looked at Sid, who, for his part, traded a glance with Darcy.

Stephanie glanced at the captain. "No further questions."

"You may step down, Dr. Odega." said Ransom.

"The prosecution rests," Stukov said.

The captain took a deep breath and held it. Once Odega was out of the room, he exhaled loudly and turned to Stephanie. "Your turn, counselor."

"Thank you, sir. The defense calls Robert Keller."

"Ms. Beaumont," the captain offered a patronizing smile. "You are well aware Mr. Keller has not surfaced at this point."

"Captain, a witness called has one hour to appear, prior to being stricken from the list."

"Very well, another call shall go out for him. In the meantime, your next witness?"

"Captain, if a given witness has testimony critical to the defense, I have the right to withhold from further questioning until the witness is located or the hour has passed."

Ransom winced. He wanted this over and done with. "Congratulations, counselor, you have your recess. Commander, make another general announcement requesting the presence of

Mr. Keller. Add to it that if he doesn't show he'll face the maximum penalty for not responding to the captain's summons."

"Yes, sir."

"Since I doubt Mr. Keller will appear at this point, we will reconvene in one hour, and counselor?"

"Yes, Captain?"

"You realize I'm going to plug this loophole at my earliest convenience."

"Yes, sir. I know that."

Ransom banged the gavel, and left, Commander Stukov immediately behind him.

"Nice," Stephanie stated in a tone that said it was anything but. She turned her chair around to face them. "When I told you tell me everything, apparently you thought I meant something else."

"I knew Ted was here," Sid exclaimed. He strained at his cuffs. "What didn't we tell you?"

"About Donald Graff, about the first time you met."

"Didn't think it was important. Anyway, we've got Odega. He just admitted he's a thief. He's lying about not trapping us here. Tear him apart. If you don't think you can, I'll do it."

Stephanie's face softened. "You don't understand. However he managed it, Dr. Odega is a citizen. That gives his word weight, where yours has none. Neither the captain nor the XO flinched when he admitted to assault and theft. Dr. Leighton and Dr. Chen, their word is gold. Your friend must know his stuff to impress them the way he has. Also explains why you've been chasing him."

"I don't see the problem," said Darcy. "He's admitted the crimes he's committed against us. Obviously he'd do anything to prevent us from taking him back."

"He doesn't have to do anything." Stephanie was exasperated. "There's no extradition from *Terpris*. In the past, people have been admitted with questionable backgrounds, provided they have something to offer. Unless he commits an offense here—"

"He has committed offenses here," said Sid.

"If they commit offenses here, there's nowhere to escape to. They'll be found, put on the barge, or splashed. He's not on trial here, you are. He's been honest about his past without needing to be. The way he behaved when he saw you, even if I…don't believe him, I feel the captain did."

"Then your captain is an idiot," said Sid.

Stephanie shot a worried glance at the guards. "Don't say that again." Her assistant chose that moment to enter the room. She shook her head to Stephanie's questioning look, and took her chair.

"So, my associate was unable to find a witness that Seaman Reid left his post. She also wasn't able to dig up any dirt on him. Given a day or two…well, no use wishing for what you can't have."

"You act as if we've already been convicted," said Lena. "I thought you were the best lawyer in *Terpris*."

"Don't sass me, girl." Her West African accent thickened and her head bobbed a bit as she said it.

In the middle of everything, it was the head bob that turned Sid on. She glanced back to him and caught his look, fleeting as it was. He knew she saw it because of the way her eyes widened, just a tiny bit.

"We still have Donald Graff," said Darcy. "When he testifies on our behalf—"

"I'm striking him from my list," said Stephanie. "There's nothing he can say that won't just do more damage on cross.

"But he's the only friend we've got on board."

"Maybe not." For the remainder of their time she questioned them intensely about Compton Pit. The people, the settlements they traded with, the political atmosphere both within and without. She could sense they were holding back in certain areas, but she moved on, not wanting to waste precious minutes picking. The hour passed all too quickly.

Ransom took his chair, folded his hands on the desk in front of him, looked towards the door when Mark. "Marshal, Mr. Keller has put his foot in it this time. You'll finally get to punish him, once he's found."

"I think he skipped town," said Mark. "Maybe this was a last score before making for places where people don't know him."

"Maybe," offered Stukov, "you people killed him and stashed his body once he helped you get below."

"Objection," yelled Stephanie.

Ransom laughed. "Councilor, we haven't reconvened." He banged his gavel. "Now we have. Go ahead."

"Yes, sir. Call Petty Officer Thomas Kunaha."

For a second, Darcy thought Seth Boomatay, Compton Pit's chief of stores, had entered. But this man, though he shared Seth's round face and Polynesian features, was stockier. His nose was wider and both his arms were healthy and fully functional. He wore khakis, though they were rumpled, and a grease stain marred one lapel. Still, the resemblance was strong. Darcy suddenly felt homesick.

"Mr. Kunaha, what is your function aboard *Terpris*?"

"I'm a pit snipe, ma'am. I direct a shift in the boiler room and perform regular maintenance on all her systems."

"Have you ever had reason to work in maintenance access 06, on the port side of the Second deck?"

"Yes ma'am. There's a number of pipe joints in there. They have to get tested."

"Tell me about the temperature in that room."

"It's a sealed compartment. Most of the pipes in there carry steam for the turbines. Because of its size, it can get hotter even than the boiler room."

"How long do you think you could spend in there, Mr. Kunaha? Let's say, on a dare, or better, on a bet."

"That's a dare I wouldn't take and a bet I wouldn't make. When she's all fired up, fifteen minutes in a place like that is twenty minutes too long. It's not just the heat, it's the noise as well."

"Tell me more about the noise."

"There's a reason above and below 06 is just storage. Over the years, we've had to use replacement pipe barely compatible with the rest of the system. When we're in port, or anchored for a few days, the pipes contract. When the steams starts going, they expand unevenly. The noise is insane. I wear ear protectors when I'm in there while we're stoking up."

"Thank you. No further questions."

"Mr. Kunaha," said Stukov, "as well as performing regular maintenance on the pipes, you also look after the hatch?"

"No, sir, not usually."

"But you did check it today?"

"Yes, sir. At least one of my men did. If there's a chance I could get stuck in there..." he shuddered. "There was nothing wrong with the hatch. Nothing at all."

"You speak of metal expanding and contracting. Is it possible for a hatch to become jammed from one side to the degree where no amount of force can open it, only to fix itself?"

"No, sir."

"No further questions."

"Dismissed," said Ransom. "Who's next, Miss Beaumont?"

"Call Dr. Timothy Leighton."

Dr. Leighton came into the room and took his chair. He was a tall, slim man, with grayish-white hair and clear, alert eyes.

"Dr. Leighton," Stephanie began, "are you familiar with Robert Keller?"

"You know I am. Yes. I know Robert Keller. I know Spider."

"How would you describe him?"

"He's an untrustworthy little scoundrel. Still, he has a knack for acquiring things once in a while."

"So you've used his services?"

"Nearly everyone in *Terpris* has...once in a while."

"Have you had any contact with Mr. Keller in the last few days?"

"No."

"To the best of your knowledge, has Dr. Odega made any contact with him in the last few days?"

"No."

"Was Dr. Odega out of your sight any time between 08:00 and 16:00 today?"

"For a minute at a time, maybe. No longer than that."

"Dr. Leighton, Timothy…in your brief experience with him, would you describe Dr. Odega as a man of integrity?"

"For what I've seen, yes."

"Has he spoken with you of his past concerning the accused?"

"At length."

"At any time, has Dr. Odega displayed signs of irrationality, of being unbalanced? In short, do you think he's watered?"

"No. I have seen no evidence to support that."

"Thank you. No further questions."

"Cross?" the captain offered Stukov.

"None, sir. The defense seems to be fighting for my side."

"You may step down, Dr. Leighton."

Sid gripped one of Stephanie's sleeves and pulled her close. "What are you doing?" he hissed.

"I'm gambling your lives, Mr. Halbert." She pulled away from him. "Call Dr. Theodore Odega."

Odega was readmitted. He made eye contact with Sid and shook his head sadly.

"Dr. Odega, given the circumstances of your departure from Compton Pit. Do you believe they would welcome you back if you chose to return?"

"No. I broke a number of laws. I'd be locked outside."

"Dr. Leighton says you had in-depth discussions concerning your previous dwelling. Is that true?"

"Yes."

"Did you mention specific names and places?"

"Yes."

"Did you physically describe people? Hair and skin color? Visible scars?"

"I may have."

"Were these conversations in private locals? Just the two of you?"

Odega pondered the question. "No. Some were in the mess hall, some in common areas."

"Dr. Odega, do you believe Sid Halbert would come all this way with the intent to do you harm?"

"No."

"Would you describe Mr. Halbert as an honorable man?"

"Without a second's hesitation."

Stukov's eyes narrowed. From the tension in his body, he wanted to object, but couldn't think of a reason to do so.

"To your knowledge has he committed any crimes for which he would have to flee Compton Pit?"

"No."

"No further questions."

Stephanie sat down, smiling at the dumbfounded expression on the face of Sid and the others.

Stukov rose and approached the witness. "Dr. Odega, did you let anyone know you were coming here when you left Compton Pit."

"No. I had no idea at the time that this was my destination."

"So in order for the accused to be here, he would have had to track you from place to place."

"Yes, I suppose so."

"So he and his group have been hunting you."

"Objection," said Stephanie. "Commander Stukov needs to brush up on his Jeopardy."

Stukov looked confused.

"I think she means phrase it as a question," Caps stage whispered.

Everybody glared at him.

"Sustained," said Ransom.

Stukov nodded. "In your past experience, is Mr. Halbert the type to give up on something?"

"Oh, no. He persists until…" Odega clamped his mouth shut.

Stukov removed a book from his bag. It was the same journal he'd pulled on Graff. He flipped through it, briefly scanned one page, then replaced the journal in his bag.

"Dr. Odega, what did Mr. Halbert do in the old world?"

"Do? I'm not sure I follow you."

"What was his profession?"

"Objection," said Stephanie. "Relevance?"

Before the captain could respond, Stukov broke in. "Character, sir. It is one question, not a line of questioning."

"I'll allow it. Dr. Odega, answer the question."

"He…he was a police officer." He sounded mystified by the question.

"A city police officer? A small town officer? What type exactly?"

"He was in the RCMP. Royal Canadian Mounted Police."

"Thank you. No further questions."

Ransom instructed Dr. Odega to step down, then raised his eyes to Stephanie.

"The defense rests, Captain."

Ransom was surprised, but not so much that he didn't raise his gavel in anticipation of an outburst from the defendants. He was not disappointed. Sid and Darcy were both quite vocal in their disgust with the way they'd been represented. He banged twice before they were silent and a third time before they sat down. Once everything was to his satisfaction, he turned to his XO.

"Ready to close?"

Stukov stood, nodded at Stephanie, then turned to the captain. "Sir, I do not need to repeat the crimes or the accuseds' version of events. The method in which they claim they gained access to the lower decks is unsupported, and therefore, irrelevant. Sid Halbert knew Dr. Odega was on board, and when his brief attempt at reaching him through legal means were met with frustration, he directed his subordinates to stowaway in order to extend the hunt. I only guess at his motivations. It may be that he intended to help Dr. Odega. It is more likely he endangered both himself and those that serve him to satisfy a personal need for success.

"Tales of the legendary RCMP came even to my country. As a child I heard stories. Wonderful stories of adventure, and in those stories, one theme was consistant: the Mountie always gets his man. As a leader, a lawmaker, this is not a bad philosophy, but in this case, following through included violating our laws. Sid Halbert and his subordinates are stowaways."

He sat down, completely satisfied.

Stephanie stood and turned to regard Stukov. She offered Mark a smile, then with a small laugh, faced the captain. "Robert Keller, Spider, earns his living listening to things. Hiding under stairwells and in the backs of closets, it's how he got his nickname, he's always in the corner. It is my contention that he eavesdropped on Dr. Odega's conversations with Dr. Leighton, and using information garnered from this, jumped at the opportunity to strip money from the accused. I do not suggest that he physically assaulted anyone, but an accomplice could have performed that end. I do not deny that the defendants ventured into unauthorized areas, but it was not their intention to stay there. Quite simply, they are not guilty of the crime with which they are charged.

"They should be considered ambassadors, guests if you will. If that will not do, consider this: Dr. Odega was granted citizenship despite his past, presumably for his skills and knowledge as a scientist. It was in the opinion of Master Chief Porter and both Doctors Leighton and Chen that he has merit and integrity, and for all intents and purposes, both you and your executive officer agree. By Odega's account, Sid Halbert is also a man of integrity. We have here experts in the fields of administration, mechanics, electrical engineering, communications and security. As such they are of equal merit.

"Dr. Odega committed his crimes mere months ago, and you have decided to ignore this. And yet Commander Stukov wants to convict Sid Halbert based on a catch phrase from a departed era. To forgive Dr. Odega, and convict these people is both a direct contradiction, and a waste of exploitable resources. Don't splash or barge these people, Captain. Offer them a chance to earn their keep until the next port. Our laws were written to protect the people, sir, not to protect the law."

32. To Protect the Law

Ransom didn't go to another chamber to deliberate, he simply turned his chair so its high back was to the rest of the room. At one point his right hand appeared from behind the chair. It signaled for coffee, or whatever was in the mug delivered by the sailor.

Commander Stukov stood and requested permission to leave. The captain granted it without turning around. The XO had no personal interest in the outcome of the case. He'd played the prosecutor because it was his duty to do so. Right now, the foremost thing on his mind was why MCPO Porter had been so negligent in his reporting of the immigration of Dr. Odega. More importantly, why had he personally accepted responsibility for admission of a potentially dangerous man? Stukov himself would have passed that one up to the captain.

Sid and his group were admonished for trying to speak to each other in even the quietest whispers. Stephanie and the Marshal seemed to know when one of them was even thinking about opening their mouths.

Sid tried to put himself in Ransom's shoes. What would he do? A man with admitted transgressions is accepted to the Pit. He'd need something very valuable indeed, and there was no doubt in Sid's mind what Dr. Odega had used to buy passage. Either he'd gotten the Mimi working independent of Gershwin, or his abilities as a salesman were greater than Sid had given him credit for. So, what to do with a group of people found locked in an empty room? It was fairly simple. Provided they'd learned nothing useful to enemies of Compton Pit, send them packing if they had a vehicle. If they didn't...under most circumstances, Sid would lock them outside. For the first time, the idea of complete failure became a solid possibility.

Lena, who'd accepted death hours before, squeezed Caps's hand and examined memories one by one, some with nostalgia, a few with regret. All in all, she had nothing to complain about. She'd achieved a position of importance and respect within her community, a position her parents would have been proud of. If they were still alive it was something they could brag about over bathtub gin and wolf-liver pâté at some cave-dweller's hobnob. She'd had ten years of life after the Change, which was a decade more than billions of people. She'd loved, and was loved by a wonderful man. Lena despaired that she wouldn't get one last chance to express that love.

Darcy put her faith in Sid. If the verdict was guilty, he would still get them out of there. Her belief in him had been shaken of late, but she put that out of her mind. No point in undermining the one thing that kept the panic at bay.

Caps was worried sick, but couldn't show it for Lena's sake. He held down the leg that threatened to tremble with the hand not clasped in Lena's, and kept his face frozen in an expression of quiet confidence.

Noah went with complete denial, augmented by optimistic fantasy. The captain was going to turn around, apologize for any inconvenience, and sail them right back to Astoria. Even better, *Terpris* would go farther up the coast and drop them off at Piper's Cove. That would be a coup, a yarn to top any of the stories the fishers had to offer.

The expression on Ransom's face when he did turn around dispelled any daydreams of out-bragging the Cove's mariners.

"Commander Stukov," the captain began, "did not need to present anything other than that you were where you were. We have one rule concerning outsiders entering unauthorized areas. We expel them. Were you discovered prior to departure, it would have saved us all a great deal of trouble.

"I've been in maintenance access 06, or a space like it, and I do not think even a swarm of wasps outside could keep me in there voluntarily for the duration you endured. I do not, however, believe that Dr. Odega had anything to do with your confinement. In the essence of expedience, I choose to take the door opened by the defense and lay the blame for this at Robert Keller's feet. The defendants will rise." They did so. "Noah Thurlow, Richard Scagling, Lena Wong, each of you will be given an opportunity to prove your worth in your chosen field. Since you have each risen to the position of chief at your settlement, I assume you'll be of some use to us. Darcy McCullough, the security detail of the Navy is full. As such—"

"Maybe he can use me," said Darcy, jerking her thumb at the Old Bull.

Stephanie groaned inwardly at the breach of protocol, but the captain didn't seem to mind.

"I can't use her," said Mark.

"Miss McCullough," the captain gained her attention, "since you are physically capable, you will be assigned duties where that is of use."

Great, thought Darcy. *I'm swabbing decks*.

"Sid Halbert, your skills would be administration and coordination of people and resources. However, considering your current situation, I do not have much faith in those skills. As leader of this group you accept responsibility for the consequences of both your own actions and the actions carried out by your subordinates. Rules were broken, rules outlined clearly to you by two officers of the civilian court. No matter what your motive, you knowingly and willingly entered unauthorized areas. The barge, one year." He banged the gavel. "Court is adjourned."

Immediately, two sailors took Sid by the arms and dragged him away.

"Wait," said Darcy, then louder, "Wait!" She tried to follow, but another sailor moved to bar her passage. He was quickly pushed aside and replaced by Mark. Even handcuffed, Darcy would have made short work of the sailor. The Old Bull was a different story and they both knew it.

"What does that mean?" she demanded of Stephanie. "What happens on the barge?"

"Don't make any trouble," ordered Sid as he was pulled through the hatch.

"I'm not going to be thrown over the side?" Lena said, disbelieving.

"Are there any cars on board?" asked Caps.

"Commander Stukov will return shortly," said Ransom as he passed them. "Councilor, good job, but you were wrong about one thing. The law must protect both the people and itself."

"Yes, sir. About my clients' restraints?"

"Marshal, remove their cuffs."

"Clients," said Caps, rubbing his newly-free wrists.

"It's no joke," said Stephanie. "Had you all gone over the side, the Merchants Guild would remunerate me. It would be a token, an honorarium. Now I'm free to charge my regular fee."

"Shouldn't you have discussed this with us before this started?" asked Lena.

"Why? Would you have refused counsel?"

"We'll pay," said Darcy, stepping up in Sid's absence. "What's the barge?"

"It's better than being splashed, that's what it is."

"That year was a formality, right?" asked Caps. "I mean, we'll all be tossed off at the next port, right?"

Stephanie shook her head. "You four will disembark at Diego. Mr. Halbert will serve the duration of his sentence, providing he survives it. After that, he'll be free to go."

"Where is this ship going to be in a year?" asked Darcy.

"An ocean away, honey. You'll be staying in the pokey again tonight. There's just nowhere else to put you." She left.

Everybody was gone now except for the Old Bull.

"You people are my problem now," said Mark. He moved behind the desk, but didn't sit, choosing instead to lean on it with his fists. With his almost seven-foot height and dangling hair, it was an effectively intimidating posture. "Listen up. These are the rules, and follow them this time. You have access to the Street, the Valley, your berthing space, when you get it, and your area of work, also mess halls one and two, and the Dirty Shirt, that's a lounge, not a laundry, plus the cramps used to get to and from these locations. Anything else is out of bounds. If you get lost, stop where you are immediately and ask for directions. You are on the tightest probation. One problem, the tiniest thing, and your stay is over. As far as the rest of the rules go, follow the Ten Commandments, but replace 'God' with 'the Bull.' "

Darcy thought he was arrogant and overbearing. Noah found him terrifying. Caps thought he was cool.

"Would you actually toss me over the side for sleeping with a married woman?" asked Caps.

"No. I'd let her husband do it. As of now you are considered guests….put your hand down, this isn't kindergarten."

Noah dropped his hand. "Do all guests get put up in the pokey?"

"It's too late to beg somebody for floor space and I doubt you can afford to book a room in the hotel."

"Of course there's a hotel," said Caps, as if he knew it all along. "Does it have a casino? What about a show room?"

"There's a stage in Tanzers, on the Street. The casino is a floating craps game, and if you find it, you can bet *I'll* find it. Don't be there when I do. I'm going to take you to sick bay now where one of our doctors will tell you to drink a lot of water. From there, one of my people will take you to the mess hall, and then back to the pokey. Obey him like I'm standing behind you the whole time. Let's go."

Master Chief Petty Officer William Porter lived in a small house in the valley. It wasn't an elaborate structure by any means. The kitchen/dining room window faced the amidships starboard opening, and occasionally sunlight spilled through and made pretty colors through the prisms hung by Mrs. Porter.

Mrs. Porter was visiting friends, and William sat in the kitchen, going over a diagram with the captain.

Ransom dragged a fingernail across the schematic, then pushed it back across the table to Chief Porter. “It means nothing to me, and therefore explains nothing.”

“Me either,” said Porter, folding the schematic neatly and placing it in his breast pocket. “But it means a great deal to Dr. Leighton and Dr. Chen, and these are just their best guesses so far.”

“This small box can repel anything? Birds, insects?”

“It has the potential. Gerry, I had no idea any of this was going to happen. The equipment is useless without the man’s knowledge. With his past bouts of paranoia, aggressive behavior, the mess he made leaving this Compton Pit place… I felt it was an acceptable risk.”

“I wouldn’t have admitted him,” said Ransom. “I doubt Mikhail would have.”

“Neither of you could afford to. That’s why I waited until we left port. If he flips out, it falls on my head, not yours.”

The captain leaned back in his chair and stared at the ceiling. The stucco had been recently redone. “Bill, I’m going to take that sword away from you, you keep falling on it for me.”

“You’ve got a visitor,” said the middle-aged sailor on night watch in the brig.

He oozed sourness and the Boss thought he knew the reason why. The lack of color on his uniform showed that at his age, he hadn’t advanced very far even in a Navy that had limited recruiting capabilities. Sid folded his arms across his bare chest, and looked up in expectation of red hair and sympathetic eyes. What he received was a guarded look, and no hair whatsoever.

Dr. Odega looked through the gray, steel bars and asked the sailor quietly, “Can you open the door?”

“No,” said Sid. “I’d rather keep something between us.”

“Put your hands through the bars,” ordered the guard.

“Forget it.”

“So you want the hose again?”

Sid’s lip curled. He looked at his shirt, hang drying off one corner of the top bunk. He stood and did as he was told.

“For your protection,” the guard said to Odega as he snapped cuffs on Sid’s wrists. He opened the cell door, and locked it behind the visitor.

“Where are you going?” Sid asked the guard’s retreating back. The hatch closed and he was alone with Dr. Odega. He put his weight on his right leg, preparing to kick if he had to.

Odega sat on the lower bunk, as far away as possible, and folded his hands in his lap. "I never meant for this to happen."

"Of course not. You meant for us to die in that room, or get thrown over the side if we didn't. You led us here, dropping crumbs behind you everywhere you went."

"Crumbs? You think I *wanted* you to follow me? All I want is to continue my research. Why do you think I signed on to this…this floating coffin? Sid, it was temporary insanity, what happened. When I came to myself again, I couldn't go back to the Pit. We both know that."

"Temporary insanity? From what I was told you were behaving quite rationally. Pearl Harbored Harpreet and Purty, killed Gandhi and even had time to destroy most of your notes. What about Remo Tyree? Trading our van to him? Pointing him right at Underbel?"

"The van's a guzzler. That was expedience. I assume Underbel purchased the van from him and then sold it back to you?"

"So it was just a coincidence that he resembled you?" his voice was heavy with sarcasm.

"You mean…Underbel didn't know, did they? You went there thinking it really was me." Odega shook his head ruefully. "Sid, I haven't had a drink in five months. Not one. I have moments of irrational anger, but I recognize them for what they are. I write down what I'm thinking, I pour my rage into the page, as it were. Afterwards, I read what I've written, and I analyze my mental condition. I'm of no danger to anyone. Not at the moment anyway."

Sid felt a part of himself beginning to believe the doctor, but the cuffs and bars let him stay hard. "You gave them the Mimi, didn't you?"

"Yes. They're no danger to the Pit, Sid. You think this bunch would stage a raid so far inland? My work must continue. That's all that's important."

"How did you do it, Ted? How did you tame the dog?"

"I did nothing to Gandhi. She—"

"You're lying. You lied on the stand, unless you're so tooth crazy, you think you're telling the truth."

"Do I seem tooth crazy to you?"

"You were a brilliant man, Ted. Now you're a brilliant lunatic."

Odega gave him a long look. "I didn't come here for this. I came for clarification, and to say goodbye. I intend to have nothing to do with you or the others. They could be years on this ship and our paths would never cross, unless I wanted them to. I don't. Guard! I wish things hadn't turned out as they did."

So heavy was Odega's face with sorrow and regret, Sid had nothing to say to it. He was stunned, all his suspicions dashed away, leaving him with nothing but his own bullheadedness and a missing dirtbag nicknamed Spider.

Dr. Odega and the guard were gone, the hatch closed behind them before Sid remembered his wrists were still cuffed through the bars.

33. Water City

August, Year of the Change

Ransom stood on the bridge, fingers traced the contours of his scars, exploring the new geography of his face, as they had done countless times since the bandages had come off. Perhaps it was his slow way of working up to being able to look in the mirror for more than a few moments. He was never a handsome man, not ugly, but never handsome. His cheekbones were too low, his chin just a shade on the weak side. It was the face of an uncle, or the neighborhood grocer. Now it was the face of a pirate, and it was applicable because that's what he was. A pirate of lost vessels, grave robber of the seas.

"All stop, Captain," said Lt. Sung. "We're right beside her."

"Good. Mr. Keiths?"

"No change, sir. Clear waters."

"Let's give it twenty minutes." Ransom took his chair.

Underwater cameras were now mounted on the bow and starboard side. Fifty caliber machine guns recovered from a French cruiser were mounted on the catwalks around the flight deck. A pair of crude catapults sat on the hangar deck, prepared to throw barrel bombs to clear the sea. The lesson of the *Rybinsk* would not need to be repeated. The carrier and her crew had since looted two tankers, a cargo ship and a luxury cruise liner. They rescued the survivors, half-mad and half-starved. Of smaller vessels, only those abandoned still floated. The general theory was that once the people were off the boat, or it held only corpses, it no longer interested anything in the deep. It was the same story each time: captains who'd chosen not to attempt landfall; who'd taken their vessels out to sea to avoid the birds and then wait for everything to calm down. The boats would run out of fuel first, then water if they didn't have purifying equipment on board.

Today's catch was a hundred-and-twenty-foot pleasure boat named *Cinnamon Audrey*. On New Wilderness Day, it was doubling as a floating stage for a high-budget porno shot on 8mm and featuring at least one actress worthy of the title. It was the seventh in a series chronicling the repetitive adventures of high-seas DEA agents Foxy Mulbush and her partner Dan Skull.

The appearance of dolphins off the stern during the filming of scene seven—Agent Foxy extracts information from a smuggler by rubbing him with her tonsils—inspired Director Wally. Looking to add an artistic touch, he ordered his actresses over the side. The actor who leapt in to save them fared no better than the cameraman perched close to the water on the afterdeck.

The captain of the boat, below deck, fondling a starlet he'd plied with heroin, heard nothing. He was on top of the girl when the birds swept his first mate and Director Wally over the side. He was halfway through his cigarette when his second mate and the surviving actor left the aft cabin to find out what all the noise was about.

Eventually, his plaything headed up to see if her three-way with Dan Skull and deckhand Donna was ready to shoot. The captain smoked a joint and had a nap. When he awoke of his own accord, not because someone had come to get him, he assumed he'd been out for less than an hour. He was shocked to see starlight through the porthole, and astounded when nobody responded to his calls. The sight of two bloodstained gulls, sleeping near the savaged body of his second mate drove him to hysterics. The gulls awoke, and attacked. The captain made it below deck with minor lacerations and ran to his communications station. The scanner, by habit always on and set to the frequency of the nearest coastguard, sang its tale of death in a medley of voices.

The handset, poised to transmit a mayday, dropped from the captain's hand.

Col. Mills's boarding party knew nothing of this. What they did know was they had a pile of camera equipment, a small cache of weapons and a large cache of heroine, which they never would have found had it not been for the corpse, belt cinched around one bicep, lying next to a hatch that, when closed, all but disappeared into the bulkhead.

The fate of the drugs became yet another point of contention during the meetings of the Ship's Council, and the contentions were many.

The Flag staff's dining room had been converted to a parliament of sorts.

Captain Ransom had, as yet, kept his place at the head of the table through intelligent debate, and when that didn't work, hard-ass bullying, made all the more effective by his new face. That the majority of his sailors were still loyal to the chain of command spoke of Ransom's capabilities and of their desperate need for order.

The civilians, initially obeisant to the commands of the Navy, now barely acknowledged its authority. In every group there were leaders and there were followers, but there were far too many leaders here for Ransom's liking. Even Col. Mills seemed to be edging for more clout.

The Russian ambassador sat with Captain Stukov at his side. As the only other country besides America with a military presence at the table, the ambassador sat tall. It was good to be a super power again.

The Japanese delegates had gotten their equal share of SatCom and HF radio time. Japan was in a truly sorry state. Snow monkeys were in every city, living in habitats by the hundreds within the city cores, running wild and pillaging homes on the outskirts. Multiple companies in Japan put food on the table installing grids and cages around people's properties. On June 10th, the monkeys showed that they knew all along how to escape the habitats, and how truly ineffectual the monkey barriers over the back yards were.

Of the Middle East, only military compounds in Israel and one outside of Riyadh, Saudi Arabia, were conversing. There were transmissions from somewhere in Iran, but all they said was that the chaos would continue until the Children of Judah were pushed into the sea.

Ambassadors from England, France, Spain, Australia and China were all in the same position. What superiors they could contact couldn't give them a plan of action because one simply didn't exist.

For the three-thousand, seven-hundred and sixty-one people on board the carrier, no matter where they'd once lived, the floating city was their home now.

"I didn't sign on to be the mayor of Waterworld," said Ransom. They were on the gallery level—the 03 deck—in the admiral's stateroom. Comfortable leather chairs, wood paneling. Ransom had once taken drinks here with Captain Huff, privilege of rank allowing them to sup nectar forbidden to the crew. Captain Huff was not the man he once was, and Ransom had taken to having his sherry with Captain Stukov.

"You get ahead of yourself, Captain," said Stukov. "Watercity, perhaps, but hardly Waterworld."

"The Arabs want to change the name of the carrier, and that bloody Englishman, Riddleford, is siding with them."

"You are English yourself, yes? You use some of their colloquialisms."

"I'm fifth generation American. When I was six, my father died in a car accident. My mother remarried. My stepfather was British. Ex-Navy, ex-boozer. He was a good man. He gave me a motorcycle when I earned my wings. Hmph. Did you hear what I just said? *Was* a good man. I have no proof he's dead."

"This is good," said Stukov, referring to his drink. "I feel guilty that you and I should sit in these soft chairs, while our loved ones hide or have already traveled through an animal's digestive tract."

Ransom liked Stukov, although the man could be excessively colorful in his ramblings.

"I don't know how much longer the men will hold out, Mikhail. If this is truly where we are to live, all of us…it's not much of a life. Most of my crew are boys, and there's a distinct shortage of women on board. We've still got over forty people incarcerated. There's talk of throwing them over the side."

"A sound idea," said Stukov, refilling his glass from a crystal decanter. "I realize…may I?" He reached for the humidor that sat between them, "…the idea may offend your sensibilities, but we do not have the resources to spare, yes? Perhaps the time for certain mercies is at an end."

"You're so full of shit, Mikhail. You waited on board your own ship to release the mutineers, or whatever it is you call them. Being merciful saved your life. Eight of those who might have to go swimming are your men, by the way."

"This level of dissention…this would not happen on a Russian carrier."

"As soon as we find a Russian carrier, you can prove that to me. In the mean time, it's not a surprise at all. In a perfect world, we'd all pull together in a nice, floating commune. We're mostly Americans on this ship, and commune smacks too much of communism."

"So give them capitalism."

"Come again?"

"Split the ship. You have enough of it. Create civilian areas. You have machine shops. Stamp out money. Make this a city in form as well as name. The foundation is already laid for you. A black market exists, as does a small brothel in pilot country." Pilot country referred to the berthing and ready rooms in the forward section of the 03 deck, once reserved for pilots only. With no air wing on board, the comparatively luxurious spaces had been filled up by senior petty officers and civilians of perceived rank.

"I had no idea. I'll have to put a stop to that."

"The black market, definitely. I would leave the brothel if I were you." Stukov pocketed two cigars. "Or at least wait until morning, yes?"

Ransom checked the humidor. The supply had dwindled to less than a dozen. "I understand Cuba's nice this time of year."

34. Slam

They spent their last night in the civilian jail. In the early hours of the morning Lena awoke in a cold sweat. It was a nightmare, but not of animals. She was a little girl on her father's first boat, a rickety twenty-six footer that taught her parents to be mechanics, carpenters and fierce dependants on prayer. Her father was explaining to her that they were on their last boat ride, that after this, she would never sail again.

The dream faded, and as she closed her eyes, she noted that the slight swaying of the deck wasn't quite as discomforting as it was before.

Dawn came and Officer Curtis Sloan opened their cells and gave them towels, some misshapen slivers of soap, and four buckets of hot water. Curtis was a large man, but had a slow quality to him Caps couldn't resist picking on. The artist tossed a couple of insulting zingers that went so far above Curtis's head, they blew past people on the flight deck.

Showering together was so ingrained in them, the four had no problem stripping down and getting to it. Curtis eyed the women until Lena shucked her leg off, then he looked away guiltily.

"I'm taking your clothes." Curtis came into the cells to do just that. "You'll find stuff in the box. We took up a collection."

The clothes they had were saturated with every drop of sweat their bodies could produce inside maintenance access 06.

They grabbed handfuls of garments from the box and stared at their prizes. Noah grabbed at what he thought were pants, but turned out to be a skirt. An ugly skirt. Frayed to tassels at the hem, purple with big yellow flowers. The others all had trousers.

"Lena," Noah held the dress out, "this might be easier, with your leg, and all."

"Nice try," she balanced easily on the prosthetic while pulling the trousers up her other leg.

"Darcy, I can't—"

"And you think I can?" She laughed at him.

"Darcy." It was a command.

She blinked. He'd never used that tone with her before, not outside a life-threatening situation, anyway. She decided not to fight him.

"Here, these are too big for me anyway." She shot a warning glance at Caps as she accepted and pulled on the skirt.

"Yeah, I'm gonna talk," he indicated his jacket. It had wide lapels and thin, alternating horizontal lines of black and white. "This is from the seventies. Civilization collapsed, but this piece of shit managed to survive. Hey Curtis, enough of this, huh? We spent the night in Quickdraw McGraw's house, now you've got us dressed up like…dude, I'm not expecting you to know this from experience, but it's better to look good than to smell good."

Curtis's cheek twitched slightly. He mumbled something at the floor, then said, "Let's go. Scagling, Thurlow, you're going to Tanzers. Wong, there's a sailor waiting for you. McCullough, the Old Bull wants to see you.

"I already said no." Mark had his feet up on his desk.

Darcy cracked her knuckles. "What's it going to take to make you reconsider? Hmm? What if I take you down?"

The office had precious little in it: the Old Bull's desk, a few chairs, some filing cabinets and a miniature basketball hoop mounted on the inside of the door.

Mark put his hands behind his head. "One, you couldn't take me down. Two, even if you could, the answer'd still be no."

"Why?" She was trying her best but her temper was coming. "I bet I'm more capable than half your men."

"Oh, I know what you can do. I was in New Portland. I watched you fight." Mark's eyes dipped to her breasts. It was a polite dip; down and right back up again.

"Then why—"

"Because you'd have to keep proving yourself. None of the barge rats would take you seriously. You'd be the worst guard ever. It would get messy."

"I don't think that—"

"If you were a foot taller and butt ugly, I'd chance it. But you ain't a foot taller and you sure ain't ugly. Well, maybe in that skirt…"

Darcy wanted to punch him. "How big can that barge be? Word'd get around. I'd put the fear of me into a couple of guys and word would get around."

"Mmhmm." Mark swung his legs from the desk and planted his feet hard on the floor. He looked out the window at the dim light of the Valley, and imagined the sun that was rising over the deck above. "Word would get around alright. Sooner or later they'd get you alone, get you with numbers. It'd go bad. You'd have extra holes by the time they were finished. No way. No barge guard job for you."

Darcy glanced at the office door. It was locked. "How long are you going to keep me here?"

"Until your boss man is on the barge."

She crossed her arms, clenched her jaw. "You're not keeping the others locked up."

"I'm not worried about the others. You? I think you'd try something stupid and I'd have to splash you."

"We were trapped here. Deliberately. This is so wrong."

"Wrong is a matter of perspective, girl. But you'll learn that soon enough."

"It's up here," said Caps, pulling Noah past a light blue hull.

"Where'd that sailor take Lena?" Noah ran his fingers around the curved structure. He glanced at the brackets and bolts that fixed the thing to the deck.

"She's going tech rep, it seems. Civilian aid to the Navy. What a joke."

The Street was laid out in three zones. Manufacturing and industry was furthest aft. Residential structures, nearly all of them small boats, filled the middle stripe. Closest to the bow stood the commercial area, shops and such, with Tanzers in the middle.

"It's not a joke to these sailors," said Noah.

"Yeah, that's what's so funny. They act like nothing's changed. Inspections, salutes, sir, yes sir! They're all cowards. None of 'em want to have to think for themselves. Every enlisted man is a sheep. Every officer is an egomaniac."

"How's it different from the Pit? We run our lives by the bells. Our uniforms are our coveralls and we have marks of rank."

"You ever see me wear marked coveralls?"

"No."

"Only person who ever told me what to wear was my mommy. And that stopped about the same time I learned how to tie my own shoes."

Tanzers was once a luxury houseboat permanently moored at an east coast dock. The red-bearded Arnold Tanzer didn't own the houseboat, but he'd spent enough time on it that he could have been considered a resident. Tanzer was the party wizard. He wasn't quite an agent, and he certainly wasn't a manager. He made it work though. He called the right band, the right caterer. He had the phone numbers of all the elbows people wanted to rub. Private performance from the latest MTV wunderkind? Done. Dog fight to go with the Dom Perignon? No problem.

Tanzer pulled the strings and he got a cut of everything, from the clarets and canapés to the call girls and cocaine.

Anchored a few kilometers out to sea, the shore a deathtrap, the ocean even worse, Tanzer had stared in awe as the aircraft carrier pulled alongside. He was one of three left alive. The woman stood beside him making strange noises in the back of her throat. The French cinematographer was inside, tied to a bed. He'd gone mad the week previous. They didn't know what to do with him.

Crane arms had swung out from above and a voice had called down, "That's a mighty fine houseboat you've got there. It's about to move up in the world."

Caps and Noah climbed the gangway to find themselves standing on what could have been an outside patio for any restaurant. The major difference was that the furniture was solid steel and bolted down. Noah turned in a circle. The ocean went on forever. "There's so much water," he said.

"C'mon," said Caps, running his gaze along the horizon. "Let's go in."

"I can't see any land. Just water everywhere."

"Yeah, yeah, and nary a bud to smoke. Whatever. Learn to look at it in increments, sun boy. You'll go tooth crazy trying to get it all at once."

The inside of the houseboat looked exactly like what it was—a nightclub. Any internal walls not necessary for structural support had been removed. The long bar took up most of the north wall, at least that's how Noah was thinking of it. North was the bow, south was the stern. He had to think in these terms. Fixed directions were important to him.

On the stage, past the small wooden dance floor, Tivoli sat at the piano wearing dress pants and a bathrobe.

"Good morning," he said, as he struck a high-pitched chord. He wiggled his fingers, then launched into the open bars of 'Morning Mood' from the Peer Gynt Suite.

"So what's the deal here?" asked Caps. "You guys adopt us or something?"

"You're a mechanic," said the cloud of red hair as it came up through a hatch in the floor. "And you're an electrician." He finished his climb but left the hatch open.

"You have a basement?" said Caps. "How much headroom is down there?" He leaned forward to glance down the steps.

"You'll find out, that's where the two of you are going. I've got dozens of appliances and things that don't work anymore. You want to eat, you'll need to change that."

Noah stooped by the hatch. "It looks kind of low."

Tivoli shifted into playing 'In the Hall of the Mountain King'.

"Jeez," said Caps. "Enough with the Smurf soundtrack, okay?"

"You see?" said Tanzer, pointing a beefy finger at Tivoli. "I'm not the only one."

Tivoli stopped playing and sighed. "Guess it was just before my time. I watched Simpsons and South Park."

"So play Simpsons," said Noah.

Tivoli shrugged a shoulder and with one finger plinked out the show's theme music.

Noah's eyes moistened and his lips curved into a wistful smile. Tivoli finished with both hands, hammering the last three chords like Beethoven in a bad mood. He winked at Noah and smiled.

"Yeah," said Caps, looking at Tivoli from the corner of his eye. "Gargamel would have kicked Homer's ass. C'mon, Noah. Let's get started."

"Dammit," said Caps, rubbing his head.

The ceiling touched Noah's hair if he stood up straight. Caps's extra couple of inches was making it tough on him. Every time he moved, he hit his head.

Noah had a disassembled coffee grinder on a table in front of him. He worked by daylight coming in through the portholes.

"Lemme see that," said Caps, picking up the blade and grind cup. He sniffed the cup and ran his finger along the blade. "This wasn't used for grinding coffee. This is a bud buster." He looked up quickly and smacked his nose on the ceiling. "Owe!" He swore a couple of times. "One of these guys has weed. I wonder how much of this junk I'll have to…heh. Will fix for a fix."

Noah pulled the bits from Caps's hands. "Who knows how long this has been sitting around. Who's going to waste electricity on cutting up marijuana?"

"I would," said Caps. "Just give me that chance."

"Do you know if we're allowed to visit the barge?"

"Uh…" Caps leaned down into a pile of gizmos and pulled out a CD/Tape player. "I could probably get what I need out of here to fix that VCR." He put the music box down on the trunk he'd chosen for a workspace. "After you guys crashed I talked to the guard about the barge a bit." He picked up a screwdriver. "The Boss's getting a real raw deal. The barge carries coal for the boilers and other stuff for civilian firewood. Anything that'll burn, practically. Like old furniture. The prisoners' job is to break that stuff down."

"Climb on," said the guard.

Sid eyed the contraption. It looked like an upside-down unicycle. At the it's top, a pulley hung over a steel cable that ran from a post at the stern of the carrier, to a post at the prow of the barge. A chain thick enough to sleep on stretched between *Terpris* and her fuel depot.

"Move it." The guard was losing patience.

Hands manacled, Sid eased himself onto a plank of wood and gripped the handlebars as best he could. *I'm not going to enjoy this*, he thought.

The guard gave him a hard shove and he was off, the aircraft carrier vanishing beneath him. The ocean far below—every inch of it a hungry mouth—unnerved him, so he looked ahead, at his new home. From his perspective it looked like he was headed for the hull, not above it. He saw himself smash into the metal, bounce out of the seat and hit the water. At least the barge would run him over before something else got to him.

Wind stung his face, he felt like he was traveling at the speed of sound. As he neared the barge, Sid understood the cause of the illusion. At the end, a man had let the cable slack, specifically to add a little extra scare. The man cranked a handle and the cable pulled taut. Sid's conveyance came to a swinging halt. Arms grabbed him and hauled him down.

"He's a healthy one," said a gruff voice.

They let him be long enough to gain his feet. There were six of them. Two wore Navy uniforms, the other four were in civy attire, though each of them wore a badge pinned to their right breast. The badges were oval in shape, stamped tin bearing the words *Terpris* Security.

The Old Bull finally let Darcy out of his office and dropped her off at Mistress Cassa's. Darcy was admitted by a middle-aged woman who said nothing and left her alone in a room empty except for a metal bucket.

The inner door was locked, and wandering around outside would probably be a breach of protocol, so Darcy waited, and waited. Finally, the door opened. A woman in her forties with long dark hair and olive skin entered. She wore a long, dark blue dress. She would have been pretty had it not been for the derision on her face.

"Why are you here?" the woman demanded.

"My name's Darcy McCullough, I was—"

"I know who you are."

"Are you Mistress Cassa, then?"

"Your duties are there." She pointed at a bucket sitting in one corner. "Do you need to be told everything?"

Darcy gritted her teeth, took a deep breath, and stopped counting ways she could send the woman to sick bay. She moved to the bucket, and noticed for the first time its contents. A tin, a piece of paper, and small brush, about the size used for scrubbing fingernails. The tin contained an abrasive powder. The paper had written on it "02, F, G, H. 03, F, G."

"What is this?" She held out the paper.

"02 deck, corridors F, G, H. 03 deck, F and G. I suppose you don't know where those are." She said it as if Darcy's ignorance was an indication of stupidity. "I'll have to give you a map then, won't I?"

Darcy understood her position here was somewhere south of bottom of the pole, but there was no call for this. "Listen, lady, I—"

Mistress Cassa stepped forward and put her face right up to Darcy's. "One word from me and you spend the rest of your stay behind bars. You will clean everything. The floor, the walls, handles, everything. You use what you've been given, nothing more. Your shift was supposed to end at 17:00, but since you've wasted an hour standing in my foyer, you will work until 18:00. Is that clear?"

Upside-down with her head in the bucket, that was how Mistress Cassa would be found. Then Darcy thought about Sid. If she was tossed into the brig, she would be in no position to help him. Biting her tongue, she stepped back, and nodded.

"Good," Mistress Cassa produced a cracked, laminated map from somewhere in the dress. "You may take a half hour break. Someone will tell you when. Will you go now, or do I need to show you where to get water?"

"No…ma'am. I'm sure I can find it." *You're going to owe me, Sid*. She thought as she stomped away from the building. *You're going to owe me big time*.

"How's it going down here?" asked Tivoli. He was the same height as Noah. He didn't have to stoop.

"I was going to fix this," said Noah, pointing at the coffee grinder. "But I couldn't do it what with Caps trying to smoke it every time he got close." He tapped a finger on the desk next to a semi-sorted pile of wires and components. "A lot of this stuff is burnt out. I'm cannibalizing parts that I think are good, but I don't trust the circuit tester you gave me."

"We'll get you a better one. Here," he held out a scrap of paper.

"What's this?"

"Go to the first place on the list to borrow some tools. Tell them we sent you. The other two are houses on the Street. Tanzer owes these two women a favor, so you're going to overhaul their solar panel arrays and check their connections to the wind generators." He climbed the steps, singing something under his breath.

"He should stick to the piano," muttered Caps. "He can't sing a note."

"He sings better than you," said Noah. "At least I could recognize the tune." He stared at the piece of paper in his hand. "This sucks. I should be building the Pit's new array right now, not tinkering with houseboats."

Caps held up the guts of a VCR. "Does this look like an internal combustion engine to you? Anyhow, no matter what they tell us to do, we're still better off than the Boss."

Sid stood naked, hands cupped protectively over his groin. A Navy man eyeballed him then said "He'll need a number."

"Good timing," said a civy guard in a leather jacket. "935 is available. They're about the same size."

"Isn't 935 Jerry Kernsey's number?" asked the sailor.

"Yeah."

"When did we lose Kernsey?"

"First thing this morning. Kernsey got smart with our new guard. Guess the fellah likes to make his point fast."

The civy's arm shot out. A jacket flew from his hand to the Navy man's, to end up in Sid's arms. It was more like an extra-large shirt than a jacket. The number 935 was stitched into the back of it. The jacket was followed by wool pants, wool shirt, socks and worn shoes.

"Do I get a blanket?" Sid asked.

"What for? Somebody would just take it from you. If you're still alive in a couple of weeks, then we'll talk blankets."

Noah lay on his back, arms stretched as far as they could go behind his head. A wooden box built into the bulkhead made getting at the coupling as difficult as possible. The owner of the system, a pasty woman with white hair, said the batteries were the problem and she couldn't afford to replace them. Noah also shouldn't expect any pay from her, because she didn't request the maintenance.

There was nothing wrong with the batteries. It was all in the configuration. Instead of being charged equally from the sources, one battery was charged and then in turn, charged the second, which charged the third. With the loss of energy in each transaction, the woman was getting less than two thirds of what the system could supply.

"How is it?" asked a man's voice.

Noah pushed himself out from under the box and sat up. Donald Graff was looking down at him, a notebook in one hand.

"A mess," Noah wiped his hands on his pants. "And the people aren't very nice here, either."

"Still, better than swimming, isn't it?" Graff flashed his yellow-toothed grin.

"Yeah, no thanks to you." Noah eyed the notebook. "What are you writing? That you think I might be planting a bomb?"

"I am sorry, but a man can't be blamed for his private thoughts. If you think about it, I did make the right decision there, not letting you know—" He stopped at Noah's scowl. "Look, if it makes you feel better to blame me for this…go ahead. I can't stop you. I might as well give you my blessing."

Noah's resentment subsided a little. "I guess this isn't your fault. You just wandering, or did you come looking for me?"

"Actually, I was looking for your chief of security."

"She was sent to some woman. Mistress something. What do you want her for?"

Graff wasn't looking directly at Noah. Instead he was scanning the air. "I keep expecting a bird to drop on me. Such an unprotected sky."

"Ah, I'm used to it," Noah pulled himself back under the wooden box.

"Used to it?" asked Graff. "Used to it how?" Graff stooped and shook Noah's leg. "Used to it how?"

"What are you talking about?"

"You've been here less time than me. How are you used to an unprotected sky?'

Noah bit his lip. *Oops.* "During the…uh…tour. We were topside for a while before…you know."

"That was at Astoria. There were at least fifty people with Double A's on patrol at all times."

"Double A's?" Noah sat up. "What do they do? Throw batteries at them?"

"Not batteries. A.A. Antiaircraft guns. A joke. They're wide-bore shotguns…I'm getting sidetracked. Look, every shadow, every piece of clothing hanging on a line that flutters in my peripheral? I hit the deck the first few times, must have looked a total fool. I've been watching you. You walk around like one of them. What's your secret?"

Only the sudden relaxation of his feet gave away Noah's relief. The writer hadn't latched onto a Compton Pit secret, he only wanted to save face. "Denial. Deny everything. Nothing bad is happening. Ever."

"Denial." Graff leaned back on his heals a mulled it over. "From a mental health point of view, that sounds rather detrimental."

"Yeah, but Caps says it's not something I'll have to worry about for at least another ten years."

"Ah, yes. Wise man, your Caps. So how's the setup here? Solar power, I mean."

"Couldn't be better. Denial. Get it?"

Graff left after that, and Noah moved on to the next building. This one was another reinforced houseboat. Larger than the first one, this one had sleek curves to the molding, the white hull and wavy blue detailing were freshly painted. Noah climbed a short companionway, stepped around a half wall, and knocked on the door. At first there was no answer. At the second knock he got a muffled "I'm coming, I'm coming," then the door was opened by a brown-robed woman yawning and knuckling her eyes. Her blond hair was incredibly long, spreading out behind her like the tail of a bleached peacock. The robe hung open, giving a generous view of shapely breasts. Her eyes were sky-blue, with fair, almost invisible eyebrows above them. Noah's cheeks flared red as he recognized her as the dancer from the Wonders of the World Show.

"Who are you?" She reached down and tugged at her robe, but instead of closing, it opened a little more.

Noah's mouth moved, but no words came out.

"You caught my show, didn't you?" She gathered her hair into a single ponytail and dragged her hands down the length of it. When she let go, it hung over one shoulder, emphasizing one breast by obscuring the other.

Noah was at war with his eyes. It felt like there was a hand inside his head trying to push them down despite his best efforts to keep them on the dancer's face. She, on the other hand, had no such compunctions. She looked him over head to toe. "Nice outfit. I hope you look better out of clothes than you do in them."

The blush, which had begun to fade, came back with reinforcements. She leaned out of the door and the robe fell completely open. She turned her head away from him. He lost the war with morality and his eyes went down and...found disappointment. Her hair, clasped in one hand near the bottom, was pulled across her chest covering all but an inch of cleavage. She waved at somebody.

Noah turned his head and caught a hint of movement as a shape disappeared behind a building. When he turned back, she'd closed the robe right up to her neck.

"Don't worry," she said. "That's just someone who watches when a stranger knocks on my door. I sent him away. So...who are you?"

"I'm here to look at your solar panel array."

"That's you? I'd expected someone a bit more skuzzy. You think stowaway, you think...well you're dressed for the part. They're up top, have fun. See you tonight."

"Excuse me?"

"At Tanzers. You are going to Tanzers, right?"

"I…uh, guess I am now."

She laughed, then placed two fingers on the middle of his chest. "You would have been anyway." Still laughing, the door closed and a latch slid into place.

Noah floated up the ladder to the panel array. Denial wasn't going to play a hand in this one. The gorgeous dancer. She was obviously coming onto him big time. His mind rushed ahead at a thousand miles-per-hour. No shared berth for him tonight. A few clever jokes at the bar, some innuendo, then three miles of hair spread out everywhere across the bed, her ankles locked behind his back, or better yet, his neck. Then he looked around the flight deck and his steam train of lust smashed into a brick wall. This was Jenny all over again. If Delilah did warm his bed, there'd be a price tag attached to it. That guy she waved to was probably her handler. Tanzer owed her, huh? Owed her for what?

Noah shook off images of naked dancers. His heart already landed him in enough trouble. He didn't need his dick adding to it.

"Mostly it's gonna be coal," said the narrow-faced sailor giving Sid an orientation. "We've got a lot of coal. That's part of the conditions with *Terpris*. If you want us to pay you a visit, you better have coal."

Sid walked along the gangway, the sailor in front and a civy guard behind. They were on the uppermost level, a narrow oval track around the circumference of the barge. Barge was a bit of a misnomer. This thing was a dry-bulk tanker. It had been cut and welded and bent and modified, but nobody pre-Change would ever have called this monstrosity a barge.

"Where do I sleep?" asked Sid.

"Wherever you collapse," said the civy.

The sailor ahead gave a mercy laugh. "You'll find a place in the nets or the mounds."

"Wait a minute." Sid stopped walking. Twenty feet below, four large hatches in the top deck opened into the cargo holds. "You mean there's no separation between living areas and work areas?"

"No," said the civy, giving Sid a shove.

"So I'm supposed to live and breathe coal dust twenty-four hours a day?"

"I'd give you a mask," said the sailor, "but somebody'd just take it from you."

A pair of civies rolled a cart towards the sternward hatch. They used a hoist to lower some barrels into the darkness. After that, they took two large crates of food and upended them, dumping their contents into the hold.

"That was your idea of serving lunch?" said Sid. "And the people below fight over the scraps."

A number of barge guards surrounded the hatch, rifles held loose but ready, watching the frenzy below.

"Yeah, well there's nothing good on TV anymore."

"You're so glib," said Sid. "Were you always this insensitive or has this job stripped away your humanity? You treat these people like animals."

"Like rats," said the sailor. "That's what you are now. You're a barge rat. Stop here." He turned and held his rifle like a bar. "Turn and face the gunwale."

Sid pivoted, putting his back to the top deck and its four dark maws.

"Off you go, rat," said the civy.

Both men put a hand on Sid's chest and shoved hard. He flew backwards off the catwalk. Staring at the sky, feet above his head, Sid made a sound no louder then a squeak. In a fraction of a second he'd hit the deck and shatter both his skull and his neck. He knew his life was about to get really bad, but he didn't think they were planning to murder him.

The expected impact didn't come.

Sid's arc carried him past the deck, through the hatch and to a much greater fall than twenty feet.

35. Farewell Compton Pit

Lieutenant Commander Vincent McCabe was immensely impressed with the woman sitting in his usual chair. One hand flew across the keyboard while the other flipped pages in a ring-bound book with plastic pages. She could not only identify the *Athena Challenger III* communications system, but was instantly comfortable with the modifications and improvisations the Navy had been forced to perform over the years. In her first hour, she waved off another officer's stilting explanation of a certain procedure, and with an air of bravado, performed the link up while simultaneously initializing a second link on the adjacent system. In her second hour, she successfully pinged a geosynchronous satellite thought lost forever by the *Terpris* crew months ago.

Twenty-two-thousand miles above the Earth, what few geosynchronous satellites remained, twisted and spun. Getting signals to and from them involved knowledge, skill, and concepts of trajectory far beyond those of the greatest pool player. Hitting them from a moving platform made it that much more difficult, but as long as Lena knew their position, their speed and heading, ricocheting invisible waves off the distant orbiters was easier for her than dancing.

Her eye caught the chronometer at the top of the panel, near her right hand. She turned to face Cmdr. McCabe. He had straw-colored hair and a round face. He made her think of the actor Sam Neil in red-framed glasses. "In a couple of minutes, I'll have about half an hour to get through to my home. You said you'd think about it."

"Go ahead. Finding that bird over Greenland earned your keep for the whole ten days, far as I'm concerned. Can you use it for this?"

"I have to, otherwise it will be ..." she ran her finger along a transparent navigation chart fastened to a short wall of glass separating the work stations. "… thirty-six hours before I can do it again. Whole different set of satellites, too."

"Good," McCabe smiled. "If the logs are questioned, it's a justifiable test of the supposedly dead bird."

Lena was surprised the Navy officers still referred to satellites as birds. They certainly weren't called that at Compton Pit. She initiated the link. Like her own system, the *Athena*'s software had been modified to allow for feedback every step of the way. As each satellite was found, it registered on the screen. Preprogrammed relay settings were a waste of time. There was no consistency up in the sky anymore. Keeping track of windows of communication was a twenty-four-hour job.

"Compton Pit, are you receiving?" she asked into the microphone.

"The Pit here, who's this?" countered a woman's voice. It sounded young.

Warmth and comfort flooded through Lena, like putting on an old familiar jacket on a cold day.

"Bethany. I put Lyle on this shift."

"Lena! Ohmygod! Hey…where the hell are you? I think there's a problem with your transmission ident."

"What problem?"

"Your positional signature. It's telling me you're coming in from around eighty west, forty-five north. That would put you—"

"I'm in *Terpris*, Bethany. Listen, I haven't got long. You have to get Sara."

"Terpris? Never heard of that island. How'd you get there? Lena, you actually got on a boat?"

"There's no time for this, hon. Get Sara now."

"Dr. White's sick, chief. I don't think she can come to the phone. I'll page Seth."

The Pit's chief of stores was on the line in less than a minute. He must have been close by.

"Seth here. Lena, there's no island where you say you are."

"I didn't say I was on an island. I said I was in *Terpris*."

"You mean the carrier? Holy cow. I'm jealous."

The black window in the center of Lena's screen flickered, and suddenly Seth's gentle face appeared. *"Can you go visual?"* he asked.

Lena got the nod from McCabe. She keyed on the camera mounted above her work station.

"Hi there," said Seth, responding to the image he was seeing. *"Where's the Boss?"*

"Indisposed."

"Whatever he's doing, you guys better come home ASAP. It's really hit the fan."

"What's the problem?"

Seth's eyes darted from side to side. Lena guessed he was trying to spot shadows, to see if there were other people at her end.

"I'm not alone Seth, but go ahead. What's wrong?"

"Underbel lost another tunnel. Looks like the whole place is going to collapse. Sanderson's past desperate. She's demanding shelter for a lot of her people. She's implied our people still there might become hostages. It's really ugly. Sara's no good. How soon can you get back?" His eyes grew wide. "Terpris *is bringing you isn't it? Damn! The Boss really can pull off anything, can't he?"*

"What's wrong with Sara?" Lena's stomach was churning.

"Headaches, dizziness. She's showing signs of dementia. Harpreet's got her sort of sedated." Seth looked away for a few seconds. *"They're dropping you off at Piper's Cove right? That's the best place. What's your ETA? I'd love to see—"*

"We're going in the opposite direction, Seth. We're disembarking in Diego. It's where San Diego used to be."

"San Diego?" Seth was shocked, then angry. *"Are you nuts? That's over two-thousand klicks away. It'll take you months to..."*

Even with the grainy image, Lena could see the color drain from his face. He realized what she had the moment Diego was mentioned, even if the others hadn't. A road trip of that length couldn't be done non-stop. The ground would be covered settlement to settlement, earning keep every step of the way. It wouldn't take months. It would take years.

"You're telling me I'm on my own here."

"Congratulations, Seth. You're the Boss of Compton Pit."

"No way! Tell Sid—"

The image vanished and was replaced by a column of numbers and a red bar along the bottom of the screen as the software attempted to reconnect.

The journey to Compton Pit was not one Lena planned to take. She'd find a place in Diego. Caps would stay with her, she was sure of it. Except through a camera, she would never see her home again. Lena's hand drifted up, fingers touching the screen. "Goodbye."

36. Leaving the Light

Sid hurtled downward, the expanse of sky now a square. Now a smaller square. The bottom of the hold was going to end him.

He hit. The deck beneath him stretched and absorbed, slowed him, then stopped. Heart pounding, breath frozen in his chest, Sid looked around. Four posts anchored the cargo net like a trampoline.

"Get him off of there," said a voice.

Hands grabbed Sid by the arms and pulled him from the net.

The hold was a cavern of darkness with pools of light. The only illumination came from the four hatches. Layers of cargo nets and ropes hung between pillars and posts. Cart rails bolted to the deck created a path between and around mounds of junk, broken furniture piled high. To the left, dunes of coal rose and fell away. Above the coal, and in every direction were hammocks, hammocks, hammocks. *How many men are in here?* he wondered. There was movement everywhere.

Two guards, both Navy, stood nearby, rifles in their hands, batons in their belts.

A handful of prisoners backed away from the net. All of them wore dust masks either across their mouths or dangling from around their necks.

Swearing and grunting, the sounds of open-mouth chewing, came from somewhere in the coal. The air was thick and acrid, pungent with rotting fish and the added tang of human stench.

One of the guards removed Sid's manacles, then both guards backed away.

One of the prisoners, half in shadow, lingered, watching.

Sid rubbed his wrists, closed his mouth and forced his nose to do its job. He'd have to get used to the smell. He looked up, involuntarily, at the distant hatches. He saw no ladders or nets reaching the top. It appeared the only way out was by hoist.

Way up high, flush to the ceiling, a caged catwalk ran around the inside of the hold. Angled metal plates thrust out from beneath the catwalk, perhaps to thwart items hurled up from below.

The lingering prisoner stepped into the light. His right eye was wide, his left demolished. The socket was caved in and healed over. He was tall, about Sid's height. Straggly brown hair hung in front of his face and down the sides of his head. His beard was thick, but patchy in parts. The number 416 was stitched above the pocket of his work shirt.

"That's a bad number," he said. "935 only died this morning. Bad luck, man."

Sid didn't reply. What wasn't bad luck right about now?

416 edged a little closer. His hands were at his sides. His shoulders bobbed up and down. It looked like nervous energy; a twitch.

"You gonna take this guy under your wing, Four-Sixteen?" asked one of the guards. "You got ten minutes, then both of you better be working."

"Yes, boss," said 416. There was a piece of fish stuck in his beard. Sid fixated on it. "I'm crumbling coal," the man continued. "You can crumble coal with me." He turned and shuffled away.

For lack of anything better to do, Sid followed.

A hulking shape moved deep in the coal, half unseen before disappearing into the gloom, like a whale in a dark sea.

"Jesus," said Sid.

"That's Atoe. Don't get on his bad side."

"He's the biggest man I've ever seen."

"He's Samoan. They grew them big in Samoa."

They walked along the tracks. Between two high mounds the light faded to almost total darkness, before they stepped out into a clearing of sorts, with work tables and hoppers on the tracks.

416 put on a pair of gloves and pulled his dust mask over his mouth and nose. He yanked a chunk from the nearest wall of coal. "Got to make it smaller." He started banging the chunk against the inside of the hopper.

Sid looked around. "Are there gloves for me?"

"Two weeks," said 416.

"Everything's two weeks. Why is that?"

"If you survive two weeks, most guys'll leave your stuff alone. Don't know how that started. It just is."

Sid moved to a coal pile. He worked a slab of the stuff loose and moved to a hopper.

"Hoists the only way out of here?"

"Yep."

"Guards mostly stay topside and in that catwalk?"

"Yep."

"How do the guards get down here if they have to get in quickly?"

416 looked at Sid's hands, holding the coal but not doing much else. Sid banged the lump against the hopper.

"They use the cargo net."

Sid looked back over his shoulder. "What if the net was sabotaged?"

"They'd throw us all into the ocean."

"That's what they say?"

"That's what they've done." 416 dropped his last two bits of coal and went to get another slab.

Sid finished crumbling his bit and looked at his hands. "Why are we doing this?"

"Pulverizers need smaller bits to process. Fuel coal and coke coal. Gotta make a powder of it. Trusted barge rats get to use tools."

"Couldn't a machine do this?"

"We are the machine."

Whistles sounded. Lunch was over. Feet tramped through the mounds. Prisoners trickled into the clearing, setting their masks, pulling on their gloves.

"How depraved is this place?" Sid whispered to 416.

The man's one eye crinkled in disgust. "What the hell do you think, man?"

Darcy clenched her teeth and limped towards the pokey. Her back ached, her wrists hurt and her chin was bruised from hitting the floor because the stupid skirt kept tripping her up when she went to crawl forward. When she arrived, Noah was waiting for her outside.

"You're late."

"Thank Mistress Cassa. What a witch. She was supposed to send someone to tell me to knock off. She didn't."

"Lena's got your berthing assignment. She and Caps are up at Tanzers. Here," he held out a fancy poker chip, blue and red striped edges with a laurel wreath stamped in the middle. "Believe it or not, it's a shower ticket. You can cash it in somewhere on the second deck."

"Is that up or down? I've got a map and I'm still confused."

"Decks are numbered down from topside to the hangar deck. 01, 02, 03. Below the hangar deck are second, third…get it?"

"How many of these do we get?" she took the chip.

"That guy at Tanzers, Tivoli, gave me two of them."

"How much did they cost?"

"Nothing, at least not yet. I think he's trying to be our friend."

"Better clothes?"

"Tivoli said he'd work on it. Should I tell everybody you'll be up later?"

"Sure. Thanks."

Noah turned to leave but she caught his arm. "Noah, could you wait for me outside the bar? I want to talk to you but I really want to shower first."

"Uh, sure. I'll be by the rail."

Noah was about to give up and go in when she arrived, hair still wet. She didn't have a jacket, but she'd scrounged a blanket from somewhere, and had it wrapped around her against the cold. The sky was clear, the sliver of new moon outshone by countless stars. Below them, and beyond them, was nothing but blackness.

"I have to apologize to you," she said without preamble. "What I said in New Portland, I mean just before the fight—"

"As opposed to the other times you were incredibly mean?"

Darcy was at a loss. "What other times?"

"I'm kidding."

"Oh. You don't…that shower was three minutes long. Did you know that's all a chip was worth?"

"Mmhmm. Tivoli told me."

"So you gave up half a shower for me. Noah…"

"It's okay about New Portland. You figured I didn't think you could take the guy and it pissed you off. I'm the one who should apologize. Friends are supposed to have faith in each other. I'm sorry I doubted you."

And just like that, all her preparation went over the side. She'd labored over what to say as she scrubbed pipes and floors. She'd braced herself to tell him everything if necessary, and with a few words he'd stripped away the need.

"You don't owe me anything," he said. "Not after spending the whole day in that skirt."

Darcy shrugged the blanket off her shoulders and wrapped it around her waist to cover the offending garment. It wasn't much of an improvement.

"Let's go in." Darcy ran her hand along the side of the boat as they moved towards Tanzers's door. "Must have been a sight when they hauled this up and dumped it on the deck."

Caps and Lena were at a table near the stage, quietly conversing with Donald Graff to the tune of soft music from the piano. At the keyboard, Tivoli looked up and smiled when Noah and Darcy took their seats. He shifted briefly into a jaunty tune that was vaguely familiar, before returning to the semi-classical piece already in progress.

Caps and Graff both laughed.

"What was that?" Darcy asked, taking the chair the cartographer pulled out for her.

"The closing theme from the 'Carol Burnet Show,' " said Caps. "You know, washerwoman, ugly skirt."

"Nice. Your idea?"

"Nope. Came up with it all on his lonesome. Hey, Donny, tell her about her new boss."

"Donald," said Graff with some reserve. "Not Donny." He patted the back of Darcy's hand. "None of this is your fault. Apparently a year or so ago Miss Cassa had herself a little tryst during a docking. The gentleman that swiped her heart, for whatever reason, was refused citizenship and couldn't afford to book passage. What do you think happened next?"

Darcy looked down at the table. "He stowed away."

"Exactly. I'm told he only lasted eight days on the barge."

"Heavy," said Noah.

"So her lover stows away and dies in prison." Darcy clicked her tongue. "And then I show up at her door. That still doesn't give her the right to treat me this way."

"Oh come now," Graff laughed. "Don't tell me you've never taken something out on someone that had nothing to do with them. If so, you're a better person than I am, Ms. McCullough."

"I know I am, *Donald*." She spoke his name like it was insult. "How did you know who we were?"

The cartographer's eyebrows went up and down a couple of times. "You told me your names when we met at—"

"But not where we came from, or what we did there. So who told you?"

"I do collect as much data as possible prior to visiting a settlement. I'm sure I must have—"

"Did you visit Gascan D'Abo?"

"Yes, well…" he stood. "I'm suddenly busy elsewhere."

"Son of a bitch," said Caps as the bar's door closed behind the cartographer. "You're right. I never would have thought of that. Aw, crap. He was buying the drinks."

"The least you could have done is taken it up with him privately," said Lena, the two fingers in the bottom of her glass suddenly far more valuable than it had been a minute ago.

"I just kind of figured it out."

Noah stared at the door. "*He* sold us out? What a doglicker. So why'd he try so hard to help us?"

"Guilt, Noah." Caps waved over the only waitress, a handsome girl with a mop of curvy, ashen blonde hair nearly as profuse as Tanzer's. "Another round please. Donald will be having the same. We've got two more at the table." The waitress left. "Yes, guilt. Guilt that would have kept us in food, drink and favors all the way to Diego if Darcy here hadn't blown it. It's like the gift that keeps on giving. And also consider that we own Gascan's reservoir now."

"No thanks to Graff." Darcy stopped herself from rubbing at a stain on the table.

The drinks arrived. Caps moved Graff's beer to the middle of the table.

Darcy leaned closer to the table and lowered her voice. "So what are we going to do here? Bribe or break, we've got just over a week to figure this place out and get Sid off that barge."

The four hatches closed and even the stars disappeared. Electric lamps, wide spaced and set high on the walls, now provided small puddles of light.

Sid tried to clear his stuffed nose. Blowing it on his sleeve wasn't working. He tried to inhale, do a hard-sniff-and-swallow routine. That wasn't going to happen either.

He was covered in coal dust. It was under his nails, in his clothes. Sid could feel it on his teeth.

"Head's that way," said 416, pointing towards the bow. "Follow the tracks in the dark."

Sid felt ill. From the dust he'd inhaled to the scrap of fish he'd manage to snatch at supper time, to the tidal wave of emotions barely kept at bay, he knew he was going to throw up.

He walked, hands out front, one foot sliding along the rail. He heard muted conversations in the darkness, mumbles and shuffling sounds. The distant lamps appeared and disappeared as Sid followed the curving track through the mounds. His shoes were a little too big. Abrasions on the backs of his heels would soon be blisters.

Nine days.

Sid had nine days to be off this tub and on the shore. He'd hook up with them in Diego and lay low until *Terpris* was well on its way. He didn't know if the Navy would waste the effort on hunting for him, but it was too early to even consider that.

The prisoners were taken topside—aloft—in groups of fifty, for fifteen minutes, twice a week. Beyond that, the ways out of the hold were limited. Sid considered making a grappling hook. There was no shortage of rope. Having the tool and being able to use it, however, were entirely different matters. The hatches opened at sunrise and closed after dark. When open, guards watched the hatches from multiple angles. As to the catwalk, a grappling hook could get Sid up to it, but not in.

Once he was out of the hold, getting to shore was another matter to consider. Swimming wasn't an option. Dolphins shadowing the carrier would chew him to pieces the moment he was out of the ship's gun range.

The shapes around him changed from rounded edges of coal to the rough angles of splintered wood.

As part of his RCMP orientation, Sid had once visited a prison that kept a special little museum in a room near the warden's office. Displays included weapons made from toothbrushes, combs and bedsprings. Convicts excelled at giving anything a business end. If a particular inmate didn't cotton to stabbing, a padlock in a sock served to put things bluntly.

In those days, with all that security and monitoring, prisoners managed to gear themselves up like a militia. On this barge prison, all a person had to do was reach into one of the piles.

I really have to get out of here, thought Sid, pulling his hand away from the wood. He took solace in knowing even now his Pit crew was out there. *They've probably got their heads together right now, planning away.*

"Skol!" shouted Caps, draining his mug.

"Gan bei," echoed Lena, doing the same.

"This isn't helping," said Darcy. She'd barely touched her beer. "Lena, you need to get them to really trust you in communications. I'm thinking we could send false orders to the barge."

Caps craned his head around as far as it would go. He signaled the waitress.

"Could you guys please stop drinking?" Darcy begged.

"Could you please start?" said Lena.

The waitress showed up. Caps held up four fingers. Noah covered his mug with his hand and shook his head.

Darcy gave Noah a grim smile. "Thank you. At least one person agrees with me."

"The fourth is for Donald," said Caps. He turned to Darcy once the waitress was gone. "Noah can't hold his liquor. He's on one and a half."

"I can hold my liquor," said Noah.

"Only by the ears, sun boy."

Lena burst out laughing.

"I don't get..." Noah started. "Oh, very funny." He caught something from the corner of his eye, and stood. "I'm crashing. Long day, and all. My berth is close to yours, isn't it?" he asked Caps.

"Don't wait up for me, Noah. I plan to close the bar down."

A few moments after Noah left, Caps noticed a lovely face heading towards them. Right away he recognized her; the stripper. She passed the table and spoke to Tivoli, who in turn nodded at their table.

"So you're the rest of them," she said, resting her hands on the back of an empty chair.

"If you mean stowaways," said Caps, "that's us. All except one. Past his bedtime."

"Welcome to *Terpris*." She smiled. "Next time you see Noah, thank him for me. It was the longest blow I've had in a long time." She winked at them, and walked away with a sway to her hips that was sensual without being tawdry.

"She means with a hair dryer," said Tivoli, taking a seat. "She's got a separate battery system just for her hair dryer. Your young friend did something that gave her forty more seconds."

Darcy could still hear piano music. She looked at the stage.

"It's a CD," said Tivoli.

The waitress dropped four more mugs on the table and grabbed up all the empties.

"I think this one needs an owner," said Tivoli, taking an unclaimed beer. He gestured broadly at the waitress, and when she arrived he said, "There's far too much empty space on this table."

She looked around. "Where'd the writer guy go?"

"Mr. Graff's credit is good whether he's here or not."

"Fine. But I ain't eating a big tab." She moved away.

"I can't just sit here and get bombed," said Darcy.

"Hey, c'mon," said Caps. "We're in shit up to our ears here. Even if we…" He glanced at Tivoli. "Once we get to Diego, we have to figure out how to cross an entire coastline."

Lena took a drink to hide her scowl.

"Tonight the booze is free," he pushed Darcy's mug closer to her. "Get drinking, Mary Poppins."

Darcy curled a fist in the material of her skirt.

"Hey," said Caps, taking a long pull of beer. "Mary Poppins had a parrot on the end of her umbrella. I'll bet it tried to eat her. That'd be a good cartoon. Whadaya think? 'Just a spoon full of kidneys helps the governess go down.' "

The barge, at least, had proper toilets. The ocean provided an endless supply of seawater to carry waste, and there weren't any pesky environmental agencies around to raise a fuss over dumping bilge.

The more time Sid spent working his way around the gently tilting deck, the more he remembered things about ships, and it struck him how much thought and work had been put into this apparently primitive brig.

At the same time as the debris lay about everywhere, it was also contained by a series of horizontal nets. Rings in pillars and brackets bolted to the bulkheads suggested emergency stowing procedures for heavy seas.

He leaned against a vertically strung net and pondered. Where was he going to sleep? How was he going to protect his shoes? He'd seen more than one pair of bare feet so far.

A short distance away, a group of men clustered together in the spill of light from a lamp.

Sid climbed the net until he was high enough to see over a number of debris mounds. All the lamps visible had similar huddles beneath them. Were they cliques? Besides 416, nobody had said boo to him. They'd eyed him, shoved him, "accidentally" shoveled coal into his face, but none of them were interested in conversation.

Sid climbed down. He'd just have to wing it. He approached the nearest huddle.

"Piss off," said one of the prisoners the moment Sid stepped into the light.

"Man, that's a bad number," said another.

"Gentlemen," Sid began, "if you would only—"

"There he is," called a voice from the darkness. Shoes slapping deck sounded as somebody dropped from a net.

Sid turned to the darkness. Motion came from behind him. He spun, prepared to defend himself but he was alone. The cluster of men had dissipated into the gloom.

Something heavy lumbered towards him from the mounds.

Sid considered the darkness but decided it was best to see his attacker. He glanced up at the catwalk, but all that was visible was occasional red lights.

In his pocket nestled a metal bracket he'd torn from the remains of a desk. The bracket was horseshoe shaped. He slipped the curl of the bracket around the middle finger of his right hand and made a fist. The ends of the bracket protruded a quarter inch from between his knuckles.

Sid could hear two more convicts inbound. He'd have three to deal with—three men with sea legs. He put his back to the bulkhead.

"You, boy," rumbled a deep voice.

A silhouette formed at the edge of the light. With a smack of wood on flesh, Atoe the Samoan stepped fully into view. A table leg, his weapon of choice, slapped palm again. Atoe smiled.

Sid got ready to punch.

***

Darcy gripped the edges of the table and told herself she was completely capable of walking, she just didn't want to right now. A lot of empties covered the table. She didn't know how many she'd been responsible for. Caps and Lena were…somewhere. She was almost certain they were still in the bar. Tivoli was back on stage with a group of people doing a sing-along. In a way, it was a lot like home. The people in *Terpris* never had to fear an animal swarm. Relaxation could be total. But Compton Pit didn't have a bar. Not an official one anyway. The Pit was a research facility, a manufacturing plant and a communications network. Sid had sold them all the notion of winning back the world if they worked hard enough. *Terpris* didn't have such lofty goals, at least not as a collective unit. For most of the people aboard, it was just their home. Nothing more, nothing less.

A gorgeous face swam into her line of sight. "Hi there," it said. "I thought you were just a day visitor."

"David, right?" She poked him gently in the sternum. "You have nice shoulders, David." Without both hands on the table, she half slid out of her chair.

"Whoa," he said, catching her. "You need some fresh air."

Strong hands under her shoulders guided her towards a porthole where Winch lounged, smoking a foul-smelling cigarette.

"What's she doing here?" asked the Neanderthal, hardly even looking at her.

"Don't know. She's had a bit too much. Be back later."

"I have to tell my friends…or Tivoli, where I'm going." Darcy pulled away from his hands. Already coordination was returning to her body.

"Tell Tiv I took her outside," David told Winch.

"I'll get right on it."

"Okay?" David asked her.

She let David take her elbow and lead her outside. There were a few people, singles and couples, spaced along the rails. David took her forward of the bar, about fifty feet from the next closest stargazer. The wind was stronger without the bar/boat's shelter, and David took his jacket off and draped it around her shoulders. "Just take a few deep breaths," he said.

She leaned on the rail and did just that. David leaned beside her, his hand an inch away from hers.

"So why are you here?" he asked. "You booked passage to Diego?"

"You could say that."

"Business or pleasure?"

She laughed. David slid his hand so it pressed up against hers. Darcy didn't pull away. She was thinking about leaning back into that broad chest, wrapping his arms around her, and drifting off to sleep. She shivered.

"Still cold?" David took her by the arm. "Let's get some shelter."

Through a break in the rail, a short flight of steps led to a catwalk below the flight deck. For a minute the cold was even worse, then he led her up steps and pulled her into an alcove behind a cargo net. It was pitch black inside the alcove, then a candle flared. It was a small area. A canvas tarp covered the deck. A thick pile of empty sacks looked comfortable enough to lie down on.

The candle sat on an oil drum. David lit a second candle. The barrel had been much used for this purpose. Multiple layers of melted wax formed a tiny alien landscape.

David sat on the sacks, put his hands on Darcy's hips, and gently pulled her towards him.

"You're 935," said Atoe, letting the end of his table leg hit the floor. "You're in trouble, boy."

Assailants two and three reached the fray. They were both of average height. Shaggy hair, thick beards. One was unarmed, but the other dangled something wrapped in sack cloth. From the shape of it, Sid figured it was chain.

"I just got the number today," said Sid. Was there a chance in hell this could actually be a case of mistaken identity?

"935 owed me money," said Atoe. He raised his club and pointed with it. "Now you owe me money. You owe me one million dollars."

It was preposterous. "How could he possibly owe you that much money?" Sid asked, unable to help himself.

"You calling me a liar?"

Ah, there it was. Inwardly, Sid chided himself. There was no right answer. "No" made him chattel. "Yes" turned him into dogmeat.

Inside the sack cloth, the chain clinked.

37. Nightlife

He stroked Darcy's hair with one hand while the other cupped her hip and turned her towards him.

"I shouldn't be doing this," she said.

"Sure you should."

His lips found her neck and one hand gripped the side of her head, the thumb lightly tracing the inner curve of her ear. Darcy put her hands on his shoulders and stroked the firm muscles underneath. A warmth she'd feared gone forever grew in all the right places. She hooked a leg over one of his and he took it as permission to go for skin. A hand worked its way under her shirt and squeezed her breast. He rolled, putting more of his weight on her. The towel fell away. With one leg, David worked her skirt up until he could rub his knee against her crotch. Her shirt slid off. Darcy kept her arms over her head and writhed in pleasure.

With one hand kneading her lower back, his tongue found a nipple.

The unarmed convict moved first. His number was 813. He was going for a pinion grip.

Sid stepped into the man, his right thundering up from the hip. The attacker tried to dodge but the punch caught him dead on the temple. It was a meaty punch and Sid's makeshift knuckleduster earned its keep.

813 fell back and Sid kicked out with his left leg before turning to see the target.

It was a good kick, going straight for the centre of the chest. But prisoner 117 sidestepped and whipped his chain across Sid's shin. The massive bulk of Atoe pressed in.

Sid lost his balance. His left leg went numb below the knee. He fell forward and all he saw was the number twelve stitched over a pocket before the table leg, held in a bunt grip, smashed into his face.

"You are so beautiful," David said between kisses to her chest.

His hands were on full roam now, squeezing and probing. She was effectively pinned down. The miles of fabric in her skirt, rolled by the motions of their bodies, particularly the knee between her legs, held her tightly bundled. Above them, the cargo net hung like a spider's web.

Her nipples glistened with saliva when David moved lower, gently bit her stomach. He was on all fours now, working the skirt down her hips.

"I can't wait to fuck you," he said.

The way he said it set off a distant alarm bell in Darcy's mind. The last two words echoed in her head. "Say that again."

"You like that, huh? I can't wait to fuck you."

"Wait." She twisted, covered her breasts with an arm and pulled away from his busy knee. "I recognize your voice. You were at my fight." She pulled the waistband of her skirt up.

"Yeah. You were good." His reached for her. She slapped his hand away.

"You said you wanted to put a paper bag over my head. Bring one? Did you bring a paper bag? Get off me."

"I don't know what you're—"

Darcy shoved him, but he stayed in roughly the same place. She looked around for her shirt. It was under one of David's legs. He saw it too and pushed it out of her reach.

"I shouldn't get drunk," she said. "I do stupid things when I'm drunk. Get off me. And give me my shirt."

"You fuckin' with me?"

"No, bagboy. That's what I'm telling you."

He grabbed her wrist hard and pulled her hand to his crotch. "Feel that? That's for you."

Darcy tried to free her wrist with a twist and a push that should have worked, but either he was too strong or she was too drunk. She punched him in the throat. David fell back and clutched at his neck, eyes going fearful when he couldn't draw breath.

"You see?" Darcy struggled awkwardly to her feet. "Stupid things. That's a killing blow if I didn't pull it and I don't know how good my judgment is right now."

He made choking noises and reached out to her with a clawed hand.

"Relax. You'll be able to breath in a few more seconds." She grabbed her shirt. "Stay away from me from now on."

***

Atoe kicked Sid in the crotch and that was all she wrote. The feared leader of Compton Pit did a half pirouette and bounced off the hull and onto the deck. His nose and one cheek bled from where the table leg had hit him. 813 was down for the count, but chain-swinger and the Samoan weren't even breathing heavy.

One end of the table leg pushed its way between Sid's cheek and the deck. With a bit of pressure, his head rolled until he was looking straight up.

"Get his chin," said Atoe.

Prisoner 117 pressed the chain up against Sid's lips and pushed down, forcing the jaw open, exposing teeth.

Atoe touched the bottom of the club against the open mouth, then raised it, ready to strike down.

"Fire!" shouted a voice in the darkness. "Fire in the hold!"

Atoe's giant, shaggy head snapped around. The pressure across Sid's mouth eased. He tried to bring an arm up. It wasn't ready to obey yet.

"Fire in the hold!" the voice repeated. "Fire in the hold!"

Cries of alarm entwined with catcalls of derision.

"What he hell is going on down there?" shouted a voice from the catwalk.

Atoe looked down. The table leg jittered in his hands. He wanted to hit. At least get the front ones knocked out. From above came metallic clatter. A hatch thrown open, maybe?

Atoe snarled and backed off.

"Fire in the hold!"

A spotlight flared on. The beam made an irregular splotch of light on the mounds.

Atoe jerked his chin at the unconscious 813. The chain disappeared. Sid turned his head to see feet slinking off into the darkness.

"Later," said Atoe. He kicked Sid in the hip, then vanished.

"Fire! Fire! Fire! Fire in the hold"

The spotlight found 416, standing on the tracks, hands cupped around his mouth and yelling for all he was worth.

Feet pounded on the catwalk. Spotlights burst into life.

"There's no fire," shouted a prisoner from somewhere. A multitude of voices echoed agreement.

One by one the spotlights found 416. He shielded his eyes and turned in a slow circle. He was so bright. A nimbus of light outlined his clothes, danced in his hair.

A jet of water struck him full in the chest, threw him off his feet, tumbled him along the tracks. The spotlights followed as high pressure seawater from above battered him until he went limp.

"That's for making me get the hose out," yelled a guard. Laughter from the catwalk followed.

The spotlights winked out, all except one. The dot of light lingered on the supine 416, then moved aft, hunting the mounds.

"That you down there, Twelve?" asked a voice just loud enough to be heard. "What are you up to, you fat sack of whale shit?"

Sid could move his arms again. Oh, happy day. At the same time as he prodded his nose, he tried to calculate how long it took for the guards to respond to the first shout of fire. What sort of vigilance did they keep? Where did they watch from?

The lone spotlight went out.

A few shouts and mumblings echoed from the peripheries. Sid rolled to one side and coughed up a dark lump of phlegm. He hoped the color came from coal, not blood.

He stood. That went okay. His groin and sides burned and the left leg wouldn't take full weight, but he was able to shuffle over to 416. The man lay in an almost fetal position, conscious and shivering.

"Thank you," said Sid, reaching out to help; not yet strong enough to do so.

"Now you owe me, Nine-Three-Five."

"Sid. The name's Sid Halbert. I have nothing to give you."

"To start with, you're going to cover my quota for the next few days. Uhnnn." His attempt to stand didn't go well. He pressed an arm to one side, put a hand to one shoulder.

"I'm not in the best shape myself." Sid tested his left leg.

"Better 'n' me. Help me up."

Sid offered an arm. "Is there an infirmary?"

416 shook his head. "If you can't work you go swimming."

"What's your name?"

"You can call me Jim."

Sid pulled him over the tracks. Jim squeezed water from his hair.

"They going to come for you too now?" Sid asked as they leaned on each other, Jim guiding them as they shuffled.

"I got the hose. I paid my due. They won't bother you again tonight. Over here." He nudged Sid towards a stand of barrels near the front starboard corner of the hold.

A vacant space lay behind the barrels. Jim lay down on top of a few blankets. Sid hunkered down on hard deck.

"What's the deal on the guy that wore this number?" Sid plucked at his shirt.

Jim coughed. "The guy was Atoe's. Atoe figure's he owns the number. So now he owns you."

Sid's head drooped. "I must have broken a mirror or something." He looked up. "I suppose I should ask you about the factions here."

Jim chuckled. It sounded painful. "Nobody's going to notice you until you last two weeks."

"So what did the former 935 do?"

"He attacked a guard. Never attack a guard. That's instant release."

"Release?"

"Over the side."

"So my predecessor committed suicide." Sid looked down at his garb, wiggled his toes in the dead man's shoes. Depression wasn't an option. He tried to picture something happy. He thought about the first time Darcy took him down while sparring.

"Nah, he didn't commit suicide," said Jim. He rustled around beneath a net, pulled out a flask of water. He took a couple choking swallows, then offered the flask up to Sid. "He was provoked. New guard beat him hard before throwing him over."

"All the guards like that?"

Footsteps rang from the catwalk above.

Jim looked up. "The guards are the worst people in here," he whispered. "They're just smart enough to play within the rules."

Sid prodded his nose again. It wasn't broken, though the skin across the bridge was cut. His cheek was more an abrasion than a laceration. That was a relief. He splashed water on his cheek but hesitated cleaning the wound with his filthy hand.

"Here," Jim pushed a rag towards him.

"What happens if a guard's provoked?" Sid asked, setting to work on the abrasion. There was a splinter in it. That hurt.

"You mean crosses the line?" Jim took the flask back. "It's their line, man. They put it wherever they want it."

"So they can do anything they want to us, anytime."

Jim made a face, as if to say, "Pretty much." He tugged at his clothes. "Help me get my pants off."

Sid put the rag down and slowly shook his head. "I'm grateful for what you did, but…"

Jim's expression was one of hurt. "Don't be an asshole. I'm freezing. I've got dry clothes." He undid the fly. "Pull them off at the ankles. They'll have bets on you."

Sid looked at him.

"The guards. They'll have bets on you. How long you'll last."

Sid craned his neck, peered up into the darkness. Somewhere above he pictured a chalkboard with his number on it, and a grid marked off with who'd bought what time of death.

***

Lieutenant Kevin Thompson was about to call it a night when a gloved hand slapped down on his desk. He looked up.

"Something I can do for you, new guy?" Thompson asked.

"You keeping book on 935?"

"Yeah." He yanked open a drawer and pulled out a manifest. He set it down on the desk and flicked through some pages until he found the right one. "There's not much left. What do you want?"

"Good." One finger tapped a vacant square on the page. "That one."

Thompson licked his lips. "You seem pretty certain. You know something I don't?"

A bag of coins hit the desk. "Just place the bet." The man left.

Thompson took a pencil and scribbled in the name.

Toffee.

38. No Escape

Toffee stood back from the Hummer and did a final check. With any luck, all this was for nothing and he could retrieve his blade and other possessions from the vehicle in a few weeks. The landslide was easy.

Toffee'd rigged rope from the ledge below the cliff so it dropped all the way to the bottom of the ravine. After blowing the charges he drove the long way around, and down into the canyon, a trip that took almost two hours. He parked the Hummer at a tilt near the bottom of the rope and piled small to medium-sized rocks on the car's side. He worked quickly, knowing that although the rockslide had driven off anything hunting in the ravine, it wouldn't last forever.

Toffee eyed the rope and sighed. From the moment he saw Darcy walk into the workshop with the PVC pipe in her hands, he knew it was only a matter of time before she put it all together. She'd convince Halbert and it'd be a done deal.

He caught movement at the far end of the ravine. It was too far away to identify exactly—probably a dog. That meant there'd be more on the way.

"Toffee?" said Sid's voice from inside the Hummer.

The hunter pulled the handset out through the window and waited. It was coming, a good-sized dog. It sounded out a rapid-fire series of yelps. Barks answered the call.

"Toffee, are you there? Over."

Toffee stood, one-armed. No blade and rifle out of reach. It was suicidal. Dread ripped through him. It was the exact mood he needed. He keyed the mic. "Halbert, I'm at Lockout Point. Get out here or I'm dead."

"What? What are you doing out at—"

"There's no time!" There really wasn't. "A rock slide hit me. I'm in the Hummer. The Hummer's on the edge. If I get out, it goes over. If I don't get out, it's going over."

"We're on our way."

Toffee let go of the mic and its stretched chord snapped it back into the vehicle. He grabbed the rope and pulled, got ten feet up as the lead dog—there were four of them now—reached the Hummer.

Now came the hard part. He'd done a lot of work to give his one arm the strength of two, pushups and pull-ups every day since he'd lost his smarter limb, but he'd never tried to climb such a distance before.

The dogs scampered about snapping at the rope. Toffee had been careful not to leave any slack on the ground.

It was an arduous climb. Slide, grab, pull. Slide, grab, pull. Each time he slid his hand up the rope there was a chance he'd fall.

Toffee learned his physical limits on that ascent. He mantled the ledge and collapsed on it as if it were a soft feather bed. He still had to haul the rope up and stash it before Sid arrived and the seconds were ticking away. Fifty feet of rope still dangled when he heard the vehicle pull up on the ground above him. In a frenzy he yanked up the remaining line and bullied it into a nook out of sight from above.

"Figures he'd bring you," he said when Darcy's head appeared over the ledge. His foot was all that hid the tail end of the rope. He was pale and covered in dirt and dust, exactly the way he should look after surviving a rockslide.

When Darcy went back to the jeep to rig the winch, Toffee piled more rocks on top of the rope.

An hour later he was sitting at the desk in his room, scratching his stump as if he felt ghost pains from the blade.

The next trip out to the lockout point was far more difficult. He hadn't counted on Darcy punching him in the nose.

In what felt like seconds, they were gone and he was alone, and then he was on his back, with one dog taken care of and another one's teeth on his throat.

The secret to killing anything, be it man or beast, with a finger through the eye, is commitment. The impossible part for most people was feeling around for the opening in the skull behind the eye.

With Toffee's finger up to the last knuckle, the dog jerked away. The animal whined once, then started thrashing. Toffee was up and moving, blood and tissue dripping from his hand.

Altitude's grace period was long past over.

If only she hadn't punched him in the nose. The teeth were coming up fast. Dogs, a cougar, it didn't matter. He ran. The cougar hit him in the back just before the cliff's edge. Claws raked him, tearing out chunks of flesh and the back of his prisoner's coveralls. The hunter rolled, the cougar stayed with him and both of them went over the side. Toffee snagged a handhold, swinging them over the ledge. He twisted in the air so the animal broke his fall, but it was a tough one and struggled beneath him. His back burned and blood dripped from his hairline down his face, either from a claw wound or an impact break.

He rolled to bring his feet to bear on the cougar. One of its front legs was broken, but it still had plenty of fight in it. Toffee kicked out with both feet and sent the animal over the ledge.

Above him, a dozen frustrated creatures looked down and snarled in rage. Saliva spattered around him on the ledge. Toffee pushed the rocks off the rope and dropped one end over the side. From the nook he then removed his last stick of dynamite, a glove, boots, and a lighter. With the boots on and the glove in place to protect his hand from rope burn, Toffee lit a long fuse on the dynamite and shoved it next to the stone anchoring the rope.

The descent was a snap compared to the climb up. In no time he was behind the wheel of the Hummer and pulling away. The dynamite went off, blowing the rope free, along with part of the ledge. Large chunks of stone fell where the vehicle had been moments before. From above, it would look as if another rock slide had occured. If somebody did come back to look around, there'd be no evidence of his escape route. With both his blade and new arm in place, Toffee leaned forward in the seat to protect his tender back, and drove out of the ravine and off to freedom.

There was nothing for him north. South, Underbel wasn't an option, and Mt. Baker was even less of one, although he'd have to ambush someone outside of one or both settlements to get fuel and ammunition. He'd stocked up well, but a man could never have enough gas or bullets. The Hummer was loaded with everything he needed; extensive first aid kit, food, water, a radio scanner, portable generator and all sorts of lovely pharmaceuticals secretly acquired on shopping sprees in Vancouver. He had enough to trade his way to Mexico if he felt like it.

That he'd forgotten his bag of teeth was a sour note. He dwelled on that, channeled his anger at it. Better that than acknowledge what he really hated leaving behind.

A little time, and a lot of distance, and he'd put her where she belonged—in the past.

By the time Toffee reached New Portland it was plain there wasn't enough road in North America to put between himself and the redheaded Chief of Security, but there was the option to put an ocean between them. He sold the generator and some drugs for an obscene amount of money, then bought citizenship in *Terpris* with a bag full of cash and a handful of pills.

He was aiming for Africa. He'd always liked Africa. Now, more than ever before, the continent was made for him.

The hunter was leaning over a rail, pondering what he'd do to thwart boredom when a headful of windblown red hair and that yammering painter walked right under his nose. And then came Lena, and the kid, and finally Halbert.

Toffee had been near death countless times, but that moment at the rail was the first time he truly believed he'd felt his heart skip a beat.

The group passed by, looking everywhere except at him. The painter was rattling on about the magician at the Wonders show, and his box full of bees.

Toffee followed them discretely, moving to eavesdropping range when an opportunity arose. When he realized their presence had nothing to do with him, he was shocked. Not because they didn't know he was there—that was expected—but shocked at his disappointment. Having a crew of people chase you to hell and back? Well, it made a fellah feel wanted.

No, the Pit crew was there for Odega.

At first the coincidence seemed staggering, but the more Toffee thought about it, the more he realized the inevitability of it all. Odega had stolen a Mimi. If he wanted to do anything with it, he'd need access to high-end technology. Outside of Compton Pit, New Portland was the closest choice, and if New Portland had good stuff, then it was a sure bet that *Terpris*, the last stronghold of the American military, would have better.

When the group split up, he stayed with Sid and Darcy, unnoticed but close enough to hear every word. After another few minutes Toffee knew he wouldn't be bored for a long time.

39. The Gliding Devil

"I've got it," said Dr. Albert Chen. "No. Yes. Yes, I've got it. I'm in." His fingers flew across the keyboard.

"Are you really?" Dr. Timothy Leighton got up from his console and moved to Chen's.

Dr. Chen was short and round. His head was round, his torso was round; he appeared to have been assembled from a collection of spheres.

A contrast to both of them, the hulking Dr. Theodore Odega loomed over the back of Chen's chair.

"Let's hope we speak its language," said Chen.

Odega stepped back from the chair and sagged with relief. He was vindicated. He knew if he could just hook his Mimi up to a network, the signal timing could be found.

Leighton and Chen had connected the Mimi to a VLAN, creating a cyberspace airlock between *Terpris's* systems and this unknown entity.

Almost instantly the device had leased an IP address from the lab router and Chen used a Secure SHell—SSH—program to say hello. Two lines of data reflected in his glasses; one of them was a password prompt.

"Is it checked access? Can we both be in there?" Leighton practically ran to his computer.

Odega traced the cable with his eyes, from the hub to the Mimi where it sat, clamped in a speaker stand, pointed at an ultrasonic transducer connected to a spectrum analyzer. The analyzer was drool-worthy from a research point of view. Drab in color, plastic and metal, it looked like a portable television from the sixties. It had a few more buttons, though, and what its small screen displayed would entertain only the most cerebral or the definitively stoned. It was a Hewlett Packard 8565E with a range of 30 Hz to 50 GHz. Leighton and Chen were very proud of it.

"Ted," said Leighton. "Over here, please." The same two lines glowed on his monitor.

"I have no idea," said Odega, looking at the prompt. "Try 'Gershwin.' "

Leighton typed it in. "No dice."

"Try 'George,' or 'Ira.' "

Clickity-clack."Nope."

"Porgy? Bess?"

*Click click click.*Leighton shook his head.

Odega threw up his hands. "How should I know? I never met Gerard Fritz. I didn't know the man."

Leighton tried various permutations of Gerard Fritz's name.

"It could be a woman he loved," said Odega. "Or his mother's maiden name. It could be something stupid like 'password' or '1234.' "

Neither of those worked either.

"I'm in," said Chen, beaming. "It was blank. He left it blank."

All three scientists stared at Chen's screen.

Within a box of asterisks, scattered words showed the final login of Gerard Fritz: notes to self, to-do reminders, and the tantalizing line, "New password for topside Mimis Gershovitz."

"Is this a 'topside' Mimi?" asked Chen.

Odega nodded.

"If he was the only one working on it," said Leighton, "I guess it makes sense he'd leave that lying around."

"Let's see what happens," said Chen. He entered a command including the suggested password and new lines appeared on the screen.

Executing/usr/bin/gershovitz…
Logging set to gershwin.fritz.pit:/var/log/mimi/mimi12.log
Logging failed! Unable to mount directory.
Logging set to localhost:/var/log/mimi12.log…
Screamer seed being set…..unable to set seed! No communication with Gershwin!

"Now it gets difficult," said Leighton.

"That's an understatement," said Odega.

A new line appeared on the screen.

Using previously obtained seed value…

"Apparently he coded in redundancies," said Chen as a final line popped up.

Running. CTRL+C to abort.

"That's it?" said Leighton. "No requests for a billion instructions we don't have to give?"

"Impossible," breathed Odega.

Chen got up and moved to the spectrum analyzer. He flipped switches, turned dials, set reference levels, resolution bandwidth and sweep rate, then stood to one side so the others could see.

The curvy green lines on the display danced and jittered.

"It's certainly doing something," said Chen.

The three scientist gathered around the analyzer.

"It seems we don't need your supercomputer after all." said Leighton.

Odega said nothing. Certainly the unit was projecting something in the ultrasonic range, but if it truly worked autonomously, if all it needed was a single command instruction, then everything Compton Pit knew about Gershwin was a lie. The Mimis didn't need to stay pinned to the Pit. They could be operated with a laptop.

The hatch swung open and a thirtysomething woman with dark skin and short hair said, "You should come to the cages. Something's got the animals good and scared. All of them."

The green lines on the analyzer's screen disappeared. Leighton and Chen turned to find Odega, the Mimi's disconnected power cable dangling from his hand.

"They should all calm down now," Leighton said to the lab assistant.

"Marissa," said Chen, "did you notice if Pinocchio was in any way affected?"

A buzzer went off near the hatch. "Dr. Leighton," said a man's voice from an intercom. "A Donald Graff is here to see you."

Graff stood when Dr. Leighton finally appeared in the ready room.

"My apologies," said the gray-haired scientist. "I was in the middle of something. Welcome to Drowntown, Mr. Graff."

"Call me Donald. Drowntown?"

"We're below the waterline. If the cetaceans ever come up with a way to pierce the hull, well, you get the idea. Drowntown is separated into two areas: animal research which nobody wants to get near, and on the other side of that bulkhead," he pointed sternward, "is *Terpris's* equivalent of a ghetto, where nobody wants to end up."

"Isn't that a security risk? Having the ship's indigent side-by-side with some of the most secure areas?"

"There is no way to enter this side of Drowntown from the other. You have to climb up to the second deck and come back down. And as I said, nobody wants to be near the animals. Dr. Chen and I do most of the work."

"Will the new addition to your department help any?"

"Ahh, Dr. Odega does not wish to be discussed."

"I see. Well, I'm sure he has his reasons."

"This way, please." Leighton led the cartographer through the side hatch, down a short cramp and to another hatch. When this one opened, the smell of kept animals flooded the corridor. "This is small-animal research. Rodents, felines and such. Entomology is also here."

Small stacks of cages lined the right wall. Racks mounted on work stations held various implements. A full video and audio recording system was in place with a camera mounted in each corner of the room. Past two workstations stood ceiling-high glass cases. The larger of the two contained a moldering stump of wood, the smaller was filled with dirt.

"Ant farm and wasp farm. Both dormant now. We regulate their temperature based on the seasons where the colonies originated."

"Learn anything I should know about?"

Leighton hesitated, then said, "Unfortunately, no."

Graff peered closely at the ant farm. "You're not worried about these getting out?"

"Constantly, Mr. Graff. A molecule would be hard pressed to escape either tank."

"What if the tanks were broken?"

"Any hatch in the science department can be sealed by remote and either filled with pesticide or incinerated."

"What if people are still inside?"

"The safety of the ship is more important than a scientist or two."

Graff stopped his hand from rapping on the glass. "Do you have even a clue what's made them hate us?"

"We have limited data, what with the hazards inherent in the research. We've eliminated visual. They don't attack pictures or mannequins. Blinding an animal makes no difference. In all your travels what have you managed to learn?"

"I've learned fire works very well on all of them."

"Quite. I'm sure you've seen enough bugs and rats."

The next room contained larger animals: some dogs, a large cat of a species Graff didn't recognize, a pair of hyenas, a wombat, some snakes and an iguana. Workstations similar to those in the previous room were stocked much the same but with the addition of a gun and a tazer resting beside racks of test tubes. In the center of the room was a metal contraption with numerous leather straps. At the far end of the room was a laser-scope-equipped rifle on a tripod. Old blood stained the table below the contraption.

"Yes, this is the room's conversation piece," said Dr. Leighton, letting a strap run through his fingers. "We call it the headbanger."

Graff walked over to the rifle and sighted on the device. "It looks like you strap an animal into this and then shoot it."

"That's exactly what we do. Let me explain. First off, do you know what people wanted Tanzer to name his bar?"

"Haven't heard this one."

"The Friendly Dog. On Fubar Day, Captain Ransom was attacked by a dog. It was his brother's. At first it tried to kill him, then it was struck on the head. When it recovered, it licked the captain's face and kept birds off him long enough for him to get to a hatch."

Graff lowered the muzzle of the rifle and looked at Leighton skeptically.

"I know, sounds impossible. The captain insisted it was the truth, not a panic- induced hallucination. So, we experimented. We cracked a lot of dog skulls to no effect, then we tried grazing them with bullets. It worked."

"Excuse me," Donald pulled a notebook from his pocket and flipped it open. "What worked?"

"We found the right balance of damage. For a few minutes, the dog was both conscious and tame. I petted it."

The notebook dropped to Graff's side. "Then what happened?"

"It died. We did shoot it in the head, after all. We've been able to get the same results on three other occasions. It appears to work only on dogs. We have nothing concrete as to why the animals respond like this and our test subjects become more rare with every passing year. Soon there won't be any left at all."

"You suggesting we're going to run out of dogs?"

"It has to be old dogs. Dogs old enough to have been domesticated prior to the Change."

"I'm a little confused. What's the difference between shooting it in the head and lobotomizing it?"

"A lobotomized animal has only its most basic functions intact. These dogs displayed both awareness and genuine affection."

"Has Dr. Odega been able to shed any light on the subject?"

"Donald?"

"Sorry. Habit. No more questions about Odega. I promise. So you can tame dogs, but only dogs?" He scribbled.

"Make sure to mention we can tame them only for a few minutes. Then they die. We've had no success with other animals. We haven't yet ascertained the exact place to shoot a cat. A horse would be impossible to control down here. Would you like to see which animals have been here the longest?" Dr. Leighton pulled a handle on the side of the headbanger. A mounting bracket with a muzzle attached to it lifted into the upright position. A number of the critters shied back in their cages.

"I understand there's an aquarium? What type of fish do you keep?"

"Why would we have fish?"

"To study them?"

Leighton frowned. "I'm surprised a man of your experience would labor under that misapprehension. The fish aren't hostile."

"Oh. I've seen people have fish tanks once in a while, but I thought once you got out into the ocean…"

"We believe the fish are too primitive to hate us."

"Reptiles are primitive. They attack us."

"Mother nature had to draw a line somewhere."

"What about sharks?"

"I suppose they could appear to be more aggressive because they're drawn by blood and a swimmer in this day and age is very likely to shed some."

Graff tapped his pen against the pad. "Okay, if the fish aren't biting, what makes the ocean so dangerous?"

"Allow me to show you."

Graff was led into a room much larger than he'd expected to see. Workstations with monitors on them lined both sides of the wide bay. Dominating the room were two large tanks, high enough that a ladder was required to reach the top. The tanks were built of sheets of glass with steel brackets every few feet. A foot-and-a-half of air separated the top of the water from a metal cover.

The dolphin in the closest tank drifted over and turned sideways so it could look at Graff with one eye.

"In case you didn't know, this entire deck once contained eight nuclear reactors. They were ditched. The glass and mountings for the tanks were scavenged from a marine research facility. This one is a female *Lagenorhynchus obliquidens*, or Pacific White-Sided Dolphin. Notice the tall dorsal fin and dark ring around the eyes. We've had her about six months. She hasn't earned a name yet. This one," he walked to the second tank, "we've had for years. His name is Pinocchio, though Dr. Chen wanted to call him Kelsey."

"Why Kelsey?" This dolphin also watched Graff with one eye.

"Because this is *Lagenodelphis Hosei.* Frasier's Dolphin."

"Ah."

The creature was certainly colorful to look at. Seven feet long with a dark blue-grey dorsal cape, light gray flanks and cream colored throat and belly, the cetacean's short beak was also dark, with a series of black lines extending to the flippers. A dark lateral stripe, starting at the head, went all the way to the tail.

The cartographer's and dolphin's staring match ended when Pinocchio rolled languidly, pushed his underside against the glass and excreted.

"He does that for every new person he sees," said Dr. Leighton. "Charming, isn't it?"

"This dolphin understands human revulsion of fecal material?"

"One of many things this dolphin understands. Terrestrial fauna are a hazard. The mammals of the ocean are a true enemy. Comparisons of audio recordings we've made over the years, in conjunction with Old World research, tell us cetacean vocal variation has increased exponentially since the change. Complex strategies require complex language. It is our hope to interpret that language."

"Do the markings have a purpose? The stripes and patches, I mean."

"It's called counter shading. They're dark on top, light down below. "From above the dolphin camouflages with the deep, from below it camouflages with the sky. The various stripes provide lateral camouflage."

"To protect it from sharks?"

"Heavens no. Not that the sharks aren't predacious upon them, but their biggest danger is other dolphins. Orcas in particular."

"That'd be a whale."

"Once again, a misconception. Killer whales, false killers, pilot whales and the amusingly named melon headed whale are all dolphins. They're referred to as whales because of their size."

Graff studied the tank for a few moments. "Why Pinocchio?"

"Because he lies."

"Explain?"

"When we need to go in the tanks, we use this." Dr. Leighton held a long pole with a fluid reserve and needle on the end. "I can show you."

Dr. Leighton moved to a computer, tapped a few keys, then played with the mouse. On the monitor, a video image appeared, a shot of the tank from above and slightly to one side. Graff moved to the computer but kept his eyes on the real tank, not the video version. He'd hoped to see dolphins, but certainly not from a few inches away.

"Watch, watch." Dr. Leighton played the video. On the screen, an Asian man leaned over the top of the tank from a ladder and stabbed a dolphin. "That's Doctor Chen. He has excellent aim." A time counter ticked up in one corner of the video. At forty-five seconds, the dolphin grew limp, then sank to the bottom of the tank. Dr. Chen unlatched a piece of flashing then descended the ladder, getting out of the way of a man in a wetsuit. A harness was lowered into the tank by a winch. "A simple procedure," Dr. Leighton clicked the mouse and the video image vanished.

"Dolphins don't float when they're unconscious? How do they sleep?"

"They half nap. They float at the surface on one side. After a while, they roll, and let the other half nap." He clicked the mouse. "Now, the next bit is...well, should I tell you or show you?"

Graff took a chair. "Show me."

Another video started. It was nearly identical to the first, except a different man was using the pole. This man was taller, with curly brown hair.

"That's Dr. Dylan." Leighton leaned back in his chair. "He was very hands-on."

Dr. Dylan handed the pole off to an assistant and removed his lab coat. Underneath he had on swimming trunks. At forty-four seconds, the dolphin began to sink. Dr. Dylan climbed into the tank. The dolphin raced at the scientist and Graff turned away from the screen. When he looked back, the surface of the water was red.

"The plunger was jammed." Leighton clicked off the video and stood. "Pinocchio never received his dose, but he behaved as if he had. That dolphin weighs just over two hundred kilograms. That would be four hundred and forty pounds. Dr. Dylan was dead in seconds. Pinocchio crushed him against the tank then bit his throat out."

"Why...why didn't you kill this dolphin then?"

"Apart from the difficulty of harvesting new specimens? We have more audio recordings of this particular cetacean's clicks and whistles than any other. We need to know their limits, Mr. Graff, and we desperately need to communicate with them. All animals hate us. Perhaps dolphins can tell us why."

40. A Star is Born

Darcy scrubbed in between the pipes and the wall fixture. On an inspection an hour previous, Mistress Cassa used a flashlight and a dentist's mirror and when she found a speck of dirt, she ordered Darcy to start from scratch.

Today's attack on grime was in a dark corridor on the starboard side of the 01 deck. The hatches led to holds, apparently storing things nobody wanted. Since she'd been led down in the morning, she hadn't seen anyone besides Mistress Cassa.

A spot on Darcy's knuckle not yet blistered scraped open on an unseen jagged edge of metal. Darcy cursed, sucked the knuckle for a minute, then went back to work. When she tried to resume the song she'd been singing, she couldn't remember what it was. When she was young and had chores to do, her Discman was her best friend. In her teens it was an MP3 player. In later years, her own voice had taken the place of those gadgets. Her ears had to have something to listen to. That she had a good voice was a definite benefit. She'd been singing all day, but what she'd been singing was just background noise to her. Mouth on autopilot, mind on the problems. She felt she might have been singing something by Black Eyed Peas, so she started up half-way through, and without knowing it, drifted into an Eagles tune her father had liked.

'What Ever Happened to Saturday Night' died on her lips and she looked around. The feeling was there again, the feeling that someone was watching her. She'd had it off and on since they'd arrived in *Terpris*, but now, as before, she looked around to find nothing. The one end of the corridor was empty, and nothing peeped around the corner at the other end. Darcy licked her lips and went back to work.

Another Eagles song and a Terri Clark medley later, Darcy heard footsteps coming towards her. She looked up, hoping it was someone to tell her the shift was over. It was David. He stopped about ten feet away from her. A fish club dangled from his hand.

"I figured you out," he said. "You like it rough."

Darcy stood and shifted into a relaxed but ready posture. She glanced at her mop but decided it would be an unwieldy weapon. "You don't really think you can take me, do you?"

"No, but I think he can."

A net dropped over her from behind and strong arms circled her torso. David darted forward and struck her with the club. Pinpoints of light darted before her eyes and her legs went weak.

Whoever was behind her, without releasing his bear hug, dropped to his knees, forcing Darcy down until she sat, pinioned from behind, legs splayed out in front.

"I think you hit her too hard, Davy," said Winch.

"As long as she's breathing, I don't care."

David's hands were under her skirt. He squeezed her legs, scratched her thighs. She felt his fingers hook the top of her underwear. Her head lolled to one side and Winch grinned from over her shoulder. He licked her nose.

David flipped the bottom of the net up and went to work at her skirt, shoving it up her legs.

Darcy's vision cleared. A knife glinted. David was in a rush. He slashed open her skirt and that was his mistake.

Freed from the voluminous fabric, Darcy's right leg snapped up and back, hitting Winch square in the forehead. Her left leg curled in and lashed out, sending David sprawling.

Darcy sprang to her feet, throwing off the small net. Suddenly the mop became a more attractive weapon. She scooped it up, right hand by the mop head, left hand just south of the handle's center. She swung, smashing David across the side of the head. In the same motion she pivoted and jabbed the handle end into Winch's oncoming gut. It sank in farther than was physically possible.

Winch grunted and lurched backward, taking the mop with him. A piece of the handle, broken off by David's head, lay at her feet. The jagged end of what remained had punctured Winch below the sternum and penetrated right to his spine. He tugged at the protrusion while blood ran down the handle to be absorbed by the mop head. Darcy spun to see how David fared. His temple was bloody and his right eye was closed. He was on his hands and knees, unsteady, but trying to rise. A few feet beyond him, underwear was bunched against the wall. He'd managed to get her panties off.

Darcy screamed, swung her foot up as high as it would go, and brought it down, heel like a mallet, to the back of David's head. There was a delicious crunch, both from her heel against his skull and his face against the deck. Behind her, Winch lay on his side, gurgling like a drain.

Feet pounded the corridors from all around her. Disoriented cries echoed back and forth as people called to each other.

Darcy stared from her hands to the two men lying on the floor. She didn't know what to do. There was nowhere to hide, and without guidance, she didn't know where to run. With no witnesses to defend her, this would see her swimming.

"I got her!" yelled a man coming around the bend. "Jesus!" He stopped short and backed up a few steps. He was wearing kitchen whites instead of security garb, and instead of a club he held a ladle.

Another man appeared with a short woman behind him. Both of them wore khaki. From behind appeared another kitchen worker, some people in civilian garb and finally a mixture of security officers both Navy and civie. They blocked the corridor at both ends, surrounding Darcy and her two assailants. One of the sailors stooped beside Winch and checked his pulse. The crowd behind Darcy parted and the Old Bull stepped through. He gave Darcy a once over, then nudged David with his boot.

"This one's dead," said the sailor standing over Winch.

Mark checked David's neck. "This one's not. Will be soon, though. Take him down to the pokey." Two of Mark's subordinates lifted the man and dragged him through the crowd.

Darcy stared speechless at all the people.

"Are you all right, miss?" asked the man with the ladle.

"Yes…I guess I am…" She turned to Mark.

"Everybody get back to what you were doing," Mark snapped. He didn't like having to repeat himself.

Everyone gave Darcy a long look before turning away, making sure for themselves that she was unhurt.

In a few moments, only the sailors, the Old Bull, and one of his deputies were left.

"They attacked me," said Darcy. "Tried to rape me. I acted in defense."

"We know," Mark nodded at the sailors. "You going to take care of him?"

The sailors backed away from the corpse. One of them held his hands up. "You got the other one. This one's yours too."

"How could you know?" said Darcy. "There's no cameras in this area."

"We heard it. The air vents carry stuff everywhere. People heard this all over the ship. Some people are listening right now. She's fine," he said loudly. "She got them both."

Incredibly, faint exclamations and patters of applause drifted down through the vents.

"H...how," Darcy stammered. "How did you hear this over everything else going on?"

"I told you. People were listening all over the ship. Listening to you sing."

"Ohmygod," Darcy squeezed her lower lip. "How many people..."

"Relax. They liked it. We had a fair idea where you were, but not exactly. Took us a bit to find you."

"You're some tough chick," said one of the sailors. He picked up the net. "Lucky they didn't get this on you."

"They did. Then the idiot cut my skirt and gave me some room to breathe."

"Lady, you breathe pretty hard." Mark took Winch's face in his hand. He gave it a shake. "David Ramsey and Winch Forester. Two of the biggest douchebags on the ship. Nobody would ever press charges against them."

"I'll press charges. And after this, do you think I could get a job with you? I'm really sick of these corridors."

Mark leaned back on one leg and looked at her. "No. This just proved my point."

"But—"

"One dead, one going over the side. If this is your usual rate we'll be down twenty men by the time we reach Diego."

"Whatever."

She snatched her panties up and pulled her skirt closed, realizing just how much leg was exposed. If the knife had cut a few inches farther, she really would have been giving people a show.

The Old Bull grinned though the bars and tried not to laugh. "It was her idea? That's what you're sticking with? I'm supposed to ask if you've drawn up your will."

"I want a lawyer." David moaned. He cradled his head while he lay on his stomach on the cell's cot.

"The PD said she was washing her hair today."

"Bullshit."

"No, really." This time he did laugh. "Half the ship heard you, Davy. Why waste time with a trial?"

The prisoner moaned. His face grew even more miserable.

The door separating the cells from the pokey's foyer opened. A sailor stuck his head through the doorway and said, "The captain says go ahead."

"That's that," said Mark. He unlocked the cell door. "Shore's to the east. Let's see how you do at the ten-thousand-meter breaststroke."

***

Darcy sat at the bar in Tanzers, a rag filled with ice pressed against her head.

Caps hummed the theme music from the third Rocky film and shadow boxed. “Mess with the best, swim like the rest,” he said, laughing.

At least the ugly skirt was gone. Tanzer had taken it from her and ripped it up for rags. Now she wore a pair of Tivoli’s pants. They were a bit too long and a makeshift rope belt held it bunched at her waist.

At the far end of the bar, her clothier and Tanzer were having a quiet but intense discussion.

“Caps,” said Tanzer, “get back to work.”

“Fine,” said the artist, heading for the basement.

“Isn’t Noah here somewhere?” Darcy asked.

Caps pointed a finger at Tanzer and said, “He’s got sun boy running all over the Street upgrading people’s power systems.” He looked down into the lower hold, then sighed and descended.

“How’s your head, girl?” asked Tanzer, taking Darcy by the chin and turning her face right and left, his expression compassionate.

“I’ll be fine, thanks.” She gently peeled his hand away.

“Me ‘n’ Tiv were talking. I’d like to offer you a job.”

Darcy looked around. The place still hadn’t been cleaned up from last night. Empties littered tables. The floor was as sticky as a glue trap. A hint of vomit lingered in the air.

“Thanks, but I’m done cleaning up after people. I don’t know what I’m going to do, but I won’t be your janitor.”

Tanzer gave Tivoli an amused look, then turned back to her. “I don’t need a janitor. I need a singer.”

Darcy said nothing for a few seconds. The bag of ice hit the bar top. “A singer.”

“La la la,” Tivoli said loudly from the stage. He sat down at the piano.

“Back in the day I was involved in the entertainment industry,” said Tanzer. “I know talent. You’ve got it. That’s a sweet set of pipes you’ve got.”

“In this instance,” said Tivoli, “he’s referring to your vocal cords.”

“You want to pay me to sing?”

“Yeah,” said Tanzer. “And dance a little. Not a lot. There’s not much room on the stage.”

Tivoli banged out a few stanzas of Joe Cocker’s ‘When the Night Comes’. “You mumbled your way through the first verse.”

Darcy shrugged. "Nobody in my family could ever figure out what he was saying. Oh my God. How *much* did you guys hear?"

"More than enough." Tanzer rapped the bar top. "Go on, get up on the stage. Let's give it a try."

The ice forgotten on the counter, Darcy cautiously mounted the stage and stood beside the piano.

"Pick a tune," said Tivoli, smiling.

With both men waiting, Darcy's entire repertoire deserted her. She couldn't have sung 'Happy Birthday' to save her life.

"Stage fright," said Tivoli, improvising a little bluegrass.

"Gimme a break. I was almost raped. I just killed a man."

Tivoli leaned into the keyboard, playing the opening chords of 'Bohemian Rhapsody'.

"Wayne's World," called Caps's muted voice from below.

Tanzer kicked the hatch shut.

"Deep breaths, hon," said Tivoli. He looked at the keyboard for a few seconds, then slowly, ever so slowly, eased into a Cyndi Lauper song he was certain she'd know. It was before her time, really, hitting the top of the charts before she was even born, but it was a song with staying power.

Recognition dawned in Darcy's eyes.

Tivoli sang the first few words. "*Lying in my bed I hear...*"

Darcy started nodding. "*...the clock tick...*"

She lost the words. Tivoli looped the music, playing the same three bars over again until her brain caught up. By the first 'Time after time,' Tivoli was beaming. By the second chorus, Tanzer's head tilted to one side, lost in a memory of waterbeds and a girl with spiked green hair.

At the song's end, Caps stood half out of the floor hatch, a forgotten rubber drive belt dangling from his hand. "Darcy," he said as Tivoli pinged the last note, "we have to get you a piano."

"There's a perfectly good one right here," said Tanzer.

Darcy looked at Caps, looked at the bar owner with hair so much redder than her own. She took in the room and imagined a full audience, faces vague from the stage lights, all of them watching her.

"I can't." She pushed away from the piano. "I'm sorry, I can't."

"That was great," said Tivoli. "You need some work but that was great!"

"Please," she stepped down from the stage. "It wouldn't work, it—"

"It's because of her stupid scars," said Caps, climbing fully out of the hatch.

Darcy rounded on him, a warning look in her eye.

Caps looked at Tanzer. “She’s got this stupid hang-up about ’em.” He snapped his fingers a couple of times.

“Shut up,” said Darcy.

“Dysmorphia.” He snapped his fingers a final time.

Tanzer considered Darcy’s face. “Yes, I see.” He stroked his beard. “I can see why you’d want to hide those from the world.”

“Oh yeah,” said Caps. “That’s going to help.”

“Tivoli, go get that box of masks.”

Caps turned his palms upward. “You want her to wear a mask? There’s nothing wrong with her—”

“Hush,” Darcy held a hand up to him. “Let me see them.”

A cardboard box was duly located and produced. The masks were of a Mardi Gras style, some very ornate. Darcy was fingering one with a feather trim when Tanzer held up his choice. “This one.”

“Why that one?” Darcy asked reproachfully. It was carved from wood, solid white with eyeholes and a slit for the mouth. The features on it were feminine, but nondescript. “I can’t sing in that. I doubt I could breath in it.”

“Not the whole mask,” said Tanzer, holding it up to her face. “We cut it. We use just enough to cover your scars.”

“Phantom of the houseboat,” said Caps. “It just might work. I think you should give it a shot.”

41. Rocking the Boat

Sid fell into the coal pile and all but slid to the deck. He came up fast, looked for whoever had pushed him.

Ten feet away stood 813, the guy who liked chains. He held up two coal-stained fingers and rubbed them across his mouth. When his hand came away, his teeth were black. He skinned back his lips. It looked like his mouth was empty save for gums. 813 winked and moved off into the mounds.

Sid looked around to see if anybody else was waiting to jump him. Not a person in sight seemed to pose a threat. He gathered up his armload from where it lay spilled across the track. His wrists burned. Crumbling coal was not an easy task.

The sun was directly overhead and motes of black dust swirled in the light.

Sid returned to his workspace and peered into the hopper. It was less than a quarter full.

"What happens if I kill somebody?" he asked.

Jim, hanging over the hopper and only looking busy, pulled down his dust mask and said, "They'd be dead."

"I mean what will the guards do?"

"Hoist the corpse out and pretend to give a shit who did it."

"So there wouldn't be random executions?"

"Nope."

Sid split a large chunk of coal in half by banging it on the edge of the hopper. "So if somebody touches the landing net, we all die, but we can murder each other all we want, and nobody cares."

Jim nodded.

"What if I admitted to the murder?"

"You'd go over the side."

It kept coming back to that. It was an easy exit. There were dozens of ways to get himself splashed. If they were close to land, or even better, docked, that just might work, provided he had a pickup.

"How do I get a message out of here?"

Jim tapped the coal against the inside of the hopper, watching tiny particles break off and drift to the bottom. "You mean to the mainland?"

"No, just to *Terpris*."

"That is the mainland."

"Oh. Okay. I get it. Can it be done?"

"Not for you. Nobody's going to help you until you've been here—"

"Two weeks. I know. I can't wait that long. Can you do it?"

Jim shook his head. "I'm not helping you with anything until you've passed your time."

"You helped me last night." Sid started in on a new slab. "Why did you help me last night?"

"Maybe I just wanted a shower."

Noah almost fell when the rope ladder he clung to started shaking.

"Hey you," said a man at the bottom of the ladder. He looked as if he was going to shake it again.

Noah climbed down a few rungs then jumped, landing on the deck beside the houseboat.

"What are you doing sticking your nose in my business?" His own nose was wide and pointed. His lower lip was twice the size of his upper and his Adam's apple occupied more volume than his chin.

Noah glanced up at the houseboat. The ladder hung down over a window. "I wasn't looking in at you or anything. I was—"

"I'm Gordon Palmer," he said, like it should mean something. "I'm the electrician around here," he clarified in response to Noah's blank stare.

"Oh." Noah considered that. "Oh! So you…" He waved an arm at the houseboats. "You look after all of these?"

"Yeah. I was sick for a couple of days and I find a stowaway in my yard."

Noah looked the man over; gauged him. Bluster or bite? He decided on bluster. Maybe it was the lack of a chin. "Where'd you learn your trade?"

"That's none of your business."

"You don't really know what you're doing."

Gordon's sliver of lower jaw quivered. "You trying to be funny?"

"You haven't used a single bypass diode anywhere. Array placement in most cases is less than optimal. You've got shading problems from the island so there's been thermal destruction in almost a quarter of—"

"Hey! I built half of these arrays."

Noah quirked one eyebrow. "Didn't the Navy techs help?"

"No."

"Do you ever talk shop with them?"

"Why would I?"

"Have you ever looked at their setups and compared them to your own?"

He planted his fists on his hips. "I'm not letting some stowaway take over my business."

"He might, too," said a jovial voice. A middle-aged man with deep dimples sat on the gangway of a nearby houseboat. His skin was brown, his shoulders round. He wore a bright red shirt stitched with patches of gold. "What do you charge, kid?"

"What does he charge?" Noah asked, glancing at Gordon. Might as well go with the joke.

The man named a price. Noah quoted a price twenty percent higher.

"Done," said the home owner.

"Carlos!" squawked Gordon.

"You should ask the kid to hire you on as an apprentice. You might learn something."

Noah looked back and forth between the two men. What had just happened?

"Hey, Gordon," called somebody from between the boats. "They're gonna splash David Ramsey."

The incompetent electrician's face went wide with wonder. "You shitting me?"

"No. C'mon or we'll miss it."

Loud cheering sounded from somewhere down the port side.

"Damn," said the newcomer. "We missed it."

"That was really David Ramsey?" asked Gordon, gazing aft. His eyes danced with joy, as if forty years worth of birthday wishes had all come true at once.

The newcomer stepped into sight. He had a thick blue jacket and long dark hair. "Him and Winch tried to get on some girl. She beat the tar out of both of 'em."

Noah forgot Gordon, forgot his tools, forgot everything. That could only have been Darcy. Where would she be? Was she alright?

"Hey guys," said Lila, coming towards them. She wore a clinging dress with a thick shawl wrapped around her shoulders. She must have been freezing.

"Hey, Lila," said Gordon, almost but not quite stammering.

Lila smiled at Noah. "I came by Tanzers last night but you were gone. I wanted to thank—"

"I have to go." Noah pushed past her and headed for the bow. From behind he could hear the long-haired fellow telling the tale. It was probably completely distorted. *One guy was already dead?* Noah turned, walking backwards, staring towards stern. They'd cheered—*joyeux de mort*—like gooseneckers at a Compton Pit lockout.

He faced front again. Tivoli would know where Darcy was. Tivoli seemed to know everything that was going on.

The door to Tanzers was locked. Noah was charged with emotion. Protective anger vied with fierce pride of the outcome. *Took 'em both out. That's my Darcy.* But she wasn't his Darcy, and it seemed no matter what he did, that was never going to change. He pounded on the door.

"We're closed," a voice called through the door.

"It's Noah."

The door cracked open. Tanzer looked out at him. "Come on, come on in."

Piano music and singing filled Noah's ears.

On the stage, Darcy leaned back on the piano, letting rip with an Avril Lavigne tune while Tivoli practically bounced behind his keyboard.

Tanzer, Caps and a waitress lounged around watching. The place was still a mess.

Noah moved to the tables. Darcy gave him a little wave. Caps kicked out a chair.

"What the hell?" Noah said.

"Tanzer's giving her a job," said Caps. "I don't think I've ever seen her look happier."

"What's that crap on her face?"

"The white stuff? Makeup. They're giving her a half mask thing. She wanted to know what it would look like so," he lifted a hand and mimed rubbing something with his thumb, "I drew it on her. Yeah. What do you think?"

"I don't know."

"I think it looks like Buckaroo Banzai infiltrated KISS." He held a hand up. "That one's so layered you'd never understand it."

On stage, Darcy was singing from her hips. One hand on the piano, the other in the air, her pelvis traced a figure-eight.

Tivoli gave Noah a devilish grin, then turned his attention back to Darcy.

"Did she really just kill a guy?" Noah asked.

"Yeah," replied Caps.

"And now she's on stage singing."

"Yeah." He threw an arm across Noah's shoulders. "Just roll with it, baby. Hey Tiv, how about a little BTO?"

"How close will we get to Diego?" asked Lena. She had two monitors streaming data simultaneously and logbooks spread out on every available surface. A half dozen other terminals were off. She'd be using them too if Lt. Cmdr. McCabe let her have the juice.

"If they've rebuilt like they say, we could come right into the docks. Open the hangar quarter deck," said McCabe.

"Would the barge dock as well?" she asked, trying not to sound too interested.

McCabe gave her a measured look. "The barge doesn't dock."

She held a finger up to McCabe and leaned over to one monitor, tapping a key to freeze the display. She pawed through logbooks until she found the right one and rifled pages. "I don't mean to offend you, Commander," she stopped at one page and flipped it back and forth a few times, "but you've got some very flawed data."

"We're perfect," said a technician flinging tiny darts at a miniature dartboard.

"Oh yes, you're perfect," said an officer, entering the room. He was of medium height and light brown hair framed a narrow face. He stopped halfway through handing off a clipboard and smiled at Lena. "You guys have been holding out on me. Welcome to the Nerd Corps, miss…"

"Back off, Otis," said the Navy tech. "She came with boyfriend attached."

"Lieutenant John Allen, at your service, ma'am. Folks just call me Otis."

Lena shook his hand. "You don't look like an Otis."

"It's because of the Myotis Bat. I'm a sonar man. Anyhow," he gave the clipboard to McCabe, "nice to meet you even if I still don't know your name."

McCabe snapped his fingers and pointed at the hatch.

"Yessir," said Otis, showing himself the way out.

McCabe scanned the clipboard, then looked at Lena. "You were saying something about flawed data?"

She flicked her monitor. "You've got a contact here two years ago on RYTH III." She offered the logbook to McCabe. "According to those logs, based on *Terpris's* position, heading and the settings on your dish, that would put RYTH III…" She scanned the room. Why was there never a globe around when she needed one? "Anyway, I lost RYTH III about that time. My last contact put the satellite a hemisphere away from where you've got it."

"Where are your own logs from that time?" asked McCabe.

"They're back at home."

"I see. So it never occurred to you that your memory might be faulty? Hmmm?"

"No." She took the logbook back and turned a few pages. "And you don't have another contact with it after that."

"Just because we lost it again doesn't mean we didn't find it. It could have drifted."

Lena gave him a look that said *you're reaching.* "That's not a drift. That's an extreme positional change. The satellite wouldn't do that autonomously. I'm not saying you didn't hit a bird, I'm just saying somebody misidentified it."

"Those are my initials on the log," said McCabe. "Let's just agree to disagree."

"How deep is your cross referencing?" She tapped a few keys, switching a terminal's task.

"It could be better."

"I think you've crossed a fixed orbit twice. This one." She highlighted a year-old contact.

"That's a Japanese bird," said McCabe coming around to read her screen.

"Actually it's Australian." Lena smiled apologetically. "The Japanese did build it, though."

"What," said the Navy tech. "FENTAN IC4?"

"That's it."

"She's right, sir. It was supposed to be integrated into the Optus network but there was some legal issue. I think they got around it by selling it to a shell corporation."

The tech ran a search, then crunched some numbers. "If it's a fixed orbital, sir, we can ping it in—"

"Two days," said Lena, without looking at her screens. She twirled a pencil between her fingers.

"Forty-seven hours, twelve minutes, give or take," said the tech.

"You must be wicked at billiards," said McCabe.

Noah clung to the top of the mast and looked out at the horizon. He was getting used to the endless gray of the sea. The home he was working on had probably been a small fishing boat, what with the booms and all. Now rings for trawling lines held wind chimes, flags and bamboo fish that trailed streamers. The solar panel mounted at the top of the mast needed a rotational base to optimize its performance. Something that could be adjusted from the bottom of the mast would be ideal. Noah figured most of what he needed was lying in Tanzer's basement. He shivered and climbed down the rigging. It was getting really cold.

"You were better coming down than going up," said Carlos. "Cashew?" He held out a cupped palm full of nuts.

"Thanks." Noah took a couple and popped them in his mouth. "Mmmm." He went for more but the palm had been withdrawn. "Do you grow these?"

"Sure." Carlos chuckled. "From a vacuum sealed tin in my kitchen." He closed his hand around the nuts and shook his fist. "Bought them in New Portland. Couldn't resist. So?" He glanced upwards.

"That panel's fine if *Terpris* is always going sort of east-west. Right now we're going south, so…I can come up with something. I'll work on it tomorrow."

"You've put in a good day's work." Carlos scarfed the rest of the cashews. "Show me what you can do and I'll tell my neighbors."

Noah packed up his borrowed tool kit and headed for his digs. It was one of two hundred in a single, really funky smelling berthing compartment. Darcy said she'd meet him there later. With everything else going on, she hadn't forgotten what was really important. She wanted to plan Sid's breakout. They had nothing to work with and some serious brainstorming was needed.

A few men blocked the closest steps, taking boxes down into the cramps. Noah waited, looked around. To his surprise he saw Darcy standing a short distance aft of him, gripping a safety rail, staring out at the ocean.

"Hey," said Noah as he approached. He realized only one hand gripped the rail. With the other, she squeezed her bottom lip like she planned to tear it from her face. "Darcy, what's wrong?"

Her head snapped around, her gaze a thousand miles away.

"Darcy…" he took her wrist and pulled, disengaging fingers from lip before she did permanent damage.

Her eyes focused. And she threw herself into him, arms wrapped around his chest, face pressed into his shoulder like she was trying to break bone.

It finally hit, thought Noah. *Take away the adrenaline and the happy piano player and the trauma of the day finally hits.* He returned her hug, feeling a bit uncomfortable out in public like this.

Darcy stifled a sob. Noah squeezed her a little tighter. He had no idea what to say. Maybe being held was all she needed. The tiny devil on his shoulder hoped the need might go a little further.

"There's a gondola thing," she said, pulling away. "It runs between *Terpris* and the barge."

"Okay," said Noah, not sure where she was going with this. "How can we use that?"

"We can't." She broke the embrace completely. "We can't ever use it. That's the thing." She backed away. "I need to be alone."

"I should—"

"I really need to be alone." She fled into the maze of crates and netting.

Noah clenched his fists and sighed. He didn't know how she felt, but he could empathize. After his brief torment in what had once been the Vancouver Aquarium, he knew what it was like to be sexually assualted. He knew what it was like to take a human life.

What he didn't know was that something much worse had happened, and David Ramsey and Winch Forester were the farthest things from Darcy's mind.

The stars disappeared. The prison ceiling was solid now. No open hatches, no hints of freedom.

Sid worked his way to the head, keeping to the mounds, staying away from the puddles of light. Clutched in his hand was the weapon. He'd discarded the idea of using a club. The Samoan had too much of a reach advantage. He didn't bother with chain. As a weapon it was too unfamiliar. Toe to toe, Sid didn't like his chances against the monster. This had to be a stealth kill—a dirty, sneaking nasty little stealth kill. In Sid's hand was a garrote, a coil of wire between two makeshift wooden handles. It was the first time in his life he'd made something for the sole purpose of taking another man's life.

He heard movement ahead. Sid leaned back into a coal mound, took one handle in each hand and crossed his wrists.

"Here, kitty, kitty, kitty," urged a voice in the gloom.

Sid waited. He could see two light spots from his position. The huddle of men scattered from one of them. Atoe stepped in view. Instead of a table leg, this time he carried a sack-wrapped chain. In his other hand was a short length of pipe.

Sid squeezed the handles of his garrote. He was so outmatched.

Whispers traveled above him and he looked up at the barge rats, dangling in their hammocks, passing the word. It was like trying to hide beneath a talking ceiling.

There'd be no element of surprise.

"Thar she blows," came a voice from the gloom. Feet moved in Sid's direction.

A loud groan came from overhead. The stars reappeared. Every spotlight came on. Whistles blew as lines and rope ladders dropped down. Guards rained from the sky. They slid down the lines or dove for the cargo net, bouncing out of it and landing on their feet.

"Game on," shouted one of the guards. He swung out from the hip, his baton catching the head of a prisoner whose infraction was not moving out of range quick enough.

Sid threw his garrote into the debris and moved to starboard, away from the Samoan.

Rifle barrels poked from the bars of the catwalk and guards ran around like overgrown maniacal children, kicking barrels, pulling hammocks, throwing blankets and clothes into the coal.

"It's a raid," said Jim, grabbing Sid's ankle. "Stay in the middle."

"I've got booze!" yelled a guard. He came up from behind a barrel with a plastic jug in his hand.

"Porn over here," called another guard, holding up his prize; three tattered pages, all that remained of a magazine.

Somebody howled in pain. A pair of prisoners ran by.

"People on the mainland," said Jim, "friends, family…they bribe guards to sneak stuff in to us."

Sid peered around the mound. The guards were really putting the boots to some guy. "That'd be these guards here?"

"Yeah. And they deliver. Have to keep the business going, right? But they keep track. When they figure there's enough stuff down here, they toss the place."

"Well looky here," twanged a loud Georgia drawl. "I found myself some money."

"They're all civies," said Sid, noting the lack of uniform.

"Oh yeah." Jim was looking over his shoulder. "The Navy would never be involved in something as corrupt as this."

Sid glanced up at the catwalk, at all the rifles. "Navy?"

"Uh huh. They'll get their cut. Keep your head down."

"Who does this money belong to?" shouted Georgia from the top of a coal pile.

"That's Bomber," said Jim. "He's like the big dog for the civies."

If he was a big dog, he was a bloodhound. Loose cheeks sagged above a thick chin. Still, he would have appeared friendly were it not for the menace in his eyes. "Come on now, this didn't just grow fins and swim in here."

"He's one of the guys who signed me in," said Sid. "Penalty for having money?"

"Over the side."

Bomber shook a skinbag. It clinked. "Well, I guess it doesn't belong to anybody. All mine then." He shoved the bag into his leather jacket.

"If you have friends or family on the mainland, Atoe, guys like him, they tax you," said Jim. "They make your people pay to keep you alive. The guards take a slice on the way in, and then after awhile they come down for what's left of the pie."

Guards were going up now, climbing the ladders or being hauled up by the cranes. One by one, the spotlights went out. One by one, the hatches closed.

Jim backed away. "You're on your own tonight. I can't take the hose again."

Sid waited for his eyes to readjust. All around him prisoners cursed or muttered threats. Gradually the noise level decreased but then a single howl split the darkness.

"Holy shit!" said a voice.

The howl repeated. Throughout the mounds, prisoners moved towards it. Sid joined the flow until he was almost back to where he'd been when the raid started.

In a strand of light, Atoe sat slumped against the wall. 813 was the howler. His arms stretched wide, he held the Samoan by the shoulders and shook him, but it was an impossible bulk to move. Only the head bobbled around a bit, eyes open and glassy.

"The whale's dead," said somebody. Then he shouted, "Raise a Goddamn flag, the whale's dead!"

Spotlights snapped on. Hatches opened and guards rained from the sky.

813 backed away from the corpse and Sid got a better look at the body. Blood stained the Samoan's shirt, left side of the belly. There wasn't a lot of blood. The big man had died fast, but there was nothing internal immediate to the wound that could result in such a rapid demise.

A guard ripped Atoe's shirt open and wiped at the blood.

Sid licked his lips. The wound was small, straight. Up under the ribs, straight into the heart. Somebody down here had a nice, long knife.

"Starboard side," shouted Bomber. "All prisoners to starboard!"

This sweep was far different from the random pilfering of the raid. This time the Navy was involved. The guards spread out, methodically herding the prisoners starboard, then aft. Every man was checked for a weapon, every hand checked for blood.

"He was a good earner," whispered Jim. "It's going to piss a lot of the guards off."

A cargo net descended from the hatch closest to the corpse.

"Well," Bomber shouted at the prisoners. "Get it on the net. Don't make me pick volunteers."

A number of prisoners rushed the corpse. It took six of them. When the corpse was stowed, the line pulled taught and three hundred and fifteen pounds of dead Samoan floated aloft.

“Just this guy,” said a guard, pulling 813 front and center. “Blood on his hands and shirt.”

“I didn’t do it,” 813 cried. “I was on his…” he looked around, “…crew.”

Sid could feel it, so could the guards. A major shift of power would occur the moment the lights went out. 813 would do poorly in that shift.

“I did it,” he said.

“Did you?” said Bomber. “Where’s the murder weapon?”

“Uh…I threw it. Over there somewhere.”

“What was it?”

“Sharpened pipe.”

No way, thought Sid, *did a sharpened pipe make that wound.*

“Good enough for me,” said Bomber. He looked up and flicked his hand. A line dropped down for 813.

“Oh shit,” said the condemned man.

Bomber gestured at a couple of guards. “Try and find the pipe. Give it five minutes.”

Rope around his waist, 813 went up to meet his maker.

A drop of something hit Sid’s shoulder. He looked up and the sweep of a spotlight blinded him. He didn’t see Toffee leaning over the hatch. He didn’t see the blood-soaked scrap of cloth, ripped from Atoe’s shirt, clutched in the hunter’s hand.

Toffee was proud of himself. Landing a squeezed drop on target from so high up? That was a good shot.

A stream of babbling highlighted by “I changed my mind,” and “I didn’t do it,” preceded a short scream. The splash wasn’t audible. Toffee was disappointed.

“We’re losing a lot of workers,” said a guard.

“Diego in a week,” said another. “We always get fresh fish when we’re in port.”

42. Dance Chaotic

"We're ready to go," said Leighton, stepping over the knee knocker and closing the hatch behind him. "Pinocchio is sedated and harnessed. Let's see what happens to the female."

"The other animals?" asked Odega.

"Half and half. Let's have a look at them." Leighton moved from terminal to terminal, flipping switches, tapping keys. One monitor stayed fixed on the smaller dolphin, lazily circling her tank. The other three monitors flipped through a handful of different cameras, showing caged dogs, cats, mice and a squirrel.

Odega plugged the Mimi in to the Ethernet. Leighton took his place at a computer and said, "Whenever you're ready."

"Almost," said Chen. He'd added an oscilloscope to the mix in order to chart the time division of the Mimi's output.

Leighton tapped his keyboard. Lines jumped across the oscilloscope's screen.

On the monitors, the animals were going crazy. Those with fur pressed themselves tightly against one side of their cages, hissing and whimpering. The female dolphin was trying each side of her tank.

"Based on orientation of the cages, each of them is attempting to get as far away as possible," said Leighton.

Odega didn't care about the teeth. He focused only on the dolphin.

"It's looking random," said Chen, his attention split between the oscilloscope and a computer next to it.

On one monitor, the dolphin was growing frantic.

"I think we should turn it off," said Odega.

"Wait," said Chen. "Not yet. Let me bring it down to x/y." He adjusted switches on the oscilloscope. The display changed, rapidly filling with points.

The dolphin was half out of the water, spinning on her tail in the middle of the tank. Suddenly she jetted to one side, smashing her beak on the glass.

"Your dolphin's going to kill itself," said Odega.

"Wait," said Chen.

"One of the cats is trying to chew through the bars," said Leighton. "Its mouth is bloody."

"Wait," repeated Chen.

The surface of the tank water frothed up as the dolphin thrashed. It looked like it was having a seizure.

"I'm shutting it down," said Odega, moving to the Mimi.

"Nononono!" Chen flapped a hand. "Not yet. Wait…wait… Okay, shut it off."

Odega pulled the plug.

A few seconds later all the animals calmed down. The dolphin flitted to the tank's bottom, came back up to the top, rolled to one side and stopped moving.

"Look at this," said Chen. "It's beautiful."

What looked like a ring floated in the middle of the screen. It appeared to be three dimensional, tubular, like a donut, or an inflated inner tube.

"So it's not random," said Odega.

"Oh but it is." Chen clicked a mouse until the image on the monitor was the same as the donut on the oscilloscope's screen. Zooming in showed the object wasn't solid but made up of a number of tight, pixilated spirals.

"Your man Fritz was brilliant," said Leighton. "Pure genius."

"It's a torus chaos attractor," said Chen. "The pattern changes even as it repeats itself. It's both random and finite; arbitrary but predictable."

"And the animals clearly don't like it," said Leighton.

"Neither do we," said Odega.

"We need to replicate it," said Chen.

"You can't," said Odega. "Take it apart, and it will never work again."

"Just because you couldn't reassemble one doesn't mean we can't," said Chen.

"There's nowhere to use it," insisted Odega.

"We could use it *everywhere*!" said Leighton. "Clearing beach landings, paths for the away boats."

"There is no place," Odega said quietly, "that you could put this, without your people living in its sphere of influence."

Leighton stood by the Mimi, a hand reaching for it, but not touching, like a devout Catholic finding Mary's image in a water stain. "Yes, yes. Ted, we believe you had a breakdown of some sort. An episode if you will, but that doesn't prove your theory that this…miracle…induces madness."

"You lived within its area of effect for years," said Chen.

"No." Odega moved to the chalkboard. He drew a rough oval, the circumference of which was made up of overlapping circles. It looked like a primitive two-dimensional representation of the three-dimensional torus chaos attractor. Odega placed his palm against the chalkboard in the empty center of the oval. "We lived here, surrounded but untouched. And everybody who's ever had prolonged and close exposure to a Mimi has gone tooth crazy."

"It could be coincidental," said Chen. "One doesn't need a fancy sound projector to go insane in this day and age."

Odega wasn't listening. He stared at the chalkboard. With his finger he erased one circle near the top of the oval. He drew in a new one that, while still overlapping its immediate neighbors, penetrated deeper into the oval's center. He pictured Compton Pit, walked familiar corridors in his mind.

All around the mess hall, people ate in near silence. Ambient conversation was hushed and brief, the weary discourse of early morning.

In a corner, under a pipe that rattled intermittently, the four of them sat, sipping coffee and picking at hard disks advertised as pancakes.

"Probably got some instant mix in New Portland," said Caps, sucking on a piece of what he'd christened breakfast puck. "They ignored the part on the directions where it says add eggs and butter."

"Ignored or despaired?" said Lena. "The barge won't be docking at Diego."

"Why not?" asked Noah. "Doesn't it need to be resupplied?"

Darcy had yet to speak. She stared at her plate.

"They'll do it with the ship's boats," said Lena. "They don't want to risk the prisoners starting some sort of riot and Diego people 'rescuing' them."

Caps groaned. "That's so stupid. All the liberals have already been eaten. The teeth can smell a bleeding heart a mile away."

"I'm the only woman in communications," Lena continued. "So it's not like I can even pretend to be somebody else and give fake orders to the barge."

"I could try," said Caps.

Lena shook her head. "You wouldn't get anywhere near the place. Very secure. Navy and tech reps only."

"You could join the Navy," offered Noah.

Caps spluttered into his coffee. "No way. Not even for Sid."

"And forget about Odega," said Lena. "We're not getting to him. Not unless he delivers himself to us on a silver platter."

"Darcy," Noah patted her leg under the table, "you were saying something about a gondola yesterday?"

She glanced at him and shook her head. "They put it up when they need it. It can move people and cargo. When they don't need it, they take it down. When it's up, it's heavily guarded at both ends."

"And there's no way you can get a job as a barge guard. Maybe I can."

"No! I mean, you're not big enough. The Old Bull will only hire big ugly men."

"Tanzer'd never let you off the hook anyway," said Caps. "He's raking in beaucoup favor points with the locals, exploiting your know-how and paying you peanuts."

Noah held up a pancake by its edge. It stayed perfectly vertical. "I wish this was a peanut."

"Listen guys," said Lena. "I contacted Compton Pit. I forgot to mention it earlier, what with Darcy's…you know. Seth says hello to everybody. I told him as much as he needed to know."

"How'd Sara take being told she was going to be Boss for a while?" asked Darcy.

"I have to go," said Lena, glancing at a wall clock. "We meeting at Tanzers later?"

"Sure," said Caps.

Lena gave him a peck on the lips and wandered off.

"Wonder what I'll be doing today." Caps stretched out and yawned. "So much junk in that basement. But that's me, saving the world one toaster oven at a time. I'm going to hit the head. Noah, see you later. Darcy you better wake your ass up. If you fall asleep on the piano, Tanzer'll fire you."

"Rehearsals," muttered Darcy.

"Guess I should get at it as well," said Noah, standing.

"Wait," said Darcy. "What's your schedule today?"

Noah took a few seconds to answer. "I'm in the Valley. There's some rewiring they want done in the sphinx building."

"Will that take you all day?"

"Doubt it."

"Then where are you going after?"

"The Street. One houseboat. Kind of a turret thingee I'm trying to come up with."

"After that?"

Noah shrugged. "I might finish my day there."

"And afterwards you'll come straight to Tanzers?"

"Darcy, what's gotten in to you?"

Her mouth quivered, but only for a moment. "I must sound like the worst nag. Lena's in communications. Caps and I will be in Tanzers all day. But you're out here alone."

"I can take care of myself."

"I'm not saying that you can't, but—"

"Look, just because you got attacked doesn't mean I will. What are you so worried about?"

"Noah, if I tell you something…" she looked around the mess hall. Tried to read faces. "Never mind. Forget it. I'm on edge, that's all."

"We'll get the Boss out. I don't know how, but we will. See you later."

Darcy watched him go; watched him like she'd never see him again.

Sid put his shoulder against the cart and pushed. It didn't want to move. He changed his stance, took a deep breath and gave it all he had. With a groan and a shriek of metal, the wheel went up over the obstacle and the cart rolled forward.

"Ahhhhh." Sid heaved a huge sigh of relief and sat down by the track. It was a rare spot in the hold. For a few feet in either direction, overhead nets created a blind spot for the guards above.

"What are you up to?" asked Jim sidling up from somewhere in the mounds.

Sid reached under the cart and withdrew a rectangular aluminum sheet he'd stripped from the bottom of a work table. "I'm glad you're here. I'll need your help for the next bit."

Sid had put the sheet on the track and used the heavy cart like a stamping machine. Parallel lines trisected the sheet lengthways into two wide parts on either side of a thin strip. Sid worked at the metal, folding it backwards and forwards along the score lines until the sheet snapped and all he had left was the thin strip.

Jim watched the entire process, puzzlement in his one eye.

Sid placed one end of the strip on the track, against a wheel, at an angle. "Push the cart," he said. After a small hesitation, Jim obeyed. Sid flipped the strip and asked for the cart to be pushed again.

The aluminum now had two new score lines, meeting at a point. Sid worked the flaps until they broke off and he was left with what looked like an arrow sign.

"What do you plan to do with that?" Jim asked.

"If I'm lucky, I won't have to do anything." He held it straight up by the blunt end. It wobbled. He laid it across his lap and considered it. Then he rested the point on one knee and propped it up, with one finger braced on the flat end. Sid applied just enough pressure that it stayed in place. "Yes, that's the look I'm going for."

"Oh no," said Jim. "You are a stupid man."

Donald Graff finished his shower and backed out of the stall. He toweled off, patted his hair dry and set about shaving his neck and trimming his beard. He was in a splendid mood. Both his evening and early morning had provided a number of fine pleasures. Graff grinned at his reflection in the mirror, seeing nothing repulsive in his uneven, yellow teeth. "I like this place," he told his image. "The mark of any good city is the gregariousness of its whorehouse."

Whistling, Graff left his fancy berth on the 03 deck and made his way down into the Valley. He was looking forward to this next interview. It did not, however, go well. The subject was too paranoid and Graff got too greedy.

"I promise I won't put it into print," said Graff.

"Get out."

"Look, it's off the record. What's the secret? Does *Terpris* use it for more than just a parlor trick, and if not, why not?"

Graff just managed to keep his balance as he was ejected forcefully from the home. It wasn't the magician who turfed him, either. It was his lithe, veiled assistant.

"Strong woman," Graff muttered as the door slammed. Curious that she wore the veil offstage as well. Lovely body on her. Something must have made hell out of her face. Maybe she'd been disfigured learning how to play with bees.

He peered at Mephisto's home. It looked to be made of bundled slats of bamboo, but that, like the magician's craft, was a façade. Under all the décor, it was a pretty ordinary sheet metal shanty.

Graff strolled the Valley, feeling the thrum of the ship beneath his feet. He truly loved all the landmarks. From the Eiffel Tower to the Sphinx, he applauded the effort put into preserving the decade-old models and pavilions. At the same time he thought all it needed was a replica of Mount Rushmore and it could have been the world's largest miniature golf course.

He stopped at the Sphinx, wondered if they'd ever considered knocking the nose off of it. He realized one of the creature's eyeballs was a face.

"Good morning, young Thurlow," he said.

Noah stared at him.

"Oh please." Graff took a step closer. "Not the silent treatment. That's really the domain of women."

"What am I supposed to say to you?"

"Look, the lot of you are still around, so you're none the worse for wear for D'Abo's incursion. You obviously survived it."

"Yeah," Noah said wistfully. "We kicked Gascan's ass."

"And gained the spoils of war, no doubt. I did you a favor, actually." The eyeball scowled at him. "I went too far with the favor bit. Alright. Look, could you come down from there? I find it odd arguing with a head in an eye socket."

Noah's face dropped away, leaving the socket dark and empty. Graff had the ridiculous notion of throwing a giant pirate's eye patch over the thing.

The Sphinx's chest opened and Noah stepped out. "One of the eye lights doesn't work," he said.

"I've done a lot of thinking about this," started Graff.

"Noah Thurlow?" said the sailor. It was more a statement than a question. There were two of them, tall, fit and stone-faced.

"Yes," said Noah.

"Good morning," said Graff, not liking that the two sailors were ignoring him completely.

"Come with us, please," said one of them.

"I'm allowed to be working down here," said Noah. "I'm working for Tanzer. Sort of."

"Come with us, please," the man repeated.

"Excuse me," said Graff. "What exactly is it—"

One of the sailors looked at him with an expression that said, *You're a bug, I'm a windshield.*

"Okay," said Noah. "Okay. I'll come. Where are we going?"

The stone-face twins stepped apart, indicating Noah should walk between them.

"Can I come along?" asked Graff. "The young man and I were having a very spirited conversation. No? Alright then. I'd probably find it pretty dull anyway."

He watched them leave. The sailors weren't touching Noah, but it was very clear that would change should he cease cooperating.

Quitting time on the barge blew in on whistles. Prisoners pulled down dust masks, slipped off their gloves and filed out of the mounds to the feeding tarp.

The hungrier barge rats moved faster, wanting to be front of the line. Sid found a good mound to sit on and wait. He picked a spot with good visibility to the parade of convicts, and low visibility for the two guards by the tarp.

He propped the aluminum arrow on his knee and met every pair of eyes that came his way.

There it is, boys, thought Sid. *It's long, it's slim, it's sharp.*

Nobody had laid claim to killing Atoe. Sure, rumors where ripping back and forth, personal beliefs had been expressed, but nobody had stood right up and said "I did it."

Sid wasn't saying it either. He was showing off his first piece of metal origami.

Most that looked his way looked away quickly. Some measured him. Only one spoke. He said, "Way to go, Queequeg."

A literate admirer, thought Sid, recognizing the name of Melville's whale slayer.

No actual murder weapon had turned up, and nobody believed the job was done with a sharpened pipe, or that 813 had been the doer.

When the guards neared, Sid stashed the fake dagger in the coal. When the last of the prisoners passed him, Sid buried it altogether. He didn't need it anymore. It would have been useless for defense.

When the stewed fish fell from the sky and splattered the feeding tarp, Sid moved through the throng easily, people jostling to get out of his way. It was good. It was working. Now he had some street cred. Now the guards might see him as a go-to guy. The guards controlled the exits. He had to get in good with the guards.

"Back it up," said Darcy.

Tivoli's hands retreated a few bars and started up again.

"Not there. To the second 'He's my man.' "

"Here?" He played a few notes.

"Yes. Can you stretch that?"

"What have you got in mind?"

She hummed something in his ear.

"Okay." Tivoli took a moment to stretch, then placed his fingers back where they belonged. "A little lead up?" The fingers danced.

Darcy came in after four notes, sliding into the chorus. She put her back to the piano, resting her hands against it. On the chorus's second 'He's my man,' she stretched 'man' out to three beats and used the time to push off the piano with a bit of shoulder and a lot of hip.

"Good," said Tivoli. He stopped playing and clapped a few times.

Tanzer, who'd been sitting at the bar watching for most of the day, put down the bit of wood he'd been chewing on and approached the stage. "Now you're putting yourself into it, girl."

Darcy blushed.

"The push off didn't work though. You've got the product but you're not selling it, somehow."

The blush receded. Her cheeks got hotter, but it wasn't from blushing.

"He's right," called Caps's voice from below.

"I'm going to give you to Lila," said Tanzer. "I'll talk to her about it."

"Excellent idea," said Tivoli. "She'll give you some moves."

Darcy's hand, resting on the piano, clawed at the wood. "Isn't Lila the stripper?"

There was a knock at the door.

"I'll get it," called Caps. Any excuse to get out of the basement. He flew up the steps, stopped to crack his back, and opened the door.

Upon seeing Lena enter, Darcy's comfort level kicked up a notch. Still missing one, though.

Tanzer moved to the bar. "Get you a drink?"

"Just water for now," said Lena.

Darcy spent the next few minutes singing on autopilot. She watched the door, looked out the windows. Tivoli caught on that she wasn't entirely with him and deliberately botched a countermelody. "Focus, sweetie."

"Okay, sorry."

The door opened. Caps had neglected to relock it.

Darcy looked over her shoulder. Anticipation changed to disappointment at the familiar face that poked in.

"Are you open yet?" asked Graff.

"For you," said Tanzer, "sure. For everybody else, another forty-five minutes. Lock the door, please." He turned to his performers. "Knock it off guys. You put in a good day."

"Well," said Graff, "I'm sorry I couldn't have dropped in earlier. I didn't know you were a singer." He watched Darcy move to the window. "Yes. The silent treatment."

"What's your poison?" asked Tanzer.

"Scotch?"

"Grog it is." Tanzer filled a mug with what his patrons called beer. His own name for it was a more accurate description.

"Now look," said Graff, taking in Caps's and Lena's glares. "I've thought long and hard about this, and my conscience is clear. I had no allegiance to you people. And don't tell me none of you have done something because you had no choice."

"Whatever," said Caps, turning away.

"It's like I was telling your friend Noah before the sailors took him away. It's not—"

"What?" said Darcy loudly.

Caps was off his stool.

"What sailors?" asked Lena.

Darcy charged at the cartographer. "Where did they take him?" She had the front of Graff's jacket bunched in both fists. "When?"

She released her grip. "Tiv, you have to find out where they took him."

Graff tugged at his jacket, straightened the lines. "I'm certain—"

"Tiv, you have to find out!" A tremor of hysteria ran beneath her voice.

"It's not like they dragged him off in chains," said Graff.

There was a knock at the door. Darcy saw the face at the window and flew across the room. She was on Noah before he'd even managed to step inside.

"Are you okay? What happened?" She was checking him out, looking for bruises or wounds.

"He just wanted to talk," said Noah.

Darcy's face drained of color.

"Darcy, it's okay." Noah took her by the arms. "Odega didn't hurt me. He's not a raving lunatic or anything like that."

"What did he want to talk about?" asked Caps.

Darcy's mouth silently mouthed the name "Odega."

"How did you guys know I was down there talking to him?" Noah let go of Darcy and approached the bar.

"We didn't," said Lena.

"They won't let *me* talk to Dr. Odega," said Graff.

Caps was watching Darcy. For a few seconds there, he thought she was going to come apart at the seams.

"Odega wanted to know if I'd shut down power to the…" Noah trailed off, stealing a glimpse at Graff. "He wanted to know if I'd shut down power to certain parts of the Pit when I first got there."

"Why?" asked Lena.

"I don't know. He didn't tell me. They made me wait in this little room for hours, then Odega asked me questions for like a minute and they brought me up and let me go."

"So Ted can have us delivered to him at whim," said Caps. "That's a cheery thought. First he traps us on board this ship, now we're at his beck and call."

Darcy looked like she was going to say something, but she changed her mind.

"I'd like to help you," said Graff.

"Not in my bar," said Tanzer. "I'm not going to stand around while you plan criminal activities."

"Not unless you get a cut," said Tivoli, closing the keyboard cover.

"I'm not going to break any *Terpris* laws," said Graff. "But I can certainly gather information."

"Couldn't hurt," said Noah.

"No," said Darcy.

"My dear Miss McCullough," said Graff, "carrying a grudge does not benefit you here."

"Maybe," said Noah, "if Dr. Odega could have me escorted to him, he could ask for Sid, too. That would get him off the barge."

"That's an excellent idea," said Graff.

"We don't want your opinion," said Darcy. "We don't need your help. This is none of your business."

"It's sure none of mine," said Tanzer. "I'm going to step out, rustle up that waitress of mine."

He left through some back door. Tivoli also left discretely.

"I don't feel particularly welcome here." Graff, putting down his mug. "Good luck in Diego," he said as he left through the front.

"He might have been useful," said Lena.

"I don't trust him." Darcy stared at the bar top.

"Paranoia's hitting you hard," said Caps.

"This is an awful place," said Darcy. "It's not a community like back home. Everybody here is out for themselves."

Sid stood beneath a hatch, just watching the sky. Lots of prisoners were doing the same. Way up there, clouds rolling by without a care in the world.

Men drifted away. Others drifted in. A guard walked noisily along the catwalk and another one, on the deck by the hatch, spat into the hold.

Sid pulled his gaze away from freedom's window and turned to go. His first step bumped him into a man who didn't move away.

"I'm on Blessing's crew," said the man. His hair and beard were solid black. One of his eyes was lazy.

"Okay," said Sid.

"Blessing said you're going to join us."

"Uh-huh."

"Blessing said you have until tomorrow." The man moved off.

Sid left the track and went for the mounds. It was time to have a talk with Jim.

"935," called a voice from behind him.

Sid turned to find a group of four men crowding the path. A fifth stepped around a pile from the front.

"I'm Pernelli," said Prisoner 672. "This is my crew."

"Hello." Sid checked his right and left. He could scamper up a pile if necessary. His location could be seen from a hatch.

"People are saying you offed Twelve." Pernelli was on the short side. Stocky, though. He had a thick moustache, but no beard. That meant he could shave. That meant he had razors.

"I'm not admitting to anything," replied Sid. Was this guy the real killer? Did he shave with the same blade used to kill Atoe?

"That's smart." Pernelli gave a half smile. "I like smart people. You should join my crew."

"Thought I had to wait two weeks."

"You found the express lane."

"I'll think about it."

"You do that. You're smart, so you'll be able to think about it fast."

A third invitation found its way to Sid a few minutes later. This one was very eloquent.

"It would be mutually beneficial to both parties were you to assist Mr. Ho in his endeavors," said 98. There was something wrong with the man's jaw. It didn't sit right. His speech was unaffected by it. "Mr. Ho offers an excellent health plan. Not working for Mr. Ho means you'll have no health…plan."

"You're an idiot," said Jim fifteen minutes after that. Once again he found Sid before Sid found him.

"I hadn't expected this," said Sid. "That's for sure."

They sat down, out of sight, backs against a broken crate.

"Dumbass stunt like that," Jim muttered. He was angry. "What are you going to do when the real whale slayer comes gunning for you?"

"I won't contest his claim." Sid pulled a sliver of wood off the crate. "I never said to anybody that I killed Atoe."

"Semantics don't mean shit down here. Open your eyes. Look where you are."

"I can see it." He tried cleaning under his nails with the sliver.

"You see nothing. There's a war coming. You're going to have to pick a side."

"Which crew are you going with?"

"None of 'em." Jim stood. "I'm Switzerland." He brushed his pants off. "You coulda been Switzerland too, but you messed that up." He shook his head. "I'm outta here. I don't waste time talking to dead men."

43. Echo of Hamlin

"That's quite a drawback," said Ransom, looking at the three scientists across his table. "But at this point it's merely supposition."

"Correct," said Dr. Leighton.

"But you've demonstrated conclusively that it does repel animals."

"Oh yes."

Odega really didn't like any of this. His breakfast plate of meat and thick hash browns lay mostly untouched. His coffee had barely been sipped. Ransom was going to give the order. Damn the torpedoes and turn the Mimi on.

"I do not understand," said Stukov, scrolling through data on a laptop. "This device's frequency range is between twenty-two and five hundred kilohertz. For humans, audible sound is?" He looked up from the screen.

"Twenty kilohertz," supplied Chen.

"Yes. So, the output of this device should have no affect on us."

"It does," said Odega. "I promise you that it does. The effect may be cumulative or it might be an acute response triggered by a change in blood chemistry: adrenalin, noradrenalin, epinephrine…it could be a level of intoxication. Or even body temperature. I don't know. On a land-settlement the Mimi is ideal as a perimeter defense, but here, leaving it running anywhere on or near the ship would be disastrous."

Ransom drained his coffee mug and looked at the empty bottom. "Why did you bring it to us?"

"It is contradictory," said Stukov. "You bring us a weapon and tell us how marvelous it is, but then say we can never pull the trigger."

Odega shrugged, a slight movement of his broad shoulders. "I didn't think about placement. And I hoped it might be possible to isolate the repulsion affect from whatever causes the mental imbalance." He shrugged again. "I still hope that."

Stukov turned the laptop towards the captain. "I can think of nothing unusual happening with the crew at the times the device was functioning. I will ask for security logs."

"A couple of quick bursts won't tell you anything," said Odega.

"Float the device on a raft," Stukov suggested to Ransom. "Place a volunteer on the raft with it." He paused. "Or perhaps a prisoner."

"Too many variables," said Leighton. "Alone on a raft in the middle of this ocean? I think the only way I'd avoid going mad is if I was sedated."

"A land-based test," said Chen. "Something secure in or near Diego."

Ransom and Stukov exchanged a look. "No," said the captain.

"We would not want this leaving the ship, I think," said Stukov. "It would be unfortunate if it did not come back."

Leighton scratched his head. "What about Hawaii?"

"Yes," said Ransom instantly. "We'll secure a beachfront. Until then, cease all testing. Is that amenable?"

Stukov started to protest but Ransom cut him off with a gesture.

Inwardly, Odega breathed a sigh of relief. Almost immediately his hunger awoke and he set in on his plate.

Chen and Leighton were clearly disappointed, but they weren't going to argue with the captain.

"Except," started Ransom. "For one more 'short burst' as you put it." He smiled at Stukov. "We want to see this Mimi in action."

The wardroom on the barge was a flurry of activity. Guards rolled in and out, dropping coins, booze, barter. Lt. Kevin Thompson's house of gambling was open for business. It was quite exciting. So many bets were available: number of casualties, rate of casualties, specific barge rats' survivability; the list went on. Of special interest was who'd come out on top. The names of the three frontrunners were marked on a grease-board along with their numbers and the house odds.

Ian Blessing, 244, 2/1
Ting Wang Ho, 77, 3/1
Christopher Pernelli, 672, 4/1

The guards were in high spirits. Serious entertainment was coming their way via the four holes in the deck. Diego was only days away and shore leave was a fine thing in a secure settlement.

"No cheating," Thompson called out to the room. "Let's have a fair race. They'll do enough damage to each other without us lending a hand."

Fat chance, thought Toffee, eyeing the grease board.

"You in?" Thompson asked the hunter.

"Nah. I don't like any of the horses."

Lena had the morning off. MCPO Porter and his staff had taken over communications in order to play hardball with Diego's powers that be. At this point only Navy personnel were involved. Security details, landing protocols, all these needed to be confirmed, but of primary importance were Diego's coal reserves.

Compton Pit relied on hydroelectricity, geothermal energy and solar power. Coal wasn't an issue for them. It should have been. Political agendas and land rights issues had been stripped away by tooth and claw, beak and mandible. Surface coal deposits were all over the Pacific Northwest.

Lena reached the flight deck and moved to the nearest rail. She studied the system of safety nets hugging the ship's circumference. It put her in mind of another system. If properly organized, they could rebuild the railways. Sure, tracks had been scavenged, but the ties could be replaced. Tracks could be cleared of debris. They could reconnect the continent with coal-burning trains.

Rick would go nuts for it. Lena could picture him with a stupid engineer's hat on his head, pulling the chord, blowing the whistle.

"Hon," Lena said to the wind, "build me a train track all the way home." She laughed. He'd say he'd do it for her too. He'd go whole hog for a few days, conceptualizing, looking for resources, but in about a week he'd have found a car to play with and all that would come of it would be a schematic or two, and a few rough sketches.

Lena moved forward, looking at the houseboats. The people inside didn't rent. They owned. Sure the real estate was mobile, but this was their property. By the laws of Terpris, relatives could inherit. There was legacy.

If the world hadn't changed, Lena would have been constantly kicking Rick's ass to improve himself. She'd have been the stereotypical nag. But if the world hadn't changed, she'd have never given Rick a chance if they'd ever met in the first place.

A scream came from close by, and something blurred in Lena's peripheral vision. She turned to watch a boy, ten or eleven, vault over the rail. She rushed to look over the side and a pair of children, a boy and a girl, were beside her instantly.

There was nobody in the safety nets. She looked left and right.

The little girl giggled nervously. The boy yelled, "Collin, stop messing around."

"Where could you hide down there?" asked Lena, not seeing any cubbyholes.

The boy jumped the rail, and fell, landing in the loose net and bouncing up to a crouch. Born to the rigging, he took a few easy steps to his left, looking all around.

The closest rope ladder up from the nets was fifty feet away. The closest on the other side looked to be seventy-five feet or more.

Even with agility on the ropy substrate, there was no way the first boy could have made the ladders before being seen.

The second boy climbed to the top edge of the net, gripped tight and leaned over, as if perhaps his playmate or brother was hanging from the underside.

Ice ran down Lena's spine.

The girl started screaming. The boy cupped his hands around his mouth and shouted "Coooollllliinnnnnnn!"

There was no other answer for it. The way the nets were rigged it was impossible to bounce out of them unless a person wanted to. The ocean had been the boy's destination from the get go.

"That's excellent," said Ransom. His heart pounded, and he felt a fire in his limbs that had been absent for a long time now. Inside the tank, Pinocchio was calming down.

Stukov stood by a pair of caged dogs, a predatory gleam in his eyes. "We've got you," he said to the animals.

"I really don't want to wait until Hawaii to proceed with further studies," said Leighton.

"After seeing this," said Ransom, "Neither do I. How soon can you build more of these? What do you need?"

"Ah," Leighton tapped his chin. "Apparently the unit self destructs if you open it. It doesn't explode or anything, but it does cease to function."

Stukov stooped to look closer at one of the dogs' paws. It was bleeding. The animal had injured itself while trying frantically to dig its way out of the cage.

With the Mimi off, it no longer struggled. It lay on the floor of the cage, alternating between licking its paw and fixing Stukov with looks of hatred.

Dr. Chen and Dr. Odega entered the room through a hatch behind the dolphin tanks. Chen's face held expectation, while Odega's was blank.

"I find it hard to believe," said Ransom, "that something that can so affect the animals would have no impact on us."

"We have lousy hearing," joked Leighton. "The cetaceans live in a world of ultrasound. They use it for navigation, finding food. Some whales use sound waves to stun their prey. The dolphins can put out, and detect frequencies up to—"

"Yes, yes," said Ransom, "One hundred and seventy kilohertz. But our own experiments with ultrasound proved of little value above the water."

"It's not the instrument," said Chen. "It's the musician. We had the overture but not the *ad libitum*."

"So you can replicate the output pattern with our own equipment?"

"Yesss," Chen dragged it out a little, as if there were a qualifier to his answer.

"How long to figure it out?"

"Years."

"It's very complex," Leighton jumped in. "The work of a genius or a madman."

"Both," mumbled Odega.

"I don't want to wait years for this," said Ransom. "I don't even want to wait days. I want you to—"

An alert buzzer sounded from an intercom. *"Bridge to the captain,"* said a voice.

Ransom moved to the intercom and pressed a button. "Go ahead."

"There's been an incident in the Street, sir. You might want to report to the flight deck."

"Can't the Marshal handle it?"

"One of our safety nets may have failed, sir."

The safety nets were the responsibility of the Navy.

"*May* have failed?"

"Yes, sir. If it wasn't net failure, a little boy just jumped over the side."

"Okay, folks," Mark boomed. "It wasn't net failure."

A number of voices rose in response from the crowd at Tanzers. Tivoli had opened the doors early, given the circumstances. The shock of it had stunned the ship. Navy and civy apparatuses were shutting down, the personnel going home or to gather with loved ones.

Mark scanned the room for Lena. He gave her a nod and left.

"This'll be their first child suicide," Lena said to Caps. "That's what the Old Bull told me." She lifted a jug and refilled her water glass.

"But the kid might have been trying to hang off the bottom and he fell?"

"The other boy said he did that once in a while."

Caps tightened his arm across her shoulders.

"It happened too fast though," Lena said thoughtfully. "That boy went over the rail, and right over the net."

Caps kept waiting for the explosion, the anxiety attack, but Lena was very calm. Sad, but calm. "You're taking this very well."

"It's not like he was my kid."

"Yeah, but you had to witness it."

Lena sighed. "I've seen worse."

There and gone; bloodless. Everybody in the world had seen worse.

The mess hall was packed. With every single child on board present, many of the parents and all of the teachers, it was hot and claustrophobic. Most of the adults felt inconvenienced by this sudden mandatory assembly, but at the same time they were comforted that both the captain and the XO felt strongly enough about the tragedy to attend. Captain Ransom sat in a chair behind the podium and Stukov leaned against a wall, near a clock and the intercom.

The children ranged from newborns to teenagers. In a closed community like this, every child knew the others. Collin Ellis was a happy kid. He was survived by his father, who now, bereft of both wife (four years ago) and only son, was very much on suicide watch.

Lieutenant Morris Dench, Navy chaplain and counselor, took the stand. He opened with an acknowledgement of shared pain and an uplifting quote from Matthew. This he followed quickly with positive spiritual beliefs from a variety of faiths.

An honor guard of sailors lined the walls.

Dench was getting ready to quote Daniel when a disturbance near the center of the room caught everyone's attention.

A small boy, seven or eight, was hitting the girl seated next to him. Not with the playful slaps of children, but with solid, determined punches.

Adults split the children instantly. The little girl keened, bleeding from cheek and lip.

The boy howled and sank his teeth into the arm across his chest. He bit with every ounce of strength his little jaws could muster.

Ransom was on his feet. He made a fast but subtle gesture at Stukov and scanned the rest of the room.

Stukov stabbed a button on the intercom and said one word: "Stop."

A pair of adults strained to remove the boy from his father's arm. It hurt so bad but he couldn't hit his son. How could he ever hit his son?

A man boxed the kid's ears and the wild child dropped to all fours, panting. Arms encircled his limbs. Children across the hall were wailing.

The boy went limp. He looked at the people holding him and began to cry.

The bitten father and the girl were taken off to sick bay. The little boy hung curled in his mother's arms, eyes dry now. He was unresponsive to her words and gentle rocking. Behind his eyes, something was broken.

Chaplain Dench saw the event as the most miserable of failures. Captain Ransom considered it an unfortunate, but complete, success.

"So it affects some children quite quickly," said Leighton leaning over the Mimi. "What are you, you devilish thing?"

"I think it's military," said Chen. "Your Gerard Fritz was German?"

"No idea," said Odega.

"How much do you know about his past?"

Odega didn't hear the question. He looked at his hands, clean and dry despite all the blood on them. He'd made a big mistake. He shouldn't have stolen that Mimi. He shouldn't have brought it here. "It needs to be destroyed," he said, coming to his feet.

"Not likely," said Leighton. He looked up, saw the expression on Odega's face. "No!"

Chen and Leighton threw themselves on the charging Odega. Odega tossed them aside like they were rag dolls. He backhanded the Mimi off its stand. The unit struck the wall with thump of metal and crunch of plastic. It hit the floor near the analysis hub.

Leighton rushed out of the room.

Chen hit Odega across the back with a chair. The hulking scientist didn't notice. He was going for the Mimi. He was going to grind it to dust beneath his heel. The next thing that hit him was much heavier, and it struck a more sensitive spot.

Odega staggered, streaks of light bursting from the back of his skull. There was a sharp pain in his hip. He turned to see a long pole, at one end of it was Dr. Leighton; at the other end was a needle piercing skin. Leighton pulled the needle out and shifted his grip on the pole so he held it more like a battle staff.

Odega lurched forward. The Mimi had to be destroyed. He fell to his knees, then to his side.

Chen looked at the treasured Hewlett Packard spectrum analyzer clutched between his hands. The screen was broken. He was breathing heavy. "How much did you give him?"

"Half what I'd give Pinocchio. Maybe a little more than half."

Odega's vision, dim overall, grew clouded at the edges. He heard scuffling, some tapping at a keyboard.

"Give me a one second burst," said Chen's voice. "Go."

A moment passed. Odega stared at a paperclip lying under a desk. His head didn't want to turn.

"That's a relief," said Leighton. "It's working. Just the case is cracked."

Toffee grumbled in disappointment. The day was winding down. Lights out was coming and he had his spot on the catwalk all picked out. His pockets were filled with small but heavy objects. The name of the game was exacerbation. Across the deck, Sid Halbert was being bundled into the motorized gondola. Getting to the barge just needed gravity. Getting off of it required a little bit more then that.

Toffee brazenly walked closer. Sid faced the aircraft carrier. It was unlikely he'd turn his head around.

"Don't get too comfortable over there," said the Navy guard. "You'll be coming right back here."

The gondola swung and bounced its way towards the carrier. Toffee envisioned a blue whale soaring from the ocean and smacking the little box, making it spin like a toy before it lost its grip on the cable and plummeted into the sea.

The hunter clucked his tongue and decided the night's dust ups could proceed without his participation. What good was watching a show when its star was away?

44. Gershwin's Orphans

Sid was muscled through the cramps, pushed and shoved at every opportunity. The sailors wanted him to know that he was still very much a prisoner, no matter where he was within the Navy's jurisdiction. The combination of leg chains and knee knockers was truly evil.

He didn't care. Anything was better than the barge. He breathed hard through his nose, drawing in air free of coal dust.

He didn't know what Darcy had done to get him brought here, or what they'd planned for his arrival. They were days out from port yet. Maybe this was a dry run. He watched the corridors and hatchways, hoping for a glimpse of one of his people; his crew, his only crew.

Down they went, past the hangar deck and the second deck. In a small room on the third deck, the sailors plopped Sid down in a chair and left, closing the hatch behind them.

In front of the chair was a table. On the other side of the table sat Theodore Odega.

"Evening," said Odega.

"Evening, Ted. You're handcuffed to your chair."

"So nice of you to notice." He raised his hands and rattled the cuffs that secured him by each wrist to the armrests. "I volunteered for these. You might say I had an episode earlier. You'll have to forgive me if I'm a little dopey."

Sid's heart plummeted. Darcy and the others probably didn't even know he was on board. This was all Ted's doing. "What do you want?" he asked.

"They're letting me speak to you alone," said Odega. He glanced at an intercom, "But certain people are listening to every word."

"That doesn't answer my question."

"We got the Mimi working. The units can function independent of Gershwin. Did you know that?"

Sid shook his head. "No. I didn't. Where is it? Is it on right now?"

"I'm not telling you where it is. It's not on at the moment."

Sid's face stayed stoic. "You really got it working?" He looked at the intercom. "And now they know. And they know the units can be moved. So what now?" He felt the deck vibrate beneath his feet, expecting a course change to occur any second. "Are they turning around? Going north? Is the Navy going to appropriate the Mimis in the interests of national defense?" The last came out bitter and resentful.

"No." Odega swallowed. "*Terpris* stays on course. Lena and the others will disembark in Diego. You're going back to the barge."

They stared at each other for a long moment.

"Why don't you allow children at Compton Pit, Sid?" Odega asked as if each word of the question caused him pain.

"Children are a drain on resources and manpower. They're an irresistible lure for certain animals."

"Don't hand me that dogshit propaganda." Odega's right hand tried to come up. The cuffs pulled taut.

"It's not propaganda, it's…Did something happen here?"

"One child jumped into the ocean. Another broke a little girl's cheekbone and took a chunk out of his father's arm."

Sid slumped a little in his chair. "You shouldn't have taken the Mimi."

"How did it go down at the Pit? Were children playing in the sound net? Really playing outside for the first time in their memories? Or maybe even their lives? What happened? How many children?"

Sid tried to meet Odega's eyes. He couldn't. He looked at the floor.

"So you figured it out." Odega thumped his fists against the armrests. "You had to choose between the children and the Mimis. You chose the Mimis. Easy for you. You had your Darcy and she was all grown up."

"That had nothing to do with it."

"But you knew. You knew what they were doing to them. To us."

"None of us were in the sound net," said Sid. "Not for extended periods of time, anyway."

"I WAS!" Odega pulled at the cuffs. The chair creaked. He took a few deep breaths, glanced at the intercom, then back at Sid. "One of the Mimis projected into my lab."

"Impossible. The animals in your zoo would have gone insane."

"It was the periphery, the very edges. Not enough to repel the animals. Maybe enough to make them edgy. They were locked in cages and tormented by humans. They'd be edgy anyway. We'd never have noticed."

Sid shook his head again, this time violently. "No, I made sure that—"

"And you saw the effect they had on us. Nobody liked guard duty in the caverns."

"The caverns are cold and dark. It means nothing."

"Nobody liked spending time in Gershwin's room."

"What does that have to do with—"

"There's a Mimi under Gershwin." Odega watched Sid's face. "Yes, you suspected even if you didn't know."

Sid shut his eyes and leaned his head back. "That's what you were doing in Gershwin's room with the dog."

"Gandhi was never repelled by the Mimis. She was an old dog, old enough to remember when humans were her friends. I believe she lived within the sound net. Who knows why she eventually approached us. Perhaps she was hungry. I talked to Noah…"

Sid opened his eyes.

"…and he confirmed he might have inadvertently shut power off to certain Mimis during his first few days on the job. When he shut off the Mimi near the zoo, that's when Gandhi turned mean. Although the ultrasonics didn't repel her, it somehow kept her tame."

"The Mimi couldn't have been off for very long."

"Long enough for the effects to wear off. I had her mostly sedated after that." Odega winced at the memory. "I couldn't bear to see her feral. By the time I'd stopped sedating her, you'd repositioned one of the topside Mimis. My lab was no longer within its area of effect."

"Then you took her to Gershwin."

"I let her out of the cage."

"And she protected you from Shangley's raiders."

Odega shrugged. "I was unconscious for that part." He turned his head. A small scar displayed where he'd been struck. "I lay next to that thing, comatose, with a crack in my skull. It's no wonder I woke up insane. And it seems I can suffer from relapses."

"We got Gandhi into the cage," mumbled Sid, not listening. "She turned mean again a few minutes later."

"She turned mean when you moved her from the room, when you moved her away from Gershwin."

Sid looked down. "I don't understand."

"Neither do we. But find me another dog that isn't repelled by the Mimis and I'll tame it. Find me any animal for that matter. They've managed to tame dogs here as well, but the procedure has limited applications, what with the severity of brain damage required. Brain damage."

"I wasn't going to lock you outside, Ted," Sid said quietly. "I'd have found a way to make an exception in your case."

"I believe you."

"Then help me. Keep me here on the carrier. Have them let me go in Diego."

It was Odega's turn to look down. "Give me something, Sid. Give me something I don't know about the Mimis. Tell me something I don't know about Gerard Fritz."

Sid thought really really hard. In the end he said, "I can't. By this point you know far more than I do. I never did understand how the Mimis worked, only what they did."

"You're certain. Absolutely certain?"

"I'm sorry to say that I am."

The hatch opened. The sailors stepped in. The audience was over. They hauled Sid to his feet.

"Wait," said Odega. "Please, a few more seconds." He breathed heavily through his nose. "If I'd been given the choice between children and the Mimis, I'd have picked the children. Damn Gershwin and take our chances with the teeth."

"It was my choice," said Sid. "I take full responsibility."

"Good, then you can take some more. I asked Dr. Leighton to bring me any transmissions Lena may have made to Compton Pit. I guess I felt a little homesick."

"And?"

"Lena's managed a couple of conversations with Seth. Whatever was going on at Underbel got worse. As of a few days ago, Underbel set out for Compton Pit with all their children."

"No!" Sid tried to take a step forward but the sailors restrained him. "They can't do that!"

"You should have told us. You should have given us the choice."

"Tell Lena," Sid insisted. "Tell her everything! She…they'll be there by now. She has to tell Sara, you can't have kids at Compton Pit."

A sailor opened the hatch and they pulled Sid out.

"You have to tell her," Sid shouted again as the hatch slammed shut.

Odega sat alone in the room for a few minutes, brooding. Commander Stukov came in and sat down. The two men regarded each other.

"I can't let you tell Lena Wong, or anybody, anything," said Stukov.

Odega nodded sadly. "I know."

"It can never be known we did something that hurt our own children."

"I know," he repeated.

"I'm afraid you will be confined to quarters until after Diego."

Odega nodded for the third and final time. "I know."

45. Twelve Steps

Sitting in Tanzers's basement, eating dried fruit and drinking beer, the four of them shared looks of frustration.

"Two days from Diego and we have nothing," said Darcy. She was looking straight at Lena.

"I'm sorry," said Lena. "What can I do?"

"You're supposed to be some master of communication and you can't get a message to a man a stone's throw away.

They sat on crates. Any surface not used for a chair was covered in screws and springs, belts and electrical components. Lena picked up a rubber washer and fiddled with it. "All I have open to me are monitored, official channels. Above board. We need to go under. I don't know who to talk to and Tanzer and Tivoli won't put their necks out."

Darcy looked at Caps.

He rolled his eyes. "Like I know how to get in with the criminal element."

"This is where we could use a guy like Toffee," said Noah.

"Go to hell." Darcy stood, threw open the hatch, climbed up the ladder and slammed it shut behind her.

Noah rubbed his forehead. "I'm not even going to try going after her."

Lena tossed the washer into the gloom.

"I didn't say we need Toffee himself," said Noah. "I just meant somebody like him."

Caps looked off in the direction the washer had flown, wondering if he needed that bit for anything. "Toffee would own this ship. He'd be like a puppeteer on crack."

"Two days to Diego," Lena whispered. She took a sip of beer.

"It's harder on her than it is for the rest of us," said Noah, needing to defend Darcy now that he'd looked after himself. "We don't love Sid. She does." He stood. "I guess I am going after her."

Noah didn't close the hatch behind him. Caps did, turning to Lena with a leer. "Alone at last."

Lena gestured at the mess. "Here? Forget it. I'm glad we're alone though."

Caps made room for himself on her crate, pushing at her hip with his. He pulled her into his arms and kissed the top of her head.

"We need to talk," said Lena.

"Tell me about it. Darcy's totally manic. She's really hitting the posts."

"Not about her. About us."

Alarms went off in Caps's head. "How heavy is this going to be?"

"Are you stoned?"

"I wish. I haven't been able to find a connection. I got a little buzz off of cleaning out a coffee grinder but that was a few days ago."

Lena turned, snuggled her back into him. She wrapped her arms around his. "I don't want to leave."

"We can stay down here for a while."

"I mean I don't want to leave *Terpris*."

"Come again?"

"I want to stay on board."

"If we can't rescue Sid?"

"I don't care if we rescue Sid. I want to stay on board."

She tried to keep his arms in place but he was too strong. He pulled away and stood up, almost banging his head. He shot an accusatory glance at the ceiling then said, "You hate the ocean."

"I love the ocean. My father always had a boat. Even now…"

"That's nuts. And what am I supposed to do?"

"I want you to stay here with me."

"I hate this stupid boat. I hate the uniforms. I hate the smells. I hate the knee knockers and that constant vibration and I really hate the millions of dolphins down there just waiting for us to spring a leak."

"This old girl is a fortress," said Lena. "Nothing in the ocean can take her down."

"Oh yeah? Where are all the other carriers, then? Why is this the only one puttering around?"

"This carrier's special, Rick. You of all people should feel that. I believe in her. And the SatCom here? The Pit's is a toy by comparison. You have no idea the places we talk to. I'm on a team here, a smart, efficient team."

"You've got a team back home."

"It's not a team. I'm den mother to a lazy idiot and three people who couldn't track a train, never mind a satellite. If I had a team I never would have had to go to Underbel. Lyle could have gone."

"But then we'd be apart."

"I know. I want us to be together. Here. I'm not going back to underground settlements. I don't want to hide in tunnels anymore. I can stand outside here. I can feel the wind. I can see the stars."

"You can do that at the Pit."

"Compton Pit is a world away, sweetie."

"Wait, wait, wait," Caps held up a finger. "Back up. First you said you wanted to stay here. Just now you said, 'I'm not going back.' " One eye narrowed. "You've already made up your mind."

Lena looked as if she was going to deny it, but stopped. Her hands were on her knees. They tightened in the fabric of her pants. "Commander McCabe says he'll sponsor me for citizenship."

"Oooohhhh." Caps backed up a step. "He knows. He knew before I did."

"Rick—"

"This fancy Navy fellah you're spending all your time with knew before I did."

"Sweetie—"

"You told him before you told me."

"Try to understand—"

"Screw this." He banged the hatch open and sped up the steps.

"This isn't about you!" Lena screamed up at him.

Caps stopped, looking around at the people he'd forgotten about. Darcy sat at the piano, slumped over the keyboard, endlessly tapping the same two keys. Tivoli cleaned mugs at the bar. Noah sat at a table spinning a *Terpris* coin. And Tanzer… well Tanzer was sitting on a chair, right by the hatch, listening to every word.

"I've been nursing this beer for an hour," Lena said, climbing up the steps. "I don't think I have more than one drink a day now. Did you even notice?"

Caps just stared at her. She wanted to keep going in public? This was not her at all. "Yeah, I noticed, but I figured you hated the booze here. I know I sure do."

"Watch it, kid," said Tanzer.

"Rick, there were days at the Pit where I was drunk by breakfast."

"No way."

"I hid it from you."

"You couldn't."

"Darcy helped me."

Caps looked towards the piano. The plinking stopped. Darcy nodded.

"You were stoned all the time," said Lena. "I could have lost my other leg and hidden it from you."

He was speechless. She hated seeing him that way. "You are a brilliant man. You can get a job in *Terpris*."

"What if I don't want to?"

"I'm staying," said Darcy.

Caps groped for a chair, fell into it. "How?"

"I'm sponsoring her," said Tanzer. "You think I'd put all this work into her just so she could waltz away in Diego?"

"We've got nothing," said Darcy. "I won't leave Sid. I can't."

"I'll sponsor Noah," said Tivoli. "Tanzer Enterprises wants to expand into the utilities market."

"Have you people lost your minds?" Caps was out of the chair. "Where do you think we're going? Haven't you been paying attention? This boat isn't taking us on a cruise to Mexico. After Diego, it's go west young man, go west. Hawaii and then we're not hitting land again until we're in another hemisphere."

The distance of travel was too far, too overwhelming. Caps couldn't wrap his mind around it. So far from home; his nice new room and his happy little motor pool where every car worked because of him and he was the world's most popular artist.

"Get a job," said Lena. "And you can get a sponsor."

"Noah?" Caps turned his head, but he knew it was pointless. Sun boy's decision was made the second Darcy announced hers.

Noah spoke volumes with a tiny little shrug.

Caps looked at Tanzer.

"Not me." The proprietor shook his head. "I've been giving you charity work. I don't have a full time job for you."

"I'm an auto mechanic."

"Cars are the jurisdiction of the Navy."

"I can learn to work on boats."

"Boats are the jurisdiction of the Navy."

He looked at Lena, pleading. "I can't believe you made this decision for both of us. What if I can't find a job?"

"Don't put me in that position." She turned her back, wrung her hands. "Don't make me make that choice."

46. Diego

The aircraft carrier didn't dock at Diego. An inspection of the facilities revealed a wide gulf between the settlement's and the Navy's concept of safe. In addition to structural inadequacies, both hymenopteran and avian protective measures were deemed unsatisfactory. This wasn't the cold northern coast of Oregon. Almost December and it was eighty-eight degrees Fahrenheit in the shade; or thirty-one degrees Celsius for the metric set; or three-hundred-and-four degrees Kelvin for Noah. He was a little strange that way.

In this part of the world, the ants never went to bed.

Terpris lay at anchor a kilometer off shore and everything that even came near her boats was inspected for ants and sprayed with pesticide regardless of insect presence.

On the starboard side of the flight deck, forward of the island, Caps stood near a hatch and watched the boats coming in. All day long they'd shuttled back and forth.

A brief flash of light from the shoreline spoke of a flamethrower being used, even as a shotgun's blast from up in the cargo cranes said the Double A's were on top of things.

A dead bird dropped from above, bounced off the rail and wound up in the safety net. A child dropped to the net and snatched up the dead gull, skipping easily along the net until he reached one of the rope ladders. A woman took the bird from him once he'd regained the deck. All along the rails bird collectors watched and waited. It was called shore harvest.

Almost everybody wore protective headgear. The Double A's were good, but every once in a while a bird got through. Anything would do in a pinch: bicycle helmets, motorcycle helmets, hardhats…it didn't have to be bulletproof as long is put a li'l something between a beak and a person's skull. Some birds liked to swoop and claw, others liked to hook and bite. Most fishing birds liked to go for the spear job. Starting their attack approaches from great heights, the feathered things were like heat-seeking lawn darts.

A tourist boat arrived. Caps'd have tourists gawking at him in a few minutes. Maybe it was the helmet he wore.

Getting a job on board the ship had been a miserable experience. *Terpris* had plenty of artisans and didn't need anymore. There were loads of full time handymen and he couldn't even get a job as a janitor. Mistress Cassa ran the cleaning business and she would only employ women. "Men can't even keep their noses clean," was her motto.

An hour before arrival at Diego it looked like Caps was going to get the boot.

"I do know one person who's always hiring," Tivoli had said.

So, feeling like he was carrying the load of six pall bearers, Caps had put in an application.

"Seaman Scagling."

Caps came to attention.

The officer looked him over. "You're dismissed."

"Thank God."

"Come again?"

"Yes, sir." Caps saluted, but with only two fingers on his right hand, he felt more like he was in Cub Scouts than any sort of navy.

He skipped away from his (Caps's gorge rose at the thought of it) *post* and pulled his disco corduroy jacket on over his uniform shirt. Khaki was so not his color. He yanked off his Navy issue helmet and combed his hair back with his fingers. A number of strands clung to his hand. A glance inside the helmet showed even more shedding.

There goes another inch of my hairline, he thought.

A series of shotgun blasts went off near the prow. Caps put his helmet back on and headed straight for Tanzers.

Closer to the bar, Caps pulled his helmet off again and looked inside. He was certain there was even more shedding in it. Rationality turned completely off, he threw the helmet at the ocean. It fell short of the rail, landing inside a coil of rope.

Grimacing, Caps went to retrieve it. He heard a familiar voice shouting obscenities from below. Looking over the side, he saw Tanzer loading something dark and heavy into a cargo net.

"Hey, you Caps?"

Caps turned to see a short man with scruffy brown hair and weather-beaten cheeks.

"Yeah."

"Tivoli told me to find you."

"Is there a problem?"

"You're looking for weed, right?"

The scruffy man instantly acquired an angelic glow.

"You better believe I am. But listen, I don't have any cash right—"

"It's okay." A hand stole into his jacket and came out with a plastic bag of green and gold and glorious. "I know you're good for it. Tiv said you got a job."

"Yeah." He could taste it already, feel its warm and loving glow. "I signed up with the Navy."

The man's eyes flicked to the hint of khaki showing through at the top of the jacket's zipper, at the helmet nestled in the rope coil. "Shit," he said. The bag disappeared.

"What? What? What? What's the problem?"

The dealer took a step back. "Didn't they tell you you're not allowed to toke in the Navy?"

"Oh come on. Yeah, of course they did. Like anybody cares."

"*They* care. They catch you high on duty they'll come after me."

Without realizing it, Caps had brought his hands together as if to beg. "I would never tell them."

"They'd beat it out of you. No way." He backed off another step. "I won't sell to you. You never met me." He split.

Caps stood, reaching into empty air, lips moving but no words coming out. He didn't understand.

"Aaaaaagggggg!" He screamed at the sky. The disco jacket hit the deck and he grabbed the front of his uniform shirt with both hands, biceps bulging. He was Bruce Banner becoming Hulk, he was going to rip the shirt to shreds. He pulled. Not even a button popped. He pulled again. The fabric slipped from his half-hand and he spun left to see the newly arrived tourists, Stephanie and the Old Bull staring at him.

A woman in a yellow helmet started clapping.

"You need to cut ovals in the back of the shirt," said Mark.

Caps snatched up his jacket, retrieved his helmet and stopped to examine the buttons. He tugged at one to look beneath it. Mixed with the threads was metal wire. *I guess buttons don't grow on trees.*

Tanzers was open but only a few people sat at tables.

"Nice uniform, sailor," called Tivoli from the stage. He'd just sat down to warm up.

Caps didn't even spare him a glance. The door opened behind him and Noah came in, wearing a construction worker's hardhat.

Intuition flared and Caps turned to see Tivoli, hands poised over the keyboard.

"Don't even think about it," Caps snarled.

The hands quivered, descended an inch, then found a safe place in Tivoli's lap. "Well, all right. But only because there's no Indian chief."

"Dammit," Tanzer cursed as he backed his way in through the door, dragging a life-size cigar store wooden Indian.

"YMCA!" sang Tivoli, fingers pounding on the keys.

Caps put his forehead on Noah's shoulder. "I'm having a really bad day."

Sid was running with Blessing's crew. Of the three, it seemed like the winning team. It was a microcosm, a university sociology experiment. It was a territory war in a box.

The war was about to end for Sid though. This time he was done.

The guards were adept at fading away. Combat wasn't restricted to lights out. Any place the guards could even pretend was a blind spot was fair battleground.

In a six-man melee close to the bow, Sid had stepped up and gone down fast. It didn't help that he had two sprained fingers and assorted bruised ribs. It didn't help that a constant ringing tone had set up shop in his right ear, and it really didn't help that Prisoner 111 was Wing Tang Ho's best man. They called him Carver. The sonofabitch even had a meat cleaver.

A stunning left cross put Sid on the deck. The cleaver was coming down and there wasn't a damn thing he could do about it. Sid closed his eyes.

And opened them.

The weapon was gone. So was its owner and Sid's skull was still in one piece. Enough mobility returned that he could clamber to one knee. A pair of men rolled on the deck behind him, punching and kicking. Carver lay prone, the top right side of his head caved in. The cleaver was a mile away. Near Carver lay a short length of very thick chain. Sid struggled over to it and picked it up by the end not clogged with hair and blood.

The floor scuffle ended. The man who got up was Sid's crewmate, Prisoner 309. His name was Martin but he went by Pop.

Through hamburger lips, Pop grinned. His smile had a new gap in it and there was blood in his beard. "Look at that." He cupped his hands around his mouth and shouted, "Carver's down." He slapped Sid on the shoulder. "Way to go, Queequeg." They were all calling him that now. Pop pointed at the chain. "Nice. Where'd you have that hidden?"

Carver moaned. His left leg kicked. One of his eyes wasn't seeing anything. He gurgled, having trouble breathing and stretched a hand out, imploring.

Sid shuffled over, reached down, and took the man's dust mask.

***

The barge mess hall was fairly packed. Civy and Navy guards sucked on brewskis—old world beer, straight from the can. It was a special treat dug up by Lt. Thompson. There was a lot of backslapping and tale telling. The war had been fun but all good things must come to an end. A full net of medical supplies had been lowered into the hold and the prisoners had been told, unequivocally, to knock it off.

"Here are the numbers," said Thompson tacking up the list of dead prisoners. "Ensign Miller is handling your winnings."

Miller was a dark-skinned Navy guard with an egg-shaped head.

"And as to the big race," Thompson pointed at the grease board. The names Ho and Pernelli had been scored over. "Those of you who backed the right pony, count your Blessings."

Hands stretched out for coins.

"It was a good run, guys." Thompson snagged the last can of beer. "I'm not happy about that cleaver getting down there, but we cleared out some room, we got a good show." He cracked the beer. "Tomorrow we take on a lot of coal, and then," he dropped into a chair, leaned back and put his feet on the table, "it's a slow ride to Hawaii."

Most of the Navy guards were on shore, or in *Terpris* performing shore-related duties. The four remaining clustered together, around Miller and his cash box.

Toffee sat with one hip on Thompson's table. "You clear a nice piece holding book on this?"

"I allowed myself an acceptable fee."

"Mmmm."

"You might cost me soon. Your boy is still alive."

Toffee watched the payouts, little bags of money, pockets full of coin. "How much did you clear from taking out Pernelli?"

"Excuse me?"

"Pernelli was shot." Toffee tapped his forehead. "From above."

The room went silent. Hands at the cash box froze mid-transaction.

"Pernelli was hit in the head with a pipe," said Thompson, sipping his beer.

"Nah. Somebody hit him in the head with the pipe to hide the entry wound. If you…" Toffee mimed holding something head-sized between his hands "…squeeze the bits together, you can see the hole. It was a soft shot. No exit wound. If you dig around in there you'd find the bullet."

The civies were getting tense, glancing at Bomber for direction. One of the Navy guards kept looking at the exit hatch.

"Pernelli was hit in the head with a pipe," said Thompson. He swung his legs off the table and planted his feet. "And even if he was shot, the bullet is in some fish's belly by now."

"I didn't throw Pernelli's body over the side," said Toffee. "I put it in the cold tank."

Bomber took off immediately. Two civies went with him.

Thompson looked at Toffee, dumbfounded. "Why?"

"I just don't like cheaters."

"This is bullsh—"

"Shut up," said one of the civies.

Hands found rifles. The Navy was outnumbered.

After a few long minutes, Bomber came back to the mess hall and threw a malformed bullet at Thompson. It missed, but bounced off the wall and landed on the table.

Thompson stared at the artifact. "Okay, okay, that's a bullet, but how could anybody have shot Pernelli? We'd have heard it, right?"

"Not with a silencer," said Toffee. "Shitty silencer. That's why the shot was soft."

"This is a frame job. Come on, you guys know my scars. This guy just showed up."

"Why would I do that?" asked Toffee. "What would I have to gain? I didn't bet on this war. And if you go down, I lose out on a big payoff in a few days."

"Check their lockers," said Bomber. "Silencer'd be a pain in the ass to get or make. If I had one, I wouldn't throw it away."

Sid sat on a coal mound holding his life savings in his hands. Three dust masks. One by one, he dropped them over his neck. The place had gone from being the frontline to a MASH unit. Everybody helped patch everybody else up. Factions, temporarily, had ceased to matter. Ian Blessing was king of the coal.

Sid checked his torso, so nicely wrapped with cloth bandages. Smaller strips of cloth held his swollen fingers to his good ones. His cuts were clean, and scraps from the master's table had included topical antibiotics.

In the calm after the storm, Sid's mind, unbidden, roamed back to Compton Pit. He watched lunatic children devolving into animals, running off into the woods to be eaten by the real thing.

"So you finally got yourself a real notch in your belt," said Jim, coming over the mound. "Or did you just stand over Carver holding the murder weapon?"

Sid watched the man but said nothing. He didn't have the energy to argue, and that's all Jim wanted to do lately.

"The guards saw a chance for some population reduction and you helped 'em out real fine."

"I did what I had to do," said Sid.

"Ian Blessing's golden boy."

Sid lay back against the mound. "Why are you so angry?"

Jim's eye flashed. "Because I thought you were different. I thought you were somebody I could…bah." He moved away but stopped and turned back. "Maybe you'll make it, you know? Maybe you'll serve your sentence and they'll let you go, but you'll have to get a job, and there's only one you'll be good for. You'll be right back on the barge, up there, placing bets."

The silencer turned up in Seaman Macomb's locker. It was an ugly thing, welded pipe and steel wool. Macomb wasn't present, but that didn't matter. None of the Navy guards did a thing without Thompson's say so. The civies held an improvised trial, short and blunt. At first Thompson maintained his innocence, but once Bomber took over the prosecution, the bookkeeping lieutenant accepted total responsibility and none of his Navy boys had to accidentally fall into the hold. Money bet on Pernelli was refunded. Thompson called *Terpris* and told his CO he was taking sick leave to recuperate from a broken arm. He didn't have to fake the broken arm.

The gondola chugged off with Thompson inside. Toffee watched from the upper catwalk.

Bomber approached, stood next to him. They were roughly the same size and height. "Good call. Those Navy boys are always ripping us off."

Toffee nodded. "Thanks." *You're next.* "Just doing my part."

"Listen, I'm heading over to the mainland—"

"*Terpris* mainland or mainland mainland?"

"*Terpris* mainland. The real land we call shore."

"Got it."

"A few of us lost large on Pernelli, so getting that back feels like free money."

"Fancy that."

"I'm hitting the brothel. You want in? My treat."

"Nah, I'm good."

"Oh. You like men?"

"Not in general."

"You into some sort of weird stuff?"

Toffee thumped his prosthetic against the rail. "My arm ain't the only place I got bit."

"Oh. Oh man, I am sorry. That sucks. You got enough left to piss with?"

"I get by."

"Well, sorry again. I'll keep that under my hat. See you tomorrow."

The gondola left. Once it had emptied, Toffee called it back and got on board.

"Who's that singing," asked the patron, his mug raised, gesturing at the speakers.

"Some CD," said Tanzer. "Don't know. I could look."

"Please."

"I'll do it later."

"What's the song called?"

Tanzer shrugged.

The patron's head turned suddenly. "Was that a Double A? They're still shooting birds out there?"

Tanzer smiled ruefully. "Some critters don't respect a man's right to drink."

"Ain't that the truth. I'm gonna go check it out." He drained his mug and left.

Tanzer nodded to himself. Nobody was shooting birds. The shotgun blast was on the tape because they'd recorded it that afternoon; Darcy singing something by Kylie Minogue.

"I think she's ready," said Caps, nursing his second and last beer of the evening. He had a curfew. A doglicking curfew.

"She can't dance yet. She's got the moves but not the feel. Whoa!" Tanzer looked at something over Caps's shoulder. "That's a surprise."

Lena sat down. Caps nearly gagged, seeing the gold bar on her collar, the stars on her cuff and epaulets. That she was wearing the jacket at all was a thing of horror.

"Leeeeennnnaaaa!"

"I had to, Rick. As a civy tech rep I could only be cleared for half the material."

Caps looked straight down at the bar top. "I want to go home." His face changed, a bit of hope, a bit of surprise. "This means we can berth together."

Lena winced. "I asked about that." She shook her head. "I'm in officer country. You're down with the enlisted."

"Yeah but there must be some provision—"

"Only if we're married."

"Oh come on!" He looked at Tanzer. Tanzer nodded. Caps did something with his face, it looked like his cheeks were trying to cover his eyes. "They still cling to that shit?" He bit his lip and nudged Lena. "So…"

"No."

"Was worth a shot."

"New brides make new widows. It's not like we lived together at the Pit."

"We had our own rooms though."

"Hey, I have to deal with a roommate."

"I've got eighty-four. Is yours a…heavy sleeper?"

"I'm not even supposed to bring you into my berth. It's against regulations."

Caps grumbled something under his breath. "I suppose Commander McCabe lives in officer country."

"Yes."

"And does he have married quarters?"

"He's a widower. He lives alone."

"What a surprise. So Darcy and Noah are still stuck in that pigsty."

"I've got a place for her," said Tanzer. "And Tiv said Noah could stay with him for a while."

"Well say hello to them for me," said Lena. "I just dropped in for a few minutes. There's some data I want to get back to."

"I have to hit the head," said Caps, sliding off the barstool and shuffling away.

The place was mostly empty. A lot of the partiers were on shore, exploring the tunnels of Diego. The place wasn't the festive bird cage of New Portland.

Diego, when it came right down to it, was a dreary, desolate hole in the ground, but Los Angeles was a write off, and some of the survivors had found their way down to Diego. The fun thing about the place was that a lot of pre-Change celebrities had wound up there, and there was something satisfying about seeing Mister Twenty-Million-Dollars-a-Picture sitting on a crate, scraping an animal hide, earning his keep like the rest of the world.

"Beer or water?" asked Tanzer.

"Water."

He filled a mug and placed it in front of her. "If I was him, I'd grow a pair and ditch you."

Lena was watching Tivoli. He was on stage again, quietly working his way through Gilbert & Sullivan's greatest hits. "Excuse me," she said, turning. "What did you say?"

"I've gotten to know that boy a little since he's been in my basement and he hates that uniform more'n I hate paying wages. He put that on for you. There's a half hour left on his curfew, and you're talking number crunching instead of taking him off somewhere private and saying thank you."

"That's none of your business!"

"Hell, you can even use my bedroom. Just strip the sheets after."

"I'm not going to go have a quickie because some bartender tells me to." She shoved the mug at him. It was still three-quarters full.

Off she went, righteously indignant, but she stopped a couple of paces away and said, "Tell Rick I'm waiting outside."

She was pink and chubby, saggy and a little bit on the ugly side, but Toffee decided he liked her eyes and the sounds she was making so he bent her over the writing desk and gave her the full meal deal.

Alternating between cataloguing the bones in the human body and a fantasy wherein Darcy performed felattio on him while playing with herself, Toffee pounded the woman into three orgasms and almost through the bulkhead.

The moment he was doing more to keep her standing than she was, he tossed her on the bed and lay down beside her.

Dazed smile at her lips, eyes cloudy with dopamine stupor, she reached for his erection.

"Don't." He pushed her hand away.

"But you didn't—"

"I'm saving it."

"For what?"

He rubbed a spot at the base of her neck.

"Ohh. Mmm." Her eyes closed. She wiggled against him.

"So tell me about your husband."

"Hush." She pulled his hand down near her face and kissed it. "I don't want to talk about him."

"I should know who he is, y'know. Help me to avoid him when I leave."

She rubbed his leg with her foot. "Don't worry. He told me he had to be on the barge all night long. Some sort of riot lockdown."

"So he's a guard on that barge thing?"

"Yeah."

"Sounds dangerous. What's his name?" He applied pressure to a spot on her lower back, rolled the heel of his hand back and forth across the muscle.

"Clifford. Mmmm. That feels really good. Everybody calls him Bomber."

"Why Bomber?" If he'd had two hands he probably could have brought her off again.

"It's this leather bomber jacket he's so proud of," she said, in between pleasure noises. "He couldn't find it one day. He ran all over *Terpris* accusing people of stealing it." She started laughing.

"You want to know where it was? Do you? Do you want to know where it was?"

"Tell me."

She stopped laughing. "Under another woman's bed."

They were silent for a minute or two.

"Tell me about Diego," she said.

"Nothing I want to say about it."

"How long have you lived there?"

"I wouldn't call it living."

"What don't you like about the place?"

"Wouldn't know where to start."

Her hand dropped between his legs. "You could apply for citizenship here. Oh, you're all soft."

His fingers traced a circle over her buttocks. "So what other stupid things has Bomber done?"

"Oh, honey, the list is endless."

A hammock hung between an upright fishing boom and the dormant radar tower on Carlos's boat. A second hammock, strung between the tower and the second boom, created a V-shaped configuration. A net tightly rigged above the hammocks offered some protection against diving birds, while a tarp facing the bow acted as a windbreaker.

Noah lay with his head at the vertex and feet towards the boom. From this position he could stare at the three little lights visible on shore. They held his attention more strongly than the millions of stars twinkling in the sky. One of the shore lights had an orange tint to it. Noah blurred his eyes until he could imagine he looked at the Enchanted Forest. In a dangling hawser he saw the cables of his solar power array. In the clanging of a hatch he heard the trapdoor that led to the battery bay of Compton Pit.

In the back of Noah's mind had always been the notion that he would one day leave the Pit, but it never occurred to him he'd ever leave North America.

A double-barreled shotgun rested in his lap, but he'd taken his hardhat off and hung it from a protrusion on the radar tower near his head.

Something shook the rigging and he looked down as an old metal helmet and a spray of red hair moved up the ratlines towards him.

"Hi," said Darcy, when her head was level with his.

"Evening. I thought you'd be at Tanzers tonight.

"They taped me earlier today and tonight Tanzer's slipping the tape in with the other canned stuff to see if anybody reacts to it. I couldn't stand to be in there for that." She climbed a little higher and surveyed his rope-and-canvas domain. "You know, when I was told you were staying at this guy's boat, I thought your berth would be inside."

"I go inside when it rains." He inhaled deeply through his nose. "I like it out here."

"So you chose this?"

"I kind of made it. He had the hammocks lying around. I rigged it up. Look." He reached for a pair of lines, then stopped. "Could you move onto the other hammock?"

She did, awkwardly, releasing her grasp on the rigging only when she was fully on the hammock. She didn't lie down. Instead she sat on it cross-legged.

"Thanks." Noah did something with the lines and the edges of the overhead net dropped down until it enveloped the hammocks on either side. "See? Completely closed in for when I want to sleep."

"Uh…you've kind of trapped me in here," said Darcy, realizing she could no longer get to either the boom or the radar tower.

Noah started pulling on the lines, working the corners of the net back up.

"No," she said. She removed her helmet. "That's okay. Leave it." She pulled her hair over one shoulder and combed it with her fingers. "Why two hammocks?"

Noah shrugged. "Symmetry, I guess."

"So you really sleep out here? You sleep outside."

"Sure. Didn't you ever do that at the Pit?"

"No."

He chuckled. "Yeah, me neither. I like it here, though. I won't be able to do it with some of the places we're going, but here there's not a lot of nocturnal bogies."

"You're picking up the lingo around here. Bogies. Who'd have ever thought we'd be calling birds bogies?" Darcy rocked the hammock gently, looked at the knots and ties and pulleys. "You've picked up the skills, too. Did your dad teach you about sailing?"

"No. We had a kayak, but I've never been on a sailboat. Rigging is just tension, angle and force." He reached into a bag strung between the hammocks, pulled out a blanket and dumped it in her lap.

"I don't need this. I'm not cold." She bunched the blanket into a ball and kneaded it with her hands. "I can't believe you're sleeping outside. It just seems so…"

"Stupid?"

"Brave."

"Mmmm." Noah felt a blush coming on.

"I'm surprised you didn't go ashore," said Darcy. "You know, a last visit."

"To that?" Noah waved at the shoreline. "Everybody I've heard talk about it say the place is a hole. Hundreds of tunnels and every section has its own alpha and set of rules. Caps said he wanted to go and ridicule some movie stars, but I don't care. It's the films I remember, not the people in them."

She made a lazy gesture at his shotgun. "You're armed?"

"I'm a citizen now." He held the firearm with both hands, raised and lowered it a couple of times like he was lifting a barbell. "All citizens of *Terpris* have the right to keep and bear arms."

Darcy looked through the net at the top of the mast. "Is that the thing you've been working on?"

"Yeah." He sat up a bit. "I used the guts of this mammoth blender. It's like Tanzer's got one of every piece of crap that was ever sold on TV. Anyhow," his face became animated, "the rotation is controlled from a crank at the bottom of the mast. I marked up a compass so it shows the best position of the panel in relation to the heading of the ship." He put his hands behind his head and lay back down. "By itself it doesn't give him much extra, but in conjunction with a couple other things I did it'll give him a few more minutes of power here and there."

Darcy tried to appreciate his contraption but it was just a dark shape to her. "So what's the deal on this other guy? The other electrician?"

"Palmer?" He let out a big sigh. "Any good technical specialists are sucked up by the Navy. Lots of incentives. The civies learn to do it themselves or pay this guy. He's not good enough to be recruited."

Darcy lifted the shotgun from Noah's lap. She checked the safety, felt the weight. "It's nice to hold one of these again. So, you going to join the Navy?"

"I don't know. I'd start as an officer. Decent pay grade, or so they tell me. I don't think I'd want to be Caps's superior, though." He stretched, rolling to one side. "And I like staying near Tanzers."

Darcy's hands paused in their examination of the shotgun. *You want to stay near me*. "How are you feeling about this?" she asked. "About, well…" She gestured west.

"Weird. It's really weird. You?"

"Not as strange as you'd think. It's like…I spent years with Sid, always moving. Some places we'd stay a week, some we'd stay a year, some we'd stay an hour. We were at the Pit for a good stretch, but now we're moving again. It almost feels more like home than home. It's just that this time, Sid's not with me, not near me." She looked off in the direction of the barge. Something caught her eye.

Down on the deck, a shape moved into a distant strand of light radiating from a lantern on a davit post. It was man; a large man. Though he was only a silhouette, Darcy knew exactly who he was, and she knew he was looking right at her. She brought the shotgun up without making the conscious choice to do so. She put him dead in her sights and her finger caressed the trigger. She wondered what choice she'd make if she held a proper rifle instead of a scattergun.

"Boom," she mouthed, and shook the gun a little to imitate recoil.

The figure remained motionless for a few more seconds, then left the light, heading aft.

"Mind pointing that at the sky?" asked Noah. "Would suck if my first houseguest got taken out by return fire."

Darcy let the weapon go limp. Her hand was going for her bottom lip, but she caught it, and, turning away from Noah, bit her knuckle. Something was going to bleed. At least she could hide her hand from him.

"What are you doing over there?" he asked.

Darcy handed him the shotgun and shifted in the hammock, gripping it as it swayed. She rotated and lay down, feet in the same direction as Noah's. She turned her head and looked at him through the mesh of both hammocks. "Do you mind if I sleep over?"

"Did you bring any s'mores?"

She patted her pockets. "I must have left them in my other life."

47. No Strings

Chief Engineer Lieutenant Bart Freeman's thick Boston accent was difficult to understand over the din. "If you look up there," he said, pointing at the ceiling, "you'll see where we cut the hole in the flight deck."

Graff looked up at the weld marks, wiping his brow with a monographed handkerchief. His red shirt was turning dark from sweat.

The boiler room, sealed away in zone three of the hangar deck, was unbearably hot and terribly noisy.

Two enormous reconditioned boilers sat side by side, taking up over half of the deck space. Whatever room remained was occupied by bins of coal dust.

Half a dozen sailors attended to the boilers, checking gauges, adding fuel.

"Why not just keep the nukes?" asked Graff loudly. "I thought the things could go decades without refueling."

"Sure," said Freeman, "if we could still get replacement parts rushed in whenever we needed them."

"I didn't think that would be an issue for you people. You trade weapons and ammunition across the world…bits and pieces of military equipment. With the caches at your disposal, how would reactor components be any different?"

"Heh. Mister, there isn't a qualified nuclear engineer alive on this ship, and we don't know any willing to get onboard."

The number three elevator was no more. Instead the aperture and the elevator's support structures had been used to mount the giant funnel that sat on the flight deck, aft of the island.

"We cut right through the decks and hauled out every scrap of them," Freeman continued. "From reactor cores to bulkheads, everything went into the sea. We stripped the funnel from a cruiser and these boilers from a Hong Kong tanker called the *Angel Lee*. It was adrift off the coast of Peru. No idea how it got there. No crew or lifeboats on board. Even the logs were missing. The boilers were set up for diesel, but we modified them."

Graff wiped his brow again and undid the top two buttons of his shirt. "So why not put these down where nukes used to be?"

"Couple reasons I guess. First off, it's easier to run the steam down to the turbines than it would be to mount a funnel from the engine room all the way up through multiple decks. The second reason is nobody wants to be down there. We got rid of anything radioactive but people don't believe that."

The cartographer could feel sweat forming puddles in his hair. Maybe that was why so many of the pit snipes had shaved scalps. "How easy was the refit?"

"Easy?" Freeman laughed. He patted a bulkhead. "Really stressful time in this girl's history. We had to do the work far from shore to keep the bogie activity down. We were weeks in the middle of nowhere, tied off to the *Angel Lee*."

"Commander, this is truly fascinating information, but I don't think I can stand another minute in here."

"It's a calling," said Freeman, leading Graff to an exit. "Meet me in the Dirty Shirt later and I'll buy you a drink."

"No later for me, I'm afraid." Graff offered his most apologetic grin. "My vehicle's packed. I'm off for Diego on the last boat. My publisher was hesitant about financing this little coastal cruise. He'd never let me off the continent."

Freeman slapped Graff on the back. "That's fantastic, man. That you have a publisher, I mean. In this day and age."

"I think it's fantastic that you have an aircraft carrier."

Graff pulled on a helmet and went straight for the flight deck. He grasped the port rail and slumped in relief at the slight breeze. It was actually hot and muggy, but after the boiler room, standing in the center of a campfire might seem cooler by comparison.

He inhaled deeply through his nose, taking in the brine, the fish, the brimstone and bird guts. One thing was for certain: the carrier wasn't boring to the nose.

Two of the starboard davits were empty, what with the ship's away boats gone to shore. Graff looked up and down the port rail, wondering where they'd put the ballast to balance out the righting arm when all four boats were up and secured.

He had everything he needed for a solid piece, finding that the largest challenge had been coming up with enough synonyms of the word "big". His time on the carrier would be the highlight of *Graff's Graphs Volume X*. On top of the social and technological wonders of *Terpris*, he'd also uncovered little intrigues that, should he print them, would make returning to *Terpris* a bad idea.

His tidbits ran from the tolerated corruption of the barge guards to certain perversities of the brothel. Apparently the redheaded proprietor of Tanzers was a bit of a sex fiend, but his own equipment had failed long ago, so now he paid others to enact his fantasies while he watched. Rumor had it that he'd also hidden cameras in his bedroom and tried to entice people into getting it on up there.

That in and of itself wasn't particularly interesting, but when the names of certain officers were hinted at as players in these private shows, well, it just added dimension, didn't it? Made people seem more human. Or maybe a little less.

For the folks who still looked for inequality to rant about, *Terpris* was very much a man's world. The Navy was over eighty-five percent male and the way the carrier dealt with female criminals left an ashen taste in Graff's mouth.

Still, people were mostly free to leave the ship at will and he'd seen no hint of cannibalism, so in that regard the place was more civilized than a few settlements he'd investigated.

At the same time as Graff was looking forward to having stable ground beneath his feet, he regretted not going farther. He had fond memories of the South Pacific. He once left a piece of his heart in Fiji. He'd have liked to have seen those beaches again, even if only the Marines and the combat-trained sailors were allowed to set foot on them.

There was one loose end, however, one tale not yet followed to its end. Taking another shot at it would require bending the rules a little, but the worst that could happen was he'd be invited to disembark a few hours earlier than planned.

"Dr. Leighton," said the guard, "Donald Graff here to see you."

Leighton came around the dolphin tank, sedation stick in his hand, surprised to see the cartographer had already been admitted to the aquarium.

"I didn't get any orders," the guard continued. "But he said he'd cleared with you."

"Yes," Leighton nodded. "Of course. Dismissed."

The guard left. Graff waited until the hatch closed, then said, "Thank you."

"I didn't do that for you. I did that for the Navy. I'd hate to see all the guards you've passed put on report just because you've got a silver tongue."

"We all have our gifts."

"What do you want?" Leighton turned towards the tank and waggled the sedation stick at the dolphin.

"It's my last day on the ship. I was hoping I could convince you to let me speak to Dr. Odega."

"No." He climbed a set of steps next to the tank and opened a section of the lid.

"I wouldn't pry into any of *Terpris's* secrets. It's actually prior to his coming here that I'd like to discuss."

"Even if I were willing to oblige you, which I'm not, Dr. Odega is currently unavailable."

Graff approached the tank and watched the dolphin watching him. "Would he be available before I disembark?"

"Not to you." Leighton checked the syringe and held it over the water. "Is there anything else?"

"I guess not." His shoulders sagged. "Since I'm here anyway, could I at least ask what it is you're doing?"

"You can watch if you like. We're going to drain the tank and clean it. This is a good time to do it since we're at anchor. We'll be hoisting the dolphins out for the duration."

He slid the syringe into the water. Immediately Pinocchio flattened himself into the very bottom of the far end of the tank. Leighton extended the pole as far as it would go, but it came up short, an inch away from dolphin flesh.

"Look at that," said Leighton, withdrawing the implement. "He's learned a new way to contort himself." He descended the steps, leaned the sedation stick against the tank and moved off to a cabinet against a bulkhead.

"Done?" asked Chen, coming in from a port-side hatch.

"No. Look at what he's doing."

Chen's expression of surprise upon seeing Graff melted into a look of indifference, then the scientist's attention was drawn fully by the tank. "You can't reach him?"

"I can with this." Leighton returned with a small crossbow. A syringe-tipped bolt was already nocked and loaded. "Pop the lid."

Chen moved to a three-button panel on the side of the tank. He pushed the uppermost button and the entire top of the tank rose up a couple of feet.

"Can he jump out of there?" asked Graff, backing away.

"The gap is large enough, but there's not enough clearance given the angle of his jumps," said Chen.

"He's tried," said Leighton. "He bangs his head and we mock him." He aimed the crossbow at the dolphin.

Pinocchio rocketed up and twisted, coming parallel with the water's surface as he popped into the air, rigid and spinning. His rotation as he hit the lid sent him sideways, towards the small gap above the tank's top. Water sprayed everywhere as the creature landed on Donald Graff.

The two scientists reacted immediately. Chen palmed an alarm button while Leighton snatched up the sedation stick and rammed it into the dolphin's side.

Pinocchio lay atop his victim like a lover. He bounced and rocked from side to side. Graff's ribs popped like kettle corn.

Chen lowered the dolphin hoist while Leighton stood back and looked on in horror. The only safe course of action was to wait for the sedatives to take affect.

The dolphin bleated at Leighton then bit off Graff's nose.

Two guards rushed into the room but Leighton waved them back. "A few more seconds, gentlemen. Be calm."

"Doctors, what is happening?" asked Stukov's voice from a speaker.

Chen grabbed a mic and said, "Medical emergency in the aquarium. And you'd better come too, sir."

"Don't!" shouted Leighton, slapping down the arm of a guard who'd brought his sidearm up.

The sailor pushed Leighton away and made as if to finish what he'd started, but the dolphin was still, sleeping peacefully upon its human cushion.

Chen pulled the sling down to the ground next to the dolphin. The two guards shoved at the creature, rolling it, forcing blood out through Graff's mouth and the wound in the middle of his face.

Beneath his clothes, the cartographer's chest was sunken, pulverized. His eyes were wild. One foot began to jerk.

Leighton studied the gap between the tank and lid. "I had no idea a dolphin could maneuver like that. He used an overhead surface for lateral movement."

"I'll bet that's the first time it's been done," said Chen. "We just witnessed a moment in cetacean history."

"Shame we had to sedate him. I'd have loved to monitor his vitals after that performance."

"Hey," said a guard. "One of you *doctors* going to do something here?"

Leighton glanced over his shoulder. "Unfortunately, he's dead."

The medical team that arrived seconds later confirmed the diagnosis. Punctured lungs, crushed chest and massive internal bleeding all contributed to trauma *Terpris* was in no way capable of dealing with, either quickly or long term.

Stukov entered the aquarium in time to see the dolphin being lowered to the surface of the tank water.

"We'll be wanting to put some grills around the sides here," said Chen, waving his hand through the gap beneath the raised lid.

"Who gave this man clearance to be here?" demanded Stukov, pointing at the corpse.

Leighton flicked his eyes at the guards, indicating a hasty departure would be wise. "It was a last minute visit," he said to

Stukov. "He came to watch us clean the tanks. I didn't expect this to happen."

"None of you will speak a word of this," ordered the XO.

The body was placed on a stretcher and covered with a sheet.

"Why him?" asked Stukov, after being given the details of the incident. "Would that monster not prefer to kill one of you?"

"Trajectory," said Chen. "Pinocchio couldn't hit either of us with that little trick. I wonder how long he's been waiting for somebody to stand in just the right the spot."

Captain Ransom felt no need to inform the community at large that their science division had allowed a celebrity to be killed by a dolphin, while standing in a hold in the deepest part of the ship.

The corpse was delivered to Diego at the last possible moment before weighing anchor. An aversion to long goodbyes was the official explanation given for the cartographer's quiet departure. A rumor concerning some vague indiscretion was "leaked" to satisfy those who'd actually met the man.

Donald Graff rolled onto *Terpris* as a headline. He rolled off as a footnote.

48. Touched

The show costume hung in strips over one arm of the loveseat. The little white Velcro dots on the fabric matched dark spots on the fingers of the disassembled mannequin on the floor. Sampson lay in a semi-disorderly pile of detached limbs, easily stored, just the way Lila liked her men.

"So," she said, "I'm waiting."

Early '90s dance music issued from a small CD player on a stand near the heap of Sampson.

Darcy felt embarrassed. The private dance lesson was uncomfortable, her normally controlled limbs felt heavy, clunky. Mostly, she hated the outfit; halter top and panties that were little more than a thong.

"It's so I can watch your muscles," Lila had said.

Darcy had a dozen tiny nicks and cuts. It had been a long time since she'd had to shave her legs.

The tempo changed as one unidentifiable techno-beat faded into another.

"Come on, girl," said Lila, clapping her hands together. "Show me what you've got."

Might as well get it over with. Darcy squeezed her eyes shut and went with the music. She tried to pretend she was on a stage somewhere, gold chain around her waist, the tops of go-go boots brushing the bottom of her miniskirt.

She did her best to go with the beat, give a little hip, shake a little ass. Darcy wasn't very good at pretending. She wasn't in a club. There were no flashing lights, no coat check or two-drink minimum. She was in a houseboat welded to the flight deck of an aircraft carrier.

"Forget it," said Darcy, arms coming down mid-sway. She turned off the CD player. "You're just wasting your electricity."

She made for the guest room where Tanzer had talked Lila into giving her a berth.

"I see what Tiv means," said Lila, stretching her legs. "You hate your sexuality."

"He said what? We are *so* finished here."

"You've got a contract with Tanzer, hon. This is part of it. Come on." She took Darcy by one hand and dragged her to a tall mirror in one corner of the room. "Stand here. Yes, like that. Look at yourself. What do you see?"

Darcy tossed her head out of reflex, bringing her hair over the right side of her face. "I see myself. What? I see a halter top that's too small for me."

"You've got a body on you, girl."

"Stop calling me girl."

"I don't mean—"

"It's not the word. It's the way you say it. Like I'm a kid or something."

"I am a bit older than you."

Darcy turned away from the mirror and looked at Lila. If they weren't the same age, then surely Darcy was the elder.

Lila laughed. "Honey, I'm close to forty. I won't say from which direction."

"Not a chance."

"Look." She raised her hands. "Look at the backs of my hands."

Darcy was surprised she hadn't noticed it before. She blinked at the wrinkles, the lines. "How do you do it?"

"Genes, honey. You ever hear of Bertram Wallis?"

"No."

"He was my grandfather. When he was antique, he looked fifty. People thought it was cosmetic surgery, but it wasn't. My dad's whole side of the family was like that."

"Hang on," said Darcy. "Wasn't Bertram Wallis the pilot that…the blast mark on the side?"

"Yes. He was a pilot. That scorch mark is his grave."

"So you've been here…"

"Since the start. I've only been dancing again since we started the Wonders of the World Show."

"Were you a stripper before the Change?"

"I call it dancing without inhibition. My mega-rich family couldn't understand it. What can I say? I'm a born exhibitionist. I made good cash too. I was always a dancer, but I was never a whore. No drugs, no adult movies. I was scheduled to do a shoot for Playboy, though. 'Granddaughter of a Legend' was going to be the title. It was so funny. Hi, my granddad achieved something in his life, so look at my tits."

Darcy laughed.

"There we go," said Lila. "Let's try something different." She removed the CD and went hunting through her collection; no jewel cases; all scratched. "Here." She popped a new one in and hit play. This music was the opposite of what had been playing before. "Spanish," she said, moving back to the mirror. "I can't get enough of the clapping. Okay, face the mirror. Come on, come on."

Darcy grudgingly obeyed.

"Right arm straight up. No, like this, watch me. Don't turn around. Watch me in the mirror." She held her arm rigid but the wrist semi-limp. "Okay, other hand on your stomach. Good. Now sway."

"What, like a tree?"

"Your hips. Keep your right hand fixed in space and sway your hips."

Darcy thought she was doing it right, but a cough from Lila suggested she wasn't.

"Here," said Lila.

It surprised Darcy when Lila pressed against her from behind, put hands on her hips. "Go," she said, "but let me drive."

Extremely uncomfortable, Darcy gave it a shot. It was very hard allowing Lila to guide her. She had an impulse to do exactly the opposite of what the hands instructed. She breathed through it, tried to relax. After a while something changed. There was a rhythm, slightly offbeat, a flow. When she caught it, a feeling went through her from her toes up to her right arm, which by now was getting pretty tired. She let the arm drop and sway.

Lila was pressed tight now, using her entire body to guide Darcy's, watching them both in the mirror.

"That's enough," said Darcy, going rigid. Cheeks burning, she crossed the room and turned off the CD player.

"Oh, girl." Lila hid a grin behind her hand. "It's okay if you were getting turned on. You're supposed to get turned on." She did a little jitter with her torso. "Okay, show me some kicks."

"You mean like Rockette stuff?"

"No. Do something martial arty."

Darcy checked headroom, put her weight on her left leg, brought her right leg up and did three snap-kicks before setting the foot down again.

"There it is," said Lila. "You're so in touch with your body, but only when you're using it for a weapon."

"Yeah, well…it's kept me alive."

"Tiv's told me your story." Lila faced the mirror and struck a pose. "But you're not in security now. Your job now is to be a fantasy." Left hand on hip, right arm held out to the side, she did a boogie roll, the circular motion starting in her pelvis and stopping at her shoulders. "It's about desire, and desire's not an easy sell anymore." She half-turned, watching the reflection of her hip as she shifted weight from right to left. "Desire's about want, and nowadays everybody wants pretty hard. They want the world to be the way it was. So to sweep the audience away with desire, you have to offer something they might want *more*."

She chainéed, throwing in some Cuban motion, a sensual writhing turn that ended with her hands above her head, crossed at the wrist. "And if you want them to want it, then you've got to want it."

Tentatively, Darcy tried to imitate the movement Lila had just done. She looked up at the end and found her hands were nowhere near each other and one of them was clenched in a fist.

"I was wrong," said Lila. "You don't hate your sexuality. You're at war with it. Hon, any idea what it'd take to call a ceasefire?"

Caps was getting better at maneuvering through the cramps. His knee knocker hurdling had improved tenfold and he was getting pretty used to the nearly vertical steps. His increase in proficiency was lost on him because he hated every second of his day. At the moment, he was playing FedEx, running things from one VIP to another. It started with a breakfast tray for a helm officer, then it was documents for MCPO Porter. It went on and on. At one point he had a pickup to do at communications. He'd hoped to get a glimpse at Lena, maybe even a smile and a wave, but he was met at the hatch, handed a disk and told to deliver it to the science lab. At the science lab he was also met at the hatch.

All these cool places he was going and he wasn't allowed to see any of them. It sucked. It all sucked.

The worst thing about going down to the science lab was the labyrinth of steps and passages that segregated Drowntown. Security doors and walls forced a person to go up a few extra decks, over and down, instead of being able to take a more straightforward route.

Caps was at the steps from the second deck to the third deck when somebody shoved him from behind. His feet left the ground completely. A brief moment of freefall ended when he struck metal. He lay on the deck, one leg on the steps. The impact made him woozy, but it was the boot to the head that knocked him unconscious.

"You've been gone a while," said Lena when Lt. Cmdr. McCabe stepped into the room.

"I needed to hunt someone down." He carried two mugs. He placed one beside Lena. "It's tea."

She looked at its golden brown color. "Is that milk in it?"

"Coffee whitener."

"Oh." She tried it. It wasn't totally disgusting. "Thank you."

They were in a smaller computer room off of the main communications hub. This room only had two terminals but it was a quiet place for her to study.

"Is this it?" Lena asked, hooking her thumb at the screen. "All these years of pillaging vessels and this is all the stuff you've logged?"

"It's everything important." He didn't sit at the other terminal. He dragged his chair next to Lena's before sitting down.

"That's not good enough. It doesn't explain anything."

"What were you hoping to find?"

"I don't know…something. A report of some giant convention of whales and dolphins plotting our downfall. Maybe a big wooden boat with a really old guy in it offering to give us humans a ride as long as we came two-by-two."

"Ah. You're one of those." McCabe folded his hands in his lap and nodded. "You thought the answer to the world was in the ocean."

"It's sure not on land. There's something else that's missing. Where are the carriers?"

McCabe's face became serious. "I'm sorry, Mr. President, I can't answer that." He chuckled. "Old Navy joke. But it is the sixty-four-thousand-dollar question, isn't it? We don't know."

"How can you not know? The carriers couldn't just disappear."

"We know what happened to a number of them." He leaned across her, tapped on her keyboard. "Here's a list of…no, that's destroyers. Here. Carriers." He sat back.

"This is sorted by?"

"Nationality. The checkmark indicates we've confirmed their destruction."

"Not a lot of checkmarks here."

"The ocean doesn't leave much evidence."

"You guys say every blue whale in the world couldn't put a dent in *Terpris*. So what sank the carriers?"

McCabe leaned across her again. "I never said they sank." He used directional keys to bring up a file. "You can't imagine how close to catastrophe a functioning flight deck could be every second of its operation. On that first day? Multiple deck impacts. And not like we had. Not like the toys the veterans were flying. There."

A grainy image appeared on the screen and McCabe leaned back.

"This was taken near Anamur. That's in Turkey. You're looking at the *Abraham Lincoln.*"

The carrier was grounded, lying in the water like a building that had fallen over on its side. Low tide exposed a great deal of her hull and a rocky beach was visible beyond the bow.

"It's hard to make out," said McCabe, "but that's the fuselage of an F-18 sticking out of the bridge."

Lena reached up and touched the little blur on her screen. She heard the tearing of metal through metal, felt the terror.

"Here's some more pictures." He clicked away, giving her a slideshow. "You can see the effects of chaos on the flight deck. It's a chain of disasters. On this one, look at where lift four should be."

"Oh my."

"Heavy munitions will do that. Upon closer examination we decided the explosion came from inside."

"Okay, I get it."

"An aircraft carrier was a floating box of jet fuel and bombs. Chaos took care of a number of them, if not the ships themselves, then a significant portion of the crews."

Lena had taken off on her own path, bringing up details on specific carriers.

McCabe sipped from his mug. "There were also confrontations. Ensign Wong, do you know where animals are superior to us?"

"Fangs, claws, acute sense of smell," she said absently. "Agility, strength, innate camouflage." Now she was ticking off fingers. "Lung capacity, wings, venom—"

"Yes, yes. Apart from all that. Most animals, within their own species, settle their differences in ways that don't involve physical harm. They know that to damage one another ultimately hurts their pack or herd, or flock, or whatever. Mankind has never understood this."

"So you're saying on New Wilderness Day, the world's navies blew the crap out of each other."

"On the day and the weeks that followed, yes. It's not all that surprising. Out of contact with your superiors, the world not making sense, and there's a foreign power in your sights, lining you up in theirs. It was never the role of a captain to determine policy. Their job was to implement it. In a case like we had? Shoot first and ask questions later. That's not even taking into account the ways the cetaceans have learned to mess with us."

"So what about the nuclear engines? You stripped them out of this carrier, but what about the *Lincoln*?"

"Oh." McCabe tapped some keys and Lena's screen went black. "We don't go near that part of Turkey anymore."

***

Tanzers was full and for a few seconds, Caps thought the big guy at the door wasn't going to let him in.

"Oh it's you," said Ripper, recognizing last week's basement dweller under his new disguise of Navy clothes and facial bruising. "What's the other guy look like?"

"I wish I knew," said Caps. He pushed past the part-time bouncer and looked around for Lena. He couldn't see her but he found Noah and saw that some chairs had been reserved.

"What happened?" asked Noah when his friend sat down.

"I was mugged." A bandage encircled his forehead and a dark bruise covered his left cheek and the side of his chin. "Don't make a big deal out of it. I thought Darcy was singing tonight."

"She's between sets. You were mugged?"

"Oh my God, Caps!" exclaimed Darcy, appearing at the table. She wore a knee-length red tube dress with spaghetti straps. "What happened to you?"

"Bad day at work. I've never seen you wear a dress before." He signaled to the waitress, held up two fingers. "Or heels. And they almost match the dress."

"He was mugged," said Noah.

"Darce," Caps plucked at a spaghetti strap, "you look fantastic."

"Thanks. I hate the heels. What was taken from you?"

"Even the mask works." It covered the right side of her face, exposing only her eye and mouth. "Makes you look mysterious. Only thing stolen was my pot pipe."

Noah was shocked. "Do you know what happens if the Navy—"

"I wasn't smoking any," said Caps. "I can't even get the stuff. I've been carrying the pipe in protest against the uniform. Secret one anyway. I had it under my shirt in a pouch around my neck."

"That pouch you took from Toffee?"

"Yeah. Don't know why I was keeping that thing. That's gone too." He suddenly winced. "Where's Lena?" He rubbed his jaw, prodded his cheek. "And oh yeah, I lost a tooth."

Darcy took a shuffling step backwards. Her eyes went wide. "Caps, I am so, so sorry."

"What for? It's not like you beat me up."

"So what's happening over this?" asked Noah. "Mugging Navy personnel must be like barge time or swimming."

"Time," called Tanzer from where he stood by the stage.

"You're up," said Noah.

On stage, Tivoli was ready to go again. Ambient conversation dropped in volume.

"I'm so sorry," Darcy repeated. "You have to believe me."

"Chop chop, hon," called Tivoli.

She stepped up onto the stage. A few people clapped.

"They loved her first set," said Noah. "She's not turning though. She doesn't want people to see the scars on the backs of her legs. So do they know who attacked you?"

Darcy mumbled something to Tivoli. He shook his head.

"Nothing's being done, Noah. I told 'em I fell down the steps and I'm sticking to my story. I'm not going to report my pot pipe stolen. That'd be even stupider than enlisting in the first place."

Darcy was shaking her finger at Tivoli now. He was trying to reason with her. She rapped a fist against the top of the piano. Tivoli consented. Darcy moved from the piano to the microphone stand.

"She's a stunner in that dress," said Caps. "How's that affecting you?"

A little smile quirked Noah's lips. "Like I'm in heaven and hell at the exact same time. Can't say I care for the mask. Buddy, you look awful."

"Where's Lena?" he asked again.

"Some sailor came and got her. She said she'd have to miss the second set."

"I guess that's okay. She'll flip when she sees me like this."

Tivoli hit a couple of chords, then rolled out a subtle, poignant melody.

Darcy took the mic in her hands and started. "*There's a saying old...*"

Tanzer wasn't happy. He stormed off towards the bar.

"Ella Fitzgerald?" Caps gave the stage a questioning look. "Second set should start with something more upbeat."

"I don't know this song," whispered Noah.

"It's called 'Someone to Watch Over Me.' " Caps looked around the room, watching people's faces lighting with recognition. Those not familiar with the song were becoming enthralled regardless.

He returned his attention to the stage. The pain in his face and the humiliation burning in his gut faded into the background. Darcy wasn't just singing the song, she was owning it. He'd never seen her like this before and it wasn't just the dress. It wasn't even like she was doing anything amazing with her body. She stood in place, swaying slightly. It was all coming from her head and shoulders.

"I wonder if she's singing about you," Caps joked to Noah.

"Sssshhh."

By the time she hit "I'm a little lamb," her eyes were wet.

"Is she singing about Sid?" Caps asked.

Noah wasn't listening. He was too busy *seeing*. Her words weren't meant for him and he didn't think they were about Sid either, though both of them might be in there somewhere. As she turned her face upwards, sang the last line, Noah felt like she was open, raw, and completely tapped out. She wasn't singing for a man. She was singing to the universe. The lyrics spoke of a missed opportunity, but Noah heard a plea for help and Darcy stood at the edge of the short stage as if she teetered over an abyss.

Tivoli finished with a gentle flourish, letting Darcy's voice carry the last few beats.

The audience erupted. Darcy gave a slight bow of her head, and left the stage. The applause continued. A few people stood up.

Tivoli closed the keyboard cover. On her premier night, Darcy's second set lasted only one song, but she wouldn't be able to top that. Her performance had been a show stopper, a real one, and thus, the show had stopped.

"That wasn't a song for her," said Noah. "That was therapy."

49. Kama'aina

"Okay, men, grease up and remember not to lick your fingers," said Major Dawson as he rolled the cart into the prep room. The cart was laden with black metals cans and rubber gloves of various colors.

As Marines approached the cart, Dawson noticed an unfamiliar face in the back of the room. "Who are you?" He asked, cutting across the room to Toffee.

The hunter looked up from where he was cinching the top strap on his left boot.

"It's okay, sir," said Sergeant Fincher. "He's one of us. He got on at Astoria."

Toffee stood up and rapped on his prosthetic. "If I still had my right forearm, I could show you a tattoo."

"Where did you serve?" asked Dawson.

"Ever hear of the Thirteenth MEU?"

"Who was the CO?"

"Col. McIntyre. Andrew McIntyre."

"What about the chaplain?"

Toffee looked up for a few seconds. "Hudson, I think. Lt. Hudson."

"The Fighting Thirteenth were in Korea on Fubar Day. How'd you get back to North America?"

"Were they? I wouldn't know. I wasn't with them at the time."

Toffee lifted a forearm protector and stared at it for a moment before offering it to the Major. "Do you mind?"

"And why weren't you with them?"

Toffee wiggled his prosthetic.

"I see."

"I already went through this with him," said Fincher. "We *are* a man short."

"Alright then." Dawson took the offered piece of armor and strapped it to Toffee's left forearm. "Can you handle a rifle?"

"He's got a really good prosthetic," said Fincher.

"Welcome aboard," said Dawson. "What are you doing in *Terpris*?"

"I'm a barge guard right now."

"Show me you're worth something today and you might have a new job."

Marines, thought Toffee as the major moved off. *The few, the proud, the gullible.* He'd never been a Marine, but the Thirteenth Marine Expeditionary Unit's presence in New Guinea had once scuttled a very lucrative operation of Toffee's, and he'd made it a point of learning everything he could about them in case an opportunity came along to return the favor.

In *Terpris* the Marines were an exclusive bunch, a faction within a faction. There were only twenty-five of them now, and of that number only ten were among the original unit doing security on the carrier.

Dawson was only a major for the same reason that Ransom was still only a captain. There was nobody higher up to promote them.

Toffee one-handed a web-belt, whipping it around his waist and catching the buckle. The gear was excellent. Flexible, with a series of metal and ceramic plates, the landing suit provide maximum bite protection while not adding tremendous weight.

"Here," said one of the Marines, offering Toffee a glove and a can. All around the room, men were smearing a reddish gunk on themselves, rubbing it into the outer fabric of their armor.

"What is this stuff?" Toffee asked, pulling the glove on with his teeth.

"Special marinade made from hot peppers and bug spray. Everything hates the taste of it. Don't get it in your eyes."

The Marine held the can while Toffee reached in with two fingers and scooped out a big, oily dollop. As he rubbed the noxious stuff into his clothes, he smiled to himself, happy about how well things were working out. Everybody who could pose a threat to Sid Halbert had either been bribed, intimidated or eliminated. Unless Halbert did something stupid, Toffee could take some time off, and avail himself of opportunities to shoot things.

Geared up, the Marines moved from their prep room to a secure portion of the hangar deck that now acted as a motor pool. A pair of vehicles, looking like armored pickup trucks with tank treads, rolled out to elevator one, where cranes on the flight deck would lift the vehicles onto one of the landing boats. The Marines called them ACV's—armored cargo vehicles; the Navy called them baggage carts.

With the vehicles cleared and the lift returned, the Marines crowded onto the platform as their landing craft descended from the davits. They hustled into the covered back of the vessel as all around them Double A's spent their ammo and deck-mounted launchers fired cheap and dirty chaff rockets into the sky.

To the west, the sunny island of Kauai beckoned with its flawless beaches and lush foliage.

Sailors, wearing similar gear to the Marines, piled into the second landing craft.

Through the hull of the boat, Toffee heard eruptions from the water. Depth charges, flung from *Terpris* and set to detonate shallow, cleared a watery path.

"Away the boats," came a voice through a speaker.

Cables raced through pulleys and the three vessels hit the water.

Levers were flipped, detaching cables. They'd have to be reattached externally, but for now nobody wanted to be outside a second longer than they had to. This wasn't hardhat weather, this was stay-the-hell-inside weather. The birds had been thick and constant for a couple of days now. Large flocks of "tuna birds" foraged far from the islands, subsisting on small prey driven to the surface water by predators. Sooty terns, wedge-tailed shearwaters and black noddies got shredded in the air, littering the Street with feathers and guts.

This close to the islands, petrels and Layson Albatrosses, nocturnal feeders, made the nights almost as dangerous as the days. That the Laysons were in their breeding season made it that much worse.

The three vessels cut through the low sea, heading for a white sand beach.

Toffee checked his respirator and goggles. These he'd be wearing under a facemask made of thick, hard wire and bugscreen. It was going to be crazy hot.

Hollow *thumps* from above announced the launch of mortar shells packed with the closest thing to tear gas the Navy was able to manufacture. It wasn't quite as strong. The Marines called it frown gas.

The vessel slowed, turned and placed its stern to the beach. The ramp-like hatch fell open and the men charged through ankle-deep surf and onto the gas-choked sand.

Toffee had locked the fingers of his prosthetic to the pump of the shotgun. He'd much prefer a rifle, but that's what they'd given him. The .357 on his hip was personal property, his oldest friend in the world. His belts and webbing carried flares and knives, a flashlight, a radio and a pair of funny little tube-shaped grenades the Navy called junior mints.

"Give me burns at eleven and one o'clock," Dawson ordered. The two men with flamethrowers moved up and took point. Ferns and koa trees charred and sizzled. Gas shells arced farther into the forest and Sgt. Fincher radioed in, "The beach is secure. Over."

The ACVs trundled up the beach and into the tree line, crushing everything in their path and giving an audio and visual focal point for men trying to find their way through goggles, mesh, wire and gas.

The sailors merged with the Marines and the combined force moved west. Relics of civilization rotted away amidst the vegetation, the final remains of a once thriving resort.

"Keep it tight," shouted Dawson.

"I golfed here once," said a Marine, voice barely intelligible through all the protection on his face.

There was no festival here, no real shore leave. Nature had cleaned out the Hawaiian Islands entirely and on Big Island, the animals had also been evicted.

Five years ago, *Terpris* had staged a landing on Big Island, gathering, among other things, a healthy supply of Kona coffee beans. This time around, the place was a giant mound of obsidian and magma. Somewhere between five years ago and the present, Mount Kilauea, an active volcano, had stopped gurgling and gone for a nice long spew.

The only mammals endemic to the islands were monk seals and a small type of hoary bat, but pretty much everything else had been imported. People kept cats and dogs and the occasional exotic. The islands were host to over forty types of ants including the red imported fire ant, an aggressive stinging ant the islands were desperately trying to get rid of long before everything went nuts. Fire ant colonies created multiple queens and some of those queens could fly. The bite was nasty and often carried with it secondary infection.

What really killed America's fiftieth state was its inability to deal with the catastrophe while cut off from the rest of the world. *Terpris* didn't know exactly what had happened at Pearl Harbor, but it was easy to assemble a probable scenario by looking at the wreckage.

If there were any human survivors on the islands, any at all, none had attempted to make contact with *Terpris*, nor had any evidence suggesting long term post-Change habitation ever been found.

The clam bakes were over, the hula dancers vanished like footprints in the sand.

"*Terpris*, we have reached the primary objective. Over," said Dawson into a radio. "Form up," he shouted. "This is where it gets dangerous."

***

Caps scrubbed like mad at a vertical pipe in a storage bay on the port side of the O3 Deck. He'd gained a great deal of sympathy for Darcy in the last few days and wondered if there was any way he could learn to sing. As he banged his knuckles on a pipe bracket for about the four-hundred thousandth time, he honestly could not decide which was worse; standing for hours at an end keeping watch over some hatch or another, or breaking his back hand-scrubbing floors and fixtures in compartments not cleaned for months.

"Having fun?" asked Lena, stepping over a knee knocker.

"Hey." Caps gave her a weary smile and dropped his scrub brush on the deck by the bucket.

She hooked a finger in the collar of his shirt, pulled him close and kissed him.

"Fraternizing with the enlisted men," said Caps, grabbing her ass. "You're such a rebel."

"I've been locked out of communications," she said, wriggling her posterior against his hand. "There's something going on in there I'm not cleared for. So I figured I'd come find you. You going to be stuck in here all day?"

"Until this section is done, yeah." He held her at arm's length and gave her a head-to-toe. He had to admit, she looked good in the uniform. Her pants fit quite nicely. "We're all restricted to the lower decks right now, though I'm pretty sure once we're away from the islands I'll be scrubbing bird guts off of anything made of metal."

Lena rolled up a sleeve, dunked her hand in the bucket and came out holding a second brush. "Okay, I'll help you. We'll get it done quicker and then we can goof off somewhere."

"Lena, you're my angel."

"I'll help you, I won't do it for you. If you start slacking off I'm outta here."

"Scout's honor," said Caps, giving her his two-fingered salute. "Start over in that corner. You look good, hon. You look really good."

"Thanks," she blew him a kiss. "You look awful. How's your jaw today?"

"I'm past the worst of it." He flattened himself against the wall and strained his arm to scrub a patch of wall blocked by the pipe.

"Rick, what would it take to secure an area large enough and long enough to play a game of football?"

"That's an odd question. You were never into sports. Hmm." He held his brush like a football, cocked his arm and imagined himself on the gridiron. "A lot. Birds would probably attack the football on kicks and passes. What would really suck is when the mascots devoured all the cheerleaders."

"In other words, it's totally unfeasible."

"Yeah, why do you ask?"

"One of the officers said the landing party was going to go play Superbowl."

"You're a blocker," said Fincher. "You're on sky. Do not track your target to eye-level. There will be zero friendly fire."

"I'm not an idiot," said Toffee.

"I never said you were. We lost last time. We're winning this time. Coverage. Your job is coverage."

"Bogies inbound," said a Marine.

A twenty-four gun salute met the diving avians, smoke and feathers everywhere.

The gas was no good here where the trees grew sparse and long-leafed three-foot high plants—*Ananas Comosus*—took over. The Marines and sailors had separated, forming up with their own kind, each group of twenty-five behind an ACV. The vehicles started forward, crushing and pulping the vegetation. Wide sprays of pesticide fanned out behind them.

Twelve Marines and twelve sailors had slung their rifles. They were the quarterbacks and needed both hands free.

Each team had twelve blockers and the final man per side raced through the green and yellow caltrop-looking vegetation, planting chaff launchers and setting them off.

"Game on," said Dawson, blowing a whistle.

The object now was to be the team that got the most footballs into their ACV. The poison wake of the vehicles took care of the ants while quarterbacks shoved their hands into the plants and picked the pineapples; delicious, golden, sugary pineapples.

Because nobody wanted to get close enough to the ACV's that they were hit directly by the spray, they'd lob the fruit into the cargo bed from a distance.

Toffee trotted forward but kept his eyes on the sky. Being able to lock his artificial hand to the gun provided a type of control that was fantastic. He felt a rare moment of gratitude. If there was still a mail service, he might have sent Neil Eggerson a postcard.

Pineapples bounced and thudded into the cargo beds. The chaff launchers tossed all sorts of crap up into the air. It dissuaded some birds, confused their approach, but others ignored it.

Toffee tried to identify each avian he blasted: red footed booby, Ala Moana heron, the great frigate. Some of them used to be on conservation lists. To those ones, Toffee ascribed a pre-Change price tag. Halfway through his ammo, he'd calculated that he alone had shredded $125,000 worth of contraband decorations and illegal entrees.

The commanding officers shouted encouragement to their men. Toffee plastered a diving fish hawk that got so close its demise splattered entrails across a half-dozen Marines.

"Dogs inbound at eight and two o'clock," shouted a sailor.

The animals were lean and shorthaired. Many generations removed from their original domesticated gene pool, these hounds subsisted on shallow-water fish, bird eggs and turtles. Now they wanted a bit more variety in their diet.

Blockers spread out north and south. Toffee slung his shotgun and pulled his sidearm. He wanted to save his scatter ammo for the birds.

Something part-terrier bounded towards him through the pineapple plants. Toffee's bullet hit the thing right in the nose, flipping it over backwards. The shot earned the hunter a nod from Dawson.

The ACVs turned, describing a wide arc that ended with them facing the beach, heading home.

One of the Navy blockers had ranged too far from the path. He came running back, covered in ants, and practically pressed his lips to the pesticide sprayer. Another sailor was off the ground, clinging to the back of the ACV. He was injured. Even with the body armor, birds got in lucky hits.

"The bleachers are getting crowded," shouted a Marine.

Feathered menaces were coming in from all directions, and something new was on its way from the forested area to the west.

"It's over, sir," called Fincher. "We woke the bats."

"Time, ladies," Dawson bellowed.

The quarterbacks gave up fruit for firearms. Everybody had to get under their masks long enough to put their respirators back in place. Dawson took an extra second to blow his whistle.

Marines hurled junior mints into the air. Tarps were thrown over the cargo beds.

"We kicked your ass," yelled a sailor.

"Get splashed," returned a Marine.

"There a prize for this?" Toffee asked Fincher.

If the sergeant replied, his answer was lost to gunfire.

"Out of ammo," called a sailor.

Gas shells went off in front and behind but they were too late to prevent the next mass dive. It was like it was raining birds.

Toffee gave up trying to put a name to anything. His ammo ran dry. Something dark and feathery hit him in the face. He took more impacts on his back and side. His foot caught a tree root and over he went, birds clawing at his armor.

A number of the birds jerked and quivered, brought down by the gas. Some were less affected than others. A hand grabbed Toffee's belt and hauled him to his feet.

The men stumbled forward, clinging to the ACVs. Chaff and toxic vapors finally did their thing and the landing party reached the beach. They staggered towards *Hugin*, *Munin*, and the *Nancy Dean*.

Dawson did a headcount and swore like a madman when he came up one sailor short.

The birds were coming through the gas now. Diving blind but hitting more often than not.

Hatches closed. The boats sped for home.

"Keep your masks on, boys," came a voice from the speaker. The compartment filled with pesticide. Nobody wanted ants finding their way onto *Terpris*. Vents opened along the top and sides and the air cleared fast.

Toffee pulled his headgear off. He was almost happy to only have one real arm because it meant a few less square feet of skin that ached. He undid a snap on his vest and tried to shrug out of it but that wasn't going to happen. His lack of strength surprised him, humbled him, maybe even scared him a little bit. The armor plates had stopped penetration but the continuous impacts left Toffee feeling like he'd been beaten with a bag full of tennis balls.

Marines and sailors were mixed in the landing craft, cliquish separatism abandoned during the retreat.

Bits of armor, belts and webbing slid off men and littered the floor.

"You're a man down?" Toffee asked Fincher. "All the ammo, fuel, munitions and a man for a few hundred pounds of pineapple? It's worth that to you?"

"The first day is always the worst," said the sergeant. "We'll be coming back for sugarcane, breadfruit and coffee. It's not like Big Island but Kauai has coffee." He fumbled at his vest buckles. "By the time we leave we'll have decimated the local fauna. By the time we're back again it'll have totally repopulated." He gave Toffee a weak slap on the shoulder. "You did good out there."

"The boats are back," said Lt. Cdr. McCabe, sliding one earpiece half off. "We're down one of our boys."

Cmdr. Stukov squeezed his eyes tight shut and lowered his head. "Who?" he asked after a minute.

McCabe paused for a few seconds before answering. "Lt. Nabikoff."

Stukov shifted in the command chair and sighed. "He was tired of this world. Perhaps he went willingly. Perhaps I shouldn't have allowed him to go."

"Can't watch them all."

"No. Now there are six of us. Six of the Russian Navy, yes? Only six." He stood and leaned over McCabe's terminal. "And the others?"

"They checked in a few minutes ago. So far, they're fine."

On a strand of beach far from where the football players had landed, Captain Ransom sat on an upended bucket and stared at the clear blue sky. No chaff, no gas blocked his view. He wore body armor, but no helmet or mask. Bobbing gently fifty feet from shore, *Terpris's* fourth landing craft, the *Enrique*, waited for a signal or a sign.

Ransom reached over and picked up his water bottle from where it sat on top of the Mimi. The unit was attached to a laptop and a battery. It was on and fully functional. In a few more minutes he'd check in again, but for now he was playing mental games. He'd run through names of his subordinates, inventoried the motor pool and the munitions supply. He'd made a chronology of the last twenty landings and estimated the ship's food stocks. So far his brain was running in perfect order. He turned on the bucket and stared at the tree line, tempted to pick up the Mimi and move inward.

Shaking off the urge, Ransom detached the radio from his belt and pressed the button. "All is well. Over."

"Acknowledged. Over."

Ransom reclipped the device to his belt and contemplated radio protocols. Then he took a trip back in his mind, wandering a virtual construct of his house in Virginia. He started at the front lobby, looked up the stairs with their polished mahogany banister. He went left, into the living room walked past the leather couches to the fireplace and the family pictures on the mantle. Through the living room was a short hallway that led to his study. In the study was a desk he never worked at for lack of room. The desktop was covered in photos of his son and daughter.

Way up in the sky, a pair of birds veered away, unwilling to descend into the Mimi's area of effect.

Ransom got off his bucket and knelt down next to the sleeping Marine. He checked pulse and breathing. All systems go, as it were. The man wasn't actually sleeping, he was sedated. But based on Odega's supposition that unconsciousness might exacerbate the effect in an adult, they'd called for a volunteer and filled up a needle.

A man waved from the *Enrique*. Ransom waved back and gave an okay sign. Everybody was nervous on this one, but the captain couldn't ask anybody to do something he wasn't willing to try himself. His senior officers had beaten out of him the concession that he wouldn't be the one sedated.

"I haven't gone insane yet," he shouted at the boat.

Ransom kicked at the sand, checked his watch, looked at the trees again.

The unconscious Marine—Lt. Woods—twitched a little. His right hand clenched into a fist.

"What dreams may come," said the captain under his breath. "He's moving," he said into his radio. "Might just be having a bad dream. Over."

"Acknowledged," came McCabe's voice. *"Standby. Over."*

The fist relaxed, then clenched again.

"Captain," said Stukov's voice, *"there should be no movement whatsoever. We'd like you to return home. Over."*

Ransom watched Lt. Woods's face begin to twitch. "Alright. Experiment is done. We're coming in. Over."

Ransom moved to where his gear lay piled by the bucket. He pulled on his respirator, then his mask and finally his helmet. He waved at the *Enrique* and a chaff rocket exploded over his head as he switched off the Mimi.

50. Illusions

"Oh come on," said Darcy, slapping the bar top with a hand. "What's wrong with 'Frosty the Snowman?' "

Tanzer eyed a bottle of tequila before setting it back in a rack. "I said no."

"There are no animals in Frosty."

From down the bar, Tivoli shook his head and looked away.

"It's the thumpety-thump-thump," said Tanzer. "In the chorus. The thumpety-thump-thump makes people think of Thumper the Rabbit, and that makes people think about Bambi. Nobody wants to think about Bambi."

"That's just stupid," said Darcy. "Now you're—"

"I said no." Tanzer hoisted a box of empty bottles and moved off to his back rooms.

"You gave it a good try," Tivoli said to the fuming Darcy. "He's never allowed Christmas carols in the place and he wouldn't start now, even for a face as pretty as yours."

"I like carols. I like caroling." She crossed her arms and gave the bar a light kick.

"Did you really do that much of it back where you come from? Compton Pit?"

"No. Not really. But I wasn't a singer there."

"Tanzer hates Christmas. He hated it before the Change and nothing he's seen has made him change his mind."

"What about 'Away in a Manger?' " she asked meekly.

"Cattle, second verse."

" 'We Three Kings.' "

"They rode camels."

"Where does it say that in the song?"

"Uh-huh, like they walked across the desert."

" 'Silent Night.' "

" 'Sleep in heavenly peace' is a death metaphor."

"I give up."

"Smartest thing you've done all day. Oh c'mon," he squeezed her shoulder. "I know what'll cheer you up. I'll show you one of my favorite things."

"What the hell do you think you're doing up there?" Noah shouted up the rigging of a houseboat.

From the top of the mast, Gordon Palmer looked down, cheeks reddening in guilt.

"I don't believe this," said Noah. "Now you're sabotaging my work?"

"I'm making up for your incompetence," Gordon yelled back.

"This boat is my customer, not yours. Get down from there."

Gordon's face grew dark. He shifted his position in the rigging and changed his grip on a wrench. It looked like he was going to throw the tool. "You just back off, stowaway."

Noah was tired and cranky. He'd been up late the night before working on a proposal for the Merchants Guild and the last thing he needed was for this nitwit to be messing around with work already completed. "Palmer," he growled. "Either you come down, or I'll come up."

A warning cry came from somewhere on the Street. It was echoed by another. Both Gordon and Noah turned to look, but neither of them saw the black dot hurtling from above.

The bird struck Gordon Palmer in the side of the head with enough force to toss him from the mast. He did two complete aerial cartwheels. It was probably the coolest-looking thing he'd ever done in his life, which ended a moment later when his neck broke on impact with the deck.

The wrench landed at Noah's boots and he gaped at the crumpled man, lying dead not twenty feet away. People came running from all directions and a panicked squawking sounded from above.

"Goddamn Wandering Albatross," said a man, looking up. Fourteen feet of white feathers were tangled in the rigging. "Albatross," the man shouted down the deck. "Albatross," he shouted in the other direction.

Heads swiveled up, searching the sky but only a few clouds could be seen.

A number of people rushed indoors.

"Are we near land?" Noah asked. He was under the impression it was open ocean until the new year, that after they'd left the Hawaiian Islands there'd be nothing solid until they reached Oceana to the northeast of Australia and New Zealand.

“Those things fly five hundred kilometers a day,” said the man. “Stupid bogies. They spend most of their life in the air. Lucky for us they’re loners. They don’t flock.”

People reappeared wearing helmets and hardhats. A voice declared Gordon Palmer dead. Somebody yelled for Double A’s while somebody else asked if they could just throw the poor excuse for an electrician over the side.

A number of people stood around, staring at the albatross, but not doing anything about it.

“So what do we do here?” one of them asked. “Draw straws?”

“We could ask for a barge rat to be brought over,” said another.

“I’ll do it,” said Noah with a tinge of disgust. The bird was completely trapped in the net and no more danger to anybody. He picked up the wrench at his feet, clambered up rigging and beat the creature’s head to a pulp. He climbed back down again, but once on the deck, the witnesses all backed away from him.

“What?” said Noah, looking at his arms and chest. “It’s just a little bird blood.” He rooted around in his toolbox for something to cut the bird out of the rigging.

“It’s really bad luck to kill that kind of albatross,” said a man. “Might be bad luck just to see it happen. I’m heading in.” He wandered off and the rest of the onlookers did the same.

“Seaman Scagling?” said the officer, coming to a halt just before the puddle of water.

“Look,” said Caps, “I’m working as fast as I can.” He shoved the mop head into the bucket hard enough to make a splash, then remembered to add, “Sir.” This particular spot of the O2 Deck was never going to come clean, ever. He could mop for days and it wouldn’t look any different.

“I understand you’re an auto mechanic?”

Caps released the mop handle. His entire demeanor changed. “Yes, sir. I’m about as good as they come. Not meaning to brag, sir.”

“Well, we’ll see about that. We have an opening in the motor pool. Clean up this water and report to zone one on the hangar deck.”

“Yes, sir!” He grabbed the mop and with more enthusiasm than he’d shown for anything in the last few weeks and set about slopping up the puddle. “Uhm, sir,” he said suddenly to the officer’s retreating back.

“Yes, seaman?”

“Uh…you expanding the staff or did somebody…was somebody promoted?”

“Died, you mean? Did somebody die?”

Caps grimaced and nodded.

"When you get served any pineapple over the next few days, take the time to really enjoy it. You'll be reporting to Petty Officer Lewis. Carry on."

"I can't let you go up there," the sailor said to Tivoli. "We had an albatross earlier."

Tivoli put his hands on his hips and searched the sky. "Nothing up there now. Wandering?"

"Yes."

"It get anybody?"

"Some civy. Gordon Palmer."

"Oh, him. He's an asshole. He okay?"

"He's dead."

Darcy had moved against the wall of the island. At least there was a catwalk over her head.

"Look," said Tivoli, "we never get more than one of those at a time."

"Orders, Tiv," said the sailor.

Tivoli whispered something in the sailor's ear. The sailor hesitated then chewed his lip. "I'm going to take a short walk to aft. I'm advising you not to ascend." He strolled away.

"I really don't think this is a good idea," said Darcy.

"Relax. Palmer ate a bogie for us. Heck, we're safer now than if he hadn't taken a bird hit."

"That makes no sense."

"Just humor me. Come on. We can grab hardhats at the Pri-Fly."

He took her up six ladders in the island until they reached the Primary Flight Control, where they grabbed hardhats from pegs by the hatch door. Through another hatch and up another ladder they stopped at a thin catwalk surrounded by six-inch-high crawl-rails.

The only things above them were radar dishes and antennae. Tivoli sat down and dangled his legs over the side. "Sit," he said, patting catwalk beside him.

With one final hesitation, Darcy joined him, gripping the crawl-rail tightly in case some unseen force pushed her forward.

Eight stories below, all four-and-a-half acres of the Street spread out beneath them. It was dizzying.

"This is one of your favorite things?" Darcy gasped.

"Sure is. Just look at it. Look at the deck, look at the ocean. Where else in the world can you sit outside this high up?"

"Assuming you'd even want to."

"Hush. Just look. Breathe it in. We're two-hundred-and-fifty feet above sea level, traveling at six knots, into the unknown."

"I'll push you overboard if you say you're the king of the world."

He chuckled but didn't reply. They sat for a while, wind scouring their faces, feet kicking in the air.

"So you pretty much get your way around here, don't you?" said Darcy.

He shrugged. "I do and I don't."

"Why don't you have any friends?"

"Excuse me?"

"I never see anybody hanging around with you. Except me, now. And Caps when he can ditch work."

"I've got Tanzer. He's got me. That's enough, I suppose. Until you lot came on board."

"And what's so special about us? You seemed to be on our side right from the get go."

"You're fun people. But I have a confession to make." He glanced at her slyly. "The moment your group came on board I took one look and said to myself, 'There's somebody I'd love to get naked with.' "

Darcy groaned. "Not you too. If it's not some drunk at Tanzers it's..." She slapped the rail. "Why does every man I meet try to get in my pants?" She pulled her legs back, tried to find a safe way to stand.

"The ego on you," said Tivoli, grinning. "It's not you. You're a honey, but you're not my type."

Darcy blinked at him a few times. "Lena? No way. Her and Caps are—"

"Not her either."

"But we're the only two..."

Tivoli scanned the deck, finally pointing at a spec of a shape in the rigging of a houseboat. "Him. I think that's him right there."

"*Noah?*"

"Mmhmm. Scrumptious."

Darcy sat back down again. "You're...but you don't..."

"Just because I don't have limp wrists and lisp? Or behave like an over-the-top, out-and-loving-it fairy? I'll let you in on a little secret: nobody's in the closet anymore. Too many rats in dark little places."

Darcy shook her head, bewildered. "Well, I guess I should've known. You do know every show tune ever written."

Tivoli just smiled, still watching the tiny figure in the rigging.

"So...you and Tanzer ever..."

"Hah! No. Not that he wouldn't. Tanzer's omnisexual. When the animals went nuts, we all lost our pets, but Tanzer lost dates. And...don't ever let on I told you this...his dick hasn't worked for years. It's actually a little sad. He's a sex addict who can't get it up."

"Too much info." She held up a hand. "Anyway, Noah isn't gay."

"You sure about that? I don't see him hooking up with any ladies."

"That's because…" she paused. "This isn't ego, what I'm about to say. Noah's in love with me."

"Uh-huh. And that's working out real well for him."

"It's…it's complicated."

"No, it's simple. It's a sham."

"Come again?"

"He's in his early twenties, right?"

"He turned twenty-one in June."

"Yeah, so a guy who looks like that, at his age, not mounting every girl that looks at him sideways? Gay."

"Noah's not like that. He—"

"Then he pretends to be in love with a woman who won't give him the time of day. It's classic repression. You're a shield, honey. He probably can't admit it to himself."

"I thought you said nobody's in the closet anymore."

"Touché. Okay, not dark closets. Your boy there carried his out into the sunlight."

"He's not gay. Trust me."

"Well," Tivoli pulled his legs back. "There's one sure way to find out."

"This is it," said Caps, patting the side of an ACV. "Just these six vehicles?"

"That's it," said Petty Officer Lewis. "But they do take some maintenance. We still need to refit the tread wheels on one of the baggage carts since Kauai."

"Wow." Caps lay down on his back and shoved himself under the vehicle. "You know there's still vegetation stuck in the undercarriage?"

"Wouldn't surprise me."

PO Lewis was a thin man; reedy almost. He had a long nose and thinning light brown hair. A scar on his forehead was the shape and size of a car key.

Caps pushed himself out and stood up. "Lift? Some sort of pit?"

"We use the cargo hoists. We lash 'em to the deck for stability. It's not optimum, but it's the system we work with."

"What's that over there?" Caps pointed at a large shape hidden under a dun-colored tarp.

"Oh, that's a civy vehicle. Some rich fellah who boarded at New Portland had the barter to pay for storage. That's strictly don't touch stuff. Not our problem."

Caps approached the tarp. "You look under this thing?"

"Yeah, I've looked at it. It's a Hummer. Nice mods on it, too. A real critter killer. I said we should buy it off the dude, but he's not selling."

"So what's he want with a Hummer on board? He going to drive around the Street?" Caps plucked at the tarp.

"He's getting off somewhere along the line. Guess he figures it's better to bring wheels with him than hope he can get some there. Hey, leave it alone, seaman."

"Okay, okay." Caps backed away. "I really know my way around a Hum-V, though. Maybe I could spruce it up a bit in my spare time."

"Off limits," Lewis repeated. "And if you've got spare time, you can spend it on the ACVs. God knows the Marines kick the crap out of them on shore."

"Tell me about it. Hunters are the same no matter where you go." Caps turned in a complete circle. "Man, I'm so happy to be here. Swabbing decks sucks."

"You're not officially here yet." Lewis held out a spanner. "Show me what you've got, seaman."

Half an hour later PO Lewis wiped his hands on a rag and grinned. "Okay, I've seen enough. Vehicle specs are in that cabinet over there. Most of them are handwritten, but I get the feeling you won't have to look at them much."

"Thanks, chief." Caps shoved some tread plates aside and lifted a wheel.

"Don't call me chief, seaman. Anyhow, keep at it. I'm going to hunt down the real chief and bring him back here. You'll be okay by yourself for a while?"

"Sure thing, skipper."

Lewis gave his head a little shake, dropped the rag on the deck and set off for a ladder.

Caps worked on the ACV tread until a crick in his back forced him to stand and stretch. He strolled between the vehicles, running his hand along metal, touching this, poking that, until his feet brought him to the Hummer. With a glance at the ladder, he took hold of one edge of the tarp and flipped it up.

His eyes took in a wheel well, a rear fender, tail lights and a curved molding into which a series of blades could be fitted. His knees buckled and he lurched back as if electrocuted.

This wasn't just a Hummer, this was *the* Hummer. His Hummer! There was no mistaking it. Caps knew every square inch of this beast. He'd practically built half of it himself and it shouldn't be here, not here on the hangar deck of a floating anachronism. This vehicle was supposed to be buried under a rockslide a hemisphere away.

Caps patted his chest where a small skinbag used to hang. His tongue found the vacant spot where he used to have a tooth.

"Dogshit," he breathed.

"So what am I?" asked Lila, "Some kind of bet whore?"

"It's not like that," said Tivoli. "We haven't made a wager or anything."

Tanzer was off somewhere and it was early yet. They had the nightclub to themselves.

Lila slid off the barstool and gave the piano player a look of disgust. "Why don't you throw your own pass?"

"I don't want to spook him."

She turned to Darcy. "So you do it."

Tivoli laughed. "Our diva here is cultivating cobwebs between her legs. Be a shame to break that up."

Darcy snorted.

"Lila, I know you like him," said Tivoli. "I've seen you checking him out."

"Well I kind of already gave him an invitation." Lila shrugged. "He didn't take it."

"Score one for my side." Tivoli poured himself a drink.

"Were you subtle?" asked Darcy. "Noah doesn't exactly do subtle."

"I flashed him some skin," said Lila. "I wouldn't call that subtle."

"Where we come from, men and women shower together."

"You've seen him naked?" Tivoli raised an eyebrow. "How does he measure up?"

"I'm not going to answer that."

"You know what? I'm in." Lila gave Tivoli a wicked smile.

"You sure, hon?"

"Yeah. You know what I always say. The hand that robs the cradle is the hand that rules the world. He's working the Street today, right? No subtle. I'll hit him in the head with a shovel if I have to. Darcy, do me a favor? Don't come home for a couple hours, okay?"

The hatch banged shut behind the dancer and Darcy stared at the empty nightclub, suddenly irritated, and underneath it, something unexpected, something like dismay.

"Don't sweat it," said Tivoli, pouring a drink for her as well. "It's not like you planned to do anything with him."

The hatch swung open. Darcy's head turned, thinking Lila might have changed her mind, but it was Caps.

"Need to talk to you," he said, with a look on his face she'd never seen before. "Alone."

Darcy took him to her little closet of a green room, and the moment the door closed and latched he was nose to nose with her.

"You didn't want Graff snooping around!" he spat. "You flip out anytime you don't know where Noah is! That raccoon is on board with us and you *knew!*"

"Caps, what are you—"

"*He* trapped us on board! *He* took my tooth! He's been here all along and you doglicking knew about it!"

"Ohmygod, Caps, shut up!" She pushed him against the wall, hand over his mouth. "Did you see him? Is that how you—"

Caps shoved her so hard it flattened her against the opposite wall. "How could you?" His eyes burned. Saliva frothed at his lips.

"I'm sorry," Darcy wailed. She threw an arm over her face. "I couldn't tell you."

"WHY?"

"I just…couldn't."

"I'm going straight to the Marshal with this!" He breathed heavily through his nose, like a bull about to charge. "Forget that. I'm going to the captain."

"You can't."

"You don't get to tell me what to do. Never again!"

He turned to the door, flipped off the hook latch.

"Caps, don't," she grabbed his arm.

"Get splashed." He pulled away from her. "Sid's stuck on that barge because of him."

"Sid's alive because of him."

Caps froze, hands on the door. "You cut a deal."

Darcy wrapped her arms around her stomach, tried to gulp back the shame. "It was all a scam. He told me the story, how he survived." In short form she explained the hunter's getaway from lockout point. "He offered me a deal. He'd keep Sid alive in exchange for…in exchange for…"

"What?"

"My silence."

"That's it?"

"Yes," she lied, looking him right in the face.

"Dogshit."

"He doesn't want us making waves while he's settling in." She reached past him and latched the door again. "Have you told Lena?"

"I can't get to her. Not until she's off duty."

"You can't. You can't tell her or Noah. If Toffee finds out he'll kill Sid."

"I don't believe you, Darcy. I don't believe you would do this to us."

"I didn't have a choice. He's a citizen here. He bought his way on board."

"Yeah, with stuff stolen from Compton Pit."

"It doesn't matter. We're not at home anymore. Here in *Terpris*…he's got more pull than we do. You can't tell Lena. You can't tell Noah. Please, Caps. Please. I'm begging you."

Caps grabbed his head with both hands. "I HATE THIS PLACE!" Then he tore the door open and stormed out, leaving Darcy alone in her green room, shaking from head to toe.

"It's in here," said Lila, leading Noah into her bedroom. She'd changed into a sundress, more of a shift. She wore nothing underneath. "Right here," she smiled and lay back on her bed.

Noah looked around the room. "Uhm, is it one of your lamps?" There were two of them. "I'm pretty sure everything here is wired up. Maybe the bulb is just burnt out."

"It's not a lamp." She licked her lips. "Don't you see anything else you can work on?"

He looked up. There wasn't an overhead light. To the best of his knowledge the two lamps and the single outlet were the only things in the room that required electricity. "Do you want me to put in another outlet? I don't know if that would be such a good idea."

She looked at him as if he'd lost his mind, then laughed, light and airy. "Let me give you hint." She wiggled down the bed, feet first. It was a very practiced maneuver. By the time she reached the foot of the bed, she'd left her sundress behind.

Noah gasped.

"Now are you getting it?" She reached for his belt. "Yes, I think you're getting it. In a minute, I'll be getting some too."

His belt came open, then his zipper. He looked down at the top of her head as she did her thing. A stupid grin stretched his mouth almost to his ears.

"Ohhhh," he sighed. If this was the bad luck brought on by albatrosses, he'd have to kill one a week. "Should we close the curtains?"

Toffee passed by the window, heading starboard.

Noah gasped again, but this time not in any sort of ecstasy. Without thinking he shoved her head away, grabbed his pants and pulled them up, half running, half stumbling for the door.

Lila stared after him, stunned. On a rare occasion she'd been turned down, but never after the deal was essentially closed.

Noah had his fly up and pants buttoned as he rushed from the houseboat. He gave up on the flapping belt. As his feet pounded across the deck he looked in every direction, but the hunter was nowhere to be seen. He rushed to Carlos's boat and climbed the rigging to get a high vantage point, completely heedless of any Wandering Albatrosses that might be lurking in the sky. From the top he was able to see most of the Street and though people walked about, none of them were one-armed, crater-nosed hunters.

All at once the insanity of it sank in. There was no possible way he'd really seen what he thought he had. It was a mirage, an illusion, some twisted vision brought on by weeks at sea, culture shock and a sudden erotic encounter.

Or maybe it was more than that.

Noah collapsed into the rigging, Lila, or anything to do with her, completely forgotten.

Up until six months ago, Noah couldn't remember an iota of his life on or prior to New Wilderness Day. He thought he'd come through that brainstorm pretty okay, but possibly he hadn't.

Some people snapped all at once. Others got to take the slow boat to madness.

Caps was so lost in fury he took the wrong way to the hangar deck. Instead of arriving at the motor pool, he found himself in the Valley. He spat a curse at the multinational structures and turned for the ladder. That was when Toffee hit him in the face.

Caps went sprawling. A hand grabbed his foot and dragged him into shadow.

"Nice to see you again, painter," said Toffee, hauling him to his feet.

Caps tried to kick or use his knees or elbows, or anything, but he was too dazed, and he wasn't facing the right direction to attack. Somehow he'd been turned around, and in the darkness under the steps an arm with the strength of two locked around his throat, cinched tight and cut off his air supply.

"I don't know," said Tivoli. "Tanzer won't like it if I let you get hammered before the evening show."

Darcy said nothing. She tapped the bar top with two fingers and glared. He refilled her shot glass and she knocked it back, then tapped the bar again.

"He might be bi," said Lila, coming in through door. "That's the best I can offer you, Tiv."

"You did the nasty already?" said Tivoli, glancing at a clock. "So much for the staying power of youth."

"I'll have what she's having." Lila took a stool next to Darcy. "We didn't do anything. He ran away."

"Seriously?" Tivoli gave Darcy a knowing look. "So you gave him an invite and he ran off?"

"I was trying to give him something alright. Out the door, quick like a bunny." She downed her shot. "He's not gay, Tiv, but he's messed up somehow."

Darcy pushed off her stool and went for the door.

"Where you headed?" Tivoli called after her.

She didn't give an answer, because she didn't really have one. She stepped out of the nightclub and wandered the Street, breathing the sea air and hating herself. Darcy looked at the tops of houseboats, not realizing she was looking for Noah until she couldn't find him.

With over two thousand people in *Terpris*, Darcy felt all alone. For the moment Lena was as unreachable as Sid, and Caps…well, she didn't know if he was ever going to speak to her again. She couldn't blame him really. She'd betrayed all of them.

She watched the men and women working the davits, pulling the lines, hauling up fish. She eyed stacked crates and coils of rope, the daily flotsam and jetsam of these people who lived this way, survived on the oceans, waiting for the day when a bird would drop from the sky and lay them out forever.

Noah was standing by a rail, watching the water so far below.

"Hi," she said, coming to a stop a few feet from him.

He looked up at her, ghosts in his eyes. He looked away again without speaking.

"What happened with Lila?" Darcy asked. It was the only thing that came to her mind.

"Huh?"

"Lila says you…I guess it's none of my business."

"Oh, great." He gripped the rail a little tighter. "What's she doing, blabbing all over the ship that I'm afraid of sex?"

"No, not the whole ship. Just me and Tiv."

Noah started to say something, then stopped, seeming to collapse in on himself. "This boat is getting to me."

Darcy edged a little closer. She didn't know what to say to him but she wanted to keep him talking. "I thought you liked it here."

"Not today. I miss the Pit. I miss everything." He clasped his hands together and leaned on the railing with his forearms. "You know I beat a guy up in New Portland? And that jerk? Palmer? He died right in front of me and all I cared about was killing the bogie before it could damage my work."

"Noah, why do you love me?" The question spilled out of her mouth before she could clamp her teeth to hold it back. She didn't know why she asked it. Maybe it was the booze.

He looked at her, searching her face, perhaps trying to formulate a dodge, a subterfuge, but something had stripped him defenseless and in the end all he said was, "Hell if I know. You're a total bitch half the time."

"But you do love me."

He nodded. "Yeah. Head over heels. Why are you asking me this? You already know. You just don't care."

She closed the distance between them and put her hand on top of his. "Would you come with me? I want to show you something."

There was a sound in the darkness, rhythmic and familiar. It didn't make sense at first, but then nothing did. Caps was standing, but that didn't add up because he was asleep. How could he be standing if he was asleep? Ah, he wasn't standing exactly; he was leaning against something. All five of his senses came alive at once. The world was dim, not pitch black. The taste in his mouth was material of some sort, shoved in tight and held in place by a gag. The smell was a combination of old wood, sweat and sulfur and the sound was a man's voice.

"...glad I was watching Tanzers this afternoon. I do that sometimes. I like to hear her sing. I don't think of it as stalking so much as keeping an eye on my investment."

A light flicked on, solving the mystery of what Caps leaned against. He was in a see-through box about three feet by three feet and seven feet high. His jaw ached, either from the punch or from being stretched around the gag. Looking down provided an answer to why he couldn't move his arms. He was wrapped up in a straightjacket.

"I guess you could say I've been visiting a lot," said Toffee, shifting in his chair. He wore a brown leather bomber jacket. "We're in the magician's storeroom, in case you were wondering."

Caps moaned into the gag and looked around. The box had a door, which was locked from the outside. The only other aperture was a small, waist-high hatch to his left.

"You enlisting in the Navy wasn't something I'd planned on." Toffee got up and slid a smaller box out from the shadows. It was mounted on wheels. "And I guess you're assigned to the motor pool, now, huh?" He rummaged around in a trunk until he found a clock. This he fitted into a bracket on top of the box.

Caps pulled at the straightjacket, felt around with his fingers for some sort of internal release.

"Yeah, I never did much like magicians." Toffee wheeled the small box until it was directly in front of Caps. "Caught this guy's show in New Portland though. Quite the closing number."

Caps threw himself against the door. It didn't budge, neither did the tiny prison shake or wobble.

"And I overheard you postulating about how he did it." He rotated the small box until Caps could see through the front—see the swarm. "I mean, how does a fellah survive being locked in a box with a bunch of bees? Let's see if we can figure it out together." Toffee pushed the bee box against the side of Caps's prison until something clicked together. He set the clock. "Think fast, painter. You've got thirty seconds."

Caps screamed involuntarily. It came out as no more than a muffled groan. He looked all about the box but there was nothing inside that he could nudge or hit or manipulate. No double layer presented itself, no gas nozzle or other orifice. The clock ticked loudly, but not as loud as the hundreds of bees going crazy inside their own little prison. He pulled at his bonds with all his might, but this wasn't a trick straightjacket, no siree, this was a government inspected, grade-A, hug-me-all-day coat.

Twenty seconds.

Caps stopped hitting the door with his shoulder and tried using his knees but there wasn't enough room.

"I'll let you in on a little secret," said Toffee, holding up a small jar. "It has something to do with this. Yep, that Mephisto guy smears it all over himself before he gets in the box. Bet you wish you had some of it in there, huh?"

Ten seconds.

Caps bit down hard on the gag and tried to shove his nose into his shoulder, but he couldn't quite reach.

Five seconds.

"This is exciting, isn't it?" Toffee put his face right to the door. "I was a decade collecting those teeth. Ten years of survival tossed away so you'd have somewhere to put your pot pipe."

Zero seconds.

The hatch fell open and the entire swarm buzzed through the opening and all over Caps.

"It's right over here," said Darcy, clambering over another crate.

"That's what you said the last three times," said Noah, following her. "Darcy, I think you're trying to do something to cheer me up, but I've had a real dog of a day and—"

"Found it. Here. I was a little drunk the first time I saw this and a bunch of stuff's been moved around. Come on."

Noah climbed off the last box and found himself standing before a darkened niche formed by a tarp thrown over a cargo net. Darcy stooped, took his hand and pulled him inside.

The barrel was still there, with its collection of melted candles. So too was the pile of empty sacks. She didn't have anything to light the candles with but it wasn't like she'd planned to ever come here again, and besides, they didn't really need any light.

"What is this place?" asked Noah.

"It's somewhere private." Her hands found his face, traced the line of his jaw, then his lips.

"What are you doing?" asked Noah, touching her wrists.

She kissed him. Not hard and passionately, but neither was it dry and chaste. Her lips molded gently to his and he stood paralyzed by shock, not even responding when her arms moved around him and the tip of her tongue pushed against his teeth.

Caps stood trembling within the Plexiglas coffin. Bees covered him from head to toe. They also covered the sides and ceiling of the box. Though the feeling of their tiny feet was maddening, not a single one of them tried to sting, or crawl up his nose or into his ears.

"Nifty, huh," said Toffee. He opened his little jar and lifted the lid on the swarm box. "They're not bees."

Caps whimpered.

"They're hoverflies. They *look* like bees. It's the way they defend themselves. It's called Batesian mimicry."

The hunter upended the jar into the box then closed the lid. The hoverflies began to cluster around the hatch, returning to their home.

"This stuff is some sort of nectar-based concoction. It attracts them. Mephisto smears it on his face and chest so they all land on him. They swarm out when the clock goes off because there's a fan in the box, but you don't hear it over the buzzing. Flip a switch," he did so, "and the fan reverses so it sucks them in instead of blowing them out."

In less than a minute the see-through coffin was devoid of insects. Toffee closed the hatches and sent the wheeled box spinning with a soft kick.

"See, painter, there are things in this world that look deadly and there are things that are deadly." He fiddled with the latch on the door. "I think you know which one I am."

The door opened and Caps fell face-forward. Toffee stepped out of the way, grinning as his toy-for-the-hour collapsed to the deck. He knelt down, putting one knee on the back of Caps's head. "Now you've got two secrets. I don't care what you do with the magician's, but mine? You tell anybody that I'm here? Anybody at all? I'll kill Lena. I won't hesitate. She'll be fish food before you've finished saying my name."

The pressure came off the back of Caps's head and he felt the straps on the back of the straightjacket being loosened.

"You're supposed to be on duty somewhere, ain't you, Seaman Scagling?" Toffee moved off into the gloom with a scuff of shoe and a creak of leather. "Better not be caught AWOL now. I hear they splash you Navy boys for that."

Noah couldn't believe what was happening. All he could smell or feel was Darcy. She'd pulled him down on the sacks and for the second time in the same day, a woman was fondling his privates. He tried to say something, but every time he opened his mouth, she covered it with hers. Some part of him resisted, though he couldn't for the life of him define why. Maybe it wasn't real at all. It could be just another illusion.

Their clothes were melting away. His pants were bunched around his ankles and she was pushing the back of his head, drawing him down her neck to her chest.

Darcy moaned, one hand in Noah's hair, the other working her pants down over her hips.

Then she was under him, a heel against his buttocks, the other on the back of one leg and he could feel her, hot and ready. Contact. He stopped just before penetration.

"Are you sure?" he asked.

"Please," she said. "Please, Noah. Make me feel clean again."

51. Sea of Wounds

"It's official, sir," said the navigator. "We're here."

Captain Ransom left his chair and moved to a window. At no instruction from him, a button was pressed and bogie bars retracted from outside the glass, moving up.

Ransom raised a pair of binoculars. On the deck below, civies and sailors alike gathered at the railings, looking in all directions, telescopes and binoculars searching.

Nine degrees north latitude, one-hundred-and-ninety-two degrees east longitude: it was where the troubles started the last time.

"All lines in," said Ransom.

"Aye, sir, all lines in." The bridge officer made a general announcement across the decks and to the barge. On both vessels, fishing lines were hastily reeled in, all nets brought up.

Ransom continued scanning the horizon. "Sonar?" he asked.

"Possibles, sir," Otis answered, eyes glued to his screen. "We'll need visual confirmation."

The timing was bad. Some people were still all stirred up by that albatross from the week before. Now there was an additional variable that hopefully none of them would ever have to know about.

"How's our girl to the north?" Ransom asked, moving from the window to the radar station.

"Out there," said the radar man. He flicked a switch and made a notation in his logbook. "Direction is constant. Speed constant. We'll be well out of her way."

The captain eyed the long-range radar screen and resumed his vigil at the window. A hurricane was inbound, moving southeasterly. As long as it didn't get any new ideas, it would cross their wake in the late afternoon, but that's all the bitch would get.

A new face for the bridge crew sat at the communications station. "Visual, sir," said Lena, tapping a finger against her earphones. "Spotter at the forecastle. Ahead, sir."

Ransom brought his binoculars back up. He saw it almost right away: a grey-and-white spec corkscrewing through the air before splashing into the surf.

"They took a drift net from us," said Seaman Creery. He was a morose man with a poor complexion and a thin, greasy moustache.

"They're kind of small, ain't they?" said Caps, lowering the telescope, then raising it again. They were on the flight deck, port side, amidships.

"It's the numbers, man. Ants of the sea."

"Yeah? What kind of school we talking about here?"

"Pod, not school," said Creery. "And this one travels in the thousands."

After the initial spotting, the spinner dolphins appeared in every direction, popping out of the water, spiraling through the air.

Caps folded and stowed the telescope then unslung his rifle. This wasn't a scattergun, it was of the long-range type; not quite a sniper rifle, but close enough. He shouldered the rifle and took aim. "Way too far off," he said, lowering the barrel.

"Oh, they know. The dolphins know. They spread the word."

"How'd they get the drift net off you?"

"It was strung from the barge. They hooked it to a wreck. Least that's the line from command."

Caps leaned out and looked down. "You mean like a shipwreck?"

"Yeah. These are funny waters. Ridges. Underwater mountains. Who knows what's lying down there. Whatever the dolphins did, it didn't give at their end. Lines snapped, davits popped. Away she went."

"Wow. You get the irony, don't you? Dolphins killing a drift net?"

"You think this is funny? You weren't there, man."

"It's only a net. Big net, but still just a net."

Creery picked up a coil of rope, held one end tight and threw the other end over the rail to Caps's left, then he moved to the right. The rope slid over to the rail until it pulled taut against Caps's chest.

"Oh," said Caps, pushing the rope down his body and stepping over it. "I get it. Crowded deck, people getting hit with stuff. How bad was it?"

Creery pulled up the rope, coiling it on the deck between his feet. "Got any memories you'd cut off a limb if it would make them go away?"

"Yeah." Caps looked at his hands.

Creery nodded. "I can still hear it. Late at night, if it's real quiet? I can still hear it." He stowed the coil of rope. "There's so much of us in the ocean. Lots of wrecks down there. All kinds of ships. Just lying there so the dolphins can study them. Learn how they work."

Caps caught sight of something to stern and slid away, leaving his partner to his Davy-Jonesian contemplation.

"Hey," said Caps, coming to Noah's side. "Whatcha thinking?"

"Surrounded by devils," he said, watching dark specs pop up and down in the distance.

Caps gave Noah's shoulder a squeeze. "You're looking in the wrong direction. Whatever. How's married life?"

Noah grinned wolfishly.

"Yeah, you're getting your rocks off, ain't you, sun boy? Still can't believe she just moved in with you like that."

"Well, her 'n' Lila aren't seeing eye to eye at the moment. It's a chick thing." And it was one hell of an ego stroke, having two of the most desirable women on board at odds over him. Not that he was bragging about it at all. He had this little fear that if it got back to Darcy he was playing cock-of-the-walk, she'd kick his ass.

Caps had his telescope out again. "At least those little bastards break up the horizon a bit. This Carlos guy doesn't mind you two rocking his houseboat?"

"Hasn't said boo about it if he does. I think maybe he likes listening. She's weird in the morning, though."

"Oh? Smells bad? Hair all over the place?"

"She's got spectacular bed head, that's for sure, but she never smells bad." Noah shook his head and imagined her scent. "Never." He lowered his voice. "I get up before she does. She gets this look on her face like…I dunno."

"Like what?" Caps had put his telescope away and taken up the rifle again.

"Like…hmm…I dunno. Sometimes I think she's keeping tabs on me."

Like I keep tabs on Lena, thought Caps. He'd been tossed from the motor pool for apparently abandoning his post. Fortunately the punishment didn't go past a reunion with his mop. He'd begged, bribed and cajoled to sync his watches with Lena's. He'd hook up with her the moment she came off duty and didn't let her out of his sight until she was safely through the hatch into officer country, and even that smidgeon of security was starting to feel like a stronghold built out of drywall. Nothing looked the same anymore. The aircraft carrier was a deathtrap as much inside as outside and every person, every skull, was a barely-sealed tub of dark, nasty secrets.

"Whoa," Caps pushed back from the rail and looked around. "It's a pocket."

Noah glanced at the people nearby, looking for some oversized pouch.

"It's gone." Caps looked right and left and turned back to the rail. "You missed it. You haven't been looking for 'em."

Noah slapped him on the back. "Congratulations, bud. You found pot again!"

Caps sighed. "No, man. And y'know what? I'm glad. I couldn't handle this stoned." He shifted his grip on the rifle, wondered if there was someway he *could* get access to the sniper gear. "It's so crowded on this ship. You live up here, so you don't really get it, but down in the cramps? Man, you're in everybody's way, and everybody's in yours. You can't get carts through there. You know what we do when we have to move a bunch of stuff? You round up a bunch of enlisted and make a bucket brigade. We're in this bastion of technology and half the crap we do is totally primitive." He tapped the rail with the gun barrel. "But there are pockets."

"You sure you haven't found some weed? You're sounding more like you than since like, Underbel."

"For a few seconds there, nobody was looking at us. All these people on the deck and not a single person could absolutely confirm we were here. For those seconds we were invisible. Pockets come and go. I see 'em once they've happened now, but if you can anticipate 'em? Move through 'em? You could be invisible all the time. That takes some creepy awareness." He aimed at the horizon, tried to keep a twirling spec in his sights. "The devil ain't out there. Those things are just dogs with blowholes. The devil lives in the pockets."

"Pod strength?" asked Captain Ransom.

"I'm estimating, sir, but eighteen hundred, give or take," replied Otis.

"Proximity?"

"Oh, we'll get them, sir."

"Audience?"

"Packed house," said an officer at a window, looking down at the deck.

"Showtime. Hit it."

"Activating the LFA, sir."

There was no explosion, no streaks of light as missiles launched to blast the waves. Nevertheless, *Terpris's* opening barrage in this encounter was titanic.

Far out at sea a nation of dolphins took to the air, crashing down, moving away at top speed and minimum depth.

Ransom didn't have to leave his chair to see the grayish plume against the horizon. It was as if a giant crescent of the ocean had turned to rubber. He wanted to dance, he wanted to sing, but that would be inappropriate. He satisfied himself by standing, clasping his hands behind his back and moving to where he could look down and see the astonished, cheering masses on the decks.

The bridge was jubilant. The Low Frequency Active sonar had finally been completed in Diego. If only the carrier had had one from the very first day. The ships that had functioning LFA back then didn't turn it on right away because it was illegal. Illegal! By the time most of them realized that didn't matter anymore, well…they didn't matter anymore, either.

"Restrict that!" said Ransom, his mood getting the better of him. "Signpost-waving hypocrites. And we had to listen to them because somebody let the hippies get money." He rested his forehead against the glass. "I wish I could rub their noses in it. Heh. Ensign Wong, hail the NRDC."

Lena looked up, confused. She'd never heard of the Natural Resources Defense Council.

"She can't, sir," said Otis. "We don't have the right satellite alignment to ping the afterlife."

It was good to laugh.

Over two-hundred decibels of sonar thundered the water below. The information return was phenomenal. When the LFA had first gone live, sonar operators, navigators and tactical officers throughout the fleets shuddered in spiritual orgasm. Then whales started beaching themselves all over the place and a population of Cuvier's beaked whales in the Bahamas sort of disappeared altogether. Turns out that repeated pulses at those frequencies, at volumes far in excess of those safe for a human ear, were kind of bad for cetaccans too. It made them bleed from their brains; it filled their tissue with bubbles. It gave them the bends.

And it makes them run like hell, thought Ransom.

Terpris had been nearly ten years building her LFA. They'd tested it once or twice since Diego, but really they'd saved it for this chunk of the blue. Ransom would have loved to have turned the thing on and never turn it off. Unfortunately, the same thing that was chasing off the dolphins also made the fish a little scarce, so that wasn't an option. Also, the components were old. The engineering couldn't guarantee the system any lifespan. It was a lot like everything else in *Terpris*. Consoles at multiple stations were reduced to light switches that did nothing, but a person flicked them once in a while anyway.

"Deck spotters reporting all clear," said Lena.

Ransom sank into his chair and contemplated taking a short nap. Contentment was such a rare and fleeting thing.

Sid gripped his chest and stomach with both arms and coughed. A real wracking cough this time, a deep wet ripping tearing hacking that sounded like a whole lung was coming up.

When the fit ended, he dry heaved.

Strong arms encircled his and dragged him from the work area.

"I'm sorry, man," said Prisoner 716. "Blessing's orders."

"I ain't sorry," said 510. "I'm tired of covering your quota."

Sid didn't try to struggle. He'd seen this. He'd participated in it. When a man on the crew couldn't pull his weight, no matter what the reason, he was gone.

"Some people just can't take the air in here," said 716. "Sucks to be you."

Every man down here would have Black Lung disease, that was a given, but theirs would take them years from now, or decades, on the slim chance they made it off the barge in the first place. For a rare person, the barge's own version of coal workers' pneumoconiosis advanced quickly and it looked like Sid had hit the numbers.

He was taken to a space along the port side, far from Blessing's territory and just out of sight of the guards at the hatches. It was a lockout, plain and simple, only in this type, the walls and gates were built of attitudes and codes of honor. For now his primary concern was keeping away from the guards, not being labeled as a man too sick to work.

They dumped Sid against a broken crate and walked away without a word, without looking back.

After a few minutes, Sid took deep breaths again. He reached for his dust mask but his hand patted empty chest. The mask was gone, slipped off sometime during the drag. His other masks were all in Blessing's nest, and therefore property of his former crew.

Prisoners passed him, but didn't speak. Some looked at him and took note before moving off.

One man, mostly in shadow, watched for an uncomfortably long while. It wasn't until he spoke that Sid knew him for who he was.

"So look at you now," said Jim.

Sid lay there speechless, breathing.

Jim pulled his dust mask down to his chin. He picked at something in his teeth with a fingernail, then looked up. "Night's coming real soon. How many of the crewless have you terrorized? Hmm? How many have you beaten? Extorted? When the lights go out?" He shook his head and walked away.

Feet moved on the catwalk above. Sid pressed hard against the hull and pulled the crate a little closer.

"Whoaaa," said Otis, flipping a couple of switches and then reaching forward and tapping his screen.

Ransom immediately brought up the station's display on one of his chair-mounted monitors. "Systems fault?" he asked.

"I don't think so, sir. I think the spinners are doing this."

The interference was getting worse. Long range sonar displayed an ocean that was quickly becoming a solid block.

Sonar display was now coming up at every station that could access it. Lena alerted central communications and all science departments.

"Sir, long range sonar is now comple—"

"It's right in front of me, Lieutenant. Can't you compensate?"

"I'm trying, sir. The cetaceans have done this to us before but never with so many voices."

"Bridge to science lab," said Ransom, stabbing a button on his arm rest. He turned to Lena. "Call the XO."

"Leighton," came a voice from a speaker.

"Doctor, are you watching what's going on with sonar?"

"Oh yes. It's quite fascinating. Look at that, we've completely lost long range. We brought such a large cannon to this fight, we forgot about their thousands of little pistols."

"Do you think this is a planned attack or an improvised response?"

"We can't answer that, Captain."

"How are they communicating? With all the noise we're making, it should be like trying to hear whispers in a wind storm."

"We've looked at some footage of the mass exodus. It's hard to be certain from such a distance, but we feel their spin patterns have become far more complex. We'll need time to analyze—"

Ransom cut Leighton off and spoke to the navigator, nicknamed Gator no matter who was doing the job. "Go over the logs, find anything out there that could even possibly be dangerous."

"Way ahead of you, sir. We're clear."

"Sir," said Otis. "There's…never mind. I thought I saw something, but I'm getting a lot of ghosting on mid-range."

Oh, the choir. The greatest acapella in the history of the world was going on around the carrier. Ransom wondered if there was a great fat dolphin out there somewhere wearing a cravat and a cummerbund.

A hatch opened and Stukov entered, coming to stand at the captain's side.

Ransom quickly brought him up to date.

"It seems a simple response then," said Stukov. "A chorus of disapproval."

"We've lost mid-range, sir," said Otis.

"So we will be blind until their throats get sore." Stukov moved to stand at the sonar station. "What was that?"

Otis looked up. "You saw it too."

"Talk to me," said Ransom.

"Sir, we may have a possible…It really could be ghosting, but…" He brought up an overlay. "Possible large contact to port. Bearing is east by northeast. It should be coming into short range any second now, if it's real."

"Give me a playback," Ransom ordered. "Define large."

"Bigger than a whale, sir. Even a blue."

"Could it be a pod cluster?"

"It could, sir. With these numbers it could be."

"There," said Stukov, finger snapping to the screen. He'd seen the edge of something pushing into short range. The next instant, short range filled up with ghosts.

"Leighton," Ransom said into his mic, "what would be the effect of dolphins swimming directly into us while the LFA is working?"

"It would be suicide," came the reply. *"Any cetaceans that did reach us would be disorientated beyond the capability to function. Even if they survived the encounter they'd be permanently damaged. Fatally so."*

"Thank you." He closed the channel just as short range became completely useless. "How long can they keep this up?" he asked Stukov.

"Captain, I suggest sounding general quarters and telling all decks to brace for impact."

"No need to panic, Commander. The whole lot of them could make a column dead ahead and all it would mean was miles of dolphin meat we could turn around and scoop up."

"If it's real, sir," said Otis, "it should be hitting us right now."

They waited. Nothing happened, no staggering impact or shudder through the floor.

"Uh…" Otis frantically toggled a switch. Across the bridge, screens went black. "Sir, we just lost sonar. All of it."

"Captain," said Leighton's voice from a speaker, *"are we absolutely certain of the topography ahead? There's something scraping the bottom. We can feel it through our feet."*

Ransom shot a look at Gator.

He held his hands up. "I swear, sir, plenty of clearance. The spinners would have to lower the ocean."

"What just happened?" Ransom shot to his feet. The vibration of the ship was an intimate voice to him, as it was to every capable sailor on board.

"We are decelerating," said Stukov.

"Sir, number three prop just shut down," said an alarmed voice at the helm.

Ransom and Stukov both rushed the station.

"Number four just went. Safety disengage."

The captain ran three steps to his chair and pressed a button. "Bridge to engineering."

"Freeman here, sir."

"What's going on down there?"

"Something's jamming the props, sir. Once sufficient resistance is reached, the drive safety—"

"I know that! What's jamming the props? Is it dolphins?"

"Not a chance, sir. That would be like a blender jamming on butter."

"Captain," said Lena, "aft spotters report chopped meat in our wake."

"We just lost prop 1, sir," said the helmsman.

There was a shudder, subtle but discordant. All power went out, only for an instant, but it was enough to make the entire bridge deaf and blind as all systems reinitialized.

Then there was nothing. No vibration, only the humming of computer fans.

"We're adrift," said Stukov.

Bright colored loading screens popped up at every active station.

"Engineering," said Ransom. "Engineering," he repeated.

"Sorry about that," said Freeman's voice. *"The safety on two was a little slow on coming off. We have a couple problems down here."*

"Damage assessment?"

"Minimal, I think, sir. Give me a few minutes. We have to know what's jammed the props, sir. I can't really proceed without that."

"LFA is not responding," said Otis. "Short range not responding. Sir, I think the sonar dome's been trashed."

"Sir, aft spotters saying there's something following us, just under the water."

"Do we have any cameras on it?"

"Patching through now, sir."

Ransom stared at his screen. "What is that?"

A massive shadow beneath the waves looked to be pressed up against the stern, matching speed.

"Deck spotters cannot confirm, sir."

"Sir, we'll need to deploy the ROV."

"The barge is requesting orders, sir."

"Bridge, Odega here. The scraping has stopped. Whatever it was, we seem to be clear."

"How long?" Ransom snapped at the navigator. "How long can we be adrift and still outrun that hurricane?"

Gator looked at his screen and shook his head.

52. More Equal Than Others

"You should be getting visual now," Odega said into the microphone.

"I see a lot of water," said Ransom's voice.

"Turning to props now, sir." Odega twiddled a pair of joysticks on a small console. He was running the remote operated submersible not because he had greater skill than the other two scientists, but because he really wanted to and he was twice their size.

Random bits of detritus sped across the screen as the ROV turned. At one time the device had arms and clamps and drills and all manner of useful things. Over time the ocean life had battered it into its current role of doing nothing more than carrying a camera. The props came into view but Odega didn't arrest the ROV's movement for a few seconds.

Dr. Chen whistled.

"Kingdom of the spiders," said Leighton.

"Dear God," said Ransom through a speaker.

The ROV drifted left, then stopped and did a slow drift right.

"How much of it do you think there is?" asked Leighton.

"Let's have a look behind us," said Chen.

Odega pitched the ROV into a downward rotation. A filthy web moved across the screen. When the submersible's attitude came to 120° from vertical, Odega rolled it, righting the perspective.

"Is that a washing machine?" asked Leighton.

"It could have come off a ship," said Chen.

It was as if *Terpris* was being shadowed by a junkyard. Appliances, chains, bits of fiberglass, broken masts…

"That's a tire," said Odega tapping the screen. "It's a car tire."

…metal drums, pipes, bottles, small anchors, cinder blocks, and other scraps so bent and twisted they could have been anything; rusted and barnacle-covered and all trapped in an endless weave of net.

"Turn it back to the props," ordered Ransom's voice.

Odega complied.

"Captain," said Leighton, "it looks as if they've gathered every net they could get their beaks on and made a giant trash bag. Then they filled it up and used us for a curb."

On the screen, the enormous props were enmeshed in garbage. Miles of netting and rope twisted between the screws. The ceramic bowl of a toilet came free from the net and dropped off-screen.

The image shook violently.

"Raise the ROV," said Ransom.

The order came too late. The submersible spun and shuddered, catching a close-up face of a dolphin for half a second, then bounced off something hard and the image turned to static.

"Well that's that," said Leighton. "The dolphins killed our camera."

Odega looked down at where his thumbs strained against now-useless joysticks. Through memory he witnessed plane after remote-control plane crashing into the ground above Compton Pit. "This wasn't my fault." He let go of the console and folded his arms across his chest.

"Will the Mimi work?" asked Stukov. "They swam right through the LFA."

"Oh yes," said Leighton. "The LFA is simply an issue of decibel level. The Mimi is something else entirely."

Seven of them sat in the war room: the captain, the XO, MCPO Porter, Major Dawson and the three scientists. The oval table was covered in printouts of the props. Leighton had cringed at the volume of paper consumed by each image.

"What would be the effect on us from deploying it underwater?" asked Ransom.

"Well," Leighton hesitated, "We don't know. We could hope the hull of the ship would protect us from ill effects, but that same hull might reverberate somehow. It's a risk."

"It is an acceptable risk," said Stukov.

"Just give the word," said Dawson. "My boys are ready to get wet. Even if this thing drives us nuts, we'll get that crap cut out the screws before we're watered."

Ransom put his face in his hands. The dolphins were out there, waiting. He dropped his hands and let his breath out through his teeth. "It is an unacceptable risk. We cannot endanger the children. If we lose them, we lose everything."

"What will it matter?" said Stukov. "Of what use is sanity if we drift out here until we die?"

"I wonder if they believe in luck," said Porter. "They must have been preparing this since the last time we passed through."

"Perhaps," said Stukov, "knowledge of the hurricane made them desperate. Perhaps that enabled them to decide on suicide."

"They must have religion," said Leighton. "Birds are stupid. Instinctual hatred overrides self-preservation, but cetaceans are reasoning creatures. For a reasoning creature to choose mass suicide—"

"That requires ideology," said Chen. "Philosophy! There's a potential here for cetacean theology. What an—"

"We're wasting time," said Dawson. "Less than four hours on the clock, Captain. If we're not going to use this Mimi thing, then we need another plan of attack. Whatever we're shooting or dumping into the water, we can't do it over our divers. How are we going to keep the spinners away?"

The captain stood up and punched the table hard enough to skin his knuckles. "There's so few of us humans left." he said. He turned to Stukov. "We're not using the Mimi."

Ransom rubbed his injured hand and explained his plan. When he was finished, six people stared at him in stunned silence.

"Bravo, Captain," Odega deadpanned. "Nice to know we're still the biggest monster in the sea."

Toffee watched incredulously as a beer cooler popped to the surface a few feet off the bow of the barge. A dozen spinners broke into view and streaked a frothing pattern across the chop before vanishing.

"This can't be happening," moaned a civy guard a few feet down the rail. "They're just dolphins! They're just overgrown fish!"

Off the starboard bow two groups of spinners skipped across the water on a collision course. One group submerged just before impact and the resulting cross of wakes made a checkerboard pattern.

Battle plans, thought Toffee. *It's aquatic semaphore.*

"This just isn't happening," the guard insisted. "Fish can't stop us. We're a damn aircraft carrier!"

Toffee backhanded the man across the face. "Get a hold of yourself or I'm tossing you over." He drew back his hand again, then thought better of it. Beneath his anger he felt a quiver of sympathy. He threw a glance over the side and said, "Dolphins with a purpose. Every time I think the world's tossed me its best scare, it comes up with something new."

Motion on the carrier caught the guard's attention. Toffee turned to look. The first of the gondolas was on its way over.

***

"This is the lock," said dark-skinned Chief Petty Officer Perez. "This is the range finder. Scagling? Are you listening, man?"

"Yeah, I am," said Caps. "Why do I need to know? I'm just supposed to be turning a wheel."

It was a catapult, pure and simple; hand cranks, ropes, metal-reinforced wooden arm.

"Everybody on the artillery crew has to know everybody's job," said Perez. "In case a man goes down."

The thing was about the size of a station wagon. The ammunition looked like small beer kegs.

"Go down?" said Caps. "It's not like the dolphins can jump this high."

Perez hefted a keg. "Hello? We're playing with explosives."

Down deck a number of hoppers were filling up with snorkeling equipment. A lineup of armed sailors had formed at the gondola launch.

Caps couldn't pull his eyes away.

"That's not your duty," said Perez, taking Caps by the shoulders and turning him away from the stern. "It's not your duty, so it ain't your business."

Tanzer stood behind his bar, ready to club the next person who tried to take a drink without paying for it.

On stage, the Old Bull looked like he was contemplating throwing the baby grand at the crowd.

"Everybody shut the hell up," yelled Mark. "I can only tell you what I've told you."

"We need compensation," said a swarthy man near the front. "How'm I supposed to earn my keep if the Navy loses my tools?"

A few people in the packed nightclub made sounds of agreement.

"*Terpris* is under a state of emergency," said Mark. "That means the Navy does what it likes, takes what it likes."

"You're a selfish prick," said a woman, but to the complainant, not to Mark. "You just pray. You pray your tools come back because if they don't, it means we've lost a man."

"There's a typhoon comin'," said Old Harry from the back, black knit cap pulled down over his eyebrows.

How could he know that? thought Mark. "Yes, there's some wind out there but—"

"That's like saying there's *some* fish." Old Harry grinned, then went back to sucking on whatever it was he had pouched in his cheek.

Mark fumbled for a response. Less than thirty people on board had been informed of the hurricane, but some of these folk had a kinship with the ocean that hadn't changed just because everything living above and below the water had.

"It's because of the albatross," said a woman.

"No," said Mark. "You shut up about that right now."

"Albatross!" cried a man.

Heads swiveled. Half the crowd looked at Noah by the bar, where he'd been lucky enough to score a stool.

Darcy, who stood behind him with arms wrapped around his shoulders, released her hug and moved to stand in front of him.

"It's him the dolphins want," said a man.

"We should be so lucky," said Tanzer, putting his club down on the bar top and taking up a shotgun.

From the piano came the first four bars of "Octopus's Garden." Mark turned in surprise, not realizing Tivoli had snuck onto the stage.

"The albatross," sing-songed Tivoli, "what rotten luck, but with everything else, who gives a—" his hands banged out an ugly chord. "Look, even if the albatross had a karmic mark of Cain at one time, it sure doesn't apply now. That's like saying it's bad luck to kill a dolphin."

This triggered a loud argument that had been raging since the day after the Change. At least it was a distraction, a direction for fear and anger to vent itself out without resulting in a walk-the-plank lynching.

An officer and two sailors had entered at some point and now forced themselves through the crowd to the bar.

"Noah Thurlow," said the officer. "You're to report to maintenance, 03 Deck. These men will escort you there."

"He's not in the Navy," said Darcy, shifting her weight to the balls of her feet. She was in protection mode. She'd have attacked a cloud of cigarette smoke if it got too close to Noah.

"He is today."

"There an electrical problem?" asked Noah.

"Many," replied the officer. "Need everyone we can get."

"Okay, I'll go."

"I'm coming," said Darcy.

"Essential personnel only, ma'am," said one of the sailors. "It's awful tight in the cramps right now."

"And you've got a job to do here," said Tanzer. He dropped Darcy's half-mask on the bar top. "You're going to get up there and sing some Simon and Garfunkle, and if that doesn't calm these folk down then you're going to break some heads."

Darcy gave Noah a hard kiss. He broke her clinch and glanced at the sailors, a little embarrassed. After he'd been taken away, Darcy slipped the mask off the bar and pulled her hair over one shoulder.

"Gimme a double," said Mark, pushing through the throng.

"It's on the house if you get Ripper in here," said Tanzer.

"No can do," he said sadly.

"Oh, hell."

"Yep. Ripper was a welder for nine years. Four of that underwater. Navy didn't have to come and get him. He volunteered."

Tanzer handed him a mug and Mark downed the works. He scanned the crowd and bit his lip. As tense as things were now, it was going to get a whole lot worse.

In the fantail, Major Dawson checked his regulator and then gave his diving vest a good shake, making sure the tank was strapped in tight. The rest of his Marines were in similar stages of preparation.

Dawson stood, flexed his muscles within the neoprene rubber, then reached into a trunk and pulled out a loose weave of chains. He wrapped the chains around his left shin, feeling like a snow tire.

A portly Arab shadowed by his two sons moved from tank to tank, wrapping glittering fabric around the octopus hoses. It was canvas and rubber, coated on one side with powdered glass.

The non-Navy in the fantail weren't civies anymore. Now they were militia, homesteaders at war. They'd improvised their gear quickly; the big fellah who did the prize fighting was winding barbed wire around his wetsuit.

A bucket brigade of sailors moved underwater cutters and grinders along to a petty officer who assigned them. There wouldn't be enough to outfit just the qualified divers, never mind the whole lot. The last of the cutters arrived, hand by hand, then the saws appeared.

"We'll be resorting to grooming scissors by the end," Dawson said to one of his men.

Farther back in the maintenance crawlways, and back along the cramps, other divers were gearing up as best they could. This was going to take multiple waves, and every wave would be more poorly equipped than the one before it.

Dawson strapped chain to his forearms, then knives over the chain. To his left thigh he harnessed a weapon that looked like a jagged short sword.

"Eyes and blowholes, people," he called out. "And stab, don't try to slash."

Four man-sized cages descended from the lip of the flight deck protruding overhead. In each cage was a spear gun and a quiver full of ammo.

Banging sounds, drifting in from the hangar deck, said the ship's boats were being unloaded.

Sid stood shoulder-to-shoulder with the prisoners on either side of him. Every one of them was topside. The holds had been emptied, the hatches closed. The Navy guards stood clustered near the bow, the civy guards forming a second cluster nearby. The upper catwalk was full of Navy riflemen, but they weren't guarding the ocean. They were facing inwards, weapons leveled at the prisoners.

Near the bow a number of hoppers stood, filled with what looked like diving gear. The upper rail had been disassembled and ramps were secured to the lower rail, so it was just a quick run and jump into the stretch of water between the barge and the carrier.

Anything out of routine for the prisoners was disturbing. The only welcome surprise had been the smattering of fruitcakes that dropped into the feeding net on Christmas Day. But apparently, even that was routine. Had to hand it to fruitcakes; their shelf life was an unparalleled scientific achievement.

"Why aren't we moving?" asked one prisoner.

The incoming gondola stopped and a small group of officers got off. Sid was pretty sure he recognized one of them as Commander Stukov.

A civy guard detached himself from his clique and moved to a microphone that had been set up on the upper port rail.

"Okay, you barge rats, settle down and shut up. Anybody talking back will be shot. The XO is going to—"

"What kind of Navy bullshit is this?" demanded a prisoner from somewhere ahead of Sid.

A rifle *cracked* from above. A small mist of blood appeared above the head of one prisoner and he collapsed. Whether or not he was the man who'd spoken, it was impossible to tell.

The guard at the microphone had his sidearm out, pointed at the front row of convicts. "We mean business. Here's the XO."

Stukov approached and took the microphone, seemingly unaffected by the violent introduction. "Prisoners, these are the captain's orders. You will follow them without hesitation. When the instruction is given, each of you will dive into the water and swim for the carrier. One minute after—"

"Are you nuts?" yelled a prisoner.

Crack.

"One minute after the instruction is given," continued Stukov, "we will open fire on any prisoner still standing on this deck." He gave that a moment to sink in, watched barge rats eye the riflemen.

Sid's mind reeled. For whatever reason, the Navy had decided on a mass execution. But why instruct people to swim for *Terpris*? Why instruct them at all?

"There are rope ladders hanging from the fantail," said Stukov. "Reach the ladder and you get to live. The first twenty prisoners to reach the carrier will win amnesty. You will be free men. The bins there have snorkeling gear. There isn't enough for everybody."

Sid was one of the first to move, pushing and shoving. He slammed his fist across the jaw of a man who didn't get out of his way fast enough. The prisoners swarmed the hoppers. Sid was able to get a mask and fins, but no snorkel. The moment more people were fighting each other for gear than there were getting it from the bins, rifles sounded off and club-swinging guards knocked the prisoners back into order.

In the middle of this, something wet struck Sid in the middle of his back. He turned quickly but nobody behind him seemed to be looking in his direction. Something dribbled down his arm. He brought his hand up and saw streaks of pink along his wrist. He contorted such that he could look at his back.

"Somebody just marked you," said Prisoner 210. He had no mask and only one flipper. "You're going to stand out like a fishing lure."

The entire back of Sid's shirt was stained bright pink. Some of the stuff had spattered on his legs.

"Looks like they threw a dye marker at you, Queequeg," said 210. "You're so dead."

A dull staccato of thuds sounded from the carrier. Barrel bombs arced through the air and exploded in the water.

"Dive," boomed Stukov's voice from the speakers.

Before Sid could strip his shirt off, he was caught up in the rush. Stumbling over his fins, the force of the charge dragged him up the ramps and over the side.

Freefall.

Some forgotten part of dive training bade him clamp a hand over his mask as the ocean rushed up to meet him. There were so many people in the water already, surely he'd land on…

He was under. Cold, wet, disorientated. His mask was filled with water. Something bumped his right side. Sid pushed the top of the mask against his forehead and exhaled hard through his nose, forcing seawater out the bottom.

The ocean around him was not an empty expanse. Below trailed a grime-encrusted net filled with debris. To his sides and above, men thrashed and twisted, getting their bearings. Sid had no way to gauge visibility. He didn't know how far out the darkness was, at least not until the shape of dolphins rushed in, giving him a frame of reference.

53. Misdirection

"They went over," said Caps. "I can't believe it. They went over."

"Scagling," shouted Perez, "eyes on the ball, man!"

Caps's hands were frozen in their task as the avalanche of prisoners sputtered its last two or three men into the water.

"Scagling!"

Caps tore his eyes away from the barge and set to turning the crank. A sailor on the other side assisted in this task. Another sailor loaded the cup, while a fourth man set the timers. Perez called range and gave the order to fire.

The catapult thundered and the little keg arced through the air and splashed down farther out than the previous bomb, which bobbed up and down in the three-foot sea.

Both of them went off simultaneously.

"Nice one," said the timer man.

"Set range seventy-five meters," said Perez.

Caps pushed against the crank. This effort was going to exhaust him fast. He wished for some sort of motor, but acknowledged that the catapult was a simple and effective means of delivering ordinance. The wizardry was in the bombs, not the launcher. They weren't trying to shell an inland village, or sink an enemy battleship. Their purpose was to create a moat, a safety perimeter of concussion and shrapnel.

Almost all the ship's boats were in the water. Only the punts weren't deployed. *Hugin* and *Munin* patrolled the outermost "corridor" within the area of the keg bombs. Inside the course of the larger boats, a trio of 26-foot MK-10s zipped back and forth, gunfire pouring from their decks into the water. Spikes and blades along the keels of the boats discouraged ramming and the more insidious attack dolphins and whales had developed whereby they rocked a vessel until it capsized. For the men and women on the MK-10's, the biggest danger was from flying dolphins. Coming up from deep down, the spinners generated enough momentum to easily clear the gunwales, knocking sailors overboard or crushing them beneath their weight. Dolphin blood and innards on the decks made even the non-slip surfaces hard to stand on.

From the fantail and the stern, a curtain of machine-gun fire covered the water above the rudders. Under the keel, the submerged Marines braced themselves on the nets and fought with knife and spear.

Major Dawson drove his short sword into dolphin flesh just below the creature's beak. He tried to pull back as fast as he could but everything was in slow motion and as the mammal twisted away, it disarmed him.

Above, below, all around him, divers worked at the nets and debris, cutting, sawing and hacking away.

Dawson pushed off of the net and drew both his diving knives. Visibility was shrinking faster than expected, filling up with filth from the nets and blood both human and cetacean.

Every time Sid's ears cleared the surface, he heard gunfire and screams. Below the water were sounds far worse. He swam fast, but controlled. While everybody around him panicked, he dropped back into the middle of the pack, to the safest place in the school of prisoners. The garbage-filled netting provided a floor, a defense from below. What it was doing there in the first place was beyond him.

To his left, a dolphin had skipped across the surface, bit into the wrist of a man and dragged him under. The creature took its victim down to the net and raked him across the debris, cutting him to ribbons as he drowned. When the dolphin released its grip, the corpse of Prisoner 161 drifted, rotating slowly before its pant leg caught on something jagged in the net. Arms and head came up, until it looked as if the corpse was reaching for the surface, surrounded by a misty red aura.

Raising his head to breathe, Sid caught sight of Jim, ahead and to the right. Mr. Switzerland had hooked onto the same survival scheme. Sid poured on a little more juice to catch up. His arms powered through the water, his legs thrashed. There was nothing wrong with his lungs. Sure, he had a bit of a cough nestled in the back of his throat, but everybody had that. What everybody didn't do was nurture theirs. It was the only way he'd come up with to escape Blessing's crew, and beyond that, the barge. If his performance was convincing enough, the guards would bring him up for an examination. His plan once he got topside was vague. There was nowhere for him to go, but that was irrelevant. Then suddenly this had happened. This...whatever this was.

It's not like *Terpris* wasn't doing its damnedest to slaughter the dolphins, but none of the weaponry was being used to protect the prisoners.

We're a diversion, thought Sid. *The net didn't come from the Navy. It came from the dolphins.*

The prisoners' right flank collapsed. A wedge of dolphins smashed and dragged its way through human flesh and now Sid wasn't in the middle of the pack anymore. His right side was completely exposed to the ocean.

From twenty feet away a spinner burst out of the waves and shot across the whitecaps straight at Sid.

"Reload," said Perez.

The catapult was primed, range set, but no new keg bomb hit the cup. The loader wasn't bringing one either; he was dismantling one.

"Wilkes, what the…" Perez moved forward.

Caps backed away. Wilkes had the lid off the keg and he fiddled around on the inside.

The other crank man was reaching for Wilkes's shoulders, then suddenly sprang back, colliding with Perez.

Wilkes stood up, brandishing a metal tube he'd removed from the keg.

"The hell are you doing?" shouted Perez.

"Do you remember?" said Wilkes. He twisted the cap off one end of the tube.

"Holy shit, Wilkes! Don't do that."

"Do you remember what it used to smell like?" He moved the tube under his nose and took a deep whiff. "It used to be in everything. It was in your clothes. You could taste it in the coffee."

"Wilkes, cap that tube and get a grip or I'll shoot you."

"Where's your purple?" Wilkes asked, hugging the tube to his chest. "You can't touch the jet fuel unless you're purple. You're not allowed."

A sailor came out of nowhere and smashed a rifle stock into the back of Wilkes's head. The loader went down, the contents of the tube splashing across the deck.

Caps felt like he'd jumped forty feet away. Jet fuel on a deck loaded with explosives; they were all going to blow sky high.

"Relax," said Perez, checking Wilke's carotid. "That's JP5. You can put a match out in it. Needs electricity to ignite. You," he pointed at the sailor who'd brought down the crazy man. "You're loading now."

The seaman slung his rifle and grabbed a keg bomb.

"All of these things have an electrical starter?" said Caps, returning to his side of the crank. "Where do you get all the parts?"

"It's not that hard. You can get a little electricity out of a potato if you know what you're doing."

"So there's potatoes in these things?"

"No. Don't be stupid. Fire!"

From where he stood along the stern, MCPO Porter snapped his fingers and signaled for a medical team to remove the unconscious Seaman Wilkes. He looked down at the ocean and shook his head. They didn't need some high-tech wonder toy to break people's sanity. All a fellow had to do to lose his mind was open his eyes too wide.

Darcy was one of the first to run when word went out that the prisoners had gone into the water. From the houseboats and the cramps swarmed civies with family or friends on the barge. A line of sailors armed with riot gear formed a barrier across the flight deck, a guard against what was just about to happen.

"Diversion my ass," yelled a black woman, dreadlocks poking out from beneath a headscarf.

The first rank of sailors held clubs. The second rank had rifles.

Darcy bunched, readying herself to break the line.

"First they'll beat you," said Tivoli from behind her. "Then they'll shoot you and throw you over the side."

"Sid's out there!" she protested. "He's in the water."

"Then he's probably already dead."

The dolphin was three feet away, half submerged and going for Sid's leg when its dorsal flesh blew apart in four meaty explosions of blood and blubber.

It disappeared as another spinner came from behind. The moment it cleared the waves, its melon came apart in chunks.

A new sound filled the above and below. Zipping sounds in the air turned to hissing underwater. Bullets peppered the sea, tracing linear splashes, shredding dolphins.

Sid looked back at the barge, but saw no muzzle flash. *Terpris* was too far away to be the source and the boats were staying close to the carrier's stern.

Trying to keep watch on everything around him, Sid looked up and to his left. There, on the gondola, a single man was at work with a heavy machinegun.

Thank you, thought Sid, but his gratitude blasted away when the track of bullets cut the man swimming next to him in half.

As the prisoner sank, Sid did something insane. He stopped and began to tread water. The bullets splashed around him in an oval pattern. The gunman wasn't protecting the prisoners, he was only protecting Sid.

"You bastard!" Sid shouted as he kicked back into motion. It was a bet. It had to be. They'd put money on anything and Sid was some guard's pony. Now that sonofabitch was up there, tipping the odds in his favor. The pink dye all over Sid's back wasn't to make him an easy target for the dolphins; it was so his benefactor could pick him out from above.

Sid kicked like mad to reach Jim, colliding with him, timing it so the sweep of machine-gun fire would be well away. Sid threw an arm over Jim's shoulder and pulled him in. "Keep close," he yelled through a mouthful of water.

Jim garbled a response and threw an elbow that connected with Sid's jaw, but not hard enough to knock him loose.

"There's bullets all around me," yelled Sid.

Through a crazed eye, Jim watched the splashes make their course. He turned to Sid and nodded, fast and vigorous, then, arms locked, both men kicked harder.

The lanky man spoke over his shoulder as he led Noah through the starboard cramps, second deck.

"So you're the new civy guy," he said. "I've heard about you."

"All lies, I'm sure," said Noah, nearly tripping over a knee-knocker.

"Join the Navy."

"No."

Electrician Warrant Officer Lowell Benning gave a quick shrug. "Well I tried. Right here."

They turned at a T-junction and moved into a darker tunnel. They had to put their backs to metal when a spontaneous bucket brigade formed up to move bundled blankets to and up a set of ladders.

"This old girl had over a hundred electricians while on deployment back in the day. Nowadays I've got six people who know what they're doing. Being a Navy electrician is an honor, son. And I treat my people right. What kind of pay grade are the civies giving you?"

"I get by," said Noah.

"Here," said Benning, turning into a cluttered stowage compartment. "Take these." He shoved a water-stained technical manual into Noah's hand. The cover was missing. "Here," he repeated, slapping a hastily scrawled list of components down on top of the manual.

"What am I supposed to be…"

"This." Benning yanked a tarp off a chest-high object shoved into a corner.

Noah gaped at the thing's screen, its card reader slot and an open cavity from which wires sprouted. "Is that a bank machine?"

"Yeah, ATM. Our last one. Get everything on that list out of it. Do it fast."

"Why do you have a—"

"It's how we got our pay." Benning punched four numbers into the dead keypad. "Back when we had over a hundred electricians."

Major Dawson rolled his body and slammed both daggers into the back of a dolphin making a beeline for a cutter. The mammal dragged him through the water a few feet before thrashing. Using one blade as a handhold, Dawson freed the second, pulled himself forward and stabbed at the blowhole. He kicked away, keeping both his weapons.

It was the light of the cutting torches that made those particular people prime targets, at least that's what Dawson had decided. The big fellah, Ripper, was moving again. He'd taken a hit or a bite, or something, but was able to shake it off.

A spinner, a child really, sped by, bleeding from its mouth. Dawson looked around and found a diver losing air. The calf's reward for severing the hose was a mouthful of powdered glass.

The diver gave a thumbs-up sign, meaning he was going to ascend. He exhaled and chased his bubbles to the surface, almost getting there when a pair of spinners streaked from the murk, bit him on an arm and leg and dragged him away forever.

MCPO Porter watched the prisoners. So few of them were left, the front runners out-swimming a dark red stain in the sea. One man was well in the lead. He'd be the first man to the rope ladders and lines. A few more meters and he'd live. Sacrificing all those men bought the cutting crews time to get into position and at least there'd be some survivors, at least the captain could make good on his promise of amnesty. The lucky lead swimmer was the first to hit the curtain of gunfire.

"Oh shit!" yelled somebody in the firing squad.

The prisoner second in line stopped short, watching the pack leader sink, staring up at the gunners on the flight deck and the fantail.

"You have to stop firing," Porter yelled at the squad leader. "Stop or you'll kill all the prisoners."

"If we stop," a sailor yelled back, "we'll kill the cutting crew."

"Watch your fire," shouted the squad leader. "Prisoners incoming." The order was echoed down the line.

The third runner up was even with the second place man and both now splashed towards the same rope ladder. They disappeared beneath the surface at the same time and neither came back up.

Then Porter spotted the pink man. “What the devil?”

“Chief,” called Perez from the nearest catapult. “We’re out of ammo.”

“Switch to rifles,” said Porter, pushing away from the rail. He saw a few of his runners coming towards him, which meant other catapults were running low or empty as well.

A prisoner made it to safety, then another and another. Running off pure adrenaline, the men flew up the rope ladders, kicking off fins, dumping masks into the water.

The firing squad was being more discreet, opening brief holes in their firing pattern to allow men to swim through safely.

Other prisoners saw what was happening. They weren’t the only ones.

Life, air, freedom all lay within sight. A few more kicks and they’d be topside. Sid couldn’t believe it. The circle of fire had carved a path to salvation. Sid didn’t know how many men had been killed in the process. Unfortunately the bullets could only protect him from the sides, close to the surface. The garbage was descending, opening up more room to attack from below. A dolphin came up from beneath and stopped a few feet short of striking range. Another dolphin moved beneath the first. They kept pace with Sid and Jim but didn’t rise to attack.

They reached the ladder. The two dolphins broke off and shot forward. At the same time Sid caught a glimpse of the props, saw the cutters at work, and understood everything.

“Go,” he said to Jim, pushing him at the ladder.

Jim didn’t need to be told twice. He hauled himself up but stopped just out of the water, looking down, watching Sid hyperventilate.

“What are you doing?”

“Go!” Sid gasped, forcing carbon dioxide out of his lungs. “Tell them that dolphins are swimming in under the prisoners.”

Jim climbed a few more rungs and looked down again.

Sid sucked in a deep breath and dove beneath the water.

“No no no no no!” shouted Toffee, watching the fins slide out of sight. “All you had to do was grab the ladder! Doglicker!”

The gondola crunched to a stop.

Toffee dumped the machine gun and dropped to the deck. A sailor got right in his face. “Just what the hell do you think you were—”

Toffee shouldered the man out of the way and jumped from the flight deck. He grabbed a line and slid down, ankles locked around the rope. When he was level with the fantail, he kicked with his legs, swung in and let go, landing next to a somewhat surprised boy holding a box of glittering rags.

"Doglicker!" the hunter shouted. He leaned over the rail, searched the ladders, then looked down again, envisioning a pink spot somewhere beneath the keel.

Sid kicked hard, amazed at what spread out before him. Four brass props, twenty-one feet in diameter, covered from screw to screw in nets. It was like capturing a skyscraper. Cutters had started from the top and were working their way down between the screws. Hanks of ropes drifted and sank, twirled in the currents and the wakes of dolphins.

An unmoving diver hung, twisted in the net, one leg bent at an unnatural angle and his octopus regulator bumping against his hip.

Sid kicked towards the corpse, looking around for a cutting tool.

He wasn't terribly surprised by his actions. All he'd thought about was getting up that ladder but when he reached it and looked up, he saw nothing. No friends or family on board waiting for him; life as a free man but an ex-convict. Probably not a lot of choice jobs open for him.

Sid had left a part of his humanity behind on the deck of this ship, but he was going to reclaim it from beneath.

He reached the dead diver, shoved the regulator into his mouth and set to work on the buckles of the diving vest. In under a minute he'd freed the BCD and flipped it up and over his head.

A chain-wrapped man with a pair of knives turned in his direction, saw the prison shirt. Through the mask, Sid watched the man's eyes go wide.

The dagger man gestured at a hacksaw caught in the net, flipped off something that might have been a salute, and turned in time to stab at a dolphin that passed just out of reach.

Sid pulled his way down the net to the hacksaw. A break in the murk showed him a diver in a cage. A spear gun lay across the cage floor, an empty quiver was secured to one side. The diver had a long pole with a blade on the end and thrust through the bars at the mammals battering the metal. The diver was being knocked around like a pinball, but still tried to fight back. A dolphin snatched the spear away, did a funny corkscrew twist and the other creatures backed off. With a snap of its head, the dolphin sent the spear at the cage. It hit metal, bounced off and sank. Another dolphin snatched it up, jetted to the cage and tried its own "throw".

This also missed. One by one, other dolphins lined up to take their turn.

“Sir,” said Lena, “*Munin* reporting a large contact on their short range. They’re patching through.”

“Got it,” said Otis.

Ransom brought the transmitted sonar up on one of his screens. “Is it another pod cluster?”

“I don’t think so, sir. I’m seeing a whale here.”

“What kind?”

“Humpback, maybe. Second contact sir, depth 1100 meters and rising.

“Did somebody order spermaceti oil?” asked Leighton’s voice from a speaker.

“You saying those are sperm whales?” said Ransom.

“Moby Dick’s coming to pay us a visit.”

“Hurry up,” said Toffee. “Hurry the hell up.”

The intimidated sailor was working the tank onto Toffee’s shoulders as quickly as he could.

The hunter tested the regulator, then yanked off his prosthetic and dropped it on the leather jacket bunched at his feet.

The sailor twisted wide of the blade as he cinched buckles.

“All he had to do was grab that damn ladder!” Toffee yelled at the sailor.

The seaman didn’t care. He didn’t care that this guy, obviously watered, was about to go over without a wetsuit. He didn’t care that the psychopath was after some animal called a pink doglicker. He just wanted the raving man with his suddenly deadly arm over the side and out of his life.

Toffee pulled his mask into place, shoved a short-hafted barbed spear under his right armpit, clambered over the rail, grabbed a drop line and slid into the sea.

54. Above and Beyond

This is the stupidest, most suicidal thing I've ever done, thought Toffee, getting angrier every inch of the way. He kicked down, seeing but not quite absorbing the gigantic props in their plankton-covered webs.

Blade pressed against his side, left arm pulling for two, the hunter descended, stopping every ten feet or so to squeeze his nose and equalize his ears.

He stuck close to the net, used the debris as his protection. These critters used echolocation as well as eyesight. All the crap, both organic and inorganic, had to be messing with their sense of direction.

Finally he saw pink through all the blood and rust. He pulled his way down to where Sid braced with one hand and sawed with the other.

Just don't have a heart attack, Halbert, thought Toffee.

Sid's arm was already tired and sore. His wrist burned and his grip kept slipping, but he persevered, switching hands when necessary. He couldn't last much longer anyway. The number of protectors was dwindling. He sensed movement above him and looked up, but it wasn't a dolphin, it was another diver. No wetsuit on this one, no chains or barbs, just the spear under his arm and...and...and that's when Sid lost his marbles.

Of all the reactions the hunter could have expected, laughter wasn't one of them. But that's what Sid was doing. His eyebrows were high and the big bursts of air coming from the regulator were accompanied by an unmistakable sound.

Sid spread his arms wide and then shook a finger as if to say, "That's what you get." Then he was laughing again.

Toffee kicked forward, snatched the spear from under his arm and drove it at the face of an incoming dolphin. The creature veered away and Toffee turned with it, thrusting out with his bladearm. He caught the mammal by a tail fluke, cutting off a small tip of it. He folded himself, bringing up the spear. The dolphins had such an overwhelming agility advantage, to win he had to think ten steps ahead.

Sid's laughter subsided to a giggle, mostly because he was starting to get water in his mouth. It was the funniest thing he'd ever seen. There was a God and his sense of humor was as wicked as his justice. Death hadn't in anyway freed the hunter from this world. He'd been assigned as Sid's guardian angel. *Ethan probably thinks he's in hell.*

Above him, the hunter impaled a spinner through the side, but lost the weapon when the creature sped away.

That an angel would need scuba gear was a little odd.

Toffee kicked into the net and raised his middle finger, giving Sid a sign that didn't appear in any diver's handbook.

"Six hundred meters and rising," said the sonar man in the *Munin*.

At the stern of the vessel, a tripod-mounted whaler's harpoon launcher was primed and loaded. Its projectile was a long thick spear with a barbed tip and an impact-actuated powerhead—sort of like a shotgun shell the size of a watermelon.

"Come about," ordered the boat's captain, one Lieutenant Commander Sheila Hatcher, the highest-ranking woman in *Terpris*.

"Three contacts now," said the sonar man. "They're coming up from way deep."

Munin and the *Nancy Dean* did their best to intercept the whales, but they couldn't keep one of the MK-10s from being smashed to fragments. The whale that did it sustained deep lacerations from the MK's keel blades, and the harpoon it took in the side blasted a huge divot of blubber from its log-like skin.

The leviathans dove deep again, all the while surrounded by dolphins that flitted back and forth along the whales' sixty-foot lengths. The smaller mammals chattered and twisted until one of the giants did a slow roll and changed direction.

"Something's wrong," said Otis. "They can't have just vanished."

"*Enrique* and *Hugin* also reporting loss of contact," said Lena.

"They're under us," said Ransom.

"Spotters reporting different species, sir," said Lena. "Other pods of dolphins are joining the spinners."

"Captain," said Leighton over the open channel, *"If the whales are under us, if they reach the props, it's over. That's fifty tons per whale bashing against the cutting crew."*

Toffee wanted to cut Sid's air hose. That'd make him give up on cutting and go for the surface, but every time the hunter thought he had an opportunity to do it, something else demanded more immediate attention. Once again a shape was coming straight at them out of the murk, but this time it wasn't a dolphin. A diver pulled along by a motorized sea scooter shuttled past, an empty spear gun trailing by a wrist strap.

A sudden force pushed upwards, like the current had somehow gone vertical. Debris raced and twirled for the surface. Toffee looked down at the garbage net, caught between the screws and the rudders.

The "floor" rose and twisted, then strands of thick rope and nylon shredded like paper. The terrible dark mass of a bull sperm whale, three times longer than any of the props, glided across the second screw, killing every cutter on it in a single pass.

Toffee had never felt so insignificant in his life.

A second whale expanded the hole in the net and dolphins swarmed up from below like boiling milk overflowing a saucepan.

Ransom stabbed a button and spoke into his mic. "Stukov?"

"Yes, sir."

"Do it."

"Yes, sir."

The captain released the button and leaned back in his chair. "Recall the boats," he ordered, then closed his eyes. "Everybody congratulate Otis and his team on repairing the LFA."

"Excuse me?" said Otis. "We didn't, sir. I don't even have short—"

"Mr. Allan," said Ransom, cracking one eye. "Congratulations on repairing the LFA."

"Uhm…okay, sir."

"Damn the torpedoes," said Leighton, hunching over his keyboard.

Odega sat, elbows on knees, head between his hands. "No. Damn the children."

Sid, clinging hard to netting still wrapped around prop three, watched his angel face down the whale. It didn't look as if he'd done a thing, but suddenly everything in the water not human spun and raced away. The whales descended, force from their tails like an underwater tidal wave. Toffee shot up into the keel as the bull sperm went down. Many of the dolphins, so coordinated in their attack, now panicked their way into strands of the very net they'd used as a weapon.

The underwater cutting crew at the props of CVN-65 had no idea how close they'd come to complete doom. They couldn't hear the Mimi, singing away in its waterproof box. They didn't see it in the murk, and nobody was unlucky enough to spy the true size of the whale pod.

Across the length of the net, cutters and protectors braced for attacks that suddenly stopped coming, and on every deck of *Terpris*, certain officers watched and waited.

"All boats returned, sir," said Otis. "We're sonar blind."

"Except for the LFA, of course," said Ransom.

"Er..."

"Captain," said Lena, "if you'd be a little more specific, I might know what you mean by 'strange' reports. Right now the only thing strange is the all clear from every single station."

"Nothing strange about that. We know why the dolphins have left."

"Captain..." Otis spoke the word like a plea for help.

"Mr. Allen, turn off your screen."

"Sir? Uh...okay." He powered down his monitor.

"Mr. Allen, according to what's in front of you, is there any indication that the LFA is malfunctioning in any way?"

"But my screen's...No, sir. Nothing I see on my screen suggests the LFA is malfunctioning."

"Good. That's what I wanted to hear."

Lt. Cmdr. McCabe entered the bridge, moved to Lena and tapped her on the shoulder. "You're relieved, Ensign."

Lena looked up at him sharply. The bridge crew had dropped into silent resignation but her curiosity was stronger than that.

One thing sprang to mind, but why keep it such a secret?

"Lieutenant Allan did a fine job, didn't he, sir?" she said.

"Yes, yes he did. I'll take your station now."

"I think he might even want a promotion out of this."

"Uhm, yes, commendable performance."

Lena stood and looked at the captain. "In fact we all might want a promotion." She took a step towards the command chair. "You know us lower ranking officers, so greedy. Always screaming me, me, me."

"Permission to speak with Ensign Wong privately?" said McCabe.

"Please do," growled Ransom.

***

At the end of a catwalk, with the wind chafing her lips, Lena pulled her jacket tighter and snarled at her commanding officer. "Odega gave you a Mimi!"

"Ensign Wong—"

"You sent all those men into the water and you had a working Mimi all along! Did Sid make it? Did my friend make it?"

"Ensign—"

"What the hell is the matter with you people?"

"LENA!"

McCabe had seen her irritated. He'd seen her cranky and frustrated, but never angry. Certainly not this angry and she was gorgeous in her fury.

"There are hazards involved with the Mimi's use."

"What hazards? We used them for years."

"Yes, but you didn't spend much time in their immediate area of effect, did you?"

"What difference would that…" she looked past McCabe's shoulder to where the ghost of a child ran across the catwalk and jumped over the side. "No…that couldn't…"

"I have to take my station. Restrict yourself to quarters. Speak to no one of this until I've had a chance to bring you into the loop. That's an order. Don't make me have you escorted."

Lena started to salute then waved him off and hugged herself as he stepped through a hatch.

"This is the captain," the voice boomed over the flight deck. *"We have restored the LFA. We have recalled the boats. All citizens please return to and remain in your quarters."*

For most, this was something worth cheering about. For others, it made the sacrifice of the prisoners that much more pointless.

"All prisoners are aboard," bellowed Porter through a megaphone. "All surviving prisoners are on board."

Some of the riot control seamen stood down.

"How many," yelled a man. The question was echoed by a number of voices.

Darcy had her hands buried in her hair. Any second now she was going to pull it out by the roots.

Porter raised his megaphone again. "An accurate headcount will be announced." (There were eighteen. Only eighteen.) "For now they're being taken down to be fed and supplied with accommodations." (The brig.) "A full list of survivors will be posted."

Mark weaved his way towards the swarm of desperately hopeful. He met Darcy's eyes and shook his head.

"Your friend Halbert didn't make it," he said, coming to her side.

For a few seconds Darcy wasn't on the deck of an aircraft carrier. She was standing in a wind tunnel, darkness at both ends. Through the rushing air she could faintly hear the Old Bull replying to questions with "no," or "I don't know." Nobody was getting a "yes," not a single redeeming "He lived. He's safe."

She screamed at the sky and fell to her knees, gut rolling over, twisting into a pretzel. A great oblivion was forming in her head, ripping and tearing as much as possible before shock could smother it under a blanket of irrational indifference. Beneath that anguish, something else was on the rise that Darcy didn't want to feel right now—relief.

55. The Real Deal

On the same day Darcy killed Winch Forester, mere hours after David Ramsey was thrown kicking and screaming into sea, Toffee stood amidst pieces of broken glass and plastic.

"Oh yeah, break something else, Red," he said. He had no idea what it had been before she'd used it as a missile.

She went left. So did Toffee. Only the table between them kept her out of reach and the intense game of Pop Goes The Weasel was great aerobics.

"Use your head," said Toffee, not falling for her feint to the right. "I'm a full citizen. You're a stowaway."

She was coming over the table, but he anticipated it. Toffee grabbed her wrist and a moment later she was pressed face down on the table, arm in a hammerlock.

"I served my sentence," he said into her ear. "You locked me out."

"And you locked us in."

Toffee released her and stepped back fast. "Prove it." He shifted into a defensive stance. "Day before yesterday you were accusing Odega of doing that."

Darcy came off the table and cocked one hip. She'd decided to break Toffee's knees.

"I'm a barge guard, Red. I'm the only chance he's got."

His right knee first. His blade was covered but he'd still lead with the right.

"I can keep him alive and in one piece." Toffee lowered a shoulder. She had exactly one second to settle down or he was going to deal out some pain.

She threw a fake at his nose, he'd be all about defending it. But he wasn't. As her leg came up for the kick he stepped in and knocked her across the room with a forearm to the chest.

"I'll ride out his whole sentence," said Toffee. "I'll baby-sit him all the way to freedom."

Darcy rolled into a crouch, then stood. Toffee was reading her. She didn't know what he watched for, but she was telegraphing somehow. The hatch was an option. She could run out, cry for help, but she didn't want to do that. If she did move to the hatch, it would be to lock it.

"How did you survive?" she hated that she had to know.

So he told her. Not once did he drop his guard, neither did she lower hers. It was an exhausting conversation.

"I've paid for my crimes against Compton Pit," said Toffee.

"You cheated."

"Now you're just being puerile."

That Toffee used a word Sid threw at her on occasion made her really wish for a shotgun. Or an axe.

"Let's say you take me down." He grinned. "You'll be caught. Happy swimming. Halbert won't have anybody and then your little gang is really lost at sea."

It was such a perfect trap. Could he have truly planned all this out or had luck been very kind?

"I won't get caught." She relaxed her right leg. A part of her had given up and bluster had moved in to fill the void. "There are other guards I can bribe."

"With what? Songs? You know me. You know what I can do."

Darcy relaxed her fists and put one hand on the table. She relaxed her spine and pelvis, then braced her stomach. "What do you want?"

Toffee folded his arms across his chest. The fake hand bent well into the cup of the opposing elbow. It almost looked real.

Darcy waited. So did Toffee.

"You going to make me say it?" His jaw clenched a little tighter.

"I'm not a mind reader."

"Uh-huh. You. I want you."

"You watch Sid's back and I lie on mine. You are so disgusting."

"And your thinking's too limited." He swallowed. "This is an all or nothing deal. I won't put a hand on you until Halbert is safe and sound onboard this ship. But after that you leave with me the next time *Terpris* lands. I don't care what continent."

Darcy stumbled back, fingernails dragging across the table.

"A life for a life, Red. Yours for his. You give yourself to me completely. And there's rules. You keep your cakehole shut about me. You tell any of the others and one of them disappears. I won't say which one. I know how you ladies like mystery."

"I'm being expelled in Diego. How can I—"

"You'll stay onboard. If you can't find a way, I will. You don't bribe any other guards. You don't interfere with me in anyway. If I see you trying to sidestep me, Halbert dies nasty. I'm holding all the cards here and you know it. Make the call. The next time I see Halbert's neck, do I save it or break it?"

"You can't touch any of the others," said Darcy, hating the quaver in her voice.

"I might want to play with them from time to time, but as long as you keep quiet, I won't do anything permanent. And until Halbert's safe, do your own thing. Sleep with the whole Navy for all I care, just don't get pregnant."

Darcy felt her gorge rising. She gripped the bench and stared at a spot on the floor. When she looked up, Toffee's expression bordered on empathy. It quickly turned to stone.

"It's a good exchange, Red. We both get something we want."

"If Sid dies, I'll kill you."

"I expect you'll try. If he makes it, you're mine."

"Deal," she whispered.

Darcy stayed alone in the compartment for a while after Toffee left. He was off for a gondola ride, he'd said. The analytical part of her mind finally mentioned how strange it was that the compartment wasn't in use. Toffee had prepared the little meeting room before hand, and somehow kept anybody else out.

The metal bulkheads transformed into the cold stone of a cavern. She heard a rat swarm skittering across the rocks. She tasted honey and felt a dozen grubby hands clawing at the waistband of her pants. A long thin blade slid up her thigh and she ran, tearing open the hatch. She rushed through the cramps, climbed steps, bashed her knees and her shoulders and moved upwards; to the open sky, away from the compartment, from the corridors and caverns.

On the flight deck she ran to the stern, stared out at the barge and watched some sort of cargo gondola carry hoppers to the carrier.

"This is a restricted area, miss," said a Navy man coming towards her.

In a fog she drifted up the starboard rail. When crates blocked her path she stopped and stared off into the dark.

"Hey," said Noah, appearing at her side. "Darcy, what's wrong?"

He didn't seem quite real. His grip on her wrist was real enough, though, and only then did she realize her lip hurt and she could taste a little blood.

"Darcy?"

Yes, he was real. Real and unchanging. She threw herself into him, felt him solid against her. She needed and he could supply the need, whatever shape it took, he'd give it to her. He would do anything for her, like take risks in restricted areas.

"There's a gondola thing," she said, pulling back in his arms. "It runs between *Terpris* and the barge."

"Okay," said Noah. "How can we use that?"

And suddenly she wanted to put Noah in a crate, wrap it in chains and guard him 24-7. "We can't." She broke free of him. "We can't ever use it. That's the thing." She backed away. "I need to be alone."

"I should—"

"I really need to be alone." She ran from him before her mouth could tell him everything and paint a bull's eye on his forehead.

56. Musical Chairs

Sid pushed hard at the saw. It kept slipping in his hand. His arms were useless lumps and cold was setting in. The angel was kind of deficient, though. Sure, he'd just driven away whales and dolphins but couldn't he toss a celestial pick-me-up?

Toffee had run out of patience. He didn't know what was responsible for the sudden retreat of the sea life, but whatever it was, he was going to make the most of it.

Dropping down the net to where Sid appeared to be almost comatose, Toffee grabbed the man's pressure gauge and held it up to his face. There was less than five minutes of air left. The hunter dropped the pressure gauge and jabbed his thumb up.

Sid nodded and followed Toffee, but the ghost-from-beyond thing was wearing a little thin. An angel wouldn't need scuba gear, it just wouldn't. Sid had gone to to Sunday School. He remembered angels with wings or not, halos or pillars of light, but none of them ever had masks or fins. And the blade thing was a little off. Surely God would have given him back his arm. Throw the man a bone at least.

As they passed the rudders, Toffee caught sight of something dangling fifteen feet below the surface, a clear plastic box containing a laptop and a very familiar piece of audio equipment.

Well isn't that interesting, he thought.

A thickening of the murk obscured the Mimi as Sid caught up. Toffee grabbed him by the back of the tank and pulled him up.

At the surface, Toffee inflated Sid's dive vest. He tugged at a horse collar and secured it around the both of them. A minute later the line pulled taut and they rose into the sky, but not in any divine fashion.

Temporary delusions drained away from Sid like the water running off his fins. This was Toffee buckled to him; a real living, breathing, locked-out Toffee.

The hunter yanked both their masks down and rocked forward, head-butting Sid hard enough to knock him senseless for a minute.

Rough hands grabbed them and pulled them into the fantail.

"I'm done with you now," Toffee growled in Sid's ear. "Stay out of my way, I'll stay out of yours."

"Holy shit," said a voice. "This guy's a prisoner."

Somebody pried the hacksaw from Sid's hand. "You were cutting, unbelievable. Here, put a new blade on this and pass it on." The hacksaw was taken away.

Another wave of cutters was suiting up to go over the side.

The dive vest and tank were pulled free and Sid took deep breaths, trying to clear his head and suppress the urge to vomit.

"I'll tell the XO you're a prisoner," said a voice near Sid's ear. "I'll tell him what you did."

Sid's head throbbed. His entire body felt like it was swollen. Hands checked his extremities and he was dragged out of the fantail and lifted over a knee knocker.

"Pink man," said MCPO Porter staring down with undisguised awe. "I'll inform the XO," he said to a seaman. "Carry on." He looked Sid over. "Are you injured?"

"I don't think so. Fatigued. Beyond fatigued. Am I a free man?"

"Oh yes. Quite free." He flicked his hand and Sid was placed on a stretcher and carried away.

"It's a bit anticlimactic, don't you think?" asked Leighton as he bounced a ball against a bulkhead and caught it again.

"Two hours, fifteen minutes," said Chen, looking at a clock. "And not a single problem."

"None that's been reported, anyway," said Odega. His left wrist was handcuffed to the armrest of his chair.

Chen stuck his head through the hatch that led from the computer room to the aquarium. He leaned back and said, "Both sleeping peacefully."

"I think we should send the female to the kitchens and acquire another specimen," said Leighton. "She's of no use. Brooding and violent. No attempt to adapt."

Stukov entered the compartment. "How are you feeling?" he asked Odega.

"How would I know? Ask them."

"He's been mostly non-threatening," said Chen. "Though he tried to bite me when I closed the cuff too tightly. I'm joking, of course."

"We've recovered the ROV," said Stukov. "It's in engineering."

"Repairable?" asked Odega.

"We don't know yet. Are you three certain the Mimi's effects are penetrating the hull?"

"Most definitely," said Leighton. "We've had to sedate everything."

"Except the rabbit," said Chen.

"Oh yes, we didn't sedate the rabbit."

"Why not?" asked Stukov.

"I don't like rabbits," replied Leighton. "How amenable would the captain be to getting us a new dolphin? I'd love to have a spinner."

Stukov's look could have withered plants.

"Never mind."

The commander crossed the room to a communications panel and did a check in with a few watch stations. When he was finished he turned to Odega. "It is the water, yes? It buffers the effects."

"It's possible. Doesn't make sense to me, though. The water amplifies the ultrasonics. Shouldn't be the hull either. A Mimi got at me through I don't know how many feet of dirt and concrete."

"Perhaps we are just lucky. Let us hope we stay lucky."

"What is the meaning of this?" McCabe demanded, bursting into communications.

At a terminal, Lena clicked away with determination.

"I told you to go to your quarters." He glared but it wasn't getting him anywhere. She barely spared him a glance. So he turned his anger on a more susceptible target. "And why didn't you stop her?"

"I tried, sir," said the curly haired lieutenant, sitting as far from Lena as the compartment would allow. "But she hit me."

That was when McCabe noticed the prosthetic leg leaning against the side of her chair. She'd detached it and had it within easy reach.

Lena snarled and started from scratch. She looked at McCabe again but he really didn't matter at the moment. She'd club him with the leg if she had to. It wasn't an optimum weapon from the point of view of dealing damage, but brandishing an artificial leg had a stark-raving-mad connotation to it that kept people at bay.

Reading her body language, seeing her need, McCabe approached slowly and looked over her shoulder. "Who are you trying to contact?" he asked. "And why?"

"Compton Pit," she looked up at him, face pale. "The last time I talked with them the nearby settlements were bringing in…" she lowered her voice to a whisper, "…their children."

McCabe's head drooped. "Is there anything I can do to help?" He snapped his fingers at the lieutenant. "You too."

Lena watched feedback play name-that-bird as her signal bounced from satellite to satellite.

"It's a long trip," said McCabe.

"We should have three viable channels."

"Which channel is this?"

"This is my second try on the first choice. None of them are in sync."

At his own terminal, McCabe brought up Lena's terminal's history and began reverse engineering her failed attempts. "Perhaps your Pit is simply unable to respond. Oh. You were a few birds short on this one."

"All of them," said Lena. "Anything near the North American west coast is gone. Three sats aren't all going to burn in or spin out at the same time."

She slammed the side of the terminal. "Dammit. Dammit!" She got up and hopped a few feet away, one arm wrapped around her stomach, one hand clutching her chin.

McCabe's empathy for her was on hold for that moment. He flipped through a few screens on his monitor, then leaned back and looked at Lena's. "Wally," he said to the lieutenant, "I want you to compile every time we've lost more than two proximal birds at the same time."

"Going back how far?"

"As far as we have data for it."

"That's going to take a while."

"Then you should get started."

"Yes, sir."

"Wally?"

"Sir?"

"Do it somewhere else."

The lieutenant gave Lena's back a speculative look, then powered down his station and left.

McCabe locked the hatch and turned to face Lena. "Could you at least put your leg back on if you're going to pace?"

She hopped back to her chair and sat down. She looked hopelessly at McCabe, then her despair turned to anger. "Why wasn't I in on the Mimi from the get go?"

"You weren't deemed necessary to the project."

"I studied the hell out of those things. I know—"

"Very little actually. Dr. Odega shared all your findings with us."

"I had limited equipment to work with. Let me use your stuff and—"

"We have people who already know how to use our 'stuff.' "

She pulled up her pant leg and fitted the prosthetic. "And what about Sid? He's rotting on the…" The leg nearly dropped from her fingers. "You should have brought Sid off the barge."

McCabe approached her and stopped, his hands clutching at the air as if he didn't know what to do with them. "Sid Halbert was questioned extensively, first by Dr. Odega and then by Leighton, Chen and Stukov. When it was felt the extent of his knowledge was reached. He was…" he nodded glumly, "returned to the barge."

Lena's face pinched tight. She held a hand over her mouth as she asked, "Did he know?"

"Halbert's information confirmed that the Mimi output has an acute affect on children."

"No."

"Circumstantial evidence," he continued, "supports the belief that long term exposure to its area of effect impairs mental functions in adults."

"No," Lena repeated, shaking her head.

"An experiment we performed confirms being unconscious close to one causes a short-term but intense delusional state."

"So what's going on right now?" she asked loudly, almost shouting. "Are kids going tooth crazy all over the ship?"

"Nothing's happening right now. That's the thing. Being underwater somehow blunts the detrimental effects."

"Ultrasonics just don't work that way."

"Leighton and Chen would agree with you but—"

"I want to see all your data."

"An ensign isn't cleared for that."

"Then you'll have to promote me."

He started to laugh, then stopped when he noticed the hard look in her eyes. "I can't just—"

"I'm smarter than everybody you've got. You know it, I know it. Where I'm from I was the head honcho, buddy. I mean sir."

"The problem, Lena, is that in today's Navy, there's too many lieutenants and not enough ensigns."

She looked away. "After today, I think you've got less of both."

"Yes, well. The Gold Coast is in for a surprise. No settlement likes us when we come recruiting."

She hugged herself. All she wanted right now was to be with Caps.

The moment nobody was looking in Caps's direction, he snapped up a rifle and hightailed it to the stern. An arriving gondola disgorged weary sailors. Just before the dangling box could return for the next load, Caps darted on board and shut the door.

He heard a petty officer third class yelling something at him as the gondola moved away from the carrier. Caps checked his rifle's breach and flipped the safety off. A strong gust of wind made the gondola shudder hard and Caps stumbled, fell to one knee, then gripped the central pole and held tight.

The conveyance, still swinging, banged to a halt at the prow of the barge. Guards and sailors rushed to steady it and as Caps got out, a group of sailors filed in.

"Ain't you going in the wrong direction?" asked one of the sailors.

Caps didn't answer him. He looked at heads and faces. Toffee wasn't there, which was good because killing the man in front of witnesses would be suicide. Not that hunting Toffee in the first place didn't suggest a lack of self preservation. Heck, just playing Toffee at a round of checkers was a dangerous thing to do.

The Navy boys were too busy leaving the barge to notice the one sailor doing exactly the opposite.

How many passages could the barge have? From everything he'd heard, the place was a big shell around a giant hold.

At the wheel house, Caps found a single sailor, an ensign, sitting at a communications terminal.

A hatch on the other side of the bridge led to living quarters. So much time spent in the cramps had given Caps a sense of ship layouts and the barge in comparison to *Terpris* was like searching a bathroom after learning the floor plan of a mansion. Twenty minutes later Caps stood in the protected catwalk and stared down into the mounds. The smell of the place nauseated him and he struggled to keep from feeling emotional echoes of prisoners who were now either on the carrier or dead beneath the waves.

Caps found his way back topside, scanned the upper walkways and then stared at the carrier. He was on the wrong ship.

Cursing, he slung his rifle and returned to the gondola launch. About fifteen sailors waited their turn. The box was halfway across the gap when the wind suddenly howled like a demon. The cable hummed and the gondola swung hard and twisted. When the pull of gravity exceeded wind force, the conveyance swung back the other way. For a few moments the air calmed and the sailor-filled pendulum rocked its way back towards equilibrium. A second hard gust set the cable screaming. The gondola twisted counter-clockwise and with a quick burst of high-pitched *pings* the cable snapped. The gondola went into the sea.

Immediately geared-up divers dropped down on lines from the carrier's fantail.

The broken end of the cable streaked for the pulley on the barge. It rounded the wheel, whipped through the air and fell into the water.

"They're screwed," said one of the sailors.

"So are we," said another. "We won't be fixing that in this wind." He looked off to the northwest. "And it's only going to get worse."

"What do you mean?" asked Caps, gripping the sleeve of the sailor turned meteorologist. "We're stuck here? For how long? I have to get back to the carrier right the hell now!"

Toffee was over there, free to do whatever his raccoon's heart desired. Caps released the man's sleeve and eyed the distance between the barge and the carrier. In no way was that an option. He'd never been a strong swimmer.

One of the divers reappeared empty handed. A second one popped up, dragging a spluttering man behind him.

At an unseen signal, more lines dropped into the water from the fantail and one by one, men ascended, pulled up from the chop.

Another drenched sailor was fished out even as divers tossed their cutting tools into a cargo net that vanished and reappeared in the swells and troughs of a five foot sea. Men had inflated their BCDs and their heads and shoulders were dark spots that rose and fell at the whim of the ocean.

In all the activity, nobody really noticed a small, tarp-covered object pulled up by its own dedicated line.

Tanzers's front door swung open and Mark stepped in. "They're recalling the divers, folks. We'll be underway soon."

The room had been filled with conversation, oaths, pleas, prayers and crying, but until that moment, it was if the bar itself had been holding its breath. Mark stepped out of the way as Tanzers exhaled its occupants into the Street. Another round of *who's alive* was in the brewing and the stakes were so very high.

With a handful of people left in the place, Tanzer locked eyes with Mark. The Old Bull lowered his chin, gave a single shake of his head, and left.

Tanzer sighed. He turned around, put his back to the room.

On the stage, Tivoli sat gripping the sides of the keyboard. His mouth was a hard line and his skin had lost some color.

Darcy approached the bar. "Who?" she asked.

"Tony Moore," said Tanzer. "You knew him as Ripper."

The floor started vibrating softly, almost imperceptibly. It was a tactile white noise, only noticed when it stopped.

Darcy couldn't have cared less about Ripper's death. It was irrelevant in the face of her own loss. She couldn't connect with Tanzer and Tivoli on it, neither could they connect with her.

She was alone in her grief. No other person within reach had loved Sid. She had an urge, a craving to do something so weak and vulnerable it seemed to be the desire of a different person. She wanted to go completely to pieces, and she realized she could do just that in Noah's arms.

"I'm taking tonight off," Darcy said.

"Uh, yeah, copy that," said Tivoli.

"Tiv," said Tanzer, looking out a porthole window behind the bar. "Let's pack up the glassware."

A gust of wind hit the back door the second Darcy opened it and it was all she could do to keep it from ripping from the hinges. She used her shoulder to close the door.

"I thought you were never coming out," said Toffee.

Darcy spun but saw nobody. She looked up. He stood on the tiny balcony of the boat's upper deck. He was black against the turbulent sky, seaman's coat whipping about, long strands of hair riding the wind, writhing like Medusa's brood.

"Halbert's in sick bay," he called down. "That's my end delivered, Red."

"Liar!" she shouted.

"Just go to sick bay. If he's dead now, that's not my problem. He was alive and free when I left him."

She glared up at him, desperate to believe, determined not to trust.

"You handle this any way you want," the hunter continued. "I'm not gonna say boo to any of them, but when we touch ground, you belong to me. Well? What are you doing standing around here? Go see Halbert."

Without thinking she turned in the direction of the nearest access to the lower decks.

"One thing," Toffee yelled at her back. "You might want to wrap things up with the kid."

Her body locked up, but only for a moment. Then she was running and she reached the hatch at the same time as the rain started to fall.

"Look," said Ensign Barnes, finding himself in the preposterous position of being the highest ranking sailor on board. "We'll just have to ride it out. We're on tight time here. *Terpris* can't stop and send the boats."

The wheel house was packed, filled or surrounded by just under thirty men.

"They should have got us before we started moving," said one of the civy guards.

"They can drop those boats on the fly," said another. "I've seen them do it."

"Not in these seas," said a sailor.

"We've got some work to keep us busy," said Barnes, raising his voice. "For one thing we have to stow the hold."

"No way," said a Navy guard. "Barnes, go take a good look at that mess down there. You want that hold stowed, you bring back the workforce we threw overboard."

Barnes turned, annoyed at being questioned by a subordinate. "If we don't do it now, it really will be impossible later."

"Why's this dipstick in charge?" asked a civy. "Where's Toffee?"

The question was echoed by a few of the guards.

Caps pushed against a wall to keep from staggering. *I don't believe it,* he thought miserably. *They think Toffee's their leader.*

57. Separation Anxiety

Darcy looked over the wounded who filled three quarters of the mess hall. Sick bay was full. Sid wasn't there, or here. Neither had he been in the brig.

She clenched her fists. Why would Toffee taunt her like this? It wasn't...she winced. Darcy hated knowing what the man was and wasn't like.

"You sing nice, ma'am," said a short man in a stained white frock.

She blinked at him.

"At Tanzers I mean. I like to hear you sing."

"Uh, thanks. I'm look—"

"For somebody. Yeah, the mix of hope and terror kind of gives you away. Name?"

"Sid Halbert. He was one of the prisoners but he wasn't—"

"Black? Scars on left cheek and neck? Of course, being on the barge he could have acquired new scars that you wouldn't know—"

"Yes that's him!" she said, wondering how the nurse had suddenly become taller. Biting her lip she released his lapels and he sank back down from his tiptoes.

"We treated him for minor injuries and exhaustion. He's currently recovering in MCPO Porter's house in the Valley."

"Porter's house? What's he doing there?"

"I wouldn't know for—"

"Oh, I don't care. What does the place look like?"

Noah crawled backwards out of a maintenance access and dropped a handful of bolts onto the inside of the toolbox's open lid. One of the bolts bounced off the plastic and slid beneath an uneven stack of deck plates.

Main power was off in the entire section. Emergency lighting was poor and he couldn't see the bolt beneath the shadows of the plates. He'd left his flashlight in the access. Noah was about to go crawling for it when a bright beam of light hit the area he was searching.

"Thanks," said Noah, reaching beneath a sharp metal edge. His fingertips brushed the object but couldn't quite reach. He started to move the plates, then the deck pitched at just the right angle and the bolt rolled out and bumped into his knee.

Noah turned to drop the bolt in the toolbox, but instead had to raise an arm to shield his eyes. "Shine that somewhere else, please."

The light didn't waver. Noah moved to one side but the light stayed tight to his face.

From somewhere off in the darkness came the sound of deck plates being scattered, followed immediately by quiet but enthusiastic cursing.

Noah dropped the bolt and hefted a wrench. "You going to knock it off with the flashlight?"

"Ah, what the hell," said a rough voice. The beam swung up until it shone straight up from under its owner's chin. "Boo," said Toffee.

Noah shrieked like a little girl, took three steps straight back and fell over a knee knocker.

"The hell was that?" called a voice down the passage. Footsteps came towards them. The flashlight blinded Noah again, then went out.

A Navy man with a pencil light mounted over one ear stepped into view.

"You okay?" he asked, giving Noah a once over. The corridor was empty, save for the two electricians. "You really have to watch the knockers in the dark. Especially if you're not used to them."

"Yeah." Noah stood up and brushed himself off.

"You're okay?"

"Yeah."

"You're looking a little shaky."

"I hit my head. I'll be fine."

"Okay." He moved off, his shape becoming dimmer until he disappeared altogether.

Noah put his hands flat against the wall and took a few deep breaths. He didn't know what exactly was happening to him, but it couldn't be a good thing. Now his hallucinations carried an audio component.

Moving carefully, he removed a voltmeter from his toolbox and pocketed the bolts. A brain tumor could cause hallucinations. "Or maybe I really am getting watered," he said out loud.

Toffee rolled out of the maintenance access and stood up. Before Noah could utter a sound or react in anyway, the hunter pinned him to the wall with a chokehold.

Toffee looked deep into Noah's eyes, searched his face.

Noah was too stunned to do anything but draw in what little air the hand on his throat allowed him.

"You don't do too good with surprises," Toffee whispered into Noah's ear. "Thought I taught you better 'n' that. I'm alive. I'm here. Deal with it."

Little black spots danced through Noah's vision.

Toffee switched to whispering in Noah's other ear. "The next time I throw a chokehold on you, it ain't coming off until you make it."

The grip on Noah's throat released and right away bright light was in his eyes. The flashlight dropped, clattered on the deck and rolled a few inches.

A hint of Toffee melted into the shadows of the corridor a couple of knee knockers aft.

Noah drew in a deep and ragged breath. His heartbeat thundered in his ears. The deck tilted to starboard. The flashlight rolled into a wall and went out.

All repair work forgotten, Noah picked up the flashlight and set off after the hunter.

"What are you doing there in the first place?" cried Lena, trying not to let her voice reach the red zone of hysteria.

There was nothing but static from the speakers for a second or two, then Caps's voice became clear. *"...and it seemed like a good idea at the time."*

Lena gripped the mic stand and wrung it like it was a neck.

A pen not yet stowed rolled across the deck behind her chair. It was snatched up by the technician at the next terminal and tossed into a drawer.

A few stations past that, a male lieutenant caught Lena's eye and gave her a finger across the throat gesture.

"Rick," she said into the mic, "we have to clear this channel."

"Hon, you have to find Darcy. Tell her where I am. Tell her I'm here alone."

"Alone? I thought there a bunch of sailors stuck on the—"

"Ensign Wong!" shouted the lieutenant.

"I have to go," she said, then cupped her hands around the mic and whispered, "I love you."

The deck's rolling was definitely becoming more severe.

One of the techs got up and ran for the hatch. From the sound outside, he made it about ten feet up the corridor before losing his cargo.

“Spires,” said the lieutenant, “get us a barrel or something in here. Something you can secure.”

“Yes, sir,” said an ensign, pulling himself to his feet.

Some more retching came from the corridor.

“Spires.”

“Sir?”

“Make sure it has a lid.”

“That’s it,” said Ensign Barnes. “Sorry folks. No more personal communications to the mainland.”

A unified groan came from the handful of men leaning against walls or gripping fixtures on the bridge.

“Ship’s business only.” Ensign Barnes tapped a couple of keys on the communications panel, then sat down in the captain’s chair. “Anybody not supposed to be here, clear out, please.”

Caps shambled his way through the hatch and along a corridor. His feet were a little confused. Uphill, downhill, uphill, downhill…it felt like walking on a demented treadmill.

Anybody who actually could do something useful had been assigned a post. Barnes didn’t really come across as an ensign. Bits of grey streaked his dark brown hair and he carried himself with the bearing of a veteran seaman. He must have held a higher rank and been demoted for something or other. Disciplinary action would also explain how he’d landed on the barge.

Caps, having no real use, had been told to get out of the way. He found his way into the civy quarters for no other reason than that they were closer than Navy country.

The pitch of the deck caught him as he stepped into a berth and he did an uphill lurch to grab and hold one of the eight bunk beds.

“Hey,” said a civy guard, hands and feet pressed to the posts of the bed like he was tied there. “Don’t throw up in here, squid.”

“Do I look like I’m going to throw up?”

“You look like you’re going to toss everything including your liver.”

Caps imagined he probably did look pretty awful, but it had nothing to do with sea sickness. The motion of the deck wasn’t really bothering him that much. If anything, it seemed appropriate.

“I’m fine,” said Caps, wrapping his arms around bedpost. “I’ll just pretend I’m in Joker’s lair from the old Batman show.”

The man offered him a look Caps was quite familiar with.

“What I mean is in the old Batman show, the bad guy hangouts all had slanted floors. You know, the camera was at angle? And all the henchmen…” He suddenly realized his metaphor was more apt than he’d intended. “So who’s this Toffee guy y’all were talking about?”

"Only my personal friggin' hero," said the guard. "Doesn't take shit from anybody and he knows how to get things done. Guess he got called over to the mainland for something. Maybe the Marines put in a call for him."

"Marines?" Caps's lip curled. Full access to the carrier's armory. Joy.

"Yeah, they came over here a couple of times to yak with him."

"Attention," blared Barne's voice from a speaker. "All free hands to the wardroom. Move it ladies."

"I knew it," said the guard. "Prick found jobs for us to do."

From bow to stern the carrier was a frenzy of activity. Small objects found drawers, boxes and lockers. Larger objects were secured to the deck, or lashed to posts and poles, anything deemed solid.

On the Street, slick black rain-jacketed teams of people hauled on lines, tightened nets and did whatever they could to protect their homes and businesses.

Down in the Valley, people gathered the more mobile components of their old world monuments. Crates were lashed or relocated and a general assortment of odds and ends amassed over time were either stowed or discarded.

The gigantic hatches port and starboard were shut tight. A section of the Valley was browned out and both flashlights and lanterns bobbed and weaved in the half gloom.

Darcy pushed through people, past the Sphinx, past the windmill and next to a Middle-Eastern-looking temple thing, she came to a wood and metal structure painted light blue. It had artificial turf for a front lawn, cordoned off by a diminutive white picket fence.

She pushed through the little gate and knocked on the front door. A few seconds later the door opened slightly and a woman's face appeared in the crack. "Yes?"

"Is this MCPO Porter's house?"

"He's not here. He's on the bridge."

"Is Sid Halbert here?"

"He's not to be disturbed."

"Please. Please. I'm his daughter."

The door opened a little more and the woman's entire face came into view. She had graying auburn hair and a firm mouth. She raised an eyebrow at Darcy.

"It was a mixed marriage, okay? My name's—"

"Darcy," called Sid from within.

The woman turned and said, "You shouldn't be out of bed, Mr. Halbert."

Darcy burst into the house, almost knocking Mrs. Porter over. She froze three feet past the threshold.

She barely recognized the man standing in the narrow corridor, one forearm against the wall. His head was bandaged. "I couldn't believe it when Chief Porter told me you were still on board." He was so much thinner than he should have been and there was a slump to his shoulders that had no business being in Sid Halbert.

But then her arms were around his chest, and his cheek was pressed tight to hers. She kissed his neck; not in a sexual way but because it was the closest skin to her mouth.

"All right, come on, come on," said Mrs. Porter. "You can stay, dear, but this man here has to go back to bed."

They put him on a cot in a tiny room across the hall from what appeared to be a kitchen. Empty hooks on the walls marked spots where pictures had been taken down.

Mrs. Porter reached under the cot and pulled out a pair of long straps with buckles on the end. She offered these to Darcy. "Things might get rough. Best you strap him down. I have things to pack up. There's a bucket tied to the bed there, if you need it."

After the woman left, Darcy stood unmoving, straps dangling from her hands. She stared at Sid, compensating for the motion of the deck without realizing it.

He gave her a weak smile and nodded at his legs. Remembering the straps, Darcy dropped one and wrapped the other around the cot and its occupant just below his knees. "Is that too tight?" she asked, checking the tension.

"It's fine."

She gathered his hands between hers, squeezed at them and resumed staring down at him. For almost a minute, no words would come. None existed that could have done the job.

"I missed you," they both said at almost the same time.

She hugged him again. "They said you were dead. They listed the prisoners that made it and—"

"I stayed in the water," said Sid. "I saw what was going on and I stayed down to help cut."

Darcy pulled away and picked up the second strap. "You're insane."

"Possibly. This next thing is going to sound really crazy, but it isn't." He gripped her shoulders. "Ethan's here. He covered my ass in the water. I think he may have protected me on the barge." He stopped and watched her bottom lip become a squeeze toy to her fingers. He misread the uncertainty in her eyes. "You have to believe me. Even I thought I was losing my mind at first but—"

She leaned back, pulled the strap taut between her hands. "He is here, Sid. He was here ahead of us. The rockslide was all a sham.

He…bad luck. I've run it through my head and all I can come up with is bad luck."

"Who else is here?" asked Sid, letting his head sink into the pillow.

"Everybody. Caps and Lena are in the Navy. Noah and I…"

"Noah and you what?"

"Noah and I…" she cupped Sid's face and kissed his forehead. "Sid, I'm so happy that you're…you have to know I am, but…I have to find Noah."

She dropped the strap on his chest, gave him another peck on the cheek and rushed out.

He'd been choosing direction by instinct. Left here, right there, up…down. Noah had no footprints to follow, no broken twigs or spoor with which to track. When he came to a set of steps that offered access to the flight deck, he took them.

The possibility of madness still lingered in the back of his mind, but the bruising on his throat was real. The flashlight in his hand was real and it wasn't the one he'd brought down with him in the first place.

I thought I taught you better….

What kind of BS was that? How could you teach anybody to respond to that kind of surprise in the first place? *No*, thought Noah, *that's not the 'first place.' The first place is what is he doing here?*

Toffee had locked them in, trapped them here, that was without question. Noah tried to be angry, tried to hate him for that, but the chain of events that followed had given him something worth more to him than anything else in the world.

Noah shoved open the hatch and wind across the flight deck tried to rip his head off his shoulders. He was instantly drenched, instantly freezing. He fought his way a few steps to where he could latch onto the starboard rail.

Everything for him, both internal and external, was in chaos.

The sky was an angry, ugly thing. The ocean roiled, fifteen to twenty-foot-high waves took the carrier across the beam.

A group of barrels had come loose and people in rain gear struggled back and forth trying to get things under control.

Noah looked around, facing the southwest so the wind-driven rain scoured his back instead of his face. That he'd lost his quarry was a definite. He didn't know what he'd planned to do if he'd caught the man at all. Maybe thank him. The chokehold was a bit rough, but heck, sometimes that's just how Toffee communicated.

How was he going to tell Darcy? She'd think he'd gone tooth crazy. *How can you be happy about this?* asked a voice in the back of his head. *The man's a murderer.* Noah dragged himself forward, towards Carlos's house boat and towards Tanzers.

He had simply too many questions, and standing outside getting drowned by the weather wouldn't answer any of them. All around, people were doing their best to lock the ship down. Noah thought about the deck plates he'd left lying up and loose down in the cramps. He couldn't worry about those right now. No, right now it was best to get home, help Carlos with the house and hope that Darcy would be there waiting for him.

The deck dropped severely to starboard.

Noah didn't hear the shouts of warning, or see the barrel until it smashed into him and knocked him over the side.

"So you miscalculated," snarled Captain Ransom, gripping the arms of his chair. As turbulent as the deck was, the bridge was that much worse. It was like sitting at the top of a metronome.

"The instrumentation is wrong," said Gator, defending himself. "The props can't be operating at full power."

Ransom looked at the radar display on the screen closest to his right hand.

A hatch opened and Lena stumbled in, doing a side-to-side dance getting to something solid and grip-worthy.

"Ensign," said Ransom, "take your station."

She looked over at the vacant chair by the communications terminal. It seemed like a long way away.

The captain watched her starts and stops across the room. He didn't have much patience at the moment and it showed. Lena was the last person who should have been called to bridge duty under the circumstances, but she was also the only communications officer not sick to the point of uselessness. Even McCabe had reached his limits.

She planted herself and logged in to the terminal.

"We have to lose mass, sir," said Gator. "If we don't, we'll take the worst she's got to throw at us."

Lena pulled on her headphones and was immediately bombarded by overlapping reports coming in from all decks. She tapped buttons, clearing things up, limiting the feed.

"Open a channel to the barge," said Ransom.

Thank you, Lord, thought Lena. "Aye, sir. I'll instruct them to prepare for evacuation."

Three different crewmembers tried to talk at the same time. Ransom cut through them all. "We are not evacuating the barge. We can't evacuate it."

"But…" *Rick!* "The people on board? You can't just—"

Ransom squeezed his armrests. He'd handled everything so poorly, always one step behind the problem. He'd already sentenced so many to an unnecessary death, what difference were a few more? He should have ordered the barge cleared and detached the moment the props started turning. The navigator felt it wouldn't be necessary and the captain didn't ask for a second opinion.

Neither ship had undergone proper stress tests in over a decade. If the carrier's capacity to withstand a full-on hurricane was slightly in question, then the barge's capacity was a question mark as big as *Terpris*.

Caps pulled himself up through the hatch just as the covered catwalk beneath his feet broke free of the bulkhead and tumbled to the bottom of the hold.

He spilled into the corridor. For a few seconds the wall and the deck tried to swap roles in the universe, then the deck tilted to port and Caps was able to clear the hatch so another seaman could slam it shut and secure it.

"That's not going to work," said Caps, back to one wall, feet against the other. "Basically, we've got no safe way into that hold."

The sailor cursed a few times then patted the hatch-cover. "It's a good thing there's no men down there. They'd be pulp by now."

A new sound joined the slams and bangs coming from the hold. It was a single, loud *clank* that shuddered through the metal.

"That sounded really bad," said Caps.

"Shit." The sailor turned on his hands and knees to face the bow.

"Bridge to all decks," crackled Barnes's voice. *"By order of Captain Ransom, we have disengaged from the mainland."*

"Shit!" the sailor repeated.

"All available hands to the main deck. Whatever we've done to secure the main hatch covers, we better do more."

The alarm blared. One of the speakers for it was directly above Caps's head. He clapped his hands to ears and shouted at the sailor, "What does that mean? What's the mainland? What does that mean?"

The man's eyes were glassy saucers. "It means we're dead."

58. Riders of the Storm

The carrier sliced ahead, like a metal splinter in the ocean's skin. The seas rose. Three men and a woman hauled Noah out of the safety net bare seconds before the alarm sounded to clear the flight deck.

Twenty minutes later a second alarm sounded. This one meant evacuate the flight deck completely. In houseboats across the Street people shoved bare essentials into waterproof bags and charted in their heads paths across the deck to the nearest access.

"What else can I do?" asked Tivoli, legs akimbo, hands gripping the edge of the baby grand piano.

"You've nailed it down with everything short of railroad spikes," said Tanzer, pulling on a raincoat. "I'm out of here. If you're staying, at least tie a rope around your waist. I've always fancied kites."

A large tarp covering cargo hoppers tore free and sailed over the deck like a giant bat. It wrapped its wings around the top of a houseboat's wind generator mast. The mast shuddered, groaned and split. Lines snapped as the tarp blew on, now trailing the mast behind it. The tarp sailed over the greenhouse. The mast decided to go through. Huge shards of glass flew across the deck and over the port side, lacerating anything in their path. Cut lines released drums and crates. A small cargo crane came loose, spinning in a circle, casting its heavy hook and cable like a fishing rod.

Inside, everything bigger than a coffee mug became suspect. People eyed cargo and pipes, hatch covers and furniture, wondering when something would come free and start crushing.

The degree to which the carrier pitched now was in excess of anything most of her passengers had experienced. Even the veterans of the sea began to feel alarmed and as bad as it was, the hurricane had so much more to give.

Darcy had been on her way up the steps to the flight deck when she'd been stampeded back down again following the "clear off" alarm.

She found herself trapped in a mess hall. All the chairs had been removed. Only the tables, bolted to the floor, remained. Civies hugged the walls or clung to the fixtures. A pair of sailors by the hatch acted as a one-way door. People were allowed in. Nobody was allowed out.

A tearing sound came from Darcy's left. A hand appeared before her face holding up a strip of shirt.

"It's for around your face," said the woman next to her. A similar strip of cloth covered her mouth and nose. "It's helps against the smell."

Darcy nodded in understanding and took the offering.

"I wish you'd do more Streisand," said the woman.

Darcy knotted the cloth behind her head and looked around, wondering if she could guess who next would succumb to nausea.

Oh, she thought as the deck tilted to starboard, *it's me. How nice.*

Darcy clawed at the knot behind her head as she crawled towards a bucket.

The sea disappeared as wind ripped the tops off waves and sprayed the water out like steam above a boiling kettle. The roar of the ocean, the thunder and wind blended into a single, all-encompassing noise.

The Sphinx's head fell off. It rolled down the Valley and stopped, embedded in the front of a single-family dwelling behind the Porter residence.

Sid looked at the Egyption icon through the window of the guest room and once more questioned his sanity.

Noah huddled under a blanket in a corridor on the 02 deck. He had only a vague idea as to his actual location. He knew that the Street had been abandoned. He hoped that included Tanzers.

Pinocchio floated serene in his habitat, the water of his world rotating around him. It was quite pleasant. Out there, in the empty, the graceless ones jerked about. Their rocks and coral broke and scattered.

The dolphin flexed its tail and rotated, fixing one eye on *her*. There was no gleam in her eye, no life to her flukes. He turned away, sorry for her loss. She hadn't heard the song. It was gone now, but for a while the song had trembled up through the rock and empty, filled Pinocchio's little world. It was not the language of his pod but he felt the meaning. Then the graceless ones had pricked him with their spine, and the dim came, and when it departed, the song was replaced by the bellowing of the great world. And for the first time since he'd been ripped from the great world and sealed in this little one, Pinocchio could relax his hate, in the presence of a fury far greater than his own.

Tanzer's second-floor balcony tore off and went for a swim. A net popped and some neglected crates launched into space, followed by a stack of empty sacks and a metal drum covered in melted wax.

The starboard-facing side of Lila's houseboat cracked open like a peanut shell. It exposed her wardrobe to the wind and for a few seconds the darkness was treated to flying silks and lingerie.

On the bridge, Lena stared at her screen, pretty much ignoring everything coming out her headphones. She could barely hear it over the storm anyway. With each toss of the ship, each second that passed since she'd lost contact with the barge, she felt her recently acquired sense of control slipping away. It started with a vague feeling of the universe being unfair and grew into a resentment that sank hooks into everything it could find: Sid for bringing them here and then dying; Sid again, because hoping to find him was the only reason she could come up with for Rick heading to the barge. She hated the captain for his choices.

Having dealt with the preliminaries, her resentment was heading for the gold. It would cocoon itself in her choice to stay on the carrier at Diego, and come out the other side with wings of self-loathing.

A text message prompt blinked on her monitor. She opened it to see the outline of a bat followed by the words, "There's Navy on the barge. We may not have a President, but we're still sailors."

She turned in her chair and looked at Otis.

"This is so messed up," said Caps. Leaning against a knee knocker (was there no escape from the things?) back to the one side of the corridor, feet pressed against the other, he shoved his fingers through the grill-like deck plating and held on tight.

"We're going to be underwater soon," said a civy guard with a blond-and-white beard. "Waves are going to come right over us. Flood the main deck."

"You done this before?" Caps yelled over the roar.

"Ayup. Done a tanker through a typhoon 'bout fifteen years back."

"On purpose?"

"Nobody takes on a typhoon on purpose."

The deck was tilting really far this time. "And this is what you do? Go straight into the thing?"

"We ain't the mainland, squid. We can't take this on our side. We have to go in, take the waves bow-on, and hope the engines don't crap out or the hatches cave in. And we hit the eye, and then..."

"And then? Then what?"

"If we make it that far? Then we get to do it all over again."

For the people in *Terpris*, the storm seemed to reach a plateau. Then it abated, slowly at first, then surprisingly quickly until the howling subsided to a petulant gasp of wind that harried the rigging and swept broken bits of houseboats down the deck a few feet at a time.

The sea was still high, but nothing like the like monster walls of water that had been coming in earlier.

A wall of fog marked the storm's edge to the east.

There was no sign of the barge. If it was still afloat, it lay within the darkness of water and lightning.

Gradually the denizens of the Street shuffled out onto the flight deck, inspected damage, calculated losses.

Tanzer looked up at where his balcony used to be. "I'll bet some water got in there," he mumbled. He entered through the back door and heard a discordant noise coming from the bar room. Tivoli was on stage, plunking away at his piano. It was out of tune, but a note came from every key.

"Happy now?" asked Tanzer.

"Relieved."

"Well, go check the stockroom. You'll have your hands on a broom before I let you near a tuning fork."

Noah looked up at the tops of the houseboats. There'd be no shortage of work for him, that was for sure. He worried there might be a shortage of materials, though.

He meandered forward. The deck still pitched, but by comparison it was quite tolerable.

From a cluster of people near the base of the island, Darcy detached herself and moved for Noah as quickly as possible given the people and the debris. She reached him and burrowed in under his blanket, hugged him tight enough to crack his ribs.

"Hi," he said, kissing her forehead.

"You look terrible," she said.

"I fell over the side. But I'm feeling much better now."

They kissed for a few seconds.

"I heard about the prisoners," said Noah, pulling back. "Did Sid? Is he..."

"He's alive. He's going to be okay. He...Noah! What happened to your neck?"

He covered the bruises with a hand and his mouth got stuck at open. He didn't know what to tell her.

"Did someone do that to you?" Pointless question; she knew what choke bruises looked like, and she could tell the difference between those made with two hands and those made with one. "Who did that to you?"

Noah could see it in her eyes. "You knew."

"We should talk to Sid."

"You knew Toffee was on board and you didn't tell me!"

"Noah, baby, we've just been through a hurricane. Let's go talk to Sid."

"I would never keep a secret from you!"

Anger flashed in her eyes. "You have. When you thought you were protecting me."

"That was *different*."

"Why? Because you were looking out for me? I can't—"

"Because we weren't living together. Because I didn't go to sleep with your head on my shoulder and wake up with your knee in my back."

"This isn't about you!" she howled, for a moment hearing the same words that came from Lena's mouth such a short time ago.

People altered coarse to avoid them. Heads turned. Darcy backed up a step to give herself screaming room.

"You think you've been lied to? You think you're hurt? I'm the one whose had to keep it a secret. How much do you think that hurts?"

"So what am I? Painkiller?"

"You tell it like it is, son," said some guy sorting through hull boards.

"I've had to keep secrets," said a woman, coming over to Darcy and putting a hand on her shoulder as if to lend strength. She immediately snatched her hand away and backed off. "Sorry to interrupt."

Noah realized something the woman had probably grasped through sheer instinct. Darcy was looking to hit something, or someone. He saw it in the way her hips shifted, how her right shoulder drew back the tiniest fraction. Violence dashed across her face.

Hello. This was Darcy when threatened. It never occurred to Noah she'd ever feel threatened by him.

"Hon," he dropped his hands, let the wind slide the blanket off his shoulders. "I just don't understand what's going on."

This was how he got her, how he slew her every time. In the face of her attack he'd go defenseless. If she'd pulled a chainsaw on him, he'd have stopped it with his heart.

"Please." She took his hand, felt so grateful to be holding it. "Let's go talk to Sid."

***

"Take us to gentler seas then hold position," ordered Ransom.

"Aye, sir," replied the pilot. "Course laid in for gentler seas."

Cmdr. McCabe entered the bridge, nodded to the captain, then moved to Lena's side.

"Don't relieve me," she said. "I won't go."

"I'm not relieving you, Ensign. Chief Porter wanted me to tell you Sid Halbert is alive and well."

She started to get up, then sank back into her seat as if pulled by an elastic. "I can't leave. Can you send him to the bridge?"

"No."

"Can you give him a message?"

"That I can do."

"Tell him I'll see him soon."

"Okay."

"And tell him—"

"I'll tell him you'll see him soon."

McCabe left and Lena returned to studying her screen, which had nothing to do with communications. She was looking at the surface radar. It wasn't telling her much of anything. Either there was too much fuzz or she simply couldn't interpret the data, but she looked for any sort of shape or blip that her instincts would say was the barge, still intact, still above water.

Stukov appeared. The captain stood and the two men shook hands, then saluted each other.

"You have the con," said Ransom.

"Aye, sir," said Stukov taking the chair. "Recommend you get some sleep, yes?"

"So noted, Commander. Meeting in my wardroom. One hour."

"Damage reports," said Stukov. "Ensign Wong?"

"Oh." She tapped some buttons and turned up the volume on her headphones. "Right away, sir."

Stukov noted surface radar was on one of the command chair's screens. He didn't change it.

A spotter saw something on the deck but didn't say anything. Captain Ransom wasn't going for a much needed nap. He'd put on a thick coat and was wandering through the Street. At one point he stopped, rubbed his hands together and helped a man load broken bits of fiberglass into a bin.

It was a difficult conversation told in snatches and restricted to harmless catch-up because the moment Darcy and Noah set foot in the house, Mrs. Porter put them to work. Noah swept up glass while Darcy put pictures back on the wall. Every few minutes Mrs. Porter would dart in and rearrange the pictures anyway.

Sid leaned in a doorway, head slightly bent because Chief Porter had put in this bit of ceiling and both he and his wife were under six feet.

At last Darcy and Noah finished everything that Lydia Porter trusted them to do, and she shuffled Sid back to bed, allowing his friends to stay with him.

They waited a few seconds, then Sid said, "Okay, cut to the chase. I'm really confused and Noah there looks a little scared."

Darcy stared at the floor and put the finishing touches on her story. "The deal was I kept quiet and he'd protect you on the barge and leave everybody alone. He needed time to put down roots here and didn't want any of us making trouble for him."

"Then why did he trap us here?" asked Noah.

"He probably thought we'd all go over the side," said Sid.

"He didn't admit to doing that," said Darcy. "But assuming he did, us getting stowaway treatment would be the best motive. Once we were here and people knew us, things got more complicated for him. Noah, it killed me not to tell you, but I couldn't risk it."

"So what do we do now?" asked Noah.

Darcy leaned towards him then shifted away. She hadn't touched him yet in Sid's presence. He thought he understood why, but he still didn't like it.

"That's what we're here to discuss," she said.

There was a knock at the door and a brown-haired, round-faced officer stuck his head in the room. He had a gold leaf on his collar. "I'm Lieutenant Commander McCabe. Mr. Halbert, Chief Porter told me what you did. Thank you. Lena Wong wanted me to inform you that she'll see you soon. Right now she's on bridge duty."

"Can't she be relieved?" asked Sid.

"Seaman Scagling, uh, her boyfriend is on the barge. Until that's resolved, I doubt she'll leave."

"What was Caps doing on the barge?" Noah turned to face McCabe. "Why did you send him to the barge?"

Darcy rubbed her forehead.

"I have to leave you now," said McCabe. "I'll make sure you're kept informed in regards to the barge."

"You're a popular man," said Mrs. Porter, looking in before shutting the door. "I always knew I'd have a celebrity in my home."

"Noah, go be with Lena," said Darcy.

"What?" He rounded on her. "She's on the bridge."

"Well get up there somehow. She needs one of us right now."

"Why me?"

"Because you're an electrician. He's an ex-con and I'm a showgirl."

Then, partly because she wanted to, but mostly because she felt he needed it, she kissed him on the mouth. "Tell her I'm with Sid. Don't tell her about—"

"I won't." He put his hand on the door. "No need to mess her up anymore than she already is." He looked at Sid. "Good to have you back, Boss." He mouthed something at Darcy and left.

Sid prodded at his head through the bandage and said, "Enough with the bullshit. What was Toffee's real price, Darce? Is it what I think it is? Are you still paying it?"

She was going to tell Sid the whole of it the moment Noah was out the door, but now, lips parted to spill the beans, her tongue froze. The back of her scalp crawled like it was going for the yellow streak down her back. She felt completely defeated. There was no way to prove Toffee guilty of trapping them in *Terpris*. He'd had the entire prison at his disposal for nearly two months. It was like a comprehensive database of every dirty secret on the ship.

"He hasn't touched me," she said. "I swear."

The hunter's act of defending the cutting crew would paint him a hero. He was untouchable. And on top of it all, the man had delivered, to the point of strapping on an air tank and diving into the maelstrom.

Toffee didn't quit. The game wasn't over until *he'd* won.

There was only one way to protect the people she loved.

Darcy closed her eyes and said, "He beat us. We don't interest him anymore."

"Do you really believe that?"

"Yes," she said quickly. "I really think he'll just leave us alone."

Sid considered her for a few seconds before patting the mattress. "Are you really a showgirl?"

She sat on the bed next to him. "I'm not a showgirl. I'm the show. Lady Mystique. I sing, I wear a mask. Somebody thinks I don't do enough Streisand."

"How much do you do?"

"None."

"That's plenty."

He chucked her under the chin. The corners of her mouth grudgingly curled up.

"Liar," she said. "You like Streisand."

"I like the one about the clowns. Anyway, it made you smile." He folded his hands across his stomach. "So. You and Noah."

"Yeah."

"And how's that?"

"It's good, Sid." She tried not to let her voice catch too much in her throat. "It's really good. He doesn't judge me. He shrugs off my tantrums."

"I guess I'd always hoped you'd end up with an educated man. Ah, who am I kidding? If he can take your tantrums he could be dumb as toast for all I care."

"Yes?" Stukov said to the disheveled-looking civy who'd stepped onto his bridge.

"Uh," Noah said. He jiggled his toolbox. "Uh…"

Lena stared at him, eyes wide, mouth open.

"Well?" Stukov started to get out of his chair.

"Sir, I told the guards I was under temporary subcontract to the Navy for some diagnostic work, and that's sort of true, but really I came up to see her." He pointed.

"You have one minute," said Stukov.

"Thank you, sir." Noah started to salute, then switched to a half bow, then shook it off and moved to Lena's side. "How are you doing?"

"Hanging by a thread," she whispered.

Noah looked into her face, saw the panic barely kept at bay. "Sid's pretty much okay," he said. "Darcy's with him now."

He didn't tell her about Toffee, but it loomed in the front of his head, threatened to slip out every time he opened his mouth. Lena didn't tell him about what Screaming Mimis do to children and try as she might, it was all she could think about each time she pictured Sid.

"Why is he on the barge?" Noah asked. "Caps I mean. Do you know?"

Lena winced. "We didn't get that far. I don't know. Cmdr. McCabe says he wasn't assigned to it. The sailors on the barge, they went over to point rifles at the prisoners and…Rick couldn't have done that."

Noah gave her leg a squeeze. She took his hand squeezed harder.

"Sir," said a lookout, "do you think this qualifies as gentler seas?"

Stukov craned his neck. "Yes. All stop and maintain position."

"Aye, sir. All stop."

"Mr. Allen, you do not actually have any sonar, do you?"

"No, sir."

"Then you are not really fulfilling a purpose here."

"Uh, I guess not, sir."

"Good. Take the con."

"Yes, sir."

Stukov got up to leave and Noah stood to do the same. Otis held up a finger. As the hatch closed behind the XO, Otis sat in the command chair and said, "That didn't feel like a minute yet. Carry on."

"Wow," said Caps. "That sucked." He stumbled up the corridor, ashen as a ghost. "I was in this truck in Vancouver filled with rats and stuff," he said to anybody who might listen. "That sucked. I thought that was the worst and…" He stared at a knee knocker, had to summon the will to step over it. "But this just went on and on and on."

"We know," said somebody. "We were there. Shut up, okay?"

They gathered at the wheel house. The wind was light and the storm was drifting away, moving southeast.

Barnes did a headcount. "We're one short," he said. "Who's missing?"

"I haven't seen Eddie since we were working the hold," said one sailor.

Caps looked over at the enormous hatches. Three were intact but the fourth was burst. One of the hatch covers was askew and the other was just gone. The upper walkway was crumpled in like foil around the lip of a pan. Water was ankle deep in the wardroom and offices. The gondola launch was gone, as were two of the cranes.

Barnes also looked at the breach in the deck. "Here's the gouge. We're through, but our communications are out. We've taken on water. And yeah, something's sprung. So we're sinking." He gestured at twisted, empty davits. "We have no lifeboats."

"Like that'd do any good," said a Navy guard. "Whole ocean of nasty down there waiting for us to set out in little boats."

As a group, they scanned the horizon. Visibility was terrible. It was like trying to peer through a cloud.

"Still nothing," said Lena's voice through the speaker.

Ransom nodded at the box as if she'd see that up on the bridge, then he thumbed it off. He placed a finger on the chart spread out across the wardroom table. "If we assume they've lost systems but are still afloat, *and* somebody capable took her helm, it would put their position somewhere around here."

Cmdr. Stukov, Lt. Cmdr. McCabe and MCPO Porter also sat at the table.

"We don't have enough fuel for a prolonged search," said Porter. "We'd strand ourselves."

"If we find the barge we have plenty of fuel," said McCabe.

"They would come this way," said Stukov, tracing a line along the chart. "We would intercept them here."

"We could run smack into them in this fog," said Porter.

"At least it would mean we'd found them," said Ransom. "Bill, bring me exact fuel stocks. Calculate maximum duration and range for a search pattern, but be stingy with the safety margin."

"Yes, sir," said Porter.

"What state could their communications be in, theoretically?"

McCabe gave a deep shrug. "Assume worst case scenario. They'll have taken waves higher than the wheel house. Everything on their roof is most likely destroyed or gone. The forward antennae tower would certainly be damaged beyond use. Maybe something on short range would get through. Very short range. Sir, we're working with flares on this one."

"Well, figure out the best time to start firing them." Ransom stood. "Gentlemen, when this is over I want you to give me a performance review. Be as objective as you can."

"Sir?" Stukov looked up, alarmed.

"I bilged this one." Ransom rapped his knuckles on the table. "There was no need to kill those prisoners. My decision cost men lives and cost us time and resources. Commander, you recommended we deploy the Mimi immediately."

"We had no of way of knowing it would be safe," cut in McCabe.

"This was a very expensive operation, men," Ransom contined, nonplussed. "In every way. I find I'm second guessing myself now. We've most likely lost the barge. I'll take us to Australia, but once there, if it is your recommendation that I retire, I will do so."

"You are asking us to give you permission to run away?" asked Stukov.

"Maybe I am. I want my board of inquiry. It's my right. It's the right of the Navy. Inquests can vindicate as much as they condemn. And as for the Mimi, if it's safe to operate underwater, we need to find out how to make a few million of the things. We could restore small vessel shipping. It would crack travel wide open. We could rebuild the fleet."

"With the same breath that you question your captain's chair, you dream of becoming an admiral," said Stukov.

"We made it through another one," said Porter. He'd found his way to the roll-top bar and made a tray with four half-filled glasses. He took a glass and watched the tray get passed around the table. "To the Big T," he said.

"To the Big T," they echoed.

When Noah returned to the Porter residence, Darcy met him at the door. She took him by the hand and pulled him through the white picket gate, away from the house. "Sid's sleeping," she said. "Let's check out what shape our own home is in."

Noah looked over his shoulder as she walked him towards some steps. "The Sphinx's head is lying behind the Porters' place. How did I miss that before?"

"Just be glad it missed Sid's little corner of the Valley."

"How's he doing? After being on the barge 'n' all."

"He's traumatized. I think he wants to forget all about it. Anything about Caps?"

"Not a thing, but the general consensus is they'd have lost radio capacity. So what are we doing about Toffee?"

"Be wary, but not proactive."

"Do you think he might just leave us alone?"

Darcy tugged at Noah's collar, touched the bruises around his throat.

"I thought I understood him," said Noah, "but I guess I really don't. Can't he find another way to amuse himself?"

They reached the flight deck. Noah looked out into the fog. "I know what Caps is going to say."

"He already said it." Darcy moved behind him, put her chin on his shoulder.

"What do you mean he…Oh. He knew. You both knew. He kept it quiet—"

"Same reason I did. More to protect Lena, though. Toffee blackmailed us. Made us pay him with silence."

"So that's why Lena doesn't know already. He threatened to hurt her. Did he tell you he was going to hurt me?"

"I don't think he expected you to…" She sighed.

"To what?"

She couldn't meet his eyes for a second or two. When she did, she said, "To mean the same thing to me that Lena means to Caps."

Standing beside the wrecked houseboat village, Noah grinned.

"Don't read too much into that." Darcy pushed him away. "I don't make leaps of faith like you do."

"You moved in with me pretty fast."

"Uh-huh, and look at what that got me." She gestured.

In the middle of the Street, Carlos stared at a chunk of catwalk sunk into his upper deck directly above Noah's and Darcy's room.

"I think it came from the island," he said when he noticed them approaching.

At the rear of the Pri-Fly, a gap marked the rightful location for the debris.

"How is it inside?" asked Darcy.

Carlos scratched his head. "With some tarps and pitch we could probably make it…completely unlivable. I'm sorry, you two."

"We could try Lila," said Darcy hesitantly. She looked off in that direction.

Lila sat before the ruin of her houseboat. She didn't have to do any actual work. A group of men stepped over themselves to do it for her.

"The Porters told Sid he could stay with them indefinitely," said Darcy. "So now he's got a berth and we're homeless."

"Tanzer'll look after it," said Noah.

"Let's go see how they're doing."

What Tanzer was doing involved a lot of shouting. "I'll not break out a bottle until I see seas flatter than my bar top," he cried at the people crowding the gangway to his front door.

"Oh come on," said one of them. "We need to celebrate."

"Celebrate that I packed away my club. Now clear off." He spotted Darcy and Noah and gestured with his head for them to go around back.

Darcy started moving then felt her wrist tug when Noah didn't follow right away. She saw the way his head was moving about. "Stop looking for him," she said. "The only way to find Toffee is to see him out of the corner of your eye."

Darcy led him to the back door. She looked up at the hole where the balcony had been torn away. *At least he'll never talk to me from up there again.*

They moved through the corridor and past the stage to where Tivoli unpacked boxes and Ethan Toffee sat at the bar.

"Good to see you two," said Tanzer. "This is our new bouncer."

"Heya," said Toffee, raising a mug.

Tanzer took in their stunned reaction. "I know, scary lookin', ain't he? The Old Bull highly recommended him."

"Mark…recommended you," Darcy stammered.

"Oh yeah, me and the marshal are like this," Toffee held up two fingers curled together.

"He was a barge guard," said Tanzer. "Might not have a job now and Mark says he's good at keeping order. I think things are going to be really stressful around here."

"You have no idea," said Darcy. She squeezed Noah's hand, hard enough that she knew she was hurting him. "Just checking to see if you guys are okay. We have to go." She dragged him outside.

"What are we going to do now?" asked Noah. "He's got the Old Bull on his team."

Darcy put her hands on either side of her head and tried not to scream. She could see him at the door each night, all big and congenial, making friends with all the patrons. Hey everybody, come look at what this guy's got on under his arm.

A pair of sailors, the tall-and-wide type, approached them as they rounded the side of the nightclub.

"Noah Thurlow?" said one of them.

"Yes." He stopped and groaned. Having Navy goons show up for him was becoming routine.

"While on attachment to the Navy, you knowingly and willingly abandoned an open maintenance access, as well as left tools and deck plates unsecured."

"What?"

"Said unsecured deck plates are believed to be the primary mechanism of injury to Petty Officer Second Class Stephen Sinclair."

"Sinclair? Was that the guy with the pencil light on his goggles?"

"You are hereby charged with dereliction of duty and negligence causing harm to Navy personnel. You will come with us, now."

They moved in fast, pinned both arms.

Noah looked at Darcy, not them. "Stand down," he said to her, not sure why he chose those particular words. "We'll get through this," he called over his shoulder as they dragged him away.

59. Turbulence

"Yeek!" Caps jerked back from the rail. He heard but didn't see the dolphin splash back into the water. "That one almost got on board."

"Yeah, maybe you shouldn't be hanging around at the rail," said the blond-bearded civy.

"You know, we just rode out death together and I don't even know your name."

Blond-beard chuckled. "Russ. For all the good it'll do you. You're?"

"Caps. Seaman Scagling. Whatever."

"You can feel the list starting now," said Russ. "Pumps can't handle it. Barge'll be underwater soon." He watched shapes form and twist apart in the fog. He raised the flare gun and fired one of the last three they had.

Caps unslung his rifle and tested the trigger. He hadn't fired it yet. They were saving their ammo for when the deck got really low.

"Is it as rough for them down there as it us for us up here? Isn't like the force of the wave under the water more than above?"

"They manage." Russ loaded the second-to-last flare.

"Why are you a barge guard? You belong in this uniform more than I do."

Russ leaned over the rail and pointed the flare gun at a dolphin peeking at him from the crest of a wave. "I like to get drunk and start fights. I don't know why. First I was here as a Navy guard." He raised and fired the gun. Green light flashed in the mist and soared up into the dark gray sky. "Then I got tossed from the Navy. The Old Bull and me cut a deal." He picked up the last flare. "Now I do my drinking alone."

A dolphin's head cleared the rail. It chattered before it disappeared.

"Ready arms," called Ensign Barnes from somewhere up the deck.

"Flare," said a bridge lookout, pointing excitedly into the mist.

"Yeah, yeah, yeah!" said the radar man, shaking his finger at the screen. "I've got 'em, Captain. Twelve-hundred meters off the starboard bow."

Ransom looked at his screen, only seeing the profile because he'd been told it was there. "Return flares immediately. Ensign Wong?"

"Nothing on short range yet, sir." It was all Lena could do not to give the radar man a lap dance.

"Let's see how your parking is," Ransom said to the pilot. "Put us within one-hundred meters."

"Aye, sir. One-hundred meters and not a centimeter more."

Noah was pushed through a hatch on the Second Deck and shoved into a chair. A light was flicked on and pointed at his face. He squinted and looked away. He was quickly learning to hate bright light.

He heard another hatch open and movement around him.

"Do you know what the penalty for dereliction of duty is?" asked a voice from the gloom.

"I'm not in your stupid Navy," said Noah.

"Yeah, and you really should be." The interrogation light went off and the main compartment light came on.

Warrant Officer Lowell Benning sat behind a desk. A group of men and one woman leaned against the bulkheads.

"You really, really should be," said Benning.

The people started to laugh. One of the goons left outright, the other patted Noah a couple of times on the head before exiting.

"So there you go." Benning put his hands behind his head and leaned back. "Join the Navy. See? We're fun people."

Noah felt his blood boil. This was so not the right time to be playing jokes. "Nobody got hurt?" he squeezed between clenched teeth.

A chubby guy with a predominantly thick upper lip raised his hand. "I'm Steve Sinclair. I think I'm okay. I secured your post. It was a hurricane, bro. Nobody's blaming you."

"Technically it was typhoon," said one of the electricians.

"Whatever," said Benning. "Thurlow, you'd have to start at ensign, but we could bump you fast."

"Ahoy the barge," a voice shouted down the corridor outside. "We found the barge."

Everybody in the compartment sighed.

Noah almost walked out right there, wanting to see the barge with his own eyes. Instead, he sat up straight and said, "If I was an ensign, that would come with quarters in officer country?"

"Listen to him," said the woman.

"Yes," said Benning.

"That's a secure area?" Noah asked.

"From civies and non-coms, yeah."

"But there's married quarters? Where civy or non-com spouses are allowed?"

"Well, yeah. You're married?"

"No."

"Then why do you—"

"I've got a girlfriend. I'll take two of the married quarters."

"Two of them?"

"I'm thinking this is a seller's market."

"Whoaaa," Benning stood and floated a look of disbelief around his crew.

"I've got a good thing with Tanzer." Noah contemplated putting his feet up on Benning's desk, but decided that would be too snotty. "And I call my own hours."

"We'll teach you things you'll never learn playing with tinker toys on houseboats."

"You've got my price. One civy, one non-com."

Benning sat down and flicked his hands. "Everybody dismissed."

There were some raised eyebrows and looks of scorn as they filed out. "You're not making any friends playing hardball, you know."

"I've already got friends and I want them looked after."

"I can't put unmarried non-coms into—"

"Fine, promote him. Then you just have a civy to worry about."

"Who is 'him?' " Benning asked, flinching at having to ask at all. But his people told him the kid worked smart and fast, especially considering the equipment was unfamiliar to him.

"Seaman Richard Scagling. If your requirement for officers is that they have a specialty, I'd bet he's the best auto mechanic on this ship. What are you? A warrant officer? That's because you're an electrical engineer. Make him a warrant officer."

"And the other officer?"

"Ensign Lena Wong."

"The new girl in comms? She has a boyfriend, huh?"

"Yeah, she has a boyfriend."

"You bucking for a promotion for her, too?"

"Nah. She can look after herself. That's a fact I'm giving you. I'm not disrespecting her."

"I can just force you to work for me."

"Only while *Terpris* is under a state of emergency and the Merchants Guild will only let you get away with that for so long."

Benning rubbed a hand through his hair.

"I know things because I ask a lot of questions," said Noah. "How'd the grid take the ride? I noticed two corridors blacked out on the way down here."

"Okay, okay." Benning sucked on his cheek. The kid looked so clean and scrubbed, the typical boy next door. Who'd have thought he'd be so mercenary? "You're right, I do need you."

Noah wasn't trying to be mercenary. He was trying to be a brat. One look from Toffee and his spine had folded like a wet noodle. Benning was giving him a rebound conflict.

"You're asking for things I don't give people already on my crew."

"That's not my problem," said Noah. "I have plenty of work to do on the Street and in the Valley. By the way, is there an insurance company on the ship?"

"I'll swing the room for you and the civy. She have a name?"

"Darcy McCullough. The singer at Tanzers."

Benning pursed his lips. "Seriously?"

Noah held his tongue and narrowed his eyes.

"Hey, no offense, man. It's just that chicks who look like that usually end up with the Marines. I'll do the room for you, but not the other. If Ensign Wong can look after herself, she can look after her guy."

Noah decided not to push it. "Okay."

"So, couple of questions I didn't quite hear the answer to. First one is, are you married?"

Sailors lined up along the starboard side, rifles swung out over the rails and searched for likely targets.

Hugin and *Munin* hung ready which was also an attention getter, but Toffee wasn't interested in them. He was at the very stern, arms crossed, leaning over the lip, watching the water behind the fantail.

Shouts from the men on the barge drifted up through mist. Toffee leaned out a little bit farther. Ah. There it was. The tarp-covered box dropped into the water. *Hugin* and *Munin* went after.

LFA my ass, thought Toffee, coming away from the rail.

Not a single shot was fired from *Terpris* as the boats pulled alongside the foundering cargo ship. Ropes dropped from the port rail, now much higher than the starboard. One by one men dropped from the barge to the smaller decks waiting below.

***

When both boats were on their way back from the barge, a bridge spotter said, "I counted twenty-three, sir."

"There were twenty-four," said Lena. "Who's the missing man?"

She got stalled between which of the two boats to reach out to, but then someone on the *Hugin* made the decision for her.

"Tell the captain," said a voice in her ears, *"that Seaman Second Class Edward Cohen is missing and presumed dead. As much of a search as was deemed possible was conducted."*

"Seaman Edward Cohen," said Lena out loud.

"Barnes was ranking officer on board?" asked Ransom, leaning towards Stukov who stood next to the command chair.

"Yes, sir."

Ransom turned to face Lena. "Tell Ensign…tell Lieutenant Barnes, 'Welcome back.' "

Toffee listened to the away boats being brought up and swung in, then he watched the magic box rise up from the sea and disappear under the lip.

He wandered up the starboard rail, watched men drop down from the boats. He noted faces of men already dancing to his tune, then got a surprise.

"Painter?" the hunter asked the wind. "What were you doing over there?"

Caps touched down and immediately scanned the deck. Toffee stepped into the edge of a stack of crates, molded himself to the outline and became completely motionless.

A sailor collecting rifles gestured impatiently and Caps reluctantly gave up his weapon. Another sailor yelled something and Caps turned and raced for the island.

Everybody was home, and they'd be planning up a storm. Toffee had some of his own planning to do. "Semper Fi," he said under his breath and marched in time for a few paces before easing back into his usual stroll.

Lena snuck Caps into her quarters and bribed her roommate a week's pay to get her to sleep somewhere else that night.

By four in the morning they lay, wrapped up in each other, a unification of need, relief and sweat.

"We forgot to go see Sid," said Caps.

Lena went dead in the eyes. "I'm sure he'll still be here later."

"There something you're not telling me?"

She glanced up at something. "Nothing I feel like talking about here."

Caps rolled onto his back and looked at the air vent. He tightened his arm around her. He gave her an expression that said, "You think?"

She shrugged in reply.

"I need to tell you something as well," he whispered. "You want to go for a walk?"

She nuzzled into him. "I'd rather go for a snooze."

"Okay, okay." His eyelids started to droop. "Maybe I should go. What happens if they catch me in here at first bell?"

"I don't care." She trapped both his legs with her one good one. "When they find us here tomorrow…" Her mouth stretched in a wide yawn, "…maybe they'll put us in the same cell in the brig."

"Baby, wake up." Darcy jabbed him in the shoulder.

He stirred enough to wrap his arms around her waist, pillow his head against her breasts, and go limp.

Darcy sighed and ran her hand along his skin, from one shoulder all the way down to where she pinched the back of his knee.

"Yow!" Noah was instantly awake and jumping from the bed.

"Sorry," said Darcy. "But you've got to go to work."

He rubbed the back of his leg and looked at the blue shirt draped over the footboard.

She watched him as he pulled on his clothes, one of her fingers teasing her bottom lip.

"What about you?" he asked, buckling his belt. "You going into work today?"

"Oh yeah. I can't let him take that from me. We let him take any one thing from us and soon he'll take anything he wants." She stretched and scratched her belly. "Besides, as long as he's hanging around Tanzers, I know he's not off somewhere messing with my friends."

Noah touched his hair, looked in the mirror over the sink, then pulled on a ball cap with an anchor embroidered into the visor.

Darcy patted the steel bulkhead. "I like Carlos's boat better."

Something fell from Noah's back pocket. If he'd ignored it, Darcy wouldn't have cared, but he covered it with his foot so fast she just had to know what it was.

Swallowing, he picked it up and handed it to her. "It's your security pass."

She read it. "Darcy Thurlow?"

"Look, you'll only have to carry it until the guards learn your face."

"Darcy Thurlow."

"It's a stupid rule. I didn't make it. You can still use McCullough as your stage name."

"Why, thank you."

"Uh-uh," he held up a hand. "No beating me up on my first day in the service." He blew a kiss at her as he opened the hatch. "Besides, now it would be spousal abuse."

Sid took a stool at the bar and looked around the room. It was tough to reconcile the place with the club he'd first entered while looking for Odega. At that point he thought he'd be home at Compton Pit by Christmas.

Darcy stepped down from the stage and took the stool next to him. She glanced at the front door, outside of which sat Toffee, unseen but definitely felt.

"He's being a model citizen," she said. "If you'd been here earlier you could have seen the Old Bull treating him to a rum and choke."

"Choke?"

"It looks like Coke. It can eat through metal. That's where the similarity ends."

"You really do have a beautiful voice. I'd forgotten. I mean, sometimes in the barge I'd pretend I could hear you singing, but it wasn't…" He turned away from her. "This tactic of his is beyond me."

Darcy's hand, which had been sliding across the bar towards Sid, stopped and withdrew. "I know. You expect him to go hide in a dark hole somewhere. Raccoons are typically nocturnal."

Toffee came in, he nodded at Tivoli, then gave the same brief, cordial tilt of the head to Sid and Darcy. He walked behind the bar as if he owned the place, lifted a metal coffee pot, sniffed it, and poured himself a mug. Then he left, taking the steaming coffee with him.

"He's not really that interesting to look at," said Tivoli, having watched them swivel in their stools, silently memorizing the new bouncer's every move. "So what's happening with you?" he called to Sid.

"Chief Porter's pushing to make me an officer. Cmdr. Stukov doesn't like the precedent. He likes the word precedent. He said it a lot. Some lieutenant took me to the stern and tested me on a few different firearms. So I don't know."

"And what's it like living with the Porters?" Tivoli plunked out some chirpy notes.

"Mrs. Porter cooks these potato dishes." Sid scratched his ear. "Except I don't think she has any potatoes."

"You're only doing one set tonight," said Tanzer, coming in from the back. "And we're closing early. Going to hold a memorial service for Ripper."

"Okay," said Darcy.

"You should come." He moved behind the bar. "You beat the crap out of him. It's only fair." He headed off for the stockroom.

Tivoli watched Tanzer from the corner of his eye, then left the stage and followed the man.

"Why haven't I seen Richard or Lena yet?" Sid asked quietly.

"It's nothing personal. Yesterday Lena just wanted to OD on Caps and now they're on watch. We're all meeting here later. I hope you-know-who doesn't try to sit with us."

In the stockroom, Tivoli gave Tanzer a knowing look. "There's a spring in your step today."

"What are you talking about?"

"You don't fool me, you old perv. You got some last night."

Tanzer said nothing but the gleam in his eye was answer enough.

"Congratulations," said Tiv, bringing his hand up. "Allow me to salute the flag for saluting the flag."

"Yeah, yeah." Tanzer shoved a box into Tivoli's arms. "Adrenalin from the hurricane, you know."

"Well let me know if you get any more adrenalin. I'll have something warm sent up from animal research."

"I thought I was prepared for this, but I'm not," said Lena. She drew back her leg and Caps zipped in front of her to keep her from trying to kick Toffee in the balls.

"I have no business with you two," growled the hunter. Then he smiled and said, "Try the shooters. They're on special tonight."

Caps shuffled her in and closed the door.

"I can have him taken care of," Lena hissed. "Nobody messes with the Navy."

Caps shook his head and tried to relax his jaw. "For all we know he's in special forces now with a covert rank of commander." He looked out over the bar. "There he is."

They came to Sid's table. They hugged him in turn, and if he noticed either of them being a little stiff, he didn't react to it.

Caps and Noah had a lengthy conversation condensed into two grimaces and a shrug.

"It's okay," said Noah, concluding the summit. "It sucks having to keep secrets."

"Yeah. Knowing things sucks." Caps pulled out a chair for Lena, then took one for himself.

They had some drinks, forced small talk and tried really hard to have a good time.

Darcy joined them for a few minutes while waiting to start her set.

"I guess I'm the fifth wheel here," said Sid, looking around the table. "Is that tour guide still with the ship? The lawyer?"

"Stephanie," said Lena. "Maybe you should look her up."

The piano chimed and Darcy slipped her mask on. She calmed her breath and tried as hard as she could to forget the man, in the corner, by the door.

When it was time for the memorial service, Noah and Darcy stayed, while the rest left as a group, staying close, finding a spot at the rail. They watched Toffee saunter off to port and disappear behind a tarp-covered houseboat.

"There's an access close to there," said Caps. "He could be staying somewhere on the 02 Deck. He's got the pull to get vehicle storage, he could probably afford digs on 02. Man, if I could get access to the motor pool again, I could really mess his ride up."

"He'll be expecting that," said Sid.

"We have to do something."

"Maybe we don't."

Caps hooked a finger in his mouth and stretched his cheek. "You see that? There used to be a tooth there." He let his mouth return to its normal shape. "He stuck me in a box of bees. At least I thought they were bees. If you think I'm going to—"

"Is your dignity wounded?" hissed Sid. "Did he hurt your pride? He bullied you a couple of times, Richard. How do you think my dignity feels. On the barge? For all I know he made every choice for me."

"Maybe you shouldn't be allowed to make choices," said Lena.

"What's that supposed to mean? And don't take that tone of voi—"

"Get splashed, Sid," said Caps. "Face the stern and wave buh-bye to Compton Pit. Lena's boss is McCabe now. My boss is just about everybody on this ship, but that *doesn't* include you."

For the briefest moment Sid's reaction was to punch Caps in the throat. He quashed it, but the threat was real to the point of his fingers closing into a fist. He'd been briefed solidly by both Stukov and McCabe. Caps shouldn't be in the loop but generally, what Lena knew, he knew.

"I told Odega to tell you," said Sid. "I begged him."

"So what happened?" asked Lena. "What was covered up? Which kids?"

"If I tell you, then you'll know. Do you really want it in your head?"

"The Navy's just as bad as you," said Caps. "Studying the thing instead of destroying it. Dr. Patel was in on it, wasn't he?"

Sid looked as if he wouldn't answer, then he raised his hands as if to say, *What difference does it make?* "Yes. Harpreet's participation was necessary. And Sara. The three of us made the call. Darcy wasn't involved, in case you were wondering. If she ever suspected she's said nothing. Willful blindness, maybe. I hope you won't..."

"She won't hear it from us," said Lena. "We still *like* her."

"Done is done." Sid shoved his hands in his pockets. "I won't have you two judging me. I can do that all by myself."

The carrier put days between itself and the battlefield, one of the away boats always running escort, providing sonar data. Under protection of the Mimi, divers had confirmed the destruction of the sonar dome. Once again they'd have to start from scratch. This was an ongoing problem for the carrier. The very first sonar dome they'd ever had was demolished during a mishandled dropping of the anchor. The next three were crushed by whales. This last one was built with serious defense in mind, but the long external spikes had provided a perfect anchor for the dolphin's garbage net. Once the net was in the screws, the entire sonar assembly ripped away.

Rehearsals began for the Wonders of the World Show. Darcy's attempt to lose herself in the work was made fruitless by the knowledge that she'd never get to perform. Every night she stayed awake after Noah would doze off. She'd listen to him breathe and wish that morning wouldn't come.

The emotional tone of *Terpris* had reached a level of constant sorrow a few notches higher than was the norm. Repairs to the houseboats had come to a standstill due to lack of materials. An electrical infrastructure already jury rigged in so many places really took a beating during the severe oscillations of the ship. Some things shaken loose didn't become a problem until days after and now places in the lower decks, always gloomy, were blacked out altogether.

Disappointment came when it was announced a number of stops were cancelled. Fiji and Samoa, Vanuatu and the Solomon Islands would have to wait until next time.

The exotic foodstuffs that could be obtained in these places would also be missed and certain botanicals lost in the destruction of the greenhouse weren't going to be replaced anytime soon.

The worst part for everybody was the view from the stern. The barge had been a stable thing for a culture where even home's longitude and latitude were variable. The horizon in all directions was normally featureless, but the aft view now seemed particularly empty.

Giving the surviving prisoners amnesty was every bit as problematic as expected. Freedom from confinement in no way mitigated behavioral tendencies that landed these men in trouble in the first place.

One of the newly freed barge rats had already been splashed. Two more sat in the brig, waiting to be expelled at the Port of Brisbane on Fisherman Islands.

"And now we're just talking in circles," said Lieutenant JG Lena Wong, shoving a bunch of charts across the table.

"Unless you can contribute something," said Odega, "I don't see the need to keep bringing you down here."

The hulking scientist just didn't go topside. He showed no desire to re-associate with his former den-mates. He'd told Lena that seeing any of them made him feel sad.

"You're looking in the wrong place." Lena eyed the thick pipes running along the ceiling. She didn't like being in Drowntown. All the compartments felt icky.

"We've gathered all the data we can acquire based on the limited testing."

Lena rummaged through the charts, selected two and held them up. "You have not. What about this?"

"Trash. Meaningless artifacts. It doesn't appear on any of the others."

Lena kept her two sheets in one hand and swept the rest of the charts aside. "These two are the only ones that could show this because everything else was done with narrower parameters."

"Those two were done with superior equipment. The spectrum analyzer we're using now doesn't go up that high."

"So use the other one again."

"We can't. It got broken." He rubbed the back of his head. "And it doesn't matter anyway. Why would there be output up around fifty gigahertz? We've established that the Mimi's upper range is five hundred kilohertz."

"You've exhausted everything you know. I've done the same. The only conclusion that we've all come to is that nothing here accounts for the Mimi's side effects, that it barely accounts for the device's efficacy at all." She placed the charts side-by-side. "You eggheads are killing yourselves trying to find an X-factor when it's sitting right here, at fifty gigahertz."

Odega pulled the sheets of paper closer and turned them around. "So, what would operate at that frequency? Supposing this is legitimate and not a glitch stain."

"I don't know, Ted. Get your fancy analyzer fixed up and take a better look."

There was an awkward pause.

"You know," said Odega, "for a minute there…"

"Yeah, it almost felt like old times."

"No word from Compton Pit?"

"'Fraid not. The callout's going the full distance now, but there doesn't seem to be anybody receiving."

Odega looked down at his hands. "I won't ask you again."

"I don't know if I'll ever try again. Maybe we're better off not knowing. Guess I'm done here for now. Call me when you get something new for me to look at."

Sid was escorted to Vulture's Row and left alone in the middle, guards at either end of the balcony. Sid looked up at the window of the Pri-Fly and wondered what the level was used for now, what with there being no air wing to command. He looked down, taking in damage to the houseboats not visible from the Street.

"Mr. Halbert," said Ransom, joining him at the rail.

"Captain."

"I heard an interesting story about how you first came to be associated with Tanzer's new singer."

Sid tried not to look offended. "I didn't realize my personal history was making the rounds of the ship."

"Chief Porter isn't a gossip. But neither does he consider dinner table conversation to be confidential. Especially not when I order him to tell me what he knows of you."

"I see."

"You were a police officer and yet on Fubar Day you'd joined an illegal protest. What to do with you, Mr. Halbert." He raised an eyebrow and shook his head.

Sid held his tongue, tried to feel like he still stood on equal ground with a settlement's leader.

Ransom made a gesture with his hand and the two guards departed. "It's a big problem," he said. "So big that my XO felt the need to kick it up to me. You're privy to information confidential at the highest level. You put yourself in harm's way for the sake of the people who sent you to the barge.

"Chief Porter's somewhat in awe of you. He wants you counted when we're handing out the medals. The Marines have also expressed interest in recruiting you. You've gone from barge rat to local hero, but based on what I know of you now, I don't see a hero. I see a crusader." He looked at Sid intensely.

"Captain, I'm not sure if that was a compliment."

"It was and it wasn't. Your dedication is without question. It's what brought you to *Terpris* in the first place. But for you I think the cause can become too malleable."

There were a lot of things Sid wanted to say in response to that, none of them polite.

"I'm going to defer your application to the Navy," said Ransom with the tone of a man summing up. "Take a good long think about where you wish to go from here. If you're still on this ship when we depart from Brisbane, you'll be given the rank of petty officer first class and assigned to Lt. Dench, Chaplain Corps."

"Chaplain Corps? Captain, somebody's giving you false information. I'm no minister."

"No, you're a crusader. Your immediate duties will be the rehabilitation of a special unit made up entirely of barge rats now receiving amnesty. If you're going to crusade on my ship, it will be for a cause the Navy approves of."

60. When the Fiddler Stops

The carrier entered into a long corridor of hard-hat weather and everybody knew it would be that way for a while. Bogie cages went up around the decks. People with routines that required long exposure to the sky had to pack it in for the duration. Huge nets dropped like screen windows over the hangar deck elevator openings one, two and four, providing proof against birds that preferred horizontal attacks to kamikaze diving.

New Brisbane had been chosen as the first Australian port of call for two reasons: the docking facilities at Port of Brisbane had been somewhat restored; and the settlement was proximal to a number of significant coal deposits that made for geographically convenient mining.

The usual deterrents existed in one form or another. Most of Australia's animals had to be respected even back when a dog would still fetch a person's slippers instead of their feet. Fire ants had a presence on the land surrounding the mouth of the Brisbane River, and word was they'd spread up and along the northern coast.

Toffee pushed into the Marine's wardroom to find the place packed with squids and jarheads surrounding two men facing off over a chessboard. He edged along the periphery of the crowd, acknowledging brief nods from the surviving Marines and returning them in kind. It was Navy vs. Marine Corps with the gyrenes represented by a skilled soldier nicknamed Rooster. Toffee caught sight of the board in passing and wondered if Rooster knew he was being forced into castling.

Major Dawson was alone in his office at the back of the wardroom. His right sleeve was pinned up at the shoulder and a crutch leaned against the wall. His hunting days were over.

"Never thought I'd see the boys so worked up over a chess game," said Toffee as he closed the door.

"High stakes. I've got a dozen spots to fill. We've got one squid volunteering but his buddies are giving him a hard time on it, so we're playing chess for him."

Toffee had a skinbag in his hand. He put it on the floor. "Back in my day we'd have arm wrestled."

"It was the Navy's idea. And we take our chess seriously. Colonel Mills drummed it into us. I've kept that up. But the squids threw us a fast one. They put up one of the Outcasts for their side."

"Outcasts?" Toffee sat down and fished a drinking flask from his jacket pocket.

"Stukov's men. They were mutineers on board his ship way back when. He never talks to them except to give them orders."

"And just because they're Russian makes them chess masters?"

"This one is. It's best out of three. We're already down one. I left because I think Rooster was nervous having me at his shoulder."

Toffee pushed the flask across the desk. "So what happens to you now?"

"Me? I'll administrate the detachment and drown my feelings of inadequacy in booze until my liver packs it in." He picked up the flask and thumbed the cap open. "Might as well get started. Thanks."

"Keep saying it, you'll end up doing it."

Dawson shrugged his right shoulder. "Guess we're both missing tattoos now."

"Nah." Toffee pulled back the sleeve on his fake arm. "Only one of us." The eagle, globe and anchor were painted on the back of the forearm.

"That's a thing of beauty," said Dawson. "And a load off my mind. You're joining us."

Tofffee pulled the sleeve down. "I just got that for a souvenir. I'm getting off in Australia."

Dawson choked on a mouthful of liquor. "What? Why?"

"Because it suits me."

"Ethan, the men need you. The whole ship does. There aren't many old warriors left. We've got plenty of big brothers, but we're running out of father figures."

"That was deep."

Dawson chewed his lip. "People can only grow if they have something to aspire to, and the bar gets lower every day."

"I can't help you."

A cheer went up from the wardroom, followed by Marines trash talking at the Navy.

"Sounds like you tied it up," said Toffee.

"You just come down here to say goodbye?"

"No, I want a couple things."

"Figures."

"I need you to hook me up with a suit of your body armor, and tranq darts. Empties are fine. I'll put my own stuff in them. I hear the Australians are kind of funny and there's a high demand for a fellah who can bring the critters in alive. I'll pay, of course, but you're the store keeper."

"I might be able to find a little surplus. You need a rifle as well?"

"No, just the darts."

"So what's the other thing?"

Toffee lifted the skinbag from the floor and put it on the desk. Dawson pulled the string and looked inside. He removed a plastic box, shook it and put it back. "It's a .357 and some shells."

"She's a good gun. I've had her a long time."

"What am I supposed to do with it?" He pulled a small card from the bag.

"The day after I leave the ship, give it to an ensign named Noah Thurlow. He's in electrical. I'd give it to him myself, but I don't want to have to see the look on his face."

"Interesting message to go with it." Dawson put the card in the bag. "You lose a bet to him?"

"Don't know yet." He extended his left hand and they shook. "It was good hunting with you, Major."

As Toffee got up to leave, Dawson patted his empty sleeve and asked, "Any advice?"

The hunter mulled it over for a few seconds, then said, "It won't grow back. The moment that hits you one-hundred percent, either get a replacement or go for a swim."

When Tanzer stomped into the bar, Darcy was onstage, hands flexing at her sides, getting into it with Lila. Tivoli sat at the keyboard with a bored look on his face.

"What's the problem now?" Tanzer asked, mood darkening even further.

"You keep changing the song on me," said Darcy.

"She's acting like a prima donna," said Lila at the same time.

"It works better faster," said Tanzer. "All we did is speed up the tempo. Sing faster."

"Oh, that's fine for my mouth," said Darcy. "But what about my feet?"

"It's a simple six-step combination," said Lila.

"Simple for you, maybe."

"Not today!" Tanzer barked.

The closer they got to Australia, the grumpier he'd become. Darcy passed it off to the increased stress of being a part-organizer of the Wonders show.

"Darcy," Tanzer approached the stage, "if the footwork problem was eliminated, then you'd be fine?"

"Yes."

"Good. Then eliminate the problem. Do what Lila tells you."

Lila had the good grace not to smirk.

"What's got you in such a prize-winning mood?" asked Tivoli.

Tanzer kept up his glaring match with Darcy for a second longer, then let her win it. "Real estate," he said. "We're going to have to carry a lot more fuel on the carrier. Everybody's losing storage space. The Merchants Guild gave half our land away." He looked at Darcy's feet. "Dance!"

Tanzer moved to the bar as the piano started up. He put some coffee on to brew and was despairing how few beans he had left when a crash sounded from the stage and the music stopped.

Darcy was on one knee, other leg twisted a little behind her. "I'm fine," she said, standing up. "I'm okay."

"Maybe we can slow that part down if I put in a bridge," said Tivoli.

"No. I can do it," Darcy said fiercely. Then softly, "Just not right now." She looked at Tanzer. "I'm too on edge. This is my last day onboard for a week. I have things to do. Cut me loose and I'll practice by myself later. I promise I'll have it nailed for tomorrow."

Tanzer's face said "no," but maybe he sympathized with being on edge because he gave a big sigh and waved a hand at her green room.

"I guess that frees me up too," said Tivoli as Darcy clicked away to trade her heels for more practical footwear.

"Not a chance," said Lila. "I've got a couple of flourishes I want to work out before the dress rehearsal."

The specialized mannequin used for the Sampson & Delilah routine was one of many things sucked out of her home by the storm. More than one man had offered to substitute for the wooden partner, but she declared Sampson irreplaceable and worked up a new dance with a ragtime theme.

She stood on one foot, pressed a heel to her buttock and stretched for a few seconds, then switched legs and repeated. "Okay, give it to me from about halfway through and," she grimaced, "slow it down just a touch at the changeup, okay?"

"Seriously?"

"I'm not getting any younger, piano man."

***

Caps talked his way into engineering and found Noah two-finger hunt-and-pecking at a keyboard. The artist looked over his friend's shoulder at a screen filled with text, read two sentences and became instantly bored.

"That looks more like economics than electrical engineering," said Caps.

"Oh, hi," said Noah. If he was in any way startled, it didn't show. "My watch ended an hour ago. This is a proposal for the Merchants Guild. I've been working on it off and on since we became citizens."

Caps flipped the ensign bar on Noah's collar. "Isn't that beyond your jurisdiction now, sir?"

"I'm moonlighting."

"You need money for something?"

"Maybe. I think we could build a hybrid system on the flight deck. Integrate the wind generators and consolidate the panels. A central array would fit right in with the new greenhouse. There's a bunch of leftover hardware from ATMs that could be used for data management. I don't know how to assemble that but I bet Lena can. The Street gets its own grid. The Navy charges for the technical labor, but the civies look after the actual administration."

Caps made snoring sounds.

Noah saved the file and powered down the terminal. "Well, you asked."

"Actually I didn't. Look, I'm sorry, but I came here for a reason." He pulled a chair out, turned its back to Noah and straddled it. "A buddy in the motor pool told me Toffee's leaving."

"How would he know?" Noah asked, staring at his reflection in the blank screen.

"The Hummer. Toffee was down this morning packing it away and giving it a real check-over. It's going out on the first run tomorrow."

"Maybe he's taking it to Brisbane to sell it."

"I thought about that, but why? He can sell it to the Navy without having to leave the ship."

"Maybe one of us should ask him."

"What for? Man, I hate that glum look you get sometimes when I bring you good news. You don't actually like having him around do you? It's running us all ragged, in case you hadn't noticed." He gave Noah's shoulder a light backhand slap. "Let me ask you this: have you had a single conversation with him since he measured your collar size?"

"One," said Noah defensively. "At Tanzers. He told me he didn't mean to kill Travis Jones. That it was meant to be sort of a joke. He said, 'Sometimes a person does a thing and it gets out of hand.' He said it like we were discussing the weather."

Caps braced himself. "He say anything else about the night Travis died?"

Noah shook his head. "He left right away. I think maybe he was trying to apologize for trapping us all here."

The chair scraped. Caps tucked his chin against his throat and tried to keep emotion out of his voice. "You ever make an excuse for that raccoon again and I'll tell you something that will make you hate him to the grave."

"What could be worse than the stories I've already heard?" Noah stood up. "We're all stressed out because of him. He scared the crap out of you and busted out your tooth, so yeah, I do hate him. But you can hate somebody and respect them at the same time."

Toffee tightened the chin strap on his helmet and legged it across the flight deck. He looked for the bogie cage closest to the number four elevator and jogged towards it, dodging to one side in order to avoid a pair of hardhat-lidded children running for a dead gull.

Toffee reached the bogie cage and pulled the door open. In a whirl of red hair, the cage's single occupant spun and leveled a shotgun at Toffee's chest. He ducked under the barrel and ripped the weapon from Darcy's hands as he hit her with his shoulder.

"Sorry," she said, regaining her balance. "I thought you were a bird."

Toffee checked the breach. "It's empty."

"I need to reload."

He offered her the weapon. "Cute."

"I thought you'd like it."

"What are you doing on Double A duty?"

"I volunteered while Tanzer wasn't looking. I needed to shoot things."

"I can relate. So? You sent for me. I'm here."

One by one, she fed shells into the magazine. "I can't go with you first thing in the morning. It just doesn't work."

"It works for me."

She finished loading and racked one into the chamber. "It's not like Sid and Noah will smile and wave and let me go."

"I can help with that."

The sky was empty for the moment, but Darcy slid the barrel out through the rifle slot anyway. "No. You've been true to your word this long. I don't want a bloodbath now."

From up the deck a blast shredded a bird that was just about to pop into Darcy's arc of fire. She grumbled.

"Unless you have an alternative," said Toffee, "I can start the bath running right away."

Darcy pulled the trigger just to hear the bang. She racked another shot, tilting the shotgun so the ejected shell hit Toffee in the chest. "You still go out first thing. I'll come later. After the show we'll go wherever you want."

"You really think I'd leave this tub without you?"

"I have a contract with Tanzer witnessed by the Merchants Guild. If I refuse to perform in the show he'll have me expelled. This stuff I do on the ship is just to make him feel classy. I really pay off for him when he gets his cut of the Wonders show."

Toffee made a face.

"Fine," she said. "Go check it out if you don't believe me. Noah doesn't get liberty until the second day. Caps and Lena on the third. I have a way to keep Sid distracted long enough to miss the last boat out tomorrow night. It'll be just you and me. I want a big head start. They can make good on this ship. I don't want them throwing that away to chase me."

"We go before the show."

"After."

"No."

She turned on him, lips tight, eyes starting to tear. "Wherever we go, are you going to let me sing? Stand up in front of people and be a performer?"

"Doubt it."

An off-white shape soared through her peripheral vision. The seabird landed on top of the cage and pecked at the metal with its beak.

As Darcy moved to bring the weapon up, Toffee grabbed it above the breach. "Careful now. Wouldn't want any accidents in here."

"I got it," came a yell from outside the cage. A sailor wearing a pilot's helmet ran up and smashed the gull with a cricket bat. He looked around for any other nearby targets, gave the two people in the birdcage a thumbs up, then trotted off.

Toffee released his grip on the shotgun.

"Please," she said. "You don't know what it's been like working on the show and knowing I won't be in it. I have a fitting and a dress rehearsal tomorrow. This is my only chance to play for a big audience. Let me have this one last thing."

"No."

"Is there nothing human in you for me to appeal to?"

"Red, you appeal to everything that's human in me."

"That's not what I meant—"

"Stop it." For a moment, anger clouded his face. "Anybody else but him? I'd have killed them already. But I'm letting you get your jollies. And as bad as I could mess the kid up? It's nothing compared to what'll happen when he finds out you've been saving the last dance for me. And that's on you. I told you to wrap it up with him. Ain't my problem if you don't."

Something flickered in her eyes and Toffee caught it.

"You're not even going to leave the kid a note. That's cold. I knew there was something about you I liked." He stroked two fingers down her cheek. She jerked away with a look of revulsion that was almost poignant.

"Get out." She racked the gun, ejecting a full shell.

"Do that a few more times."

Her lip curled but she emptied the magazine.

"Thanks. I've changed my mind. If we leave before the show you'll be missed too fast. We'll go after, but don't try to pull a fast one or linger with any of your 'fans.' "

Toffee left the bogie cage and hurried to starboard, making sure that before she could reload, he was well out of "accident" range.

61. Curtains

With *Enrique* running escort, *Terpris* navigated the Spitfire and East Channels, ever mindful of the narrow safety margin between the channels' true depths and the carrier's draught. Moreton Island passed by on the port side, a wind-deposited landmass of pure white sand. Scribbly Gum and Pink Bloodwood comprised the bulk of the island's forestation. It was once a national park, hosting fresh-water lakes, an inland desert, and "mountains" that were essentially giant overgrown dunes. Tourists came for the purity of its nature, as well as the thousands of migratory birds that flocked there between September and April. The tourists were gone, but the birds were still there and every single one of them took a run at the carrier. It got particularly bad when the transition from Spitfire Channel to East Channel brought them within spitting distance of Moreton's beaches.

Pushing into Moreton Bay, *Terpris* altered her heading to south by southwest and dropped anchor, three minutes after midnight, off the northwestern tip of the Fisherman Islands and the Port of Brisbane.

Darcy sat astride Noah, the heels of her hands digging into his chest. He was finished—they both were—but she wouldn't let him withdraw. From the first time under the cargo net she'd been passionate, but tonight she seemed desperate; pushing harder, squeezing tighter, as if her goal was to permanently weld her body to his.

Noah stroked her sides, took her wrists and kissed her palms, then swept her hair back with his fingers so he could see her whole face. He always wanted to see her entire face.

She collapsed over him, forehead to forehead, giving him all her weight. She knew he liked that. "Who made you so perfect?" she whispered. "Who made you so perfect and sent you to me?"

He slipped out. She tried to hold on but it only quickened the process. She straightened her legs and slid off him enough to bury her face in his neck.

"Darce?" He touched her cheek the same way Toffee had, stroking with two fingers. "Are you crying?"

There were three little words she hadn't said to him yet. She'd barely let herself think them, never mind let them pass her lips. There was something she could tell him, though. "I was thinking about Travis."

"Oh." His body went rigid.

"And how much better this is."

For about three seconds he tried to be restrained in his reaction, then he kissed her until she was laughing and slapping at him to stop. They fumbled their way into another session of lovemaking and Noah drifted off with a smile on his face.

Darcy didn't sleep a wink. She lay curled up to him, ear to his chest, trying to memorize his heartbeat the way she would a song.

The sun rose a little after 5:00 am and the fireworks started shortly after that. Chaff pods banging, shotguns blasting, the boat crews prepped the *Munin* and the *Nancy Dean* while under the additional weight of body armor and facemasks. It was a good day for sky fishing and people played their deadly game, rushing about, scooping dead birds off the deck.

At 5:45 am, the five of them, punchy and weary eyed, stood in the Valley at the elevator two opening and watched the Hummer descend to the deck of the *Nancy Dean*. At 5:55, the transport boat was on its way to the Port of Brisbane.

A few minutes later, the *Munin* hit the water and followed. They'd seen Toffee get on board with their own eyes. He didn't even wave goodbye. When the boats came back they inspected both of them from stern to prow.

"No way," said Caps. "He's really gonc. No Hummer. No Toffee."

"What did you say?" Darcy grabbed Caps's wrist.

"I said he's really gone."

Lena gestured at the *Munin's* comm officer. He wandered over and said, "He got off, got in his vehicle and drove away. Was there something else you expected him to do?"

"No. No. Thanks, Mitch."

"Whatever. I'll be doing the next run on the *Munin.* You on the bridge?"

"Second watch."

"Okay. Talk to you then." He walked away.

Darcy's fingers slid from Caps's wrist to his hand and squeezed. "Thank you."

He squeezed back. "Sure, okay."

"Still plenty of boats coming and going," said Sid. "We'll have to figure out a way to watch them all."

"And he could still try to pick us off onshore," added Caps.

"Oh stop it," said Noah. "We're just not worth his effort. Don't you guys get it? He's done with us. I mean he's off the ship and you're still talking about guard duty."

"The last time I thought that man was gone forever," said Sid, "he came back."

"That time he left on our terms. This time he left on his." He gave Darcy a quick kiss. "I have to get to work. I'll see you before you go ashore?"

"I'll make sure of it," she said, a hand pressed to his chest. "And I'll have something to say to you."

"I have to go too," said Caps. "I'll swap my way into a starboard birdcage. I'll watch the boats coming in."

"So long, men," said Lena. "I'm going to have a nap. A nice fear-free nap."

"So I got a job," said Sid once the others were gone.

"Navy come through?"

"No, I signed on for show security."

"You didn't."

"I'll be with you the whole time."

"I wish you hadn't done that, Sid. I'm not going over there and I don't want you there either."

"Excuse me?"

She clenched her fists. "I'm going to break a leg."

He looked confused.

She lowered her voice. "More specifically, I'm going to break my ankle." She pulled him deeper into the Valley, away from the busy activity of the elevator. "I'll do it at the dress rehearsal. There's a six-step combination with a tough pivot. If I hit it right I can blow out my ankle. It'll make a good sound."

"What the hell's going on?"

She gripped his arm. "I'm not leaving this ship."

Sid's face held a mixture of fear and anger. "Tell me."

"This never gets back to Noah."

"Darce, what did you do?"

Telling the whole truth was such a relief she had to lean against him. "So I'm breaking more than my ankle," she concluded. "I'm breaking my word."

"He'll come back on the ship."

"It doesn't matter. Caps said it. No Hummer, no Toffee. He can't get the vehicle back on board and keep it as his. There's no room. I won't be able to walk until after *Terpris* has left Brisbane.

In a choice between me and the Hummer, he'll take the Hummer. I'm sure of it."

She expected him to be furious. Instead he just looked sad. "This is all my fault."

"Sid, I realized something. Right now I've got about as good a life as I could possibly hope to have in this world. I want to keep it. All of it."

"When I taught you how to break bones, it wasn't so you could do it to yourself. We should at least prepare Richard and Lena."

"No. I want their shock and sympathy to be genuine. Tanzer can't suspect for a moment I did this on purpose and Toffee has to think he was disappointed by circumstance."

"Why would he even want you in the first place? He must know you'd cut his throat the first time he fell asleep next to you."

"I don't know, Sid. He'd probably keep me tied up most of the time until he'd decided I was broken or…" She shook her hands on either side of her head as if warding off a swarm of flies. "I don't even want to think about it."

Sid took her by the shoulders. His grip tightened until it hurt. "Why are you just telling me about this now?"

She grimaced. She was trying so hard to keep it together but her right eye was twitching and that hand was going for her bottom lip.

"Stop." Sid pulled her into a tight hug. "Sssshh. Bad enough you'll have a swollen foot. You don't need puffy eyes. Toffee didn't do jack for me. I know who saved my life. Sssssh. I know who saved my life." He pushed her out to arm's length. "Okay, you go break your ankle and I'll find you a get-well present."

She took his hand and pressed it to her cheek. "I have a fitting first."

Sid watched her leave, then turned to look out at the Fisherman Islands.

She wanted to keep it all. That wasn't going to happen. A person was lucky to keep a sliver of something worthwhile. Darcy deserved more than most. She'd still have Noah and her job on the ship.

Keeping track of every boat on and off would be a nightmare. They'd have to screen every tourist, open every large crate, and even then the hunter might slip in somehow and express his displeasure.

Sid was going to go to Brisbane that night. He didn't require planning or subterfuge. Witnesses ceased to be a complication when the problem was simplified. Ethan Toffee didn't need to be killed in secret. He just needed to be killed.

"If you're bored," said Tanzer, "you can grab a broom and sweep."

Darcy finished the yawn and let her head droop forward. She was sitting on the piano bench, leaning back against the keyboard. "Where's Tivoli?"

"I sent him ashore."

"Oh yeah. I even watched him get on the boat earlier. Sorry. I was up late practicing." She looked at her wrist where she didn't have a watch but kept expecting to find one. "When's this fitting?"

"As soon as *Mistress* Ruth gets here."

"The rehearsal's soon." She looked at all that booze behind the bar. A bottle or two would surely dull the pain, but the problem was it would dull everything else. If she wanted to break her ankle with the minimum necessary damage, she had to do it unimpaired, and she was already overtired.

"We've got time. Coffee?"

"I'd love some."

The front door opened. The head of wardrobe rushed in, a bag slung from her shoulder. She didn't take her helmet off until the door was closed and she was halfway across the room.

"Took your sweet time," said Tanzer.

"Well if you'd brought her to me instead of making me come up here to you…"

"I don't like going down below."

"Hello, Darcy." Ruth dropped her bag on the stage. She was of medium height and a little plump and everything she did, she seemed to do in a hurry. "I've got all three here." She pulled outfits from the bag. "Evening gown, sun dress and slut."

"Slut?" Darcy eyed the small pile of black lace and red silk. "I'm only doing two numbers which one is—"

"It's for the Madonna number," said Tanzer, as he circled the room, pulling curtains over the windows.

"What Madonna number?"

Ruth held the bustier up to Darcy's chest. "Try this on first. It will probably need the most work."

"An important person in New Brisbane put in a special inquiry for any Madonna memorabilia we might have," said Tanzer. "It will curry favor if we give him a live performance."

Darcy pushed the lingerie away. "Are you sure he's not a devout Christian? What song? When do we have time to do the blocking?"

"You can learn it five minutes. Shake your ass and lick your lips a lot. It'll be fine. Now hurry up and give me my fashion show."

Darcy gathered up the outfits and headed for her green room. "This is exploitation," she said.

"Just one of many perks."

The top was too tight across the chest. Tanzer said it was fine. The short shorts felt like they were designed by a wedgie fetishist. Tanzer said they were fine. The other two outfits fit perfectly. Tanzer said nothing.

Ruth folded the outfits and arranged them in the bag. She pulled on her helmet with a scowl at Tanzer and left.

Happy to have her pants and sweater back on Darcy sat on the stage and looked around the bar. She wouldn't be seeing it for a little while.

"You don't have to do the Madonna thing every night," said Tanzer, putting a fresh cup of coffee down beside her. "Little reward for your patience. That's the good stuff. It's not too hot."

She took a belt. "Yuck. This is the good stuff? It tastes worse than the bad stuff."

"It's not good for the taste. It's good for the kick. You look completely washed out. Get it in you."

She took a good swallow, forcing the stuff down her throat. "Like I said, I was up all last night."

"You and me both," he said, almost too quietly to hear. "You're a remarkable talent." He walked to the front door and made sure it was locked. "In the old days I could have made some calls. You would have been famous."

"Thanks," she blushed, feeling a little guilty.

"A diva."

"I wouldn't go that far."

"It's a real shame."

She heard him speak, but couldn't quite remember what he'd said. "I'm sorry, could you repeat…"

"I mean it. It's a real shame we'll have to delay your debut."

How did he know that? The deck was tilting. Bad weather must have sprung up. No. The deck wasn't tilting. She was sliding off the stage. She heard the back door open and close.

"When it's over you won't remember a thing. I'm a bartender. I'm good with doses." He looked down the corridor to the back door and said, "Make sure you lock it."

Darcy slumped completely off the stage.

Tanzer moved behind the bar. "I thought this thing had gone south until I saw you at the window. What'd you do? Never leave in the first place?"

Toffee came around the corner and looked Darcy over. He wore a long coat and loose trousers. He carried a large bag over one shoulder. Keeping an eye on Tanzer, he crossed to her and nudged her with a toe. "How long will her eyes stay open?"

"Maybe another ten minutes." Tanzer moved behind the bar.

Toffee took a metal tin from his pocket. He placed it on the bar top, thumbed it open, showed the little blue Viagras inside, then closed the lid. "There you go. Eighty-nine ways to dance."

"The deal was for ninety."

"The one I already gave you was a taste, not a freebie."

Tanzer moved a few feet away, looking anywhere but at the pill canister.

"How's about..." Toffee moved closer, sliding the tin across notched mahogany, "I paint them silver and just give you thirty?" He grinned. "Kidding. Don't hate yourself for having needs."

The tin disappeared into Tanzer's pocket and he leaned on the bar with both hands. "Get on with it."

"Here?" Toffee said incredulously. "With you watching?"

"Bad enough I'm going to have to keep her delirious for a few days and get it diagnosed as brain fever. I'm not taking the risk of you leaving bruises or cuts."

Toffee started to undo his coat. "Or maybe you just like to watch."

"If I do, that's my own business."

Toffee fumbled at the coat button above his waist. "How 'bout you pop one of those beauties right now? You'll be ready to go by the time I'm finished."

Tanzer's eyes went flat and hard. "I would never do that to her."

"I love a man with ethics." Toffee's hand flicked out. A fat dart appeared in Tanzer's shoulder.

"What the..."

"You'll wake up in about an hour," said the hunter. "I'm good with doses too."

Tanzer yanked the dart out and lunged for where he kept his shotgun. Toffee vaulted the bar and kicked him in the chest. When the bartender tried to get up, he couldn't. Then he couldn't focus, and finally couldn't do anything at all.

Toffee pulled off his coat, boots and pants. Underneath he wore a wetsuit. He dumped the clothing on top of Tanzer and pulled on a mask and snorkel.

He put his fake arm in the bag. The right sleeve of the wetsuit was already cut and tied off above the blade. With the bag slung, he grabbed Darcy by the front of her sweater and, as gently as he could, hoisted her over his shoulder. He popped his head out the back door, looked both ways, then carried Darcy and his bag to the rail, where he threw them both over.

Toffee clambered over the rail and dropped, landing in the safety net. A coil of rope was rigged to the net with some carabiners. He pushed the bag through a long slit in the net. It hit the water and sank. Checking above and finding no eyes on him,

Toffee tied the rope around Darcy's waist and pushed her through the slit. Feet braced, gloved hand cramping up, he lowered her until she dangled with her hands and feet in the water. With that done, he put his feet through the hole, grabbed the rope once more and slid down. A few feet above Darcy he placed his bladearm against the rope and sawed through. Everything splashed into the sea.

Using the rope around her waist, he dragged her down the side of the hull. It went another thirty-five or so feet but he only needed to reach a large bundle fifteen feet down and secured by wire to a clump of barnacles.

This was the hairy part, the bit that just might not work. Being underwater in of itself wasn't the least bit dangerous. Oh yes, this was shark and dolphin water, but for a few days this was also Screaming Mimi water. With repair crews on rotation checking the rudders and the screws, another team on the sonar dome, and all the boats going back and forth, that magic little box was going to be on constant deployment. If Toffee hadn't seen it go into the water earlier, he'd have aborted. If he hadn't seen the repair crews go to work, he'd also have aborted. But the Mimi went down and the repair crews gave him a way to get back in *Terpris*, wrapped up in rubber and wearing a mask.

He pulled Darcy to the bundle and clipped her to it. An air tank, a sea scooter and a vest knocked about as Toffee pulled a full-face dive mask over Darcy's head and depressed the button, filling the mask with air and forcing the water out. That done he popped the spare regulator in his own mouth and watched her. After a painfully long few seconds, she coughed up a little water and breathed normally.

Toffee pulled on fins, then after checking the straps on Darcy's mask, left her there and swam down until he found his bag on the ocean floor, twenty feet deeper than the bottom of the carrier.

The keel was so big, another hundred divers could have been down there and he'd still have found places not to be seen.

He swam back up to Darcy, put the spare regulator back in his mouth and struggled into the dive vest.

A dead bird splashed into the water above their heads.

Toffee unclipped Darcy from the cable, bent her over his shoulder, started the sea scooter and let it pull them away, muscling it one-handed.

Dull thumps carried down from the air above followed them to shore.

Toffee kept them at a shallow depth. He didn't want to risk damaging Darcy's eardrums. In waters like these he would easily be spotted from above, but not so clearly that anybody would know for sure what they were looking at. A long dark shape in shark water shouldn't be a rare thing.

With the ocean floor at a depth of seven feet, Toffee dumped the air tank and the scooter. He kicked hard against the current, shoving Darcy the last few meters to shore. Once there he ran, hauling his bag, dragging her. The Hummer was parked a short distance away, hidden beneath a camouflage net. He'd needed a burn circle to get things set up but departure would be much quicker. The net pulled away, he laid Darcy across the back seat, got in the front and started the engine.

Toffee angled the rearview mirror so he could look at her. "I'm just doing you a favor," he said, stepping on the gas. "I'm helping you keep your word."

Acknowledgements

I would like to thank:

My mother, who, after reading my work, still claims maternal pride instead of staging an intervention.

Dwight Hill for suggesting I might find a use for an aircraft carrier somewhere in my world.

My proofreaders. There are too many to list, but they happily waded through a ton of typos. I know. I made 'em.

Various members, past and present, of the Everquest guild Grey Hawke, with whom support, humbling and therapy is always just a few mouse clicks away.

Bill Richards for his unique and compelling art style.

Storma Sire, for opening her umbrella when I really needed a Mary Poppins.

Tom Bulmer, for getting worked up about things so I don't have to.

Ron Heron, for his ability to use only as many words as are needed.

Jason Olson, for nitpicking, a wardrobe suggestion, and talking quietly to Mimi, when all she wants to do is scream.

Douglas Corp, for teaching me how not to sink an aircraft carrier, and managing to stay afloat in my sea of questions.

Dr. John Q. Pinkney, who might one day build the things I ask him to design on paper, and then we'll all be in a lot of trouble.

And finally Fiona Prince, who thinks she's doing nothing when she simplifies a problem just by being in the room.

About the Author

Indigenous to Western Canada, Brian S. Matthews is a large furry member of the chipmunk family. Though typicaly nocturnal, he sometimes ventures out during the day and can occasionaly be spotted renewing his insurance or trying to order fast food in Klingon.

Brian's dating history includes such highlights as being stood up by a hooker. He is illiterate in over a dozen languages and once lectured at the University of Queensland, Australia to a group of post-grads even more baffled by it than he was.

His debut novel, *New Wilderness,* was critically acclaimed internationally and was a finalist for the 2006 Ippy Award for Science Fiction.

The author may be contacted at
newwilderness@shaw.ca

Book III of the New Wilderness Trilogy

The Last Walkabout

Brian S. Matthews

In a land held deadly long before the Change, in a place where the sun kills faster than the teeth, six people must test the very limits of their will to survive.

Settlements are few. Technology is nonexistent and the last known tribe of Aboriginal People warns that a worse change is coming.

Between myth and truth, between science and superstition, lies the answer to the mystery, and the final days of all mankind.

December 2006

Aydy Press

www.ingramcontent.com/pod-product-compliance
Lightning Source LLC
Chambersburg PA
CBHW020625020726
47494CB00001B/48
9781897242230